MICHAEL MOORCOCK

"A myth-maker,
an epic fantasist"
The London Times

JERRY CORNELIUS

Crusading against the forces of ritual evil—
Hurling through the gateways of the myriad alternate versions
of Earth—
Fondling the diamond, ruby, and sapphire controls of his
Phantom VI Gilian Packard convertible—
Hanging around in a subterranean coffin–
Jerry Cornelius is the mind-blown Spirit of the Age.

THE CORNELIUS CHRONICLES

The Past transforms the Future in a world which is an
anagram of today, in which time reels backward
and forward, and which Jerry Cornelius assaults in an
assortment of sexes, avatars, and colors.

THE CORNELIUS
CHRONICLES

MICHAEL MOORCOCK

**THE FINAL PROGRAMME • A CURE FOR CANCER
THE ENGLISH ASSASSIN • THE CONDITION OF MUZAK**

AVON
PUBLISHERS OF BARD, CAMELOT, DISCUS AND FLARE BOOKS

THE FINAL PROGRAMME was first published in Great Britain in 1969 by Allison & Busby Limited.

THE CONDITION OF MUZAK was first published in Great Britain in 1977 by Allison and Busby Limited.

AVON BOOKS
A division of
The Hearst Corporation
1790 Broadway
New York, New York 10019

Introduction copyright © 1977 by John Clute
THE FINAL PROGRAMME Copyright © New Worlds
1965 and 1966
Copyright © U.S.A. Michael Moorcock, 1968
A CURE FOR CANCER Copyright © 1971
by Michael Moorcock
THE ENGLISH ASSASSIN Copyright © 1977
by Michael Moorcock
THE CONDITION OF MUZAK Copyright © 1977
by Michael Moorcock
Published by arrangement with the author.
Library of Congress Catalog Card Number: 77-78116
ISBN: 0-380-00878-5

First Avon Printing, August 1977

AVON TRADEMARK REG. U.S. PAT OFF. AND IN
OTHER COUNTRIES, MARCA REGISTRADA, HECHO EN
U.S.A.

Printed in the U.S.A.

OP   10   9   8   7   6

CONTENTS

CONTENTS

The Repossession of Jerry Cornelius

Once upon a time a rather unremarkable composer and music publisher named Anton Diabelli composed a rather unremarkable waltz—simple to hum and easy to remember—which gave him an idea. As he was always looking for material to publish, especially music that could be played by amateurs on the piano, why not (he thought) take this waltz around to as many composers as possible (eventually he found fifty of them) and have them each write a variation on the thing? Then he could put the fifty-one pieces into what was commonly called (at this time, 1823) a *pasticcio,* a collection of works by various hands, all in the style of some original composer, and then hawk his *pasticcio* far and wide. Which is more or less what happened. But what if Diabelli had been a trickier, more formidable composer? What if he had given his fifty composers not the simple-hearted waltz history records, but only a variation of the *real tune?*

Rather more recently, in January 1965, a young writer and editor named Michael Moorcock, who seemed rather unremarkable at the time, composed a regular waltz of a novel called *The Final Programme,* excerpts from which caused some comment when published soon after in *New Worlds,* the sf magazine he had then been editing for about half a year. Easy to read, linearly plotted, full of sf twists and turns, this novel introduced to the sf world (and in fact seemed to donate to some of its writers) a new kind of infinitely malleable template for myth-making called Jerry Cornelius, simple to hum and easy to remember, a sexually ambivalent, amoral (but exceedingly oral) portmanteau anti-hero who was part saint

and part devil, an instant myth of the pop sixties whose
tastes in music, clothes, cars, drugs, wombs, technology
and apotheosis all seemed to make him an authentic
emblem of Swinging London and (more narrowly) of the
New Wave in sf which Moorcock had instigated by
giving space to its writers in his magazine, which soon
became notorious. As did its mascot. Moorcock encouraged his fellow writers to use Cornelius as a template in
stories of their own. There may not have been fifty of
them, and *New Worlds* hardly became a *pasticcio*, but all
the same it was pretty clear—indeed advertised—that *The
Final Programme* was being used, sometimes very compe-
tently, as the initial theme for a whole series of mytho-
poeic variations, whole multiverses of riffs—on Jerry
himself; on Miss Brunner, his collaborator in instant
Messiah-hood; on Frank, his shifty, scrounging brother;
and on Catherine, the sister he's deeply in love with. But
what if *The Final Programme* turned out not to be the
basic template tune at all? What if it was only a variation
on the real tune?

The fate of Diabelli's theme is well known, for the
poor devil had the singular luck to approach Ludwig van
Beethoven with his little template waltz. Sick, deaf, and
aging, the great composer slammed the door in his face at
first, but later, somehow intrigued by the tune, he told
Diabelli that he would undertake the task after all. He
rather exceeded his brief, as it turned out; instead of one
variation he wrote thirty-three—they comprise his final
and perhaps greatest work for solo piano. They last an
hour. You could call them the real tune.

What happened with Michael Moorcock is rather different. After seeming to give Jerry Cornelius to the world
as a pop saviour, he went and took him back, just as
though he were Beethoven. The final result, after a long
wait, is before you, all thirty-three variations. Though
it's been published in separate volumes over the past
decade—*The Final Programme* (by Avon) in 1968, *A
Cure for Cancer* in 1971, *The English Assassin* in 1972,
and *The Condition of Muzak* only in 1977—what you
are now holding is a single novel, and a very fine formidable novel it is, too. Like most books whose structure is
most easily described in musical terms, the meaning of

The Cornelius Chronicles only comes clear as the end is neared. What seems theme turns out to be only variation; for a decade now we've been reading fragments of Cornelius, and only now have we been told the real tune.

Or that's how I read it.

That basic theme, as I read it, Jerry Cornelius's fundamental obsessive concern through all his various incarnations, is simply the problem of how to acquire and maintain an identity strategically capable of constituting urban life, because identity in the city is a costume drama. The presentation of self in everyday life in the inner city is a form of theatre, where identity is role and where entropy is high, for time is passing. Jerry Cornelius is the paradigmatic native of the inner city; his roles constitute a genuine paradigm set of strategies for living there. His inner city is London (but could be New York), his patch is Ladbroke Grove. His real story (I believe) runs from about 1965 to about a decade later, a period during which London has been destroying itself as a place to live, hence the rapacity of his need for safety and solace. It is for this reason that the various masquerades and venues which make up his story read as a series of precariously achieved enclaves, or wombs. To shift the metaphor, Jerry's life is a constant series of *auditions*. His constant failures are the failures of the city (circa 1975) where ultimately there are no enclaves, no permanent wombs, for time rots them. No music stays fresh. Jonathan Raban speaks to something of the same general point in his socio-literary study of the meaning of urban life, *Soft City* (1974):

Sociology and anthropology are not disciplines which take easily to situations where people are able to live out their fantasies, not just in the symbolic action of ritual, but in the concrete theatre of society at large. The city is one such situation. Its conditions effectively break down many of the conventional distinctions between dream life and real life; the city inside the head can be transformed, with the aid of the technology of style, into the city on the streets. To a very large degree, people can create their cosmologies at will, liberating themselves from the deterministic schemes which ought to have lead them into a wholly different style of life. To have a platonic conception of oneself, and to make it spring forth, fully clothed, out of one's head, is one of the most dangerous and essential city freedoms, and it is a freedom which has been ignored and underestimated by almost everyone except novelists.

Michael Moorcock is one of those novelists. His main gloss on Raban may be that the city in our time, being deeply entropic, life within it therefore tends to the condition of Muzak.

But he's also an sf writer, and the whole of *The Final Programme* is sparkling good sf. Being the most extended single riff on the basic theme of identity maintenance in the entire *Chronicles,* it is consequently the most easily assimilated story, very remote from the darker, more complex, virtually Edwardian verisimilitude of later pages, grimmer times. *The Final Programme* is a constitutive image of the sunshine of surviving at a time (1965) when (perhaps for Moorcock, too) London bore an air of slightly pixillated ebullience. London swung. The story reflects this. Jerry and Miss Brunner (here a computer technician with enormous powers—it's only in the final book that she's revealed for what she always was in the city, a tight-assed schoolma'arm from Ladbroke Grove) clash and conspire from here to Lappland and Angkor Wat (to be similarly grounded as a dream of Derry & Toms department store half-choked in its own overgrown roof garden), and eventually get their computers and their super-science formulae together in a womblike cave where they merge themselves into a new hermaphrodite Messiah for whom the world is "tasty," so it eats the world.

Altogether there's a lot of vampirism in both *The Final Programme* and succeeding parts of the *Chronicles;* part of the time it's an sf energy-transfer, a countervailing response to the loss of usable energy in this venue or that; ultimately it reads as an analogue of the use people make of each others' images (or life-forces) in coping with the interplay of dramaturgies that constitutes social life in the deep city. In any case, Jerry Cornelius as polymorphous Messiah could be said to constitute the false theme of the tetralogy, the spunky little Diabelli waltz; for though it makes a nice story (and helped fuel the New Wave's own wry messianism), generally speaking Jerry is anything but . . .

In *A Cure for Cancer,* which is a kind of negative scherzo on the pattern of the first book, he has polarized into a black with white hair, and continues to vampirize those about him to maintain his own image-stability. A couple of years have passed in the real world, the scene has darkened, witness the headlines and news reports and arms advertisements that appear more and more frequently in the text and whose function is not to make editorial points about the world (they'd date very quickly), but to demonstrate some of the ways in which the world acts as a shaping, controlling input on its victims (us, Jerry); headlines are like executive memos in the Castle. War has come, American "advisors" have turned Europe into something very like the news reports of life in Viet Nam. We are inundated with media. Jerry Cornelius makes to dance in step, to keep alive, to recover his beloved sister. He runs a transmogrification service which forcibly does to others what the media do to all of us, thus maintaining a kind of intricate balance. He goes to a strange Amerika (perhaps Kafka's), continuing a conflict with the newly introduced, loathsome Bishop Beesley, who with Miss Brunner seems to represent the only kind of officialdom Moorcock is willing to deal with directly: their life-denying "orderliness" constantly threatens Jerry's identity and the enclaves of aesthetic harmony he and his compatriots try to inhabit.

We meet most of these compatriots in the next volume, *The English Assassin,* where the action broadens and deepens significantly. We are into the 1970s in the city, and Jerry has retreated very far indeed within the action. Having gone into a fugue of horror at the collapse of the century, he spends most of the novel in a coffin, beneath the surface of the newly ornate narrative, whose Edwardian cadences depict a turn-of-the-century dream of the romance of Empire at its hectic Jubilee peak. *The English Assassin* is also full of nostalgia for Edwardian visions of what the future might hold, dreams of a time when art deco flying boats and zeppelins would crisscross a balkanized Europe with fin-de-siècle lords and ladies, a time when all the weapons and appurtenances of technological progress would make up a glorious raree-show. Every single invention would be fixed still in time long enough to be memorized, the great Duesenberg would not turn to junk before we had a chance to make a symbol of it, every surface of the steam yacht would be polished and legible and reflect our faces. Into these scenes of nostalgia for an endurable future are introduced various lords and ladies, *The Cornelius Chronicles'* remaining important characters, who dance out their roles on Jerry's coffin: Sebastian Auchinek, the two Nyes (Captain and Major), Colonel Pyat, Prinz Lobkowitz, and most importantly Una Persson (stage singer and dancer, revolutionary, Catherine's lover and Jerry's) and Mrs Cornelius (his appallingly greedy, vulgar, foul-mouthed libidinous mother, who seems to represent an earlier form of city life—a sly, savage, indomitable, wise Cockney survivor of everything the century can throw at her). These lords and ladies are alive in their own right, but also represent Jerry's desperate attempts to apply fixative to the Empire and to time, so as to maintain himself in a lousy era.

Of course it doesn't work. The Edwardian vision of Empire is deeply tubercular; the Edwardian dreams of the future are hopelessly innocent, hopelessly prewar. The bright clothing and the jamborees rot, like Jerry in his coffin. The entropic decay of the British Empire mirrors the entropic decay of Jerry's attempts at constituting images of survival in dehumanized London as the sixties turn sourly downwards into the seventies. A dozen futures have died for us sf readers before we could breathe them to life. Golems stalk the council flats. *The English Assassin* ends in fire and death. There is a lot of aging going on: It's the nature of the catastrophe.

And so we reach *The Condition of Muzak*, which repossesses Jerry Cornelius from messiah-hood and other intoxications by retelling his earlier lives in its own complex terms, as phases in a harlequinade. In *The Final Programme* and *A Cure for Cancer* Jerry has seemed to be Harlequin himself, the dominant figure of all the show, manipulating costumes and plot at will so as to reach a point of stable bliss with Columbine, who is his sister Catherine. He snaps his fingers at incest, and the world shrivels at his dancing feet. But of course it doesn't work. In *The English Assassin* he has gone to earth, and as we reach the dense heart of *The Condition of Muzak* (the chapters leading up to his final Ladbroke Grove party, which this time is a genuine masquerade) we find him undergoing a strange metamorphosis. He is deeply withdrawn (therefore London is deserted), but manages to struggle back to the roof garden at Derry & Toms as to a tropical womb, where he settles into a foetal position and, umbilically tied by earphones to music emblematic of his past lives, sinks into near coma, which is no way for Harlequin to act. The whole department store is covered with roots and vines and undergrowth, but finally Major Nye and Hythloday (the Professor Hira of *The Final Programme*, whose first meeting with Jerry thus anticipates his last) discover Jerry and drag him to safety in a nearby house, where he lapses into catatonia, only to be ultimately aroused, and reborn, as Pierrot. It must be a great relief. Deep within he has always been incapable of the coercive manipulations his roles as Harlequin have laid on him. Deep within he has always really been Pierrot the Weeper, helplessly in love with Columbine, and always at risk of losing her to the genuine Harlequin, who is Una Persson.

Indeed everyone is relieved. There is a fugue of joy. Though Jerry is only a figurehead now, the Empire in all its parti-colored glory returns to honor him as the King of London in a coronation parade lasting hours in the bright sun. The dream of Empire has come true. Time passes in this dream. Chistmas is nigh. In an extraordinary sequence that marries Dickens and Wells in a description of a London heartbreakingly clement and legible as the snow falls and everyone sings carols, Harlequin leads us through gaily bedizened streets to the Ladbroke Grove party, whose zone of peace has spread this time throughout the town. Jerry is there as Pierrot, Catherine as Columbine is in a magic sleep, Harlequin awakens her lovingly (Una Persson loves Catherine too), but gives her up to Pierrot. In a London prepared to rejoice with him at such a moment, Jerry Cornelius has won his heart's desire.

But of course it doesn't work.

Framing the rest of *The Condition of Muzak* are several chapters of another complexion entirely, also set in the Ladbroke Grove area of London, Jerry's mythical home, but no longer is Ladbroke Grove mythical. Jerry Cornelius is a teenager who lives with his gluttonous mother and his seedy brother Frank in a slum flat. He is rather seedy himself. He spends much of his time in a "tiny balcony formed by the house's front porch," which he plans to turn someday into "an ornamental conservatory with semi-tropical plants," and suddenly we realize with a sort of horror that this imaginary conservatory grounds the roof garden at Derry & Toms in the same way that that roof garden grounds most of the exotic locations (like Angkor Wat) of the entire tetralogy. It is a shocking discovery. Jerry Cornelius is a grubby little daydreamer. Worse follows. He is a rock musician, or hopes to be one, but his taste isn't really very secure, he's not much on the guitar, and when he finally gets the chance to perform in public (at an amateur gig under an elevated highway) he's too spaced out to make any sense at all. It's the real world, in which time passes, taking us down. For Jerry, as the years pass, life seems to be a series of bad auditions. Most of his fellow denizens of Ladbroke Grove are in no better shape than he is; the Edwardian tapestry of lords and ladies (with two exceptions) turns out to be a klatch of petty entrepreneurs; Auchinek is a music agent, for instance, while Frank sells fake antiques to tourists at the Portobello Road market. Gradually Jerry achieves some success, on the stage, acting Harlequin; he has teamed up with his sister and Una Persson (she remains vital) and they all have sex together; they play games with themselves. His mother is also unchanged, or so it seems. She remains all appetite, she remains indomitable; because she survives the Cornelius clan survives. Then, in the last pages of the novel, she dies. Her death is not like the play-deaths earlier in the tetralogy. She is dead. She is dead. As the novel closes—for she is dead—Jerry is on his way to tell his pregnant sister the terrible news of the real fact of death.

There is no enclave secure against time. No style has a permanent lock on the shape of the world. No tune can last, certainly not as played on Jerry's dismal guitar. If you ask whether or not it is possible to maintain homeostasis in a decaying world, the answer is that all art constantly aspires towards the condition of Muzak. Entropy rots your heart out. There is a lot of aging going on.

But that's not the final point of the novel, for Jerry Cornelius has, after all, survived the lacerating light-shows of our portion of the century, and in the intensest of venues; and at times his Pierrot heart fills with love that transcends his sustaining self-pity. From his scummy little balcony, he speaks to us at these times. Sf, which is the least urban of genres, likes to tell us how to live in the Wild West, in case the need arises, and loves to show us how to hate Utopian city-states constructed by Utopian city-haters who live in suburbs behind hedges. In *The Cornelius Chronicles* Michael Moorcock has tried to tell us how to stay alive in the places where so many of us truly live. He has tried to tell us how to live here, in the deep cities of this world, in the years of their dying.

—London
February 1977
John Clute

THE CORNELIUS CHRONICLES

The Final Programme

Illustrated by Malcolm Dean

For Alfred Bester

PRELIMINARY DATA

In Cambodia, a country that lies between Vietnam and Thailand on the map, between n and zero on the time chart, is the magic city of Angkor, where once the great Khmer race lived. In the nineteenth century a French explorer rediscovered it in the jungle, and it was subsequently resurrected by French archaeologists. The simple-living inhabitants, descendants of the Khmers, had two theories about the city—that it had been built by a race of giants and that the city had created itself when the world was created. Writing about Angkor in *The Sunday Times* (10/1/65) Maurice Wiggin said: "Did the citizens of Angkor have the future they wanted? Hardly. Yet they seemed adaptable, switching pragmatically from Hinduism to Buddhism, building to last. ('The most impressive ruins in the world.') But the great kings of Khmer are dust."

Built not merely to last but to exist for its age, towering over the huge statues and ziggurats of Angkor, stands the Angkor Hilton. According to the simple-living descendants of the Khmers, it is the chief evidence for the second theory.

On the roof of the Angkor Hilton is a glass conservatory or observatory, not unlike a miniature version of the old Crystal Palace. The greenhouse-like building is the particular property of one of the hotel's regular customers. It contains a bed, a metal locker, a large astronomical telescope, and a marine chronometer dating from the eighteenth century. The chronometer is beautifully made, of steel and brass, and is probably one of the original clocks constructed in 1760 by John Harrison, the first man to make a really accurate marine chronometer. It stands on top of the locker, and below it, hanging from the handle, is a calendar. The year is 196–.

The owner of this equipment, Jerry Cornelius, was not in the observatory at that moment. He was wandering the grassy paths that wound among grey and brown statues or below the leafy branches of big trees where monkeys peered down at him and chattered. Cornelius was dressed incongruously for the place and climate, and even in the West his clothes would have had a slightly old-fashioned look about them; the high-heeled elastic-sided boots, for instance, were not at all in style, nor had they been for several years.

Cornelius was on his way to keep a date.

Serene and carved in ancient rock, the faces of Buddhas and the three aspects of Ishwara looked from terraces and archways; huge statues, bas-reliefs—probably the greatest clutter of deities and devils ever assembled in one place. Beneath an extravagantly bloated representation of Vishnu the Destroyer, one of Ishwara's three aspects, a tiny transistor radio played. It was Cornelius's radio. The tune was "Zoot's Suite" by Zoot Money's Big Roll Band.

Beside the radio, in the green-gold early-afternoon sunshine, a man sat at leisure while mosquitoes buzzed and gibbons chattered, leaping from one half-reconstructed terrace to another. A Buddhist priest passed by, shaven and saffroned, and a group of brown children played among the massive statues of forgotten heroes. It was a pleasant afternoon, with a slight breeze fanning the jungle. A good time for idle speculation, thought Cornelius, sitting down beside the man and shaking hands.

They sat in the fallen stone palm of some minor Hindu divinity and took up the conversation where they had left off earlier.

Jerry Cornelius was a young man, with long, fine black hair that flowed to below his shoulders. He wore a black, double-breasted car coat and dark grey trousers. His tie was of black wool and his white shirt had a high collar. He was slim, with large, dark eyes and large, long-fingered hands. The other man was an Indian, owlish

and pudgy—perpetually smiling, no matter what he said
—in shirt sleeves and cotton trousers.

Jeremiah Cornelius was a European of many parts;
the Indian was a Brahmin physicist of some reputation, Professor Hira. They had met that morning while
touring the city. It had been love at first sight.

The Brahmin physicist patted at the mosquitoes settling
on his arms. "The Gnostics possessed a cosmology very
similar, in many ways, to the Hindu and Buddhist. Interpretations varied, of course, but the figures were very
close."

"What figures exactly?" Jerry asked politely.

"Well, for instance, the mahayuga. Both Hindus and
Gnostics give the figure as 4,320,000 years. That is an
interesting coincidence from any point of view, eh?"

"What about the *kalpa?* I thought that was your word
for a time cycle."

"Ah, no, that is a day and night of Brahma; 8,640
million years."

"As little as that?" said Jerry, without irony.

"The *mahayuga* is divided into four *yugas,* or ages.
The current cycle is nearing its end. The present age is
the last of four."

"And what are they?"

"Oh, let me think. . . . The *Satya Yuga,* the Golden
Age. That accounted for the first four-tenths of the
cycle. Then we had the *Dwapara Yuga,* the second Age.
That took care of another 864,000 years. The Third
Age—the *Treyta davapara Yuga*—can you hear the echoes
of an ancient common language?—lasted for only two-
tenths of the whole cycle. I think that's right, don't
you? How much we rely, these days, on our calculating
machines. The *Kali Yuga,* of course, is the current age.
It began, as I recall, on February 18, 3102 B.C."

"And what is the *Kali Yuga?*"

"The Dark Age, Mr. Cornelius. Ha! Ha!"

"How long is that supposed to last?"

"Just one-tenth of the *mahayuga.*"

"That gives us plenty of time."

"Oh, yes."

"Then at the end of the *manvantara* the cycle repeats itself, does it? The whole of history all over again!"

"Some believe so. Others think that the cycles vary

slightly. It is basically an extension of our convictions concerning reincarnation. The strange thing is that modern physics begins to confirm these figures—in terms of the complete revolution of the galaxy and so on. I must admit that the more I read of the papers published these days, the more confused I become between what I was taught as a Hindu and what I have learned as a physicist. It requires increasing self-discipline to separate them in my mind."

"Why do you bother, Professor?"

"My career, old man, at the University, would suffer if I let mysticism influence logic."

The Brahmin spoke slightly sardonically, and Jerry smiled. "Yet the cosmologies mingle and absorb one another," Jerry said. "There are people in Europe who believe that the *Vedas* describe a prehistoric civilization as advanced, or more so, as our own. That would tie in with your first age, wouldn't it?"

"Some of my friends have wondered about that, too. It is possible, naturally, but not likely. Exquisite parables, Mr. Cornelius, but nothing more. Not the mythical vestiges of a great science, I fear. The embroidered remnants of a great philosophy, perhaps."

"Pleasant embroidery."

"You are kind to think so. Perhaps I should not say so, but it occasionally crosses my mind to wonder why, in all the mystic cosmologies, even in some of the modern so-called parasciences, our own age is always described as the age of chaos and contention. A comment, my logical side argues, on why people turn to mysticism. The past age was always better."

"Childhood is the happiest time of life except when you're a child," said Jerry.

"I understand you. True."

"Whereas your philosophers produced beautiful metaphors that were not true, maybe?"

"You are pushing me too far; but you have studied the *Vedas?* It seems that more Westerners study Sanskrit than we. And we read Einstein."

"So do we."

"You have more time for everything over there, old man. You are at the end of your *manvantara*, eh? We have begun a new one."

"I wonder."

"I do not speak seriously—as a Hindu—but there are shorter cycles within the ages. Several of my more metaphysically inclined acquaintances have predicted that we are at the end of such a cycle."

"But our affairs diminish in significance compared with a span of even 432,000 years."

"That's a Western idea, Mr. Cornelius." Hira smiled. "What is Time? How long is a millisecond or a millenium? If the old Hindus were right, then we have met in Angkor before and shall again—and the date will always be today's, October 31, 196–. Will anything have changed, I wonder, in the next *manvantara?* Will gods walk the earth? Will man be—?"

Jerry Cornelius got up. "Who knows? Let's compare notes then. I'll be seeing you, Professor."

"This time next *manvantara?"*

"If you like."

"Where are you off to now?" The Indian also rose, handing Jerry the little transistor radio.

"Thanks. I'm going to Phnôm Penh Airport and then to London. I want to order a guitar."

Hira followed him through the ruins, climbing over slabs of stone. "You're at the Angkor Hilton, aren't you? Why not stay one more night at the hotel?"

"Well, all right."

That night they lay in bed together, talking and smoking. A heavy mosquito net had been drawn round the bed, but they could see through it, and through the glass beyond, to the still sky.

"It makes you wonder just how close we are to finding the great equation." Hira's voice hummed like an insect through the warm air. Jerry was trying to get to sleep. "The total equation. The final equation. The ultimate equation, drawing all the information together. Will we ever?"

"The climate seems right," said Jerry sleepily.

"In your terms it is time for a new messiah—a messiah of the Age of Science. I suppose that is blasphemy. Has the genius been born yet? Will we recognize him when he comes?"

"That's what they all wonder, don't they?"

"Ah, Mr. Cornelius, what a bewildering, topsy-turvy world this is."

Jerry turned over to his side, his back to the professor. "I'm not so sure," he said. "The world seems to be steering a fairly straight course at last."

"But to where?"

"That, Professor, is the snag."

"She was talking about the final equation, this woman I met in Delhi last year. A passing affair, you know, and I'm glad it was. She gave me some very interesting food for speculation, this Miss Brunner, old man. She seemed to know . . ."

"Bully for her."

"Bully? Yes . . ."

Jerry Cornelius fell asleep.

PHASE 1

1

It was raining.

The house was in South-East London, in Blackheath. It stood back from the main road, looming out of its overgrown garden. The gravel drive was weedy, and the house needed painting. It had originally been painted a light mauve. Through the grimy ground-floor windows Jerry Cornelius could glimpse five people seated in the big front room. It was full of dark furniture and poorly lit, the fire giving more light than the standard lamp in one corner. The faces were all shadowed. On the mantelpiece stood a baroque figurine of Diana holding two candlesticks; there were two candles in each stick.

The garage door slammed, and Jerry made no effort to become any less visible, but the bulky, tweed-coated man didn't notice him as he patted water from his heavy black beard, took off his hat, and opened the door. He wiped his feet and went inside. Jerry had recognized him as Mr. Smiles. Mr. Smiles owned the house.

After a moment Jerry went up to the door and took out his key ring. He found the right key and opened the door. He saw Mr. Smiles enter the front room.

The hallway smelled a little damp, in spite of the radiator burning close to the hat rack; and the walls, each painted a different colour (tangerine, red, black, and blue), were all cold as Jerry leaned on first one and then another.

Jerry was dressed in his usual black car coat, dark trousers, and high heels. His hair was wet and did not fall as softly as normal.

He folded his arms and settled down to wait.

"What's the time? My watch has stopped." Mr. Smiles entered the room, shaking rain off his Robin Hood hat and still patting at his beard. He walked to the fire and stood there, turning the hat round and round to dry it.

The five others said nothing. All seemed introspective, hardly aware of his arrival. Then one of them got up and approached Mr. Smiles. His name was Mr. Lucas. He had the decadent good looks of a Roman patrician. He was forty-five and a successful casino owner. Except for Mr. Smiles (who was forty-nine), he was the oldest.

"Twelve-forty, Mr. Smiles. He's late."

Mr. Smiles concentrated on drying his hat. "I've never known him not to do something he said he'd do, if that's any comfort," he said.

"Oh, it is," said Miss Brunner.

Miss Brunner was sitting nearest to the fire. She was a sharp-faced, attractive young woman with the look of a predator. She sprawled back in her chair with her legs crossed. One foot tapped at the air.

Mr. Smiles turned towards her.

"He'll come, Miss Brunner." He gave her a glare. "He'll come." His tone was self-assuring.

Mr. Lucas glanced at his watch again.

Miss Brunner's foot tapped more quickly. "Why are you so certain, Mr. Smiles?"

"I know him—at least, as well as anyone could. He's reliable, Miss Brunner."

Miss Brunner was a computer programmer of some experience and power. Seated closest to her was Dimitri, her slave, lover, and sometime unwilling pimp. She wore a straight fawn Courrèges suit and matching buttoned boots. He also wore a Courrèges suit of dark blue and brown tweed. Her hair was red and long, curving outward at the ends. It was nice red hair, but not on her. He was the son of Dimitri Oil, rich, with the fresh, ingenuous appearance of a boy. His disguise was complete.

Behind Miss Brunner and Dimitri, in shadow, sat Mr. Crookshank, the entertainers' agent. Mr. Crookshank was very fat and tall. He had a heavy gold signet ring on the third finger of his right hand. It gave him the common touch. He wore a silk Ivy League suit.

In the corner, opposite Mr. Crookshank, nearer the fire, sat dark Mr. Powys, hunched in his perpetual neurotic stoop. Mr. Powys, who lived comfortably off the inheritance left him by his mine-owning great-uncle, sipped a glass of Bell's cream whisky, staring at it as he sipped.

The fire did not heat the room sufficiently. Even Mr. Smiles, who was usually unaffected by cold, rubbed his hands together after he had taken off his coat. Mr. Smiles was a banker, main owner of the Smiles Bank, which had catered to the linen trade since 1832. The bank was not doing well, though Mr. Smiles couldn't complain personally. Mr. Smiles poured himself a large glass of Teacher's whisky and moved back to the fire.

None of them were well acquainted, except with Miss Brunner, who had introduced them all. They all knew Miss Brunner.

She uncrossed her legs and smoothed her skirt, smiling up unpleasantly at the bearded man. "It's unusual to find such confidence these days." She paused and looked round at the others. "I think . . ." She opened her handbag and began picking at its contents.

"What do you think?" Mr. Smiles spoke sharply. "When I first put this deal to you, Miss Brunner, you were uncertain about it. Now you're impatient to get started. What do you think, then, Miss Brunner?"

"I think we shouldn't include him in our plans. Let's get going now, while he's not expecting anything. He could be planning some kind of double cross. We stand to lose too much by hanging about waiting for Cornelius. I don't trust him, Mr. Smiles."

"You don't trust him because you haven't met him and given him the Brunner Test, is that it?" Mr. Lucas kicked at a log sticking from the fire. "We couldn't get into that house without Cornelius's knowledge of those booby traps of his father's. If Cornelius doesn't come, then we'll have to give up the whole idea."

Miss Brunner's sharp teeth showed as she smiled again. "You're getting old and cautious, Mr. Lucas. And Mr. Smiles, by the sound of it, is getting soft as well. As far as I'm concerned, the risk is part of it."

"You silly cow!" Dimitri was often rude to Miss Brunner in public, much as he loved to fear her. Public insults; private punishments. "We're not all in it for the risks; we're in it for what old Cornelius hid in his house. Without Jerry Cornelius, we'll never get it. We need him. That's the truth."

"I'm pleased to hear it." Jerry's voice was sardonic as he entered the room rather theatrically and closed the door behind him.

Miss Brunner looked him over. He was very tall, and that pale face, framed by the hair, resembled the young Swinburne's. His black eyes did not seem at all kindly. He seemed about twenty-seven and had been, so they said, a Jesuit. He had something of a Church intellectual's decadent, ascetic appearance. He had possibilities, she thought.

Jerry dropped his head a trifle as he turned and gave Miss Brunner a slightly amused stare, half-chiding. She crossed her legs and began tapping. He walked gracefully towards Mr. Smiles and shook hands with a certain degree of pleasure.

Mr. Smiles sighed. "I'm glad you could make it, Mr. Cornelius. How soon can we start?"

Jerry shrugged. "As soon as you like. I need a day or so to do a few things."

"Tomorrow?" Miss Brunner's voice was pitched somewhat higher than usual.

"In three days." Cornelius pursed his lips. "Sunday."

Mr. Powys spoke from behind his glass. "Three days is too long, man. The longer we wait, the more chance there is of someone getting to know what we're planning. Don't forget that Simons and Harvey both backed out, and Harvey in particular isn't well known for his tact and diplomacy."

"Don't worry about them," Cornelius said with finality.

"What have you done?" Miss Brunner's voice was still sharp.

"Nothing much. They're taking a cruise on a tramp bound for New York. It'll be a long trip, and they won't mix with the crew."

"How did you get them to go?" Mr. Lucas dropped his eyes as Cornelius turned.

"Well," said Jerry, "there were one or two things they wanted. On condition that they took the trip, I fixed them up."

"What things?" asked Mr. Crookshank with interest. Jerry ignored him.

"What have you to do that's so important?" Miss Brunner inquired.

"I want to visit the house before our trip."

"Why?"

"For my own reasons, Miss Brunner."

Mr. Powys's brooding Welsh face didn't look up. "I'd like to know just why you're helping us, mind you, Mr. Cornelius."

"Would you understand if I told you that it was for revenge?"

"Revenge." Mr. Powys shook his head rapidly. "Oh, yes. We all have these grudges from time to time, don't we?"

"Then it's revenge," Jerry said lightly. "Now, Mr. Smiles has told you my conditions, I think. You must burn the house to the ground when you've got what you wanted, and you must leave my brother Francis and my sister Catherine unharmed. There is also an old servant, John. He must not be hurt in any way."

"The rest of the staff?" Dimitri waved a questioning hand. It was an impolite gesture.

"Do whatever you like. You'll be taking on some help, I understand?"

"About twenty men. Mr. Smiles has arranged them. He says they'll be sufficient." Mr. Lucas glanced at Mr. Smiles, who nodded.

"They should be," Jerry said thoughtfully. "The house is well guarded, but naturally they won't call the police. With our special equipment you ought to be all right. Don't forget to burn the house."

"Mr. Smiles has already reminded us of that, Mr. Cornelius," said Dimitri. "As have you. We will do exactly as you say."

Jerry turned up the wide collar of his coat. "Right. I'll be off."

"Take care, Mr. Cornelius," said Miss Brunner smoothly as he went out.

"Oh, I will, I think," he said.

The six people didn't talk much after Cornelius had left. Only Miss Brunner moved to another chair. She seemed out of sorts.

2

Beat music filled the Cadillac convertible as Jerry Cornelius drove towards the Kent coast—Zoot Money, the Who, the Moody Blues, the Beatles, Manfred Mann, and The Animals. Jerry played only the best on his built-in tape machine.

The volume was turned up to full blast. There were three speakers in various parts of the car, and it was impossible for Jerry to hear even the sound of the engine. In the spring clip near the steering wheel the contents of a glass danced to the thud of the bass. From time to time Cornelius would reach for the glass, take a sip, and fix it back in the clip. Once he put his hand inside the glove compartment and brought it out full of pills. He had not slept for the best part of a week, and the pills no longer stopped him from feeling edgy; but he crammed his mouth with them, just the same, washing them down. A little later he took out a half-bottle of Bell's and refilled the glass.

The road ahead was wet, and rain still beat at the windscreen. The two pairs of wipers swished away in time with the music. Though the heater was on, he felt cold.

Just outside Dover he stopped at a filling station and had the Caddy fed while he rolled himself a thin cigarette out of licorice paper and Old Holborn. He paid the man, lit his cigarette, and rode on in the general direction of the coast, turning off on to a side road and eventually driving down the main street of the harbour village of Southquay, strains of guitars, organs, and high voices drifting in the car's wake. The sea was black under the overcast sky. He drove slowly along the quayside, the car's wheels bumping on cobbles. He switched off the tape machine.

There was a small hotel set back from the road. It was called The Yachtsman. Its sign showed a smiling man in yachting gear. Behind him was a view of the harbour as seen from the hotel. The sign moved a little in the wind. Jerry backed the Cadillac into the hotel's courtyard, left the keys in the ignition, and got out. He put his hands in the high pockets of his coat and stood stretching his legs by the car for a moment, looking over the black water at the moored boats. One of them was his launch, which he'd had converted from a modern lifeboat.

He glanced back at the hotel, noting that no lights had gone on and that no one seemed to be stirring. He crossed to the waterside. A metal ladder led down into the sea. He climbed down a few rungs and then jumped from the ladder to the deck of his launch. Pausing for a moment to get his sea legs, he made straight for the well-kept bridge. He didn't switch on the lights, but by finding the instruments by touch got the motor warming up.

He went out on deck again and cast off.

Soon he was steering his way out of the harbour towards the open sea.

Only the man in the harbourmaster's office saw him leave. Happily for Jerry, the man was quite as corrupt as the six people who had been at the house in Blackheath. He had, as they used to say, his price.

Steering a familiar course, Jerry headed the boat towards the coast of Normandy, where his late father had built his fake Le Corbusier château. It was an ancient building, built well before the Second World War.

Once outside the three-mile limit, Jerry switched on the radio and got the latest station, Radio K-Nine ("The Station With Bite"). There was some funny stuff on; it sounded like a mixutre of Greek and Persian music very badly played. It was probably by one of the new groups the publicity people were still trying in vain to push. They were completely non-musical themselves, so still found it a mystery that one group should be popular and another unpopular, were convinced that a new sound would start things moving for them again. All that was over—for the time being at least, thought Jerry. He changed stations until he got a reasonable one.

The music echoed over the water. Although he was

careful not to show any lights, Jerry could be heard half a mile away; but when he saw the faint outline of the coast ahead, he switched off the radio.

After a while his father's fake Le Corbusier château came in sight, a large six-storey building with that quaint, dated appearance that all the "futuristic" buildings of the twenties and thirties had. This château had a dash of German expressionism in its architecture to boot.

To Jerry the house symbolized the very spirit of transience, and he enjoyed the feeling he got from looking at its silhouette, much as he sometimes enjoyed listening to last year's hits. The house stood, in its corny old way, on the very edge of a cliff that curved steeply above the nearest village, some four miles distant. A searchlight was trained on the house, making it look rather like some grotesque war memorial. Jerry knew the house was staffed by a small private army of German mercenaries, men who were as much part of the past as the house and yet intratemporally reflected something of the spirit of the 1970s.

It was November 196—, however, as Jerry cut the engine and drifted on the current he knew would carry him towards the cliff beneath the house.

The cliff was worse than sheer. It sloped outward about a hundred feet up and was loaded with alarm devices. Not even Wolfe could have taken it. The nature of the cliff was to Jerry Cornelius an advantage, for it hid his boat from the tv scanners in the house. The radar did not sweep low enough to find his launch, but the tv cameras were trained on any likely place where someone might attempt a landing. But Jerry's brother Frank didn't know of the secret entrance.

He moored the boat to the cliff by means of the powerful suction cups he'd brought for the purpose. The cups had metal rings in them, and Jerry tied his mooring lines to the rings. He would be away again before the tide went out.

Part of the cliff was made of plastic. Cornelius tapped lightly on it, waiting a couple of moments as it inched inward and a gaunt, anxious face peered out at him. It was the face of a lugubrious Scot, Jerry's old servant and mentor, John Gnatbeelson.

"Ah, sir!"

The face retreated, leaving the entrance clear.

"Is she all right, John?" Jerry asked as he eased himself into the metal-walled cubicle behind the plastic door. John Gnatbeelson stepped backward and then forward to close the door. He was about six feet four, a gangling man with almost non-existent cheekbones and a wisp of chin whiskers. He wore an old Norfolk jacket and corduroy trousers. His bones seemed barely joined together, and he moved loosely like a badly-controlled puppet.

"She's not dead, sir, I think," Gnatbeelson assured Jerry. "It's fine to see you sir. I hope you've returned for good this time, sir, to kick that brother of yours out of our house." He glared into the middle distance. "He had . . . had . . ." The old man's eyes filled with tears.

"Cheer up, John. What's he been doing now?"

"That's what I don't know, sir. I just haven't been allowed to see Miss Catherine for the past week. *He* says she's sleeping. Sleeping. What kind of sleep lasts for a week, sir?"

"Could be a number of kinds." Jerry spoke calmly enough. "Drugs, I expect."

"God knows he uses enough of them himself, sir. He lives on them. All he ever eats is bars of chocolate."

"Catherine wouldn't use sleepers voluntarily, I shouldn't think."

"She never would, sir."

"Is she still in her old rooms?"

"Yes, sir. But there's a guard on the door."

"Have you prepared for that?"

"I have, but I am worried."

"Of course you are. And you've switched off the master control for this entrance?"

"It seemed unnecessary, sir, but I have done it."

"Better safe than sorry, John."

"I suppose so, aye. But there again, it would only be a matter of time before . . ."

"It's all a matter of time, John. Let's get going. If the control's dead, we won't be able to use the lift."

"No, sir. We must climb."

"Off we go, then."

They left the metal chamber and entered a similar, slightly larger one. John lit the way with his torch. A lift cage became visible, the shaft rising above it. Paralleling the cables and running up one side into the darkness was a metal ladder. John tucked the torch into the waistband of his trousers and stepped back. Jerry reached the ladder and began to climb.

They went up in silence for more than fifty feet until they stood at the top of the shaft. Ahead of them were five entrances to corridors. They took the central entrance. The corridor twisted and turned for a long time. It formed part of a complicated maze and, even though the two men were familiar with it, they sometimes hesitated at various turnings and forks.

Eventually, and with some relief, they entered a white, neon-lighted room, which housed a small control console. The Scotsman went to the panel and clicked a switch. A red light above the panel went off and a green one went on. Dials quivered, and several monitor screens focused on various parts of the route they had just taken. Views of the room at the bottom of the shaft, the shaft itself, the corridors in the maze—now brilliantly lit—came and went on the screens. The equipment operated in silence.

On the door leading out of the room was a fairly large ovoid of a milky greenish colour. John pressed his palm against it. Responding to the palm print, which it recognized, the door slid open. They entered a short tunnel, which led them to an identical door. This John opened in the same way.

Now they stood in a dark library. Through a transparent wall to their right they could see the sea, like black marble streaked with veins of grey and white.

Most of the other three walls were covered with shelves of pink fibre-glass. They were filled mainly with paper-backs. The half-dozen or so books bound in leather and titled in gold stood out incongruously. John shone his light on them and smiled at Jerry, who was embarrassed.

"They're still there, sir. He doesn't often come here; otherwise he might have got rid of them. Not that it would matter that much, for I have another set."

Jerry winced and looked at the books. One of the titles was *Time-Search Through the Declining West* by Jeremiah Cornelius, MAHS; another was called *Toward the Ultimate Paradox,* and beside it was *The Ethical Simulation.* Jerry felt he was right to be embarrassed.

Part of the library wall, naturally enough, was false. It swung back to show a white metal door and a button. Jerry pressed the button and the door opened.

Another lift cage.

John stooped and picked up a small case before they got in and went up. It was one of the few lifts in the house that, as far as they knew, did not register on one of the many control panels located in the château.

On the sixth floor the lift stopped, and John opened the door and looked cautiously out. The landing was empty. They both left the lift, and the door (a wall-length painting reminiscent of Picasso at his latest and tritest) slid back into place.

The room they wanted was in a passage off the main landing. They walked silently to the corner, glanced round, and ducked back again.

They had seen the guard. He had an automatic rifle crooked in his arm. He was a big, fat German with the appearance of a eunuch. He had looked very wakeful—hoping, perhaps, for an opportunity to use his Belgian gun.

Now John opened the case he'd been carrying. He took out a small steel crossbow, very modern and beautifully made, and handed it to Jerry Cornelius. Jerry held it in one hand, waiting for the moment when the guard would look completely away from him. Shortly, the man's attention shifted towards the window at the end of the passage.

Jerry stepped out, aimed the crossbow, and pulled the trigger. But the guard had heard him and jumped. The bolt grazed his neck. There was only one bolt.

As the guard began to bring up his gun, Jerry ran towards him and grabbed the fingers of his right hand, hauling them off the gun. One finger snapped. The guard gurgled and his mouth gaped, showing that he was tongueless. He kicked at Jerry as John came in with a knife, missed his neck, and stabbed him through the left eye. The blade went in for almost its entire six inches, driving downward and coming out just below the left ear. As the German's CNS packed it in, his body was momentarily paralysed.

It softened as Jerry lowered it to the floor; he reached

down and slid the knife out of the German's face, handing it to John who was as limp as the corpse.

"Get away from here, John," Jerry muttered. "If I make it, I'll see you in the cliff room."

As John Gnatbeelson rolled off, Jerry turned the handle of the door. It was of the conventional kind, and the key was in the lock. He turned the key when the door resisted. The door opened. Jerry took the key out of the lock. Inside the room he closed the door quietly and locked it again.

He stood in a woman's bedroom.

The heavy curtains were drawn across the big windows. The place smelled of stale air and misery. He crossed the familiar room and found the bedside lamp, switching it on.

Red light filled the place. A beautiful girl lay in a pale dress on the bed. Her features were delicate and resembled his own. Her black hair was tangled. Her small breasts rose and fell jerkily, and her breathing was shallow. She was not sleeping at all naturally. Jerry looked for hypodermic marks and found them in her upper right arm. Plainly she hadn't used a needle on herself. Frank had done that.

Jerry stroked her bared shoulder. "Catherine." He bent down and kissed her cold, soft lips, caressing her. Anger, self-pity, despair, passion were all there then, flooding up to the surface, and for once he didn't stop them. "Catherine."

She didn't move. Jerry was crying now. His body trembled. He tried to control the trembling and failed. He gripped her hand, and it was like holding hands with a corpse. He tightened his grip, as if hoping pain would wake her. Then he dropped it and stood up.

"The shit!"

He pulled the curtains back from the windows and opened them. The night air blew away the odour in the room.

On her dressing-table there were no cosmetics, only bottles of drugs and several hypodermics.

The labels on the bottles were in Frank's tiny printing. Frank had been experimenting.

Outside, someone shouted and began to bang on the metal door. He stared at it uncomprehendingly for a moment, then crossed to it and shot bolts at top and bottom.

A sharper, colder voice interrupted the yelling.

"What's the trouble? Has someone been boorish enough to enter Miss Catherine's room without her permission?"

It was Frank's voice, and Frank doubtless guessed that his brother Jerry was in the room.

There were confused shouts from the guards, and Frank had to raise his voice. "Whoever you are, you'll suffer for invading my sister's privacy. You can't get out. If she's harmed or disturbed in any way, you won't die for a long time, I promise. But you'll wish you could."

"As corny as ever, Frank!" Jerry shouted back. "I know you know it's me—and I know you're shit-scared. I've more right here than you. I own this house!"

"Then you should have stayed and not turned it over to me and Catherine. I meant what I said, Jerry!"

"Send your Krauts off and come in and talk it over. All I want is Catherine."

"I'm not that naïve. You'll never know what I fed her, Jerry. Only I can wake her up. It's like magic, isn't it? She's well turned on. If I turned her off now, you wouldn't be so keen on hopping into bed with her after ten minutes." Frank laughed. "You'd need a dose of what I've got out here before you'd feel up to it—and then you wouldn't want it any more. You can't have your fix and make it, Jerry!"

Frank was in high spirits. Jerry wondered what he'd found to pep him up. Frank was always after a new synthesis and, as a good chemist, usually came up with a nice new habit every so often. Was it the same stuff as Catherine had in her veins right now? Probably not.

"Throw in your needle and come in with your veins clear, Frank," Jerry shouted back, joining in the spirit of the thing. He took something out of his pocket and waited, but Frank didn't seem willing to rise to this. Bullets began to rattle on the door. They'd soon stop as the ricochets got too much for Frank. They stopped.

Jerry went to the bed and heaved his sister off it. Then he put her down again. It was no good. He wouldn't have a chance of getting out with her. He'd have to leave her and hope that Frank's mind didn't turn to thoughts of mur-

der. It was unlikely. Slow death was the only good kind in
Frank's book.

From the inside pocket of his coat Jerry brought out a
flat box like a snuff box. He opened it. There were
two small filters there. He packed one into each nostril and
clamped his mouth shut, sealing it with some surgical tape
from another pocket.

Then he unbolted the door and slowly turned the key.
He opened the door slightly. Frank stood some distance
away, talking to four of his storm troopers. Frank's skin
was grey, drawn over his near-fleshless skeleton like a lifeless film of plastic. They hadn't yet noticed that the door
was open.

Jerry tossed the grenade into the passage. They saw it
fall. Only Frank recognized the nerve grenade for what it
was, and he dashed off down the passage without stopping
to give the guards the benefit of his knowledge.

Jerry stepped swiftly out of the room and closed the door
tight behind him. The guards tried to aim at him, but the
gas was already working. As they jerked like epileptics and
fell down to bounce about spasmodically on the floor, Jerry
gave them an amused, appreciative glance.

Jerry Cornelius went after Frank Cornelius and saw
Frank pushing the button of the lift that went down to the
library. When Frank saw Jerry, he swore and ran towards
the end of the passage and the stairs. Jerry decided that he
didn't want Frank alive any more, and he drew out his
needle pistol. The air pistol could hold a magazine of a
hundred sliver bullets and was just as effective at short
range as any small-calibre pistol—and far more accurate.
Neither was it messy. Its only drawback was that it had to
be repressured after every volley.

Jerry ran after his brother. Frank was evidently unarmed. He was scuttling down the spiral stairs now. Leaning on the banister, Jerry took aim at Frank's head.

But when he put his arm down, he realized that he'd
caught a sniff of the nerve gas himself, for the arm jumped
twice and he involuntarily pulled the trigger. The needles
went wide, and Frank had left the stairs on the third floor.
He was now out of sight.

Jerry heard voices and noisy feet and knew that Frank
had called in another section of the militia. He had no more

nerve bombs with him. It was time, perhaps, to be leaving.

He ran back down the landing. The lift was waiting for him. Frank might assume that it wasn't working, since he'd had no luck himsef. He got into the lift and went down to the library. It was empty. In the library he paused and hauled his books off the shelf. He opened the door in the window and stepped out on to the balcony. Then he flung the books into the sea, re-entered the library, closed the door carefully, and knocked on the other entrance. It slid back. John was here. He still looked pale.

"What happened, sir?"

"Maybe he'll never guess completely, John, so you might get away with it. He's fazed, I think. Now it's up to you. On Sunday you must somehow get Catherine away from the house and into the lodge on the village side of the grounds. There'll probably be enough confusion and you'll be able to do it easily. Don't make a mistake. I want you both at that lodge. And Sunday starts at about 10 pm, I'd guess."

"Yes, sir—but . . ."

"No time for details, John. Do it. Don't bother to see me out."

Jerry Cornelius went through the control room, and John shut off the equipment again.

Then Jerry was on his way, torch in hand, back to his boat.

Within twenty minutes he was looking up at the house as his launch throbbed towards the English coast. The house was full of light now. It looked as if the residents were having a party.

It was still an hour until dawn. He had a chance of making it back to Southquay before the new man came on watch at the harbourmaster's office.

3

On Sunday morning Miss Brunner and Dimitri left for Blackheath. She locked the door of her Holland Park house and tucked the note for the milkman into an empty bottle on the step. Dimitri had the Lotus 15 ready and running by the time she had put on her gloves and walked daintily down the path.

Later, as they waited for the Knightsbridge traffic to move, Miss Brunner decided that she would drive, and she and Dimitri changed places. They were used to changing places; it held them together in these uncertain times.

"Mr. Cornelius had better be there," Miss Brunner said obsessively as she drove down Sloane Street, which was less crowded than it would have been on a weekday.

Dimitri sat back and smoked. He'd had a tiring night, and he hadn't enjoyed himself as much as usual, particularly since Miss Brunner had insisted on calling him Cornelius the whole time.

Let her work it out, he thought. He was rather jealous of Cornelius, all the same; it had taken him two cups of strong coffee when he'd got up to convice himself that he was not in any way Jerry Cornelius. Miss Brunner, on the other hand, had evidently not been so easily convinced, and she was as bad today as she'd been since Thursday.

Well, with luck it would all be over by Monday, and they could begin the next phase of their plan—a much more sophisticated phase that involved thought and little energetic action.

It was a pity that attacking the house was the only way. He hadn't liked the idea at all when it was first proposed, but since he'd had time to think about it, he was half looking forward to it. The fact disturbed him.

Miss Brunner drove the throbbing Lotus 15 over Westminster Bridge with gusto and entered the maze of streets beyond, then went down the Old Kent Road.

She had decided that she must have Jerry Cornelius, but she knew that this was one situation in which she must act for herself and not rely on Dimitri. A savoury chick, she thought, a nice spicy chick. She began to feel better.

Mr. Crookshank, the entertainers' agent, kissed Little Miss Dazzle goodbye. Little Miss Dazzle was quite naked and did not appear on stage like that, if for no other reason than that the public would see that she was in fact equipped with the daintiest masculine genitals you ever saw.

It was not yet time, Mr. Crookshank had decided, to reveal that particular secret; not while Miss Dazzle was still smoothing up to the number one spot in the Top Ten Girl Chart within three days to a week with every disc she cut. When number five came to be her ceiling, then a few rumours might start. Then perhaps a marriage, he thought, though he'd hate to lose Miss Dazzle.

Mr. Crookshank's Rolls, complete with chauffeur, waited downstairs outside the entrance hall to Miss Dazzle's Bloomsbury flat.

The chauffeur knew the way.

Mr. Crookshank lit a panatella as the car cruised off in the general direction of Blackfriars Bridge. He switched on the radio and, as luck would have it, Little Miss Dazzle's latest hit on Big Beat Call, the non-stop pop programme, was playing. It was a moving song, and Mr. Crookshank was duly moved. The words seemed to be for him.

> *I am a part of you, the heart of you,*
> *I want to start with you,*
> *And know . . .*

The beat changed from 4/4 to 3/4, and the guitars tumbled into the fifth when she sang:

> *Just what it is,*
> *Just what it is,*
> *Just what it is,*
> *I want to know.*

He looked out of the window as the car went down Farringdon Street towards the bridge. The Sunday workers all seemed to be moving in the same direction, as if the voice of the lemming had been heard in the land. In a philosophical mood, Mr. Crookshank decided that it had been heard indeed, through the whole of Europe.

Mr. Powys was running late, for Sunday was normally his day of rest, and he had got up early only after he had realized that he was due in Blackheath that morning. He left his Hyde Park Gate maisonette with a shaving cut on his face and yesterday's shirt on his back. He got his blue Aston Martin from the garage round the corner and put the top down so that the wet breeze would wake him up as he drove.

He switched on the radio for the same purpose, though he was too late to hear Little Miss Dazzle's "Just What It Is." Instead he came in on the middle of Tall Tom's Tailmen singing "Suckers Deserve It." If Mr. Powys had a destiny, then Tall Tom's Tailmen were singing its tune—not that it occurred to Mr. Powys, but then he was like that. The only thing the song did for him at that moment was to make him feel hungry, though he didn't know why. His thoughts turned to Miss Brunner and Dimitri, both of whom he knew intimately. In fact, it was extremely unlikely that he would have agreed to this venture if he hadn't known them so well.

Miss Brunner and Dimitri had a persuasive manner. Except in moments of extreme sobriety, they were usually mingled together in his mind, Miss Brunner and Dimitri.

Mr. Powys was a baffled, unhappy man.

He drove through the park under the impression that the air was clearer there, turned left, and entered Knightsbridge, London's fabulous thieves' quarter, where every shop doorway (or, to be more accurate, every shop) held a thief of some description. Sloane Street was also his choice, but he went over Battersea Bridge and realized only after he'd reached Clapham Common that he'd made a mistake and was going to be later than ever.

By the time all the cars had crossed the river, Mr. Smiles was having breakfast in his Blackheath house and wondering how he'd got into this in the first place. His knowledge of the information (probably on microfilm) to be found in old Cornelius's house had come from a friend of Frank Cornelius, a successful drug importer who supplied Frank with the rarer chemicals for his experiments. In a high moment Frank had let something slip, and Mr. Harvey, the importer, had later let the same thing slip to Mr. Smiles, also in a high moment.

Only Mr. Smiles had fully realized the significance of the information, if it was correct, for he knew the City better than it knew him. He had told Miss Brunner, and Miss Brunner had organized it from there.

Mr. Smiles had then got in touch with Jerry Cornelius, whom he hadn't seen for some time—not, in fact, since the day he and Jerry had robbed the City United Bank of some two million pounds and, with a million each, split up. The investigation by the police had been very half-hearted, as if they were concentrating on the important crimes of the day, realizing that the inflating pound was no longer worth attempting to protect.

Mr. Smiles could read the signs, for he was something of a visionary. He could see that the entire Western European economy, including Sweden and Switzerland, was soon to collapse. The information Mr. Harvey had kindly passed on to him would probably hasten the collapse, but it would, if used properly, put Mr. Smiles and his colleagues on top. They would hold pretty well nearly all the power there was to hold when anarchy at last set in.

Mr. Smiles toyed with a fried egg, wondering why the yolks always broke these days.

In his permanently-booked room in The Yachtsman, Jerry Cornelius had woken up at seven o'clock that morning and dressed himself in a lemon shirt with small ebony cuff-links, a wide black cravat, dark green waistcoat and matching hipster pants, black socks and black hand-made boots. He had washed his fine hair, and now he brushed it carefully until it shone.

Then he brushed one of his double-breasted black car coats and put it on.

He pulled on black calf gloves and was ready to face the world as soon as he slipped on his dark glasses.

From the bed, he picked up what appeared to be a dark leather toilet case. He snapped it open to check that his needle gun was pressured. He put the gun back and closed the case.

Holding the case in his left hand, he went downstairs; nodded to the proprietor, who nodded back; and got into the newly-polished Cadillac.

He sat in the car for a moment, looking out over the grey sea.

There was still a quarter of a glass of Bell's in the clip on the dashboard. He took it out, wound down the window, and threw the glass to the ground. He reached into the glove compartment and found a wrapped, fresh glass, fixed it in the clip, and filled it half full from his bottle. Then he started the engine, turned the car around, and drove off, switching on the tape machine as soon as he was on Southquay's main street.

John, George, Paul, and Ringo serenaded him with the old standard "Baby's in Black" from all three speakers.

"Oh dear what can I do, baby's in black and I'm feeling blue . . ."

They were still his favourite group.

"She thinks of him and so she dresses in black, and though he'll never come back, she's dressed in black."

Halfway to Blackheath he stopped off at a newsagent's shop and bought himself two Mars Bars, two cups of strong black coffee, and a pound or two of newsprint labelled NEWS SECTION, BUSINESS SECTION, LEISURE SECTION, ARTS SECTION, POP SECTION, CAR SECTION, COMIC SUPPLEMENT, COLOUR SUPPLEMENT, NOVEL SUPPLEMENT and HOLIDAY ADVERTISING SUPPLEMENT. The News Section was a single sheet and the news was brief, to the point, uninterpreted. Jerry didn't read it. In fact, he didn't read anything except part of the Comic Supplement. There was plenty to look at, though. Communications were taking the form of pictures more and more these days. Jerry was well catered for.

He ate his sweets, drank his coffee, and folded up his sections and left them on the table, less by way of a tip. Then he went back to his car to continue the journey to Blackheath.

He found that he didn't need to eat much, because he could live off other people's energy just as well, though it was exhausting for them, of course. He didn't keep many acquaintances long, and Catherine was the only person off whom he hadn't fed. Indeed, it had been his delight to feed *her* with some of his stolen vitality when she was feeling low. She hadn't liked it much, but she'd need it when he eventually got her away from that house and back to normal again, if he could ever get her back to normal.

He would certainly kill Frank when they raided the house. Frank's final needle would come from Jerry's gun. It would give him his final kick—the one he kept looking for.

Only Mr. Lucas hadn't arrived by two o'clock, and they gave him up, feeling annoyed with him—which wasn't quite fair, for Mr. Lucas had been stabbed to death in Islington the previous evening and robbed of the best part of his casino's takings by a much-embittered all-time loser who, by the following Monday, would fall downstairs and kill himself while taking his money to the bank, such being the fate of all-time losers.

Miss Brunner and Dimitri, Mr. Smiles, Mr. Crook-shank, and Mr. Powys were all looking at a map, which Mr. Smiles had laid out on the table. Jerry Cornelius stood by the window smoking a thin cigarette and half-listening to them as they talked over the details of the expedition.

Mr. Smiles pointed one of his strong fingers at a cross that had been drawn roughly in the middle of the English Channel between Dover and Normandy. "That's where the boat will be waiting. The men were all hired by me in Tangier. They answered an advertisement. At first they thought they were going to shoot Africans, but I managed to talk them round. They consist mainly of white South Africans, Belgians, and French. There are a couple of British ex-officers. I put them in charge, of course. Apart from the South Africans, they got keener when I told them that they'd be fighting mainly Germans. Amazing how some people manage to hang on, isn't it?"

"Isn't it?" Mr. Powys was, as ever, a trifle uncertain. "They'll have been waiting for us, will they?"

"We thought that was best, you know. Actually, coast-guard patrols aren't seen about as often as they were. We won't need to worry too much."

Miss Brunner pointed at the village near the Cornelius mansion. "What about this?"

"An advance force of five men will isolate the village communications-wise. They'll be able to see something of what will be going on, of course, but we don't anticipate any bother from them. All outgoing radio and telephone calls will be scrambled."

Miss Brunner looked up at Jerry Cornelius. "Do you expect any trouble before we get into this cliff-opening place, Mr. Cornelius?"

Jerry nodded.

"Boats about as big as your hoverlaunch, plus my own, are almost bound to be spotted. They've got radar. My guess is that my brother will still rely mainly on the traps in the maze and so on. But the house will have some other surprises. As I told you, we'll have to get to the main control room as soon as we can. That's in the centre of the house. Once there, we can shut it down, and it will be straight fighting until we have Frank. I estimate that if you keep him off his junk for a couple of hours, he'll tell you exactly where the microfilm is."

Miss Brunner said quietly, "So we must preserve Frank at all costs."

"Until you have your information, yes. Then I'll deal with him."

"You *do* sound vengeful, Mr. Cornelius." Miss Brunner smiled at him. Jerry shrugged and turned to the window again.

"There seems little else to discuss." Mr. Smiles offered them all his cigarettes. "We have an hour or two to kill."

"Nearly three hours to kill, if we're leaving at five," said Miss Brunner.

"Is it three hours?" Mr. Powys glanced about.

"Three hours," said Mr. Crookshank, nodding and looking at his watch. "Almost."

"What's the exact time?" Mr. Smiles asked. "My watch seems to have stopped."

"I see that lire are thirty cents a million." Mr. Crookshank lit Miss Brunner's cigarette with a large gold gas lighter.

"They should never have backed out of the Common Market," Miss Brunner said pitilessly.

"What else could they do?"

"The mark's still strong," said Mr. Powys.

"Ah, the Russo-American mark. They can't go on supporting it at this rate." Mr. Smiles smiled a satisfied smile. "No, indeed."

"I'm still not sure that we were in the right." Mr. Powys sounded as if he were still not sure of anything. He glanced inquiringly towards the Scotch on the sideboard. Mr. Smiles waved a hostly hand towards it. Mr. Powys got up and poured himself a stiff one. "Refusing to pay back all those European loans, I mean. I think."

"It wasn't exactly a refusal," Dimitri reminded him. "You just asked for an indefinite time limit. Britain certainly is the black sheep of the family today, isn't she?"

"It can't be helped, and if we're lucky tonight, it will all be to our advantage in the long run." Mr. Smiles rubbed his beard and walked to the sideboard. "Would anyone like a drink?"

"Yes, please," said Mr. Powys.

The rest accepted, too, except for Jerry, who continued to look out of the window.

"Mr. Cornelius?"

"What?" Dimitri glanced up. "Sorry." Mr. Powys gave him a baffled look. He held a glass of Scotch in each hand. Miss Brunner glared at Dimitri.

"I'll have a small one." Jerry appeared not to have noticed Dimitri's mistake, though, as he took the glass from Mr. Smiles, he grinned broadly for a moment.

"Oh, we are living in an odd kind of limbo, aren't we?" Ever since the weary lemming image had occured to him, Mr. Crookshank had retained his philosophical mood. "Society hovers on the point of collapse, eh? Chaos threatens!"

Mr. Powys had begun trying to pour one full glass of Scotch into the other. Whisky ran on to the carpet.

Cornelius felt that Mr. Powys was overdoing it a bit. He smiled a little as he sat down on the arm of Miss Brunner's chair. Miss Brunner shifted in the chair, trying to face him and failing.

"Maybe the West has got to the quasar stage—you know, 3C286 or whatever it is." Miss Brunner spoke rapidly, half angrily, leaning away from Jerry Cornelius.

"What's that?" Mr. Powys sucked his fingers.

"Yes, what is it?" Mr. Crookshank seemed to dismiss Mr. Powys's question as he asked his identical one.

"Quasars are stellar objects," Jerry said, "so massive that they've reached the stage of gravitational collapse."

"What's that got to do with the West?" Mr. Smiles asked. "Astronomy?"

"The more massive, in terms of population, an area becomes, the more mass it attracts, until the state of gravitational collapse is reached," Miss Brunner explained.

"Entropy, I think, Mr. Crookshank, rather than chaos," Jerry said kindly.

Mr. Crookshank smiled and shook his head. "You're going a bit beyond me, Mr. Cornelius." He looked around at the others. "Beyond all of us, I should say."

"Not beyond me." Miss Brunner spoke firmly.

"The sciences are becoming curiously interdependent, aren't they, Mr. Cornelius?" said Dimitri, whose statement seemed to echo one he'd picked up earlier. "History, physics, geography, psychology, anthropology, ontology. A Hindu I met—"

"I'd love to do a programme," said Miss Brunner.

"I don't think there's a computer for the job," Jerry said.

"I intend to do a programme," she said, as if she'd made up her mind on the spot.

"You'd have to include the arts, too," he said. "Not to mention philosophy. It could be just a matter of time, come to think of it, before all the data crystallized into something interesting."

"Of Time?"

"That, too."

Miss Brunner smiled up at Jerry. "We have something in common. I hadn't quite realized what."

"Oh, only our ambivalence," Jerry grinned again.

"You're in a good mood," said Mr. Powys suddenly to Jerry.

"I've got something to do," Jerry answered, but Mr. Powys was staring at his Scotch again.

Miss Brunner felt extremely satisfied. She returned to the subject. "I'd like more information. You know that this computer could be built. And what would it, in turn, create? Where are we heading?"

"Towards permanent flux perhaps, if you'll forgive the paradox. Not many would have the intelligence to survive. When Europe's finally divvied up between the Russians and Americans—not in my lifetime, I hope—what expertise the survivors will have! Won't they be valuable to their new masters, eh? You should remember that, Miss Brunner, if ever events look like exceeding their present speed." Jerry tapped her playfully on the shoulder.

She reached up to touch his hand, but it had gone. He got up.

"Can Time exceed c?" She laughed. "I'm sliding off, Mr. Cornelius. But we must take up this conversation again."

"Now or never," he said. "Tomorrow I'll be away, and we shan't meet again."

"You're very certain."

"I have to be." He no longer grinned as he went back to the window, remembering Catherine and what he must do to Frank.

Behind him, the conversation continued.

Miss Brunner was in a savage, exhilarated mood now.

"And what's your philosophy for the coming Light Age, Mr. Powys? You know, the c age. That's a better term, on second thoughts."

"Second thoughts?" Mr. Powys could summon nothing else. He was now on his fifth thought, trying to equate it with his fourth and, as he remembered it, his third.

Mr. Powys was busily disintegrating.

Mr. Smiles kindly filled his glass up, there being some good in all of us.

4

Jerry steered the boat towards the light that had suddenly flashed out from a point near his port. Illuminated by the greenish glow from his indicator panel, his face looked stranger than ever to the others who waited on the deck outside his cabin.

Miss Brunner, most prone to that sort of thing, reflected that the conflicting time streams of the second half of the twentieth century were apparently mirrored in him, and it seemed that the mind behind cried forward while the mind in front cried back.

What had Cornelius been getting at? Time disintegrating? She'd never read one of his books, but she'd heard of them. Didn't some of them talk about cyclical time, like Dunne? The ultimate point in the past would therefore be the ultimate point in the future. But what if something interrupted the cycle? An historical event, perhaps, of such importance that the whole pattern was changed. The nature of time, assuming that it was cyclical, would be disrupted. The circle broken, what might happen? It would certainly make Spengler look silly, she thought, amused.

If she could get her computer built and start her other project as well, she might be the person who could save something from the wreckage. She could consolidate everything left into one big programme—the final programme, she thought. Idea and reality, brought together, unified. The attempt had never succeeded in the past; but now she might have the opportunity to do it, for the time seemed ripe. She would need more power and more money, but with a bit of luck and intelligent exploitation of a shaky world situation she could get both.

38

Jerry was bringing the boat up alongside the bigger hoverlaunch. He watched as his passengers boarded the vessel, but he didn't join them, preferring to have his own boat waiting for him when the expedition was over.

The hoverlaunch whispered away towards Normandy, and he began to follow behind it, positioning his boat slightly to one side to avoid the main disturbance of the launch's wake. The launch belonged to Mr. Smiles, who, like Jerry, had invested his money in tangibles while it had still had some value.

Bit by bit the Normandy coastline became visible. Jerry cut his engine, and the hoverlaunch followed suit. Jerry went out on deck as a line was shot to him from the hoverlaunch. He made it fast. It was a cold night.

The hoverlaunch started up again, with Jerry in tow. It headed towards the cliff where the fake Le Corbusier château stood, a silhouette in the moonlight.

There was a slight chance that the bigger boat wouldn't register on the mansion's radar. Jerry's boat didn't, but it was much lower in the water. The hoverlaunch's central control bridge, a squat tube rising above the passenger disc and power section, was what might just blip on the radar.

Old Cornelius's microfilms were buried deep within the château, in a strongroom that would not resist a high-explosive blast but would, if attacked in this manner, automatically destroy the film.

The information the intrepid band required was probably there, but the only sure-fire means of getting the film was to open the strongroom in the conventional way, and that was why Frank, who knew the various codes and techniques necessary, had to be preserved and questioned and, with luck, made to open the strongroom himself.

The whole house was designed around the strongroom. It had been built to protect the microfilms. Very little in the house was what it seemed to be. It was armed with strange weapons.

As he looked up at it, Jerry thought how strongly the house resembled his father's tricky skull.

Virtually every room, every passage, every alcove had booby traps, which was why Jerry was so valuable to the expedition. He didn't know the strongroom combination, but he knew the rest of the house well, having been brought up there.

If he hadn't gone off after that night when his father had found him with Catherine, he would have inherited the microfilms as his birthright, since he was the elder son, but Frank had got that honour.

The wind was up. It whistled through the trees, groaned among the towers of the château. The clouds ripped across the sky to reveal the moon.

The hoverlaunch rocked.

From the house, searchlights came on.

The searchlights were focused mainly on the house itself, lighting it up like some historic monument—which, indeed, it was.

The lights blinked off, and the another one came on, a powerful beam, moving across the water. It struck the hoverlaunch.

The other lights came on, concentrated on the house, particularly the roof.

Jerry shouted, "Keep your eyes off the roof! Don't look at the towers! Remember what I told you!"

Water splashed against the sides of the hoverlaunch as they waited.

From the roof three circular towers had risen. They began to rotate in the blue beam of a searchlight. The colour changed to red, then yellow, then lilac. The towers rotated slowly at first. They looked like big round machine-gun bunkers, with slots located at intervals down their length. Through these oblong slots shone bright lights, geometric shapes in garish primary colours, fizzing like neon. The towers whirled faster. It was almost impossible to take the eye away.

Jerry Cornelius knew what the giant towers were. Michelson's Stroboscope Type 8. The eye was trapped by them and so were the limbs, the will. Pseudo-epilepsy was only one result of watching them for too long.

The wind and the hissing towers produced a high-pitched, ululating whine. Round and round, faster and faster, whirled the towers, with bright metal colours replacing the primaries—silver, bronze, gold, copper, steel.

First the eye and then the mind, thought Jerry.

He saw that one of the mercenaries on the boat stood

transfixed; glazed, unblinking eyes staring up at the huge stroboscopes. His limbs were stiff.

A searchlight found him, and, from two concrete emplacements on the cliff, machine-guns smacked a couple of dozen rounds into him.

His bloody body was thrown violently backward; it softened and collapsed. Jerry was still yelling at him to take his eyes away from the stroboscopes.

Jerry stopped yelling. He hadn't expected such a display of violence so soon. Evidently Frank wasn't taking chances. He crouched behind the cabin as the boats drifted towards the cliffs. The overhang offered them some shelter.

Within a minute the towers were no longer visible. They had been designed primarily for use against land attack.

As his boat bumped against the hoverlaunch, Jerry glanced at the body of the dead mercenary. It represented the start of an interesting anarchic process.

He leaned over and got a grip on a handrail, hauling himself aboard the hoverlaunch. He took out his needle gun and held it in his gloved right hand.

"Welcome aboard, Mr. Cornelius," said Miss Brunner, her legs astraddle, her hair blowing back from her head.

Jerry walked forward as the hoverlaunch knocked itself against the cliff. Behind him a mercenary jumped to the deck of his boat and made it fast.

Another mercenary—darkly tanned, with oiled, wavy hair—came forward holding a suction mine intended to destroy the door. The man steadied himself and bent to attach it to the spot Jerry indicated. They backed up the deck as the mine exploded, bits of wreckage pattering down.

The door was open.

Jerry led the way forward, put his foot on the handrail, and pushed himself into the opening. He began to walk down the short passage.

The main force of mercenaries, dressed in the lightweight khaki they were never without, followed him with their machine-guns ready. Behind them, not so swiftly, stepped Mr. Smiles, Miss Brunner and Dimitri, Mr. Crookshank, and Mr. Powys. They all carried their big machine pistols awkwardly.

An explosion rocked the cliff. They looked back as fire spread over the water.

"Let's hope they don't spend too much time on the boats," Mr. Smiles said, speaking adenoidally because his nostrils were stuffed with the filters that Jerry had issued to them all.

Jerry reached the inner room and pointed at two places on the walls. The leading mercenary raised his gun and shot out the two cameras. From the control chamber above, the lights were switched off by way of retaliation.

"Frank's found this entrance, anyway," Jerry said. It was really only what he'd expected.

The mercenaries now unhooked heavy helmets from their belts and fitted them on their heads. The helmets were equipped with miners' lamps. One mercenary had a long coil of nylon rope over his shoulder.

"Perhaps the lift's still working?" Mr. Powys suggested as Jerry set foot on the ladder.

"Probably." Jerry began to climb. "But we'd look great if they switched the power off when we were half-way up."

They all started to climb. Miss Brunner went last. As she put her foot on the first rung, she said thoughtfully, "Silly. They forgot to electrify the ladder."

Jerry heard some sounds above. He looked up as a light went on in the shaft, making him blink. A hard-faced German was looking down at him, sighting along his automatic rifle.

Jerry snapped up his needle gun and shot the German full of steel. He paused, arm curled around the ladder, to repressure the gun, shouting, "Look out!" as the guard rolled off the edge and fell down the shaft.

As the guard's body thumped to the bottom, Jerry reached the top, his needle gun ready, but no one was there. Frank had spared only one guard here, being sure that the maze would serve him best.

Everyone else scrambled up, and they all stood at the entrance to the maze while the soldier with the rope paid it out to them. They roped up.

Knotting her bit of the rope around her waist, Miss Brunner looked uncomfortable.

"I don't like this sort of thing," she said.

Jerry ignored her, leading them into the maze.

"Keep your mouths tightly shut," he reminded them. "And whatever happens, keep your attention on following me."

Their helmet lights lit the way as Jerry walked cautiously ahead, pointing out television cameras to the mercenaries, who shot them as they passed.

Then the first wave of gas hissed into the passageways. It was LSD gas, refined by old Cornelius. The nose filters, sophisticated by his son, could cope with it if they got through it fast enough. Old Cornelius had invented or modified all the hallucinatory protective devices in the house. Frank had added the guns and guards.

Hallucinogenic gases had been old Cornelius's speciality, though an offshoot had been his hallucinomats such as the rooftop stroboscopic towers.

Old Cornelius had exhausted and killed himself searching for the ultimate hallucinogenic device ("total dissociation in under one second" had been his aim, his war cry), just as his son Frank was destroying himself fairly slowly by looking for the ultimate kick in the veins.

Someone began to giggle, and Jerry looked back.

Mr. Powys had his arms high and was shaking all over, just as if someone were tickling his armpits. Every so often he would stretch out his arms in front of him and make pushing motions at wisps of gas.

Then he began to skip about.

Mouths thin and firm now that they had seen the example of Mr. Powys, Mr. Smiles and Mr. Crookshank stepped in, striving to hold him still.

Jerry signed for the expedition to stop, unhooked the rope from his belt, and went back to hit Mr. Powys on the back of the neck with his pistol barrel.

Mr. Powys relaxed, and Mr. Smiles and Mr. Crookshank hefted him up between them.

In silence they walked on through the faintly yellowish gas that clouded the air of the maze. Those who had absorbed a little of it thought they saw shapes in the writhing stuff: malevolent faces, grotesque figures, beautiful designs. Everyone was sweating, particularly Mr. Smiles and Mr. Crookshank, who carried Mr. Powys who would soon have breathed enough LSD to kill him.

At a junction Jerry hestitated, his judgment slightly impaired. Then he was off again, taking the gang down the tunnel that branched off to the right.

They moved on, the silence sometimes interrupted by the sound of a rifle shooting out a camera.

It was a little ironic, he thought, that his father should have become so obsessed with the problem of the increasing incidence of neurotic disorders in the world that he himself had gone round the bend towards the end.

Now Jerry rounded the last bend and the door of the control chamber was ahead of him. He was quite surprised that so far there had been only two casualties and only one of those actually dead.

About fifteen yards before they got to the door Jerry gave a signal, and a bazooka was passed down the line to him. Leaving Jerry and his loader, the remainder of the party retreated down the passage a short way and stood in a disorderly knot waiting.

Jerry got the bazooka comfortably on to his shoulder and pulled the trigger. The rocket bomb whooshed straight through the door and exploded in the control room itself.

A booted foot came sailing out and hit Jerry in the face. He kicked it to one side, his mouth still tightly shut, and waved the others on.

The explosion had wrecked the control panel, but the opposite door was still intact. Since it would open only to the thermal code of someone it knew, they could either blast through into the library or wait for someone to blast through to them. Jerry knew that armed men would definitely be waiting in the library.

The other members of the expedition were unhooking their ropes and dropping them to the floor. It was unlikely they would be leaving by the same route, and therefore they wouldn't need the ropes again. Jerry pondered the problem as Miss Brunner squeezed into the room and studied the wreckage of the panel.

Her big eyes looked up at him quizzically. "A nice little board; and this is only a minor control panel?"

"Yes. There's a large roomful in the cellars—the main console. That's got to be our objective, as I told you."

"You did. What now?"

Jerry smoothed the hair at the side of his face. "There's an alternative to waiting for them. We could try the bazooka. But there's another door behind this one, and I doubt if a rocket would go through them both. If it didn't, we'd get the worst of the explosion. They must be waiting there—probably with a grenade thrower or a big Bren or something. It's stalemate for the moment."

"You should have anticipated this." Miss Brunner frowned.

"I know."

"Why didn't you?"

"I didn't think of it," Jerry said with a sigh.

"Someone else should have." She turned to look accusingly at the others.

Dimitri was kneeling beside Mr. Powys, trying to revive him.

"Not for Mr. Powys," said Mr. Crookshank, unable to restrain a slight smile. "The LSD always gets you in the end, eh?" "You too," he said. "Looks as if poor old Mr. Powys has had it."

"I thought it had been too easy," said Mr. Smiles.

"I've got it." Jerry looked up. Over the door was a metal panel, secured by wing nuts. He pointed to it. "Air conditioning. A grenade thrower, a single neurade and a good eye should do the trick if the grille at the other end isn't closed."

He put his hand on the arm of a big South African. "You'll do. I'll stand on your shoulders. Hang on to my legs when the recoil comes. Who's got a grenade attachment?"

One of the Belgians handed him the attachment. He fitted it to the automatic rifle and detached the ammunition clip. The Belgian handed him a different clip. He fitted this to the rifle, too. Then he took a neurade out of his pocket and popped it into the thrower's basket.

"Someone give me a hand up," he said. One of the British mercenaries helped him climb on to the South African's broad shoulders. He pushed back the metal panel and began to bash in the wire grille with the gun butt. He could see down the pipe to where the lights of the library shone. He heard muted voices.

Shoving the rifle into the pipe, he put it on his shoulder. The space between the fan blades was just big enough. Now if the neurade wasn't deflected by the grille at the other end, which wasn't likely, they'd have a chance of getting the guards there in silence and have time to blast open the doors with small charges of explosive before anyone realized that the detachment in the library was out of action.

He squeezed the trigger. The neurade shot down the pipe, was missed by the fan blades, and burst through the grille.

He smiled as voices at the other end shouted in surprise. He heard dull thumps and knew that the neurade had exploded. Then he started to lose his footing on the South African; half-jumped, half-fell to the ground; and handed the Belgian's gun back to him.

"Okay, let's get these doors open. Hurry. And keep your mouths closed again."

The charges burst both locks, and they were through. On the floor of the library beside an overturned machine-gun three Germans jerked limply, mouths in rictus grins, eyes full of tears, muscles and limbs contorted as the gas worked on their nerves. It seemed a mercy to bayonet them; so they did.

They tumbled out of the library and into the ground-floor hall as the ceiling suddenly rose and the walls widened out, light glaring like magnesium, blinding them for a moment. Jerry fished goggles from his pocket and put them on, noticing that the others were doing the same.

They could now see shapes flickering around them, like a colour-film negative. Traceries of deep red and luminous blue veined the walls.

Then the lights went out and they were in pitch blackness.

One wall became transparent all at once. Behind it a huge black-and-white disc began to whirl, and a rhythmic boom swam up the decibel scale, almost to pain level. It seemed that the enlarged room swayed like a ship as they staggered after Jerry, who was none too steady on his pins himself, heading straight for the disc.

Jerry grabbed a gun from one of the dazed mesmerized mercenaries, switched it to full automatic, and fired an entire magazine into the wall. Plastic cracked, but the disc continued to whirl. As he turned to take another gun, Jerry saw that all of them were now transfixed by the disc.

Another burst and the plastic shattered. The bullets struck the disc, and it began to slow down.

Behind them the far wall slid upwards, and half a dozen of Frank's guards stood there.

Jerry ignored them as he kicked a larger hole in the wall and smashed at the big disc with his gun butt until it crumpled.

"Throw down your arms!" ordered the chief guard.

Jerry flung himself through the hole. Aiming between Miss Brunner and Dimitri, who were beginning to blink back into wakefulness, he killed the chief guard.

The shot seemed to be enough to bring the others round quickly. Almost before Jerry knew it Miss Brunner had jumped through the hole, her high heels catching him on his buttocks.

Firing broke out generally, but Mr. Smiles, Dimitri and Mr. Crookshank all got through safely, although several of the mercenaries, including the big South African died.

They fought back until they had killed all Frank's guards. It was fairly easy from their cover.

They were in a small room, now bathed in a soft red light, a sound like the swish of the sea in their ears.

Something dropped from the ceiling and bounced on the floor until its sides opened up.

"Nerve bomb!" Jerry yelled. "Cover your mouths!"

He knew there was an exit somewhere to the right of the smashed disc. He edged in that direction and found it, using his gun to pry it open. If they didn't get out shortly, their nose filters wouldn't help them.

He went through the doorway, and they followed him.

The next room was yellow, full of soothing murmurs. A remote-control camera panned around close to the roof. One of the mercenaries shot it. A normal door, unlocked, opened on to a flight of stairs leading upward.

There wasn't another door. They ascended the stairs. At the top three men waited for them.

"Frank's spreading his guards thin," said Jerry.

Their first burst missed him but shot the head of one of the Belgians to bits. Feeling panicky, Jerry hugged the wall, raising his needle gun and shooting a guard in the throat.

Behind him the leading mercenaries opened up. One guard fell at once, blood spurting from his stomach. The second fired down the stairwell and got two more mercenaries, including one of the Britons.

Jerry, rapidly repressuring his gun, shot him, too.

On the first-floor landing everything was silent, and Jerry relaxed his pursed lips. The mercenaries, with the civilians behind them, moved up on to the landing and looked at him questioningly.

"My brother's almost certainly in the main control room," Jerry said. "That's two floors down now, and there'll be extra guards turning up at any moment." Jerry pointed at a television camera near the ceiling. "Don't shoot it. He isn't using it at the moment for some reason, and if we put it out he'll know we're here."

"He must have guessed, surely," said Miss Brunner.

"You'd think so. Also, he would have sent some reinforcements here by now. He could have a trap waiting somewhere for us—wants us to relax a little. This landing's equipped with a Schizomat in a panel in that wall. My father's crowning achievment, he always thought."

"And Frank isn't using it." Miss Brunner tidied her long red hair.

"I had to leave Mr. Powys behind, I'm afraid." Dimitri leaned on a wall. "This house certainly is full of colourful surprises, Mr. Cornelius."

"He'll be dead by now," said Jerry.

"What could your brother be planning?" Miss Brunner asked.

"Something funny. He's got a rich sense of humour. He may have cooked up a new ploy, but it's not like Frank to be subtle at a time like this. It's just possible that he's run away."

"And all our efforts have been wasted," she said sourly. "I hope not."

"Oh, so do I, Miss Brunner."

He walked along the landing, with them following him. Jerry led them through the quiet house until they reached a point where they looked down, through what was evidently a two-way mirror, into the partitioned hall where the nerve bomb had exploded. Stairs led down alongside the far wall.

"These stairs normally lead to the basement," Jerry told them. "We might as well go back the way we came now. There's no obvious danger as far as I can see."

They began to descend.

"There are steel gates farther down," he said. "They can shut off any part of the stairs. Remember what I told you: Use your guns to wedge them, stop them fully closing."

"No rifle's going to stop steel," Mr. Crookshank said doubtfully.

"True—but the door mechanism's delicate. It'll work."

They passed openings in the walls where the steel gates were housed, but none of them closed.

They reached the first floor and entered a curiously narrow passage, obviously created by the widening of the hall walls earlier. At the far end Mr. Powys suddenly appeared and came staggering towards them.

"He should be dead!" exclaimed Mr. Smiles, offended.

"It's haunted! It's haunted!" moaned Mr. Powys.

Jerry couldn't work out how he'd got there. Neither could he guess how Mr. Powys had survived the LSD, not to mention everything else.

"It's haunted! It's haunted!" Mr. Powys repeated.

Jerry grabbed him. "Mr. Powys! Pull yourself together."

Mr. Powys gave Jerry an intelligent look that was suddenly sardonic. He raised his thick eyebrows. "Too late for that, I'm afraid, Mr. Cornelius. This house—it's like a giant head. Do you know what I mean? Or is it *my* skull? If it is, what am I?"

"I know whose bloody head this house is," Jerry said, shaking him! "I know, you bastard."

"Mine."

"No!"

"What's the matter, Mr. Powys?" Dimitri slid up. "Can I help?"

"It's haunted. It's my mind haunted by me, I think. That can't really be right, Dimitri. You are Dimitri. I'd always thought . . . It must be my mind haunting me. That must be it. Oh, dear!" He rocked his poor head in his hands.

Dimitri looked at Jerry Cornelius. "What do we do with him?"

"He needs a converter." Jerry Cornelius smiled at Mr. Powys, raised his gun, and shot him in the eye.

The party stopped.

5

"It was for the best," Jerry said. "His brain was already badly damaged, and we couldn't have him running around."

"Aren't you being exceptionally ruthless, Mr. Cornelius?" Mr. Smiles took a very deep breath.

"Oh, now, now, Mr. Smiles."

They pressed on until they reached a big metal door in the basement. "This is where he should be," said Jerry. "But I can't help thinking he's cooked up a big surprise." He signalled to the surviving Briton and a couple of Belgians. They saluted smartly.

"Have a go at that door, will you?"

"Any particular method, sir?" asked the Briton.

"No. Just get it down. We'll be round the corner."

They retreated while the soldiers got to work affixing things to the door.

There came a loud and unexpectedly violent explosion (obviously far bigger than the soldiers had planned). When the smoke cleared, Jerry saw blood all over the walls, but very little recognizable of the soldiers.

"Great lads," he laughed. "What a good thing, their thing about orders." And then they were all stumbling backward as a sub-machine-gun began to bang rapidly from within the room.

Peering through the smoke from behind the cover of a

South African, Jerry saw that Frank was in there, apparently alone, with the machine-gun cradled in his arms, firing steadily.

Mr. Crookshank got in the path of one of the bursts, making a ludicrous attempt to duck the bullets even as they danced into his chest. Two soldiers collapsed on top of him.

Frank chuckled away as he fired.

"I think he's gone barmy," said Mr. Smiles. "This poses a problem, Mr. Cornelius."

Jerry nodded. "Stop this nonsense, Frank!" he shouted, trying to make his tone firm. "What about a truce?"

"Jerry!"

"Jerry!"

"Jerry!" sang Frank from the room, firing more sporadically. "What do you want, Jerry? A Time Fix?

"Tempodex is my remedy for everyone. It'll turn you on lovely, sport—can't you feel those millions of years just waiting in your spine—waiting to move up into your back brain—"

The gun stopped altogether and they began to move cautiously forward. Then Frank stooped to pick up an identical, fully-loaded weapon. He began emptying it.

"—your midbrain, your forebrain—all your many brains, Jerry—when the tempodex starts opening them up?"

"He is in a jolly mood," said Miss Brunner from somewhere well behind the front line.

Jerry just didn't feel like doing anything except duck bullets at that moment. He felt very tired. Another couple of mercenaries piled themselves up neatly. They were running out of help, Jerry thought.

"Can't we throw something at him? Isn't there any more gas?" Miss Brunner sounded vexed.

"Well, look here, he's got to run out of bullets sooner or later." Mr. Smiles believed that if you waited long enough, the right situation always presented itself. A thought struck him, and he turned angrily to the mercenaries. "Why aren't you retaliating?"

They began retaliating.

Mr. Smiles quickly realized his mistake and shouted: "Stop! We want him alive!"

They stopped.

Frank sang and kept his finger on the trigger.

"He'll get an overheated barrel if he's not careful," said Mr. Smiles, remembering his mythology. "I hope he doesn't blow himself up."

Miss Brunner was picking her nose. She discarded the filters. "I don't care if there is any more gas," she said, "I'm not having the filthy things up there any longer."

"Well, look," said Jerry, "I've got one neurade left, but it could kill him, the state he's in."

"It wouldn't do *me* much good now. You might have warned me." Miss Brunner scanned the floor.

Another mercenary groaned and went down.

The sub-machine-gun stopped. The last bullet ricocheted off the wall. There came the sound of sobbing.

Jerry peered round the corner. Among his guns, Frank sat weeping with his head in his hands.

"He's all yours." Jerry walked towards the stairs.

"Where are you going?" Miss Brunner took a step after him.

"I've done my bit of group effort, Miss Brunner. Now there's something else I've got to do. Goodbye."

Jerry went up to the first floor and found the front door. He still felt nervous and realized that not all Frank's guards had been accounted for. He opened the door and peered out of the house. There didn't seem to be anyone about.

Gun still in his hand, he walked down the sloping drive towards the lodge where John ought to be with Catherine.

The lights were out in the lodge, but he didn't think it strange in the circumstances. He looked down the hill towards the village. All the lights were out there, too. Mr. Smiles had paid someone to fuse the power supply. Jerry found the lodge door open and walked in.

In a corner, a bag of bones gave him a welcoming groan.

"John! Where's Catherine?"

"I got her here, sir. I—"

"But where is she now? Upstairs?"

"You said after ten, sir. I was here by eleven. Everything went smoothly. She was a weight. I'm dying, sir, I think."

"What happened?"

"He must have followed me." John spoke with increasing faintness. "I got her here. . . . Then he came in with a couple of the men. He shot me, sir."

"And took her back to the house?"

"I'm sorry, sir . . . ."

"So you should be. Did you hear where he was taking her?"

"He—said—putting her—back to—bed, sir . . . ."

Jerry left the lodge and began to run up the drive. It was odd how normal the house looked from the outside.

He re-entered it.

On the ground floor he found the lift and discovered that it was still operating. He got in and went up to the sixth. He got out and ran to Catherine's bedroom. The door was locked. He kicked at it, but it wouldn't budge. He reached into his top pocket and fished out something that looked like a cigarette. Two thin wires were attached to it, leading to another object the size of a matchbox. He uncoiled the wires. He put the slim object into the key-hole of the door and walked backward a yard or so with the box in his hand.

It was actually a tiny detonator. He touched the wires to the detonator, and the explosive at the other end burst the lock with a flash.

He pushed at the wrecked door and walked in to find Frank already there.

Frank did not look at all well. In his right hand was a needle gun, twin to Jerry's. There were only two such guns; their father had had them made and given them one each.

"How did you get away?" Jerry asked Frank.

Frank's answer was not a direct one. He put his head on one side and stared at Jerry unblinkingly, looking like an old, sick vulture.

"Well, actually I was hoping to get *you*, Jerry. As it was I got all your military friends, though I think I missed some of the others. They're still wandering about, I think. I'm not sure why I bothered with the shooting—probably just because I enjoyed it. I feel much better now. But if you'd crossed into the room you'd have found that a couple—ha, ha—of my men were on either side of the door waiting for you. I was the bait, the bait to the trap."

Frank's head seemed to be sinking deeper and deeper into his shoulders as he talked, his whole body screwed up in a neurotic stoop. "You certainly made a good try at getting our sister, didn't you? Look—I've woken the sleeping beauty up."

Catherine, looking dazed, was propped on pillows.

She smiled when she saw Jerry. It was a sweet smile, but it wasn't all that confident. Her skin was more than naturally pale, and her dark hair was still tangled.

Jerry's gun hand rose a trifle, and Frank grinned. "Let's get ready, then," he said.

He began to back around the bed in order to get on the other side of Catherine. She was now between them, looking slowly from one to the other, her smile fading very gradually.

Jerry was trembling. "You bastard."

Frank giggled. "That's something we all have in common."

Frank's junkie's face was immobile. The only movement in it came when the light caught his bright, beady eyes. Jerry didn't realize that Frank had pulled the trigger of his gun until he felt the sting in his shoulder. Frank's hand wasn't as steady as it had seemed.

Frank didn't repressure his gun at once. Jerry raised his arm to shoot Frank.

Then Catherine moved. She reached out towards Frank, her fingers clutching at his coat. "Stop it!"

"Shut up," said Frank. He moved his left hand towards the pressure lever of his needle gun.

Catherine tried to stand up on the bed and fell forward in a kneeling position. Her face was full of wild fear.

"Jerry!" she screamed.

Jerry took a step towards her.

"That needle could work into your heart, Jerry," smiled Frank.

"So I'll need a magnet."

Jerry fired and ran towards the window as a needle grazed his face. He repressured and turned. Frank ducked; Catherine rose, and Jerry's needle caught her. She collapsed, Jerry repressured and discharged another needle at the same time as Frank. They both missed again.

Jerry began to feel puzzled. This was going on far too long. He jumped towards Frank and grabbed at his body. Frank's weak fists struck him on the head and back. He punched Frank in the stomach, and Frank groaned. They stepped apart. Jerry felt dizzy; saw Frank grin and wheel.

"You had something in those needles . . ."

"Find out," grinned Frank, and he sprang from the room.

Jerry sat himself down on the edge of the bed.

He was riding a black ferris wheel of emotions. His brain and body exploded in a torrent of mingled ecstasy and pain. Regret. Guilt. Relief. Waves of pale light flickered. He fell down a never-ending slope of obsidian rock surrounded by clouds of green, purple, yellow, black. The rock vanished, but he continued to fall. World of phosphorescence drifting like golden spheres into the black night. Green, blue, red explosions. Flickering world of phosphorescent tears falling into timeless, spaceless wastes. World of Guilt. Guilt—guilt—guilt. . . . Another wave flowed up his spine. No-mind, no-body, no-where. Dying waves of light danced out of his eyes and away throught the dark world. Everything was dying. Cells, sinews, nerves, synapes—all crumbling. Tears of light, fading, fading. Brilliant rockets streaking into the sky and exploding all together and sending their multicoloured globes of light—balls on an Xmas tree—x-mass—drifting slowly. Black mist swirled across a bleak, horizonless nightscape. Catherine. As he approached her she fell away, fell down like a cardboard dummy. Just before his mind cleared, he thought he saw a creature bending over them both—a creature without a navel, hermaphrodite and sweetly smiling . . .

He felt weaker as his head cleared, and he realized that some time must have passed. Catherine lay on the bed in much the same position in which he'd seen her earlier. There was a spot of blood on her white dress, over the left breast.

He put his hand on it and noticed that the heart wasn't beating.

He had killed her.

In agony, he began to caress her stiff.

Meanwhile, Frank was also in agony, for he had been trapped by Miss Brunner and she was giving his genitals a cruel squeeze. They were in one of the rooms on the second floor. Dimitri and Mr. Smiles stood at his left and right, holding his arms.

Miss Brunner knelt on one knee in front of him. She squeezed again, and Frank grimaced.

"Look here," he said. "I've got to get myself fixed up."

"You get the fix when we get the microfilm," snarled Miss Brunner, hoping he wouldn't give in right away.

Smiles got the joke and laughed. Dimitri joined in, somewhat vacantly.

"This is serious," said Miss Brunner, and she gave Frank another squeeze.

"I'll tell you as soon as I'm fixed up."

"Mr. Cornelius, we can't allow that," said Mr. Smiles. "Come along, let's have the information."

Mr. Smiles hit Frank clumsily on the face. Discovering a taste for it, he did it several more times. Frank didn't seem to mind. He had other things to worry about.

"Pain doesn't have much effect," Miss Brunner said thoughtfully. "We'll just have to wait and hope he doesn't become too incoherent."

"Look, he's slavering." Dimitri pointed in disgust. He let go of Frank's arm.

Eyes unblinking, Frank wiped his grey mouth. A great shudder brought his body briefly to life. Then he was still again.

After a moment, while they watched in curiosity, he shuddered again.

"You know the microfilm is in the strongroom?" Frank said between shudders.

"He's coming through!" Mr. Smiles smacked his leg.

"Only you can open the strongroom; is that right, Mr. Cornelius?" Miss Brunner sighed rather disappointedly.

"That's right."

"Will you take us there and open the strongroom? Then we will let you go and you can get your fix."

"Yes, I will."

Mr. Smiles bent Frank's arm behind his back. "Lead the way," he said firmly.

When they had reached the strongroom and Frank had opened it for them, Miss Brunner looked at the ranks of metal files lining the walls and said, "You can go now, Mr. Cornelius. We'll find what we want."

Frank skipped off, out of the littered room behind the strongroom and up the stairs.

"I think I'll just pop after him and check he hasn't got something up his sleeve," Mr. Smiles said eagerly.

"We'll be waiting."

Dimitri helped Miss Brunner lift the files from their shelves and cart them into the room. When Mr. Smiles had disappeared, Miss Brunner began to stroke Dimitri. "We've done it, Dimitri!"

Dimitri had soon forgotten the boxes and had become totally absorbed in Miss Brunner.

Mr. Smiles came back a short time later, looking upset. "I was right," he said. "He's left the house and is talking to his guards. We should have kept him as a hostage. We're not behaving very rationally, Miss Brunner."

"This isn't the time or place for that sort of thing," she said as she searched through the box files.

"Where's Mr. Cornelius?"

"Jerry Cornelius?" she murmured abstractedly.

"Yes."

"We should have asked Frank. Silly of me."

"Where's Dimitri?"

"He gave up."

"Gave himself up?" Mr. Smiles looked bemused. He glanced round the strongroom. On the floor, in a dark corner, lay a neatly folded Courrèges suit, a shirt, under-pants, socks, shoes, tie, valuables.

"Well, he must have gone for an early-morning swim," said Mr. Smiles, trembling and noticing how healthy Miss Brunner's skin looked.

It was dawn as Jerry walked down the stairs. On the second floor he found Miss Brunner and Mr. Smiles going through the big metal box files. They were sitting on the carpet with the files between them, studying the papers and microfilm they had removed.

"I assumed you were dead," said Miss Brunner. "We're the only survivors, I'm afraid."

"Where is Frank?"

"We let him go after he'd opened the strongroom for us. It was a mistake." She looked petulantly at Mr. Smiles. "They aren't here, are they?"

Mr. Smiles shook his head. "It doesn't look like it, Miss Brunner. We've been fooled by young Frank. At the rate he was trembling and drooling, you'd have thought he was telling the truth. He's more cunning than we guessed."

"Instinctive," said Miss Brunner, her lips pursed.

"What happened to Dimitri?" Jerry looked at Miss Brunner. For a moment, in the dawn light, he had half-mistaken her for the Greek.

"He disappeared," said Mr. Smiles. "After I went to check on Frank. I didn't realize the strength of character your brother had, Mr. Cornelius."

"You shouldn't have let him go." Jerry kicked at the papers.

"You told us we mustn't harm him."

"Did I?" Jerry spoke listlessly now.

"I'm not sure he *was* lying," said Miss Brunner to Mr. Smiles. She got up, dusting off her skirt as best she could. "He might really have believed the stuff was in there. Do you think it exists any more?"

"I was convinced. Convinced." Mr. Smiles sighed. "A lot of time, energy and money has been wasted, and we're not even likely to survive now. This is a great disappointment."

"Why not?" Jerry asked. "Likely to survive?"

"Outside, Mr. Cornelius, is the remainder of your brother's private army. They've ringed the place and are ready to shoot us. Your brother commands them."

"I must get to a doctor," said Jerry.

"What's the matter?" Miss Brunner's voice wasn't sympathetic.

"I'm wounded in a couple of places. One in the shoulder—not sure where the other one went in, but I think it must be very bad."

"What about your sister?"

"My sister's dead. I shot her."

"Really, then you must—"

"I want to live!" Jerry stumbled towards the window and looked out into the cold morning. Men were waiting there, though Frank couldn't be seen. The grey bushes seemed made of delicately carved granite, and grey gulls wheeled in a grey sky.

"By Christ, I want you to live, too!" Miss Brunner grasped him. "Can you think of a way we can all get out?"

"There is a chance." He began to speak calmly. "The main control chamber wasn't destroyed, was it?"

"No—perhaps we should have . . ."

"Let's get down there. Come on, Mr. Smiles."

Jerry sat limply in the chair by the control board. He checked first that the power was on; then he activated the monitors so that they had a view all round the house. He locked the monitors on the armed men who were waiting outside.

His hand reached for another bank of switches and flipped them over. "We'll try the towers," he said.

Green, red, and yellow lights went on above the board. "They're working, anyway." He stared carefully at the monitors. He felt very sick.

"Towers are spinning," he said. "Look!"

The armed men were all gaping at the roof. They could not have had any sleep all night, which would help the process. They stood transfixed.

"Get going," Jerry said as he got up and leaned on Mr. Smiles, pushing him towards the door. "But once out of the house, don't look back or you'll be turned into a pillar of salt."

They helped him up the stairs. He was almost fainting now. Cautiously, they opened the front door.

"Go, tiger!" he said weakly as they began to run, still supporting him.

"How are we going to get down to the boats?" asked Miss Brunner when they had helped him round the side of the house facing the cliff edge.

Jerry didn't care. "I suppose we'll have to jump," he murmured. "Hope the tide hasn't dropped too low."

"It's a long way down, and I'm not so sure I can swim." Mr. Smiles slowed his pace.

"You'll have to try," said Miss Brunner.

They stumbled across the rough turf and got to the edge. Far below, water still washed the cliff. Behind them a strong-minded guard had spotted them. They could tell this because his bullets had begun to whine past them.

"Are you fit enough, Mr. Cornelius?"

"I hope so, Miss Brunner."

They jumped together and fell together towards the sea.

Mr. Smiles didn't follow them. He looked back, saw the stroboscopes, and could not turn away again. A smile appeared on his lips. Mr. Smiles died smiling, at the hand of the strong-minded guard.

Jerry, now unaware of who or where he was, felt himself being dragged from the sea. Someone slapped his face. What, he wondered, was the nature of reality after all? Could all this be the result of mankind's will—even his natural surroundings, the shape of the hand that slapped his face?

"You're going to have to steer, I'm afraid, Mr. Cornelius. I can't."

He smiled. "Steer? Okay." But what sort of place would he steer into? The world he had left? This world? Or another altogether? A world, perhaps, where killer girls roved metropolitan streets in bands, working for faceless tycoons who bought and sold hydrogen bombs on an international level, supplying the entire market with H— Hydrogen, Heroin, Heroines . . .

"Catherine," he murmured. Miss Brunner was kindly helping him to the cabin, he realized.

Tired but happy, unconvinced by the reality of his hallucination, he started the boat and swung out to sea.

Hi-Fi, Holiness, a hope in hell . . .

He would never have a memory of what happened until he cried "Catherine!" and woke to find that he was in a very comfortable hospital bed.

"If you don't mind my asking," he said politely to the lemon-faced woman in uniform who entered after a while, "where would I be?"

"You're in the Sunnydales Nursing Home, Mr. Cornelius, and you are much better. On the way to recovery, they say. A friend brought you here after your accident at that French fun fair."

"You know about that?"

"I know very little about it. Some trick gun went off the wrong way and shot you, I believe."

"Is that what happened? Are all nursing homes called Sunnydales?"

"Most of them."

"Am I receiving the very best medical attention?"

"You have had three specialists at your friend's expense."

"Who's the friend?"

"I don't know the name. The doctor might. A lady, I think."

"Miss Brunner?"

"The name's familiar."

"Will there be any complications? When will I be fit enough to leave?"

"I don't think any complications are expected. You will not leave until you are fit enough to do so."

"You have my word of honour—I shan't leave until I'm fit enough. My life's all I've got."

"Very wise. If there are any business matters you need arranging—any relatives?"

"I'm self-employed," he said self-consciously.

The nurse said, "Try getting some sleep."

"I don't need any sleep."

"You don't, but it's easier to run a hospital with all the patients sleeping. They're less demanding. Now you can do me a favour. Groan, beg for medical details, complain about the lack of attention we give you and the inferior way we run the hospital, but don't try to make me laugh."

"I don't think I could, could I?" said Jerry.

"It's a waste of time," she agreed.

"Then I wouldn't dream of it."

He felt fresh and relaxed and he wondered why he should, considering his recent activities. He'd probably have plenty of time in which to work it out. He knew he'd be fighting trauma on all fronts, and the long coma had equipped him to fight well.

As best he could, he began putting his mind in order. During the weeks in the hospital, all he asked for was a tape recorder, tape, and an earbead so that there would be no trouble when he turned up the sound in moments of heavy concentration.

PHASE 2

6

Better equipped for the world than before he'd arrived at the hospital, Jerry offered a grateful hand to the doctors who had saved him; gave the rest of the staff a graceful bow; got into his Cadillac, which had been delivered from town; and drove through the weary streets of London's southernmost suburbs, heading for the important centre: the hot, bubbling core of the city.

He parked the car in the Shaftesbury Avenue garage he used and, stepping light, sallied out into his natural habitat.

It was a world ruled these days by the gun, the guitar, and the needle, sexier than sex, where the good right hand had become the male's primary sexual organ, which was just as well considering that the world population had been due to double before the year 2000.

This wasn't the world Jerry had always known, he felt, but he could only vaguely remember a different one, so similar to this that it was immaterial which was which. The dates checked roughly, that was all he cared about, and the mood was much the same.

Recently converted from a cinema, jangling on thirteen fun-packed floors, Emmett's Coin Casino was the place to go, Jerry decided. He turned a corner and there it was.

Its three visible sides were entirely covered with neon of every possible colour: neon words and neon pictures with six or even ten different movements. And the music didn't blare out; it came out faint and flattened—soft, muted tones that really only suggested music.

An early-twentieth-century mystic might have thought he'd had a vision of heaven if he'd seen it, thought Jerry as he made his way slowly towards it.

It sparked and flashed, rolled and smoked, and high above everything else, seemingly suspended in the dark sky, was the single golden word EMMETTS.

At the coruscating entrance foyer, attended by young girls in military uniforms with imitation rifles with which they jokingly pretended to bar his way, Jerry changed a bundle of notes into a bag of counters for use in the fun machines. He went through the tall, shining red-and-blue turnstile and trod the thick, jazzy carpet into the first gallery, which was at ground level.

Beams of soft pastel light roamed through the semi-darkness of the hall, and money-operated machines clattered, spoke, and sang. Jerry began to descend the short flight of steps, listening to the laughter of the young men and women who wandered among the machines, or lingered by them, or danced to the free music from the giant juke box that filled the best part of one wall.

Jerry spent a few tokens on the Ray Range, operating a simulated laser beam that spat light at targets. If the ray of light struck a specified zone, you won a prize. But his score was low; he was out of practice. This spoiled his state of mind, and he began to think that if he hadn't worried so little about marksmanship, he wouldn't be in this mental limbo now. Catherine—or rather the lack of Catherine—had given his life the only dynamism it was likely to have. Now he lacked her for good. It was over.

Aimlessly, he wandered among the pin tables and fruit machines, bent over by happy young men who worked them excitedly, hand in hand. Jerry sighed and thought that the true aristocracy who would rule the seventies were out in force: the queers and the lesbians and the bisexuals, already half-aware of their great destiny which would be realized when the central ambivalence of sex would be totally recognized and the terms *male* and *female* would become all but meaningless. Here they were. As he wandered, he was surrounded by all the possible replacements for sex, one or several of which would become the main driving force for the humanity of *circa* 2000—light, colour, music, the pin tables, the pill dispensers, the gun ranges—scarcely substitutes for sex any more, but natural replacements.

The birth rate, which if it had continued at the speed predicted in the early sixties would have produced by

4000 a planet consisting, core and crust, of nothing but human beings, was a dead pigeon to modern statisticians in Europe. Europe as usual was ahead of the world.

Most of those who hadn't been able to stand the pace had emigrated off to America, Africa, Russia, Australia, and elsewhere where they could wallow in the nostalgia produced by American fashions and television shows and mass opinion, African rural life, Russian moral attitudes, and Australian cold mutton. The flow had been two-way, of course, with the passengers for 1950 going one way and the passengers for 2000 coming the other. Only France, Switzerland, and Sweden, temporal and temporary bastions, hung back and stood soon to be shaken to pieces in the imminent pre-entropic wash of crisis. It was not a change of mood, Jerry thought, but a change of mind.

Jerry no longer had any idea whether the world he inhabited was "real" or "false"; he had long since given up worrying about it.

By the spinning Racette, where you could back a model horse named after your favourite winner of the season, Jerry met Shades, an acquaintance.

Shades was a killer from California who had once told Jerry that he could prove he'd assassinated both Kennedys. When Jerry, who had believed him, had asked why, Shades had replied rather self-consciously, "The thrill of big game, you know. I'd considered having a go at your Queen, but it wouldn't have been the same. I got the biggest. The world cried for Jack Kennedy, you know."

"And Valentino. You could have led up to him."

"No, if I'd done that the trauma wouldn't have been so great—people would have been half-ready. I got me the Sun King. What a charge. Oh, boy!"

"What did you do it with? Mistletoe?"

"An Italian Mauser," Shades had told him, offended by his levity.

Shades had two girls with him: a redhead of about sixteen and a brunette of about twenty-five. Shades's lamp-tanned face turned to grin at Jerry. He was naked apart from a pair of shorts and a bolero. His real clothing, his essential clothing, was his dark glasses. He looked out of place. The girls both wore tweed trouser suits. Their hair was short, and their green-highlighted make-up glinted under the coloured beams.

The older girl had a newssheet in her hand. Jerry looked at her. "You're Swedish?"

She didn't seem surprised at his guess. "Ja—and you?"

"No. I'm English."

"Ja so!"

Jerry leaned forward and took the sheet from the Swedish girl's hand. "Anything new lately?" He'd been wondering if the raid on the house had reached the sheets. It was unlikely.

"Britain's in some sort of debt," said the young girl. "It's something to do with the crime-rate doubling."

Jerry glanced over the sheet, then reversed it to look at the comics. Instead there was a photo covering the whole side: a mass car smash with mangled corpses everywhere. Jerry supposed that the picture sold sheets.

"Well, Shades," he said, handing the sheet back to the girl, "what are you up to these days?"

"Pianotron at the Friendly Bum. Why don't you come along and sit in?"

"Good idea."

"I'm not due till the third set around three. What do we do in the meantime?"

"Help me get rid of these tokens, then we'll talk about it."

The Swedish girl attached herself to Jerry, and they made a happy circuit of the tables. The girl chewed gum steadily, and Jerry was slightly put out by this, but was mollified as her little hand tentatively touched him up. It was a nice thought, he felt, as he restrained her.

A stooped old man passed between the tables. He had long white hair almost to his waist; a long white beard to match; a pink, soft skin; and a small brief-case under his arm. He was stooped almost horizontally, and his little pale blue eyes seemed as bright as the bulbs on the pin tables. He nodded at Jerry and stopped politely.

"Good evening, Mr. Cornelius. We haven't seen much of you lately, or is it me who's been out of touch?" His voice was breathy.

"You're never out of touch, Derek. How's the astrology business?"

"Can't complain. Want a chart done?"

"I've had too many, Derek. You'll never work it out."

"There's something very odd there, you know. I've been doing charts for sixty years and never come up against one like yours. It's as if you didn't exist." His laugh was breathy, too.

"Come off it, Derek—you're only forty-six."

"Oh, you know that, do you? Well, thirty years, anyway."

"And you only took up astrology ten years ago. Just before you gave up your job in the Foreign Office."

"Who've you been talking to?"

"You."

"I don't always tell the truth, you know."

"No. Where's Olaf?"

"Oh, he's about." Derek looked sharply up at Jerry. "It wasn't you, was it?"

"What?"

"Olaf's left me. I taught him the lot. I loved him. And it's rare for a Sagittarian to love a Virgo, you know. Scorpios are all right. Olaf ran off with some crackpot star watcher I've never heard of. I just wondered. Do you know, when I first started up professionally there weren't more than six what you might call real astrologers moving around the way I do. Know how many there are now?"

"Six hundred."

"You're almost right. I can't count them all. On the other hand, custom's gone up. But not really proportionately."

"Don't worry, Derek. You're still the best."

"Well, spread it around. No, you see, I'd heard Olaf was here. I'm sure once he sees me—in the flesh, as it were—he'll realize his mistake."

"I'll keep my eyes open."

"Good lad." Derek patted Jerry's arm and sloped off.

"Is he very wise?" asked the Swedish girl.

"He's sharp," said Jerry. "And that's what matters."

"Every time," she said, taking his hand. He let her lead him back to where Shades was lying across a table with his nose pressed to the glass as little balls smacked against little coils and bounced about at random until they hit other little coils. Shades's hands gripped the edges of the table, and when a bell rang the knuckles whitened.

"*This* is what I call conditioning, Jerry," he said, not looking up. "Get a load of me. I'm Pavlov's poodle!"

"Let's see you dribble, you old-fashioned sweetie," Jerry smiled, taking it easy. He was relaxing now, moving with the tide. He pinched Shades's bottom, and Shades kicked backward with a low-heeled cowboy boot.

"You riding me?"

"Not tonight, honey."

This was more like it, thought Jerry, taking a deep breath of smoke, scent, and incense. He felt on top again. Just on top of himself.

Shades laughed. He had been concentrating on the little steel balls.

Looking about, Jerry recognized Derek's Olaf having a go on the Killagal range. You had ten shots in which to knock down six out of ten life-size plastic nude girls with something made to look like a harpoon gun. He wasn't doing too well. Olaf was a slight, pinch-faced lad who gave the impression that someone had had him filleted. He put down the gun and went over to the machine that read palms. He put his money in and laid his palm limply on the section made of pulsating rubber. As Jerry approached, the machine cut off and a little card appeared in a slot. Olaf removed it and studied it. He frowned, shaking his head.

"Hello, Olaf. Derek's looking for you."

"That's none of your business." Olaf's voice was contentious and whining. It was his normal voice.

"No. Derek asked me to let him know if I saw you."

"I suppose you want something from me. Well, I just spent my last guinea, and I don't have anything to do with Aryans."

"You're not a Jewish boy, are you?" Jerry said. "Don't mind my asking, but you're not, are you?"

"Shut up!" Olaf's voice stayed at the same pitch and tone, but became more precise. "I'm sick and tired of people like you."

"No offence, no offence, but . . ."

"Shut up!"

"I only thought, since you said . . ."

"You can't take the mickey out of me, you know." Olaf turned his back. Jerry skipped round and got in front of him again. "Now, *look*," said Olaf.

"Did anyone ever tell you you had a beautiful body, Olaf?"

"Don't try to make up for it now," said Olaf, his voice becoming slightly less precise and a trifle softer. "Anyway, you're an Aryan. I *can't* have anything to do with Aryans. It would be disastrous."

"Got to keep pure, Olaf, eh?"

"Don't start that again. People like you are scum from the lowest pits. You've got no understanding of what it's like to be a real, spiritual human being, *knowing* the infinite—" Olaf gave a thin, superior smile. "Scum from the lowest pits."

"That's what I mean. You don't *sound* like a Jewish boy."

"Shut up."

"All right—go and see Derek."

"I want nothing to do with that pervert!"

"Pervert? Why pervert?"

"It's nothing to do with *sex*—you see what I mean about having no understanding?—it's to do with his ideas. He's perverted the whole science of astrology. Have you seen the way he draws up his charts?"

"What's wrong with it?"

"His charts? Haven't you seen his charts? He'll do anything for money."

"Oh, not anything, Olaf."

"Where is he?"

"I last saw him over there." Jerry pointed through the cloudy semi-darkness.

"He's lucky I'll still speak to him." Olaf squiggled off. Jerry leaned against the palm-reading machine, watching him. The Swedish girl came up.

"I don't know *how* long we'll be," she said. "Shades still has many tokens left. He has been winning."

"We could go and smoke something at a *schwartzer* club I know where we wouldn't be unwelcome and the drumming is great. Only if I want to play tonight, it won't help by the time I get to the Friendly Bum."

"You mean marijuana, I think. I don't want to do that. Are you a 'junkie'?"

"Not generally speaking. I leave that up to my brother. We could just go there."

"Where is it?"

"Ladbroke Grove."

"That's far."

"Not that far—only just out of the Area. The other side of no man's land."

"What did you say?"

"Nothing." He glanced over to where Shades was banging a machine. The TILT sign flashed on.

"Fixed!" wept Shades. "Fixed!"

A very cool Negro attendant in a white suit glided into sight. He was smiling. "What's the matter, sonny?"

"This table is fixed!"

"Don't be childish. What else you expect?"

Shades appeared to be glowering behind his tired sunglasses. He shrugged rapidly several times. The Negro put his head on one side and grinned, waiting.

"You put the odds pretty high in your favour," snarled Shades.

"It's what you got to do, man. Any man's got to do something like that these days, you know. Eh?"

"This whole damned country's crooked."

"You just discovering that, my friend? Oh dear, oh dear."

"It's always been crooked. Sanctimonious crooks."

"Oh, no. They're pretty straightforward these days. They can afford to be—or thought they could . . ."

Jerry looked on, amused, as the two ex-patriots talked their cheap philosophy.

Shades shrugged once and turned away. The Negro strode off, proud of himself.

Shades's little girl friend trotted across the floor and joined him. He put an arm around her and steered her towards Jerry and the Swedish girl.

"Let's go, Jerry."

"All right."

They spent the last of Jerry's tokens on coffee and pills and set off for the Friendly Bum in Villiers Street, which ran off Trafalgar Square alongside Charing Cross Station, elbowing through the gay night life of the city.

Dragsters, m & f, thronged the Friendly Bum, which was as packed with people as it was with beat, and it was filled to capacity with both. Behind the spotlights, which were turned on the audience, a group could just be made out. A vast amplifier formed the back of the low stage, and a beautiful blend of Hammond organ, pianotron, drums, bass, rhythm and lead guitar, and alto and baritone saxophones, swam out of it, playing "Symphony Sid" with a slow, fugal feeling.

On the low ceiling revolved an old-fashioned dance-hall globe made of faceted glass. The lights caught the green, the red, the violet, the gold, the silver, and the orange. Light struck it from all directions and was reflected back again so that the photons fairly flew in the Friendly Bum.

They squeezed through a crowd that was all one mass from which heads and limbs seemed to protrude at random. It was almost unbearably hot.

On the left of the stage was a bar. On the right was a coffee counter. Both were busy. Leaning against the bars were West Indians, elegant in Harlem styles like chorus boys from *Porgy and Bess*. They almost all had thin moustaches and contemptuous looks mainly reserved for the other, less well-dressed West Indians who clapped their hands to every beat but the one the drummer was using.

As they reached the coffee bar on their way to a door behind it marked PRIVATE, Jerry recognized one of the spades as a musician he had once played with. It was "Uncle" Willie Stevens, who played flute and tenor and had once done vocals with a since disbanded group called The Allcomers. The group had become popular when it was playing at the Friendly Bum, and the news had spread, until the place had been filled with nothing but groupies and journalists.

"Hello, Uncle."

"Hi, Jerry." Stevens's expression didn't change as he extended a large hand and let Jerry shake it. "What's been happening?"

"This and that. Are you working?"

"Convincing that National Assistance is working. They're getting tougher and tougher every day. They threatened to send me back last week. I said if the NA was more obliging in Birmingham, I'd go back."

"So no scene."

"Oh, there's a good scene, but it's not my scene. You playing here tonight?"

"I hope so."

"I'll be listening."

Jerry walked through the door marked PRIVATE. Shades

and the two girls were already in the back room. Shades was getting into his frilly uniform. The other members of the group he played with had theirs on. The guitarists were tuning up. Jerry borrowed the lead guitar, a beautifully made piece of solid polypropylene plastic studded with semi-precious gems with a silver tremolo arm and amplification controls of amethyst. He struck a swift, simple progression of A minor, F, D7, and C. "Nice," he said, handing back the box. "Shades said I could sit in."

"Suits me," said the lead guitar, "so long as you don't want paying."

"I'll wait a couple of numbers until I've heard the group."

"Okay."

"Symphony Sid" was just finishing. Shades and the group went out as the previous group came in. The sixteen-year-old left with Shades. The Swedish girl stayed behind with Jerry. The group who'd just come off were sweating and pleased.

"Let's see if the bar is within arm's reach," Jerry said.

They were lucky. As Shades's group took off on a Lennon/McCartney standard, "It Won't Be Long"—not one of their best—Jerry and the Swede found space at the bar. She was drinking Beaujolais with crème de menthe chasers because she liked the colours. He had a Pernod for old time's sake. He didn't like Pernod, but he'd always drunk it at the Friendly Bum.

"Every day we'll be happy I know, now that I know that you won't leave me no more," merrily sang the lead guitar, warming up for the take-off into improvisation. He had a high voice that never missed a quaver. It provided excellent counterpoint for the throbbing organ.

The mass seemed to bubble like a cauldron in time to the music as the clients danced.

Smoothly, the group went straight into "Make It," an instrumental with the pianotron featured. Shades was playing better than Jerry remembered. He and the Swede got up and joined the dancers. The sense of being part of the mass was a delicious feeling. He and the girl and the others around them seemed fused together with a total absence of individual identity.

"Make It" made it, and Shades shouted into his mike, "Jerry!"

Jerry left the floor, crossed the spots, and stood on the stage. The lead guitarist handed him his instrument and went towards the bar with a grin.

Jerry played a few chords to get the feel of the amplifier and led off with one of his favourites—another Lennon/McCartney number, "I'm a Loser."

"I'm a loser and I'm not what I appear to be," he sang.

As he sang, he saw Miss Brunner come down the steps into the Friendly Bum and look around. She probably couldn't see him behind the lights. She took a step towards the bubbling crowd and then hesitated. Jerry Cornelius forgot her as he began the instrumental improvisation. Behind him Shades changed from 4/4 to 6/8, but Jerry kept on a 4/4 beat and liked it like that. The thing began to move now.

Jerry watched the time, careful not to let it go on too long, but close to every stopping point something new occurred to him, and the clients seemed to be enjoying themselves. The piece lasted a good half-hour and left Jerry tired.

"Great," said Shades—praise indeed—as Jerry climbed through the spots and took the lead guitarist's place at the bar. The Swedish girl had been absorbed into the crowd long since.

"Hello, Miss Brunner." A Pernod would suit him now; long and cool, with lots of ice. He ordered one. She paid for it at the same time as she paid for her Scotch.

"What were you playing up there?"

"Instrument or number?"

"Instrument."

"Lead guitar. Not bad, eh?"

"I haven't got a very good ear. It sounded okay. When did you leave Sunnydales?"

"This afternoon. Don't pay them a day past it."

"I won't. I had a hard time getting you there, what with one thing and another. I should think I saved your life."

"Very kind of you. Thanks. I am grateful. I think that does it, don't you?"

"Strictly speaking, yes. Mind you, your thanks could take a more positive form."

"It could."

"Are you still worried about killing your sister?"

"Naturally. And that does that one. What have you been doing with yourself?"

"I advertised for a replacement for Dimitri. I've got a girl on trial. I've got to meet her later. I've been checking some data on the new Burroughs-Wellcome. I didn't realize you were the Cornelius who'd published that unified-field theory."

"You've been digging, Miss Brunner."

"I have."

Overhead the glass ball revolved, and the light struck Miss Brunner's face until it became a flashing assortment of colours. It seemed to offer a clue to her real identity, the total identity that Cornelius had been worrying about since they had talked earlier in Mr. Smiles's house at Blackheath. He saw her now as a prism, and through the prism Miss Brunner ceased to be a woman at that moment. She was speaking.

"A noble price? Ah, I'm just an amateur. It wasn't fair to take it."

"It was your chance of immortality—you may never have another."

Around them mingled sound, light, and flesh.

"There is a flaw, you know," she said, "in quite an early equation."

"You spotted it. Are you going to shop me?"

"It could mean immortality for me."

"I think you already have that, Miss Brunner."

"Kind of you to say so. What makes you think it?"

Jerry wondered if he were in any danger. Not at this stage, he decided. "Far better mathematicians than you have checked it and found nothing wrong. You couldn't possibly know—not unless . . . ."

Miss Brunner smiled and sipped her Scotch.

"Unless you had direct experience of what I suggest in my theory, Miss Brunner—unless you *know* better."

"Ah—you are a clever one, Mr. Cornelius."

"Where's all this leading to?"

"Nowhere. Shall we go somewhere quieter?"

"I like it here."

"Is there somewhere quieter you like to go?"

"There's the Chicken Fry in Tottenham Court Road."

"Every item on the menu guaranteed vitamin-free. I know the place."

"You are a clever one, Miss Brunner."

As they left, the performers began to destroy their instruments.

"Miss Brunner," he said, leaning over his chicken and fries, "if I hadn't been through my theological phase, I'd be identifying you as first suspect for Mephistopheles."

"I haven't got a pointed beard. Not with me."

"I can't fit you in with *Homo sapiens.*"

"I don't fit in easily anywhere." She stabbed herself a forkful of chips.

Jerry leaned behind him and fed tokens into the juke box. He pressed buttons at random.

"You're sure you're barking up the right tree?" She spoke with her mouth full.

"For a long time I haven't been sure of anything. We'll let the whole thing ride."

"The House of Cornelius still stands," she said. "We didn't get a chance to set it on fire. Does that bother you?"

"Not much. Frank is currently the random factor."

"I have it on good authority that he's in Lapland. To be more accurate, he is two days' trek north-west of Kvikjokk—a small village well beyond Kiruna."

"That's a long way north."

"The French police, I believe, wrote off the incident of our expedition—an accident due to an experiment that got out of hand."

"Quite right. Frank?"

"Are you that interested?"

"No." He sat back and listened to the music.

"Frank is living in a disused meteorological post in the wilds. We could get there by helicopter."

"I've got a helicopter and a plane."

"You've got a lot of things like that."

"Anticipation. I still want to get my hands on a private oil well and a small refinery. Then I'm set up."

"You look ahead."

"I look around. Ahead's here already."

"Frank, I suspect, not only has the microfilm your father left. He also has the Newman manuscript."

"Telepathic powers, Miss Brunner, yet!"

"No—an educated guess. A lot of people have heard that Newman wrote a book after he came down from that capsule last year and before he committed suicide. I'd heard that a rep of Newman's widow was looking for Frank. I found the rep, but all he'd tell me was where Frank would be."

"Newman was rubbed out by Security, I thought. Indirect suicide, I suppose. Do you know what was in the book?"

"Some say the complete objective truth about the nature of humanity. Some say a lot of crackpot ideas. It must be one of those books."

"I'd like to read it none the less."

"I thought you might. Then we have something in common again?"

"Yes. Where did you say he was near?"

"Kvikjokk—close to Jokmokk."

"Get away with you." Jerry rose. "I'll need some good maps, then, will I?"

"I suppose so. Can we make it by helicopter?"

"That depends. I've got one of those new Vickers long-range copters and fuel caches all across Europe, but the last one's near Uppsala. Lapland's a long way from Uppsala. We could probably get there but not back."

"We'll *float* back, Mr. Cornelius, if what I suspect is there."

"What do you suspect?"

"Ah, well—I'm not sure. I've just got a feeling."

"You and your feelings."

"They've never done you any harm."

"They'd better not, Miss Brunner."

"It would be a good thing to start tomorrow morning," she said. "How do you feel?"

"I've been in the hospital, remember. I've made up a lot of ground. I'll last."

"Got you," she said. She picked up her handbag, and they walked out into Tottenham Court Road. "I've got to meet this new girl of mine," she told him. "Her name's Jenny Lumley. She was doing sociology at Bristol until they closed the university down last summer."

"Where are you meeting her?"

"The Blackfriars Ring."

"The wrestling stadium. What's she doing there?"

"She likes wrestling."

They walked to Shaftesbury Avenue, where he got his

car out of the garage and drove her to the Blackfriars
Ring. It was a big, modern building, specially built for
wrestling bouts. Outside, and somewhat jerkily, two neon
wrestlers played out a throw time and time again.

There was a big foyer lined with framed pictures of
men and women wrestlers. Some of the women even
looked nice, but Jerry didn't fancy any of the men. There
were three box offices—one on either side and one in the
centre. From loudspeakers above them came the relayed
roar of the crowd.

Miss Brunner went to the central desk and spoke to the
cute little man there. "Miss Brunner—you should have
two tickets reserved for me. Our friend's already inside."

He sorted through a small pile of buff envelopes printed
with the name of the promoter-owners of the Blackfriars
Ring.

"Here we are, dear. Good seats—C 705 and 7. You'd
better hurry up—the main bout's beginning in a couple
of minutes.'"

"Have you ever seen one of these, Mr. Cornelius?" she
asked as they walked up the plush stairs.

"Not my speed. I've seen a little on TV."

"Nothing like the real thing."

They went up three flights and walked round the gallery until they came to a door marked 700. The doors
must have been well soundproofed, because when they
opened them the noise that hit them was loud, a ululating
roar. The smell matched the sound. Sweat, perfume, and
after-shave.

The stadium was about the same size as the Albert
Hall, with banks and banks of seats rising into semi-
darkness. It was packed. Below, as they looked for their
seats, they could see two women throwing each other
around by their long hair. There were two referees—one
in a chair suspended over the ring and one outside the
ring, with his face close to the canvas.

The people in the seats were not all intent on the bout.
Many had rid themselves of most of their clothes, and some
were entertaining the surrounding fellow spectators better than the pair in the ring.

Looking up and behind him, Jerry noted that there
were a lot of children in the cheaper seats. They *were*
watching the wrestling. Amplifiers above the banks of

seats picked up the groans and shouts of the two contest-
ants as they twisted about in a way Jerry could admire
but not understand.

Here and there people were masturbating. "Quite like
the old Roman arena, isn't it?" said Miss Brunner with a
grin. "I sometimes think that masturbation is the only
sincere form of sexual expression left to the unadventur-
ous, poor souls."

"Well, at least they don't bother anyone."

"I think I can see Jenny. You'll like her. She's from the
West Country originally—Taunton. She's got those lovely
dark West Country looks. Don't they? I'm not so sure.
Yes, it is Jenny. And *you* can talk, Mr. Cornelius."

"What are you getting at?" They had to push past four
or five people to reach their seats. The people didn't get
up.

"Oh, nothing. Hello, Jenny, my sweet. This is Mr.
Cornelius, an old associate of mine."

Jenny looked up with a cocky smile. "Hello, Mr. Cornelius." She had long black hair, as fine as Jerry's; a
simple shift dress of dark pink; and a red-trimmed leather
jacket. She had large dark eyes and was as Miss Brunner
had described her. She was also, it seemed, pretty tall.
"You got here just in time."

"So we were told." Jerry sat down next to her, and Miss
Brunner sat on the other side. Jerry was a sucker for girls
like Jenny. When it came down to it, he thought, enjoying
her being so close to him, they were the only kind he could
go for. There just weren't enough to go round. He smiled
to himself. It might be an idea to get her away from Miss
Brunner.

It was intermission, and everybody was relaxing as the
MC shouted something about the winner and the contest-
ants in forthcoming bouts.

"Who was it said that sex was just two people trying to
occupy the same body?" Jenny got a bag of butterscotch
from her pocket and handed it round. Jerry liked butterscotch best. "I'm sure I read it—I don't think anyone said
it to me. I think it applies just as much to wrestling, don't
you, Miss Brunner?"

Miss Brunner's right cheek bulged as she bit her butterscotch.

"I've never thought about it, dear."

"I don't just enjoy the social side of wrestling," she said. "I like the violence and everything too."

Jerry just sat and ogled her while her head was turned to Miss Brunner. Miss Brunner noticed him and raised her eyebrows. Jenny's head shot round and she looked at Jerry, caught him half off guard, and gave him a cheerful wink. Jerry groaned silently. It was too much. It wasn't as if he often met a girl like this. He wished he hadn't come.

The rather garbled voice of the MC came through the amplifiers.

"And now, ladies and gentlemen, the main contest of the evening. In a specially prepared ring we bring you six of our biggest stars in an all-out tag match. Just to add excitement and extra thrills to the contest, we are filling the ring with thick whitewash, as you can see—" Having brought in a special tray that occupied the whole of the inside area of the ring, attendants were now pumping in the thick whitewash.

"Only one of the best can win this match, ladies and gentlemen. And who is to be the best of the six best? Let me read out the names."

The MC now flourished a large piece of paper.

"Doc Gorilla!"

Cheers from supporters.

"Lolita del Starr!"

Enthusiastic shouts.

"Tony Valentine!"

The volume rose . . .

"Cheetah Gerber!"

. . . and rose . . .

"The Masked Crusher!"

. . . and rose . . .

"Ella Speed!"

. . . and rose. There were screams and cheers and boos and a wild, raving sound that was a combination of all the voices.

Jerry looked up, hearing a strange shrilling noise above him. One of the cables leading from the ceiling to the ring held a ski chair, which was speeding downward. In it sat a heavily built woman in her late twenties. She wore a leopard-skin bikini and had nice legs. As the chair reached the ring, she jumped from it lightly and sent up a spray of whitewash. She held her balance in the slippery stuff and grinned and waved at the audience. The chair returned, and Jerry could just see the gallery far up near the roof where another small figure was climbing into the chair. It swished down bearing a gross masked man in black long johns and bowling shoes. He too bounced from chair to ring and waved briefly to the audience before flexing at the ropes. Down came the next—a slim girl with long blonde hair in a white one-piece costume. Jerry wondered how she would get the whitewash out of her hair when the bout was over. While she blew kisses at the audience, the older woman suddenly leaped on her, knocking her flat into the whitewash. The crowd moaned and booed. One of the referees on the ground shouted something, and the older woman surlily helped the younger one up. A huge black-bearded, hairy-chested man—evidently Doc Gorilla—was the next arrival. Then a tall, slim, well-muscled woman arrived. She had a handsome, heavy-boned face and dark hair almost to her waist. Lastly came a broad-shouldered, slim-hipped youngster with very short blond hair and white shorts and boots. He smiled at the audience.

Now the overhead referee was moved out to his position above the ring. Four other referees took their places outside the ring, one on each side.

The match began.

It gave Jerry no kicks, but he watched with some amusement at the whitewash-covered tangle below, at the ecstatic crowd. When Jenny gripped his hand he felt pleased until he saw that Miss Brunner was gripping her other hand.

The young blonde in the white one-piece was having her arm twisted by her old enemy. Probably Lolita del Starr and Cheetah Gerber, Jerry decided. Doc Gorilla, the hairy one, looking like the Old Man of the Sea with his beard covered in whitewash, was in a tie-up with the other girl, Ella Speed, and handsome Tony Valentine. Somewhere out of sight beneath them was the Masked Crusher, who didn't seem to be doing much crushing.

Though he couldn't summon up the same enthusiasm as the rest of the audience, Jerry sat back and relaxed. Soon all the wrestlers were so covered in whitewash that it was impossible from where he sat to recognize who was who.

He shouted in Jenny's ear, "You can't tell the men from the women, can you?"

She seemed to hear and shouted something back, which

he missed the first time. She shouted it again. "Not these days, no!"

The match went on, with people dancing about, being bounced on ropes, flying out of the ring, climbing back in again, performing acrobatics and contortions of odd complexity.

As a finale with a twist, Tony Valentine and Ella Speed jumped up and grabbed the overhead referee's legs, hauling him into the ring. Then the ref sped round the ring hurling all the wrestlers out over the ropes. The crowd cheered.

Winners were announced and the ring cleared of its whitewash tray.

"And now, ladies and gentlemen, that famous folk group, whose songs have heartened the oppressed all round the world, will entertain you during the intermission. Ladies and gentlemen—The Reformers!"

The Reformers were clapped into the ring. Two men and a good-looking girl with a pointed, self-indulgent face and fair curls. The two men held Spanish guitars. They began to sing a slow song about out-of-work miners. The audience seemed to be enjoying it as it tidied itself up and bought refreshments from the girls who were now trotting round.

"God, aren't they awful," said Jenny. "They're *ruining* the song. It's one of Woody Guthrie's, you know—very moving. They've sugared it horribly!"

"Oh, I don't know," said Jerry. "Wasn't the group originally the Thundersounds—one of those rhythm-and-blues groups that had one record at the top a couple of years ago? Social conscience, Jenny, it's a good gimmick."

"It's all wrong."

"You're right, love. When pop stars started getting a social conscience, that was the beginning of the end for the social-conscience business."

She gave him a baffled look.

"Are you being contentious, Jerry?" Miss Brunner leaned across the girl.

"Oh, you know . . ." he said.

"Would you mind if we left now, Jenny?" said Miss Brunner.

"There's only two more matches, Miss Brunner," said Jenny. "Can't we stay and see them?"

"I'd rather we went home now."

"I was looking forward to the match between Doc Gorilla and Tony Valentine."

"I think we ought to go, Jenny."

Jenny sighed.

"Come along," said Miss Brunner, firmly but kindly.

Jenny rose resignedly. They filed from the arena and walked out of the stadium. Jerry had left his car in the nearby lot. Miss Brunner and Jenny got in the back. Jerry started the car and reversed into the street. "Where now?"

"Holland Park. Quite near you, I think." Miss Brunner sat back. "If you go to Holland Park Avenue, I'll direct you from there."

"Okay."

"If we're leaving first thing in the morning, it would be a good idea if you spent the night at my place," Miss Brunner said after a bit.

"Or you at mine."

"Out of the question; I'm sorry."

"Why? Afraid of the gossip?"

"I've got things to do. All you've got to do is pack a bag and come round. We've got a spare bedroom. You'd be quite safe. It bolts on the inside."

"That sounds comforting."

"You're not joking, are you?" Jenny sounded a little surprised.

"No, love."

They reached Notting Hill and drove along Holland Park Avenue. Miss Brunner told him to turn off to the left, and he did so. Another turning, and they were outside a smart, countrified house.

"Here we are," said Miss Brunner. "What do you think of my suggestion? If you popped round to your place and packed a bag, you could be back in a quarter of an hour and I'd have some coffee for you."

"You can produce better inducements than that. Okay." Jerry was still riding with the tide.

As he drove back to Holland Park Avenue and his own large house, he realized that Miss Brunner had been doing a lot of checking. He knew he hadn't told her where he lived.

He left the car standing in the street and went up to the steel gate in the high wall. He said very quietly, "This is a raid." Responding to the sonic code, the door swung open and closed again as Jerry walked up the overgrown path to the house. Another murmured code opened the front door.

Less than a quarter of an hour later, bearing a large suitcase, he left the house and got into his car, put the case on the seat beside him, and returned to Miss Brunner's house.

He rang the bell, and Jenny let him in. She looked as if she'd been taking some rough mental battering while he'd been away, but it might have been just the different light. She gave him a small, nervous smile, and he patted her arm reassuringly. Obviously Miss Brunner wasn't planning to take Jenny with her to Lapland, and when they got back he'd make a strong attempt to take Jenny away from Miss Brunner. Jenny didn't realize it but her knight was already plotting her rescue. He hoped she wanted to be rescued. She'd better.

Miss Brunner sat pouring coffee from a Dunhill Filter finished in electric red. It went with the rest of the room, which was mainly red and grey but pretty featureless—just a long couch and a coffee table.

"How do you like it, Mr. Cornelius?"

"How it comes. I always like it how it comes."

"So you say."

"My helicopter is quite conveniently sited near Harwich. If we started really early we should be able to drive down without too much trouble."

"That suits me. What time—seven?"

"Seven." He took the cup of coffee, drank it down, and handed back the cup. She poured him another expressionlessly and gave it to him. He leaned on the wall—slim, serene, and elegant.

Miss Brunner looked him over. He had natural style, she thought. Maybe it had once been studied but it was natural now. Her mouth watered.

"Where's this safe bed?" he asked.

"Upstairs, first one you come to at the top."

"Fine. Want me to give you a knock around six?"

"I don't think that'll be needed. I'm not sure I'll be sleeping."

"It must be chess and it can't be bridge. I can see I'm not necessary."

She looked up at him. "Oh, I wouldn't say that."

When Jerry entered the room, he closed the door behind him, locked it, and pulled the bolt. He still didn't feel quite right. There was a shower in the room, and he used it, got into bed, and went to sleep.

He was awake at six, showered again, and dressed. He decided to go down and make himself some coffee if Miss Brunner and Jenny weren't up yet.

Downstairs he heard a noise in the living-room and went in. Miss Brunner, dressed as she'd been the previous night, was lying on the couch with her arms flung back and her legs asprawl. Jerry grinned. The noise he had heard was her breathing, deep and ecstatic. At first he guessed that she was drugged, but there wasn't any evidence a-round. Then he saw a neatly folded deep pink dress, a red-edged leather jacket and a pair of black tights and pumps. Jenny's clothes. Where was Jenny?

He looked down at Miss Brunner's face and felt funny.

He felt even funnier when the eyes popped open and she stared up at him with a quick but dreamy smile.

"What's the time?"

"Time for you to change while I make the coffee. What happened to Jenny?"

"She won't be coming with us—or maybe . . ." She swung herself into a sitting position, straightening her skirt. "It doesn't matter. Okay, you make some coffee, then we'll be off."

Jerry looked at Jenny's clothes and frowned. Then he looked at Miss Brunner and frowned again.

"Don't worry, Mr. Cornelius."

"I've got a feeling I ought to."

"Just a feeling? Ignore it."

"I've got a feeling I ought to do that too." He went out of the room and found the kitchen. He filled the kettle, let it boil, put coffee into the filter, added the water, and put the pot on the stove. He heard Miss Brunner go upstairs. He sat down on a stool, not so much puzzling over Jenny's disappearance as trying not to. He sighed, feeling cold and rough.

7

"You know what Jung thought, don't you?" Jerry tilted the copter up into the clear winter sky. "He reckoned history went in 2,000-year cycles and that the current cycle started with Christ."

"Didn't he work flying-saucer sightings into that theory too?"

"I believe he did."

"It was all so fuzzy—all that stuff written ten or more years ago."

"There were a lot of hints."

"There are more now."

"And something to do with the zodiacal signs—that thing of Jung's."

"Yes. According to him, we were entering a cycle of great physical and psychological upheavals."

"That isn't hard to spot."

"Not with the Bomb already developed."

The helicopter was nearing the coast, with Holland as the first stop.

"You think it could be as simple as that—the Bomb as the cause?" Miss Brunner looked down at the land and ahead at the sea.

"It could be, after all," he said. "Why does the Bomb have to be a symptom?"

"I thought we had agreed it was."

"So we had. I'm afraid my memory isn't as good as yours, Miss Brunner."

"I'm not so sure. For the last few weeks I've been having hundreds of *déjà vu* experiences. What with your ideas on cyclic time—"

"You've been reading my books?" He was annoyed.

"No. Only about them. I haven't been able to get hold of a copy of anything. Privately printed, were they?"

"More or less."

"Why aren't there any around?"

"They disintegrated."

"Shoddy jobs, then."

"No. Built-in obsolescence."

"I'm not with you."

"I'm not with you; that's more to the point." He was still brooding about Jenny. He felt a pretty useless knight now.

"You're talking like that because you don't understand."

"You should have gone to bed last night; you're getting pretty corny."

"Okay." She shut up.

He felt like crashing the copter into the sea, but he couldn't do it. He was afraid of the sea. It was the idea of the Mother Sea that had put him off Celtic mythology as a boy. If only Brother Louis hadn't brought up the same image, he might still be in the Order.

So Miss Brunner was having *déjà vu* hallucinations too. Well, it was that kind of old world, wasn't it?

He realized he was getting morbid, reached over, switched on his radio, and put the bead in his ear. The music cheered him up.

Thirty miles north of Amsterdam they landed in a field close to farm buildings. The farmer was not surprised. He came hurrying out with cans of fuel. Jerry and Miss Brunner got out to stretch their legs, and Jerry helped the farmer, whom he paid well, to fill the tanks.

Five miles east of Uppsala they had to land and carry the fuel themselves from a barn to the copter. The snow, deep and crisp and even, got in their shoes, and Miss Brunner shivered.

"You might have warned me, Mr. Cornelius."

"I'd forgotten. I've never been this way in winter, you see."

"Elementary geography . . ."

"Which, apparently, neither of us possesses."

They entered a blizzard after a hundred miles, and Jerry had difficulty controlling the copter. When it was over he said to Miss Brunner, "We can get ourselves killed at this rate. I'm going to put her down. We'll have to find a car or something and continue the journey by land."

"That's foolish. It will take three days at least."

"All right," he said. "But another storm like that one and we walk if necessary."

There was not another bad storm, and the copter performed better than Jerry had expected it to. Miss Brunner read the map, and he followed her precise directions.

Below, black scars winding through the snow showed the main roads. Great frozen rivers and snow-laden forest stretched in all directions. Ahead they could just see a range of old, old mountains. It was perpetual evening at this time of year, and the farther north they went, the darker it became. The white lands seemed uninhabited, and Jerry could easily see how the legends of trolls, Jotunheim, and the tragic gods—the dark, cold, bleak legends of the North—had come out of Scandinavia. It made him feel strange, even anachronistic, as if he had gone back in time from his own age to the Ice Age.

It was becoming increasingly difficult to make out what lay beneath them, but Miss Brunner persevered, scanning the ground with night glasses and continuing her directions. Although the copter was well heated, they were both shivering.

"There are a couple of bottles of Scotch in the back," said Jerry. "Better get one."

She found a bottle of Bell's, unscrewed the cap, and handed the bottle to him. He gulped some down and handed it to her. She did the same.

"That's cheered me up," he said.

"We're getting close. Go down. There's a Lapp village marked on this map and I think we just passed it. The station isn't much farther."

The station seemed to be built of rust-red sheets of steel. Jerry wondered how they had got the materials there in the first place. Snow had been cleared round it, and a metal chimney blew black smoke into the air.

In that odd twilight, Jerry landed the copter on the snow and switched off the engine. A door opened, and a man stood there holding a portable electric lamp. It wasn't Frank.

"Good afternoon," Jerry called in Swedish. "Are you alone?"

"Absolutely. You are English by your accent. Were you forced down?"

"No. I understand that my brother was here."

"A man was here yesterday before I arrived. He went towards the mountains on a snowmobile, by the signs. Come in."

He led them into the cabin, closing the triple doors behind him. A stove blazed in the room they entered. Another room led off it.

The little man had a slightly Asiatic cast of face, reminding Jerry, too, of an Apache Indian. He was probably a Lapp. He was dressed in a large, heavy coat that covered him from neck to ankles. It looked like tawny wolf skin. He put the lamp on a deal table and waved towards some straight-backed chairs.

"Sit. I have some soup on the stove." He went to the range and took a medium-sized iron saucepan off it. He put it on the table. "I am Marek—the local pastor to the Lapps, you know. I had a reindeer team, but the wolverines got one of them yesterday, and I couldn't control the other and had to let it go. I expect a villager will discover it and come and look for me. Meanwhile I am warm here. There are provisions. Luckily, I am allowed a key to the place. I replace the supplies from time to time, and they allow me to use it on such an occasion as this."

"My name is Cornelius," said Jerry. "This is Miss Brunner."

"Not English *names*."

"No. But Marek isn't a Swedish name," Jerry smiled. Miss Brunner looked vexed, unable to understand the conversation.

"You are right, it is not. You know Sweden?"

"Only as far as Umea. I've never been this far north—not in winter at all."

"We must seem strange to someone who sees us only in the summer." Marek reached into a locker over the stove and took out three bowls and a loaf of rye bread. "We are not a summer people—winter is our natural time, though we hate it!"

"I'd never thought of that." Jerry turned to Miss Brunner and told her the basic details of their conversation as Marek poured the soup.

"Ask him where Frank might be going," said Miss Brunner.

"Is he a meteorologist?" Marek asked when Jerry put the question.

"No, though I think he's got some knowledge of it."

"He could be going to Kortafjallet—it's one of the highest mountains near here. There's another station on the summit."

"I can't see him going there. Anywhere else?"

"Well, unless he was going to try to get through the Kungsladen to Norway—it's the pass that runs through these mountains—I can't think. There are no villages in the direction he took."

Jerry told Miss Brunner what Marek had said.

"Why should he want to go to Norway?" she said.

"Why should he want to come *here?*"

"It's remote. He probably knew I was after him, though he thought you were dead. Maybe someone told him otherwise."

"Frank wouldn't come to somewhere as cold as this unless he had a real reason."

"Was he working on anything that would involve his being here?"

"I don't think so." Jerry turned to the pastor again. "How long would you say this man had been here?"

"A week or longer, judging by the low state of the supplies."

"I suppose he left nothing behind him?"

"There was some paper. I used some of it to light the stove, but the rest should be in his bin." The priest reached under the table. "Aren't you going to eat your soup?"

"Yes. Thanks."

When they were sitting down eating, Jerry smoothed out the quarto sheets of paper. The first contained some doodles.

"Frank's in a bad way." Jerry passed it to Miss Brunner.

"That's the interesting one." Miss Brunner pointed at the doodle with the lettering. "It gives our position and, I'd guess, his destination. But what's it all about?"

Jerry studied the other three sheets. There were some figures that he couldn't make sense of and more neurotic symbols. There was a pattern there, but he didn't feel like digging too deep. Knowing Frank, he was more disturbed by these doodles than he normally would have been.

"The best way of finding out is to follow him and locate this cave. Maze symbols, womb symbols. It's Frank's signature, without a doubt. He's developed a nice fat persecution complex."

"I'm not sure," said Miss Brunner. "You couldn't blame him, really. After all, we have been persecuting him."

"It's about even, I'd say. I don't feel up to going any farther tonight. Shall we stay here?"

"Yes."

"Do you mind if we spend the night here?" Jerry asked Marek.

"Of course not. It's a strange place for you, no doubt, to celebrate the season."

"The season? What's the date?"

"The twenty-fourth of December."

"Merry Christmas," said Jerry in English.

"Merry Christmas," smiled Marek, also in English. Then he said in Swedish, "You must tell me what things are like in the rest of Europe."

"Pretty good."

"I have read that inflation exists almost everywhere. Your crimes of violence have risen steeply, as have mental disorders, vice . . ."

"IBM has just perfected a new predictor-computer, using British, Swedish, and Italian scientists; all kinds of books and papers are being published full of new observations about the sciences, the arts—even theology. There have never been so many. Transport and communications are better than they ever were . . ." Jerry shook his head. "Pretty good."

"But what of the spiritual state of Europe? We share most of your problems, you know, other than the economic and political ones—"

"They'll come. Be patient."

"You are very cynical, Herr Cornelius. I am tempted to believe that Ragnarok is almost with us."

"That's an odd thing for a Christian minister to say."

"I am more than that—I am a Scandinavian Lutheran. I have no doubt of the truths inherent in our old pagan mythology."

"I am a British atheist and I share your opinion."

"Herr Cornelius, I would very much like to know your real reason for coming here."

"I've told you. We are searching for my brother."

"There is much more than that. I am not an intellectual, but I have an instinct that is generally quite astute. There is at once something *less* and something *more* in both you and your companion. Something—I am not normally guilty of coming to such a stern assumption—something evil."

"There's good and bad in all of us, Herr Marek."

"I see your face—and your eyes. Your eyes look boldly at much that I would fear to look at, but also they seem to hide from things that do not frighten me."

"Could it be that we are ahead of you, Herr Marek?"

"Ahead? In what way?"

"In *time*." Jerry felt unusually angry with the pastor. "These old-fashioned rules no longer apply. Your sort of morality, your sort of thinking, your sort of behaviour—it was powerful in its day. Like the dinosaur. Like the dinosaur it cannot survive in this world. You put values on everything—values . . ."

"I think I can see a little of what you mean." Marek lost his composure and rubbed at his face. "I wonder . . . is it Satan's turn to rule?"

"Careful, Herr Marek, that's blasphemy. Besides, what you are saying is meaningless nowadays." Jerry's hair had become disarranged as he talked. He brushed it back from the sides of his face.

"Because you want it to be?" Marek turned and walked towards the stove.

"Because it *is*. I am scarcely self-indulgent, Herr Marek—not in present-day terms."

"So you have your own code." Marek sounded almost jeering.

"On the contrary. There is no new morality, Herr Marek—there is no morality. The term is as barren as your grandmother's wrinkled old womb. There *are* no values!"

"There is still one fact we can agree on. Death."

"*Death? Death? Death?*" There were tears in his eyes. "*Why?*"

"Have you decided to start from scratch?" Marek was rising now to Jerry's challenge. Jerry was disconcerted and miserable.

"D—" Jerry paused.

"What's goin on?" Miss Brunner stood up. "What are you two quarrelling about?"

"The old bloke's round the twist." Jerry voice was low.

"Really? Can you ask him where we sleep and if there are any spare blankets?"

Jerry relayed the request.

"Follow me." Marek led them into the adjoining room. There were four bunks there, two pairs. He lifted the mattress off one of the bottom bunks, pulled back a panel and began lifting out blankets. "Enough?"

"Fine," said Jerry.

Jerry took the top bunk, Miss Brunner the bottom, and Marek slept in the bottom bunk opposite them. They all slept fully clothed, wrapped in blankets.

Jerry slept badly and woke in darkness. He looked at his watch and saw that it was 8 am. The pastor's bunk was empty. He leaned over and peered down. Miss Brunner was still sleeping. He unwrapped himself and jumped down.

In the other room, Marek was cooking something on the stove. On the table were an opened tin of herrings and three plates and forks.

"Your brother took most of our provisions, I'm afraid," Marek said as he brought the pot to the table. "Sill and coffee for breakfast. I apologize for my behaviour last night, Herr Cornelius. My own bewilderment got the better of me."

"And mine of me."

"I considered what you had said as best I could. I am now inclined . . ." Marek got three enamel mugs from the locker and poured coffee into two. "Is Miss Brunner ready for coffee yet?"

"She's still sleeping."

"I am now inclined to believe that there is a certain truth in what you say. I believe in God, Herr Cornelius, and the Bible—yet there are references in the Bible that can be interpreted as indications of this new phase you hint at."

"You shouldn't let yourself be convinced, Herr Marek."

"Don't worry about that. Would it, I wonder, be an intrusion if I accompanied you on this quest of yours? I believe I know the mountain your brother headed for— there is one with a cave. The Lapps are not very superstitious, Herr Cornelius, but they tend to avoid the cave. I wonder why your brother should be interested in it."

"What do you know about this? I didn't mention it."

"I have a little English. I read the map your brother drew."

"Could you make sense of the rest?"

"It made some sort of sense to my—well, my instincts. I don't know why."

"You can lead us there?"

"I think so. This is hardly the weather . . ."

"Will it be too dangerous?"

"Not if we take it carefully."

"I'll wake Miss Brunner."

Through the white twilight of the Artic winter the three people moved. On the higher parts of the ground stood a few silver birches, and on their left was a frozen lake, a wide expanse of flat snow. A little snow drifted in the air, and the clouds above were dense and grey.

A world of perpetual evening which would for six weeks in the year, Jerry knew, become a lush and glorious world of perpetual afternoon when the sun never went below the horizon, where lakes shone and rivers ran, animals moved, trees, rushes, gorse flourished. But now

it was a moody, unfriendly landscape. By this time the
station was out of sight behind them. It seemed that they
were hardly on earth at all, for the grey day stretched
in all directions.

They followed Marek on the snowshoes he had found
for them. The landscape, silent and still, seemed to impose
its own silence on them, for they spoke little as they
walked, huddled in their clothes.

At long last the mountains came in sight, and they
picked up the faint tracks of Frank's snowmobile winding
ahead of them. The mountains were close, but they hadn't
seen them until now because of the poor visibility.

Jerry wondered again if Miss Brunner's telling him that
Frank had the astronaut's testament was a ruse simply to
get him to go along with her. He was not alone in wanting
to see what Newman had written. There was something
unusual in the way in which he had been silenced, the few
wild public statements he had made before that, the fact
that he had done more orbits in his capsule than had been
originally announced. Would there really be some observation in the manuscript that would clarify the data?

The ground rose and they began to climb awkwardly.

"The cave is quite close," Marek said, his breath
streaming out.

Jerry wondered how he could be so sure in this almost
featureless country.

The cave mouth had recently been cleared of snow.
Just inside they could see the runners of a snowmobile.

Miss Brunner held back.

"I'm not sure that I want to go in. Your brother's
insane—"

"But that isn't your reason."

"I've got that 'I've been here before' feeling again."

"Me too. Come on." Jerry entered the dark cave. Its
far wall could not be seen. "Frank!"

The echo went on and on.

"It's a big cave," he said. He took his needle gun from
his pocket. The others entered behind him.

"I forgot to bring a torch," Marek whispered.

"We'll have to hope for the best, then. It will mean
that he won't be able to see us."

The cave was actually a tunnel sloping deeper and deeper into the rock. Clinging together, they stumbled on, uncertain of their footing. Jerry lost all sense of passing time, began to suspect that time had stopped. Events had become so unpredictable and beyond his control that he couldn't think about them. He was losing touch.

The floor of the tunnel and the hands of his companions became the sole reality. He began to suspect that he wasn't moving at all but that the floor was moving under him. He felt mentally and physically numb. Every so often vertigo would come and he would pause, swaying, feeling outward with his foot to find the chasm that was never there. Once or twice he half-fell.

Much later he was able to see the luminous dial of his watch. Four hours had passed. The tunnel seemed to be widening all the time, and he realized that it was much warmer and deeper and there was a saline smell in his nostrils as if of the sea. His senses began to wake and he heard the echoes of his own footsteps going away into distance. Ahead and below he thought he saw a trace of blue light.

He began to run down the incline, but checked his speed when he found he was going too fast. Now the light was good enough to show him the dim figures of his companions. He waited for them to catch up, and they went on cautiously towards the source of the light.

They came out of the tunnel and were standing on a slab of rock overlooking a gloomy, steamy gallery that stretched out of sight in all directions. Something had made the water slightly luminous, and this was the source of the light—a lake of hot water probably created by some underground hot spring carrying phosphorus. The water boiled and bubbled, and the steam soon soaked them. The floor of the gallery nearest to them was under water, and Jerry could distinguish several objects that looked out of place there. He noted that the rocks on his right led to this beach, and he began to slide down them towards it. The others took his lead.

"I had no idea that there could be a cave system of this size. What do you think caused it?" Miss Brunner was panting.

"Glacier, hot springs carrying corrosives looking for a way out. . . . I've never heard of anything quite like it.

Certainly nothing as big." They walked along the slippery, mineral-encrusted rock beside the lake. Jerry pointed. "Boats. Three of them. One of them looks fairly recent."

"These caves must have been known for at least a hundred years." Marek inspected the most dilapidated of the boats. "This is that old." He peered inside. "God save me!"

"What is it?" Jerry looked into the boat. A skeleton looked back at him. "Well, Frank certainly found something. You know, I think I've got an idea about this place. Did you ever hear of the Hollow Earth theory?"

"The last people to place any credence in it were those Nazis," said Miss Brunner, frowning deeply.

"Well, you know what I'm talking about—the idea that there was some sort of entrance in the Arctic to a world inside the earth. I'm not sure, but I think the whole idea was Bulwer-Lytton's—an idea he had in a novel. Didn't Horbiger have the same idea, or was he just for Eternal Ice?"

"You seem to know more about it than I do. But this tie-up with the Nazis is interesting. I hadn't thought of it."

"What tie-up?"

"Oh, I don't know. Anyway, I thought the Nazis believed the world was actually embedded in an infinity of rock—or was that someone else?"

"They gave serious consideration to both. Either theory would have suited them. Radar disproved one, and they could never find the polar opening, though I'm sure they sent at least one expedition."

"They were certainly triers, weren't they?" Miss Brunner said admiringly.

Jerry picked up the skull and threw it out over the water.

8

One of the boats looked quite recent. Jerry inspected it. "It's seaworthy, I'd say."

"You're not going out over *that?*" Miss Brunner shook her head.

"It must be the way Frank went. What do you think these boats mean? They weren't dragged here for nothing—they've crossed and come back."

"Crossed to what?"

"I thought you wanted to know what Frank was after. This is the way to find out."

"Do you think he believes this Hollow Earth idea?"

"I don't know. Isn't it even possible?"

"It's been disproved hundreds of ways!"

"So have a lot of things."

"Oh, come now, Jerry!"

"What do you think, Herr Marek? Do you want to see if we can cross the hot lake?"

"I am beginning to think that Dante was a naturalistic writer," said the Lapp. "I am glad I decided to come, Herr Cornelius."

"Let's get this boat launched then."

Marek helped him push the rowboat towards the water. It slid along easily. Jerry put one foot in the water and leaped back. "It's hotter than I thought!"

Miss Brunner shrugged and joined them as they steadied the boat.

"You get in first," Jerry told her. Unwillingly, she clambered in. Marek followed her, and Jerry got in last. The boat began to drift out over the phosphorescent water. Jerry unshipped the oars. He began to row through the steaming water, his features, caught in the oscillating radiance, looking like those of a fallen angel.

Soon the wall of the great cavern was obscured, and ahead of them was only vapour and darkness. Jerry began to feel drowsy, but continued to row with long strokes.

"This is like the River of the Dead," Marek said. "And you, Herr Cornelius, are you Charon?"

"I wish I were—it's a steady job, at least."

"I think you see yourself more as Cassandra."

"Cassandra?" Miss Brunner caught a word she understood. "Are you two talking about mythology still?"

"How did you know that was what we'd been talking about?"

"An educated guess."

"You're full of them."

"It's to do with my job," she said.

Marek was in high spirits. He chuckled. "What are you talking about?"

"I'm not sure," Jerry replied.

Marek chuckled again. "You two—you are an ambivalent pair."

"I wish you were wrong, Herr Marek."

Miss Brunner pointed ahead. "There is another shore —can you make anything out?"

He turned. The shore ahead seemed studded with regularly spaced and perfect cubes, some about two feet high and others ten feet high.

"Could that be a natural formation, Herr Cornelius?"

"I don't think so. In this light you can't even see what they're made of."

As they rowed nearer, they could see that some of the cubes were not on the shore at all but partially immersed in water. Jerry paused by one and reached out to touch it. "Concrete."

"Impossible!" Marek seemed delighted.

"You can't say that until we know more about this place." The bottom of the boat scraped the shore and they got out, hauling the boat after them.

They were surrounded by the black outlines of the concrete cubes. They approached the nearest.

"It's a bloody bunker!" Jerry entered it. There was a light switch inside the door, but it didn't work when Jerry tried it. He couldn't see anything of the interior. He went outside and walked around the bunker until he came to the machine-gun slit. The gun was still there, pointing out over the underground lake. He grasped the the gun and took his hand away covered in gritty rust. "They're not new. What is it—some abandoned Swedish project to guard against Russian attacks? All the roads into Finland have posts like these, haven't they, Herr Marek?"

"They have. But this is Lappish land—the government would need Lapp permission. They are very particular about the rights of the Lapps in Sweden, Herr Cornelius. I think the Lapps would have known about it."

"Not if there were security reasons. This place would be perfect as an H-bomb shelter. I wonder . . ."

Miss Brunner called through the gloom. "Mr. Cornelius, I don't think this was a Swedish project."

They went over to where she stood beside a light armoured car. The paint had partially peeled off it, but the remains of a swastika could be seen.

"A German project. But the Swedish government was neutral during the war, and this couldn't have been built in complete secrecy." He translated for Marek.

"Maybe just one or two people in the government knew and covered up," Marek suggested. "The Swedes were not always Anglophiles."

"But why should they build it?"

Through the regular rows of bunkers they moved—living quarters, offices, radio posts, a complete military village hundreds of feet below ground. Abandoned.

"That expedition of Hitler's may not have found the land at the earth's core," Miss Brunner was saying, "but evidently they thought this place worth using. I wonder what purpose they had for it."

"Perhaps none at all. For a people who burbled all the time about purpose they were great ones for forgetting their reasons for doing things."

The rock began to slope upward, and the light from the phosphorescent sea began to fade behind them.

"Those Nazis were born out of their time." Jerry led the way. Though the blue light had faded, there was still light of a new quality which seemed almost like daylight. Larger buildings came into sight on the crest of the slope, and Jerry, looking upward into the distance, saw tiny rays of light like stars in a black sky. "I think that's the open air beyond the roof. I think this cavern is only partially natural and the rest was hollowed out. Fabulous engineering."

The larger buildings had probably been the private quarters of officers. Behind them they could just distinguish a long series of structures unlike any of the rest, some sort of scaffolding bearing heavier objects. "Gun emplacements, could they be?" Miss Bunner asked.

"That's probably it."

"Your brother does not seem to be here after all." Marek looked about him.

"He must be. How did he know of this place, though?"

"Frank got around," Miss Brunner pointed out. "He had all sorts of acquaintances. Even I had heard rumors about the entrance to the underground world. This is what started them, I'd guess."

"Why should he come here? It's lonely, disturbing. Frank never liked being lonely or disturbed."

"Jerry, I am now not lonely and I am relaxed. Glad you could make it." On the roof of one of the buildings Frank stood giggling, his needle gun pointing in their general direction.

"Show-off!" Jerry dived straight into the entrance of the building before Frank could shoot. He got his own gun out.

Frank yelled from the roof. "Come out, Jerry, or I'll shoot your friends."

"Shoot them, then."

"Please come out, Jerry. I've been thinking what to do. I'm going to stitch your balls to your thighs. How about it?"

"Who told you I had any?"

"Please come out, Jerry."

"You're a sadist, Frank—I just realized it."

"One of many pleasures. Please come out, Jerry."

"What are you looking for here? Steamy, uterine seas, warm caves. Revealing, Frank."

"You're so common."

"I am indeed."

"Please, please come out, Jerry."

"You're frustrated, Frank, that's all that's wrong with you."

He heard footsteps scramble on the roof, and a hatch opened above him. He fired up as Frank fired down. "This is ridiculous," he said as they repressured. They had both missed. "Do you really want to kill me, Frank?"

"I thought I *had*, Jerry. I don't know."

"You're all the family I have left now, Frank." He laughed, fired, and missed again.

"Whose fault was it that Catherine died?" Frank asked as he also missed. "Yours or mine?"

"We're all victims of circumstance." Jerry fired and missed. He had a lot of needles left.

"Yours or mine?"

"Fault, Frank? Blame?"

"Don't you feel guilty, Jerry?" Frank missed.

"On and off, you know."

"There you are, then! Missed!" Both statements were triumphant.

"Missed!"

"Missed!"

"Missed!"

"Missed!"

"Jerry."

"What is this place, Frank? How did you find it?"

"It was on Father's microfilm. The one your friends were looking for. Come to think of it, they tortured me, didn't they?"

"I believe so. But what has it got to do with the European economic situation?"

"It would take someone who knew about those things to say I can't."

"Have you got the Newman manuscript with you?"

"Yes. Missed!"

"Can I see it?"

"You'd laugh if you did. It would suit you down to the ground."

"It's interesting, is it? Missed."

"Oh yes—aaah!"

"Got you!"

Frank's feet stumbled away over Jerry's head. Jerry ran out of the building and bumped into Miss Brunner and Marek. He paused and then ran round the building

Frank was limping down towards the shore.

They ran after him.

Frank ducked behind a bunker, and they lost sight of him.

"Look here," said Miss Brunner firmly, taking a .22 from her bag, "we're not going to lose him again."

"I wounded him. We'll find him." They searched among the bunkers, emerging on the shore.

"There's your brother." Marek pointed. He didn't understand the game, but he was joining in enthusiastically.

Jerry and Miss Brunner fired together as Frank tried to push his boat out over the steaming lake. He turned, howled, and fell with a splash. He screamed, thrashing in the boiling water.

He was dead by the time they reached him and dragged him out. "Done to a turn," said Jerry.

There was a briefcase in the bottom of the boat. Miss

Brunner covered Jerry with her gun as she stopped and picked it up. Resting it on her knee, she opened it with one hand and reached in. She came out with a micro-film spool and put it in her pocket. She put her gun back in her bag and handed him the briefcase. There was a thick cardboard file containing a typescript. In Frank's handwriting were the words *The Testament of G. Newman, Major, USAF, Astronaut.* Jerry flicked off the rubber bands holding the manuscript together. He sat down on the damp rock and opened the file and began to read.

Ha ha ha ha ha ha ha ha ha ha ha ha ha ha ha ha ha ha
ha ha ha ha ha ha ha ha ha ha ha ha ha ha ha ha ha ha ha
ha ha ha ha ha ha ha ha ha ha ha ha ha ha ha ha ha ha ha
ha ha ha ha ha ha ha ha ha ha ha ha ha ha ha ha ha ha ha
ha ha ha ha ha ha ha ha ha ha ha ha ha ha ha ha ha ha ha
ha ha ha ha ha ha ha ha ha ha ha ha ha ha ha ha ha ha ha
ha ha ha ha ha ha ha ha ha ha ha ha ha ha ha ha ha ha ha
ha ha ha ha ha ha ha ha ha ha ha ha ha ha ha ha ha ha ha
ha ha ha ha ha ha ha ha ha ha ha ha ha ha ha ha ha ha ha
ha ha ha ha ha ha ha ha ha ha ha ha ha ha ha ha ha ha ha
ha ha ha ha ha ha ha ha ha ha ha ha ha ha ha ha ha ha ha
ha ha ha ha ha ha ha ha ha ha ha ha ha ha ha ha ha ha ha
ha ha ha ha ha ha ha ha ha ha ha ha ha ha ha ha ha ha ha
ha ha ha ha ha ha ha ha ha ha ha ha ha ha ha ha ha ha ha
ha ha ha ha ha ha ha ha ha ha ha ha ha ha ha ha ha ha ha
ha ha ha ha ha ha ha ha ha ha ha ha ha ha ha ha ha ha ha
ha ha ha ha ha ha ha ha ha ha ha ha ha ha ha ha ha ha ha
ha ha ha ha ha ha ha ha ha ha ha ha ha ha ha ha ha ha ha
ha ha ha ha ha ha ha ha ha ha ha ha ha ha ha ha ha ha ha
ha ha ha ha ha ha ha ha ha ha ha ha ha ha ha ha ha ha ha
ha ha ha ha ha ha ha ha ha ha ha ha ha ha ha ha ha ha ha
ha ha ha ha ha ha ha ha ha ha ha ha ha ha ha ha ha ha ha
ha ha ha ha ha ha ha ha ha ha ha ha ha ha ha ha ha ha ha
ha ha ha ha ha ha ha ha ha ha ha ha ha ha ha ha ha ha ha
ha ha ha ha ha ha ha ha ha ha ha ha ha ha ha ha ha ha ha
ha ha ha ha ha ha ha ha ha ha ha ha ha ha ha ha ha ha ha
ha ha ha ha ha ha ha ha ha ha ha ha ha ha ha ha ha ha ha
ha ha ha ha ha ha ha ha ha ha ha ha ha ha ha ha ha ha ha
ha ha ha ha ha ha ha ha ha ha ha ha ha ha ha ha ha ha ha
ha ha ha ha ha ha ha ha ha ha ha ha ha ha ha ha ha ha ha
ha ha ha ha ha ha ha ha ha ha ha ha ha ha ha ha ha ha ha
ha ha ha ha ha ha ha ha ha ha ha ha ha ha ha ha ha ha ha
ha ha ha ha ha ha ha ha ha ha ha ha ha ha ha ha ha ha ha
ha ha ha ha ha ha ha ha ha ha ha ha ha ha ha ha ha ha ha
ha ha ha ha ha ha ha ha ha ha ha ha ha ha ha ha ha ha ha
ha ha ha ha ha ha ha ha ha ha ha ha ha ha ha ha ha ha ha
ha ha ha ha ha ha ha ha ha ha ha ha ha ha ha ha ha ha ha
ha ha ha ha ha ha ha ha ha ha ha ha ha ha ha ha ha ha ha

ha ha ha ha ha ha ha ha ha ha ha ha ha ha ha ha ha ha
ha ha ha ha ha ha ha ha ha ha ha ha ha ha ha ha ha ha
ha ha ha ha ha ha ha ha ha ha ha ha ha ha ha ha ha ha
ha ha ha ha ha ha ha ha ha ha ha ha ha ha ha ha ha ha
ha ha ha ha ha ha ha ha ha ha ha ha ha ha ha ha ha ha
ha ha ha ha ha ha ha ha ha ha ha ha ha ha ha ha ha ha
ha ha ha ha ha ha ha ha ha ha ha ha ha ha ha ha ha ha
ha ha ha ha ha ha ha ha ha ha ha ha ha ha ha ha ha ha
ha ha ha ha ha ha ha ha ha ha ha ha ha ha ha ha ha ha
ha ha ha ha ha ha ha ha ha ha ha ha ha ha ha ha ha ha
ha ha ha ha ha ha ha ha ha ha ha ha ha ha ha ha ha ha
ha ha ha ha ha ha ha ha ha ha ha ha ha ha ha ha ha ha
ha ha ha ha ha ha ha ha ha ha ha ha ha ha ha ha ha ha
ha ha ha ha ha ha ha ha ha ha ha ha ha ha ha ha ha ha
ha ha ha ha ha ha ha ha ha ha ha ha ha ha ha ha ha ha
ha ha ha ha ha ha ha ha ha ha ha ha ha ha ha ha ha ha
ha ha ha ha ha ha ha ha ha ha ha ha ha ha ha ha ha ha
ha ha ha ha ha ha ha ha ha ha ha ha ha ha ha ha ha ha
ha ha ha ha ha ha ha ha ha ha ha ha ha ha ha ha ha ha
ha ha ha ha ha ha ha ha ha ha ha ha ha ha ha ha ha ha
ha ha ha ha ha ha ha ha ha ha ha ha ha ha ha ha ha ha
ha ha ha ha ha ha ha ha ha ha ha ha ha ha ha ha ha ha
ha ha ha ha ha ha ha ha ha ha ha ha ha ha ha ha ha ha
ha ha ha ha ha ha ha ha ha ha ha ha ha ha ha ha ha ha
ha ha ha ha ha ha ha ha ha ha ha ha ha ha ha ha ha ha
ha ha ha ha ha ha ha ha ha ha ha ha ha ha ha ha ha ha
ha ha ha ha ha ha ha ha ha ha ha ha ha ha ha ha ha ha
ha ha ha ha ha ha ha ha ha ha ha ha ha ha ha ha ha ha
ha ha ha ha ha ha ha ha ha ha ha ha ha ha ha ha ha ha
ha ha ha ha ha ha ha ha ha ha ha ha ha ha ha ha ha ha

Not a variation on 203 neatly numbered pages of manuscript. Jerry sighed and tossed the book into the water.

PHASE 3

9

He rowed away, leaving Marek and Miss Brunner standing close together on the shore. He was very tired, and he had a long trip ahead of him.

Halfway up the sloping cavern, he lay down to sleep. When he woke up, he climbed on until he reached the cave's mouth. The cold did not bother him as he inspected Frank's snowmobile.

It seemed easy to operate, and the grey tracks it had made coming here were not completely obliterated by snow.

Sad and scared, he followed the tracks back to the station. He sighed deeply all the way, and a few tears even wetted his big black eyes when he stopped the sleigh by the rust-red meteorological post. He went in and opened a tin of herring. The stove had gone out, but the hut was still warmer than it was outside. He ate the herring and went to fetch his bottle from the copter. He sat in the pilot's seat drinking whisky and trying to warm up the engine. He had finished the Scotch by the time it caught. He slid the door open and tossed the bottle out. The copter was a good one. There was probably enough fuel left to get him to one of the Baltic ports. Before he took off, he rummaged in the back and found his passport. There were only a few days to go before it expired.

He dumped the copter outside Lumea and was able to buy a ticket on a cargo ship leaving that night. He convinced the officials that someone must have forgotten to stamp his entry visa in his passport and headed for Southampton, via Hamburg.

In London he opened his town house. The hotel-sized building on Holland Park Avenue stood well back from the street and was surrounded by a high wall topped with electrified spikes.

It was time, he decided, for a spot of exterior meditation. He would get a big party going and lose himself in it. With luck it would help him to work a few things out.

But first he filled himself with sleeping pills and took to his bed to sleep a dreamless sleep for three days and nights. When he awoke his energy was low and people were even more urgently needed.

After his bath, he dressed in a high-collared white Bastille-style linen shirt, a black terylene cravat, black suède trousers, and black doeskin jacket. From a wardrobe containing some fifteen of them, he took a black, double-breasted car coat and laid it on the chest near the window. He pulled on a pair of black boots with low cuban heels. He studied his pale features in the mirror that covered the far wall, brushed his hair and was satisfied. He was feeling very hungry and rather weak. He picked up the coat, took a new pair of gloves from the chest, and left the dressing-room. There were actually two dressing-rooms, one containing clothes he would probably never bother to wear.

The house was mid-Victorian, with six floors and two very large main rooms on each floor. Every room was sparsely furnished and gave the impression that the occupant was in the process of moving either in or out.

Jerry walked down the wide stairs until he reached the basement, where the kitchens were. Although they shone with mechanical equipment, the kitchens had hardly been used. Great cupboards were filled with canned and dehydrated food. The cellars below, apart from containing a vast selection of wines and spirits which he never drank, also contained a commercial cold-storage room filled with a mixed herd of carcasses. The whole collection, here and below, made Jerry feel sick when he thought about it. He mixed himself a pot of instant coffee and ate a packet of chocolate digestives.

There were two cars in the garage behind the house. One was a little Toyota mini-sports that the Japanese had just started to put on the market. The other was the oldest thing Jerry owned—a three-ton supercharged 1936

Duesenberg limousine, bigger than his Cadillac, with upholstery of electric-blue silk. Custom-built for a successful
Midwestern police chief, it had bulletproof glass and
steel shutters operated by the push-button window control and automatic lubrication every seventy-five miles
and did ninety in second gear. Jerry normally liked
plenty of bonnet in front of him when he drove. His
other car, the Cadillac, was back in the Shaftesbury
Avenue garage. His own garage was large enough to house
several double-decker buses, and most of it was taken
up by drums of fuel. There was also a small petrol reservoir below.

The door slid out of the ground and closed behind him
as he drove the Toyota down the asphalt drive into
Holland Park Hill, turned left towards Kensington High
Street, and had a fairly clear drive until he reached the
main street.

He played· the radio and relaxed in the great solid
stream of traffic as it flowed slowly along. Within an hour
and a half he had parked the Toyota in his reserved
space in the Piccadilly Sky Garage and breathed the rich
air of the centre with pleasure. He never felt really
comfortable unless he had at least fifteen miles of
built-up area on all sides; and here he was happiest,
walking towards Leicester Square and the Blue Boar
Tavern for a quick cocktail. It wasn't natural, he felt,
for a man to have to live any other way.

In times of change, the Blue Boar did not change. The
small blue neon sign still glimmered outside, the plastic
trees on the way down to the cocktail bar still twittered
with artificial bird song, the plastic coats-of-arms still
adorned the leatherette-upholstered walls, and the lighting
was still low. It was quiet and pleasantly vulgar, and
the cocktails were inexpensive.

A small, pretty, dark-haired girl brought Jerry a
Woomera Special—milder than the name implied: bourbon with ginger ale. A couple were sitting in the corner,
and they paid little attention to Jerry or each other. Once
or twice the man asked an abrupt question in German
and was answered abruptly. Jerry could rarely speak
German.

Leaving the Blue Boar, he went into the Beat City
showrooms round the corner to see if his guitar was

ready. He had ordered it after his return from Angkor.

The man took him into the basement to see it. It had an oval belly and a 24-fret neck. The strings went up to the top of the neck into a small transistorized sensitizer which automatically kept them in tune. Six pick-ups were ranged between bridge and neck, and there was a control for each one, with a tremolo switch and echo play and fuzz buttons. It was one of the best pieces of musical engineering Jerry had seen. The cost was £4,200 plus £1,400 tax. They plugged it into their amplifier so he could test it. It was beautiful, sound as a bell. He gave them a cheque and took it with him.

In a Welbeck Street coffee bar Jerry put in his junk order, buying The Man's entire stock. "If your regulars are put out," he told The Man, "tell them my address and tell them it's free."

At beat clubs, at Emmett's, at bars, in bookshops and boutiques, hairdressers, grills and record shops, Jerry toured and spread the word that an open party was about to start at his Holland Park house.

When he got back to the house, carrying his heavy guitar in its flat case, he was just in time to let in the first truckload of food from the catering firm that had agreed to supply the party with almost everything it would need.

As the white-coated men began to lay the stuff out, Jerry locked the doors leading down to the basement. They were steel, eight inches thick, and would open only to a specific vocal command from him.

On the ground floor, the two rooms could be opened out into one. The only furniture was cushions scattered about on the carpet and a large stereo tele-radiogram-tape-recorder combination. Ten-inch spools of tape were ready, and Jerry switched them on to test them. They relayed music through speakers everywhere in the house.

He began to feel depressed.

He opened the guitar case and took out the instrument. He plugged in the lead and plugged the other end into the combination's amplifier, switching off the tape.

He played a brief E-flat progression, trying out a simple tune based on Rufus Thomas's "All Night Worker". It didn't come out properly. He adjusted the pick-ups and tone controls and tried again, this time in B flat. It had nothing in it. He sighed.

He tried out a number of other basic progressions. Nothing was wrong with the guitar, but there was something wrong with him.

He put the guitar away, switched on the tapes again, and went upstairs to change.

The Man and a couple of friends were the first arrivals. "I thought I'd avail myself of the facilities," said The Man, taking off his heavy raincoat. He wore a high-collared green corduroy jacket and hamlet tights. He looked a wow.

The flood was on, and half-suspicious guests got the mood of the place before they let themselves relax. There were Turkish and Persian lesbians with huge houri eyes like those of sad, neutered cats; French tailors, German musicians; Jewish martyrs; a fire-eater from Suffolk; a barber-shop quartet from Britain's remaining American base—the Columbia Club, in Lancaster Gate; two fat prudes; Hans Smith of Hampstead, Last of the Left-wing Intellectuals—the Microfilm Mind; Shades; fourteen dealers in the same antique from Portobello Road, their faces sagging under the weight of their own self-deception; a jobless Polish french-polisher brought by one of the dealers; a pop group called the Deep Fix; a pop group called Les Coques Sucrés; a tall Negro; a hunch-backed veterinarian named Marcus; the Swedish girl and a juicy youngster; three journalists, who had just finished spending their golden handshakes; Little Miss Dazzle, whom one of them had discovered in El Vino's looking for Mr. Crookshank; an Irishman called Poodles; the literary editor of the *Oxford Mail* and his sister; twenty-seven members of the Special Branch; a heterosexual; two small children; the late great Charlie Parker, just in from Mexico under his alias Alan Bird—he had been cleaning up for years; a morose psychiatrist from Regent's Park named Harper; a great many physicists, astrologers, geographers, mathematicians, astronomers, chemists, biologists, musicians, monks from disbanded monasteries, warlocks, out-of-work whores, students, Greeks, solicitors; a self-pitying albino; an architect; most of the pupils from the local comprehensive school, who had heard the noise and come in; most of their teachers; a market gardener; less than one New Zealander; two hundred Hungarians who had Chosen Freedom and the chance to make a fast buck; a sewing-machine salesman; the mothers of twelve of the children from the comprehensive school; the father of one of the children from the comprehensive school, though he didn't know it; a butcher; another Man; a Displaced Person; a small painter; and several hundred other individuals not immediately identifiable.

Jerry, suffering from a little paramnesia—a recurrent but brief condition to which, like Miss Brunner, he was subject—had the impression that he had met everyone before but couldn't place most of them. He also had the impression of having said everything before, but he recognized what was happening and paid no attention.

("So you've been in Lapland,") one of the journalists said. "So you've been in Lapland."

("Yes.") "Yes."

("What for?") "What for?"

("You won't believe me.") "You won't believe me."

("Tell me a convincing lie.") "Tell me a convincing lie."

("To study the similarities between the Ragnarok theme and the second law of thermodynamics.") "To study the similarities between the Ragnarok theme and the second law of thermodynamics." Jerry's mind jerked back on to its normal wave length. "You know: the gods and men against the giants; fire against ice—heat against cold. *Ragnarok and the Heat Death of the Universe,* my next paper."

The journalist giggled, patted Jerry's bottom, and moved off to tell the embroidered anecdote to his colleagues.

The Swedish girl saw him. "Jerry! Where did you go?"

Jerry was in a gallant mood. "Sweden—I thought that was where you had gone."

"Ha, ha!"

"You're getting too close."

"What do you mean?"

Jerry gulped. "It's time that phrase was melted down for scrap."

"Jerry, this is Laurence." She brought the juicy young-ster forward. He gave Jerry a juicy smile.

"Hello, Laurence." Jerry squeezed the youngster's hand, which immediately began to sweat. "Hmmm, fast reactions."

"Laurence has been streamlined," the Swedish girl said mockingly from behind the youngster. "No frontal lobes."

"That's the stuff to give 'em. Shall we dance?"

"If you don't think we'll look too conspicuous."

"Heavens to Betsy, what should it matter to us!"

They danced the chaver, a rather formal measure with minuet and frug influences. Jerry thought of Mr. Powys's last moments and felt he could sense the tiny figures of Marek and Miss Brunner having it away in the caverns of his mind. He got out as fast as he could, back to the wild world.

"You dance very gracefully," she smiled.

"Yes," he said. "What's your name?"

"Ulla."

"You're not chewing gum tonight."

"Not tonight."

He began to feel randy. He rolled his eyes. She laughed.

"It's a big party," she said. "Why so big?"

"Safety in numbers."

"Is it all for me?"

"As much as you can take."

"Aha!"

He began to feel blissful. He closed his eyes. Up and down went his long legs, round went his body, in and out went his hands, and they danced together. He chewed at her flavoured hair and stroked her thighs. They danced apart, pirouetting. He took her hand and twirled her again. Then he led her from the room. They climbed over the people on the stairs, pushed through the throngs on the landing, found the next flight less densely crowded all the way to the top, where there were only a few people holding glasses and talking. In his bedroom there was just enough space for the door to open. The rest of it was taken up by the *bed*.

He closed the door and threw many bolts. The room was in complete darkness. They fell to biting each other.

"Oho!" she cried as his hand swam up her leg.

"Ha, ha!" he whispered, and he began softly to punch her warm body. They rolled about laughing and groaning. She was a bit of all right. He kissed her cheek. She tickled him on the chest. Then they lay back, exhausted and content.

It was nice in the darkness with the girl beside him. He rolled her a cigarette and lit it for her. He rolled one for himself.

When they had finished, he pinched the cigarettes out and put his arm around her, cradling her head. They fell asleep.

But he dreamed of Catherine, of Catherine. He dreamed of Catherine. Cath-er-ine. He merged into her and he *was* Catherine. Catherine with a dart in her heart, a minutely feathered dart. Catherine himself, and when Frank came along, red as a lobster, he arched her body for Frank. When Frank had joined them they walked in a summer garden, the three of them peaceful in her body.

"How many can one body take?" He woke up before the dream became too crowded. He began to make love to Ulla.

When they arose the following afternoon, they found the party beginning to warm up. They washed in the bathroom adjoining the bedroom, and Jerry left her to unlock his dressing-room and put on fresh clothes.

They breakfasted on pâté and rye bread which the caterers had just brought in. Then they parted. Jerry picked up a discarded horror-film magazine and took it into the ground-floor room, where he sat on a cushion and read it. Next to him lay a cold Man with closed eyes. Someone had stepped on The Man's dropper. Someone else had removed his tights. He looked pretty funny.

When he had finished the magazine, Jerry wandered through the house and found the corpses of two Special Branch men. This intrusion annoyed him, and he kicked at the bodies for a moment. One of them had been garrotted, and the other didn't have a mark on him. Hans Smith, rather drunk, holding a bottle of wine, pointed at the unmarked Special Branch man. "Shock, old boy, shock. The rate it's taking them off they ought to set up a British Shock Research Institute, eh?"

"How long have you got, then?" asked Jerry.

"The doctors say a year, but I think less."

"It's best to."

"I don't think much of your friends, seriously, old boy. I had to ask one or two of them to leave—on your behalf, since I couldn't find you."

"Thank you, Mr. Smith."

"Thank you, old boy."

In a corner the self-pitying albino was talking to Charlie Parker. "I was thinking of changing my name myself," he was saying. "How would you like to be called White?"

Two of the warlocks had assembled the best part of the comprehensive school teachers, pupils, and parents. They wanted a virgin for a symbolic sacrifice. "Only *symbolic*, you understand."

The fourteen antique dealers from Portobello Road were enjoying the Polish french-polisher in a gang bang.

The Turkish and Persian lesbians sat straight-backed on cushions and looked on.

The Deep Fix were backing Little Miss Dazzle, and her small, true voice sang "Just What It Is," the melody weaving round and above the general noise of the party, counterpointing the screams and giggles and grunts and low moans. Jerry paused and listened to her.

She saw him and finished the song.

"This is your house?"

"Yes. That was nice."

"You're Mr. Cornelius?"

"I am."

"Mr. Cornelius I believe you know Mr. Crookshank, my agent. I haven't been able to get in touch with him for *weeks*."

Jerry felt sorry for Little Miss Dazzle, she looked so upset.

"I haven't seen him for some time either."

"Oh, dear. I've had offers from other agents, and I'll need to get someone soon or my career will be finished. But I —well, I got on so well with him. Where on earth is he?"

"The last I saw of him was in France—Normandy—the coast."

"He's abroad!"

"You could've fooled me." And, of course, she had. "I'm going out for a ride. Want to come?"

"Well—I came with three men. I met them on Fleet Street.

"I'm sure they won't mind if you're away for a few hours."

She gave him a sweet smile. "Oh, all right." She hooked her arm in his and they went out of the back of the house down to the garage. Jerry decided to use the Duesenberg.

In Battersea, as he drove toward the park, Jerry discovered the truth about Little Miss Dazzle. "Oh, well . . ." he said and put a comforting arm round her shoulders. She cuddled up.

The months of the party went by and Jerry circulated. The Suffolk fire-eater, who had experience in show business, took Little Miss Dazzle off his hands and became her agent, just in time.

Guests died or left and new ones came. Spring arrived, green and lovely, and the guests oozed into the garden. The catering firm first of all refused to accept a cheque for their monthly account; then they refused paper money, and Jerry had to pay them in sovereigns. He paid them with a secret grin.

The party continued to be catered for. The trucks, Jerry noted, drove through clearer streets, and there didn't seem to be as many people about as usual.

Jerry went back in one day and checked his calendar. He was puzzled. It wasn't right. Not yet.

He took the calendar down and tore it across with a frown.

The morose psychiatrist from Regent's Park was looking at him.

"What's the trouble?" He spoke sympathetically but morosely.

"Time," said Jerry. "Something wrong with the time."

"I don't follow you."

"It's moving too fast."

"I see."

"Don't bother," said Jerry, walking back into the main room, picking his way over the guests.

"I'd like to listen to what you're getting at." The psychiatrist followed him. "Honestly I would."

"Maybe you can tell me why so many people seem to have left London so soon."

"So soon—were you expecting them to leave?"

"I expected something like it."

"When?"

"I expected the first signs in a year or so."

"The first signs of what?"

"The breakup. It was bound to come, but . . ."

"Not so soon. An interesting idea. I thought we were bound to get straight again. Surely the economic crisis was only temporary. Europe's resources, manpower, *brain* power . . ."

"I was more optimistic." Jerry turned and grinned at the morose psychiatrist from Regent's Park.

"I see you have recovered your self-possession."

Jerry waved his hand round the room. "I wouldn't say that. You see most of what I possess."

The psychiatrist frowned.

"Well, what's your explanation?" Jerry asked him.

"I thought it was a temporary solution, as I said. This land rush I've heard about . . ."

"What's that?"

"Apparently there's been some sort of back-to-the-land movement, you know. From what I hear, the Scottish Highlands are like Blackpool beach in August, with everybody staking a claim. People seem to have lost faith in the pound and the government, such as it is."

"Very sensible. So the stockbrokers are stockbreeding and raising wheat."

"That seems to be about the size of it. Not that you can raise much wheat in the Highlands. But the same is true all over rural Britain—more people in the country than in the towns these days."

"Aha. This shouldn't have happened yet."

"Have I been missing out? Did anyone else anticipate this?"

Jerry shrugged.

"Maybe you've heard of this atom-bomb rumour?" The psychiatrist plugged on.

"Atom-bomb rumour? No, nothing." Jerry felt surprised. "Atom bombs?"

"One of the sheets reported a rumour that a maniac was threatening to bomb the European capitals."

"Go on!" Jerry jeered.

"I know—but these days you just don't know what to believe."

"I *thought* I did," said Jerry.

Soon London began to stink. There were power failures and failures of many other kinds. Jerry wasn't sufficiently concerned to check, but it seemed that the seat of government had been moved to Edinburgh. London, it appeared, had been abandoned. Jerry was prepared for this, and soon his private generators were going—years too soon, in his opinion. When the water was on, he pumped as much as he could into specially prepared roof-top reservoirs. Chemical toilets replaced the others. His guests increased for a few weeks, and then a hard core took up residence. Few left. There were few new arrivals.

What had happened to the country? The coalition government seemed ineffectual, unable to deal with anything at all. For a while it was a talking point, and then the party settled down again until July.

In July, Miss Brunner and Marek turned up at the party. Marek looked much younger and more ingenuous than Jerry remembered. At first he put it down to the Lapland winter and the poor light. But then he realized that Miss Brunner had found Dimitri's replacement.

"Congratulations," he said, leading his friends through the hall. It was full of marvellous perfume. "Where have you been all this time? By the looks of things, Miss Brunner, you made good use of my father's secret."

She laughed. "Full use. The *gold* I've been converting recently. Anarchy reigns, Mr. Cornelius!"

"Or entropy, is it?" Marek smiled secretly.

"The process is getting going sooner than I thought . . ." Jerry led them to the second-floor bar and got them drinks.

"It is indeed, Mr. Cornelius." She raised her glass. "And the toast is to Hermaphrodite!"

"Spare one for my father. He was some help to you."

"To Herr Cornelius the Elder and Hermaphrodite!" She called the toast in perfect Swedish.

10

"And what, for the record, was my father's powerful secret?"

"Something he learned in the war," she told him. "As you know, he was a talented man, part of the British scientific team that followed the Allies into Germany. They were very keen to discover just how far certain German scientific projects had got. They were relieved to find they hadn't got as far as they thought. But your father, with his eye on the main chance, discovered something that none of the others discovered."

"The underground cave system?" Jerry didn't know much about the war.

"No—this was much closer to home, although the caves were part of it. The Germans were working on an atomic reactor. At one stage, according to the records, they had been forced to decide whether to aim for an atomic engine or an atomic bomb. They decided on the engine—their resources, particularly the supply of uranium, were much more limited than ours, don't forget. The reactor was originally located in Berlin, but moved away when things began to get hot. It was captured by the Allies. That is the official story."

"The unofficial one?"

"There were two reactors, two projects—one for an engine and one for a bomb. They had produced bombs by the end of the war. They had decided on the Lapland caves—discovered by their 1937 expedition—as an ideal site for covering Russia and America. Those 'gun emplacements' you didn't bother to look at were launching pads for twenty A10 rockets fitted with atomic warheads.

The microfilm was detailed and proved it. Copies were sent round Europe with a letter. They were authenticated. I was able to blackmail virtually every country in Europe without any of the others knowing."

"Why not Russia and America?"

"I wasn't interested in them, and they weren't psychologically prepared for it the way Europe was. Anyway, Russia captured the other reactor and must have known that there was a launching site somewhere—they might have guessed."

"Why weren't the missiles launched?"

"Hitler killed himself and the general in charge got cold feet, pulled out."

"So you got your hands on a lot of gold."

"Yes. It's back in circulation now, of course, but it did its job—and the confusion has precipitated the process."

"With you owning a lot of power."

"And a lot of people. I'm over here recruiting scientists, bringing work to hundreds—thousands, what with the industries concerned."

"You're building the computer?"

"In the Lapland caves."

"What about the bombs?"

Miss Brunner laughed. "Apart from the fact that the rocket machinery was corroded, accelerated by the vapour from the hot lake, the uranium in the warheads had been hastily refined—you know the trouble they were having with their heavy-water systems."

"They wouldn't go off."

"They didn't have a chance to test them, you see."

Jerry laughed and laughed.

"I see you've got a lot of scientists and technicians here," she said. "Do you mind if I do a bit of quiet recruiting while I'm at it?"

"Help yourself. The party's all yours. I've finished with it now."

11

ABIOLOGISTS (3), ACAROLOGIST (1), ACOLOGISTS (2), ACROLOGIST (1), ADENOLOGISTS (5), AESTHOPHYSIOLOGISTS (6), AETIOLOGISTS (2), ALETHIOLOGIST (1), ALCHEMIST (1), AMPHIBIOLOGISTS (10), ANATRIPSOLOGIST (1), ANDROLOGISTS (10), ANGIOLOGISTS (4), ANORGANOLOGISTS (3), ANTHROPOLOGISTS (4), ANTHROMORPHOLOGIST (1), ARCHAEOLOGISTS (4), ARCHOLOGISTS (6), AREOLOGISTS (2), ARTHROLOGISTS (4), ASTHENOLOGISTS (2), ASTROLITHOLOGIST (1), ASTROLOGERS (7), ASTROMETEOROLOGIST (1), ATMOLOGISTS (2), AUDIOLOGIST (1), AUXOLOGISTS (6).

"Your want list." Jerry studied the pages. There were twenty-six categories, corresponding to the letters of the alphabet.

"I've filled most of it," she said. "I heard of your party through a histologist I hired—one of his colleagues was at it."

"So you came along to try to complete the list. Some ark you're building, t o."

She looked ecstatic. "Not the ark—the deluge! DUEL is its name, Mr. Cornelius, and it'll be completed within the year. I've had the hot lake roofed over, laboratories and plants put up. It's the most marvellous thing you've ever seen!"

"Why DUEL?"

"Decimal Unit Electronic Linkage. It will fill half the cave system. At this moment it has the capabilities of any machine in existence, except that it's much faster. We'll complete the assembly in another year. And that's when the real work will begin!"

"What's so different about it?"

Marek grinned at Miss Brunner. "It incorporates a number of unprecedented features," he said. "To begin with, each of its units, instead of being a simple on/off switch, is capable of ten magnetic states, so that the computer operates on a decimal instead of a binary basis. This is what gives it its already tremendouly increased power. In addition to this, it utilizes ingenious linkages which apparently," he chuckled, "not even the designer of the human brain thought of! This can open up an entirely new investigation of the material world. Hints of all kinds of unexpected relationships are appearing from the computer's calculations. Ultimately DUEL will probe beyond the root of matter itself. Miss Brunner has forged—"

"A scientific tool—not a glorified abacus!" Miss Brunner folded her want list. "DUEL is much more than a computer, Mr. Cornelius."

"Yes indeed, Miss Brunner," said Marek.

"I couldn't contribute." Jerry winked at her.

"Couldn't you?"

"Ah, Miss Brunner, you're at it again!"

"Would you have it any other way?"

"All other ways. You want more than information from DUEL, Miss Brunner."

"I don't want information from DUEL—not ultimately. It is DUEL who wants information. I want—a result. Conclusive data, and more."

"You are ambitious."

Marek's eyes shone. "But what an ambition, Herr Cornelius!"

Jerry looked sideways at her little familiar. "I'll decide later, baby."

"You want to come to see DUEL?" Miss Brunner seemed unusually eager.

"You seem unusually eager," said Jerry.

"Aha!" Marek's eyes watered.

"I think I'd like to leave London for a bit. The smell."

"The smell," she said. "I suppose we are indirectly responsible for that."

Jerry grinned at her somewhat admiringly. "Well, yes, I suppose you are. It hadn't occurred to me."

"This was a gift-wrapped, throwaway age, Mr.

Cornelius. Now the gift wrapping is off, it's being thrown away."

"It's certainly perishable." Jerry wrinkled his nose.

"Oh, *you!*"

"I won't join you just yet," Jerry decided. "I haven't been in to the centre of town for a while. I'll see what things are like there. If they're better, I'll stay for as long as I can."

After Jerry had left, Miss Brunner and Marek ranged the party, mixing in but always staying close together.

After a bit they found Jerry's bedroom and went in.

"He does himself well," said Miss Brunner, sitting on the bed and bouncing up and down.

"Why did you let him go?"

"He hasn't been downtown lately. It will do him good."

"But you might lose him."

"No. There are a limited number of places he will go to. I know them all."

She reached out and pulled Marek toward the bed. He crawled up it towards the pillows and then lay on his back, staring at the ceiling. His face was blank as Miss Brunner flung herself on top of him with a throaty cry.

"Time for a last coming together, my tender," she whispered as she nibbled his ear.

Marek let out a great sigh, expelling all the air from his lungs.

A short while later, looking better than she had, Miss Brunner supervised the men she had hired. They were rapidly crating up Jerry's threads and taking them down to a waiting van.

While she supervised, the small painter passed by wearing Marek's clothes. She gave him a swift glance. He noticed and turned, smiling rather wistfully. "I found them in the bedroom. Nobody seemed to own them, so . . ." He fingered the cloth. "Are they suitable?"

"Oh, I should think so," she said.

Jerry felt uneasy driving the Duesenberg through the ill-frequented streets. London was littered, London was grey, though here and there a crowd, extravagantly dressed, would give beauty to the picture. To Jerry, as he passed them, each crowd seemed a single unit, a composite creature, many-limbed and many-headed. Nearer the centre of town the crowds were bigger creatures, getting bigger as he came close to Piccadilly Circus. Jerry felt alone, and the crowd-creatures seemed menacing.

In the Chicken Fry he found that chicken was off. It was eat poorly flavoured algae and like it. He didn't bother. The big place was poorly lit, and he sat near the back in shadow. He was the only customer—the only person, except for the Maltese counter-hand, who never looked up.

As the light grew fainter, a crowd came in, its thick, snake-like body squeezing through the glass double doors and flowing out to fill the interior. It frightened Jerry, and Jerry loved crowds. But he was not in this one and did not want to be. It flowed forward and detached part of itself at him. He got up quickly, drawing his needle gun. At that moment, he wanted a gun with plenty of dum-dum bullets. The Part grinned slyly, and the rest of it mirrored the grin, all its heads turned towards him.

Jerry drew a number of shallow breaths, and tears filled his eyes as he stood there looking into the face of the crowd.

The Part sat down where Jerry had been sitting, and Jerry recognized it then.

"Shades?" he whispered.

"Who?" whispered back The Part.

"Shades!"

"No."

"Who are you?"

"What?"

"You!"

"No."

Jerry shot The Part in the white throat. Spots of blood made a necklace round the pale flesh. The crowd gasped and began to undulate. Jerry pushed through it. It broke and re-formed behind him until he was in the centre. Then, when he tried to push on, it gave like the walls of a stomach but it didn't break. It began to press inward.

He shot some more needles into it and hacked and clawed his way towards the door. Outside was the big, safe Duesenberg. He wept as he made the street, turned, and saw a hundred white faces, all with identical expressions, pressed against the glass staring at him.

Trembling, sick, he climbed into the car and started it up. The crowd did not follow him, but its heads turned to watch him until he was out of sight.

Jerry had pulled himself together by the time he had reached Trafalgar Square. He was not going to give up until he had tried the Friendly Bum.

He heard the music at the entrance where the dead neon sign drooped. It was slowed-down music, dragging, monotonous, introspective. Tentatively he stepped down the stairs. The spot-lights had been turned on to the stage and there sat the heavy-eyed group, moulded on to or around its instruments. The pianotron played deep, sonorous, oversustained chords. In the centre of the place stood a tired pyramid of flesh that moved to the slow rhythm, near quiescent, and the temperature of the place seemed sub-zero.

It hadn't lasted, Jerry thought. It should not have reached this stage until he was at least forty. He was a fool to have helped Miss Brunner to accelerate the process. It left him adrift.

Had Miss Brunner know this would happen to him? How long had she included him in her plans? How much was he a factor in her programme? He had been on top, right on top, at the beginning, when they had first met. She had become wiser, then? Or he had underestimated her.

"You have lost the advantage, Mr. Cornelius," she said from behind him. He turned and looked at her standing at the top of the stairs, her legs as widely spaced as the tight skirt would allow, her long red hair drawn back behind the ears of her pointed face, her small, sharp teeth exposed. "You have a choice," she said, and she spread her hand towards the pyramid.

"Where is Marek?"

"Where Dimitri is. And Jenny."

"He didn't die at the house?"

"He will never die."

"You won't take me in like the others." He smiled nervously.

"A good try, but you can do even better. I won't—not like the others. I promise."

He knew he was about to vomit. He tried to stop himself then he turned and his body shook mightily as he spewed. He felt her touch him and was too weak to shake her off. His head ached with the intensity of a migraine attack. "Get it out of your system," he heard her say distantly as she led him up the stairs.

12

He drove the car according to her quiet instructions and obeyed her when she sat him in the cabin of her plane, a handy Hawker-Siddeley executive jet.

"You will soon be almost your old self," she promised as they flew towards the North Pole.

They landed on the lush, swampy plain dominated by a huge sun, a swelling circle of blood on the horizon. It was hot, and mosquitoes swirled in thick clouds round them as she led him along a wooden catwalk through the marsh. She comforted him and calmed him as they moved towards the mountains. She fed strength to him through her hand, which tightly clasped his. He was duly grateful.

"I've had your entire wardrobe shipped here," she told him.

"Thank you, Miss Brunner."

By the time they reached the cave he had dropped her hand, and he followed her with a jauntier step into the forcefully lighted cavern. It was large and high, though not so large and high as he had thought when he had first traversed it in darkness.

Farther down, buildings were being erected and gangs of men moved busily. The cavern moaned with all the voices of all the power tools, large and small.

"You own a lot of talent." It was the first comment Jerry had made since their meeting at the Friendly Bum.

"You're feeling better. Good. Do I seem less of a threat now?" They walked on.

The hot-lake cavern had a sheet of steel-hard plastic

material as its floor. Great slabs of neon ranged its walls, and fat pipes curled among the neon lamps like the World Snake at rest. The roof was still hard to make out, the more so since it was obscured by cables, pipes, and gridworks. Dwarfed by the cavern, hundreds of people darted antlike, about.

"It's rather like an old Fritz Lang film, isn't it?" She paused to look around her. He didn't understand the reference. "Or the one they did of *Things to Come*." Another reference that escaped him. She looked into his face. "I saw them as a child," she said.

It was the first defensive comment she had made since their meeting at the Friendly Bum.

"Yes, I'm beginning to feel better," said Jerry, and he grinned at her suddenly.

"There's no need to be rude," she said. "Give a man an inch . . ."

Jerry loosened his muscles and drew a deep breath. "You almost had me that time."

"What makes you think I wanted you?"

"You want something from me."

"You should be flattered. I have most of the best brains in Europe working for me—and as many from other continents as I could hire or make enthusiastic."

"A noble enterprise. Directed where?"

"Would you be surprised to learn I had a son, Mr. Cornelius?"

"Encore!"

"How do you feel?"

Jerry didn't know. He felt odd, but he wasn't going to say so. "But you look so *young*." He sneered.

"I keep myself young, one way and another."

"You could follow it up, Miss Brunner, if you're as well informed about me as you appear to be."

"Your father got around."

"So do you."

"What do you want me to say, Mr. Cornelius? The man I'm referring to did have a connection with your father—Leslie Baxter."

"The so-called psychobiologist my father took under his wing. He's a nut. I heard that the government had even stopped subsidizing his research."

"They stopped a great many subsidies around that time."

"So Leslie Baxter's your son. He picked my father's brains, didn't he?"

"If you mean he learned everything your father could teach him and then went off to do better on his own, yes."

"Have it your way. Why did you tell me?"

"That's a very direct question for you. Did I say something to upset you?"

"Go stuff yourself."

"In time, Mr. Cornelius, we'll see about that."

"Well, why?"

"Look," she pointed. "We've torn down all those Nazi buildings—jerry-built stuff."

"You should have preserved them for posterity. Why?"

"I have a different kind of posterity in mind."

"I feel in a limpet mood. Why?"

"I've forgotton the question."

"Why did you tell me Baxter was your son?"

"How patient you're becoming. Are you mellowing, Mr. Cornelius? Be a trifle more patient and I'll explain."

"All right. What happened to Dimitri and Jenny and Marek?"

"They weren't the only ones."

"They were the only ones I knew. What happened to them?"

"They became absorbed in something—and forgot me."

"Oh, shit . . ."

She laughed. "Come and look at DUEL—the pride of Laplab."

DUEL was huge. Its great, angular, nearly featureless bulk stretched upward for nearly 200 feet. It was growing round the three walls of the far cavern in a green semi-circle covering at least a third of a mile. At its base, teams of technicians sat, like a pool of office girls, tapping out data and feeding it in.

"Nothing coming out, I see," said Jerry, leaning back to look up at it.

"Oh, not for a while yet," she said. "There's another cavern, you know—one you didn't find on our first trip."

The entrance was small, barely higher than Jerry. A steel air lock had been fitted into it. "To keep a constant pressure inside," she said, "and shut out smells and noise."

They went through. On the other side of the air lock was a cave about 200 feet high and 500 feet in diameter. It was lighted with yellow simulated sunshine, and part of it had been cultivated into a flower garden. The air was fresh and pleasant. In the centre stood a white, terraced building that looked familiar. It was extravagant, baroque, with a twin-towered Byzantine-Gothic appearance. There were crosses on top of the towers.

"A touch of vulgarity in my personality, I suppose," she said as he stared at it smiling. "Do you recognize it?"

"I think so."

"It's Hearst's palace of San Simeon. I had it transported from the States stone by stone. He was almost as big a collector as I am, though with different tastes on the whole."

"These things come and go, you know. Want to see the inside?"

They walked up the steps and through the huge doors. They walked through the high, bare rooms. There was no furniture at all on the ground floor.

"I thought you were doing a Chinese-box trick—you should have had a smaller house inside this one."

"That's an idea. I might do it—we could probably get two more in and there I'd be, cosy in a three-roomed bijou, right at the centre."

"Is that how many layers you need?"

"I don't need any *layers*, Mr. Cornelius. Your brother Frank was of that bent. Do you know I found some more of his papers? He believed that the human race originated inside the globe. How's that for a big womb fixation? He didn't come here just to check what he found on the microfilm, you know."

"You don't like caves yourself, though. You didn't want to go on, as I remember."

"You're right. This isn't a womb for me, Mr. Cornelius —it is a womb for DUEL and what it will create."

"What will it create?"

"The ultimate joke."

"Fine words." He followed behind her as she walked up the great sweeping staircase.

"Do you know what you'll find soon behind the blank wall of that computer?" He paused and turned, leaning on the banister.

"Not a giant abacus—you told me at the party."

"Living human brains that can function for hundreds of years if I need them that long. That's the sort of sophistication going into DUEL!"

"Ah, that's corny. Is that your ultimate joke?"

"No, it's just part of the food routine."

"You're getting earnest, Miss Brunner."

"You're right. Come on."

In a smallish room on the third floor she showed him his wardrobe. He inspected it. "All here," he said. "You work fast."

"I arranged it as soon as you left your house."

"If you don't mind, since you've been so thoughtful, I'll have a bath and change."

"Go ahead. We've got hot water and central heating laid on by nature."

"I bet that's all."

"More or less."

She showed him to a bathroom and stood watching him wash himself. He wasn't embarrassed by her clinical once-over, but it didn't help him to relax much.

She followed him back to the room where his wardrobe was and helped him on with his jacket. He felt better.

"What you need is a good home-cooked meal," she said.

"Play it your way."

The food was delicious and the wine perfect. He had never enjoyed a meal so much. "The calf is fatted," he said as he sat back.

"You're becoming naïve."

"Now you're trying to worry me again."

"You had a big supply of food and drink at your place in Holland Park."

"I won't use it now. The breakdown was too fast."

"But the buildup will come sooner, Mr. Cornelius."

"That hasn't got anything to do with me—you forced the pace. I was a creature of my time; now I've no natural environment. That's what you've done to me."

She looked at her watch. "Let's go and meet someone you know."

They left San Simeon and returned through the air lock, passing DUEL and going out on to the surface covering the hot lake, towards one of the new buildings.

"The quarters are not austere," she said. "I think we'll find this mutual friend at home."

Inside one of the blocks they climbed stairs, Miss Brunner apologizing that the elevators weren't working yet. On the second floor she led him down a corridor and knocked on one of the simulated-wood Formica doors.

After a short wait, it was opened by a man dressed only in a turban and a towel round his waist. He looked like a fakir. It was Professor Hira. "*Hello*, Mr. Cornelius!" He beamed. "I had heard you were in these parts. old man. Good afternoon, Miss Brunner. An honour! Come in!"

The bed-sitting-room was bright with Swedish furniture —bed, desk, chairs, bookcase, a couple of scatter rugs. The Hindu sat down on the bed and they took the chairs.

"What are you up to, Mr. Cornelius?" He slipped the towel off and sat back comfortably on the bed. Jerry looked at him and smiled to himself. Hira was a kind of link unit between himself and Miss Brunner. Was it significant?

"I'm just an observer," Jerry said. "Or you could even say I've come seeking sanctuary."

"Ha, ha! What a magnificent example! I cannot tell you how delighted I was to be offered a position here by Miss Brunner. That you should think of me, Miss Brunner, still baffles me."

"I haven't forgotten Delhi, Professor," she said. "You have special talents."

"Good of you to say so. Perhaps I will be able to make better use of them shortly. There hasn't been much for me to do so far—a few interesting equations, a little speculation; I am not yet in my stride."

"Don't worry, you soon will be."

He snorted, amused. "My God, I never thought I would have to brush up on my Sanskrit for professional reasons. That old man in the next flat—Professor Martin—he is a better scholar than I!" He pointed a finger at Jerry. "Remember what we talked about in Angkor last year?"

"Very well, now you mention it. We must both have precognition, Profesor. I find it a little disturbing here and there."

"Yes—I know what you mean. But we have faith in Miss Brunner, eh?" He leaned back, smiling and shaking his head at Miss Brunner, who smiled at him, a little faintly.

"Oh, I'm just administration." Her smile broadened.

"You said it!" Jerry introduced a wrong note.

"It's time we were leaving." She got up. "I hope the three of us will be able to get together later, Professor."

"Oh, I certainly hope so too, Miss Brunner." He saw them out. "Au revoir!"

"Au revoir, Professor," said Miss Brunner.

"And now where?" Jerry asked.

"Back to San Simeon. You must be tired."

"I'd like to know if I can leave when I want to."

"I'm hoping your curiosity will make you stay for a bit —and you've nowhere else to go, have you?" They went down the stairs.

"No. You've really got me where you want me, I suppose."

"That's where you're wrong."

As they left the block and began to walk back towards DUEL he sighed. "I thought I'd remain comparatively static while my surroundings were in a state of flux. But I appear to have been caught in the flux. It's just no good making preparations. On the other hand, I don't like being aimless while the world is aimless, and my old aim is gone."

"What was that?"

"To survive."

"I might be able to supply an aim or two if you're keen."

"I'll listen, Miss Brunner, at any rate." As she operated the air-lock control, he suppressed an urge to reach out for her. "Things are becoming peculiar," he said as he followed her into the opening. "What will I think of next!"

"You're talking to yourself, you know," she pointed out. They emerged on the other side, and the smell of the flowers was exquisite.

"Haven't I always? But whose internal monologue is this? Yours or mine?"

"You're getting warmer, Mr. Cornelius. I like you better than I did."

"Ah, well—after you've known someone for a while . . ."

"We're a finely balanced pair, Mr. Cornelius. Have you thought about it? Neither of us keeps the upper hand for long. I'm not used to it."

"I know what you mean."

"That's fine."

Jerry became thoughtful, as best he could. He was beginning to feel pretty good.

"This is our bedroom." She stood in the doorway behind him. There were shutters on the windows and they were closed. The bed was a four-poster with curtains drawn. She shut the door.

"I'm not sure," he said. He wasn't scared and he wasn't particularly randy—he just wasn't sure, in a cool kind of way.

She moved towards him and pressed herself against his back, stroking his stomach with her long, pale hands. He stood there passively for a moment, then said, "Did you know you haven't any sex appeal at all? I've wondered how you made out—with Dimitri and Marek and the others."

"No sex appeal," she murmured. "That's the whole secret."

"And here I am." He glimmed the room. "What does it make me? A sucker, a patsy, a fall guy . . ."

"You underestimate yourself, Mr. Cornelius." She walked over to the bed and pulled a cord. The curtains parted and there, spread out on the eiderdown, was the loveliest white bridal gown he had ever seen.

"Who's it for? You or me?"

"That choice, Mr. Cornelius, is entirely up to you."

He shrugged and took his jacket off as she unzipped her skirt and stepped out of it.

"Let's toss for it, Miss Brunner."

"That suits me, Mr. Cornelius."

He found a coin in his pocket, flipped it. She called: "Incubus!"

"Succubus," he said. "Lucky old me."

Two weeks later and hand in hand they walked among silver birches beneath the hot blue sky beneath the big red sun. The shining lake stretched away out of sight, and the land was green and brown, at perfect peace. The only visible life, apart from themselves and the mosquitoes, was a large partridge circling high, guarding her nest.

Miss Brunner waved a hand behind her to indicate the ancient mountains that hid her mighty projects.

The mountains were streaked with glaciers, topped with snow, time-begrimed and worn.

"We had some trouble on Number 14 Section's subsidiary circuits. That's Professor Hira's section. I had to do some fast calculating—the correlation monitors started improvising. Too much feedback potential there, I think."

"No kidding. You expected some setbacks—I mean, it's a big project, DUEL . . ."

"The biggest, Mr. Cornelius." She squeezed his hand. "The," she sighed, "total sum, the quintessence of all human knowledge, the definitive data. Yum, yum. And that'll be just the start."

They wandered, this shepherd and his lass—though neither was quite sure who was who—beside the lake. Fish were jumping and the gorse was high. The world was warm and restful and an infinity of mountains, forests, and lakes where night could not fall and it was always day, hazy and lazy.

The mosquitoes enjoyed it too as they sat on the arms and faces of their hosts, inserting their probosces through the skin and into the veins, drinking the thick, rich blood to satiation, raising little hard hillocks on the flesh as monuments to their visitation. The living was easy and the flesh pounded warmly on the bone, the veins and arteries functioned smoothly, nerves and synapses did their stuff, organs performed their proper duties, and nobody would have guessed, least of all the mosquitoes, that skeletons lurked under cover.

"The start of what, though?"

"You're still not with me?"

"Oh, I am, I am."

"The funniest thing," she replied. "Think about it. Think what's beyond this green and pleasant land, these uninhabited pastures. The world crumbles to sand—cold sand—and the sixty-minute hour is a thing of the past, the twenty-four-hour day has been devalued. There has to be a bridge, Mr. Cornelius, between now and the past-future. That's what I intend to build—the bridge."

"Blow me down. And what's my part again?"

"I didn't say. Don't worry, Mr. Cornelius, you're fixed up destinywise. Drift, drift . . ."

"If I don't?"

She turned and looked into his face. "Will you do something—a favour?"

"Things are moving again. What?"

"My son dreams of glory. He has only a small part of my resources and information, yet it is that small part I need, by God. He refuses to give it up—the last piece in the jigsaw. Would you go to England, to the Wamering Research Institute, and secure me that piece?"

"It's a long trip. Why should he hand it over to me?"

"Oh, he won't. You would probably, in the long run, have to kill him to get it."

"Kill him?"

"Yup."

"I wouldn't mind killing him."

"No."

"Oh-ho, Miss *Brunner.*"

"Don't wag fingers at *me,* Mr. Cornelius!"

"I'll kill him, then. What do you want there?"

"Nothing much—nothing heavy. A few notes. He published prodigiously, but he kept those notes back. They're the fill-in data I need."

"I'm far too tired to go by myself. I want a chauffeur all the way. I'll need to conserve my energy."

"You're getting lazy."

"Weary, weary, weary. I like it here." He stretched and stared out over the glinting lake.

"I've got you a good little gun," she wheedled. "The Smith and Wesson 41 Magnum Manstopper."

"You've been collecting catalogues. What the hell is that?"

"Spoilsport. It's a handy gun—not too heavy, not too light. Just the trick."

"Is it noisy?"

"Not very."

"Does it kick hard?"

"Not much."

"Well, I'll use it. But I'm scared of gunpowder guns."

"You lost your other one."

"I know I did."

"Let's go back. I'll show it to you and you can try it out. Blam! Blam!"

"Oh, Jesus, those gleaming eyes!"

"Har! Har!" She began to run towards the mountains. He paused for only a moment or so before he loped off after her.

Disappointed mosquitoes saw them disappear into the caves.

14

Jerry huddled in his coat as the pilot taxied the plane off the small private runway a couple of miles beyond Kiruna. The Iron Mountain, source of Kiruna's wealth—source, indeed, of Kiruna—was soon below them as they headed south.

In Kent they landed and a Dodge Dart and driver were waiting for them. The driver, as silent as the pilot, drove Jerry through a land of drifters, smoke, and disturbance, a warped landscape that he only glimpsed as he hunched in his seat and let himself be carried towards the Wamering Research Institute. The place was on the South Coast, just outside a rundown seaside resort. Jerry had memories of the place—whitewashed Regency and the sweet smell of spun sugar and frozen custard, cold promenade and green railings, pale lights at night and the silhouette of the pier, faint music, blue cafés and open-top buses. Even as a child he had disliked it all, had turned inland when left to himself.

The Wamering Research Institute stood on a slope of the Sussex Downs. On the top of the hill was an estate that seemed to have been built during the war. It still had a temporary look about it. The road took them through its concrete streets—a small grid of blocks with two-storyed houses, white walls and dull red roofs. Puzzled eyes looked out of hollow faces at them. The people stood in family groups—a Father, a Mother, a Son, and a Daughter—arms folded, heads turning a little as they passed. A stunned, wronged place.

"Have you got Mr. Pipe the Plumber?" Jerry turned to the driver.

"Nearly there, sir." The driver kept his eyes on the road.

Depressed and in a killing mood, Jerry let the driver drop him off at the gates of the institute's grounds. The buildings—some of metal, some of plastic, some of concrete—could be seen painted grey and green in weatherproof paints. The concrete ones looked the oldest. The institute seemed to have been established before Leslie Baxter had taken over the buildings.

Jerry trod the tarmac towards the institute, gun in pocket. He reached the main building, rough concrete with a steel door fairly recently installed. He pressed the bell and heard a faint buzzing within. The battery was running low.

A girl answered the door, sliding a Judas window.

Her head looked up and down. "Yes?"

"Joe sent me."

"What?"

"I'm Jerry Cornelius."

"Come again?"

"Cornelius. Dr. Baxter will recognize the name. I would like to see him. I have something that my father should have given him before he died."

"Dr. Baxter is very busy—very busy indeed. We are doing some important experiments, sir. It is vital work."

"Vital, eh?"

"Dr. Baxter believes we can save Britain."

"With hallucimats?"

"I'll give him your name—but we have to be careful who we let in."

"Cor-ne-li-us!"

"Hang on a minute."

"Tell him that my plan will radically alter his research."

"You're serious—he will know you?"

Jerry tired of his joke. "Yes."

He waited for more than twenty minutes before the girl returned. "Dr. Baxter will be pleased to see you," she said, opening the steel door.

Jerry padded in to a square reception hall and followed the girl down a corridor like any other corridor. The girl looked strange to him, with long curly hair and a full skirt, seam-free stockings and high heels. It was a long time ago when he'd last seen such a sexy girl. She was a positive anachronism and made him feel slightly sick. He restrained himself from hauling out his gun.

A door was labelled DR. BAXTER; the room contained Dr. Baxter. Nice and neat.

Leslie Baxter was only slightly older than Jerry. Well dressed and kept, tall and pale, gaunt and haunted. His body was bigger than Jerry's, gave out a greater impression of power, but even Jerry noticed that they were quite similar in appearance.

"You are Dr. Cornelius's son, I take it? I'm glad to meet you." His voice was tired, vibrant. "Which son?"

"Jeremiah, Dr. Baxter."

"Oh, yes, Jeremiah. We never—"

"—met. No."

"You were always away—"

"—from home while you were there. Yes. So you never met Frank either?"

"Only your sister Catherine. How is she?"

"Dead."

"I'm so sorry—she was very young. Was it—"

"—an accident? Of sorts. I killed her."

"You killed her? Not deliberately?"

"Who knows? Shall we discuss the matter I came about?"

Baxter sat down behind his desk. Jerry sat on the other side.

"You seem distraught, Mr. Cornelius. Could I get you a drink, something like that?"

"No, thanks. Your receptionist said you were doing some very important work. Work—vital to the nation?"

Baxter looked proud. "Perhaps to the world. I give your father credit for all the original work, you know."

"But you're getting the positive results, eh?"

"That's about the size of it." Baxter flashed Jerry a puzzled look. "Our research into useful hallucinogens and hallucimats is reaching a conclusion. We shall soon be ready."

"Useful in what way?"

"They will reproduce mass-conditioning effects, Mr. Cornelius. Mass conditioning that will make people sane again—saner, in fact, than they have ever been before. Our machines and drugs can do this—or will be able to within a few months. We are, in fact, largely beyond the research stage and are producing several models that have proved absolutely workable. They will help to turn the world on to a sane track. We'll be able to restore order, salvage the nation's resources . . ."

"It's got a familiar ring. Don't you realize it's a waste of time?" Jerry's hand stroked the butt of his S&W .41. "It's over—Europe only points the course of the rest of the world. Entropy's setting in. Or so they say."

"Why should that be true?"

"It's Time—it's all used up, I'm told."

"This is metaphysical nonsense!"

"Very likely."

"What's your real purpose here?"

"Your mother wants the missing data—the stuff you didn't publish."

"Mother—? What should she want with—? My *mother?*"

"Miss Brunner. Don't mess about, Dr. Baxter." Jerry smoothed the gun from his pocket and flicked off the safety catch.

"Miss who?"

"Brunner. You've got some secret stuff you haven't published, haven't you?"

"What's that to you?"

"Where is it?"

"Mr. Cornelius, I don't intend to tell you. You are disturbed. I will fetch the receptionist."

"Hold it."

"Put the gun—"

"—away, Mr. Cornelius. It's like doing the Junior Crossword. No. Miss Brunner wants that information. You have refused to let her have it. She has authorized me to collect it from you."

"Authorized? What's your authorization?"

"You fell into that one." Jerry laughed. "This!" He waved the gun. "Where's that information?"

Baxter glanced towards a filing cabinet on his right.

"There?" Jerry queried a little petulantly. Was Baxter

going to give in so easily? Baxter looked away hastily. Yes, it was probably there.

"No," said Baxter.

"I believe you. Then where is it?"

"It—was destroyed."

"Liar!" . .

"Mr. Cornelius. This is farcical. I have really important work to do . . ."

"It's all farce, Dr. Baxter." Jerry levelled the gun at Baxter's stomach as the man rose to reach for a phone. "Freeze. Don't move. Stay exactly where you are."

"This *is* a joke. What did you say?"

"Freeze. Don't move. Stay exactly where you are."

"It wasn't what you said—it must have been your tone of voice."

"That happens. My main assignment from your mother was to get those documents. My main intention is to kill you."

"Oh no. We had those steel doors installed to protect —we were safe—I had to let you in! Mr. Cornelius—I'm sure you have never met my mother."

"Miss Brunner?"

"The name is only vaguely familiar, I assure you."

"You're sweating," said Jerry.

"I'm not—well, wouldn't you be? I don't know a Miss Brunner!" He screamed as the gun banged and the slug splatted into his belly. "Mr. Cornelius! It isn't true! My mother couldn't—I was born in Mitcham—my father was in the Home Guard!"

"A likely story." Jerry shot him again, *bang*!

"And my mother worked in the margarine factory Mr. and Mrs. Baxter—Dahlia Gardens, Mitcham. You can look them up."

Bang!

"*It's true!*" Baxter seemed to realize that he was full of large bullet holes. His eyes glazed. He fell forward over the desk.

The girl was hammering on the door. "Dr. Baxter! Dr. Baxter! What is it?"

"Something's gone wrong," Cornelius shouted back. "Just a minute."

He opened the door and let her in. "Were you the only

one who heard the noise?" He closed the door as she gasped and stared at the body on the desk.

"Yes—everyone else is in the lab. What—?"

Jerry shot her in the back at the base of the spine. She was silent for a moment. Screamed. Blacked out or died at once, you could never be quite sure.

Jerry crossed to the filing cabinet, pocketing the gun. It took him half an hour of careful leafing to find the files he wanted. But Dr. Baxter, for all his faults, had been a tidy chap.

Jerry went out of the room with the file under his arm, a natty figure in his black car coat and tight black trousers, down the passage, through the reception hall, out of the main door and down the drive. He felt considerably better, in spite of the unpleasant smell of cordite in his nostrils and the bruised feeling of his right hand. He hadn't liked the shooting part very much.

The Dodge Dart, electric blue and powerful, was waiting. The driver had the engine running as Jerry climbed in.

"Any trouble, sir?"

"No. With luck they'll never have a suspicion of who we were. Hadn't we better go fast now?"

"No sense in going too fast on these roads, sir."

"But someone may come after us."

"That's not very likely, sir. There's a lot of violent death about, sir. I mean, take me. I'm an ex-policeman. You can't blame the police, sir. They're an over-burdened body of men."

"I suppose they must be."

They went back to the airfield in silence.

15

"No, of course he wasn't my son." Miss Brunner leafed eagerly through the file. They were in her office at Casa del Grande. Jerry sat on the table watching her.

"You're just saying that now." He swung his legs.

"Try not to be so bitchy, kitten." She grinned as she extracted a document and scanned it. "This is the real stuff. Good for you."

"Good for me, eh? You and your bloody gun!"

"It wasn't my finger that was on the trigger."

"Don't be so sure."

"Calm down, Mr. Cornelius. You're not the Jerry Cornelius *I* knew."

"You can say that again. You and your bloody gun!"

"Blam! Blam!" She put the papers down. "You're just tired, Mr. Cornelius. I had to get you to go. You were the only person who would recognize the stuff I wanted."

"You should have been more straightforward about it!"

"I couldn't be. Could you?"

"It's not right."

"You're whining, feathers. Whining."

"Sod me, you'd be wh—" He pulled himself together. "I'm not sure I'm happy, Miss Brunner."

"What's happiness, Mr. Cornelius? You need a change."

"I don't need any more. Miss Brunner. That's for sure."

"A change of scenery, that's all. There's nothing more for you to do here for a while. I have everything ready. It's just donkey work for a few months. I might come along too, when I've tidied up."

"Where do you want me to go?"

"Nowhere. It's up to you."

"I'll think it over."

She walked up to him and cupped his face in her hands. "How can you? What have you got to think with? Your tapes are stale, your clothes are tired—there's only *me!*"

He took her hands away from his face. "Only you?"

"You're failing fast. Not enough people, not enough stimuli. What have you got to live on, you bloody little vampire!"

"Me a vampire! You—Dimitri, Marek, Jenny and how many others? Me too, maybe . . ."

"Some realist you are, Mr. Cornelius. Look at you— all self-pity and emotion!"

"It's catching, then?"

"Don't lay it at my door."

"You're pretty hip yourself." He dropped off the table, feeling limp. "By God, I don't like it!"

Her voice became soft, and she began to stroke his arm. "I know some of it's my fault. Calm down, calm down. Cry if it helps."

He did; it didn't. He was being suckered skilfully, and he knew enough to know it. He broke away weeping and ran for the door. As it closed softly, automatically, behind him, she picked up the empty Smith and Wesson with a sigh that was half disappointment, half satisfaction.

"He's giving me too much credit," she said aloud. "I only hope things stay on schedule or we've all had it."

Jerry drove a Snow Trac at its top speed of 15 mph over the uneven countryside towards the distant village where he might get a place on a tourist bus. He drove south, away from the sun.

To him, Europe beyond Sweden had become not Miss Brunner's cold sand but a boiling sea of chaos soon to spread through Finland and Denmark, if it had not done so already. Not only was he physically enervated, but his mind was out of gear and exploding on all systems. It was awash with dark colours and fragments of dreams and memories. Only a small portion still operated logically, and logic had never been his strong point. He was neither fleeing nor going anywhere; he was simply moving—perhaps questing for prey like the mosquitoes buzzing round the outside of the cab, perhaps not.

The dreams and memories conflicted, and occasionally he would feel ill and weaker than ever as the thought came that they might all be wrong—even Baxter; that there was a simpler reason for it all. Yet if it were madness they had, then they shared it with too many others, and Miss Brunner had the power to make her fantasy reality. It had happened before. He remembered the families he had seen on his way to Wamering, and this image was superimposed on that of the pulsating pyramid of flesh he had seen in the Friendly Bum.

He reached Kvikkjok and there were no buses—just a couple of students from the tourist hotel driving a borrowed Volvo back to Lund. He found some sterling in his pockets and offered it in return for a lift to Stockholm. They laughed at the money.

"It's worthless. But we'll give you a lift."

The students were clean and tall, with short haircuts and well-pressed trousers and sports jackets. They were patronizing and pleased to have him as a toy to display. He knew it. He minded. He ignored it as best he could. His long hair and his pretty clothes amused them, and they called him Robinson Flanders, like well-educated lads. They stopped at the lakeside city of Ostersund and decided to rest there for a couple of days, since they felt inexplicably tired. Jerry, on the other hand, felt much better.

By the time they reached Uppsala, Jerry had seduced both the young Swedes without either's knowing about his seduction of the other. They hardly realized they were so much in his power until he drove their Volvo off, leaving them in the city of the twin spires deciding not to say who had stolen their car.

The pickings were better in Eskilstuna, where he took up with a young female teacher who lived in the town and had hitched a lift from him. He began to straighten out. He half-regretted what he had done to the two students, but it had been an emergency. Now there was no panic, and the girl was proud of her delicate English lover—took him to parties in Eskilstuna and Stockholm. He got work reading the proofs of scientific papers published in English by a Stockholm academic press. It

was light work and quite interesting and allowed him
to have some new clothes made to his own specifications,
buy some records, and even pay something towards the
girl's rent. Her name was Maj-Britt, and she was as tall,
frail, and pale as he was, with long blonde hair and
large light blue eyes. A pretty sight they made together.

They became very popular, Jerry Cornelius and
Maj-Britt Sandström. The young people with whom they
mixed—students, teachers, lecturers, mainly—began to
imitate Jerry's styles; and he appreciated the compliment, began to feel much more at home.

By way of a gesture of gratitude, after he had been in
Eskilstuna for almost a year, he married Maj-Britt. His
earlier working-over had softened him more than he realized, and even though he'd recouped pretty well, he
was almost in love with her and she with him. He played
guitar with a semi-professional group who called themselves the Modern Pop Quintet—organ, bass, drums, alto
—and made enough to pay his way like a good husband.
The group was in demand and would soon go full
time. It was becoming like the old days, with the difference that he was not, as he'd been in London, remote and in the thick of crowds. Here he set the pace
and got his name in *Svenskadagbladet* and the other papers. He shared equal space and appearances with the
streams of analyses of what was rotten in the state of
Europe. He was generally mentioned in these too. He'd
become a symbol.

Drunk with nostalgia, publicity, and hangers-on, he
dreamed no more of Laplab and Miss Brunner and
congratulated himself that he had found himself an island that could last him, with luck, until early middle
age. He had taken the precaution of keeping the name
the students had given him, Robinson Flanders.

Miss Brunner kept her data up to date. She read the
papers in her private cavern-palace.

16

So naturally the time came when Jerry's flat at
Konigsgaten 5, Eskilstuna 2, Sweden, was visited. He
came home from a session to find his pretty wife talking
politely to Miss Brunner. They were both sitting on a
couch sipping Maj-Britt's excellent coffee. The room was
sunny, small but pleasant, neat but not gaudy. He could
see them from the front door. He put his guitar case
in the hall and took off his coat of fine cord, put it on
a hanger, hung it in the cupboard, and walked in, hand
outstretched, to greet his old friend with a confident smile.

"Miss Brunner. You're looking well. A little tired,
maybe—but well. How's the big project?"

"All but completed, Mr. Cornelius."

He laughed. "But what do you do with it now?"

"There's the rub," she smiled, putting her white cup
on the low table. She was dressed in a plain black sleeve-
less dress of good, rough stuff. She wore a perky hunting bowler on her long red hair and had a man's
tightly rolled umbrella leaning beside her against the
couch. Also beside her were a black leather briefcase and
a pair of black gloves. Jerry had the feeling she had
dressed for action, but he couldn't decide what sort of
action and whether it directly involved him.

"Miss Brunner arrived about half an hour ago,
Robby," Maj-Britt explained softly, not quite sure now
that she had acted wisely. "I told her I was expecting
you shortly and she decided to wait."

"Miss Brunner was a close business acquaintance in
the past." Jerry smiled at Miss Brunner. "But we have
little in common now."

"Oh, I don't know." Miss Brunner returned the smile.

"You bitch," said Jerry. "Get out of here—back to your caves and your farce." He spoke rapidly in English, and Maj-Britt missed the sense, though she seemed to get the message.

"You've found something to keep and protect at last, eh, Jerry? Albeit a travesty of something you lost?"

"Excuse me, Miss Brunner," said Maj-Britt, somewhat coldly, in her husband's defence, "but why do you call Herr Flanders 'Jerry' and 'Mr. Cornelius'?"

"Oh, they are old nicknames we used to have for him. A joke."

"Ha-ha! I see."

"Don't kid yourself, Miss Brunner," Jerry continued. "I'm fine."

"Then you're kidding yourself more than I'd guessed."

"Miss Brunner." Maj-Britt got up tensely. "It seems I made a mistake asking you to wait . . ."

Miss Brunner looked the tall girl up and down. One hand curled round the handle of the umbrella. She frowned thoughtfully.

"You and Professor Hira," she said. "A good pair of connections. I could go for you, dear."

Jerry moved in. He grabbed the umbrella and tried to break it over his knee, failed, and tossed it aside. He and Maj-Britt stood over Miss Brunner, both with fists clenched. Miss Brunner shrugged impatiently.

"Jerry!"

"You'd better go back to Laplab," he said. "They need you there."

"And you—and this." She pointed at Maj-Britt.

They were all breathing rapidly.

After a few moments of silence, Miss Brunner said, "Something's got to happen."

But Jerry waited, hoping for the almost inevitable break in tension that would weaken him but leave him out of the situation he could see Miss Brunner wanted to create.

The break didn't come. He did not glance at Maj-Britt, afraid that she would looked scared. Things were getting worse. Outside, the sun was setting. The break must come before the sun went down altogether.

The break didn't come. The tension increased. Maj-

Britt began to stir. *"Don't move!"* he shouted, not looking at her. Miss Brunner chuckled warmly.

The sun was down. Miss Brunner rose in the grey
light. She reached toward Maj-Britt. Jerry's eyes filled
with tears as he heard a deep, desperate sound come
from his wife.

"No!" He moved forward, gripping Miss Brunner's
arm as she took Maj-Britt's quivering hand.

"It—is—necessary." Miss Brunner was in pain as his
nails squeezed her flesh. "Jerry!"

"Ohhhhhh . . ." He took his hand off her arm.

Maj-Britt stared at him helplessly, and he stared helplessly back.

"Come along," said Miss Brunner kindly but firmly,
taking their hands and walking between them. "It is all
for the best. Let us go and find Professor Hira." She led
them from the flat to her waiting car.

PHASE 4

17

Five days later, sitting at a table on the terrace, warmed by artificial sunlight, nose and eye delighted by the profusion of flowers below, Jerry listened to Miss Brunner talking. It was a square table. On the other three sides of the square sat Miss Brunner, opposite Jerry; Maj-Britt to his right; and Professor Hira to his left.

"Well," Miss Brunner was saying cheerfully, "we've all got to know one another pretty well, I think. It's amazing how quickly you settled in, Maj-Britt."

Jerry glanced at his wife. He and she were the beauties here without a doubt, both elegant and delicate-seeming, she if anything paler than he. She smiled sweetly at Miss Brunner, who was patting her hand.

Professor Hira was reading a two-day-old *Aftonbladet*.

"The only snag as far as I can see is this business of the police believing that you kidnapped Mr. and Mrs. Cornelius, Miss Brunner," said the professor. "They have traced you to Lapland and must have found the outer signs of our establishment by now—this paper being out of date, you see."

"We do have defences, Professor," she reminded him. "We can also seal off sections of the cave system if necessary. G-day is tomorrow, and after that we shall be finished within forty-eight hours. Even an all-out attack on Laplab, which isn't likely, would not be successful unless nuclear weapons were used; and I can't see the Swedes doing that, can you?"

"Would it not help if Mr. Cornelius went out and spoke to the police searching the area?"

"No, Professor. Positively not. We cannot afford the slightest chance of losing Mr. Cornelius at this stage."

"I feel flattered," said Jerry with a touch of bitterness. "On the other hand, you could let a few in and I could speak to them. They needn't come far—they wouldn't see DUEL at all."

"They wouldn't ask to. Don't forget, Mr. Cornelius, that this land belongs to the Lapps under the protection of the Swedish government. They would be more than anxious to inspect us—particularly with the international situation in its present state and the Russian border close by. This is entirely the wrong time to hope to stall a nervous administration."

"I could go." Maj-Britt spoke hesitantly.

Miss Brunner stroked the girl's hair. "I'm sorry, my darling, but I cannot trust you sufficiently. You are still a bit of a weakling, you know."

"I am sorry, Miss Brunner."

Jerry sat back, folding his arms. "What, then?"

"We can only hope for the best, as I said."

"There is another alternative." Jerry unfolded his arms. "We could send some men out to see what's going on, disguise the cave entrance, and, if they get the chance, lure any search party inside and dispose of it."

"That would not really solve the problem, but I will have it done." She rose and walked into the room, picking up a telephone. "Then at least we shall be able to question a few of them and find out exactly where we stand." She dialled a two-digit number and spoke some instructions into the mouthpiece.

"And now," she said pleasantly, beckoning them in, "let us continue with our experiments. There is not much more to do, but there is little time before G-day."

"And then, I hope, you will tell us just what 'G-day' is, Miss Brunner. We are all very curious—though I have had a few hints, I think." Professor Hira laughed excitedly.

Vibrant, pulsing with enormous energies, flushed and lightheaded, Jerry began to fold Maj-Britt's clothes and place them on top of Professor Hira's. He felt totally fit, totally purified, totally alive. What was more, he felt replete, warm, at ease and at peace; like a great tiger in its prime, like a young god, he thought.

Miss Brunner lay on the bed. She gave him a knowing wink.

"How?" he said. "I didn't realize until it was over."

"It is power," she said luxuriously, "which many have potentially. You had it. It is natural, isn't it?"

"Yes." He lay down beside her. "But I've never heard of anything like it. Not physically, anyway."

"It is a trick. There's been a lot written in some form or other. The world's mythologies, particularly those closest to source, Hindu and Buddhist, are full of references. The secret was saved by overinterpretation. No one, however dedicated, would believe in the literal truth."

"Ahhh."

"You regret nothing now?"

"I'm content."

"There is more to come. The connections brought us closer—"

The telephone was ringing.

She got up at once, walking swiftly from the room. More slowly, he followed her down to her office and entered as she replaced the receiver.

"Your plan worked. They have six policemen in the far cavern. They are talking to them. So far they have stalled them with a story about secret research sponsored by the Swedish government. We must go and talk to them now while they are still comparatively unsuspicious. Let's get dressed."

The policemen were polite but uncertain. They were also, Jerry noticed, armed with revolvers.

Miss Brunner smiled at them. "I am afraid I shall have to keep you here until we have checked with Stockholm," she said. "I am director of the establishment. Our work is highly secret. It is a great pity that you stumbled upon us—and inconvenient for you. I apologize."

Her foolproof Swedish, brisk and polite, made them relax a little.

"The area is not marked on our maps," said the oldest man, a captain. "It is usual to mark restricted areas."

"The work we are doing here is of maximum importance to Swedish security. We have guards on patrol, but we can't afford too many. Great numbers would attract attention."

"Of course. But in that case—" The captain paused, scratching his right hand with his left. "—why locate such an establishment here? Why not in Stockholm or one of the other cities?"

"Could such vast natural caves be found in a city?" Miss Brunner waved a hand back at the cavern.

"Would it be possible for me to contact my superiors whilst you are checking with yours?"

"Out of the question. It is a puzzle to me that you are in this area."

"We believe that an Englishman and his wife—" He stopped short, staring for the first time at Jerry.

"Bugger me, why didn't we think of that?" said Jerry under his breath.

"But this is the Englishman," said the captain. His hand went to his holster.

"I was not brought here by force, Captain," said Jerry hurriedly. "I was contacted by your government to help . . ."

"That is unlikely, sir." The captain drew his revolver. "If that were the case, we should have been notified."

The four technicians who had brought the policemen in were unarmed, and so were Jerry and Miss Brunner. Apart from that, they were evenly matched, six against six. Miss Brunner's tough boys were out of earshot. Things looked dicey.

"An oversight surely, Captain?" Miss Brunner's delivery was a bit rough now.

"I cannot believe that."

"I don't blame you, frankly," said Jerry, noting that only the captain had actually drawn his gun. The rest of them were still trying to catch up on what was happening.

Jerry's body was full of power.

He jumped for the gun. Two yards.

The gun went off once before he had disarmed the captain and covered the suprised policemen.

"You had better take over, Miss Brunner." Jerry's voice was thick. From inordinate energy he had sunk to exhaustion, dizziness. As she took the gun from him and covered the Swedes, he glanced down.

The bullet seemed to have entered his chest just above the heart. Lost of blood.

"Oh, no. I think I'm going to die."

In the distance, Miss Brunner's tough boys came running. He heard Miss Brunner shouting orders, felt her arm supporting him. He seemed to be growing heavier and heavier, sinking through the stone.

Was it muffled gunfire he heard? Was it hopeful imagination that made him think he caught the sound of Miss Brunner's voice saying, "There is still a chance—but we must work rapidly"?

His mass became greater than that of the stone, and he found he could walk through it with some difficulty, like pushing through air that had the consistency of thin, liquid tar.

He wondered if it were tar and if he would be found in millions of years perfectly preserved. He pushed on, knowing that this theory was stupid.

At length he emerged into the open, feeling light and fit.

He stood on a plain without a horizon. Far, far away he could make out a huge crowd of people gathered round a rostrum on which stood a single still figure. He heard the faint sound of voices and began to walk towards the crowd.

As he got closer, he recognized that the crowd, thousands strong, consisted of all Miss Brunner's scientists and technicians. Miss Brunner was on the rostrum addressing them.

No one noticed him as he stopped at the back of the crowd and listened to her speech.

"You have all been waiting for the time when I would describe the ultimate purpose of DUEL. The biologists and neurologists may have guessed—and then decided that their guesses were too incredible and dismissed them. But they were right. I do not believe that our project can fail—unless Mr. Cornelius should die, which now seems unlikely—"

Jerry was relieved.

"—and I believe in it sufficiently to be, with Mr. Cornelius, the raw material."

Jerry worked out that he must be experiencing some sort of hallucination crossed with reality. The vision was dream; the words were actually being spoken. He tried to haul himself out of the dream but failed.

"DUEL's purpose was twofold, as you know. The first job was to feed it the sum total of human knowledge and have it systemize and relate this knowledge into one comprehensive integral equation. This was at last achieved three days ago, and I congratulate you.

"It is the second part that mystified most of you. The technical problem of how to feed this programme directly into a human brain was overcome with the help of notes donated by Dr. Leslie Baxter, the psychobiologist. But what sort of brain could accept such a fantastic programme? That question is answered as I answer the question you have all been asking. DUEL's ultimate use is to satisfy an aim which, whether we realized it or not, has been the ultimate aim of all human endeavour since *Homo sapiens* first evolved. It is a simple aim and we are near achieving it. We have been working, ladies and gentlemen, to produce an all-purpose human being! A human being equipped with total knowledge, hermaphrodite in every respect—self-fertilizing and thus self-regenerating—and thus immortal, re-creating itself over and over again, retaining its knowledge and adding to it. In short, ladies and gentlemen, we are creating a being that our ancestors would have called a god!"

The scene wavered, and Jerry heard the words less clearly.

"The conditions in modern Europe proved ideal for this project—ideal in every respect—and I believe that we succeed now or never. I have destroyed my notes. The necessary equipment has been constructed. Bring Mr. Cornelius forward, please."

Jerry felt himself being lifted up and floated through the ghostly crowd.

He drifted behind Miss Brunner as she walked away towards a large oval metal chamber. Then they were inside it together, in darkness. Miss Brunner began to make gentle love to him. He felt her, closer and closer, drawing into him. It was like the dream he had had before.

Deliciously he felt himself merge with Miss Brunner, and he still wondered if this, too, were a dream inspired by his wound. And yet his body had breasts and two sets of genitals, and it seemed very real and very natural that this should be so. Then he felt tiny pricks of pain in his skull, and his memories and Miss Brunner's, his identity and hers, merged for a moment and then slowly dispersed until his mind was blanked out and DUEL began to do its stuff.

18

The technician looked sharply at his watch. Then he looked at the metal chamber and at the dials thereon. Every dial was now still. Slowly, a green light blinked on and off.

"This is it," said the technician crisply to another technician very like him.

The chamber had been rolled on casters close to DUEL. The great semi-circle of the computer was joined by a huge semi-circle of scientists and technicians, making a full circle.

A spotlight had been turned on the oval chamber. Scientists came forward to check that the indicators all registered correctly. They backed off, satisfied.

The middle-aged dietician who had won the honour through an elaborate draw spun the handle of the chamber.

All was still, silent.

A tall, naked, graceful being stepped out. It had Miss Brunner's hair and Mr. Cornelius's eyes. Miss Brunner's predatory jaw was softened by Jerry's ascetic mouth. It was hermaphrodite and beautiful.

The scientists and technicians murmured in awe, and some of them began to clap and whistle. Others cheered and stamped.

"Hi, fans!" said Cornelius Brunner.

The cavern reverberated with a massive shout of exultation. The scientists and technicians capered about, clapping one another on the back, grinning, dancing.

They surged towards their smiling creation, lifted it high, and began to march round the computer singing a wordless, victorious chant which became a christening name:

"Cor-nee-lee-us Ber-un-ner!"

Cornelius Brunner was making a big scene.

"Just call me Corn," it grinned, and it blew kisses to one and all.

Distantly at first, growing louder, a siren or two began to sound.

Corn cooked an ear. "The enemy is at our gates!" It pointed a slender finger towards the outer cavern. "Forward!"

Lifted on a rolling tide of its jubilant sycophants, many thousands strong, Cornelius Brunner sat their shoulders as they flooded forward.

Across the great hall of the hot lake, up the slope towards the cave mouth, onward they moved, their roaring thunderous, their exhilarated bodies swift.

The door of the cave opened for them, and they rushed into the open air. Cornelius Brunner laughed as it rode their backs.

A small detachment of military was there. A few light guns and armoured cars.

The tide did not notice as the soldiers first backed away and then tried to run and then were engulfed, guns and cars and all, as the huge crowd coursed ahead in triumph.

Cornelius Brunner pointed to the south-west. "That way—to Finland first!"

The flow changed direction but not its speed, and away it went in its entirety.

It streamed over the border, it swarmed down the length of Finland, it flocked through West Germany, and it gathered greater and greater numbers as it moved on, Cornelius Brunner high in the centre, encouraging it, urging it, praising it. The thousands became millions as the new messiah was borne across the continent, whole cities abandoned and the land crushed in its wake.

The vast swarm reached Belgium and, at its controller's behest, decimated Liège, depopulated Brussels, and carried half a nation with it when it crossed into France.

Its exuberant voice could be heard a hundred miles from Paris. The reverberation of its feet could be felt two hundred miles away. The aura of its presence rippled outward over the world.

The millions did not march along—they danced along. Their voice was one melodious song. Their densely packed mass covered fifty square miles or more, increasing all the time.

"To Paris!" cried Cornelius Brunner, and to Paris they went. Not once did they pause, aside from those who died from excitement.

Paris was passed, and its four remaining inhabitants gathered to watch the disappearing deluge.

"Unprecedented!" murmured the Chief of State, scratching his nose.

"Perhaps, perhaps," said his secretary.

The tide rolled on and roared through Rome, leaving the Pope, its sole resident, sunk in meditation and speculation. After some time, the Pope hurried from the Vatican Palace and caught up within an hour.

All the great cities of Italy. All the great cities of Spain and Portugal.

And then, with a slight note of boredom in its voice, Cornelius Brunner gave the last order.

"To the sea!"

Down to the coast, on to the beaches, and tide met tide as the gigantic assemblage poured into the sea.

Within six hours, only one head remained above water. Naturally, it was the head of Cornelius Brunner, swimming strongly back towards the beach.

Cornelius Brunner stretched out on the well-churned sand and relaxed. The waves lapped the peaceful shore, and a few birds cruised the blue sky.

"This is the life," yawned Cornelius Brunner, whose skull contained the sum of human knowledge. "I think I might as well kip down here as anywhere."

Cornelius Brunner fell asleep, alone on an abandoned beach.

Night fell and morning followed, and it awoke.

"Where now?" it mused.

"To Normandy. There's some unfinished business."

"To Normandy, then, and the House of Cornelius."

It rose, flexed its body, turned, and loped inland over the quiet, deserted countryside.

TERMINAL DATA

The world's first all-purpose human being tucked the detonator under its arm and walked slowly backward, unwinding the wires that led to the cellar of the house. At a safe distance it set the box down and pulled up the plunger.

"Five!"

"Four!"

"Three!"

"Two!"

"One!"

Cornelius Brunner pressed the plunger, and the great fake Le Corbusier château split, flared, and boomed. Gouts of flame and smoke erupted from it. The cliffside trembled, rubble flew, and the flames roared high, the black smoke hanging low and drifting down to obscure the village.

Arms folded, head set back, Cornelius Brunner contemplated the burning wreckage.

It sighed.

"That's that."

"Nice and tidy."

"Yes."

"What now?"

"I'm not sure. Perhaps the Middle East first."

"Or America?"

"No, not just yet, I think."

"I need some money. America might be the best place to get it."

"I feel like going east. There is still work to be done."

"The rainy season will have begun in Cambodia."

"Yes; I think I might as well walk, don't you?"

"There's plenty of time. Don't want to hurry."

Cornelius Brunner turned and looked down the slope of the cliff, turned again and looked back at the guttering house, looked out to sea, looked at the sky. "Ho hum."

A man, unshaven, clad in a ragged uniform, was panting up the slope. He called. "Monsieur—ah!"

"Monsieur-Madame," Cornelius Brunner corrected politely.

"Are you responsible for this destruction?"

"Indirectly, yes."

"There is still some law left in the land!"

"Here and there. Here and there."

"I intend to arrest you!"

"I am beyond arresting."

"Beyond?" The official frowned.

Cornelius Brunner moved in. It began to stroke the official's arm.

"What's the time, monsieur? My watch has stopped."

The official glanced at his wrist, exposed by a tear in his sleeve. "Ah! Mine also!"

"Too bad." Cornelius Brunner crooned and looked into his eyes.

A sweet and gentle smile crossed his lips, and he flushed in ecstatic fascination while Cornelius Brunner removed his trousers.

The trousers were flung away. Cornelius Brunner turned the official round, smacked his bottom, gave him a gentle pat on the back, and sent him running back down the slope. He ran joyously, the smile still on his face, his ragged jacket and shirt tails flapping.

A moment later, the world's first all-purpose human being strode eastward, whistling.

"A tasty world," it reflected cheerfully. "A very tasty world."

"You said it, Cornelius!"

Michael Moorcock
Notting Hill
January 1965

A Cure
for Cancer

Illustrated by Malcolm Dean

ACKNOWLEDGMENTS

Parts of this novel originally appeared in FATE, PREDICTION, RECORD MIRROR, NEW WORLDS, BILLBOARD, HEADQUARTERS DETECTIVE, TRUE LIFE CONFESSIONS, THE VILLAGE VOICE, GUNS & AMMO, SCIENTIFIC AMERICAN, TIME, INTERAVIA, MOTORCYCLE MECHANICS, TV AND MOVIE PLAY, MAN'S MAGAZINE, SCREEN AND TV ALBUM, NEW MAN, SILVER SCREEN, TITBITS, THE OBSERVER, REVEILLE, THE PLAIN TRUTH, SCIENCE HORIZONS, DAILY SKETCH, VOGUE and other British and American magazines and newspapers to whom acknowledgments are gratefully made.

Note to the reader:
This book has an unconventional structure.

For Langdon Jones

1.

DIAGNOSIS

"Terror is the most effective political instrument . . . I shall spread terror by the surprise employment of all my measures. The important thing is the sudden shock of an overwhelming fear of death."

Adolf Hitler

Preliminary Consultation

"HERE on the top of a modern and reputable London store lives a garden of incredible beauty one hundred feet above Kensington High Street—the shopping centre of the Royal Borough of Kensington—The gardens embrace some 1½ acres, and comprise an Old English Garden, Tudor Courts and flower beds, and a Spanish Garden with Moorish pergolas and a Court of Fountains."

Derry & Toms Famous Roof Garden

1. A TROLL ACROSS THE ROOFTOPS

The time might be July 31st 1970.

London, England. Cool traffic circulates. A quiet, hot day: somewhere in the distance—a bass tone.

In High Street, Kensington, where the trees of Hyde Park creep out among the buildings, stands the age-old structure of the Derry and Toms department store. Tier upon impressive tier, it is proud among its peers.

On the roof of the store, in a lot of rich earth, grow shrubs and trees and flowers, and there are little streams and ponds with goldfish and ducks. Who better to describe this roofgarden than those who built it? In the 1966 edition of their brochure, Derry and Toms said:

"They are the only gardens in the world of such large dimensions at so great a height, over 100 ft. above ground level, overlooking London with St. Pauls in the distance. The gardens are 1½ acres in extent and comprise an Old English Garden, Tudor Courts and Flower Beds and a Spanish Garden with Moorish Pergolas and A Court of Fountains. The water for the fountains, the river and the waterfall, is drawn from our Artesian Wells 400 ft. deep. The depth of the soil averages 2 ft. 6 in. and the distribution of weight of this and the masonry used was arranged by the Company's architect when planning the Derry and Toms building. The Gardens took three years to build and were opened in May 1938 by the Earl of Athlone, K.G.

"From the balconies that adjoin the gardens you have the opportunity of enjoying the most magnificent views of London. You can see the spires and towers of the Kensington Museums, the great Dome of St. Pauls, Westminster Abbey and Westminster Cathedral—the Albert Hall, Albert Memorial, etc."

In order, the captions to the pictures read:

1. A delightful view of the Court of Fountains
2. The water for the fountains, the river and the waterfall is drawn from our artesian wells four hundred feet deep. The depth of soil averages 2 feet 6 inches and the distribution of weight of this and the masonry was arranged by the company's architect when planning the Derry and Toms building.
3. The Spanish Gardens
4. Fully matured fruit-bearing trees stretch up towards the sky.
5. Aerial view of the Spanish garden where palm-trees and grape-vines live the year round.
6. Corner of the Spanish garden showing the Well of St. Theresa in a cobbled court—with vine-covered walls.
7. Another view of the Spanish garden—showing the spire of St. Mary Abbots Church in the background.
8. *(Opposite)* The magnificent Court of Fountains
9. Flowers bloom in profusion and green lawns flourish.
10. *(Below)* The Tudor Gardens
11. Views of the Spanish Gardens
12. The campanile and convent with fountain in foreground—so typically Spanish in atmosphere.
13. Vine-covered archways leading to the Court of Fountains—all this one hundred feet above the traffic of London!
14. *This garden has a world of pleasure in't*
    (SHAKESPEARE)
15. The Tudor Gardens
16. Entrance to the Tudor Gardens—you go back through history to the beginning of the sixteenth century.
17. Henry VIII might well have wandered through this garden and plucked a red rose for Anne Boleyn.
18. Another view of the Tudor Gardens and its carved stone archways and red brick paving.
19. *A waterfall feeds a meandering stream.*
20. Ducks on the Woodland Garden lawn
21. The Sun Pavilion Restaurant with its umbrella-

shaded balconies—a modern restaurant in the quiet setting of an English garden.

22. The waterfall—shaded by quiet trees alive with the gurgling of water and the twittering of the birds—like a rendezvous in the country.

23. Again the Sun Pavilion Restaurant—here you will find peace and pleasure—high above London—overlooking the Woodland Gardens.

On summer afternoons ill-clad ladies wander through the gardens; they wear felt and fluffy nylon hats, suits of linen or rayon or double jersey, bright scarves tied cowboy fashion about their throats. The place is the last retreat in London of the female of an old and dying English race—the "Waitesdwellers" as they have often been called, although many live in pre-Waites communities and some do not always own Austins. She comes here when her shopping is done in Barkers, Derry and Toms or Pontings (they are all next to each other in the High Street) to meet her mates. Only here may she with some certainty take her middle-class tea.

There are walls about the retreat. One wall has a locked gate. The key to the gate is owned by the man who secretly owns the chain of stores on this block, who secretly owns other similiar substantial properties throughout London.

Now, below, we hear the sound of drowsy mid-afternoon traffic. The banner of D&T hangs limp against its staff. Not far away is the Kensington Gardens Hotel and the Kensington Strip, with its bazaars and eateries and bright lights. Not far from the Strip, to the west, is secluded Kensington Palace Gardens, vulgarly called Millionaire's Row, the avenue of the Embassies, running beside Kensington Gardens where the statue of Peter Pan still plays its pipes near the sparkling Serpentine. Derry and Toms faces towards North Kensington, the largest and most densely populated part of the Royal Borough, the most delicious slum in Europe.

It is almost tea-time.

2. "BROKEN BLOSSOMS" LOVER IN
GARDEN SEX FEST!!!

Within the vine-covered walls of the Dutch garden the sultry sun beat down on colourful flowers and shrubs.

There were tulips like blue velvet, tulips of red, yellow, white and mauve; daffodils; pink and scarlet roses, chrysanthemums, rhododendrons, peonies. All the flowers were bright and all the scents were sweet.

The air was hot and still; there was not a trace of a breeze; but in one part of the garden a patch of cream daffodils began to move; they soon became violently agitated, as if invisible stallions galloped through them. Stems bent and broke. Then the daffodils stopped moving.

Almost immediately a nearby field of white and red tulips began to shake and thresh.

There was the smell of lilac, very heavy on the air, and the tulips groaned, leaves slapping against leaves.

When they had stopped, the roses in the next bed fluttered and bent, scarlet petals falling fast, thorns tearing, branches shuddering.

Finally, when the roses were calm again, a huge bed of mixed snap-dragons, pansies, meadowsweet, ivy-leaved toad-flax, irises, hollyhocks, narcissi, violets and sunflowers burst into life; petals shot into the sky, leaves erupted in all directions; there was a great, wild, lush, ululating noise; then silence.

Lying between damp, ivory thighs, Jerry Cornelius sighed and smiled into the unseeing face of Captain Hargreaves, member of the U.S. military advisory commission in Europe. The captain was a good, greedy girl.

Jerry's skin, as black as a Biafran's, glistened, and he thought about all the kinds of girls he had known as he looked at the flowers above his head and then down at Flora Hargreaves's slowly cooling eyes. He rolled like the surf and reached across the soft earth for a cigarette.

A bass tone. He glanced at the sky. It was clear.

When he looked back Flora's eyes had closed and she was sleeping, her auburn hair burnishing the pillow of crushed petals, her perfect face at perfect peace, the sweat drying on her sweet body. He bent and lightly kissed her left breast, touched her smooth shoulder, got up and went to find her uniform where she had folded it beside the patch of cream daffodils.

A man in his late twenties, with a healthy, muscular body, a large Liberty's neo-Art Nouveau wrist-watch like a bangle on either wrist; his skin was ebony and his hair not blond but milk white. Jerry Cornelius was a revolutionary of the old school, though his stated objectives seemed different.

Humming an early Jimi Hendrix number ("Foxy Lady"), Jerry looked around for his own clothes and found them on the grass close to Flora's olive duds. On top of the pile lay his chromium-plated vibragun which he now picked up and holstered, strapping the holster to his naked body. He pulled on his lavender shirt, his red underpants, his red socks, his midnight-blue Cardin trousers with the flared bottoms, the matching double-creased high-waisted jacket, smoothed his long white hair, took a mirror from his pocket and adjusted his wide purple tie, looking at his face as an afterthought.

A very *negative* appearance, he thought, pursing his lips and smiling. He picked up Flora's uniform and laid it near her; then he walked through the sunlight and flowers, knee-deep, towards the garden gate.

3. WILD WHIRLYBIRD IN ONE MAN WAR!!

Beyond the wall the middle-class woman walked the pleasant paths, glancing nervously or with disapproval at the creature who locked the gate behind him as if he owned the place. They mistook him for a dandified Negro, and thought it likely that he was responsible for the increasingly loud bass tone, for he carried something that looked rather like a transistor radio.

Jerry put the key in his pocket and wandered in the direction of the Woodland Garden which, with its streams and shady trees, was flanked by the Sun Pavilion Restaurant which was not yet open.

He passed several black doors marked *Emergency Exit* and paused by the lift, murmuring a word to the attendant and the ticket girl. They nodded. The girl entered the lift and with an air of finality it descended.

Jerry turned back to the Woodland Garden. As he reached it the bass tone sounded very close and he looked up and saw the helicopter, moving in low, up over the outer wall, its rotors thrashing, the leaves of the trees whipping off their branches, the petals of the flowers flung about in all directions.

The women screamed, wondering what to do.

Jerry drew his vibragun. He knew an enemy helicopter when he saw one.

The chopper was huge, over forty feet long, and flying close to the tops of the trees, its deep-throated motor full of menace, its shadow over the gardens.

Jerry moved swiftly across the open space towards the tree-shaded lawn of the Woodland Glade, the leaves stinging his face.

A machine gun hissed and slim bullets bit the concrete.

Jerry rested his vibragun across his bent right arm and took aim, but he could hardly see his great target for the whistling petals and leaves that lashed his face. He stumbled backwards into a pool, slipped and found himself waist-deep in cold water. There were almost no leaves on the trees now as the rotors flicked round and round.

Someone began to shout through a megaphone at him. "Fuckpig! Fuckpig! Fuckpig!"

The old ladies gasped and ran about in panic, finding the lift out of order and the emergency exits blocked. They huddled under the arches of the Tudor Garden or threw themselves flat behind the low walls of the Spanish Garden.

Some of the copter's bullets hit a group of noisy ducks and blood and feathers mingled with the flying leaves. Jerry fired back rather half-heartedly.

The chopper—a Westland Whirlwind with the 750 h.p. Alvis Leonides Major engine—banked slightly until it was hovering over a clear space in which a fountain splashed. It began to drop lower, its 53 ft. rotors barely missing the trees.

The machine gun hissed again and Jerry was forced to fling himself under the water and slide along until he could crouch beneath the small stone bridge. A man jumped from the copter, cradling the gun in his arms. He began to trudge towards the point where Jerry had gone down. There was blood on the surface, but it was the blood of ducks and doves.

Jerry smiled and aimed his vibragun at the man with the machine gun. The man began to tremble. The machine gun falling apart in his hands, he shook violently and collapsed.

The copter was beginning to rise. Jerry dashed for it.

"Easy," he called. "Easy."

There could be as many as nine people in the copter, apart from the pilot. He dived through the hatch. Save for the fallen megaphone, it was empty. Above him, the pilot stared at him through goggles. The copter gained height.

Jerry put his head out of the hatch. Frightened ladies, their hats like so many coloured dollops of cream, wailed up at him.

"We're stranded! We can't get out! We'll starve! Hooligan! Go back to your own country! Help!"

"Don't worry," Jerry called as the copter climbed. He picked up the megaphone. "The restaurant opens soon. Please form an orderly queue. It will assist everyone if you try to behave in a normal manner! In the meantime . . ." He flung his taper to the soft ground. It began to play a selection of George Formby's greatest hits, including *When I'm Cleaning Windows*, *Fanlight Fanny* and *Auntie Maggie's Remedy*. "And don't forget Old Mother Riley, Max

Miller and Max Wall! It is for them that you suffer today!"

As the helicopter thrummed out of sight, the ladies murmured among themselves and their lips curled in disgust as George Formby sang about the tip of his little cigar, but they formed a long, disciplined queue outside the restaurant.

Eight days later they would still be standing there, or sitting, or lying where they had fallen. Through the glass walls of the restaurant they had been able, every day between three o'clock and five o'clock, to see the waitresses laying out the little sandwiches, scones and cakes and later clearing them away again. If a lady signalled a waitress the waitress would wave, smile apologetically and point at the notice which said that the restaurant was closed.

One plump middle-aged housewife in a blue paisley suit hugged her handbag to her stomach in disapproval. The George Formby songs, rather scratchy now, were still going. "I feel filthy," she said. "It's wicked . . ."

"Don't start a fuss, dear."

On the lawn, quacking cheerfully, forgetful of their earlier upsets, jolly ducks waddled about.

4. SING TO ME, DARLING, IN OUR CASTLE OF AGONY

"Drop me off at Earls Court, would you?" Jerry asked, stroking the pilot's neck with his vibragun.

Pettishly the chopper sank towards the flat roof of the Beer-A-Gogo, recently built on the site of the old Billabong Club, and hovered there with undisguised impatience.

Jerry opened the hatch and jumped out, falling elegantly through the thin asbestos sheeting and landing with a bump on mouldy sacks of flour that filled his nostrils with a sour smell. Rats scattered and turned to watch him from the shadows. He sighed and got up, dusting his suit, watching, through the jagged hole, the helicopter disappearing into the sky.

Jerry left the storeroom and stood on the landing listening to the lusty sounds from below. The migrants were celebrating "Piss on a Pom" week, getting drunk on home brewed beer or "pickling Percy's plums" as they put it.

Jerry could hear them laughing a great deal as the jokes flew back and forth: "That's a beaut drop of *beer,* mate!" /"I'm telling you, drong, that sheila was like a flaming glass of cold *beer!*"/"Watch you don't spill your fucking *beer,* sport!"

Some of the lusty singing was also about beer or its absence. The migrants seemed fully absorbed. Jerry walked softly downstairs and sneaked past the main room. He was momentarily dazzled by the electric blue drape suits (Kings Cross Blues) but managed to make the front door into Warwick Avenue, full of Dormobiles, Volkswagen minibuses and Land Rovers covered in pictures of kangaroos, emus and kiwis, all marked FOR SALE.

Jerry tossed a silver yen to a Negro boy with a face daubed in white clay. "Can you find a cab?"

The boy swaggered around a corner and came back at a run. He was followed by a skinny horse drawing a Lavender Cab, its bright paint peeling to reveal old brown varnish and its upholstery cracked and bursting. The gaunt young man on the box wore a long beard and a fur hat; he signalled with his whip for Jerry to climb into the hansom which rocked and creaked as Jerry got aboard.

Then the whip cracked over the jutting bones of the horse; it lurched forward, snorted and began to gallop down the street at enormous speed. Jerry clung on as the cab rocked from side to side and hurtled across an intersection. From over his head he heard a strange, wild droning and realised that the driver was singing in time to the rhythm of the horse's hooves. The tune seemed to be *Auld Lang Syne* and only after a while did Jerry realise that the song was a favourite of the 1917-20 war.

"We're here because we're here because we're here," sang the driver, "because we're here. We're here because we're here because we're here because we're here. We're here because we're here because we're here because we're here. We're here because we're here because we're here because we're here. We're here because we're here because we're here because we're here. We're here because we're here because we're here. We're here because we're here because we're here because we're here. We're here because we're here because we're here because we're here. We're here because we're here because we're here because we're here. We're here because we're here because we're here because we're here."

Jerry pushed up the trapdoor in the roof and shouted at the singing, glassy-eyed face, giving his address. The driver continued to drone, but gave a sharp tug on the reins and the cab turned, flinging Jerry to his seat and making the trap shut with a thud.

"We're here because we're here because we're here because we're here. We're here because we're here. We're here because we're here because we're here because we're here." Through the west London streets, all desolate and beautiful in the soft tree-filtered sunlight, to the high walled fortress in Ladbroke Grove that had once housed the Convent of the Poor Clares, a closed order. Jerry had bought it from the Catholic Church shortly before the reformation. Behind the heavy metal gates topped by electrified barbed wire came the sound of the Beatles singing *Back in the U.S.S.R.* Jerry got out of the cab and before he could pay, the driver had whipped up the horse and was off towards Kilburn, his high voice still singing.

"Dear Prudence, won't you come out to play," began as Jerry rested his palm on the recognition plate and the gate opened. He glanced, as usual, at the slogan "Vietgrove" painted on the north wall of the convent. It had been there for two years and continued to puzzle him. It didn't seem to be the work of the regular slogan painters.

Crossing the elm-lined courtyard to the bleak, brick house, Jerry heard a tortured scream coming from one of the barred upper windows and recognised the voice of his latest charge (whom he had come to take to the country), an ex-chairman of the Arts Council of Great Britain, well-known in the early forties as a heavy playing opposite Humphrey Bogart, and now awaiting a crash transmog.

A tricky customer, thought Jerry.

5. MYSTERY OF YOWLING PASSENGER IN SNOB AUTO

Jerry drove the Phantom VI convertible at a rapid lick. The controls of the car, beautifully designed in diamonds, rubies and sapphires by Gilian Packard, responded with delicate sensuality to his touch. In the back, in his chamois leather straitjacket, the transmog case continued to scream.

"EEEEEEEEEEEEEEEEEEEEEEEEEEEEEEEEEEEEHELP MEEEEEEEEEEEEEEEEEEEEEEEEEEEEEEEEEEEEEEE."

"That's what we're trying to do, old man. Hang on."

"Aaaaaaaaaaaahh! Why? Why? Aaaaaaaaaaaaaaaaaaaaaa aaaaaaaaaaaaaaaawhyaaaaaaaaaaaaaaaaaaaaaaaaaaaaaaaaaaa aaaaaaaaaaaaaaaaaaaaaaaaaaawhyaaaaaaaaaaaaaaaaawhyaaa whyaaaaaaaaaaaaaaaaaaaaaaaaaaaaaaaaaawhyaaaaaahhhh! YOU WON'T GET AWAY WITH THIS, YOUNG MAN! Yaaaaaaaaaaaaaaaaaaaaaaaaaaaaaaaaaaaaaaaa! You'll regret thisaaaaaaaaaaaaaaaaaaaaaaaaaaaaaa! WHY! WHY! WHY! AAAAAAAAAAAAH! Yaaaaaaaaaaaaaaaaaaaaaaaaaaargh! Yaaaaaaaaaaaaaaaaaaaaaaaaaaaaaaaaaaaaaaaaaaaaaargh! THE AUTHORITIES WILL SOON CATCH UP WITH *YOU*, MY FRIEND! OOOOOOOOOOOOOOOOOOOOOOO OOOOOOOOOOOOH. URSH! YAROOOOOOOOOOOOO! I SAY, STOP IT, YOU ROTTERS! OOOOOOOOOCH! GAARR! EEEEEEEEEEEEEEEEEEEEEEEEEEEEEEEEE EEEEEEEEEEEEEEEEEEK! *DO YOU KNOW WHO I AM*??????"

"Do you? That's what we're trying to fix. Be quiet, there's a good chap."

HHHHHHHHH! said the ex-chairman defiantly.

Jerry pursed his lips and touched the ruby stud of his taper, adjusted sapphire and diamond controls for balance, and turned up the volume. Soon the passenger's voice was more or less drowned by *Everybody's Got Something to Hide Except Me and My Monkey.*

Jerry winked at his black face in the overhead mirror.

6. DANGEROUS DUDE'S DREAM OF DESTRUCTION

"Don't worry, we'll soon have him in the fuzz box," smiled the kindly old matron as Jerry said goodbye to her at the main door of the Sunnydale Reclamation Centre. The matron had formerly been a Greek millionairess, famous for her escapades, and had known the new client in the old days when he had holidayed aboard her yacht *Teddy Bear*. She handed Jerry the latest issue of *The Organ (A Quarterly Review for its Makers, its Players & its Lovers)*. "This came for you today—at the house."

"No other mail?"

"Not to my knowledge."

Jerry put the magazine in his pocket and waved goodbye. In the peaceful grounds of the Centre the day was warm and beautiful. His silky pink Phantom VI stood in the drive, contrasting nicely with the grey and yellow gravel. Pines and birches lined the drive and behind them Jerry could see the red roof of his little Dutch mansion which he'd had shipped from Holland in the days before the blockade.

He leapt into the Phantom VI and was away, touching seventy as he passed the gates and hurtled into the road in the path of a slow silver Cadillac that pulled up sharply as he turned and zoomed off towards the metropolis, his milk-white hair streaming in the wind.

The sweet music of a thousand hidden radio transmitters filled the countryside and brought heavenly sound to the pastoral landscape. Such harmony, thought Jerry contentedly, that only the Beatles could achieve; such a perfect combination. From the circle of U.S. and Russian Navy radio ships surrounding and protecting Britain, the same synchronised record played to all the people everywhere. Was there ever such a Utopia? he wondered as he left the subsidiary road and hit the main drag, joining the racing rainbow stream of cars on the multilane highway.

Overhead, like birds of paradise, swarmed the flying machines, the little helicopters, gliders, rocket chairs, pediplanes, air taxis, light aircraft of all varieties, belonging to the comfortably off (and who was not in these delightful Home Counties?), all flowing towards London where gleaming towers of all colours could be seen in the distance.

Was it fair, Cornelius asked himself, relaxing for a moment, to scheme the destruction of so much of this life, happiness and colour? It was a shame that his mission in life conflicted with it; but he was a man of will and integrity, not without a marked moral sensibility, and his first loyalty was to his organisation. He was a total convert and he couldn't afford to relax until there were a few more around.

And his adventures were really only about to begin.

Tissue Sample

Clean air and economical electricity are two good reasons to celebrate Nuclear Week. Here are four more.
Clean air from clean energy.
Economical energy, too.
Nuclear-powered egg-poacher.
Suddenly it's 1980.
Nuclear crime detection—a fifth reason.
Nuclear Week for your kids—three more ways to celebrate.

Headings, Con Edison ad

1. 50,000 VICTIMS OF KILL-CRAZY PRINCE CHARMING

Beale, claws together under his chin, eyed Jerry Cornelius only for a moment then moved suddenly, rising and falling across the room on his flamingo legs, the woollen frock coat, which was Burton's latest autumn offer, rumpling and floating.

The room was long, lined with books, the ceiling so large and heavy that it seemed about to fall with a thud. Cornelius glanced upwards and settled warily into the swivel armchair, knowing that, if the ceiling did fall, even he would not have a chance of surviving.

"Which book? We have fifty thousand." Beal's sibilant voice took a long time to reach Jerry.

"The names," murmured Jerry, ready to slip hand to vibragun if the situation demanded.

"London, the city of dolorous mist," hissed Beale. "The names, Mr. Cornelius, yes; the confidential names. You say he's called S?"

"According to Okharna."

"Nothing else?"

"Something in code about a mouse strangler of Munich, I'm told. But that could be a reference to an anagram of Mephistophilis . . ."

"Catching, Mr. Aserinsky, hmph," Beale said, as if in reply to a question, and began to cough.

"Not in my book, general. It's oh, oh, five and wild skidoo."

"Unused—unusual . . ." Beale began, puzzled, as well he might be.

It was only a ruse on Jerry's part to get into the library,

but he could not move yet, could not be certain that the ceiling would not fall; and he suspected the chair.

He got up. Beale gasped, hastily reaching for a book.

Jerry knew it was now or never.

He drew the chromium-plated vibragun from its silken holster and pointed it at Beale who fell on his knees and began to shake.

When Beale had shaken to pieces, Jerry slid the warm gun back in place, stepped over the corpse, checked doors and the many windows, and got to work, pulling the books from their shelves until every last one was on the floor. Wading through this rubble, he picked up a volume at random and opened it. As he expected it contained six months' issues of the Sunday Times Colour Supplement. It would do to start with.

From his pocket he extracted matches and a tin of lighter fluid, squirted the fluid over the book and lit it. The rest of the fluid he squirted at random over the piles of books.

Someone was coming.

He ran to the door and drew the bolts; ran, stumbling, to the doors at the far end of the gallery and bolted those too. The fire was beginning to take hold. It was getting warm. He drew his vibragun and gave the huge central window a touch of ultrasonics so that it shattered instantly and he was through it, peering down into the misty street.

Swinging himself onto the ledge, he began to slide down the drainpipe, scraping the heel of his right hand quite nastily, and reached the ground where his Phantom VI, its motor turning over, waited for him.

Two or three streets away, he stopped for a moment and looked back and upwards to where he could see the white stone of the library building and the orange flames and rich, black smoke that whipped and boiled from the window he had broken.

Sabotage was only a sideline with Jerry Cornelius, but he prided himself that he was good at it.

"What do you achieve," a girl had once asked him, stroking the muscles of his stomach, "what do you achieve by the destruction of the odd library? There are so many. How much can one man do?"

"What he can," Cornelius had told her, rolling on her.

Jerry glanced at the huge green-dialled watch on his left wrist. 14.41.

He sent the Phantom VI racing forward, heading away from the City, his headlamps changing the colour of the mist rather than piercing it. Muscles and silk rippled together as he raised one jet-black hand to smooth his white hair from the jet-black forehead. He swung the wheel suddenly to avoid the back of a bus, hooted his horn as he passed on into the mist, finger-tips on wheel. Tower Bridge was ahead, open to traffic, and he raced over it, made the Elephant and Castle roundabout, whisked round it and reached eighty miles an hour as he passed over Waterloo Bridge where the mist was thinner, and the West End, whose great, jewelled towers were the city's distinctive feature, was ahead of him.

"Oh, *psychedelic!*" he murmured.

He had to be in Greek Street in five minutes. He would make it easily now.

He had to meet Spiro Koutrouboussis, his chief contact with the organisation.

Koutrouboussis, one of a number of handsome young Greek millionaires who belonged to the organisation, was dark-haired and slender, from Petrai originally, but now a refugee, a nationalised Israeli subject, proving just how far-sighted he was.

Leaving the thrumming Rolls in the street outside the Mercury Club, Koutrouboussis's favourite meeting place, Jerry stepped over the mist-silvered pavement and entered the warm, neon-lit club where he was greeted with some enthusiasm by the doorman who gratefully received the twenty dollar tip.

Cornelius ignored the dining part of the club, where people sat in red plush seats and ate off golden plates the finest French cuisine available anywhere in the world.

He took the stairs two at a time and bumped into Koutrouboussis who was waiting there. Koutrouboussis rubbed his side, his eyes looking rapidly from Jerry's right foot to his left and back again.

"The same old shoes, I see," he said spitefully, and wheeled about to lead Cornelius into the private room he had on permanent hire.

2. EX-BANK CLERK SLAVE GIRL IN PRIVATE SIN PALACE

"How did you manage to get through this," Koutrouboussis asked, burying himself in the shadows of a leather armchair by the fire while a sequined girl poured them Pernod from a gleaming decanter on her hip, "time?"

Jerry stroked his glass. "They thought I was a visiting disc jockey from France. It worked well enough and long enough." There were few long-range aircraft and, to its joy, the nation was blockaded by the radio ships. Jerry downed the yellow drink and held out his glass. The girl was an organisation convert and very successful and very happy; she smiled sweetly at Cornelius as she filled his glass; she had once been a clerk in a bank, had worn a green overall and counted money. Her place had been taken by another convert who had originally worked as a hostess just round the corner. The organisation was very neat, on the whole.

Koutrouboussis's eyes glowed from the shadows as he darted a look of jealousy at Cornelius. The poor man had sacrificed himself for others, but he could not help resenting them from time to time.

"Ah," he said.

"The organisation got the French delivery?" Cornelius said. "Thirty two. Fifteen men, seventeen women?"

"Oh, yes. In good time," Koutrouboussis said with a secret in his mellowing eyes.

"That was important," Cornelius murmured. "I'm glad. You were to settle here."

"It's been arranged. Sixty-four thousand pounds in hard yen in your London account under the name of Aserinsky. Well worth it."

Jerry worked on a strict commission basis. It preserved autonomy and had been part of the original contract when he had surrendered admin control to the Greeks. "Have they been processed yet?"

"A few. It should be a successful batch, I think."

Jerry held out his glass for another drink; Pernod was the only alcohol he really liked and in this he was a child.

"But we're having trouble," Koutrouboussis added. "Opposition . . ."

"That's not—"

"—unusual, I know. But in this case the opposition seems to realise what we're up to. I mean, they understand what we're doing."

"A tip-off?"

"Could be. But does—it doesn't matter."

"No."

"This group," continued Koutrouboussis, "is an international one with its headquarters in America . . ."

"Where else? Official?"

"I don't know. Perhaps. The difficulties . . ."

"Difficult for them to operate and for us to reach them, of course. But do you . . . ?"

"We don't want you to go there."

Jerry leant back in his chair. He looked nervously at the flickering fire in the grate nearby, but it offered no danger. He relaxed.

"It's the German chapter that seems to be offering us the serious threat at this stage," Koutrouboussis cleaned his nails with a toothpick. "We know one of them—a woman. She's a dental surgeon living in Cologne. Already she's deconverted some half-dozen of our German people."

"Turned them on and turned them back?"

"Exactly. The usual method. But much smoother."

"So she's got a good idea of our process."

"To the last detail, apparently. Some Russian source, I think—the leak. Maybe the Patriarch himself, eh?"

"You want me to kill her?"

"How you work is up to you." Koutrouboussis fingered his lips.

Jerry's black face glistened in the firelight. He frowned. "We'd prefer a conversion, I suppose."

"Always. But if you can't save a soul, get rid of it."

Koutrouboussis smirked with self approval (although normally he did not at all approve of his self).

"The organisation isn't in agreement on that issue," Jerry pointed out. "Repent or die."

"Quite."

"Well. I'll see what I can do." Jerry stroked the girl's pelvis. "And I go to Cologne, eh?"

"It might be an idea," Koutrouboussis said uncertainly. "To get yourself fully in the picture—but you needn't do anything there. She's coming to Britain, we gather, shortly, to organise the British chapter."

Unsettled by the Greek's somewhat puritanical attitude (natural, he supposed, for a man who had given up so much), Jerry drank another glass of Pernod, feeling a trifle light-headed. The flavour of the liquorice was firmly on his palate now. If he were going to enjoy his dinner, he had better stop.

"Bring me a glass of ice-water, darling, will you please?" He patted the girl's thigh.

"That would be the best time to strike," Koutrouboussis suggested. "Off her own territory and on yours."

Jerry reached out for the water and drank it slowly. "What's her name?"

"Name?"

"What's she called?"

"Name."

Koutrouboussis made an urgent, spasmodic gesture with his right hand. He breathed heavily.

"Doctor . . ." he began. "Karen—Karen . . ."

Jerry reached up and pulled the girl to him. They kissed each other firmly and pulling off their clothes lay down on the floor and fucked with hot and hasty passion.

". . . von . . ."

Snorting and quivering, they came.

". . . Krupp."

"What was that again?" Jerry did up his trousers.

"Dr. Karen von Krupp. It's a lot to remember."

"Got it."

Jerry felt only pity. For some men, immortality was not enough.

"Her address in Cologne?"

"She lives outside Cologne. A small town to the west. Nibelburg. Look for the old Gothic stone tower. That's where she has her surgery."

"So I go to her and ask her to check my teeth." Jerry tapped his whitened choppers.
  "She'll guess who you are."
  "Will she try to detail me?"
  "Make sure she doesn't," Koutrouboussis said nervously. "Not you, Cornelius. We can't afford it."
  Jerry smiled. He could smell the first course, *moules marinière*, just before there was a knock on the door and the waiter pushed the trolley into the room.

3. U.S. NAVY SHIPS TURNED "PIRATE"!!!

Koutrouboussis had given him his route plan, but how he crossed from Dover to Ostend was his own affair. It was more than twenty miles of sea, and three miles out was the tight circle of well-armed U.S. "pirate" radio ships.

Jerry's Phantom VI, a streak of pink power on the white, sparkling road, roared through the clear sunlight of the autumn afternoon, making for Dover.

Wearing his Panda-skin coat and a white silk turban in which was set a jewelled clasp supporting a spray of peacock feathers, Jerry stretched comfortably in his seat. He was disguised sufficiently to fool a casual observer and he hoped, too, that Karen von Krupp would not immediately recognise him for what he was.

Jerry saw the bright ruin of the silver bridge that had once spanned the sea between England and France and which had collapsed in a tangle of flashing strands shortly after it had been built. Above it a metal ornithopter wheeled.

Now he could see the sea ahead, the little blue waves glinting in the sun, and the road began to slope towards it. Jerry decelerated gradually, switching controls in the convertible until, when the road slid into the sea, the Phantom VI had become a speedboat.

Gracefully, and without slackening speed, the Rolls cut across the water and before long the outlines of the ring of ships could be seen. Jerry touched another control.

This was his first opportunity to try out the car's new feature, for which he had paid a hundred and fifty thousand marks.

There was a soft, muttering sound and the Rolls Royce

began to sink beneath the ocean. It was capable of sub-
merging only a matter of feet and for short distances, but it
would probably see him through.

His speed had decreased considerably now. He peered
through the murky water, looking upwards, and soon saw
the keels of the radio ships ahead. Their sonar was bound
to detect him and they would begin dropping depth charges
almost at once, but with luck they would detonate well below him and a vessel as small as his would be hard to pin-
point with any great accuracy.

They had a fix.

He saw the first charge plunge into the water on his right
and fall towards the ocean bed.

Then another fell close to it, and another on his left, another behind him.

He watched them sink.

One by one the shock waves rose, threatening to blow
him to the surface under the Yankee's guns.

The car rocked. Its forward course was deflected by a
further series of shock waves.

Jerry kept firm control of the wheel, letting the car move

with the waves, waiting until they had died before pressing on, beneath the ships' keels and beyond them.

More depth charges struck the water and floated down.

One of the blue steel cannisters brushed the side of the car and he swung violently away as, below him, it exploded, catching the rear and almost turning the Rolls end over end.

Jerry was thrown forward against the wheel. Another charge went off. The water was cloudy. He lost his bearings.

The car spiralled to a dangerous depth; he managed to switch on the interior lights and regain control as he began to somersault.

Checking the instruments, he judged he was out of range. He began to rise.

Breaking through the waves, the limousine continued its stately way across the surface. Looking back, Jerry could see the ships behind him.

A few guns blew black smoke from their muzzles, he heard the roar as they fired, saw the shells splash into the sea and burst on either side of him, spraying the canopy of the car with water and momentarily making him lose visibility.

He smiled. Before they got his range, he would be over the horizon.

Until the radio ships thought of putting down anti-sub nets, the car would be useful.

Dashing like a dolphin through the warm water, the Rolls Royce was soon in sight of Ostend and a similar concrete roadway. It hit the road smoothly under Cornelius's control, reconverted and was bowling along the road to Brussels without a moment's interruption.

He bought a paper at a roadside kiosk, saw that Israel had annexed Bulgaria and that another hundred thousand U.S. military advisors had been flown into European H.Q., Bonn.

And the sun was setting.

The act of running the radio-ship blockade had tired him a trifle and he planned to spend the night at an organisation-approved hotel in Brussels.

Soon Brussels lay ahead, all baroque red and gold in the sunset, sweet city of nostalgia.

Blood Sample

At Mach 3 ordinary tires start to melt.

Goodrich   ad

1. DOPE PUSHING PREACHER WAS
   PEEPING TOM

Bishop Beesley popped a bar of Turkish Delight into his large, wet mouth, smiled as he chewed the soft chocolate and jelly, and unwrapped another bar. He swallowed, licked his lips with his grey tongue, and picked up his pen.

In the lounge of The Golden Orrery, one of the best hotels in Brussels, he was polishing up the newspaper article he was writing. It was called *Heroin: A Cure for Cancer?* and would appear the following Sunday. He had written for the *Sunday Messenger* for some years. Before the dissolution of the clergy, he had done the regular *From My Pulpit* feature, and afterwards, when the *Messenger* had to change its policy to fit in with modern trends, had changed the name of his column to *From My Viewpoint*. Journalism, however, did not pay him sufficiently and was really just a useful sideline.

From where he sat, Bishop Beesley could see the main entrance of the hotel and he looked up as the glass doors swung open. Through them came a man carrying a light grip and dressed in a black and white fur coat. The man appeared to be an Indian, for his skin was black and he wore an elaborate turban and what the bishop considered a rather vulgar silk suit. The man walked to the reception desk and spoke to the clerk who handed him a key.

The bishop popped the unwrapped bar of Turkish Delight into his mouth and resumed work.

It did not take him long to complete the article, put it into an envelope, address and stamp the envelope and walk to the hotel's mail-box where he posted it.

He looked at the clock over the reception desk and saw that dessert would be being served about now. He walked across the foyer to the dining room and entered it. The dining room was half-full. Two or three family groups sat at tables along the walls, a few business men with their wives or secretaries ate at other tables, and at the far end sat the Indian who seemed to have chosen pheasant, the hotel's speciality.

Bishop Beesley hated the whole idea of meat. He hated the whole idea of vegetables, for that matter, but the orange bombes were unmatched anywhere and it was for them that he came to The Golden Orrery.

With a great deal of dignity he sat his full buttocks down on the well-stuffed chair and put his pale hands on the cloth.

There was no need to order.

Very shortly a waiter appeared with the first of the six orange bombes that the bishop would eat tonight, as he ate every night when in Brussels.

The bishop picked up fork and spoon and bent his nose over the dessert, his eyes watering with delight.

Although absorbed in pleasure, the bishop could not help noticing the Indian when the man got up and walked past his table. He walked so lithely, there was such a sense of physical power about him, that the bishop wondered for an instant if he were all he seemed to be.

Though he had paused only a split second in his eating, it was enough to bring the bishop back to his fourth orange bombe with added relish.

Rising, at length, from the table, he decided to get an early night. He had a busy morning to look forward to.

Jerry Cornelius took off his turban and flipped it onto the chair beside the bed. The girl looked a little surprised by the colour of his hair; her full lips parted and she moved her body on the bed.

Like a big, black boa constrictor he slid from his silks and came slowly towards her, taking her shoulders in his strong hands, pulling her so that her pink breasts pressed against his ebony chest and she drew a deep breath before his lips touched her rose-soft mouth, his tongue stroked hers and love boiled in their bodies, rising, rising, rising in volume with the glory of the very finest Gregorian chant; tempo increasing, flesh flush against flesh, mouth against mouth, hands moving, bodies fusing, teeth biting, voices shouting fit to wake the dead.

He lay beside her with the smell of her body in his nostrils, trying not to breathe too heavily so that the smell would stay there as long as possible. He put an arm around her shoulders and she settled against him, her long, fine dark brown hair brushing his skin. For a while they lay still and then he took his cigarettes from beside the bed and lit one each for them.

He had not expected to meet another organisation operative in The Golden Orrery: Koutrouboussis had said nothing about it. But Polly Fass had recognised him in the corridor outside his room, though he did not know her.

"What are you doing here?" he'd asked.

"Looking for you." She took her opportunities while she could.

Now he said it again.

"I've just delivered a consignment," she told him. "On my way back to England now. It was a touchy job—all kinds of trouble. Are you looking for potentials here?"

"No."

"Oho," she said knowingly.

He slid the flat of his hand over her thighs and hips, up her torso and over her right breast, stroking the nipple until it was hard; he put his cigarette out in the ashtray by the bed, took hers from her fingers and put that out too. Her excellent teeth delicately nipped his tongue as they kissed.

It was a shame they hadn't put the light out. Bishop Beesley, peering through his spy-hole in the room above, frowned. He had recognised Cornelius.

2. DANGER! HITCH-HIKERS WHO POSE AS JOURNALISTS!

Leaving the hotel the next morning, Cornelius was stopped by a shout from the corner of the street. Turning, he saw a fat figure in the gaiters and frock-coat of a clergyman. The man was waving a small attaché case and waddling just as fast as he could.

"A moment, sir! A moment of your time!" The words were panted in a tone reminiscent of sewage warbling underground.

Cornelius paused by the Phantom VI. "Ha," he said. "A moment, eh?" He wondered if this were an organisation contact nobody had warned him about.

The clergyman reached him, breathing heavily, leant against the car and hastily pulled a paper bag from his pocket, taking something that looked like a chocolate cream from it and cramming it into his mouth. It seemed to help him recover.

"Birmingham," he said.

"Indeed," Cornelius replied.

"Beesley—from Birmingham. We met there the Easter before last."

"I never go to Birmingham if I can help it," said Jerry fastidiously. "I haven't been there in four years."

"Mr. Aserinsky." Bishop Beesley spoke with prim accusation. "Mr. Aserinsky! Come now. Birmingham. The Easter before last."

"Before last, before last." Jerry pursed his lips. "Before last . . ."

"Aha!" Beesley grinned and patted his forehead with one finger. "Aha! Memory playing tricks."

"Certainly not!"

"Can't remember where one was at any particular moment—can one? Eh? Or, might I say, *who* one was, hm? Ha, ha!"

Cornelius put himself on his guard, ready to drag his vibragun from its holster in a split second. But Beesley was leaning forward with a knowing smile. "Trust me, Mr. Aserinsky. We have much in common, you and I."

"Are you from the organisation . . ." Cornelius said, "at all?"

"No, Unfortunate. But I understand the aims. And I endorse them, Mr. Aserinsky."

"I'm leaving now." Jerry put hand to handle.

"I was going to ask you a favour."

A yellow, single-decker tram went past on the other side of the street. Cornelius watched it from the corner of his eye.

"What was that?"

"I believe you are on your way to Germany. You'll be passing through Aachen?"

"That's for me to say." Jerry relaxed a little as the tram turned a corner.

"Could you, perhaps, give me a lift? I am only a poor journalist and the rail fares are so dear, as you appreciate, I'm sure."

"Journalist?"

"Churchman? Unfortunately that profession is a dead one these days. Progress, Mr. Aserinsky, has scant sympathy for the redundant . . . I mean," the bishop reached into his coat pocket and took out a bar of chocolate which he put into his mouth, "I mean—one must survive. There was little else I was trained for. Consolation was my trade. I still pursue it as best I can."

Jerry watched a thin trickle of chocolate leave Bishop Beesley's mouth. It looked rather like blood.

"I don't trust you," he said.

"Forgive a trace of self-pity." The bishop spread his hands and shrugged in despair. "But my appearance is doubtless disturbing to you. Can I help that? My clothes— they are all I have. My poor, coarse body: glands. My method of approach: urgent necessity, if I am to earn the pittance that will support me for another week or two. And there is the plague to consider. Rats have been seen.

You, Mr. Aserinsky, *are well dressed, handsome, rich too . . ."*

"Too rich." Jerry opened the door and threw his grip into the back of the car. He slid into the driving seat, closed the door of the car and started the engine.

Soon he was driving from Brussels, on the Aachen road.

Not too far behind him, his face set in an expression of moral outrage, came Bishop Beesley, stiff-backed at the wheel of a silver Cadillac, his jaw moving rhythmically and, from time to time, his hand moving to meet it. Beside him on the seat was a large paper bag containing almost a pound of walnut fudge.

Bishop Beesley turned to walnut fudge in moments of crisis.

Analysis

> La liberté ne sera recouvrés,
> L'occupera noir, fier, vilain, inique,
> Quand la matière du pont sera ouvrée,
> D'Hister, Venise fasche la republique. (5.29)

In his book *Prophecies on World Events by Nostradamus*
(Liveright Publications Inc., 1961) Stephen Robb tells us
that Hister is an old name for the Danube. But the
passage of the centuries, he says, has brought it up to
date. He believes that it was an obvious word for the
prophet to use, for it meant the Danube and also served
as an anagram of Hitler. Mr. Robb says that in the 16th
century anagrams were as popular as crossword puzzles
are today. *Hister,* therefore, with one letter change gives
us *Hitler.* Mr. Robb says that the change of one letter
was permissible in anagram writing (see *Dictionnaire de
Trevoux*). What other word, asks Mr. Robb, can serve
better than *Hister* to specify both the name, and the place
of origin of "the bold, black, base-born, iniquitous man"
who was to "occupy liberty"?

Michael Moorcock, A Cure for Cancer

1. BLONDE MISTRESS OF NIBELBURG'S TOWER OF TERROR!

Jerry passed through Aachen listening to Olivier Messiaen's *Turangalîla Symphony* on his headphones. He frowned self-critically as the seventh movement began. His Ondes Martenot playing was dreadful. He hardly noticed the F111A nose-dive into a nearby field until the sight of the flames made him stop the car and watch as the U.S. Marines arrived in three Shawnee whirlybirds and, automatic weapons at the ready, ringed the wreck. One of the advisors jerked his thumb at Jerry to continue down the road. He waved, wound back to the beginning of the movement and was once again on his way to Nibelburg with a couple of hours to go and by this time aware of the Cadillac on his tail. The bishop was apparently making no attempt to hide the fact that he was pursuing Jerry.

Cornelius waited until the marines were out of sight and then decided to give Bishop Beesley the slip.

At the touch of a button the Phantom VI sprouted stubby wings and tail section, the turbo-jet engine whirled into life and the car took off at great speed from the almost deserted autobahn. It circled the baffled bishop once and then climbed rapidly into the calm, cloudless sky of the autumn afternoon.

A little later Jerry dropped altitude as he made out the impressive steeples of Cologne Cathedral. He checked his map and then began to descend towards the road that would take him to Nibelburg. To the west he thought he could just see the tall, stone tower where Dr. Karen von Krupp lived, worked and schemed for the destruction of the organisation and all it stood for.

The car touched down on the highway; its wings and

tail section were retracted and it whipped along the
concrete road until Jerry saw the sign saying he was
about to enter Nibelburg.

Nibelburg was a few two- or three-storied houses and
shops of grey and red brick, a little railway station, a
larger police station with a great many motor-bikes parked
outside it, and a church which had recently been converted
into a dance hall.

Over the tops of the elms and poplars lining the fields
beyond Nibelburg, Cornelius made out the tower he had
seen from the air. He decelerated, began to whistle the
Chant d'amour from the recently-finished symphony,
and consulted his guide. The tower was reached by an
unmade road about half a mile out of Nibelburg.

He stopped just before he came to the road, and he
concentrated his attention on his mouth until he had a
passable ache in one of his left molars. Feeling unhappy,
he restarted the engine and turned into the side road,
ignoring the Black Rat sign and bumping along for a
quarter of a mile until he stopped outside the seventy-
foot tower with its Gothic doorway, windows and battlements high above. The stone, which seemed to date from
the earliest Gothic period, was extremely clean, with hardly
a trace of a stain of any kind. It was pitted with age, and
worn, especially around the lower parts of the wall, but
nonetheless it was as well-scrubbed and looked after as a
carefully kept tooth. Cornelius wondered if he climbed to
the battlements he would find they had been filled with
amalgam or even gold.

He parked the car neatly at the side of the tower. Only
one other car was there, a Volkswagen sports, which, he
gathered, belonged to the doctor.

He walked up the gravel path and raised the heavy
iron door-knocker, letting it fall with a thump that fled
away into the tower's interior.

The door was opened almost instantly by a beautiful
blonde girl of about sixteen. She had blue eyes of a largeness
that was accentuated by her use of mascara. There was a
smile on her wide, full mouth; her hair was long and
straight, covering the back and shoulders of a short-
skirted dress of rich white brocade that was probably a
Biba copy. She wore matching brocade tights and Granny

shoes. Her arms were almost entirely bare and her skin
was as sweet and soft as the silk of Jerry's suit, the colour
of the first warm streaks of a spring sunrise.

"Ja?" she said, a depraved look appearing momentarily
in her eyes.

"Do you speak English," said Jerry lazily, "Southern
English?"

"Ja, of course." She looked him over slowly and with a
certain amount of awakening surprise, as if she had not
at first been struck by his black skin and his turban. What
had been her first impression? Jerry wondered.

Cornelius put his hand to his cheek. "I was going
through Nibelburg," he told the girl, "when I was overcome with toothache. I enquired at the police station and
they told me that I would find a dentist here."

"And more," said the girl mysteriously, standing aside
to let him enter and gesturing vaguely with the dildo in
her left hand.

When he stood in the polished oak hall, she closed the
door with a crash and popped the dildo into the umbrella
stand, folding her hands under her breasts and looking
down at the floor.

"You wish to see Doctor von Krupp?" she said at
length.

"I believe that is the name I was given."

The girl raised her perfect eyebrows. "But your first
name?"

"It's Michael," he said. "I call myself Mike."

"This way." She began to walk along the hall, paused
at the stone, oak-banister stairway until he had caught up
with her, and then began to ascend.

On the fourth landing, the girl stopped and knocked
gently at the only door. A voice came from the other side.
Jerry couldn't hear the words. The girl turned the handle
and they wandered in together, into a high-ceilinged surgery with a large window of rich, stained glass—a pastoral scene from the sixteenth century. The glass was
exquisite and Jerry stared at it for several seconds before
he saw the luxurious dentist's chair, the chrome-finished
instrument stand, the dentist, at a desk in one corner,
looking through a stack of index cards.

"Herr Michael von Krupp," said the girl gently. "A
toothache."

"Aserinsky," said Jerry.

Doctor von Krupp smiled condescendingly and spoke in German: "You must leave, *liebchen*." The girl glanced through narrowed eyes at Jerry and then went out.

Dr. Karen von Krupp was about thirty in a stiff, black and white paisley overall, black net stockings and purple charley boots. Her hair was a deep, dark red, very thick and wavy, worn at shoulder length. Her face was strong, with pronounced cheek-bones, intelligent and attractive. Her lipstick almost matched her shoes and her eyebrows were pencilled thin to match her hair. She spread back her overall to put her hands on her hips and revealed a dress of layered chiffon that was predominantly bottle-green, its hem six inches above the knees of her long, well-shaped legs. Her taste, thought Jerry, was dreadful, but splendid.

"It is Herr Michael Aserinsky?" the woman asked, smiling once.

"It is." He admired her figure. "A toothache."

"*Ja, ja.*" She turned and began to pack the index cards into a box on the desk. Jerry took off his coat.

"Will you go and sit in the chair, please."

"Well." Jerry wondered why he was here.

"And remove your—*hat,*" she said firmly, then laughed.

"No," he said.

"But you must." She looked over her shoulder, staring hard, smiling again. "Otherwise, you see, I cannot get a proper grip on you."

"My political convictions . . ."

"You have some?"

"Forbid me, doctor, from removing my turban in the presence of a woman. I hadn't realised . . ."

"Ah," she closed the lid of the box, "So," began buttoning up her overall. "Still, Herr Aserinsky, you must decide whether you would feel in health in this world or suffer a moment or two somewhere else."

Jerry's hand began to move towards his vibragun, but he stopped it with great self-control. "Well, perhaps you could first look at the tooth and tell me what you think needs work. Then we can decide."

"But you could be making me waste my time." She shrugged. "Very well, into the chair, sir."

He clambered warily into the chair and rested his head back so that he was looking at the upper part of the stained glass window and a section of the drilling rig.

"You like my window?" She picked up a barbed tool from the tray of instruments. "Open wide, please," and she began to poke and scrape at his teeth. "What do you think about cocaine?"

He blinked.

When she stepped back she was smiling. "Black teeth. Like black marble. Curious."

"You noticed?" He tried to rise. "The pain's gone now. Psychosomatic, I suppose."

"You're an expert at that, aren't you?"

"Um," he said.

"Why have you got black teeth, then? Painted with white enamel by the look of it . . ."

"Bored with them. . . ."

"I think not. Re-born, perhaps."

Jerry's hand fled into his jacket and grasped the butt of the vibragun. "Dancing was never more digusting than when done by Kelly, eh?"

"I'm with you there."

He felt sick. He poised himself to jump from the chair, noticing how beautiful she was. He fell in love with her.

"Why did you come here?" She replaced the hooked instrument on the tray and looked down into his eyes. She did something to the chair and he was tilted back even farther. His fingers fell limply from the gun-butt. Her face came closer, the lips opening to show large, even teeth (two of them gold) and a huge, curling tongue.

He dropped his hand away from the gun altogether. It went out, instead, to grasp her thigh, feeling the ridge of a suspender belt beneath the thin material of dress and overall.

She kissed him coarsely.

"Oh," he said. He still felt sick. He was breathing heavily.

"Ah," he said as she drew back. "Who cares?"

An unpleasant whine from outside. The blonde girl came in. "Rockets," she said.

There was a crash from below.

"No warheads," said Jerry, getting up, drawing his gun and putting his arm around Karen von Krupp's shoulders. "Pack a bag, doctor." He pulled on his coat.

"That's real Panda, isn't it?" she asked, fingering it. "Where did it come from—Moscow or London?"

Another rocket whined in and grazed the roof.

"Ouch," she said. "Perhaps my husband . . ."

"Pack a bag. We'll go to Paris."

"Wait a moment, then."

2. PRESIDENTS IN PARADE SCANDAL!

"Time flies," said Jerry.

"And who, these days, knows his name?" smiled Karen von Krupp tenderly as the crystal city became distinct ahead.

Left fingertips on her knee, right on the wheel, Jerry cruised at ninety towards Paris. "There is something," he said, "concerning Russia. But what about America?"

"I don't know what you mean, darling." She drew on her long cigarette holder one last puff and threw the whole contraption from the window. "Well, that's over."

"Something's going on," he said.

"Always. And was it not you, anyway, who engineered the Moscow thing?"

"Possibly," said Jerry frowning desperately, glancing behind him at the blonde girl who, pouting disinterestedly, lounged in the back seats. "You'd better change into an ankle-length skirt. You know what they're like in the Three Republics about that sort of thing." He touched a stud and the glass partition slid down, allowing her to crawl into the back of the car. The blonde girl moved over and looked out of the window.

While she changed he looked at his map for the best route into Paris.

In the rearview mirror he noticed that Bishop Beesley had caught up with him again for there was the silver Cadillac spinning along behind them, a fat, pasty figure at the wheel. Jerry blacked out the back windows.

"That's clever," she said, struggling into a long, bottle-green skirt. He wondered if all her skirts were bottle-green and all her shoes purple. It indicated an interest in Ouspensky, at very least.

In Paris they were just in time to watch the presidents ride by, their white horses wading, sometimes swimming, through the watery streets, sending up a fine, bright spray in the pale sunshine.

Along the Champs-Elysées the procession made its way, some of it on foot, some in barges, some in carriages, some on horseback.

As best they could the presidents waved to the few soaked spectators (survivors of the plague) who shivered on both sides of the wide street, knee-deep in water. The presidents led the Three Republics of France, Spain and Portugal (there had been four before the Israeli annexation of Greece) who had resisted offers from the U.S. wanting to send in some advisors.

Old age had made the presidents almost identical, with the same vacant eyes, drooling mouths, yellow, wrinkled skins and near-hairless heads. They were strapped firmly to horses almost as old as themselves. They were said to be very sentimentally attached to their horses.

A little behind them laboured the band; each musician up to his waist in water. The bass drums were muffled and every time the drummers struck a beat they sent a fountain of water into their own faces. There was water in all the brass, but they marched resolutely against the current, playing a burbling *La Marseillaise*.

"Touching," said Karen von Krupp stroking his leg.

Jerry leaned back in the moored Phantom VI, his arm comfortably around Dr. von Krupp's shoulders. She smiled and the car rocked gently in the wake of the presidential passing.

"Shall we go to the Assembly and hear the speeches?" She glanced back at the blonde girl. Jerry shook his head.

He cast off and began to turn the car into the current.

There was a tabac on his right and Jerry looked at it nervously as he went past. Someone was peering at him from the first floor window. He recognized the thin, intense nose.

It was Zhazhda, chief of the organization's Moscow

agency and an Okharna operative. What was he doing in Paris? Jerry pretended he hadn't seen him and pulled the car's throttle full out, boiling down the Champs-Elysées as fast as he could go.

Behind him ploughed Bishop Beesley's silver Cadillac, hood barely above the water.

"Ubiquitous," Jerry murmured and stopped outside the Hotel Aspiration. "Hurry, my dear, before he turns the corner. Leap," he said, opening the door, "to the step there. I'll bring our bags in later."

Dr. von Krupp leapt. The blonde girl leapt after her. Jerry started the car up and thrummed away down the narrow street, his wash slapping against windows on both sides. But Beesley was in too deep water and had given up the chase. Soon Cornelius was able to return, moor the car in the hotel's garage, and join his love in the lobby.

"It's just a front," he said, pressing a bell on the reception desk. The floor fell away with them, bearing them deep into the ground.

"Underground," he told her, indicating the musty darkness. "Safe and sound."

"A trap," she said.

"Not so."

As the section of the floor rose back to join the rest, he switched on lights and green brilliance filled the room. She studied the lust in his face.

"I must be careful," she said. "My husband . . ." Then she yelled with excitement as he fell upon her.

"It has been too much for me," he growled, "today."

And they rolled about all over the Dunlopillo flooring while the blonde girl sat in the corner looking on with boredom.

3. TRANSVESTITE ORGY IN PARIS HOTEL

"Husbands and wives, sisters and brothers, mothers and sons," said Bishop Beesley, adjusting his mitre and grinning at Jerry who was spreadeagled against the wall. Karen von Krupp, wearing an ermine-trimmed cape of red velvet and an elaborate crown, crossed her legs and leaned back moodily in her throne. Bishop Beesley reached out with his crook and pushed up Jerry's skirt, tickling the balls that bulged in the black lace knickers they had dressed him in while he was unconscious. "White pubic hair. I hadn't expected that, Mr. Aserinsky."

"And I hadn't expected this, bishop."

"Well, well—you can't just go around screwing another chap's wife like that and expect to get away with it, can you? There's some decency left in the world, I hope."

"So, what's your plan?"

"A restoration job, Mr. Aserinsky, on you. For your own good. Actually, I bear you no malice."

"My name isn't—"

"Aserinsky. So you say."

"It's Jerry Cornelius."

"So you say."

Someone moved in the shadows and began to wade across the Dunlopillo. It was Zhazhda, his thin face concerned.

"It's Alan Powys, isn't it?" said Zhazhda.

"So you say," said Jerry.

"Mitzi!" Bishop Beesley snapped his fingers as best he could. "Mitzi Flynn."

"This is getting to be a drag. Use the machines for heaven's sake," murmured Karen von Krupp.

"I hate artificial methods," said Jerry.

"Connie Nuttall."

"Colvin," said Jerry. "Connie Colvin. Tragic wasn't it?"

"What's in a name?" The blonde girl appeared. She had hoisted up her dress and was strapping on a black dildo.

"Fuck that," said Bishop Beesley. "I do apologise." The blonde girl began to bugger him.

Jerry glanced at Karen von Krupp, but she looked away. He was dressed in the full set: curly red wig, make-up, white lace blouse, falsies, girdle, suspender-belt, fishnet stockings, high-heels, a tight, black skirt.

Bishop Beesley's head was close to the floor and his shout was muffled. "Don't worry, sir. We'll soon have everything back to normal. You'll feel a new person once this is over!"

"How did you get down here?" Jerry asked Karen von Krupp.

"They followed you. Zhazhda pressed the button."

"Somebody has to," said Zhazhda.

"You got the dope while you slept."

"I thouht you were on my side," Jerry said to Zhazhda.

"I am. You'll realise that one day."

"I don't fancy this. It's like something out of the political age."

"Not all of us have your faith in the future, Comrade Cornelius."

"Well, there's no time like the present."

Zhazhda pulled down his pants. "That'll have to be dealt with." He turned to Karen von Krupp. "You're a surgeon, aren't you? Could you do it?"

She shrugged. "I've done it before."

The bishop rose from his hands and knees. "Now, let me see."

Jerry wondered if he were losing his patience. "Bishop— I don't know whether you realise . . ."

"I understand. I understand. This is your home and we were not invited. But these are troubled times, my dear. Needs must, as it were."

"Mitzi," said Karen von Krupp.

The blonde girl stepped forward.

"Snap the staples off. Let our friend join us."

Mitzi freed Jerry.

The bishop glanced curiously at Karen von Krupp. "You want to . . .? A party?"

"Why not?"

A strobe began to flash and the room filled with sound. It was Jimi Hendrix's *Voodoo Child* distorted because of the volume, but they couldn't be expected to know that, particularly since they were reeling about. Jerry strode through the strobe-light and took Karen von Krupp by the arm. She was vomiting spasmodically. He saw his clothes in a corner with his gun on top. There was only time to get the gun and aim it at the wall.

"Cheer up," he told her. "It's going to be worse before it's better. This is a bit of an emergency."

"Where are we going?"

"Through the Shift. I always keep one handy."

The wall fell away and Jerry hefted up his skirt and stuck the gun in his girdle.

Somewhere a mammoth screamed.

4. OUR NIGHT OF HORROR

Around them the air was jewelled and faceted, glistening and alive with myriad colours, flashing, scintillating, swirling and beautiful. She clung to him. "What is it?"

"The multiverse. All layers of existence seen at once. Get it?"

"Philosophy isn't my bent."

"This is physics, dear."

"Where are we?"

"Ah, that's the chance you have to take. Keep walking."

The air cleared. They stood on a green plain close to a clump of oaks. In the shade of the oaks stood a small man with a goatee and rimless glasses. He had a large black metal box under his arm.

"Would you believe it?" Jerry said with some excitement. "The bugger's got it."

"That looks like . . ."

"That's right. Good old comrade . . . Hey!" Jerry began to run towards him, hampered by Karen von Krupp, who refused to let go of his arm, and by the tight skirt and high heels.

A wave of jewels without substance washed over them. "My machine!" shouted Jerry and his voice echoed for a long time. "Oh, well. Some other time. I thought it was too good to be true."

"What machine?"

"That'd be telling. Unless you already know. I suspect Bishop Beesley does know and that's what he's after—ultimately speaking, at any rate."

They were now walking through the streets of St. Petersburg in the early morning. It was very romantic. Jerry pointed out the little cluster of figures staring at them from the top of an office block in Bronstein Prospekt. "*Homo habilis* by the look of them. Funny little sods, aren't they?"

Down the middle of the prospekt galloped a brontotherium herd.

"It's very quiet," she said.

"Yes, it would be."

"What's the time?"

"Not sure. Post-political, I'd say. But you can never be sure. This could be a complete mix-up. I wish I had a fix."

Bishop Beesley confronted them, threatening them with some sort of insect spray.

"We know all about you, my dear Mr. Cornelius," he said. "You and your women friends. Oh, God, it's disgusting! This *is* 1970! You're so primitive!"

"You think I should feel guilty?" Jerry got a grip on his vibragun. You could never be sure.

"I think someone should, dear."

"Where we can we talk?"

The bishop bent down and picked up his attaché case, tucking his equipment inside. Then he held the case to his chest with all the affection an old woman might give to her parrot.

"I've got a marvellous little latty here," he said. "Taste! You've never seen the like."

"Sounds sweet. But this'll do."

The three of them sat down at the sidewalk table, under the big umbrella. A surly waiter took their order.

"It's time to make up, Mr. Cornelius," said the bishop. "I've such a horror of tension. I can't bear it."

"Not yet, bishop."

"But this is *Denmark*. So *neutral*."

"I see I've caught you at a weak moment." Jerry got up. "Come on, Karen. I'll be seeing you, bishop."

"Cruelty! The world is full of cruelty!" The bishop tucked into their strudels.

They strolled on through the multiverse. "Where did he come from?" she said. "What was the conversation about?"

"What are conversations ever about? He seemed to know. Doubtless we'll meet again, either before or after, or not at all. Keep walking."

"The sooner we get back to the sane world, the better," she said waspishly.

"You're just sore because you didn't get your coffee."

They were walking on concrete. Ahead of them was the huge silhouette of a Lockheed SR-72 Mach 3 two-seat interceptor and strategic reconnaissance aircraft framed against the dawn. "Would you believe it? Maybe it's something you said."

"I feel funny."

"You probably do. It's all magic, really. We're out of the tunnel—or nearly. Run."

They tripped on their high heels until they reached the aircraft. "Hop in," he said. "I think you must have a talent, Fraulein Doktor."

"Do you know how to fly these monsters?"

"Oh, come off it."

5. FLY YOUR EGGS RIGHT DOWN THEIR STACKS!

"I've had very little private life since all this started," explained Jerry as they took off from Orly airport and were momentarily pursued by some Starfighters that fell to pieces behind them. He spoke through the intercom. "You look beautiful in that helmet." He guided the plane towards the Channel.

"Thank you." She put her hand on the portion of his thigh that was bare between his stocking and suspender belt. He decelerated.

"I don't want to fly at maximum speed," he explained, "because I've got eight AIM-174s to get rid of and they're not really suitable for the job I've got in mind."

She accepted his apology with a polite little smile.

The 95 ft. aircraft soon reached the Channel and flak began to appear as the pirates tried to hit it. Jerry angled the plane towards them, hoping for the best, and released all the air-to-air missiles in rapid succession. There were a few explosions, then they had passed the ships and were circling off the coast. "Stand by to eject," he said and putting the plane into a steep dive yanked the ejector lever.

They drifted down towards the cliffs. He leaned over and kissed her. Water gouted as the plane hit the sea.

They landed gently and got out.

"You don't look too jolly, Herr C," she remarked.

"Light or square, I suppose it's all the same to me, Doktor Krupp." He smoothed his skirt. "Well, that wasn't too bad, was it? Sure the velocity didn't bother you?"

"It's something you get used to."

"Of course you do." He squeezed her hand affectionately.

Result

"In every war in history there must have been a considerable flow of genes one way or another. Whether the genes of the victors or of the vanquished have increased most is a debatable point."

Papazian, *Modern Genetics*

1. AMERICA TAKES "NON NONSENSE" LINE

Curled in deep leather armchairs beside a comfortable fire in the sitting room of Jerry's Ladbroke Grove H.Q. Jerry and Karen von Krupp listened to Groucho Marx singing *Father's Day* while they caught up with the newspapers.

It seemed that Israel, having annexed Turkey, Greece and Bulgaria, was putting it about that Rumania and Albania were threatening her security. U.S. President Teddy "Angel Face" Paolozzi had increased the number of military advisors sent to Europe to three million. They were under the command of General Ulysses Washington Cumberland whose mission was to keep order in Europe and seek out "certain fifth column elements." The British parliament, both government and opposition, had been arrested as their jumbo Trident was about to take off for Gibraltar. President Paolozzi had sent a diplomatic note to Israel that read *Stay off of our turf, Israel, or else*. A riot in Prague had received universal censure from the European press. "Uncool" was the *Daily Mirror* verdict. Bubonic plague remained unchecked in Berlin and Lübeck.

Jerry stopped reading. Evidently, there was little news of any relevance.

"What now?" said Karen von Krupp as Jerry took her hand and pulled her down to the rug. He tore off her clothes, tore off his own knickers and made fierce love to her. Again and again she came and when he fell back, his wig askew, his skirt torn and his stockings laddered, she sighed. "Ach! At last—a man who is a man!"

2. HIS CHOICE: DIE NOW OR
   ROT TOMORROW!

Jerry looked past the bars and glass of the window at the houses in the street beyond the wall. Grey rain fell. Through the rain ran a pack of girls, few over five feet, with narrow, stooped shoulders and cheap see-through blouses and tight little skirts stretched over mean thighs. He sighed.

The Animals, The Who, Zoot Money's Big Roll Band, The Spencer Davis Group, The Moody Blues, Georgie Fame and the Blue Flames, Geno Washington and the Ram Jam Band, Chris Farlowe and the Thunderbirds, The Steam Packet, Manfred Mann, Jesus Christ and the Apostles. Where were the groups of yesterday?

Behind him, Karen von Krupp listened moodily to Ives's *Symphony No. 1 in D Minor*. He wondered if that wasn't the key to the whole thing.

"Still here," he said.

She nodded.

"And getting more so."

"There's something on your mind," she murmured.

"Something indigestible. I've been too long in the wilderness, honey."

"Don't say that, Jerry."

"I've got to face it."

"You can make it."

"Sure. I can make it."

"Are all your relatives dead now?"

"I sometimes think they must be."

"What are you going to do?"

"I'll decide soon. The world is ruled by bad poets. I must do something about it."

"That's your mission?"

"More or less, honey. More or less."

"Are you asking or telling?"

3. MY DEADLY MISSION

"It's a question of polarities," he told her as they slid about in the bed. "A problem of equilibrium."

"I told you. I don't understand philosophy."

"I told you. This is physics."

"What will become of you?"

"I'll probably die. I almost always do."

"Don't die on me, *liebchen.*"

"A lot depends on the next movement."

"Denn wovon lebt der Mensch?"

"Maybe. It's all a *dreckhaufen* really."

"Isn't that the way you like it?"

"Sure."

"You'll never die."

"Not in that sense, of course. Still, it gets boring."

"Then why don't you stop?"

"Ich möchte auch mal was Schönes sehen . . ."

4. SING HIGH, SWEETIE—FOR TONIGHT YOU FRY!

His brain cleared. The process took a few minutes.

From somewhere there came a faint hissing sound. "My programme," he murmured, smiling back in the darkness.

5. AMNESIA: WHY YOU GET IT

An early postcard showing Loch Promenade, Douglas, Isle of Man, with a single-deck open-sided omnibus drawn by a horse. The people wear Edwardian clothes. The tower clock in the foreground says 11.22. The card is post-marked Liverpool, 31 May 1968. The message and address are partially obscured—"We may arrive Sunday anyway see you soon! Julia pp JRC." 79 *Tavistock Road, London, W.11.*

6. WHAT WAS SECRET OF "THING IN THE CELLAR"?

It was a machine of intense beauty consisting of delicate red, gold and silver webs, strands of which brushed his face and had the vital warmth of human skin.

The webs rustled as he entered them, and they began to sing. He relaxed. Beesley's plan had almost worked and the Shift, in this instance, hadn't really helped, either. Still, the machine would set all that right. They certainly needed each other.

Refreshed, sobered, he contemplated the possibilities.

2.

EMERGENCY OPERATION

**IF YOU LIKE TO HUNT OR
SHOOT . . . YOU BELONG
IN THE N R A**

All these benefits for only $5.00

HUNTING SERVICE. NRA Hunter
Bulletins and *American Rifleman* articles
cover game availability, shooting preserves,
gun and game laws. NRA Hunter Awards
are issued for deer, antelope, elk, big horn
sheep, bear and moose. Marksmanship
improvement programs are conducted by
NRA affiliated clubs, including a nationwide
"Sighting-in-Day" as a public service to
hunters.

FIREARMS INFORMATION SERVICE.
Qualified men give practical answers to
queries related to guns and shooting. Plans
for shooting ranges are also available to
members and member clubs.

RECREATIONAL SHOOTING SERVICE.
Matches and leagues are provided, using
.22 caliber and high power rifles, shotguns
and all calibers of pistols. Competition
continues through state, national and
international tournaments. A Classification
system insures equal opportunities for winning
awards. Qualification courses, fun matches,
plinking courses, and informal
shooting games are provided the year
round.

GOVERNMENT EQUIPMENT SALES.
NRA members are eligible to purchase from
the Army, such firearms as are declared
surplus from time to time. Spare parts and
targets are also available.

FIREARMS LEGISLATIVE SERVICE.
NRA members receive monthly gun
legislation information through the
American Rifleman. Bills requiring
emergency action are reported to
members concerned through special
bulletins.

YOU CAN BE PROUD TO BELONG.
NRA is the largest, oldest organization of
sportsmen devoted to preserving your right
to keep and use firearms for lawful
purposes. More than 800,000 hunters and
shooters enjoy NRA's many benefits.

Ad, *Guns & Ammo* magazine

Anaesthetic

"Along with the Smothers Brothers and Rowan and Martin, (Mort Sahl) is part of that radical fringe who try to tear down American decency and democracy."

Howard Miller, WCFL, Chicago

1. LYNDA BIRD TO WED GEORGE HAMILTON?

The next day Jerry and Karen went to the pictures. They sat in the front seats of the Circle and ate popcorn as they watched *Drums Along the Mersey*. Sir William Harrison played the moody, introverted explorer, Ina Shorrock was the proud Queen of Port Sunlight and Eric Bentcliffe emerged in one of his best roles as the rascally trader from the interior.

2. MY TEENAGE WIFE WON'T LET ME OUT OF HER SIGHT

Leaving the cinema they walked hand in hand down Westbourne Grove in the late sunshine. A West Indian with a tray around his neck . sold Jerry a pot of Chaulmoogra, guaranteed as treatment for leprosy.

A squadron of M-60 tanks, mounted on guarded flat-cars, went past them towards Queensway. A crowd of dancing children followed the tanks. The grinning soldiers threw Hershey Bars and Tootsie Rolls to the children.

3. HOW A BANANA ENDANGERS THE LENNON SISTERS

Jerry signalled for the gate of his Ladbroke Grove H.Q. to be opened. A Corporation Dustcart turned the corner.

Balanced on the cab was a man in a fur jacket and a fez. His right hand clung to the truck's canopy and he shouted vigorously through a megaphone.

"Bring out your dead! Bring out your dead!"

4. WHY CONNIE THREATENED EDDIE WITH A LAWYER

Jerry poured himself a Pernod and handed the glass of Tio Pepe to Karen von Krupp. They were dressed in identical velvet suits of violent violet from Mr. Fish. The effect was a little more pleasing than a Pre-Raphaelite painting. Their flies were undone.

5. THE SECRET MIA WON'T TELL FRANK

They lay naked on the red plush bed cover staring up at the blue plush canopy of the brass four poster. Their skins, black and pink, shone with health.

"Fresh air," he said. "That's it."

"Why?"

"It'll be necessary to go to the country sooner or later. We've been in London a fortnight, you know."

"And nothing's happened. Are you worried by the stillness?"

"I suppose so. There's a shipment tomorrow. It could go straight out again." He sniffed at her hair.

She began to stroke the skin of his inner thigh.

"It's too good to be true." She nipped his forearm with her teeth.

First Incision

Newly and/or unexpectedly imposed tyranny can make people commit suicide.

Tomáš Masaryk

1. HOW MUCH LONGER CAN THIS LAST ? ? ? ?

Having left one Phantom VI in Paris, Jerry didn't feel up to using another. Besides, he was in no hurry. "We'll go by river, I think."

He drew his vibragun and went upstairs.

When he next passed the door he was herding a group of sullen transmog patients in front of him. They all wore strait-waistcoats and most of them would have looked handsome or pretty if they had been able to manage a smile or two. Karen von Krupp patted her hair.

Jerry reassured her as they reached the cool main hall. "They'll soon be laughing on the other side of their faces."

It was a lovely day.

Waiting in the courtyard was a white hovertruck with red crosses painted on its sides. When he'd stowed the passengers comfortably at the back Jerry joined Karen in the cockpit and started the engines. Whining, they lifted up and began to move forward through the open gates.

Soon they were whistling down the road, passed the scarlet gloom of Chelsea, and reached the Thames Embankment. "Oh, it is *wunderbar!*" Karen von Krupp looked out at the wrecks of the tankers poking up through oil that shone with dozens of bright colours.

"You can't beat it," Jerry agreed affectionately.

They crossed Waterloo Bridge with the siren going and were waved through by a Marine with a sensitive earnest face who leaned one hand on the butt of his Navy Colt and held a cigar in the other. The white hovertruck sang onwards into the ruined roads of South London that were full of colombine, ragged robin, foxglove, golden rain, dog rose, danewort, ivy, creeping cinquefoil, Venus's Comb, deadnettle, shepherd's purse and dandelion, then turned towards Greenwich where Jerry's cruiser was moored.

As Jerry directed his patients up the gangplank Karen von Krupp pointed to a battered, broken-looking building in the distance. "What is that, Jerry?"

"Greenwich Observatory," he said. "It's a bit redundant now, I suppose."

She came aboard and he cast off.

In a moment they were chugging away from London, moving strongly against the current.

The banks of the river and the fields and ruins beyond them were carpeted with flowers of every description. While Jerry switched the boat over to automatic steering, Karen stretched out on the deck, breathing the warm summer air, staring up at the deep blue sky and listening to the bees and the crickets on the shore.

When they were sailing through a forest of oaks and elms Jerry came and lay down beside her. From the cabin came the faint strains of Ives's *Symphony No. 1*.

"That is a favourite of yours, I would say," she said.

"In a manner of speaking."

"This is the life, is it not?"

"Which?"

"Which do you like?"

"Oh, all of them really."

The prow pushed on through the rainbow oil and every so often a quaintly-shaped fish would leap out and rest on the surface until the ripples opened the top up and it would fall back under again.

The river turned out of the forest and they sailed between fields and old, ruined farmhouses, deserted villages and abandoned pubs. Once, as they moved under a bridge, an armoured car roared over their heads and moaned off down the road. A little later a scrawny young woman threw stones at them from the bank and screamed incoherent insults. Jerry caught a few words. *"Pantalones— el jardin zoologico—la iglesia inglesa! Lavabo—negra*

*—queremos un—vino dulce—de oro, plata, platino, dia-
mantes, rubies, zafiros, esmeraldas, perlas . . ."*

"American immigrant, poor cow."

Karen cocked her head, brushing back her long red
hair. "What was that? Not bees."

The woman had disappeared into the undergrowth.

Jerry listened.

"Hornets?" Karen suggested.

Jerry shook his head. "Westland Whirlwinds. I'd better
just . . ." He jumped up and ran to the bridge. Karen got
up and then fell over on her bottom as a small missile
launcher purred from the forward hatch. She crawled to
the bridge. He was watching the radar.

"About eight of them," he said. "Hard to say whose
they are." He peered through the window. "They've seen
us. They're coming to take a closer look."

"Are they ours, Jerry?"

"No, I think they're yours. Perhaps your husband . . ."

"My husband?"

"Maybe."

Jerry switched on the laservision and tuned it to the
radar. Now he had a close-up of the leading Whirlwind
and its pilot.

The pilot was thoughtfully chewing a chocolate layer
cake as he stared down at Jerry's boat.

"I wonder where he's been," Jerry's hand went to the
launcher's controls. "I wouldn't like to hurt him."

"Does he know this is your boat?"

"I shouldn't think so. It's registered in the name of
Beesley."

"A peculiar coincidence."

"What's peculiar about it?"

But now the helicopters had spotted the launcher and,
even though equipped with superior Nord S.S. 11 air-to-
surface missiles, began to bank away.

"Velocidad maxima, I think . . ." Jerry murmured.

"What?"

"The sloop. Time to be on the move."

"Saints . . ."

The helicopters vanished over the horizon.

"They're heading for London," she said. "I think we
got away just in time."

"You could be right."

"Do you think I'm wrong?"

"Well, they weren't carrying their full complement of missiles, but they were lying rather heavy on the air, wouldn't you say?" He depressed a button and his own launcher disappeared into the bowels of the boat.

2. IT'S A FAD, DAD!

Jerry took over the steering as they turned into the Urzel tributary and moved slowly along beneath a canopy of tall aromatic grass. It was evening now and the sun was low, but a little light filtered through to them.

Since the departure of the helicopters, Karen von Krupp had become introspective and had stayed beside him in the cabin, repeatedly playing the Ives piece. Something was bothering her. Finally, as they approached a wooden landing stage, she said, "Is this, do you think, the answer to our relationship?"

"Of course not." He squeezed her hand and steered the boat in. "It's merely the key to the future. Possibly not even that. Don't worry about it."

With a pout she took the mooring line and jumped to the landing stage, winding the line round and round the oak capstan as he guided the boat into its position. He cut the engines.

"Now let's get those lubbers ashore." Drawing his vibra-gun he kicked open the stern hatch. "All right, mates, out you come. Slowly now."

Blinking in the last of the sunlight, the transmog patients stumbled on deck and trooped down the gangplank that Karen von Krupp had erected for them.

They all set off along the landing stage towards a field of corn.

"Have you ever wondered about the morality of what you are doing?" she asked. "These creatures never asked . . ."

"They prayed. We heard. We merely serve the people, Karen."

"Beesley says . . ."

". . . he does, too. I know. Beesley knows what's good for them. I simply do what they want me to do. There it is. I'm all for equilibrium."

They walked along a small path through the corn. A rabbit ran away from them and a partridge whirled into the sky. The roof of a large house could now be seen in the distance. It was Sunnydale Reclamation Centre. Welcoming smoke rose from the chimneys. "Not much further now," Jerry told the transmog patients who tramped ahead, looking at the ground.

"You never question . . ."

"What is there to question?"

"I . . ."

"I do what they want me to do."

"It's like prostitution."

"It's a lot like prostitution, isn't it?"

"You see nothing wrong . . .?"

"The customer's always right."

"And you have no," she shuddered, "ethics?"

"I give the public what it wants, if that's what you mean."

"You have no sense of mission! Ach! At least Beesley has that!" She laughed harshly. "Hà!"

"I thought it was the same as mine."

"*Nein.* It is different. He knows that people want a sense of security."

"Of course. Do you smell burning?"

"*Ja,* I do."

3. THE EROTIC GHOSTS OF VIET NAM

Sunnydale was burning. The staff stood about in the grounds staring helplessly at the Reclamation Centre. Incendiary rockets had done their worst.

"What about the patients?" Jerry asked Matron.

"All gone, Doctor Finlay. Kidnapped. Months of work! Och . . ."

"Calm yourself, woman," said Jerry with gruff kindness. "Was it the Westland Whirlwinds?"

"Aye, doctor. Eight Mark Tens. We didna have a chance tae activate the defences. We lased London. Mister Koutrouboussis is on his way. He said he'd try tae bring ye with him."

"I'm ahead of him. Is the laser still working?"

"Noo . . ."

"Then you'd better get off to Soho as fast as you can, Janet. Tell them the choppers were heading for London when last seen."

"Aye, doctor." Matron ran for the one hangar still intact. Soon a small OH-6A turbine-powered copter moaned upwards, its pilot hastily pulling on her American uniform to conform with the machine's markings. It flew away over the fields of flowers.

The sun set and the fire went down.

"The damage isn't too bad, considering," said Plemmy, one of the male nurses, vainly trying to brush off the black patches on his smock with a limp hand. "All the East wing is okay."

"They had these big bazookas and stuff," said Mr. Fowles, the Transplant Chief. Mr. Fowles was a tall, pale man with unhealthy hands, a sweaty nature. "We didn't stand a chance. We were rounded up, marked in this stuff," he pointed to the blob of green paint on his forehead, "and herded into the garden. Then they took away the patients."

"Their leader . . .?" Jerry raised a finger to his nose.

"Dressed in clerical gear. He stole the birthday cake Matron had made for the ex-chairman of the Arts Council, the poor cunt had lost so much weight!"

"You've had the cake, I'm afraid," said Jerry, "but I'll see if I can get the patients back. Miserable things. They must be in a state."

"To say the least, sir." Mr. Fowles tucked his hands under his arms. "Timid little creatures at that stage, you know. Don't understand. Couldn't tell you their own names, half of them."

"You'd better get this lot into the East wing." Jerry

indicated the new batch. Most of them had seated themselves on the ground and were staring moodily at the
Centre's smoking skeleton. "I'll be over at my place if you
want me. Come on, Karen."

He led her across the lawns to his little Dutch mansion
and stopped under the carved portal.

"Open, als't u blieft!" The door swung open.

They stepped inside.

"Waar is de nooduitgang?" asked Karen absently as
the door shut behind her. Jerry turned on the lights.

"You're getting very tense," he said.

"Ik hank det wel . . ."

"Sad . . ."

"Ja, das i seben schade . . ."

They walked along the hall. All the wood was dark
and shiny with polish. A clean old man rounded a corner
and tottered towards them. "Ah, sir! Ah, sir!"

"What have we got to eat, de Vossenberg?"

"Gekookte eieren, kaas, fazant . . ."

"Fine. We'll have it in the parlour, I think."

The parlour had walls of the same dark, panelled
wood. The armchairs were deep and old-fashioned, covered in loose folds of floral material. The room was full
of clocks in painted wooden cases, each keeping perfect
time.

They sat in the chairs and said nothing.

After a while de Vossenberg wheeled in the dumb
waiter. "Ah, sir."

He gave them trays then he gave them plates then he
served them with cold pheasant, cheese and boiled eggs.
Then he opened a bottle of Niersteiner and poured it into
two long-stemmed Czech hock glasses.

"What is going to happen now?" asked Karen von
Krupp. "You have lost most of your victims."

"I suppose we should try to get them back."

"Your duty?"

"Well . . ."

"But Beesley will take them to Amerika!"

"How do you know?"

"I just think he would."

"He told you."

"No."

"You knew."

"*Ja . . .*"

"Losing—lost—gone . . . Now it makes sense."

There was a knock at the front door. They heard de Vossenberg shuffle to answer it. They heard voices.

"Koutrouboussis," said Jerry as the Greek, sour-faced, entered the room and glanced disdainfully at the food. "A bite?"

"A fish, eh?"

"No, a mistress. Doktor von Krupp and I are together now."

"I'm getting suspicious of you, Cornelius."

"No need, Mr. Koutrouboussis. I'll be off to the States shortly."

"You heard about the converted Concorde, then? All we got from Beesley was the bang. We've a responsibility to those poor bloaters, Cornelius. You must get them back. They're neither fish, nor fowl, nor good red herring as they are."

"We'll leave in an hour or two."

"Immediately."

"We've got to book seats, Mr. Koutrouboussis. That's a civilised country. You can't just go sailing in there in one of your own planes. It would cause a scene. We'll have to take a scheduled flight."

Koutrouboussis accepted this. "There's a Pan Am airbus leaving in the morning or a VC 10 charter taking off at midnight from Gatwick. It's one of those refugee flights, but we could get you on it."

"Karen will be with me."

Koutrouboussis darted Jerry a tortured look. "Okay. I'll arrange the booking for both of you. You'll have to travel as a monk and a nun."

"Naturally. I've got the necessary gear upstairs."

"Things are becoming crucial, Jerry. I think. You know how crucial? If only you could get back that machine."

"It means going into the Shift, almost certainly."

"You haven't any other way of contacting him?"

"He's a hard man to get hold of. For God's sake—he doesn't even exist. It takes time to contact people like that."

"I know. Keep trying. With that machine, we could achieve everything . . ."

"Beesley's aware of that. He tried to get it off me in Paris. He's sure I have it."

"You haven't . . . ?"

"Oh, fuck . . ."

"He thinks, then, that we're much more powerful than we actually are?"

"Sure."

"I thought this bloody raid had a note of desperation! Oi moi! Oi moi!"

"Chin up, Mr. Koutrouboussis. Keep fishing."

"Look at the state of the nets!"

Infection Exposed

"But many other changes are beginning to affect *your* life and mine! These new trends concern us all! Student revolt in 20 countries—VIOLENCE exploding on college campuses (but *not* on our Ambassador College campuses). It's shocking, but some universities are beginning to allow unmarried men and women students to sleep together in college dormitories! Then look at this NEW phenomenon—rebellious Hippies lolling aimlessly about, taking to drugs and unbridled sex.

"Look at the unhappy marriages, the increasing divorce rate, the tragedy of juvenile delinquents. All about us racial strife, mass demonstrations, riots, VIOLENCE —MURDER! Men in the public eye assassinated! Add to all this the population explosion—the deterioration of our cities—the fear of nuclear WAR that could erase all humanity from the earth!

"These things are now striking close to YOUR life, and mine! You read of them in newspapers and magazines —you hear of them on radio, and see them on television. BUT *WHERE* DO YOU FIND THE *ANSWERS!* Where the *SOLUTIONS?*

"Not only news stories and magazine articles—but whole books have pictured and described these NEW problems of humanity. But The PLAIN TRUTH gives YOU UNDERSTANDING—makes plain the AN-SWERS! Many see and describe WHAT is *WRONG* in the world—The PLAIN TRUTH gives you the CAUSES, explains the REAL MEANING, reveals the ANSWERS, tells HOW these problems will be solved!

"To KNOW what's happening in the world is important. *OTHERS* report the news. But it's FAR *MORE* IM-

PORTANT to understand what these happenings and changing conditions all around you REALLY *MEAN!* And WHERE they are taking us! And *WHAT* are the ANSWERS AND SOLUTIONS! That's why the PLAIN TRUTH is so different.

"The PLAIN TRUTH is UNIQUE among publications.

"To bring you a true perspective, sound understanding, and the right answers, The PLAIN TRUTH draws on sources and worldwide resources unique to it alone."

Herbert W. Armstrong, Editor, The PLAIN TRUTH

1. I DIED ON THE OPERATING TABLE

As the VC 10 landed at long last at Kennedy, Jerry yawned and put down his champagne glass. They had been queuing for a landing space for two hours and it was dark again.

The red, blue and orange neon of the airport had all the richness of a late Walt Disney and everything was defined very sharply in the manner of Burne Hogarth. It was just right.

They disembarked with the Poor Clares and the Benedictines. Karen von Krupp looked lovely as a cool Mother Superior and Jerry was a slick abbot from a fashionable monastery.

Their passports showed Karen's occupation as Dental Surgeon and Jerry's as Heart Specialist, but then all clergy had been re-categorised.

The passport control officer flipped through Jerry's papers. "It says here you're Caucasian, mister."

"That's right."

The officer pushed back his cap and held the passport out in front of his eyes in a theatrical manner. "Well, your picture's okay . . ."

"I've been out East a long time."

"Israel?"

"India."

"All right. I guess you refugees have got special priorities. I hope they know what they're doing."

Jerry and Karen collected their baggage off the conveyor. They had identical expensive suitcases of black leather with gold clasps.

Customs men in smoothly styled uniforms waved them

through. They joined the other nuns and monks who had gathered around a group of shallow-eyed men and women in grey woollen suits and gaberdine coats who shook their hands and welcomed them to America. The leader of the welcomers, a Mr. Silver, had a tanned, tight face and all his buttons were done up. He spoke grimly.

"I'm sure you're all mighty tired, friends, and want to get some shuteye. We have reservations for you at a near-by hotel. Tomorrow we'll meet you and tell you where you're being assigned and how you're going to get there. Might I say how much we admire our British cousins. Follow me, please."

They trooped after Mr. Silver and his committee, crossed a metal bridge over the road that ran beside the air terminal and saw an eight storey building advertised in gold neon as the Hotel Nixon.

"It hardly seems fair," murmured Karen. "Kennedy got an airport and a bloody launching site."

"They weren't expecting a run," said Jerry reasonably.

They went through the swing doors and into the featureless lobby. Mr. Silver stepped over to the checking-in desk and spoke to the clerk who handed him a sheet of paper and a bunch of keys.

"This way, friends." Mr. Silver led them to the elevators. "We're all on the sixth floor. Keep together, please."

Mr. Silver entered the first elevator with eight of his charges. A middle-aged woman, Mrs. Bronson, wearing a belted suit and no make-up save her very red lipstick, herded Jerry, Karen and six monks into the second elevator. Peering at her sheet she started to hand out the keys.

"You're 604, Father Abbot. 605, Brother Simon. 606, Brother Peter. 607, Brother Mathew. 608, Brother John. 609, Brother Thomas. You're in 610, Holy Mother."

When it stopped, they rushed out of the elevator and looked at the signs telling them where to find their rooms. "I'll abandon you here if you don't mind," said Mrs. Bronson, "and we'll meet again at breakfast. Sleep well. It must have been awful . . ." She descended.

"This way, brothers," said the abbot.

Led by Jerry Cornelius and Karen von Krupp the monks trudged off down the corridor. They turned right, turned left and found the rooms. All the doors were painted turquoise with yellow numbers.

Jerry stopped outside his door.

Karen stopped outside her door.

The monks put their keys into their locks and opened their doors and went inside, closing the doors.

"See you later," said Jerry.

She shrugged.

Jerry entered his room and turned on the light.

It was a small, narrow room with a couch that converted to a bed, a single window at the far end with turquoise drapes. He switched on the set and got the time, the temperature and the humidity. He adjusted his watches, pulled off his cassock and checked his blue silk suit for wrinkles. It had survived pretty well.

The bathroom was near the door. It had a shower, a sink and a lavatory. The towels were turquoise edged with gold. The shower curtains were yellow. The soap was turquoise. The tiles were green and orange. Jerry turned on the shower.

He went back into the room and took off his clothes, carrying his holstered vibragun with him to the bathroom and hanging it on the towel rail. He stepped under the boiling shower, soaping himself all over and humming Jimi Hendrix's *May This be Love* to himself.

As he dried, Jerry called room service and ordered the quart of Jack Daniel's Black Label, the Onion Soup au Gratin Mouquin, the Sautéed Calf's Liver with Smothered Onion, Hickory Smoked Bacon and Home Fried Potatoes, the piece of Old New York Cheese Cake, the Two Flavor Jello with whipped cream and the Pot of Steaming Freshly Brewed Coffee. He gave his room number and his name as Father Jeremiah Cornelius.

He called the main desk.

"This is Father Cornelius. Has Bishop Beesley checked in, do you know?"

"I'm sorry, sir. No Bishop Beesley."

"Thank you. God bless you."

Room service arrived. There was something to be said for civilisation, really. Jerry set to eating.

When he had finished the food, he poured himself a large glass of bourbon and drank it down.

There was no doubt about it; America was the last decent country to eat in.

Now he was ready for almost anything.

He unwrapped the towel from his waist and pulled the cassock over his head.

The sign on his door warned him to lock it carefully in case of prowlers. He ignored the sign and crossed to Karen's door.

He turned the handle. The door wasn't locked. He opened it a crack. The light was on. He slipped inside.

At first all he noticed were Karen's legs tightly wrapped around the heaving buttocks of Brother Thomas. She looked over the monk's white shoulder and raised her eyebrows.

"You can go off people, you know," she said.

"Oh, fuck," said Jerry miserably.

2. HE WON'T HAVE TO BEG ME—
   TONIGHT

Jerry pulled up the blind, yearning for music, and stared out at the American morning.

It wasn't all beer and skittles. Even the educational channel was playing Gilbert and Sullivan. He had been sick twice in the night and had finally turned the television off.

Abandoning the cassock, he clad himself in yellow silk with a wide red tie knotted under the flowing collar of his white shirt. His soft calf boots, by Raviana, enclosed his feet and the vibragun cheered him up a little. Perhaps it was time to kill someone.

He combed his milk-white hair in front of the mirror, sweeping it down and then up to form two wings framing his graceful black face.

"Astatic," he murmured cheerfully before his thoughts returned to Karen.

As he entered the corridor, he glanced across at her door, hesitated and then continued towards the elevators.

He wasn't often in love, after all. Not that sort of love. Could it be that that was giving him the identity trouble? It was worse than he'd expected. There had been a certain difficulty in focussing ever since he and Karen had left London. A certain mistiness, a feeling of fragmentation.

He patted his vibragun under his jacket as he reached the elevator. It was his only link with reality, with the machine in the cellars at Ladbroke Grove.

Koutrouboussis . . .

The name came and went.

Memories of Soho faded.

He put his hand into the inside pocket of his jacket and pulled out a postcard. On it was a slightly out of focus picture of a Tompion clock in an engraved steel case. On the other side was an address, JERRY CORNELIUS, AMERICA, and a message: HANG ON.

He thought of Baptise Charbonneau and Kit Carson, of Humphrey Bogart and Kirk Douglas, of George Washington and Franklin D. Roosevelt, of Herman Melville and Dashiell Hammett, and he thought particularly of Charles Ives, Leadbelly, Woody Guthrie and Nina Simone.

Tears came to his eyes and he leaned heavily against the wall until the elevator arrived. America, the shattered dream, the broken promise . . .

At breakfast he couldn't eat his scrambled eggs, and his English Muffin also went untasted. He drank a lot of coffee and for an hour read Jack Trevor Story's *Hitler Needs You* which cheered him up, as he had known it would.

The monks and nuns were all seated at another table, staring at him incredulously. Karen was nowhere in sight, but Jerry saw a face he recognised.

It was Protz. A Russian agent and almost certainly a double agent for the Israelis. Could the archaically dressed man be interested in him?

Protz tripped from the crowded restaurant almost as soon as Jerry had spotted him. Remembering his encounter with Zhazhda of Okharna, Jerry began to feel nervous.

Mr. Silver appeared behind him. "Father Abbot? The arrangements . . ."

It wasn't like Jerry to lie. It surprised him as he said shiftily, "Not 'abbot' if you don't mind, my dear Mr. Silver—Chuzzlewit—I'm afraid there are enemies who have succeeded in following me to this—even this—sanctuary . . ."

"The police?"

"What could they prove? No, no. I thank you for your concern, but do not worry. I have friends, you see, in New York. They'll pick me up later. Bishop Beesley . . ."

"Oh, Bishop Beesley! Good hands. God bless you." Mr. Silver backed secretively away.

"God bless *you*, Mr. Silver . . ."

"No, God . . . Nice of you, father—Chuzzlewit—thanks again . . ." Mr. Silver dropped his eyes. "God . . . thank you, Mr. . . . ."

Jerry whirled on his heel and went softly away from the

restaurant, bought some Marlboros in the lobby and returned to his room.

He turned on the television and changed channels until he got the hotel's own closed circuit channel. It showed a broad view of the road outside the main exit. The road led across the plain to Manhattan. There was surprisingly little traffic. The channel was vision only and the room itself was sound-proofed. A sense of isolation overwhelmed him.

He went to the window and saw a Pan Am 727 shimmer into the sky.

If Protz were in the States, then Zhazhda could be here, too. Zhazhda would tip off Beesley. Beesley would come to the hotel.

Why was he waiting for Beesley to come to him? Impulsively he went to the mirror. His skin had turned a deep brown, his eyes were uncomfortable.

If he hired a car he could be in New York in a half hour. He would be all right in New York. But Karen wouldn't come with him.

In the distance, the sun beat on the towers of the shining city.

There was no escape.

He took off his jacket, switched channels, watched five minutes of *The Good, the Bad and the Ugly* before the quality of the colour upset him, poured himself a glass of Jack Daniels, sipped it, put his jacket back on and went out of his room and opened Karen's door.

She had gone. Her suitcase was gone.

Jerry took his lighter from his pocket and tried to set fire to the messy bed. But the sheets were too sweaty. They wouldn't burn.

3. A PSYCHOLOGIST REVEALS
THE SEXUAL OVERTONES OF
THE MONSTER MOVIES

For three days Jerry stared at the television and the view of the street. On the highway there were increasing numbers of motorcycle cops in unfamiliar black uniforms and helmets. Frequently, during the day or night they would arrest a driver.

Once he switched to a news programme. Someone referred to the European disease that was sweeping the country. "The only answer to it is the European cure . . ."

His meals were now brought to his room, but he had lost his taste for hotel living. When he had last appeared in the restaurant it was to see Karen with Protz. She had looked bored. On her way out he tried to trip her up but failed.

He had watched her bottom for a sign, but got nothing.

The lack of music was beginning to disturb him much more than Karen. A flutter of brushes on a skin, a whine or two from a Martin, a thud from a Fender bass; anything would have helped. But there wasn't a note in the entire hotel. Nothing, anyway, that wasn't offensive quasi-music, such as the Gilbert and Sullivan.

His vague feelings of discomfort had grown by the fourth day. The police arrests seemed increasingly arbitrary.

He turned on the television to a news broadcast for the second time.

President Paolozzi had disappeared and had been replaced by his Vice President, Konnie Agonosto, who was promising to restore order as quickly as possible.

A little while later President Ronald Boyle, elected by emergency vote, announced that his special militia were already getting the country back on a safe, sane, orderly footing, ready to honour her commitments anywhere at home or in the world.

Jerry packed his case and put it near the door. He hurried into Karen's empty room and picked up the phone. "Can you give me Mr. Protz's room number?"

Protz was in 805. Jerry went up by the service stairs, found 805 and knocked on the door.

"Was is das?"

"Karen. It's Jerry. We're in trouble I think. You'd better pack."

"Please go away, Jerry. I'm not going to be tricked . . ."

"Okay."

He walked down the corridor. Everywhere there were open doors and he could see people hastily pushing their possessions into their luggage. He went back to 805, kicking fiercely at the door.

"Karen. Everyone's getting out."

"Go away. Why?"

"Something's up. A change of government." Down the hall came a few bars of Chuck Berry that were rapidly cut off.

Jerry began to pant. Karen knew what she was doing. Koutrouboussis . . . How elaborate was the plot? There had never been so much pressure before. He was out of his element. Everything was threatened.

George Catlin—Mark Twain—Henry Ford. It was no good. The postcard in his pocket was thin and wrinkled. As he touched it, it crumbled.

The door opened. Zhazhda stood there. His eyes were sardonic. "What sort of thing, Comrade Cornelius, is up?"

"The poor sods," said Jerry. "The poor bloody sods. Is this your doing? You traitor . . ."

"Think of Frank, Comrade Cornelius. Your brother. What would he have done?"

"Uncle Frank . . ." Jerry's brain misted over again. "Where's . . . ?"

"You look out of sorts, comrade."

"You were the one, weren't you? You set the trap?"

"Nonsense. I'm merely an advisor over here."

"Tell Doktor von Krupp I'll wait in my room for her."

Jerry walked as steadily as he could to the stairs and began to climb down them. His teeth were aching.

4. THE BEAUTY THE REDS CAN'T FORGET

On the TV Jerry watched the people hurry from the hotel and be scooped up by formations of Boyle's militia. It was rather like watching a ballet.

Three black Cadillacs, their windows gleaming black one-way glass, came down the road towards the hotel. Things looked sticky for the visitors.

"Jerry."

He turned.

Karen had her case with her. Jerry picked up his own. "Got your passport? We're going back."

"So soon?"

"I know it's disappointing . . ."

The corridors were empty. They took the elevator to the main lobby where a few people, with anxious, bewildered faces, stood about.

A small man in a brown leather trench coat bent his swarthy, severe face over people's passports. It was Mr. Silver or someone very much like him. He was obviously in charge now.

Jerry strolled to the desk. "I'll pay if I may."

"Of course, sir. 604 and 610, is that right?" The brunette leafed through a desk file.

"That's right."

"There you are, sir." She handed him the bills. "Two hundred fifty dollars, please."

"I can give you American Express traveler's checks."

"I'm sorry sir."

"Carte Blanche . . . ?"

"Cash only, sir. It's the new rule."

Jerry slipped his hand into his back pocket and saw that the man in the trench coat was appproaching Karen, a triumphant look in his eyes.

Jerry gave the girl his last three hundred dollar bills.

"Keep the change."

"I can't do that, sir." She gave a prim gasp.

"It's all shifting backwards, pilgrim." Jerry got to Karen before the man who looked like Mr. Silver. If it was Mr. Silver he pretended he didn't remember Jerry.

"Let me see your passports."

"We're foreign nationals . . ." Jerry realized that this was no longer protection. They were on their own. But then, hadn't he always been on his own? He frowned.

"You don't look well," said Mr. Silver. "Anything worrying you?"

"How should I know?"

"What are you calling yourself?" A look of disdain crossed Mr. Silver's face.

"Jeremiah Cornelius. Jeremiah Cornelius."

"Okay. You're suspected of aiding agents of forces hostile to the United States government. We'll have to search your luggage."

"Go ahead." Then Jerry noted the expression on Karen's face.

Silver signalled to two tall men in plastileather trench coats. "Taylor. Dunlop." They picked up the expensive bags.

"The keys?" Mr. Silver held out his damp hand.

"They're unlocked."

Taylor opened Jerry's case first and pawed disgustedly through the coloured silks. When he looked back up Jerry knew he didn't have a chance.

"What about her?" Jerry indicated Karen. "Let her on the plane, won't you? She's just a girl who came along. A secretary . . ."

"You employ her, do you?" Dunlop laughed.

"She's not your wife, is she?" Mr. Silver curled his lip. "You aliens! Check her case."

Jerry hung loose. He lit a Romeo y Julieta.

"That's a nice cigar," said Silver sniffing. He nodded as his men brought something out of Karen's bag. "You've got it. I like the smell of a good cigar." It was a small gold model of an Apollo rocket. "Okay. Now let's see those passports."

Karen glanced at Jerry as she gave her passport to Silver. Had she been conned by Protz and Zhazhda?

How elaborate was the set-up? Silver knew there were
ambiguities but wasn't admitting it. He was going after
them merely because he didn't like them. That was
how things were.

"German," said Silver. "And British, eh? Where you
from, bwah?"

"Britain."

"Before that?"

"Heaven?"

"That in the West Indies?"

"My father didn't say."

"I'll keep the passports. They look like crude forgeries
to me. Your picture's in negative, even."

"Check it."

"We will. Taylor. Dunlop. Get them on the bus with
the rest."

The two tall men took Jerry and Karen by the arm
and guided them through the lobby, then through the
swing doors to where a big airport bus waited. There
were a lot of people already inside.

As they came out on the sidewalk Jerry saw people
run and cars swerve as a Boeing 707 swung off the
runway and, jets screaming, taxi between the airport
buildings to cross the highway at an angle and slither
across a field.

"You boys certainly have everything working for you."
Jerry threw his cigar in the gutter.

"On the bus," said Taylor.

Jerry and Karen climbed aboard. The bus was decorated in chrome and light blue. All the seats were full
of nervous people, mostly middle-aged and middle-class.
That was something, thought Jerry.

One well set up man in a grey topcoat and hat held
an expensive briefcase against his chest. He wore brown
leather gloves. "I'm Feldman," he said. "Feldman. I'm
Feldman."

"That's it," Dunlop told the driver. "You can close the
doors."

Feldman dashed forward as the doors began to shut.
Taylor hit him in the face. Feldman staggered back, his
nose bleeding.

The bus moved out with Jerry and Karen clinging to

the slippery central pole. From the hotel came the sound of Thompson sub-machine guns.

The bus reached an intersection and turned inland, away from New York.

Soon they were on Interstate 80.

Jerry felt a tugging at his jacket and he looked down into the heavily made-up face of an old woman with a blue rinse who sat in the nearest seat. "Young man," she whispered, "is this the Ithaca bus?"

"You'd better ask the driver, ma'am," Jerry told her. "I'm not sure we're going that far."

Extent Estimated

The Lance battlefield missile can go anywhere the Army needs to go.

It's rugged, it's accurate. It's easy to operate.

And . . . it's mobile.

It can be moved into action by helicopter, air-dropped by parachute or carried by ground vehicles over rough terrain under all weather conditions.

The Lance light-weight launcher can be towed by some of the smallest vehicles in the inventory, down to the ¼-ton size. The basic launcher frame and missile frame and missile fit into a full-tracked carrier for land or water surface mobility.

And, it only takes a six-man crew to operate each Lance system.

It is propelled by a storable, pre-packaged liquid propulsion system—the first Army missile so powered.

Lance is almost as portable as its ancient namesake, the basic weapon of the warrior since time began.

'Lance mobility,' LTV ad

1. MAIL ORDER BRIDE FROM PENNSYLVANIA

Somewhere in Pennsylvania, in thickly wooded hills overlooking the Delaware, the bus stopped by a tall barbed wire fence bearing a wooden notice board that said KEEP OUT—GOVT. PROTECTED EXPERIMENTAL NATURE RESERVE.

"Okay, everybody." The driver took a Swiss M11 Carbine from under his seat. "Here's where you spend your vacation."

Taylor and Dunlop glanced at him disapprovingly. The blue doors hissed open and the passengers piled out into the narrow dirt road that ran beside the wire.

Jerry's spirits were rising. As he left the bus, he tipped the driver a dollar.

"This way," said Dunlop.

Struggling with their heavy suitcases, the passengers followed Taylor and Dunlop until they reached a decorative wrought-iron gate in front of a small Bavarian-style lodge from which three armed militia men, in the black uniforms, the mirror sunglasses and the motorcycle helmets, emerged.

A fourth militia man poked his head out of the whimsically carved doorway. "Wait there. I'll call the camp."

Jerry gripped two curling bits of black metal and peered through the gate, breathing in the gentle scent of pines. A wide track led between the trees on the other side of the wire and disappeared over a rise. Beyond the rise a diesel engine whined and a big Ford articulated freight truck came bumping into sight and, sounding the twin golden horns on its roof, swung round in the clearing near the ledge. The driver jumped down from his cab and ran to open the sliding doors of the truck.

One of the militia men unlocked the wrought-iron gate. "Okay. Come on through."

The passengers trudged up to the freight wagon and got awkwardly aboard.

Jerry helped the old lady clamber in.

"It stinks of meat." She leaned on his shoulder. "Of animals. What the hell is the company doing to us?"

"It's only a short ride, ma'am." Jerry assisted Karen, relishing the texture of the rough tweed on his palm. "We'll soon be there."

As the doors of the car slid shut and the engine started up, Jerry crouched in a corner in the semi-darkness and they bumped through the woods. Five minutes later the truck braked and the outside air rang with cheerful shouts until it moved on a few yards, stopped again, and cut off its engine.

They blinked as the doors slid open to reveal a surly sergeant who waved them out with his rifle.

Mr. Feldman had recovered slightly. He stood in the yard dusting himself down as his fellow passengers disembarked and looked incuriously round at the long wooden huts and the triple fence of barbed wire that had armed observation towers every thirty feet. "Who's in charge here?" demanded Mr. Feldman. "I have some questions to ask."

"You want the Camp Governor," the surly sergeant told him. "He'll be talking to you in a few minutes."

Jerry began to whistle. Karen looked at him with a mixture of contempt, suspicion and panic.

There was a chance of a break, after all.

2. HOW SOON LEGAL POLYGAMY?

The new arrivals stood in a long line facing the main hut and there was only the sound of the pine cones cracking in the heat until the door marked CAMP GOVERNOR creaked open and a tall, elegant man came out and saluted them.

The Camp Governor wore a uniform cut from fine, black needlecord and his cap was at just the right angle above his mirror sunglasses which were as black and as bright as his highly polished jackboots.

"Good afternoon, ladies and gentlemen. I am Captain Brunner, your governor. It is my duty and pleasure to ensure that you are properly looked after during your stay here. As you are no doubt aware, under the present emergency conditions laid down by our president, Mr. Boyle, an in-depth and far-thinking piece of social experimentation is taking place and you are privileged to be part of the experiment which touches, to a degree, on the problems of over-population in this nation. You will, of course, be well treated and all your basic needs will be catered to. Western . . ." He reached languidly for the clipboard which the sergeant handed him. "We can assure you, however, that your internment will be as short as possible. We aim for a quick release." He turned his attention to the clipboard. "Now, could all professional men and wives of professional men over forty please raise their hands?"

Only Jerry and Karen von Krupp did not raise their hands.

"Excellent," said Captain Brunner. "You are all—or almost—" he glanced disapprovingly at Jerry and Karen— "entitled to priority service. Are there any questions I can answer for you?"

Mr. Feldman raised his hand. "My name is Feldman. Can I call my wife and tell her where I am?"

"Even better, Mr. Feldman—we are tracing your wife and she should be joining you soon. Yes, ma'am."

"My name's Mrs. Meriel McCarthy."

"Yes?"

"I want to know what I am doing here."

"Your maiden name?"

"Sullivan."

"I see. Well, it's hard to explain in a word, Mrs. McCarthy. It's all part of President Boyle's Law and Order Campaign. You believe in Law and Order, I hope?"

"Of course."

"Then I'm sure you will be prepared to suffer a little inconvenience for a short time so that the president can make sure there's plenty of Law and Order in the future?"

"I guess so."

"Fine. Well, I suppose you're all tired and dusty after your journey and want to wash-up. Leave your bags here and they will be taken to your accommodation. The sergeant will show you to the ablutions hut."

The new arrivals followed the sergeant towards the hut with the tall chimney. Jerry and Karen were left standing among the abandoned suitcases.

"I'll deal with you two in my office." Captain Brunner hung the clipboard on a hook by the door. "Step inside, please." He sauntered through the door which swung shut behind him.

Karen looked towards the disappearing line of people and then at Jerry. "You seem in better shape," she said.

"Not part of the plan, eh?" Jerry pushed open Captain Brunner's door. "Come on in."

Hesitantly, Karen followed him in. The office was beautifully furnished, with leather panelling and matching furniture. The view through the window showed a school yard in which happy children in little white smocks were playing.

Captain Brunner sat at his desk lighting a cigarette in a long, ivory holder. He had a sensitive face and long-fingered, almost delicate, hands. He removed his sunglasses and regarded Jerry through sardonic crimson eyes.

"Well, well, well . . . And what brings you to Camp Resurrection?"

"A series of circumstances, Captain Brunner. This is Doktor von Krupp."

"Your mistress?"

"My ex-mistress."

"How could that be possible? It seems, at this moment, Mr. Cornelius, to be a question of accretion more than anything else."

"It does indeed."

"We'll see what we can do about it. Soon. Why are you in the U.S.? Looking for me, I hope."

"I thought I was looking for a Bishop Beesley, but it's possible that I came to lose myself, as it were. Not anticipated, of course."

"You can't run away from yourself, Mr. Cornelius."

"I hope you're right, captain. I feel better already."

"So you should. You're in the shit, really, if you don't mind me telling you . . ."

"That was my impression." Jerry tapped his skull. "I was a bit out of sorts. When this Beesley pinched a batch of our best transmogs . . ."

"Still fishing, eh? Well, I know how it is. The last I heard of Beesley was at a party a week ago. He was in San Francisco, I gather, with his yacht."

"With my patients?"

"Almost certainly. His main headquarters are nearby— in Los Angeles."

"Is he working for your boss? This Boyle?"

"Good heavens, no. Beesley may be crude, but he's not that crude. He has nothing to do with the creation of Greater America. Is the name Emil familiar?"

"No."

"Well, he's vaguely connected with that name in some way. A faustian character, your Bishop Beesley, really."

"I wouldn't say that," said Karen von Krupp.

"Doubtless you know him better than I." Captain Brunner removed his cap and placed it neatly on the desk. His short hair was as white as Jerry's. He undid his tunic collar.

Karen von Krupp was frowning. "Are you responsible for this situation, Captain Brunner?"

"Indirectly, yes. Now, Jerry, we'll have to think of getting you out of here, won't we?"

"I suppose so."

"It's obvious you can't stay. You'll have to escape and perhaps you'd better kill me at the same time. I presume you've a needle-gun with you."

"Vibragun."

"So it's vibraguns now, is it? Well, well. That'll do, anyhow. It will be a relief."

"To both of us."

"Yes, indeed."

"I was wondering if there was a Shift Tunnel handy."

"In America? You must be joking. This is a stable country, Mr. Cornelius. Even I can't produce miracles!"

Jerry laughed. "A helicopter, then? Or a light plane?"

"The best I can offer is that diesel truck. Unless . . ." he raised his hands in a helpless gesture. "We're in the sticks, here, Mr. Cornelius."

"Okay. What shall we do now?"

"Wait in my office until I return. There are very few books, I'm afraid. Watch the children playing. Aren't they sweet? Do you love children as much as me?"

"Naturally."

3. THE OLD HOLLYWOOD SPIRIT
   NEVER DIES

Captain Brunner soon came back. "I'd forgotten I wouldn't be needing the Duesenberg. You can take that, if you like."

Jerry nodded. "Why had you forgotten?"

"It was returned just this morning. My chauffeur borrowed it and got caught on a carefree driving rap. He was shot yesterday. Even I couldn't get him off that one."

They laughed together.

Karen von Krupp sucked at her teeth. There was a tiny spot of blood in the middle of her lower lip. She had tense hands.

"I don't know," said Jerry, "whether to go to Frisco and risk it or try to make for somewhere else, under the circumstances. You'd know best."

"True enough. But I don't want to influence your decision, Mr. Cornelius. See how it works out."

"Certainly. Now, are we going to make this a spectacular?"

"Why not?"

"Okay. Don't look so defeated, Karen. You can't win them all. Are you coming with me?"

"I'm staying here."

"Is that a good idea, do you think? Beesley . . ."

"Failure is failure. I'm staying."

"In what capacity?" Brunner asked politely.

She shrugged and her looks faded. "I don't much care. It's peaceful here."

Jerry gave her shoulder a sympathetic pat. "You know, I should really shoot you. It's the policy."

She continued to suck at her teeth.

"That adds a new wrinkle." Jerry winked at her.

A tear fell out of her eye.

"Let her stay here," Captain Brunner suggested. "I'm sure she'll go far, when she gets over it."

"But Beesley . . ."

"Will it make a lot of difference?"

"Time's silting up."

"You're right, I suppose." Jerry grinned. "Sweet dreams, Karen."

"Off we go, then." Captain Brunner danced for the door.

"Off we go."

Off they went, with Jerry pushing Captain Brunner ahead of him with his vibragun and Captain Brunner calling in a delicious treble, "Do as he orders! Do as he orders!"

The big Duesenberg—three tons, supercharged, built 1936 with its bullet-proof windows and steel shutters—was outside.

They climbed in.

Captain Brunner drove and Jerry Cornelius pointed the vibragun at his head.

Black uniformed guards milled around in excitement, trying to think of something positive. Then the wind took a turn and thick, yellow smoke from the chimneys got into their eyes and throats and made them cough. As they opened the gates of Camp Resurrection, most of them just looked embarrassed.

Standing outside the governor's office, Karen von Krupp waved almost sadly to Jerry.

"Good, old Karen," said Jerry.

Captain Brunner settled himself comfortably at the wheel as they drove through the pines that filtered the last of the evening sunshine.

"I must admit I'd prefer Casablanca," he said. "But that's all in the past now, I'm afraid. Or present. It depends which way you look at it." He took a swig from the bottle of Bell's Cream Whisky in the clip by the steering wheel. "The last bottle. It's just as well, in the circumstances. You don't mind if I go part of the way with you, do you, my dear boy?"

"Heaven forbid!" said Jerry. "Of course not."

They reached the next fence and the lodge. Someone

had phoned the guards, for they had their guns ready but couldn't think of a use for them.

"Put the plates up, could you, Captain Brunner?" Jerry smiled at the guards.

Captain Brunner touched a button. The steel shutters moaned upwards and they were in darkness. Captain Brunner switched on the light.

"Now," said Jerry. "If you wouldn't mind . . ."

"Say the word."

"Consider it said."

"And the word . . ."

Jerry smiled. "Captain Brunner—you're a card, after my own heart."

The plate on Jerry's window opened up until there was a hole five inches in diameter in the very center. Jerry poked his gun through and took aim. The guards shook to pieces. He turned the gun and the gates quivered and creaked and fell down. They roared through.

"Hey ho for the open road," sang Captain Brunner, turning the car in the general direction of Buffalo. "Where were you thinking of for the honeymoon?"

"Where else?"

With a spontaneous gesture of affection, Captain Brunner flung his arm around Jerry's shoulders, hugged him tight, and stepped hard on the accelerator.

Transfusion

1. HOW THE ISRAELI WAR SOLVED A RAPE MURDER!

The house was a splendid example of Carpenters Gothic, covered in turrets and eccentric dormer windows, with pointed towers and jigsaw scrollwork and shadowed verandas made to resemble a monks' walk. A somewhat tasteless note was the more recent cobblestone chimney.

Inside, the hall was dark and filled with a huge umbrella stand, a hat rack and a mirror that seemed to reflect the darkness. From the parlor came the damp, musty smell of horse-hair and mahogany, of marble, artificial flowers and antimacassars. On the other side of the hall the living room was full of mission furniture in oak and leatherette. Leading off the living room was the dining room with its table and chairs of golden oak and its view from the window over the Falls.

The house was still occupied.

Outside the empty streets echoed the whimpering roar of the water. The hotels and motel cabins, the souvenir shops, the restaurants and movie houses blended with the trees, the shrubs and the weeds. Sometimes the wind would move a yellow newspaper or a rusty can.

On their way to the border Captain Brunner had steered nostalgically through streets blocked with twisted automobiles. "Ah, fickle fashion." Most of the buildings had been looted, stripped and burned.

At the dining table they ate the individual TV Steak Chateaubriand Dinners Captain Brunner had brought up from the cold room in the basement.

"And how did you leave Europe?" Captain Brunner

unbuttoned his uniform jacket to show a yellow shirt of Sea Island Cotton.

"Much as I hope to find it." Jerry pushed his dinner away and took another sip of his Californian Riesling. "It's an uphill struggle."

"Perhaps it always will be, Jerry."

"One door opens. Another closes."

"Isn't that for the best?"

Jerry raised a jet black hand to a jet black face and rubbed his right eye. Captain Brunner smiled.

"The illusion of power," said Jerry. "It sometimes seems too sweet for words."

"Or actions, for that matter."

"Sure."

"You've got rid of the déjà vu now, have you?"

"Not altogether."

"Well . . ." Captain Brunner stacked the half-eaten trays. "I'll put these in the kitchen. Do you want to take a walk this afternoon?"

"A last walk . . ."

"If you wish."

"It's really up to you, you know." Jerry turned to look at the Falls.

"I'm getting a bit reluctant to go. That's the trouble."

"I know what you mean. Do you want to do it yourself?"

Captain Brunner picked up the empty bottle. "That wouldn't be according to the rules."

"The rules are very strict."

"Stricter than you could believe."

"All right. Mind you, I could do with some bloody music." Jerry stood up.

"The victrola's over there."

Jerry went into the living room to look at the big phonograph with its oak-veneered cabinet. He opened the cupboard at the bottom and pulled out the cumbersome 78s. They rattled in his hands. He opened the lid, wound the handle and put a record on the turntable.

When Captain Brunner came back into the room George M. Cohan was singing *Yankee Doodle* and Jerry lay on the mission couch staring up at the beams in the ceiling.

"I believe there's some good Al Jolsons and the

whole of *Green Pastures* in there." Captain Brunner hesitated on the threshold. "That's going back a bit."

"Before my time," said Jerry.

"And mine."

They listened to George M. Cohan with intense, clinical concentration.

"What does it tell us?" Captain Brunner stroked Jerry's hair.

"It's not a code we could ever hope to understand." Jerry shrugged sadly.

"No."

Systematically they broke the records and stacked the pieces inside the cabinet.

2. WHY ARTISTS ARE GOING BACK TO REALISM

"What must be must be," said Captain Brunner.

It was dawn and the sun shone through the lace curtains of the bedroom.

He turned his head on the pillow and looked tenderly at Jerry who had just opened his eyes.

"This morning," said Jerry.

"It's overdue."

"Okay."

Captain Brunner rose and stretched his beautiful body then, kneeling on the mattress, reached up and straightened the GOD BLESS OUR HOME pokerwork on the wall.

"You're looking old," said Jerry. "Used up."

"Wouldn't you?"

"I guess my time will come."

"We all become redundant. It's the one snag, really. Still, I'm glad I served a purpose."

"An important one. Only you . . ." Jerry swung out of bed. Purposefully he began to dress. "I've got work to do."

"I don't think I'll wear anything today." Captain Brunner opened the door. "I'll see you downstairs."

Jerry strapped on his shoulder holster and checked his gun. He went along the landing to the bathroom and splashed cold water over his face. He dried himself and descended to the kitchen where Captain Brunner had already prepared coffee.

"I'll feel much happier in myself," said Jerry.

"And so will I. It's kind of you to have borne with me."

"I can guess what it's like."

"Of course."

They finished their coffee and left the house, walking slowly through the deserted streets towards the Falls.

At last they stood on a promontory overlooking the huge mass of descending water. Spray splashed them. Drops of water brightened Captain Brunner's body. He took a deep breath.

Jerry's eyes filled with tears. "Relationships are awkward."

His voice was drowned, but Captain Brunner nodded.

Jerry slipped the gun from under his coat. The water crashed down. It foamed and was blue-green, shining in the sun.

Suddenly Captain Brunner turned, shouted, pointed, and leapt off the ground in a perfect dive. Jerry watched him fall. Then he looked back.

Bishop Beesley, dressed in the full robes of his calling, held to his shoulder a Remington 1100 with a shell-flame maple stock. The rifle was pointed at Jerry. "I'll have your gun, Mr. Cornelius."

"This is an inconvenient moment, bishop."

"I apologise."

From the cream and yellow Lincoln convertible behind him emerged the blonde girl Jerry had first met in Nibelburg. She held an identical Remington 1100 on her thigh and wore a mustard Feraud gym-slip dress of Terylene/wool worsted crêpe, a matching hat with a chocolate band and a wide, floppy brim, narrow net Lurex stockings, chocolate-brown Marano boots buttoned to the knee with pearls and a small bag of brushed calf hanging by a gold chain over one crooked elbow. Her white kid gloves were by Pittards.

"I wonder where you've been," said Jerry.

"Bond Street," she said. "I'll kill you if you don't hand him the gun now."

Jerry offered the vibragun by its barrel. Bishop Beesley lowered his own rifle, pushed back his mitre, wiped his brow with his free hand and then came forward to take the gun. "I'm obliged."

Jerry glanced back at the leaping foam. The noise from the Falls now seemed barely audible. He frowned.

"You've certainly given us a chase, Mr. Cornelius," Bishop Beesley said. "We've come a long way to find you, you know. We thought at first you must have changed your identity. Would my good lady be with you?"

"I'm afraid not."

"I'm sorry your friend rushed off . . ."

"It's all one, really."

"Was it a close friend?"

"He's been a father and mother to me in his time."

"I admire your philosophy. Well, come along. We've a fair journey ahead of us. Mitzi, if you'll drive I'll keep an eye on Mr. Cornelius."

Mitzi looked moodily at Jerry. Bishop Beesley handed her the vibragun and curled his fat finger around the trigger of his Remington. He poked at Jerry with it. "The car, Mr. Cornelius. You can sit next to the driver."

Mitzi put her rifle under the seat and started the car. Jerry went round to the other side and got in. Mitzi was wearing Miss Cardin cologne and he breathed it in with some pleasure. After Beesley had heaved himself into the back of the car, she put it into reverse, then swung it round and headed west away from the house.

"You're going to take my word about Karen, then?" Jerry said.

"Why not?" Bishop Beesley unpeeled a Tootsie Roll. "Besides, we checked the house."

Mitzi drove with a sureness that Jerry found relaxing. He leant back and watched the buildings disappear.

"You're not going over the border, then?"

"Not by the bridge, Mr. Cornelius. Not under the circumstances."

"What are the circumstances?"

"Why—you're being sought by government officials. There is even a reward for your arrest as an escaped prisoner. You are in hot water!"

"I wouldn't be too sure of that," said Jerry reminiscently.

Bishop Beesley's mouth was full, so he shrugged.

Soon Jerry noticed the Welland Canal. It was choked with small private craft, most of which had apparently been scuttled. Others bore shell-holes. There were still people aboard some of the houseboats. He scratched his head as they drove along beside the canal.

The Bishop chewed noisily. "They had nothing to fear but fear itself," he said between mouthfuls. "Poor things."

"That's something to be afraid of." Jerry saw black smoke in the distance. He wound down his window to smell it, but it was too far away.

"Would you mind shutting the window?" Bishop Beesley rustled a paper bag. "I'm subject to chills."

Jerry wound the window back up.

"We could have the air-conditioning, if you like." Beesley tapped Mitzi on the shoulder. "Put it on, would you, dear."

She reached out with her gloved hand, exposing several inches of pink flesh, and depressed a button. There came a whispering sound from below the dashboard.

"That's better, isn't it?" Bishop Beesley adjusted his hold on the rifle. "Much better."

"Every time." Jerry settled back and closed his eyes. It had been a tiring week.

Stitching

LISTEN TO THE SOUNDS OF CRISIS!

Tune in to today's news as it actually happens!
Hear what goes on during an emergency. Monitor communications channels of police and fire departments. State Highway Patrols, Civil Defense Agencies, Coast Guard, and emergency services.
"ACTION!!" NEW PORTABLE POLICE RECEIVER $129.95.
Riot, armed robbery, homicide, major fire, high speed chase . . . the sounds of action and crisis are going on all around you every minute of the day. Now you can tune in on the police and fire radio frequencies in your area and actually hear the same communications as the police dispatcher and the men in the patrol cars and fire trucks. You'll hear the news as it's being made.

Nova-Tech ad, True Police Cases

1. ASHAMED—WHEN HE SAW THE MARKS ON MY BODY

When Jerry woke up it was late afternoon and the car was still moving down the wide, deserted highway. He saw a sign. They were heading for London.

"Is that where we're going?" Jerry asked Mitzi. She didn't reply.

"Don't disturb the driver, Mr. Cornelius. You should know better than that." Bishop Beesley tapped Jerry on the shoulder with a Mars Bar. "No. We shan't be stopping at London. We've got a long way to go yet."

Jerry looked at Mitzi's perfect features. "She's got a lot of stamina," he said admiringly.

"Mr. Cornelius . . ."

Jerry noticed that they were almost out of fuel.

London came in sight. Part of the city was burning and a strange wailing noise filled the air. The car began to slow.

"Pogrom," said Bishop Beesley. "It's so close to the border, you see. We'd better transfer. Over there, Mitzi." He pointed to the roadside which was now lined with low buildings. Most of them were stores. The neon signs were dead.

A Plymouth Barracuda, its nearside wheels on the sidewalk, its doors open, was what the bishop had his eye on. Mitzi stopped the Lincoln. "Have a look at the fuel gauge," Bishop Beesley said.

Mitzi got out and peered in at the Plymouth's dashboard. She looked back and nodded; then she glanced at her dress. It clashed with the bright red Plymouth. She shook her head.

"Try the next one, then."

Mitzi opened the door of a white Dodge Polara. "Full up," she said.

"Out you get, Mr. Cornelius."

Jerry opened the door and swung his legs from the car. He got up and stretched. It was almost dark. The flames lit the city and the wailing was louder.

"Civil disturbance is nothing to worry about." Bishop Beesley pushed him forward with the tip of the Remington. "But Europe's in real trouble. No thanks to you."

There was the noise of pistol fire and the bishop ducked. "Hurry along, please, Mr. Cornelius. Mitzi, will you get our stuff?"

After Bishop Beesley had climbed into the back Jerry sat in the front seat. More shots came from somewhere on the roofs above them, possibly from the liquor store with the half-lit neon sign, L N N I S L N N L Q R BEST.

Mitzi got the Dodge's trunk open and crammed the gear in. Jerry saw her weigh his vibragun in her hand and then put it in her handbag.

She climbed hurriedly into the driving seat and her skirt

rose up showing Lurex thighs. Jerry took a deep breath. She tossed a white paper bag to the bishop.

Mitzi turned the key in the ignition. Jerry placed the tips of the fingers of his right hand on his knee and trembled. The car started. Mitzi spun the wheel. Jerry felt a tightness about his ribs and undid the buttons of his jacket.

Soon they had left the wailing city behind and the headlights glared on the wide, white road. Jerry clenched his hands together. "You share the same faith, I take it?" He winked at Mitzi.

"More than that, Mr. Cornelius." Bishop Beesley's voice was slurred.

"There were a lot of planes," Mitzi said quietly. "But they seem to have disappeared."

"They were going somewhere, my dear."

"And tanks and so on . . ."

"Those, too." Beesley laughed. "You'd think there was an invasion or something!"

"A general mobilisation?" Jerry lit a Punch Manuel Lopez, his last.

"You could say that. We must hand it to the Americans. When they set out to do a thing, they don't waste any time. President Boyle and his Greater American Party will soon have the planes landing on schedule."

"Don't you feel something of a hypocrite?" Jerry glanced back at the bishop. "I mean, you should hand me over to the authorities, by rights. I can't help feeling a bit guilty."

"Things will take a while to settle down, Mr. Cornelius. I am doing what is best for everyone. America will soon be on her feet again. And she will be cleaner."

"I thought they were doing okay before."

"You would. Not that I don't understand your views, of course. I do not mean to criticise. I believe in everybody having a say. Free will, Mr. Cornelius. That's what the good God gave us, heaven help us."

"Amen."

"But there is a difference between free will, I would point out, and insane nihilism."

"Naturally."

"And anarchy. We are put on this earth to order it. The rhythm of the spheres, you know."

"I could do with any bloody sort right now."

"Wait till we get to San Francisco."

"*Buenas noches.*" Jerry fell asleep again.

"Everywhere seems red tonight," Mitzi spoke with faint disapproval and woke Jerry up as she put the handbrake on.

"Where are we?" Jerry sat up.

"Port Huron. If you wouldn't mind, Mr. Cornelius, I should like to leave the car." Bishop Beesley moved and there was a crackle of paper wrappings. The back seat was a mass of litter.

Jerry opened the door and got slowly from the car, pulling back the seat to allow Bishop Beesley to heave himself out.

The car was parked on a wharf. Tied up at the wharf was an elegant steam yacht of about 700 tons and about 180 feet long. Jerry made out the name.

"*Teddy Bear,*" he said. "That's a nice name."

There were no lights on the wharf. Water lapped against the ship.

"Shall we go aboard, Mr. Cornelius? Mitzi?"

Mitzi took the bags from the trunk and carried them towards the gangway. Jerry followed her. Bishop Beesley came last.

On deck Mitzi put down the bags and went forward to the bridge. From the shadows a tall, emaciated sailor appeared. He was dressed in a yellow uniform with a yellow cap and a flat, sallow face. He made a hasty salute that was half a bow. "Evening, captain," he whispered.

"Evening, steward. I believe you know Mr. Cornelius."

"Please to meet you, sir." The steward looked shiftily at Jerry.

"You're one of ours, aren't you?" Jerry glanced chidingly at Beesley. "The ex-chairman of the Arts Council, as I live and breathe. Jesus, Beesley, is this the best you can do?"

"He's not queer any more, at any rate!"

The steward gave a guilty grunt.

"He's not rich, either." Jerry rubbed his nose. "At least he was rich."

"The meek, Mr. Cornelius . . ."

"You're a bit inept in my opinion, Bishop Beesley."

"We've had to use inferior equipment, thanks to you."

"You're not kidding."

"Well, don't blame me, Mr. Cornelius. Who started it, after all? It's you people who meddle. Transmogrification. It's a farce!"

"Excuse me, sir," whispered the ex-chairman of the Arts Council, "but shall we slip out of port now, as you instructed?"

"Quietly, steward. Yes, yes."

"People are happier," said Jerry.

"Happiness? What's that? Happiness should come from a sense of self-fulfilment!"

"I'd have thought so."

"Are you happy?"

"Am I complaining?"

"Well, we're going to help you."

"Not that drag again?"

"That wasn't my idea. I agree it was crude. It was an emergency. A cruise is what you need."

"Where's my cabin?"

"The steward knows."

"Aren't you going to tell me?"

"Why should I?"

"Lead on, steward."

"You're not in Europe now, Mr. Cornelius. We're in control here, you know!"

"I'm famished." Jerry followed the ex-chairman of the Arts Council along the deck.

"You'll get something to eat in a moment," Beesley called. He had gone red.

"Not that kind of famished." Jerry felt sleepy again. It was his only comfort.

2. I'LL MAKE HIM PAY FOR WHAT HE DID TO ME

They were on Lake Superior by the time Jerry, somewhat revitalised, but by no means himself, went up on deck and breathed in the stink.

"Why don't you stop fighting us, Herr Cornelius?" Mitzi leaned on the rail and stared out at the distant Michigan shore. The yacht was making good speed through the slime.

Mitzi wore an embroidered night-sky-blue cotton waistcoat tied with tiny black threads, dark and light blue flower-printed harem hipster trousers, sea-blue necklace, braided necklace with yellow tassels, blue Giselle silk scarves bound into a bandanna around her head, golden diamanté belt, turquoise and gold pin and armlets by Cadoro, with silver block-heeled sandals on her lovely little feet.

Her only makeup was her lipstick: Guerlain's Gremoble if Jerry wasn't mistaken. She smiled. "Cheer up." She handed him a set of filters for his nose.

"You look like a dream of Jamaica. Did I say I felt cheerless?"

"Well, you are our prisoner. What did happen to Karen von Krupp, by the way?"

"To the best of my knowledge she went into the catering trade. In Pennsylvania somewhere. It was all a bit complicated. We both had problems."

"I can understand that. I expect she's too embarrassed to look us up." Mitzi turned her face towards the pale blue sky and sniffed the wind. "I don't bear her any grudge. Who could?"

"Who?"

"The planes have stopped."

290

"You noticed that two nights ago."

"Did I? Which planes? Do you have a personality problem, Herr Cornelius?"

"From time to time."

"You would say that." She laughed.

"I wish there was some bloody sustenance around here." Jerry looked over the rail at the foaming algae. "It's hard going, Mitzi, I don't mind telling you."

"What's your favourite food? Liver?"

"Not since they killed all the buffalo. It's not for me to say."

"Are you really Jerry Cornelius?"

"Ah." Jerry took a pace along the rail and gave her a wary wink.

"Aren't you an impostor?"

"Oho."

"We're going through the new St. Croix Canal, you know."

"And then?"

"Along the Mississippi down to New Orleans."

"You're very forthcoming."

"Into the Gulf of Mexico. Through the Panama Canal and into the Pacific until we berth in San Francisco."

"I get it."

"Why don't you stop fighting us, Herr Cornelius? You know in your heart that we're right."

"When does the next jolly boat leave?"

"The *Teddy Bear* has no jolly boats."

"I am in a pickle, aren't I?"

"How do you feel?"

"Sleepy."

"The long voyage will do you good."

"I wish I could have stopped off in New York."

"New York's rather hectic."

"I have quite a lot of urgent business, you know."

"It won't seem so urgent by the time we get to San Francisco."

Jerry shook his head. "I could do with a change of scenery."

"You won't get it. You'll grow to like this scenery."

"Christ!"

"Really, Mr. Cornelius!" Bishop Beesley came waddling down the deck.

"What the fuck do you know about it?"

"That's a nice thing to say!"

Jerry looked at the algae again.

"It's a long way, Mr. Cornelius."

"Yeah."

"I don't think you'd make it."

"No."

Mitzi folded her arms. "You're not much of a catch."

"I'm not the catch I'm worrying about. My patients . . ."

"I've almost lost mine, Mr. Cornelius." Bishop Beesley smacked his lips over a Walnut Whip.

"I wish that was true. I'm going back to bed."

"You'll have to wake up sooner or later."

"Says who?" Jerry went down the companionway, opened the door of his neat, white cabin and fell on his bunk.

He was in a spot.

He'd have to try and bide his time. St. Paul was his only hope.

3. MY SLEEP-TALKING SHOCKED MY HUSBAND

Abbott; Abbey; Abell; Abercrombie; Abernethy; Ablett; Abraham; Abram; Absalom; Acheson; Acker; Acklam; Acres; Acton; Adair; Adam; Adcock; Adkins; Adlam; Adlard; Adlum; Adney; Adrain; Aga; Agate; Aiken; Alan; Alban; Albert; Alden; Alexander; Alfred; Alison; Allard; Allibon; Alsop; Ambler; Ambrose; Amos; Ampleford; Anderson; Angel; Anstey; Applegarth; Arkle; Armistead; Armstrong; Arrowsmith; Ashe; Aspinal; Attwood; Auger; Austin; Aylmer; Aysh; Babbitt; Bailey; Bairnsfeather; Baker; Bancroft; Bank; Barbary; Barclay; Bardell; Barker; Barlowe; Barnes; Barnett; Bartholomew; Barton; Barwick; Bateman; Batt; Baxter; Beach; Beauchamp; Beavis; Beckett; Bedwell; Belcher; Bell; Bellhanger; Bennett; Berrington; Beverley; Beynon; Biddulph; Bigg; Bingley; Birtwhistle; Bishop; Blackadder; Blackmore; Blackshaw; Blackwell; Blackwood; Blagrave; Blake; Blanchard; Blanchflower; Blandamore; Blenkinsop; Blennerhassett; Blight; Blood; Bloomer; Blunt; Blythe; Boatswain; Bolinbroke; Bond; Booth; Bouverie; Bowen; Bowie; Brabazon; Bradbourne; Bradbury; Brand; Brannan; Breakspear; Brereton; Brewer; Bridger; Brigham; Bristowe; Broadbent; Brockless; Brown; Bruce; Buchan; Buckmaster; Budd; Burgess; Burnes; Burstall; Burton; Bury; Butler; Buxton; Byford; Byron; Bywood; Caborne; Caesar; Caffin; Caldecott; Calder; Caldwell; Calver; Cambridge; Campbell; Cannan; Capstack; Carter; Cary; Caswell; Catchpole; Catmur; Catton; Chamberlain; Chandler; Charlton; Charteris; Chatterley; Cheetham; Chenevix; Childe; Chivers; Cholmondeley; Christey; Christian; Christin; Christmas; Christopher;

Chrystal; Church; Churchill; Clachar; Clapham; Clarewood; Clarke; Clayton; Cleave; Clement; Clifford; Cock; Coffin; Cole; Coleman; Coleridge; Combe; Constantine; Cooke; Copperthwaite; Cordiner; Corfe; Corley; Cornelius . . .

Aaron; Abel; Abigail; Abraham; Absalom; Ada; Adalbert; Adam; Adela; Adelaide; Adeline; Adolphus; Adrian; Aeneas; Afra; Agatha; Agnes; Alexis; Alice; Almeric; Aloys; Alphonsus; Amyas; Andrew; Angus; Ann; Anthony; Archibald; Arthur; Audrey; Augustus; Aylmer; Baldwin; Basil; Belle; Benedict; Bernard; Brian; Camilla; Candida; Caspar; Catherine; Chloe; Christabel; Christopher; Clara; Clovis; Constance; Cosmo; Cyriac; Cyrus; Daisy; Daphne; David; Deirdre; Dennis; Dinah; Dolores; Dominic; Doreen; Dorothy; Douglas; Duncan; Ebenezer; Edgar; Edwin; Eileen; Elias; Elizabeth; Elric; Emily; Emmanuel; Ena; Enoch; Eric; Ermentrude; Eustace; Ezra; Fabian; Faith; Fanny; Felix; Fergus; Freda; Fulke; Gabriel; Gareth; Gavin; George; Gertrude; Gervase; Gladys; Grizel; Gustavus; Gwyneth; Hadrian; Hamish; Harriet; Heloise; Henry; Herbert; Hercules; Hester; Hezekiah; Hilary; Hope; Hubert; Humphrey; Hyacinth; Ian; Ida; Igor; Ingeborg; Ingram; Isabella; Isaiah; Israel; Ivan; Ivy; Jabez; Jack; Jacob; James; Jane; Jasper; Jean; Jedidiah; Jenny; Jeremiah . . .

JEREMIAH (Yah is high, or heals, or founds)
CORNELIUS (probably related to L. *cornu,* horn.—
        Dims. Corney, Corny.—Fem. Cornelia)

JEREMIAH CORNELIUS.

His mouth was dry and his eyes were dim.
Environment trouble.
Identity trouble.
Registration number: 1
Parents: Dead or whereabouts unknown.
Relatives: Dead or whereabouts unknown.
Residence: No fixed address.
Physical characteristics: Mutable.
Associates: Variable.
Psychological situation: Weak.

Position: Threatened.
Emotional situation: Desperate.
Recommendations: Hang on.

JEREMIAH CORNELIUS.
The ship rolled.

JEREMIAH CORNELIUS.
He was sick.

JEREMIAH CORNELIUS.
Inside and out.

JEREMIAH CORNELIUS.
Hang on.

JEREMIAH CORNELIUS.
Get out.

4. THE RAPE-GOON WHO TOOK A NAP WITH A CORPSE!

Jerry opened up his eyes. He had lost all track of time, but there was daylight coming through the porthole. Lying alongside him was Mitzi's soft, warm body. She was pressing his hand to her privates.

"Do you mind?" said Jerry.

"Not if you don't."

He pulled himself together. He still had some strength left, but it couldn't last much longer.

He saw her clothes were strewn across the cabin floor and there was her little handbag.

"Where are we?" he murmured, stroking her parted lips with his dark finger.

"Minneapolis is in sight."

"In a pig's eye!"

"Oh! I saw it!"

"Okay. What's the time?"

"Eight p.m."

He twisted in the bunk and wound first his right watch and then his left. "Did Beesley send you?"

"I came because I have fallen in love with you—or, at any rate, with what you might become . . ."

"Does that hurt?"

"Yes."

"And that?"

"Yes."

"Well, let's get at it, then."

It was dark when Jerry peeled back the encrusted sheets. Moonlight now came through the porthole. She murmured sleepily and held out her arms to him.

Jerry gave it to her on the point of the chin and fell forward to lie on top of her, breathing hard. He rested for a moment and then slid over her and fell to the floor, rolled and reached out for a rail, pulled himself up and staggered towards the middle of the cabin and kneeled down to pick up her heavy handbag. He opened it with an effort and closed his fingers over the butt of the vibragun. It was his only link with the cellar in Ladbroke Grove.

As his strength returned he sighed. With pleasure, he stood up and looked down at Mitzi. She was stirring.

He glanced at his gun, then at his right watch.

Somewhere a piano began to play.

He slipped into his silks, buckled on his shoulder holster, put the gun into it, and then began to tear up her clothes until he had several long strips of cloth. As he tightened the gag her eyes opened so he turned her over and trussed her up, patting her bottom affectionately.

"So long, Mitzi." Was it a setup? he wondered.

He opened the cabin door and went up on deck. The lights of St. Paul were on the larboard as the ship moved slowly past the city. On the starboard Minneapolis was in darkness.

"Mr. Cornelius, sir!" The whisper came from the bridge. He looked. The ex-chairman of the Arts Council, his worried face pale in the reflected light from the water, hissed at him. "You shouldn't be on deck alone, sir."

More in sorrow than in anger, Jerry drew his gun and shook the steward down. He turned at a sound.

Moving towards him from the stern came a fat silhouette. A Remington banged.

"Stop!"

Jerry holstered his gun and leapt for the rail.

Another bang.

"Mr. Cornelius! Really! How did you get your gun back?"

"You'll find out. Your bum trouble makes you forget some details, bishop. Cheerio!"

He plunged down into the cold water and began to strike for the bank.

There were a few more bangs but they soon stopped.

Jerry swam as fast as he could because he disliked dark rivers and this tasted particularly foul, so much so that he feared for his suit. He swam along the wharf until he reached some iron steps and climbed out.

A couple of longshoremen ran towards him but he stopped them in their tracks by waving his gun at them. He looked around.

He was in front of a line of low sheds. Beyond the sheds came the sounds of a busy road. He backed along an alley between two sheds until he came to a high fence. He shook a hole in the fence and stepped down a grassy embankment until he got to the road.

Speeding cars filled all the lanes.

Jerry waved to a cruising police car and it slowed. The car had two cops in it. The one who wasn't driving leaned out of the window. "What's your trouble, sir?" He grinned at his companion.

"Fell off a boat," Jerry gasped. "You gotta help me, boss."

"Calm down, sonny. How'd you come to fall off of a boat?"

"Yes, sir."

The cop opened the door and climbed with studied slowness out, pulling a notebook from his tunic pocket. "You wouldn't be running away from anyone, would you?"

"No, sir." Jerry rolled his eyes as best he could. "No, sir!"

"Because we've been having a lot of trouble with runaways of one sort or another just recently."

"Yes, sir."

"You got an identity card?"

"A what, boss?"

"An identity card, boy. Everybody's got an identity card unless he's an outlaw or escaper or injun or something."

"Identity. Nope, sir. I guess I ain't."

"Uh huh. Then I think . . ."

Jerry lined him up and watched him shake. Then, as his companion began to drag his pistol from its holster, Jerry turned the gun on him and he shook, too.

He stowed them in the back seat as a curious Cadillac slowed down, then he got in, started the car, turned on the siren and got rapidly up to a hundred, heading out of town along Interstate 35E.

By morning his suit had dried nicely and the dirt had fallen off it. He had switched cars twice. Now he was driving a handsome golden Chevrolet Caprice and was on Interstate 90, making for the badlands of South Dakota, having crossed the Missouri at Chamberlain. There weren't many cops about. The explanation, for what it was worth was in the two-day old edition of *The Pioneer Press* he had found in the Caprice. There had been a massive draft of all able-bodied men and women over the age of eighteen. Even those who had previously been designated as performing necessary public offices had been drafted.

At the Totanka Yotanka Motel he stole some gas and was soon in the badlands on a lonely, dusty highway where, at about seven in the evening, he saw the first Sioux.

The war chief was mounted on a black and white pony that had elaborately beaded and painted buckskin trappings. It stood stock still on the rise while its rider gave Jerry's car the once-over.

The warrior was probably an Oglala. He carried a bow-lance decorated with red, white and yellow feathers; on his left arm the round buffalo hide shield had a picture of an eagle surrounded by stars. His bleached, fringed buckskin jacket and leggings were embroidered with coloured beads and shiny red and yellow porcupine quills and his neck was heavy with beads and medallions. His head-dress of curving stag antlers had a feathered train that spread over his pony's rump. There was a knife and a tomahawk at his belt. His high cheekbones, deep-set eyes, prominent nose and long, thin mouth was the distinctive modern American face. It was in full warpaint, with yellow orange, blue and white bands, circles and triangles.

Raising his bow-lance the war chief summoned his war party to join him on the rise. They appeared to be a mixture of Oglalas and Hunkpapas, most of them wearing a great many feathers.

Jerry kept going when he saw the short bows and the bark quivers crammed with arrows, but he knew they'd get him at the next bend.

When he reached the next bend they were waiting for him.

Arrows thudded into the convertible's roof and he heard their howls as they hurled their mounts towards him at an angle to the highway. The car hit a pony and the war chief fell forward onto the hood, glaring through the windscreen at Jerry who skidded and went off the highway, hit a rock, stepped on the brake, bounced the Indian off the hood onto the ground, wound down the window and drew his vibragun.

The other Sioux lined up along the highway, bows ready, watching to see what he would do as their leader picked himself up and tried to pull his tomahawk from his belt. "You killed my fucking pony."

"You put it in front of my fucking car. I had the right of way."

"Watch your language, schvartze."

"What are you going to do about it?"

The Indian rubbed his nose and looked around. He straightened the polished bones of his breastplate and slapped the dust off his leggings. "Besides, we didn't know you was a schvartze. We got no fight with you."

"I'm not a schvartze."

"Sure, and I'm not a fucking Oglala."

Jerry opened the door and got out. "Are you trying to prove something?"

"MAYBE." The war chief at last got his tomahawk free and went into a crouch, his eyes narrowing.

Jerry kicked him in the face. He fell over and Jerry picked up the tomahawk. It was very ornamental.

The war chief looked up with an expression of puzzled resignation. "I wasn't expecting that. You win. What's now?"

"I think we should become blood brothers or something." Jerry helped him up. "Isn't that the custom?"

"What the hell if it isn't. It sounds okay to me. We'll have a ceremony at the big council. That's where we're going to now. Iron Mountain."

"Sounds fine. It's on my way."

"Great. Baby, we're in this together. We already got a few schvartzes riding with us. Honorary members, I guess. We got to pick up what we can where we can." He held out his hand. "I'm Flaming Lance." He blushed.

Jerry said generously: "Call me Buffalo Nose."

Flaming Lance shouted to the others. "He rides with the Sioux!"

"Hoka hai," said Jerry.

5. THE GAME'S THE SAME, THE PLAYERS CHANGE, BUT THE STAKES ARE STILL YOUR GUNS

During the next couple of weeks their numbers grew and they raided several farmhouses on their way through Wyoming, Colorado and Utah. Jerry wore a sparsely feathered war bonnet, blue and yellow paint, bone bow, quiver of arrows, hunting knife and a tomahawk, but he hadn't given up his silk suit. He rode a pinto pony and was beginning to regret it.

Near Iron Mountain they waited. Then from the West came the Bannock, the Shoshoni, the Paviosto, the Pyute. From the East came the Osage, the Pawnee and the Omaha. From the North came the Cree, the Blackfoot, the Gros Ventre, the Flathead, the Assinboine. And from the South came the Cheyenne, the Kiowa and the Comanche.

The councils began. All night there were dances and drumming, pipe-smoking and wampum-passing, and the medicine men cast their bones or necromantically raised up the ghosts of the great dead braves who appeared in the red smoke of the fires—Geronimo, Red Sleeve, Chief Joseph, Osceola, Cornplanter, Red Jacket, Rain-in-the-Face, Red Cloud, Sitting Bull, Crow, Black Kettle, Crazy Horse, Roman Nose, Little Wolf, White Antelope—all the heroes of the High Plains, the forests, the valleys and the mountains. And during the day there was the Sun Dance, or the dances of the warrior societies, or the women's dances, like the White Buffalo Dance. And they would listen to their Paramount Chiefs as they spoke of the glory that would soon be theirs as all the Indian Nations united and claimed the land that was theirs by right.

Jerry caught up with his sleep as best he could. He had mingled blood with Flaming Lance and felt he had done his bit. The council grounds were becoming a bit crowded and smelly as thousands more Navahos, Chiricahuas, Mescaleros, Wichitas, Chickasaws, Shawnees, Kickapoos, Santees, Cayuses, Modocs and Nez Perces flooded in.

It was time to be off.

He left unostentatiously in an old Thunderbird that had brought the Paramount Chief of the Choctaws. He made it to St. George by morning and drove through the rubble. Scalped corpses were everywhere.

Soon he was on Interstate 15, heading for Las Vegas where he hoped he might pick up a plane that would get him to San Francisco.

He was becoming extremely concerned for his patients.

6. LIVE, WORK, FISH AND HUNT IN NATURE'S WONDERLAND!

Las Vegas was quiet in the afternoon glare. The signs flashed to a steady, soothing rhythm that blended with the sounds of the one-armed bandits and the blackjack tables. Las Vegas was one of those sleepy towns where nobody bothered you much as long as you didn't make trouble. It had all the old virtues of rural American life. Jerry felt at peace here. He made for Circus Circus and wondered if Murphy still owned it.

He went inside and began to cross the vast hall filled with gaming tables. A few old people were playing, a few performers were on the high wire above the hall, but nobody noticed him as he located Murphy's office and went in.

Murphy seemed pleased to see him.

"Jerry! What brings you to civilisation?"

"I thought you might like to know that the tribes are massing. It looks like war."

"We don't need to worry about a few Indians, Jerry. The army'll look after them."

"The army seems to be busy elsewhere."

"Why should they want to attack us?"

Eugene Murphy had known Jerry in London. Ex-president-turned-motion-picture-star-turned-casino-owner, Murphy had a battered, cancerous face and a big cigar.

"They're attacking everything," said Jerry.

"What are they riled about?"

"Most everything or nothing in particular. You know the Indians."

Murphy nodded. "Well, I'll bear it in mind. Is that why you came to Vegas?"

"I came to borrow a plane. I lost mine out there."

"Sure. You can have your pick. I've got a lovely little LTV C-150A tiltwing turboprop that should suit you fine. Have something to eat and then we'll go and take a look at her. What d'you say?"

"Sounds fine."

"Great! I bet you're glad to be somewhere you can take it easy, put your feet up. All that trouble. All that burning. Washington, Atlanta, Kansas City, Philadelphia, Salt Lake City, Houston. I sometimes wonder if it's worth it, Jerry." Murphy poured them both large glasses of rye. "And it's not good for business, either. I can tell you that for nothing. You must have come through the place. Not that I'm complaining. Not yet."

Jerry peeled off his war-bonnet. "I think they'll make for Carson City and take over the mint first. They were still in council when I left."

"I'm part Indian myself, you know," Murphy said proudly.

7. COPS WHO ARE HELL ON PILLHEADS

Jerry climbed into the cockpit of the LTV C-150A and ran his fingers over the controls with a sigh of relief. He settled himself and switched on. Slowly the wings tilted upwards and the propellers sang.

Jerry sat back and took her up.

She rose neatly into the air and at five hundred feet he tilted the wings forward and headed, at a comfortable 350 mph, for California.

As he flew over the Sierra Nevadas he saw that they were black with riders. A Mayday message came in on the radio. It was Sacramento.

"This is General Partridge, Sacramento Control Tower."

"Come in Partridge, Sacramento."

"We're completely surrounded. I've hardly got a man left. We can't get a message through for reinforcements. Will you relay a message?"

"What's the problem?"

"The problem! Indians is the problem. They're howling round and round and round. Fire arrows . . ."

"How long can you hang on?"

"Another hour. We need paratroopers. A regiment at least. Half the tower's on fire. Can you get through to Hollywood?"

"I don't think so."

"Well, get through to someone. There must be a thousand of the devils out there at least. My head's spinning. Round and round. Nobody warned me."

"It's a fast world, general."

"No kidding."

"I'm on my way to San Francisco. I'll inform the authorities when I arrive."

"If we hadn't had guerilla experience, we wouldn't be here now. It's Dien Bien Phu all over again."

"That's the way it goes. Over and out, general."

Jerry could see the blue Pacific. He began to hum.

Jerry brought the plane down over the mellow ruins of Berkeley and headed for the recently built Howard Johnson's where he had a large steak with all the trimmings and a Quadruple Pineapple Astonisher with hot fudge sauce topped with grated nuts. It set him up. He left one of Murphy's thousand dollar bills under his plate and began the long walk to the bridge. The bay was blue, the bridge beautiful and the distant city had almost died down. A few buildings were still standing, a few reconnaissance copters hung about in the sky but most of them were heading back to the Hollywood base, not the Greater American operations centre.

An old man joined Jerry as he reached the bridge. "Mind if I walk along with you a taste, son?" He wore a dingy brown fedora and dirty overalls and he had a cheroot between his wrinkled lips. "Going in for a loved one?"

"Something like that." The bridge swayed, Jerry looked down at the boats leaving the bay. Most of them were cruisers from the ruined port.

"I hail from Kansas. I was on my way to join up in L.A., but then the truck broke down. Thought I'd do some fruit-picking instead."

Jerry stopped and peered through the bars. He recognised the *Teddy Bear*. She was going full steam and she was loaded with patients; he saw some of them staring up from the forward hold just before the hatches were battened. Beesley must have moved the yacht overland in a hurry. Now they were heading out.

"There's a lot of fruit to pick," said the old man. "So I hear."

Jerry sighed.

"I'll be seeing you," he said, and he jumped, swung through the struts, poised, dived, hit the salty water not three feet from the yacht, sank, somersaulted, struck for the surface, saw above him the keel, the churning pro-

pellers and grabbed the rope that trailed in the foam,
hauling himself up the side.

When he climbed aboard he had his vibragun in his
hand and Bishop Beesley and Mitzi had a nasty shock
when they saw him.

"That was just a warning." Jerry smiled apologetically.
"I seem to be in and out of water all the time." He waved
them towards the rail over which he'd climbed. "It's your
turn for a dip now."

"Good heavens, Mr. Cornelius! This is piracy!"

"Well, I see it another way, bishop. After all, it's my
crew."

"That's a moot point, sir!"

"Jerry." Mitzi's eyes were full of adoration. "Let me come with you. I'll be . . ."

"I'd like that, Mitzi, but I have to remain impartial at the moment. You've used up so much of my time, do you see. You know how it is."

She tripped to the side, pulled her tight, white skirt over her creamy thighs and straddled the gleaming brass rail.

With a wave she disappeared.

"Now you, bishop."

"A boat, at very least . . ."

"Come along, now."

The bishop moved reluctantly and looked down at the sparkling water. "When I asked you for a lift . . ."

"Don't make me feel guilty."

"I shouldn't think it would take me . . ."

"Bishop."

"A bag of provender. A Bounty bar?"

"Not even a coffee cream."

"I don't like coffee creams." Blowing like a great white whale, Bishop Beesley heaved himself over the rail. Somewhere a building toppled and crashed.

Jerry walked up and pushed him on his way. With a yell the bishop whirled his corpulent arms and fell on the water. He lay there, bobbing up and down in the yacht's wake, his arms and legs waving gently, his red mouth opening and closing, his bulging eyes staring at Jerry in pained outrage. Mitzi appeared, shaking water from her hair, and began to tow the bishop shorewards.

"Bye, bye, bishop. It's like a game of dominoes in many ways."

The bishop honked pathetically.

Jerry climbed up the companionway to the bridge and checked his charts and instruments, plotting his course.

Within half an hour they were bound for Sumatra where the organisation had an emergency Reclamation Centre, and Greater America had disappeared below the horizon.

3.

SECOND OPERATION

COMING EVENTS

The Dream
Four years ago I dreamed that I
stood in a room behind, and to the left of,
a young man I did not know. He was
younger than me. On his left, but in front
of us, stood my brother, and beside him
stood an old man whom I did not
recognize. On our right, two large cream-
painted doors were closing. I thought that
my brother and this other man were in
some way assessing this younger man, who
I felt was either my husband or my
intended husband. Since then, I have
without any doubt met this young man.
The dream is troubling me, as I fail to
understand its meaning. Never before have
I dreamed so clearly of something so far in
the future.
The Meaning
We may accept the above as a good
example of what is called precognitive

311

dreaming. Instances of dreaming ahead of time crop up fairly often and some of them get on to this page. As to what the brother and the old man are doing, that comes under a different head altogether. The earliest objects of a girl child's physical affection are her father and her brother. Any later male attachment is a result of these early, though unlocalized, sex objects. The question the reader is asking in her dream is how far the later object of affection stands up to the early ideal of childhood. The result rests with the dreamer's own nature. The old man is a father symbol; the closing doors represent the flight of time.

Dream Meanings, *Prediction*, March 1969

Lights

OUTER SPACE: IN THE BEGINNING, A BIG BANG?

Fantastic things are being discovered in outer space. Some astronomers believe they have located cosmic bodies of cataclysmic force that might indicate a primeval Big Bang. And a hiss located in outer space may be an echo of this explosive Creation, coming from thousands of millions of light years ago. Next week, in an exciting new series, we explore the new ideas which may lead to a complete overhaul of our thinking about the universe and our place in it.

Observer Colour Magazine, 26 January 1969

1. UFOs ARE UNFRIENDLY, UP TO NO GOOD, AND SOME OF THEM ARE TRULY DANGEROUS

A quick trip to the cellar, then Jerry moved easy in soft browns and yellows and a gold silk tie out into the mellow sunlight of an early autumn in Ladbroke Grove, on his way to Chelsea.

Kings Road was a healthy step away.

He strolled along, savouring the day, swinging his sonic cane and listening to the music in the handle, turned down Elgin Crescent, shaded by old oaks, and trod the length of Clarendon Road until he came to Holland Park Avenue with its tall trees and its huge, hollow, empty houses.

Pulled by two shetland ponies, a red and green baker's cart moved slowly through the falling leaves. The lean driver stretched on his seat in the soft warmth of the day, listening to the lazy drone of distant aircraft. Jerry stopped and bought a bun.

"It's a mild sort of day," said the baker.

"Not bad." Jerry bit his bun. "How's the wife?"

"Not so dusty."

"Finished your round?"

"For what it's worth. Very little bread, of course. Just the eclairs and custard tarts and stuff."

"I suppose it's for the best."

"Wouldn't have it otherwise."

Jerry headed for the park. His cane played *The Fool on the Hill*.

A few children ran about in Holland Park as he passed through. An old man fed the peacocks and pigeons and guinea fowl from a big tub of peanuts at his belt. Jerry paused by Holland House and looked at its white façade, but the Elizabethan mansion was silent so he kept going until he reached the cricket pitch and the burnt-out skeleton of the Commonwealth Institute that faced Kensington High Street where the traffic moved slowly.

He had a feeling in his bones.

On the corner of Earls Court Road, he climbed into his parked Maybach Zeppelin convertible, pushed back the top to let the breeze get to his hair, drove rapidly towards Chelsea and stopped outside *The Purple Parrot* where he had arranged to meet Spiro Koutrouboussis to discuss the past, present and future over lunch.

The lobby of the club was hung with gilded cages full of mynah birds, canaries and cockatoos who called to each other in several languages and dialects. The receptionist, dressed in elaborate quills, looked like a Polynesian chief in ceremonial robes. She smiled at him. "Your table's ready, Mr. Cornelius. Your friend's in the Linnet Room."

Spiro Koutrouboussis sat by himself on a stool by the bar, staring pensively at a cage of sulky wrens. A thrush perched on his curly black hair, a Marguerita lay between his well-scrubbed hands. "Ah, Cornelius."

"Sorry if I'm late. I had rather a rough time in the States."

"I told you so."

Jerry sniffed.

"That Karen von Krupp—she trapped you. I knew she would. You never listen . . ."

The thrush began to sing. Koutrouboussis brushed at it absently but it dug its claws in.

"It was an experience." Jerry ordered a Pernod. "Nothing like experience."

"The *time* lost!"

"That's something you can never do anything about. Come now, Koutrouboussis. Let's see a smile, eh?"

"Cornelius. We are in danger. Our whole project is in danger—*your* project, after all. If you have double-crossed . . ."

Jerry reached for the menu on the bar. "What have we got?"

"The duck's very good today," said Koutrouboussis. "So I'm told. Or the Chicken Apollinaire."

"Too heavy for me. I'll start with *paté de foie,* I think."

Jerry stroked the tip of his nose. "I miss the food. Still . . ."

"Is Karen von Krupp out of the picture now?"

"I should imagine so."

"Well, I suppose you were successful, essentially. But there's still Beesley. Particularly under the circumstances."

"Which circumstances are those?"

"President Boyle has increased the military advisors. There are three million on the Continent, seeking out certain fifth column elements."

"Surely nobody's worried."

"Not about that. Nobody but the Three Presidents, anyway. And maybe Israel. You heard what happened yesterday? A fleet of Israeli helicopters landed in the Vatican City and arrested the Pope. Admittedly, they had a lot of aggravation."

"I've been a bit out of touch."

"I'm not blaming you for that."

They walked into the restaurant. It had been converted from an old orangery and its pillars were covered in vines, its windows looking out onto a white paved courtyard with a Regency fountain in which sparrows splashed.

Jerry ordered his hors d'oeuvre and chose roast quail as his main dish. They decided to drink Blue Nun.

"I think the machine should be found, you know." Koutrouboussis chewed his chicken. "After all, we're not in a very strong position without it, are we? Our chances are slim."

"I don't much fancy the Shifter at this stage." Jerry picked up a little leg.

"You might not have to go into it. We've got something of a lead. Does the name—?" Koutrouboussis choked on an asparagus spear. "Does the name," he took a sip of his Liebfraumilch, "Gordon mean anything to you?"

"Flash Gordon?"

"Gordon Gavin?"

"That's right." Jerry nipped at a quail's breast. "The last I heard of him, he had twenty-two offences behind him. For flashing."

"Ah. Well, be that as it may, he got in contact with me a little while ago. He'd heard about our conversion scheme."

"So he's at a centre."

"Not yet. You know how timid these people are. He made an appointment but didn't keep it. Then he phoned again to say he had a message for you from a gentleman concerning an invention of yours that got lost during a test run. The machine, obviously."

"I've lost a lot of inventions."

"I'm sure he meant the machine. It could be our salvation, Cornelius."

"Get away."

2. IGNORE ADVICE TO STRIP AT HIGH SPEED

Koutrouboussis crossed the street heavily and entered the gates of the Pheasantry where he had an apartment. Jerry followed him down the crazy paving between the crumbling statues and into a dark hall full of varnished doors and unseen fluttering wings.

They went along silent corridors, across quiet court-yards and up stairs until they were deep in the Victorian complex. Koutrouboussis stopped by a door on a second floor balcony overlooking a rock garden full of finches. The door's wood had been stripped and a thin yellow undercoat had been laid on the top half.

"Here we are."

They went into a sunlit studio. On the raised floor to the right stood a brass bed with a large, loud, enamelled bird of paradise as its headboard. The bed also had a Turkish counterpane in dark red, yellow and blue.

The raised floor to the left had deep white cupboards containing Koutrouboussis's sink, stove and supplies.

An Old Gold fitted carpet covered the floor and the steps; by the far wall a large light screen was full of flowing colours that frequently changed shape.

In the corners, close to the ceiling, were four stereo speakers. In the middle of the floor kneeled two girls wearing lace and feathers, pale make-up, lots of big rings, and richly decorated eyes.

As the girls looked softly at him, Jerry remembered them.

"Hello, Jerry," murmured Maureen the Groupie.

"Hello, Jerry," murmured Barbara the Groupie.

"Maureen and Barbara are staying with me for a bit."

Koutrouboussis loosened his tie. "They're between groups at the moment."

Maureen had honey-coloured hair and Barbara had chestnut-coloured hair; they stood gracefully up and went to the kitchen where they collected two tins and brought them back.

Maureen put an old Zoot Money record on the deck. The sound came softly through and the light screen shifted its shapes and colours.

Barbara kneeled to make cigarettes. She took the ingredients from the tins with her delicate fingers and rolled fat, full fags. She lit two and handed one to Jerry and the other to Koutrouboussis. The men sat down on the ostrich plume cushions and smoked.

Maureen came back and kneeled beside Barbara; she drew on her cigarette with vague dignity. Then both girls titled their impassive faces and directed their inturned eyes at the skylight until someone should ask for something.

"Now if it wasn't for the beans that come out the can, the peas, the beef, the rice and the spam, you can get going down to the grocer's store, really I couldn't eat no more. Let me tell you, my wife—now she can't cook and if I thought she could I wouldn't bother, but all she can do is fuss and holler, she don't even know how to boil water," sang Zoot Money.

"Nineteen sixty five." Koutrouboussis took a long pull. "So long, long, long . . ."

"If you leave me, I'll go crazy."

Jerry smiled reminiscently at Maureen the Groupie who smiled back, sharing the secret that only kindness made them keep.

"Jump back, baby, jump back . . ."

Koutrouboussis lay down and closed his face.

Maureen's warm lips framed the words as she and Jerry looked matily into each other's eyes: ("Sweet   little rock   and   roller. . .")

It was too much for Jerry.

He got up and grasped Maureen and Barbara by their small, soft hands and led them across the Old Gold carpet, up the three steps to the bed with its bird of paradise and began to pile the lace and feathers and rings they handed him. They were so fine and their style was so nice; and their agile, graceful, malleable bodies moved to their mutual pleasure.

When the record was finished, Barbara went and put on another. It was Zoot Money's *Zoot!*

Jerry looked across to the middle of the room.

Koutrouboussis's eyes were alive in a frozen, fading frame.

"Pigs."

3. THE NEW RM TOP 50 CHART EXPLAINED

Jerry, Maureen and Barbara left the Pheasantry and went in Jerry's car to the Ball Room in Wardour Street, Soho, where, in a spot that shifted through all the shades of blue, Sneaky Jack Slade whined wildly his signature tune, played on his smooth sitar.

"I'm the sneaky guy, don't deny my name. Yes, I'm the sneaky guy, don't deny my name," he sang.

When Sneaky saw the new arrivals come in he scuttled off the little stage to be followed by Jonni Jane in platinum wig and rosepetal suit.

Jonni's hands flung themselves about. "Now it's time for our newest, bluest—let me introduce you—twelve or eight to the bar—to the bombshock blues of the junkiest, funkiest, wailingest picker of the year—get ready—he's coming — it's Clapham — George — *Foulsham!*" Jonni trolled off and on came Clapham George to play his latest composition, *Ma Belly's Fulla Sour Milk*.

"Mean ol' U.D., brought sour milk to me. Oh, that mean ol' U.D., brought sour milk to me . . ."

Leaving Maureen and Barbara by the Coca Cola stand, Jerry went to look for Lionel Himmler, the proprietor.

He found him, all sorrow and shit, in his little office behind the bar.

"And what brings you out in the daytime, Mr. Cornelius?" Lionel lifted a glass of Bull's Blood to his pale lips. "Not a blunt needle, I hope."

"How's business, Lionel?"

"We're going over to strip shows more. You've got to

321

get the customers from the suburbs, you see. Out of the
Stockbroker Belt into the Suspender Belt, eh?" A cigar
reared in his mouth.

"Soho isn't what it was."

"Let me be the judge of that, Mr. Cornelius."

"I felt like working."

"It's your mortgage."

Jerry opened a dark brown cupboard and took out his
Martin 206. He checked it and turned it.

"Sorry about the dust," said Lionel.

His guitar under his arm, Jerry walked back into the
room. Clapham George had gone and a stripper tow-
elled herself in the strobelight. Jerry flickered to a table,
sat down and ordered scotch and milk.

Maureen and Barbara brought their cokes over and
joined him. He felt happy with them, but they all knew
the scene was patched.

When the stripper went backstage, Jerry played *Dutch
Schultz* and then sang *Back Door Man* and Lionel came
out to play the Hammond and Jerry plugged in on the
stage and things moved a little as the audience went and
only Maureen and Barbara, two old, old ladies, listened
as Jerry mournfully finished with *My Baby Rocks Me*,
which got them all going, so they left.

Jerry blew a kiss to Lionel. He didn't notice. He was
playing a John Patton number, probably *Fat Judy*.

Off they went. Through the cold grease of the crowd
on the pavement and down the street to where his car, a
1935 Phantom III Continental Rolls Royce with its
involved V-12 engine and its independent front suspen-
sion and its fixtures of the purest silver, including the
radiator, was parked.

"Maybe it should have been a Shadow," said Barbara,
giving Jerry's arm a friendly hug. "Or is that perverse?"

The girls climbed in the back with the Martin and
Jerry started the car.

Wardour Street, all frozen brightlights and vague expressions, led to Shaftesbury Avenue, walled by brown
shops, to Piccadilly Circus, and its green spot.

Soon Jerry was out of all that, driving down Pall Mall,
round the palace, along beside the park, past the Victory
Arch, into Knightsbridge, bowling along, singing a song,

while the girls, huddled in each other's arms, fell asleep.

The music was going.

Koutrouboussis was right. He had to find the machine. He would drop the groupies off at the Pheasantry, get the whereabouts of Gordon Gavin and make an early start in the morning.

4. MY HUSBAND IS A "SPEED FREAK"

Jerry rode the 750cc MZ motorbike straight down the middle of Hammersmith Road. The hog began to hammer as it reached 130.

Jerry's milk-white hair stood out straight behind him, his black silks were pasted to his body, his visor threatened to buckle as he leaned and took the roundabout and throttled down to a comfortable ton when he neared the Cromwell Road Extension and passed a funeral procession.

Three Austin Princesses followed the hearse, their debased lines and lumpen finish offering some loathsome insult to the coffin's contents.

Lying forward on the tank, with his arms stretched out to grasp the chopper's low racing bars, Jerry weaved in front of the Princesses in a dance that was at once graceful and obscene.

The gesture made, he accelerated again and screamed towards Brentford Market.

The Austin Princess was bad for his cool.

He turned into Kew Bridge Road, leapt over the bridge and headed along Kew Green for the big main gates, designed by Decimus Burton and erected in 1848, of the Royal Botanic Gardens. He went through the wrought iron gates that bore the golden Royal Crest, and reduced his speed to seventy, passing the John Nash Aroid House, the Chambers Orangery, the Filmy Fern House, his bike leaving a churned scar across the autumn lawns until it hit Broad Walk and zoomed through the fresh, early morning air towards the Burton Palm House that glistened, all glass and girders, by the

Rose Garden, roared between the Australian House and
the Temperate House, gunned through flower beds and
lawns, wove between the quiet cedars and skidded to a
stop outside the 163ft. Red Pagoda that overlooked the
cedars.

The metal plates on each of the pagoda's ten roofs
reflected the sun, as did the glass domes that covered the
bronze dragons at each corner of each of the octagonal
roofs, exactly as they had been placed in 1761 by Sir
William Chambers on Princess Augusta's approval.

Jerry let his hog fall and shielded his eyes to peer upward.

There in the shadows of the sixth storey balcony stood
a figure which, as he watched, came and leaned over
the rail. The figure was dressed in a long, dirty raincoat
buttoned to the neck.

It could only be Flash Gordon.

Jerry opened the door and began to climb the central

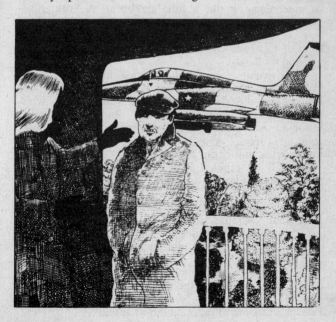

iron staircase that wound up between the bare floors of varnished oak planks. Dust sparkled in the sunlight slanting through the dirty windows.

As he reached the sixth floor, Flash climbed through an open window and stood limply waiting for Jerry to approach.

The large, brown, shallow eyes, set in the red, unhealthy face, stared shiftily at the silk suit, and the blotched fingers stroked the buttons of his mackintosh as if the urge to undo them would get the better of him at any moment.

Below the raincoat Jerry saw a pair of thick, grey socks and boots heavy with mud and blakeys.

"Er, how do, Mr. Cornelius, er." Flash moved his thick lips in a flabby smile.

"Good morning, Gordon. Kew's a bit off your usual manor, isn't it?"

Flash brightened up. "Ah, well. I'm fond of plants, you see, Mr. Cornelius. I had a little garden. I do a little gardening. I'd like a little shrubbery. A little greenhouse. I'm fond of plants. All kinds. I look after these now, as best I can. There's no one else will. That's the state of this little country."

"And it's handy."

"Very handy." As Flash dropped his lids over his suddenly heating pupils his hands went convulsively into his pockets. "And warm. Winter's coming," he whispered. Then he cleared his throat. "But I need a good bit of oil. And oil doesn't grow on trees. Well . . . not on most . . . trees." Avoiding Jerry's eyes Flash moved to the staircase and began to climb down. "Shall us?"

"It is a bit exposed here," agreed Jerry unpleasantly as he followed Flash down.

They walked along the golden Cedar Vista towards the distant Australian House.

"It's spring in Australia, of course," Flash murmured.

"I wouldn't count on it. Not these days."

"I suppose not, no."

Flash took a key from his pocket and opened the door. They went into the hot, bright atmosphere and strolled among the eucalyptus, banksias, Kangaroo Paw, Sturt's Desert Pea, mimosa and acacia.

"You told our Mr. Koutrouboussis you had some information about some stolen property," Jerry said as they paused to admire the purple flowers of a rhododendron.

"Perfectly correct."

"Hard or soft information?"

Flash gave him a startled look. "Er, hard, er."

"And you want a transplant job in return?"

"Ah, well, that's it, isn't it? No. You see, I'm happy here. I like the plants and they like me. And I can move about in them, can't I, waiting for the visitors?"

"So you can."

"Therefore, Mr. Cornelius, by and large, that problem's settled. Over and done with. It's a different problem. I'd give you the info for nothing, you know that. For old time's sake. But I've got to have the oil, you see."

"Well, we could guarantee you a regular supply. Oil's one thing we had a bit of foresight on."

"That's what I understand."

"And, of course, we'd have a guarantee that way, wouldn't we?"

"That's right. If my info's duff, you stop the supply. I hope it isn't duff, though." Flash looked anxiously at his Kangaroo Paw. "I wish you hadn't done that to my lawn."

"I wasn't to know, Flash."

"Fair enough. It'll grow over. That's something I've got to face, sooner or later. There'll be a good deal of growing over."

"It won't be a bad thing."

"I didn't say it was. But it's *different,* isn't it, I mean?"

A squadron of low-flying Northrop F-5A Freedom Fighters made the glass buzz in the frames. Flash looked up and shook his head. "There's been a lot of parachuting going on," he said. "Over Barnes way mostly. You should see what *they've* done to the grass and the trees on the common."

"They've got our interests at heart," said Jerry.

"But what about the little saplings and that!"

"You have to make some sacrifices, Flash."

Warm tears dropped from Gordon's eyes. "Well, I used to like Barnes Common. Sorry, Mr. Cornelius, but I did. That's where I first met you, wasn't it?"

"That info you were on about," said Jerry.

"Oh, yes. Yes. Just a minute." Flash's hand moved in his raincoat pocket and eventually emerged with a scrap of paper. "The swine."

He handed Jerry the piece of paper. "It is a deal, isn't it, Mr. Cornelius?"

Jerry looked at the paper. "It's a deal. Where did you get this?"

"Off the bloke that wrote it."

"That bugger," said Jerry. "Would you believe it?"

"It's all go, isn't it?" said Flash.

Jerry looked at the piece of paper again:

"He said he'd made an appointment for you. Buckingham Palace. This afternoon." Flash stroked a eucalyptus leaf. "Is that all right?"

"It'll have to do."

Cut One

Frightened mothers welcome the avenging police.

Police in Rio de Janeiro and Sao Paulo were tired of seeing criminals get away scot free. So a few of them organised 'death squads'—which operate only during the coppers' off-duty hours.

So far the deaths of more than 100 criminals have been attributed to the Rio squad. The bodies were stamped with a skull-and-cross-bones, which is the trade mark of the killer cops.

The Sao Paulo squad is believed to consist of nine officers, five of them university-educated. Their grudge is the abolition of the death penalty in Brazil and the lack of adequate police facilities.

One squad member, who preferred to be nameless, said: "We were fed up with going around with our hands tied. We decided to use unconventional methods."

Honest people among the ten million who live in the two cities welcome the unorthodox justice.

One frightened mother wrote to a local newspaper: "It is good to know we are being protected."

The men marked for death are those considered habitual criminals by the squads.

Many are drug traffickers. The squads seek maximum publicity, feeling that this will be a deterrent to crime.

The official police stations receive regular calls from a squad 'public relations officer,' who reveals where the latest body can be found.

Titbits, 1 February 1969

1. ECOLOGICAL EFFECTS OF THE VIETNAM WAR

Jerry pulled his Phantom VI up outside the gates of Buckingham Palace and lowered the window as two sergeants of the 5th Marine Division in the modified uniforms of the Grenadiers, complete with helmets and horsehair plumes, came to check him over.

"I've an appointment with Frank Cornelius," Jerry told them.

He was wearing his wide-brimmed lilac hat, with his hair knotted under it. His midnight blue shirt was trimmed in matching lace and his toreador trousers were in an even deeper blue. Around his waist was a wide patent leather belt with a huge brass buckle and a holster holding his vibragun. A flowing yellow bandanna had been tied around his throat.

The sergeants tried to keep their faces expressionless as they inspected his papers, but their lips trembled.

"Wait here, sir." One of the sergeants brushed at his new moustache and went and spoke to a man who stood in the shadows of the main entrance to the palace building.

The other sergeant rested his hand on the roof of Jerry's car and watched his companion intently until he emerged from the shadows and waved. The sergeant slammed the flat of his hand on the roof and Jerry drove through into the courtyard.

The first sergeant ran up to the car, his sword and forty-five slapping against his white buckskins.

"I'll park your car, sir."

"Don't bother." Jerry got out and locked the Phantom VI. "I'll leave it here, I think."

"We can't do that. Cars outside headquarters are forbidden. They ruin the view. Sir."

Jerry pointed up at the flagstaff on the roof of the palace. "I see General Cumberland's in residence."

"Yes, sir."

"It's a proud banner."

Jerry walked into the hall and gave his card to a dapper lieutenant who placed it on a silver tray and bore it up the staircase, passing the portraits of Elizabeth I, James I, Charles I, Charles II, James II, William III, Mary II, Anne, George I, George II, George III, George IV, William IV, Victoria, Edward VII, George V, Edward VIII, George VI, Elizabeth II, Helen, and Ulysses Washington Cumberland (C-in-C; U.S. Defense Forces, Western Europe) who had occupied the building after Helen had left to run a small riding school in Guildford, Surrey. The most recent of the portraits were by Aldridge, the last true Court Painter, in the mouth-and-foot manner that he had made so markedly his own.

Jerry admired the old-fashioned luxury, the archaic splendour of the guards who stood at attention with drawn sabres at every door.

"They certainly have dash." He nodded at the guards as the lieutenant returned.

The lieutenant eyed him up and down. "Major Cornelius is ready to see you. This way."

They climbed the plush and gold staircase until they reached the second floor and walked between the panelled walls and bad Romneys until they came to a white door with panel decorations picked out in black; the name MAJOR FRANK CORNELIUS, *Special Aide, C-in-C*, inscribed in red, and two splendid Royal U.S. Marine Grenadiers on either side. Their swords clashed as they ceremoniously barred the portal then returned their weapons to the slope.

The lieutenant knocked on the door.

A faint but unmistakable Afrikaaner accent answered: "Come."

The lieutenant saluted and marched off. Jerry opened the door and walked into a room decorated and furnished entirely in a style as ugly as anything by the Adam Bros.

Frank stood by the fussy fireplace looking at a little lyre clock that was of the German fake Directoire variety but

quite pretty. He was dressed in the sharply cut uniform of
a major in the U.S. 8th Airborne, one hand in his pocket,
one arm on the mantelpiece. He looked very pale and his
black hair was clipped close to his shoulders. He smiled at
Jerry.

"Long time no see, old chap."

"You've been out in South Afrika, then."

"Good for the constitution, Jerry."

"Or reconstitution."

Frank laughed loudly. "Good old Jerry!"

"I wish you wouldn't keep using that word. You seem
to be doing well for yourself."

"It's a mission."

"I saw Mr. Gavin. I gather you have some idea of the
whereabouts of a piece of property I own."

"Your invention, you mean."

"You could put it that way."

"Well, I haven't got it here, you realise."

"Where would it be?"

"Let's discuss it later. Time for refreshment first?"
Frank touched a bell and a ravaged girl with long chestnut
hair came through a side door. "This is my secretary. Do
you know her? Rose Barrie, my brother Jerry. Rose is a
civilian auxiliary." Frank smiled. "They call you
Bombhead Rose, don't they, Rose?" He winked at Jerry.
"Rose knows . . ."

Rose smoothed her cherry dress and raised a hand to
her garish face. "Wh. . . .?"

"Something to cheer us up, Rose. Good gal, eh?"

Rose went away again.

"She got smacked for speeding," Frank said. "But she's
my type. You know. I couldn't let her down."

"You're too good."

"It's too sweet."

Rose returned with a white tray on which various
bottles, ampoules and instruments were laid.

"Now—let's see," said Frank. His hand hovered over
the tray. "Anything you fancy, old boy?"

"You go ahead. Unless you've got anything in blue."

"Rose had the last of the rozzers last night, didn't you,
Rose?"

"Y . . ."

"She'll tell you. Nothing in blue."

"Then I'll let it go."

"As long as you're sure." Frank picked up an ampoule with the fingertips of his left hand, a needle with the fingertips of his right. "I've been experimenting too, you know, in my own field. Something that might even interest you, though I know you haven't my obsession with chemistry. A synthesised DNA, with something added." Frank rolled back his well-cut sleeve and applied the needle. He smacked his lips. "Tasty. The trouble is, I found, that it's virtually impossible to manufacture in large doses. With your physics and technical know-how, we could be in business."

"You shouldn't diversify too much, Frank."

"That's rich advice from you, old man!"

"Besides, it's not a lot to do with my work. Not if you mean transfusions."

"Transfusions are what I had in mind. A little from that source, a little from this, mix 'em together and see what happens."

"Schitzy!"

"Quite."

"But it still isn't my scene. Now, if you could hand over the machine. Or maybe let me know where . . ."

"Ah. Well, you see, it's Rose that knows where it is. She told me all about it the other day, didn't you, Rose?"

"I . . ."

"It was a vision of some kind, I believe."

"I . . . wish . . . I . . ."

"Anyway, I checked her out."

"I . . . wish . . . I . . ."

"And she was right."

"I . . . wish . . . I . . . was . . ."

"So I got in touch with you."

"I . . . wish . . . I . . . was . . . pretty . . ."

"So it's around here somewhere is it?" Jerry frowned at Rose "In London, I mean?"

"I . . . wish . . . I . . . was . . . pretty . . . again."

"Oh, it's in London, old sport." Frank smiled, turned Rose round and pushed her towards the door. "That's why I contacted you. I mean, there wouldn't be much time, would there? The way things are working out."

"You mean . . ."

"The Op, old son. The rationalisation program. That's

why my boss and I are here, naturally. There's a conference of all European commanders . . ." he checked one of his watches . . . "in about ten minutes. General Cumberland has taken emergency measures already, but I don't think they'll contain anything for very long. Berlin, Geneva, Luxembourg are now negative threats and I expect reports on Helsinki and Milan any moment."

"Bombed?"

"Out of their *minds*, old bean!"

There was a knock on the door.

"Come."

The lieutenant entered and drew himself up in a salute. "Sir. The native commanders are in the conference room. The general hoped you'd entertain them until he can make it."

"Of course. Well, Jerry, if you'll ask Rose for anything you need . . . I'll be back in a little while. Take it easy. You look beside yourself!"

"I wish I were."

"Chin up." Frank, one hand on the butt of his own neatly stashed needle-gun, struck off towards the door. "Wise yourself up to the situation, if you like."

He pulled a cord as he left and the wall over the fireplace glowed and became a map. "I never forget, you see. You taught me how to do that."

Jerry glanced at the bright relief map on which little spots of light flickered where cities had been. It was a bit of a bore. He wondered if you could change the channel.

2. GALLAGHER TO FORM LABEL IN THRUST OVERSEAS BY MCA

Jerry found a button and pushed it.

The map gave way to a scene somewhere in the palace; evidently the conference room. At the long table sat the generals and the field marshals of every European country (with the exception of the Three Republics and the one or two who were still having trouble with the Israelis). They chatted cheerfully among themselves, looking up when Frank, his seamed face set in a smile, came in.

"Gentlemen. I am Major Frank Cornelius, the general's special aide in the European Theater. Please call me Frank."

He put down a slim file on the table and took his place near the top. "General Cumberland regrets he has been delayed, but will join us shortly. In the meantime," he spread his hands, "I'm here to answer any minor questions you might like to put."

The Norwegian field marshal cleared his thin throat.

"Field Marshal Lund?" said Frank.

"I was wondering if you could give us a brief run-down on which areas have been—um—"

"Depersonnelized."

"Ah. Yes."

"Capitals — Helsinki, Berlin, Geneva, Luxembourg, Vienna. Major conurbations—Milan, Munich, Strassbourg . . ." Frank's pencil paused over his file.

The commanders politely accepted the information.

"Of course, news is coming in all the time. We'll keep you up to date."

"Thank you." General von Chemnitz nodded his burly head. "We realise we are not up to date . . ."

"These are rapidly changing times, general. Who can hope to cope with so many events?"

"Indeed, so . . ." The red fat at the back of General von Chemnitz's neck trembled a little. "And what will you be needing our forces to do?"

"Work with our boys I should expect, general." Frank laughed and glanced at all their faces. "Seriously—we'll be needing your men to clean up any pockets of subversive activity after our first wave has gone over your particular areas. The details of that are what we're here to discuss just as soon as General Cumberland gets here."

"There's the question of looting," General de Jong of the Netherlands raised his elegant pen.

"Reclamation of goods. We have two basic categories here, gentlemen. Perishable commodities and non-perishable commodities. Most perishable commodities may be used by the divisions that come across them. Non-perishable commodities should be stored safely until a committee of senior officers has conferred as to their use and distribution. We have had the leaflets prepared which tell you how to cope with that problem. There are also leaflets available on Sexual Intercourse By Force, Sexual Intercourse By Consent, Sexual Intercourse By Unnatural Methods, Sexual Intercourse Between Members Of The Same Sex, Sexual Intercourse With Animals, Sexual Intercourse With Minors, Sexual Intercourse With Enemies Or Those Likely To Be Potential Enemies Or Enemy Sympathisers, Sexual Intercourse While On Active Military Duty, Conditions Under Which The Use Of Torture May Become Necessary, Conditions Under Which The Orders Of A Commanding Officer May Be Disobeyed, Conditions Under Which Allies May Be Killed Or Confined, and so on and so forth. General Cumberland and his staff have thrashed all these matters out to save you time and trouble. General Cumberland wrote most of the leaflets himself, in fact. He is a man of immense energy and thrust. An inspiration."

Field Marshal Lord Martell glanced at his wizened wrist. "Good Lord! Look at the time! I say, do you mind if I bow out on this one? I promised a fellow a game of golf in a quarter of an hour. You'll keep my staff up to date, I take it."

"Of course, Field Marshal."

Martell shook hands with some of the other generals, saluted and hurried off the scene. Two or three others got up and made their apologies.

"I'm sure we can leave it with you." General Groente of Belgium lifted his belly over the edge of the table. "The wife . . ."

"The children . . ." said the youthful Field Marshal Denoël of Switzerland.

"The car . . ." said pale General Ingrid-Maria Stafstrom of Sweden.

"Well, I guess this is cosier anyway." Frank's eyes hardened.

"But you are so capable of 'running the show'. It is a compliment." General von Chemnitz clicked his heels. "Ah, here is . . ."

They stood up as General Cumberland came in. He wore light battle-dress, his tunic open all the way down and his shirt unbuttoned to show his chest and medallion. Dark combat goggles were pushed up over his cap and his light blue eyes were steady in his weather-beaten face. He looked younger than fifty and he did not seem at all anxious about his immense responsibilities. As he shook hands with the other commanders he shuddered every time his flesh touched theirs.

"Now, gentlemen." He sat down at the head of the table. "I hope Frank's filled you in on the basics, uh?"

"I think they're in the picture," said Frank.

"Great. But I'd like to briefly reiterate the ideology behind all this again for you. See, we've been sent over here because we heard you needed some help with a few of your problems. And we didn't just say we'd help—we put our money where our mouths were.

"And we sent you the guys to help you out. Well, I guess you needed more guys, and you got 'em. You got 'em without even having to ask. And you're welcome. We know the trouble you have and that's what we're here to put a stop to. We know what the Israelis are up to and we think we can maybe give 'em something to think about—so they'll damn well *stop* what they're up to before they do something really foolish.

"We know that your armies, your intelligence outfits and your civilian communities are riddled through and through with fifth columnists—with traitors—and we're

doing something about that, too. When action's called for—
we're the guys to call."

He put his teeth together and smiled. "Let me just read
you something I got from back home the other day." From
his tunic pocket he took a clipping which he carefully unfolded and spread before him on the table. Then he began
to read in a quiet but declamatory tone:

"Let's start looking at the situation in which we and the
rest of the free-world forces involved find ourselves. It is
not complex, not obscure, not hard for anyone to understand.

"We are losing the war.

"So many of the people on our side are being killed that
the rest of them are thinking about quitting.

"That definition of losing, incidentally, is not only my
own. It was taught to me by Admiral Bull Halsey before I
covered the battle for Iwo Jima, the first time I saw mortal
combat. The actions in the Rhine Valley now are no less
obscene or exalting or decisive than were those in the grey
sands cradling Mount Suribachi twenty-five years ago.

"Even the hideous casualty totals are in the same mag-
nitude, though they have taken days instead of years to in-
flict; the fighting in Europe between the forces of our side
and those who would bury us has cost more than 100,000
lives. Of the dead, only several hundred have been Americans.

"Of those, seven were men beside whom I had walked or
parachute jumped or river forded or shared a stint of guard
duty on a sandbagged emplacement at some place whose
name we could not pronounce till we got there.

"Almost all U.S. casualties are from the small group
of Americans serving in active combat. Most U.S. uniformed personnel do not actively risk their lives. Out of
every five or six sent overseas, only one is exposed to
actual daily fighting while the others serve in supporting
roles. So those three millions of our men now in Europe
add only several thousand to the active European armed
forces which, including militia, now total more than twelve
million.

"Those few exposed Americans, though, have accomplished something by their sheer character that no other
Americans have been able to do in more than a decade.

They have forced a major enemy to change tactics as a response to what they are doing.

"This is in utter contrast to what happened to free-world forces in Hungary and Algeria and Cuba and Formosa and Laos, where our side did all the second-guessing and did not once win.

"The fighting in Europe marks the first time that our side *in the eyes of the enemy* has been applying a system of force so effectively that the other side considers we must be halted at all costs lest we start winning the war.

"What we have been doing right, of course, is to provide some superb leadership to the tough European fighting man.

"I have watched the workings of the practice during fourteen months in the field with nine different combatant forces. The enemy fear it so greatly that killing Americans now is their priority tactical objective.

"The erstwhile ranking target used to be any European community leader; in September, almost a thousand mayors and provincial representatives were assassinated or abducted.

"Somehow, this fact seems not to have become known to most Americans and they impatiently ask what defect of will in the European people prevents formation of a stable democratic government.

"The facts as I saw them in the region where most Europeans live, the suburbs and the countryside, were not mysterious at all; there just haven't been enough surviving politicians, thanks to enemy raiding and the attendant atrocities.

"But beginning this fall, enemy tacticians issued orders that were a little different from their previous ones. And shorter, too. *Get the Americans.*

"These orders are not being disobeyed. Out of forty-two American mentors attached to European combat units, who happened to be billeted in one headquarters in the heart of Bavaria's most strategic area, nineteen were killed or wounded in two months. I know: I too was quartered there then, and the count is my own, not that of any public information officer back in Bonn.

"By the grisly economy of war, this change in enemy targeting is the ultimate stamp of effectiveness on what we at home have been taught cynically and incorrectly to call the 'advisor system' of military aid to Europe.

"Obviously, it is more than that. 'Advisors' do not become prime enemy targets.

"I submit with great pride that these Americans are not only advising; they are not just fighting in self-defense. Without any trappings of command—indeed, without even a shadow of command authority—they are leading.

"They are leading foreign troops simply because that's the way the troops want it. Why? Because each of these men, in the European troops' opinion, is the best soldier around and hence the leader most likely to bring them through victorious. And to put it bluntly, bring them back alive.

"In short, though the U.S. seems to have hidden its virtue, the details of the honorable course it has taken in Europe, the Europeans know and salute it when the chips are down.

"Why 'honorable'? Consider our defense treaty; it pledges to supply Europe whatever she lacks to win over communism. When it developed that in fact military leadership was a prime lack, we began delivering just what we'd promised.

"Well, then, why is there still a question about the outcome? Why aren't we winning?

"In my judgement, simply because we haven't sent *enough* of this leadership.'"

The general paused, looked up and spoke softly. "Well, gentlemen—that's the kind of support you're getting from the folks back where I come from. I'll skip most of the rest—but I'll read you the last bit:

"All of which puts the determination of tomorrow's history where I have every confidence it best belongs: squarely into the hands of the people of the United States.

"It is for each of us to decide what we want to do and to give the government we have elected freely some clear evidence of our will to win, lose or draw.

"After all, it is not that administrative abstraction we call a government that will bear the final bloody consequence if we choose badly.

"It is us and our sons and daughters.'"

General Cumberland looked reverently at the clipping

as he folded it carefully and when he glanced up his eyes were chips of blue steel.

"That's how we feel. You know you can rely on us. The only way to win a war is to fight it. The road ahead will not be smooth or offer easy traveling. But the road map we're using today is a heck of a lot better than it has been. In the words of Patrick Henry as he stood before the Richmond Convention and delivered his famous address—'They tell us, sir, that we are weak; unable to cope with so formidable an adversary. But when shall we be stronger? Will it be the next week or the next year? Will it be when we are totally disarmed, and when a British guard shall be stationed in each house? Shall we gather strength by irresolution and inaction?'—of course we will not! The United States will accept a decent negotiated peace in Europe. But it will not go, umbrella in hand, like Neville Chamberlain, to the aggressor, and let him write the settlement on his own expansionist terms. There can be no complaint about U.S. Marines being sent to Europe, except that they might have been sent sooner. For years the Europeans—with token assistance from the United States—have been trying to defend themselves against raids, murder by stealth, sabotage and subversion. The results have been a mounting loss of American and European lives—no progress at all in ridding the continent of the invaders. Now the Europeans and the U.S. have taken to offensive strikes of their own . . . hitting where it hurts! And that's the way it's going to be, gentlemen, until the last enemy is destroyed and Europe can settle down to building the continent she wants in the way she wants to, without fear of attack from without or within. There's a wave back there and it's coming in fast—and that wave is American strength, gentlemen. American strength, American manhood, American know-how, American guts; American money, American dynamism, American bullets, American guns, American tanks, American planes, American freedom, American efficiency . . ."

Frank took notes and the European commanders stared in faint surprise at the C-in-C. Those nearest the door were already leaving and the others were rising from their chairs.

"American love, American humor, American health, American beauty, American virility . . . ."

The last general quietly closed the door behind him

and General Cumberland raised his head at the sound.

"Have they deserted us, Frank?"

"I think they got the picture, general. I think their confidence is won."

"I hope so, Frank. I tried to raise their morale. It sometimes seems to be the hardest job. They're all fairies, of course. Decadence is a terrible thing to witness. But maybe if we improve their conditions—give them a chance . . ."

"They'll pull through"

"God willing, Frank."

3. IT'S KLM'S 50TH ANNIVERSARY. WE THOUGHT YOU'D LIKE TO SHARE A FEW HAPPY MOMENTS

When Frank came back Jerry was still looking at General Cumberland whose lips moved as he scribbled rapidly in a notebook.

Frank stood beside Jerry and watched for a while. Then he turned the general off.

"It's rotten for him, really." Jerry was sympathetic.

"He takes it well. The responsibility." Frank crossed to the window and peered in the direction of St. James's Park. "Sometimes it seems there'll never be an end to it, Jerry. Or a beginning, in one sense, I suppose. There's so much to do—and so little time."

"True."

"I hope you're not brooding on our differences any more. After all, if brothers can't fall out occasionally, who can?"

"It all depends, a bit, on your position, Frank."

Frank shrugged and spread his thin hands. "You know me, Jerry. It's easy for you."

"It is easier. You've got the heat death to contend with. I've always granted you that, Frank."

"After all, what is a memory?"

"Perhaps nothing more than a hologram."

"Exactly. Remember that dream of mine when we were young? A hologram on every billboard. A billboard the length of every street. A grid of streets that covered the globe . . ." Frank shrugged. "But it didn't prove to be as simple as that, did it, Jerry?"

"That's the difference between you and me. Where's my machine?"

"It's a question of cycles, I suppose."

"Or equilibrium." Jerry rested his hand on his vibra-gun. "Come along, Frank."

"You'd never get out, Jerry. And you'd lose a lot of potential friends."

"I don't need friends."

"You don't need enemies, either. I only want to strike a bargain with you. It could make us both rich—and extremely powerful. You've got to look to the future, old man."

"I'm not too happy about these artificial divisions, Frank. I want to look to it all at once. I don't like the way you and your allies slice up time."

"Somebody's got to do the dirty work."

Jerry drew his gun. Frank drew his gun.

Jerry sighed. "There doesn't seem a lot of point. Couldn't you just tell me where the machine is?"

"You tell me what it is, then."

"It's a simple diffusion device," lied Jerry. "A randomizer. Nothing complicated."

"It replicates conditions in the Shifter, is that it?"

"That's it."

"Well, it wouldn't suit me, Jerry. I've never had much sympathy for that sort of thing. You know me—live and let live—but it wouldn't . . ."

Jerry raised his gun.

"Well, it wouldn't! Christ—there are much better ways of having fun."

"Where's the machine?"

"Derry and Toms Famous Roof Garden."

"Thanks," said Jerry and waited until Frank had put his gun back. "Let me know something I can do for you." He holstered his own vibragun.

"Nothing at this stage," Frank said, riding swiftly into the new situation. "You haven't got much of a chance of getting to that machine or of getting out of London alive. But if you should manage both things, then it's quite likely I'll be in a difficult position and you'll owe me a favour, won't you?"

"You've mellowed, Frank."

"I'm coming apart, Jerry. I'm desperate."

"It seems to be doing you good." Jerry grinned. "You're more mature."

Frank sniffed. "Call it what you like. I call it caution. You have to look after yourself when you get into my condition."

"Well, let's hope I make it to Derry and Toms."

Frank glanced at his watch. "You just might, if they don't get around to that sector right away. I'm off to Milton Keynes in a few minutes. That's our new base. The general thinks it's cleaner. No population, you see. They never had a chance to fill it."

"Sure. Well, don't take any wooden nickels."

"Not from you, Jerry."

"I'll be off, then."

Jerry opened the door and the swords clashed under his nose.

"Let him through," said Frank in a peculiar voice.

Jerry closed the door and looked up and down the corridor. He frowned as he contemplated the rigid guards and then came to a decision.

It was just as well to be on the safe side, to give himself some sort of edge. Frank was so shitty.

"If you ask me," he said quietly, "he's not what he seems to be. He's all bits and fucking pieces."

He trod the soft carpets. The sunlight poured through the big window at the far end of the corridor and through it Jerry could see the green and gold of the quiet autumn trees.

It looked a nice day for a picnic.

Cut Two

POLARIS NUCLEAR SUB!

How proud you will be as commander of your own
POLARIS SUB—the most powerful weapon in the
world! What hours of imaginative play and fun as you
and your friends dive, surface, maneuver, watch the enemy through the periscope and fire your nuclear missiles
and torpedoes! What thrills as you play at hunting-sunken
treasures in pirate waters and exploring the strange and
mysterious bottom of the deep ocean floor.

HOURS AND HOURS OF ADVENTURE

Sturdily constructed . . . Comes complete with easy assembly instructions. Costs only $6.98 for this giant of
fun, adventure and science. (Because of the POLARIS
SUB's giant size we must ask for 75c shipping charges.)

MONEY BACK GUARANTEE

Order today and we will rush your POLARIS NUCLEAR
SUB to you. Use it for 10 full days. If you don't think
it is the greatest ever—the best toy you ever had—
just send it back for full purchase price refund.

Real Confessions ad

1. SCREAM AND DIE, EUROPEAN COMMIE HOMOS, IN YANK "CLEANSE AND BURN" OFFENSIVE

It wasn't far to Derry and Toms, but the napalm was coming on heavy as Jerry drove west to the sound of Ronald Boyle's recorded voice booming in even tones from loudspeakers mounted in every flying thing.

BURN OUT THE CANCER
BURN OUT THE CANCER
BURN OUT THE CANCER
BURN OUT THE CANCER
BURN OUT THE CANCER
BURN OUT THE CANCER

The day was grey; the sunlight blocked by the planes whose steady roar echoed through the city.

BURN OUT THE CANCER
BURN OUT THE CANCER
BURN OUT THE CANCER
BURN OUT THE CANCER
BURN OUT THE CANCER
BURN OUT THE CANCER
BURN OUT THE CANCER

The napalm sheets kept falling.

BURN OUT THE CANCER
BURN OUT THE CANCER
BURN OUT THE CANCER
BURN OUT THE CANCER
BURN OUT THE CANCER
BURN OUT THE CANCER
BURN OUT THE CANCER

Jerry waited impatiently at Knightsbridge for the lights to change. Several buildings, including the recently re-built barracks of the Royal Horse Guards, were beginning to burn.

BURN OUT THE CANCER.
BURN OUT THE CANCER

BURN OUT THE CANCER
BURN OUT THE CANCER
BURN OUT THE CANCER
BURN OUT THE CANCER
BURN OUT THE CANCER

He decided to go through the park and turned right.
As he did so the first B52s came in low, streaming clouds
of defoliant and making a thick fog that reduced visibility to a few feet.

Jerry slowed down and switched to his own air supply,
turned his most powerful lamps into the swirling white
mist, and kept going. He could see just far enough
ahead to avoid hitting any large obstacles. Derry and
Toms was in Sector D-7 and this was Sector G-6. Depending on their sweep, he had a little time before they
started on D-7.

He was, as ever, impressed by the efficiency of the
strike. By tomorrow, London should be completely Triple
A Clean. His brother, with his liking for systems and
his knowledge of London, had probably had a lot to do
with the planning.

As the mist thinned a little he looked up, recognising
the hazy silhouettes of a squadron of General Dynamics
F-111As lumbering across the sky followed by Mc-
Donnell F-4B Phantom IIs, F-4C Phantom IIs, RF-4
Phantom IIs, F-101B Voodoos, F-101C Voodoos, Re-
public F-105 Thunderchiefs, Ling-Temco-Vought
(Chance Vought) F-8U Crusaders, Convair F-106
Delta Darts, Lockheed F-104 Starfighters, Convair F-
102 Delta Daggars, Northrop F-5A Freedom Fighters,
Ling-Temco-Vought A-7A Corsair IIs, North American
F-100 Super Sabres, North American FJ Furies, Doug-
las F-6A Skyrays, Grumman F11A Tigers, McDonnell
M-3B Demons, Northrop F-89 Scorpions, North Ameri-
can F-86D Sabres and, very much behind the others,
Republic F-84F Thunderstreaks doing their best to keep
up.

The planes passed and the helicopters chattered by.
As far as Jerry could make out they were all heading
due north, which meant that Derry and Toms, if it had
so far missed the strike, would probably be okay for
a little while.

He took a bearing off the Albert Memorial and

bumped over the dying grass until he splashed into the Round Pond by accident and had to operate the screws for an instant as he crossed the pond and at last got to The Broad Walk near the London Museum, drove down the The Broad Walk and came out onto a Kensington Road that was red with reflected firelight, but seemed as yet undamaged, though clouds of sodium cacodylate mixed with free cacodylic acid, water and sodium chloride drifted in the streets.

Elsewhere Jerry recognised n-butyl ester, isobutyl ester, tri-isopropanolamine, salt picloram and other chemicals and he knew that the park had got everything—Orange, Purple, White and Blue.

"Better safe than sorry." He pulled up outside Derry and Toms.

Business appeared to have fallen off badly in the last few hours, though it was relatively peaceful here. In the distance Jerry heard the sound of falling buildings, the scream of rockets, the boom of the bombs, the shouts of the dying.

A boy and a girl ran out of the smoke, hand in hand, as he entered the store; they were on fire, making for the drinking fountain on the corner of Kensington Church Street.

The fire would probably help cope with the plague. There was nothing like the chance of a fresh start.

2. THE MAN BEHIND THE FACE THAT 350 MILLION TV VIEWERS KNOW AS THE SAINT

Although the defoliants hadn't yet reached the roof garden, there was a strong chemical smell as Jerry used his vibragun to shake down the door of an emergency exit and emerge into the Tudor Garden.

He wondered at first if the machine's batteries had started to leak. They had been manufactured hastily, for the machine had originally been intended only as a prototype. It was Jerry's fault that he had tried it out in the Shifter and had lost it in the ensuing confusion.

Jerry placed the odour at last. It was Dettol.

The disinfectant had been used to hide another smell which he now recognised as the smell of corruption. It would have been good for the garden, of course, if things had been left alone. He wondered who had been here recently.

Everything was tidy and there wasn't a trace of an old lady. Jerry noticed with disappointment that the ducks had flown.

He wandered across to the Spanish Garden, watching as the blue heaven gradually filled with black smoke, and climbed the wall to look at the burning city and the insane jets wheeling about the sky in their dance of death. Napalm fell. Rockets raced.

"Out of time, out of touch," murmured Jerry. It was what his father had always taught him. He didn't often feel this complacent. "Goodbye, America."

"Europe," said a voice with a thick Russian resonance, "can become the ultimate possibility pool. You're slowing down, Comrade Cornelius."

Jerry shifted his position on the wall and looked down at the little man standing among the flowering ferns and dwarf palms, tugging at his goatee. "You've been taking speech training."

The man looked embarrassed and removed his rimless glasses. "I can't stay long."

"Is my machine here?"

"That's what I came to tell you about, comrade. I didn't think it was safe. I gave it to a friend of yours to look after. She was here until recently."

"Captain Hargreaves?"

"I didn't realise, until she put on her uniform, that she was with the defenders."

"Do you know where she is?"

"Presumably with the rest of her comrades, wherever that may be."

"You've never been able to do anything right, have you, you old softie." Jerry jumped down from the wall. "Ah, well. It was nice of you to tell me."

"I'm sure everything will work out all right. Won't it?"

"Keep your fingers crossed, comrade."

The little man extended his hand. "Well, if I don't see you again." He vanished.

Jerry yawned. He was getting behind on his sleep. He left the roof garden as the first wave of planes arrived in Sector D-7, leapt down the stairs as the building began to shake, and reached the street as spluttering napalm flooded through the store.

He drove down Kensington High Street as fast as he could. He hoped Koutrouboussis and the rest were okay. If they'd been able to get out they should be safe enough at the Sunnydale Reclamation Centre.

He didn't feel particularly disappointed. After all, things had gone very easily up to now.

He made for Milton Keynes.

Extraction

Jews get out of Palistine it's not your home anyway!
Moses was the first traitor and Hitler was the Messiah!!!
Black militant placard, Harlem

352

1. OUTLAW IN THE SKY

Jerry left the burning city behind and headed up the M.1. It was a wide, lonely road, through the hushed countryside.

He turned on the radio and tuned it to Radio Potemkin. It was playing the Yardbirds. The Moquettes, The Zephyrs, Mickie Most, The Downliners Sect, Rey Anton and The Pepperment Men, The Syndicats, The Cheynes, The Cherokees, Cliff Bennett and The Rebel Rousers. Unable to bear either the nostalgia or the quality, Jerry switched over to Radio John Paul Jones which was in the middle of putting over *The Vibrating Ether Proves The Cosmic Vortex*, the latest hit by Orniroffa, the Nip Nightingale. All art, thought Jerry, aspired to the condition of Muzak. What would William Morris have thought?

It was at times like this that the brain needed balming. He turned to his taper and selected Schoenberg's Quartet No. 2, left the M.1 and took a winding lane towards Oxford.

Soon he could see the white shell of the city shining in the distance. The concrete roof was good for anything except the H-Bomb.

He slowed as he reached the opening of the tunnel and drove through to emerge in the shadowy darkness of Magdalen Bridge.

The dim light from the central lamp at the highest part of the roof was reflected by the spires of the city. Power was failing, but Oxford survived.

Jerry felt the cold. The High was full of a strange, sticky dampness and black-cloaked figures crept miserably along beside the walls, while every so often hollow, echoing shouts and clatterings broke the stillness. The hissing noise of his own car seemed menacing.,

Stopping the Phantom VI in the car park of the Randolph Hotel he walked to the Ashmolean Museum, pushed open the heavy wooden doors and paused. A few candles in brackets on the walls lit a sinister avenue of Tompion and Knibb longcase clocks which had all stopped at a quarter past twelve. He began to walk.

The sound of his footsteps was like that of a huge pendulum, regular and ponderous. He came to the locked door at the end of the avenue and took a key from his pocket, turned it in the lock, opened the door and descended the stone staircase, lighting his way with his torch.

Climbing downwards for half-an-hour he at last reached a tunnel which led to another door. Unlocking this, he came to a room containing a small power plant. He crossed to the plant and depressed a lever.

The plant whispered and then hummed softly and steadily. Lights went on. Jerry switched off his torch, passed through two more empty chambers until he came to a fourth room which was lined on three sides with cupboards that had mirrors set into their panels. The cupboards had been imported from Sweden nine years earlier. The mirrors were more recent.

The room was carpeted with a deep, red, Russian rug. On it stood a couch draped with white mink covers and yellow silk sheets. It was unmade. Against the wall near the door was a neat console operating a series of small monitor screens and microtronic indicator boards, all slightly archaic in design and function but still in good working order. Jerry had not been here since he had left the seminary.

Sitting on the couch, he tugged off his block-heeled boots; he removed his jacket and his shoulder holster and dropped them on the floor, pulled back the pillows and touched a stud on the control panel set in the low headboard. The console activated, he lay and watched it for a bit until he felt up to visiting the morgue.

The room had become unfamiliar, yet a lot of things had happened here. The Shifter gateways had been

erected, the earliest prototype of the machine had been
built, the Web completed and, of course, those ridiculous
books had been written. It had been a rapid development
really, from priest to politician to physicist, but it had
been necessary and, he supposed, inevitable.

He was drained. He smiled and shrugged. Perhaps he
had better visit the Web before he went to the morgue. It
was still very cold in the room. It would take a while for
the place to warm up.

This had been his grandfather's complex originally, before the old man had moved to Normandy, and his father
had inherited it, passing it on to him. His father had built
and stocked the morgue, too.

He got up shivering, opened one of the mirrored panels
and stepped through into a well-lit corridor with four steel
doors on each side and another steel door at the end. He
rested his palm against the fourth door on the right and it
opened. A peg behind the door supported a clean black
car coat. Jerry put it on and buttoned up. The schizophre-
nia had been bad at first, his father had said. He had
been lucky not to inherit the worst of it.

There were ten drawers set low into the far wall. Each
drawer was labelled with a name. Jerry opened the first
drawer on the left and looked down into the eyes of the
pale, beautiful girl with the tangled black hair.

He touched the cold skin of her breasts.

"Catherine . . ."

He stroked the face and drew a deep breath.

Then he bent down and picked her up, carrying her
from the morgue and back to the bed chamber with the
console.

Placing her in the bed, he stripped off the rest of his
clothes and lay beside her, feeling the heat flow out of his
body into hers.

His life was so dissipated, he thought. But there was
no other way to spend it.

"Catherine . . ."

She stirred.

He knew there could only be a few seconds left.

"Catherine."

The eyes opened and the lips moved. "Frank?"

"Jerry."

"Jerry?" Her perfect brow frowned slightly.

"I've got a message for you. There's some hope. That's the message."

Her eyes warmed, then faded, then closed.

Trembling with a terrible cold, Jerry began to cry. He staggered from the bed, fell to his knees, got up and lurched from the chamber into the corridor, pressing his frozen palm against the first door on his left.

The door opened stiffly, almost reluctantly.

Jerry leaned against it as it closed, peering through his blurred eyes at the rustling machine before him.

Then he flung himself at the singing red, gold and silver webs and gasped and grinned as they enmeshed him.

Why was resurrection so easy for some and so difficult for others?

2. BEYOND THE X ECLIPTIC

When he had filed Catherine again, Jerry whistled a complicated piece of Bartok and returned, radiant and replete, to his cosy room to look at himself in the mirrors.

Time to be moving; moves to be timing.

He opened a cupboard and regarded his wardrobe. The clothes were somewhat theatrical and old-fashioned but he had no choice. His nearest wardrobe to Oxford was now in Birmingham, the only major city in the area which had not needed cleaning, and he had never fancied Birmingham much at the best of times.

He selected a military-style green jacket, a suede shako with a strap that buttoned under his chin, matching suede britches, green jackboots and a shiny green Sam Browne belt with a button-down holster for his vibragun. A short green pvc cape secured by a silver chain over one shoulder, and the ensemble was complete.

He left the little complex and closed the door behind him.

Shining the torch up the stone staircase he climbed to the top and opened the surface door. Then, stopping at each and winding them up, he walked back down the avenue of long-case clocks. The gallery was soon filled with their merry ticking.

As he strolled away from the Ashmolean towards the carpark of the Randolph Hotel, he heard the clocks begin to strike nine o'clock.

He started the Phantom VI and turned the car into the Broad, switched the taper to Nina Simone singing *Black Swan*, and lay well back in the driving seat until he reached the Western airlock which he passed through without difficulty. He blinked as he broke into the bright, warm morning.

Soon he could see Milton Keynes.

The new conurbation rose out of the greenish ground mist, each great tower block a different pastel shade of pale chrome yellow, purple, gamboge, yellow ochre, chrome orange, vermilion, scarlet, red (ost), crimson, burnt sienna, light red, cobalt, cerulean blue, turquoise, ultramarine, prussian blue, mauve, leaf green, emerald, sap green, viridian, hookers green, burnt umber, van-dyke brown, orange (ost), ivory black and grey (ost).

Entering the quiet streets of the great village, with its trim grass verges and shady trees, Jerry was filled with a sense of peace that he rarely experienced in rural settlements. Perhaps the size of the empty buildings helped, for most of them were over eighty feet high, arranged around a series of pleasant squares with central fountains splashing a variety of coloured, sparkling water or with free form sculptures set in flower gardens. There were terraced gardens with vines and creepers on the buildings themselves and the air was full of butterflies, mainly red admirals and cabbage whites.

Jerry drove at a leisurely pace until he came to the middle of the conurbation. Here were the main adminis-tration buildings and shopping arcades, the schools and the play areas, and here were parked the armoured ve-hicles, the tanks and the helicopters of the advisory force. Neat, newly painted signs had been put up and it was easy for Jerry to park his car and make for General Cumberland's headquarters in the tall, domed building that the planners had intended for the town hall and which now flew the Stars and Stripes.

As Jerry climbed the steps, a detachment of unhappy marines broke from the building and surrounded him with a ring of sub-machine-guns. "I was hoping I'd find Frank Cornelius here," Jerry said mildly.

"What you want with Colonel Cornelius, boy?"

"I have some information for him." A faint shock ran from the left hemisphere to the right of Jerry's brain.

"What sort of information, fella?"

"It's rather secret."

The marines sniffed and rubbed their noses with their forearms, keeping their steely eyes fixed on him.

"You'd better tell the colonel I'm here, I think."

"What's your name?"

"He'll know who it is if you describe me."

One of the marines broke away and trotted inside. The circle closed up. Jerry lit a Romeo y Julieta and dropped the aluminium tube on the ground. Still staring unblinkingly at his prisoner's face, a marine with pursed lips kicked the tube violently away.

Frank hurried out.

"Jerry! You made it! Great!"

The marines withdrew behind Jerry and came to the salute with a crash of boots and armour.

"Did you have any luck with the machine?" Frank put a cold arm round Jerry's shoulder and guided him into the new town hall.

"I can't complain." Jerry spoke through his cigar. "And are you satisfied?"

"*Relatively,* Jerry. Look, we'll go to my private quarters. That's the best idea, eh?"

They went through a glass door, crossed the open quadrangle and entered the building's northern wing. "It's just here." Frank stopped, unlocked his door and led Jerry into an airy, pleasant room in which Rose Barrie was arranging flowers on a sideboard.

"That's fine, Rose, thanks." Frank smiled. The girl left.

"You're pretty loathsome, Frank." Jerry took a golden chrysanthemum from the vase and smelled it.

"So would you be. I was never the favoured son, Jerry. I had to fight for what I wanted. You had it easy."

"Until you fought for what you wanted."

"Oh, that . . ."

"I've just been to see Catherine."

"How is she? I was wilder in those days, Jerry."

"She's keeping pretty well."

"Our family always were great survivors." Frank grinned. "Do you want a . . . ? No, I suppose not. But let's face it, Jerry. You got where you were by luck— by intuition, if you like. I had to do everything by thinking. Hard thinking. Logical thinking."

"It made you tense, Frank."

"That's the price you pay."

Jerry put the chrysanth back. Then he smashed the vase from the sideboard and looked at the fallen flowers, the spilled water and the broken glass on the carpet.

"Don't lose your temper, Jerry." Frank was laughing. "You are a hothead! What's wrong, old sweat?"

"I'd love to be able to kill you, Frank. Kill you, Frank. Kill you, Frank."

Frank spread the fingers at the end of his extended right arm. "Jesus, Jerry, so would I . . ."

"I'd love to be able to kill you, Frank."

"That's a remote possibility."

"It's all too fucking remote."

Jerry swayed from the waist, eager for his gun.

"Calm down, Jerry, for Christ's sake." Frank snapped his fingers at his sides. "You'll need removing. Is this the time? Is this the place?"

"Space is all you ever fucking think about."

"Somebody has to. Listen, Jerry, I've got a moral responsibility. I never had that. I *have* changed. I could lose it all. Split. I'm going to keep it. The power's building up."

"You'd have thought Einstein had never happened!"

"Maybe he shouldn't have happened. It's running too wild. We need something concrete—definite—solid. Something hard."

"I want something easy."

"Exactly. Connect, Jerry—just for a moment."

"Shit . . ."

"Technology is potential freedom from brutality. I should know. The old can't riot and have no power. We must forfeit the right to breed in order to retain the right to breathe. Immortality is just around the corner!"

"Mortality is *space*."

"You've got too much imagination. That's what I mean."

"What's the matter with you, Frank? You . . ."

"I'm older. You can never be that."

"Piss . . ."

"Man is the only animal with the imaginative characteristic developed to any degree. No competition, see? The trait has become *over-developed*. A survival characteristic turned into an anti-survival characteristic. We must limit imagination. Destroy it, if necessary, in the majority, limit it in the rest. Jerry, it's our only chance to get back to something worthwhile. To normality."

Jerry stared vaguely at his brother. "Get back? Get back? But we're moving on. The abstract . . ."

". . . can only destroy civilisation . . ."

". . . as we know it."

"You see."

"See? Death."

"Death—and life."

"Sure."

"Then . . . ?"

"Kill you, Frank."

"No!"

Jerry felt faint. "You're fouling things up, Frank. You were nicer when you knew it."

"Forget Time." Frank slapped the sideboard. "That's what's important right now. A cleaning up. A getting back to fundamentals."

"Forget Space."

"Jerry—when I returned I decided there had to be some constructive action. We mustn't fight."

"Catherine. You killed our sister."

"You killed her."

"You made me."

"Who's the guilty one?"

"Guilt? There you go again." Jerry relaxed. "Well, I suppose you just saved your life. Boredom is a great preserver." He stretched. "So you've decided to think ahead? I can't see it myself."

"You won't give yourself a chance. You won't give me a chance."

Jerry began to pick up the pieces of broken glass and put them on the sideboard. He gathered the flowers into a bunch and crossed the room to a mock Tudor table which had an empty vase on it. He put the flowers in the vase. "It's a question of identity, Frank. What the hell. A wild environment, an integrated identity."

"We're clearing things up. Tidying the world."

"You might just as well be in the political age. You can't bring it back, Frank."

"We will."

"Not for long."

"You'll see."

"But you know what I'm out to do, don't you?"

"Randomise."

"More or less."

"You won't succeed. History's against you, Jerry."

"That's the difference between you and me, Frank. I'm against History."

"Where are you going?"

Jerry made for the door. "I've got to look up an old flame. You don't mind me hanging around for a while, do you?"

"I'd rather you did. Have you got the machine with you?"

"No."

"Then I'd rather you did."

"I'll be seeing you soon, Frank."

"Bet on it."

3. THE PRISON OF THE STARS

Jerry found Flora Hargreaves by the fountain, behind the M-60 tanks.

"You're just as I remember you," he said.

She smiled, smoothing her olive uniform. "You never told . . ."

"No."

"Thanks."

"You met a friend of mine in London, didn't you? He gave you something to look after."

"That's right, Jerry."

"I need it now."

"You do? You'd better come back to my quarters. I've got a nice place. There's plenty of space for everybody."

"Everybody who needs it."

"Yes."

They walked between the tanks and crossed the square to the violet building opposite the town hall. All around the square the marines were relaxing, chatting to the WACs, smoking, sipping soft-drinks, cleaning their Navy Colts.

"It's been pretty tough for them," said Flora. "But I guess they know how to take it."

"They can take anything by the look of them."

"Almost anything." Flora straightened her shoulders. She winked at him. "It's gotten to be a rotten war, Jerry. I sometimes wonder what you people make of it. It can be hard, sometimes, to take the overall view when your own country's . . . well . . ."

Jerry sucked in his breath. "It has to be this way.

Maybe if the CIA were still around things would be better."

"I guess."

"They've nothing against—you know—consorting?"

"If you're here, Jerry, you've had security clearance. That's all they want to know. It's my leave. I can do what I like."

They entered the building and climbed the concrete stairs to the first floor, walking along a cool, shady corridor until they came to her room. She turned the handle and threw the door open with a sweeping gesture. *"Après vous!"*

Jerry padded in and eyed the room. It was very feminine. There were a lot of soft toys on the bed, posters of British beauty spots on the walls, a helmet and battle overalls hanging over a chair, a .22 in a holster on a stack of Penguin paperbacks, a neat kitchenette through an archway. The room was sunny. Flora drew the blinds.

"The machine," said Jerry.

She went to her wardrobe. There were three print dresses in it. She bent and Jerry looked at her thighs. She straightened, holding something black, square and heavy, and Jerry looked at her eyes. She widened them. "Is this it?"

"This is it." Jerry laughed with relief. "Put it down. Aha!"

As she put it on the floor he seized her, running his hand up her leg and down her regulation drawers; kissing her wide, soft, hot, damp, lively mouth; running his other hand through her sweet auburn hair; guiding her to the bed and fucking her with enormous joy and energy.

"Well, that was nice," she said. "I alway knew . . ."

"Come off it." He gave her one of her Kents and lit one for himself.

"Is the box valuable?"

"It means the world to me."

"It just looks like some sort of geiger counter—something like that."

"It's a bit more versatile than that."

"Tell me what it is, Jerry." She curled a leg over his leg and licked his left nipple.

"There's no real word for it. Nothing—*authentic*. One of its functions is as a sort of randomiser. It can produce all the alternatives at once. There's a lot of power in that little box."

"A computer? Multivalue logic?"

"Not a computer. Far from it. Almost the opposite, in one sense. It breaks down the barriers. It lets the multiverse—well—'in'."

"That isn't a proper word."

"It's everything."

"What's everything?"

"You're everything, Flora. But now you can be mirrored by your environment. It creates a human environment for a human being. It can also speed up various basic processes."

"That's an explanation?"

"Explanations shouldn't be necessary between us, Flora."

There was a cool breeze and a neigh.

Frank stood in the open door, his upper lip curled like a mule's, his needle-gun in his hand. He came in and closed the door, crossing to the black box. "I thought so."

"You're so fucking high-minded." Jerry climbed over Flora and sat on the edge of the bed, pulling on his underpants and socks. "You can't destroy that machine without risking the whole bloody universe going wild."

"Isn't that what you want?"

"Moderation in all things, Frank."

"You're a traitor, Captain Hargreaves. Consider yourself under arrest."

Flora shrugged and pushed the bedclothes back with her feet.

Jerry crossed to the chair and picked up his shirt, pulling it over his head. "Well, Frank, I think a certain equilibrium's been achieved, don't you?"

"You can talk of equilibrium with this—" Frank kicked at the black box— "in existence. This chaos machine."

"Oh, come now, Frank. We're not even sure if it has an entropic effect or not. It's an experimental model. That's how I came to lose it in the first place—I created the field and then couldn't find the machine in it." Jerry laughed. "Ironic, eh? I've got to test it. Find out exactly what it does do."

"At the expense of society."

"Well, that's how you see it."

Jerry put on his other clothes and buckled his Sam Browne belt. "That's better. You're always catching me with my pants down."

"It used to be nice. But you know what happened the last time. What has this machine to do with Catherine?"

"Work it out. It's the creation of all possible worlds. It can channel energy—re-divert it—re-form it . . ."

"Bloody romantic," said Frank.

"Who's Catherine?" said Flora.

"My aunt . . ."

"Our sister," said Frank.

"Have it your way." Jerry licked his lips. "Still, this has nothing much to do with the current situation."

"What is your relationship?" Flora frowned.

"It's become a little ambiguous of late," Jerry told her. Frank had swung the needle-gun into line with his heart. "I suppose it boils down to a matter of identification, in the long run."

"Identity!"

Frank snarled and squeezed the trigger as Jerry dropped behind the chair and drew his vibragun.

"If either of us hits that machine," said Jerry, "we might find out a lot about identity."

Frank hesitated then lowered his gun. "All right, Jerry. Let's talk like rational men."

"I'm not sure how it's done."

Flora Hargreaves rose suddenly and threw the bed-clothes over Frank's head. Jerry jumped out and thumped his relative on the back of his neck with the barrel of the vibragun. He fell down heavily. Jerry took the needle-gun out of the tangle of sheets and handed it to Flora. "He couldn't bear it if you shot him."

"Why?"

"Oh, well. It's all a matter of ritual, you see." Jerry uncovered Frank whose face had aged. He began to shiver, rubbing nervously at his arms, passing his hands over his head.

"I'm losing heat, Jerry. I'm losing heat, Jerry. I'm losing heat, Jerry."

"And dynamic, I suppose." Jerry pushed at Frank's chest with his vibragun. "Move along there, Frank. Can you manage the box, Flora?"

"I'll have to get some clothes on first. And pack."

"Wear your uniform. Pack your dresses. Okay?"

"Okay."

Flora quickly got ready and lifted the heavy box. Jerry pushed the cringing Frank forward. "We'll make for my convertible. We'll take you along with us, Frank. This environment isn't doing you any good at all."

They descended the stairs, then descended the steps that led them into the square. Marines still stood about in the sun, taking a well-deserved rest from the dirty business of war. Jerry hid his vibragun with his cloak and the three of them walked slowly to the car. Flora got in the back with the box. Frank sat beside Jerry as he started the Phantom VI up.

"Where are we going?" Flora asked.

"Our first duty is to get Frank into a rest home. It's not far from here. A couple of hours drive. I think he'll last until then."

Flora sniffed. "You think so?"

"He is beginning to niff a bit, I must admit."

Saturation

Female Auto-Erotic Practices

Out of print for years. By Havelock Ellis, M.D., world's most famous sexologist. New illustrated edition.

Subjects include: initiation; auto-erotic practices with males; masturbation as the cause and cure of frustrations in marriage, various technic employed (both clitoral and vaginal); objects used for vaginal and urethral masturbation.

The use of artificial penes; mutual masturbation (both homosexual and heterosexual); psychological factors; fantasies, erotic dreams; incestuous masturbation (between brother/sister, uncle/niece, father/daughter as well as a case of initation involving mother and son).

Auto-eroticism among dis-satisfied wives, girlhood experiments (with both sexes); initiations of boys by older women, nurses, etc.; club contests; public masturbation; breast stimulation; modern concepts of masturbation; primitive concepts; etc.

Illustrations include: artificial penes (both single-ended and double-ended for lesbian activities); other masturbatory devices; auto-erotic humor; auto-erotic symbols; childhood postures as well as women depicted in various auto-erotic attitudes. $3.00.

Futura Books ad, *TV & Movie Play*

1. BIZARRE FATHERHOOD TRAP
   EXPOSED!

When Jerry, Flora and Frank arrived at Sunnydale Reclamation Centre, Matron greeted them with some eagerness.

"You've done the place up nicely." Jerry gave the rebuilt centre the once-over as they stood in the drive by the car.

"What with all the emergency cases coming in during recent months, Mr. Cornelius, we had to work quickly. Och, we've been that understaffed! Working with no proper instructions from administration . . . There's no much left of your wee mansion, o'course."

"We have to cannibalise where necessary." Jerry glanced sadly at Flora and past her to where he saw the shell of his little Dutch mansion.

"It's a shame," said Flora.

"And what's yon wee chappy so upset aboot?" Matron looked professionally at the crumpled figure of Frank who sat in the front seat covering his face with his thin hands and mewling to himself.

"Another emergency, I'm afraid, Matron. A special case . . ."

"Aye. That's what they all say."

"Could you put him in a blank tank right away?"

"Is it wise, Mr. Cornelius?"

"It's urgent."

"A rather crude . . ."

"Don't worry. He's a rather crude patient."

"If you say so, sir. I'll get a couple of the lads tae take him in." Matron went back through the main door and reemerged with two assistants who picked Frank up and bore him, tightly foetal now, off.

Koutrouboussis, in an elegant blue mohair lounge suit with matching shirt and tie, his face and hands bandaged, came out of the door after Matron had gone in. He glanced sourly at Jerry. "Having fun?"

"Can't complain. You appear to have left London in a hurry. How are Maureen and Barbara?"

"They were bubbled up," Koutrouboussis said thoughtfully.

"Ah. This is Captain Hargreaves. Captain Hargreaves, this is Spiro Koutrouboussis. He's a member of my organisation."

"You run an organisation?" Flora raised her eyebrows.

"Six of one, half a dozen of the other."

"How do you do?" Koutrouboussis gave a tiny, stiff bow, winced with pain and seemed to have difficulty turning his eyes on Jerry again. "Did you get the machine?"

"Flora had it. It's in the back of the car."

"So we can begin work. About bloody time. I'm sick to death of my particular role. I need a break."

"We could all benefit from a change."

"Can we get down to the lab now?"

"You can if you like. I'm a bit anxious about the inner man." Jerry looked enquiringly at Flora. "Could you do with a bite?"

She laughed. "You know I could!"

Jerry escorted her into the cool, sweet-smelling interior of the reclamation centre.

2. DOCTORS PROVE SEX GUILTS MAKE YOU IMPOTENT!

Jerry walked between the rows of blank tanks in the long, hushed ward.

Each tank had its indicators, its curled, black figure, its tube running from the head to the surface to the connections along the edges. He studied the coded plates on the base of each tank and eventually found Frank. He was hanging in the exact centre of his tank. Nothing moved. Every dial registered zero.

Jerry turned to the engineer who walked slowly down the other side of the aisle checking readings against sheets on a clipboard.

"Number 30005. Any anticipation yet?"

The engineer shrugged.

"Too early."

Jerry licked his lower lip.

"Fair enough."

3. THE NYMPHO COSSACK QUEEN OF THE BLOODY STEPPES

Catherine, in all her sweetness, stared at him through the darkness of the room and he sat up in the bed, his hand clawing into Flora's right breast so that she screamed and Catherine disappeared and Jerry slapped her mouth and punched her stomach and shrieked and ran from the room, and staggered through the galleries until he came back to the blank tank ward and reached Frank and smashed at the glass with his fists so his hands streamed with blood and the fluid from the tank bathed them.

Frank sank.

4. I TRAINED THE NUDE GIRL BOXERS OF BANGKOK

Naked, Jerry went back to the bedroom and gathered up his gun while Flora wept.

"It's not your fault," he said. "But it's terror time, I'm afraid."

5. SWAMP LUST!

Jerry crossed to the lab wing, holding his gun tight against his thigh. There were lights. He opened the door. Koutrouboussis looked up red-eyed.

"You may be black," he said, "but you look juicy to me."

"Any results?" asked Jerry.

"We needed you. You were fucking about."

"Well, I'm not fucking about now." Jerry tied his gun by its trigger guard to a lock of his hair so that the weapon rested against his neck.

The black box stood on the bench. A score of fine leads ran from it and were connected to other instruments. Jerry pulled them out.

"You won't need those. It's to do with instinct, you see." He flexed his fingers.

"There's more than one way of skinning a cat," said Koutrouboussis mildly.

6. JUST FOUND: $10,000,000 IN PIRATE TREASURE! MILLIONS STILL UNTOUCHED!

"That ought to do it." Jerry straightened up and closed the lid of the box. "Ready to go, Mr. Koutrouboussis."

"Glad to hear it."

There was a wet sound behind them. Flora Hargreaves supported a bleary Frank who had his needle-gun in his hand.

"You look nice in rubber," Jerry said, "but it's all that's holding you together."

Frank groaned. "I've a moral duty to perform, you filth."

Jerry tilted his head so that his gun swung onto his shoulder. Frank steadied his hand.

"Why are you involving yourself in this, Flora?" Jerry folded his arms across his chest.

"I give back what I get, you bastard."

"Then you'd better give me Frank." Jerry laughed. "You know very well what will happen if you hit the box, Frank."

"Well—Jerry—I don't—have to—take the—risk . . . " Frank drooled.

"I suppose not."

"You're the only—one—who knows which—button—to press . . ."

"Well. Mr. Koutrouboussis . . ."

Koutrouboussis screamed as Frank's gun moved and the needle hit him in the knee.

"Good," said Frank thickly. "It's . . ." He squeezed the trigger again but Jerry was sliding across the floor and taking cover behind a rustling hallucimat, untangling the vibragun from his hair and brushing the cobwebs from his nose just as the door opened again and Bishop Beesley and Mitzi, closely followed by a man wearing the red robes of a Roman Catholic cardinal, entered the room. They all wore crossed bandoliers of bullets and carried Italian Mausers. Mitzi took Frank's needle-gun away from him and darted a disgusted look at Flora who was nursing her injured breast.

"By the way, Mr. Cornelius," said Bishop Beesley as he frisked Frank for pleasure. "You'll be happy to know we've taken Karen into the fold again, poor thing."

"How is she?"

Beesley shook his head. "She's not the woman you remember, I'm afraid. Is that the box? Would you mind, cardinal?"

The cardinal hung his gun over his shoulder and lifted the box in his arms.

Mitzi glanced at Flora, then at Jerry, and with a gesture of compassion plugged Frank in the heart. Frank slapped down on the floor.

"Just a minute!" Jerry was offended. "That was my bloody brother!"

"He was going to kill you, Herr Cornelius."

"Still, it's my job." Jerry stayed behind the hallucimat, his vibragun raised. "You'd better put that box down, Cardinal."

The cardinal turned his swarthy, questioning features in Bishop Beesley's direction.

"Oh, Mr. Cornelius knows his weapon would seriously upset his machine's mechanism." Beesley lowered his rifle. "It's not our intention to destroy either you or your invention, Mr. Cornelius, as you well know. We intend to save both—for everybody's benefit. We have a great deal of work to undo yet, haven't we?"

Jerry sighed.

"I've got a good mind to . . ."

"Of course you have. You're so impulsive."

"You couldn't operate it."

"Perhaps not."

"Oh, take the fucker."

Mitzi looked at the needle-gun. Then she frowned at Flora and, by way of an experiment, stitched a line of slivers across Flora's throat.

As the blood sprang out, Flora put her hand up, then let it fall again, then toppled backwards. Mitzi laughed and shot Koutrouboussis while she was at it.

"Do you believe in premonitions?" Jerry asked as they left.

"It depends on the source, Mr. Cornelius." Bishop Beesley rummaged in his pocket and found a large piece of walnut fudge. "We'll be seeing you soon, I hope."

4.

FINAL OPERATION

Guilt and fear are amongst the most
soul-destroying, fatal and disintegrating
emotions and experiences that come to
man. Guilt because of wrong doing,
unconfessed, unrepented of, and uncleansed
causes havoc and must be got rid of by
Jesus alone. Psychiatrists have their couches
to handle this, but they are helpless for
only Jesus can meet this need. Did you
know that it has now been revealed that
there are more psychiatrists that commit
suicide than any other profession, so it is
obvious they do not have the answer. Jesus,
alone, upon full, whole-hearted, and honest
confession, is able to deal with a guilt
complex and cleanse and deliver utterly.

Len J. Jones, *The Evidence*, December 1967

Radiation Treatment

End result: CANCER OF THE CERVIX

The March issue of *McCalls* reports that "Cancer of the cervix seems to be linked with the early loss of virginity and promiscuity on the part of young girls, according to three recent reports . . . patients with cervical cancer . . . had a greater number of sexual partners than comparable women who did not develop cancer . . . Monogamy in sex appeared to reduce the risk of cancer."

Newsweek (October 21, 1968) reports that: "Researchers have long suspected that cancer of the cervix, which afflicts some 40,000 women per year, is a venereal disease . . . most common among promiscuous women."

. . . "Enlightened modernists," cry for more sexual freedoms to undo the repressive sexual inhibitions of society and make people better off. How could these self-impressed, lawless intellectuals explain the fact that the large majority of students who need psychiatric help *have already experienced this sexual freedom?*

They simply IGNORE these facts. They rant about sexual permissiveness and sexual looseness. Proof? They don't need it. Satisfy the animal lusts of the people and they will all flock to your side.

The PLAIN TRUTH, January 1969

1. COME AWAY MELINDA

Jerry didn't mind the bombs as much as the rock scene. He wouldn't care what they sent so long as it wasn't Simon and Garfunkel.

It was like something out of 1962.

He switched off the radio.

Time to turn the lamp on bright.

2. YOU'RE EASY TO LOVE

A killing scene from now on. You couldn't stay smooth forever.

He began to assemble his gun again, ignoring Matron's panicky knock on the door.

He picked a scarlet shirt with a huge rolled button down collar and frilly cuffs, scarlet velvet bell-bottoms, crimson suede boots, vermilion frock coat, scarlet cord cap. He combed his milk-white hair and crooned a tune to himself, clipped on his yellow chamois shoulder holster and stepped out into the soft night and his smooth car.

As he drove, he considered the stars. It would all be over in a flash.

3. SISTERS OF MERCY

Somewhere a clock had stopped.

Jerry checked his watches.

They were running slow, but they were running.

He checked the car clock. It ticked painfully on.

Overwhelmed by a sense of urgency Jerry took the car up to a hundred and fifty. As it flew towards the dawn, he sighted Oxford's dreaming dome.

The day brightened. The sun appeared. Jerry glared at it with tears in his eyes. His heart beat rapidly, but he was filled with a growing stillness.

Was it too late?"

Was Beesley's shit hitting the fan?

He roared into the concrete cavern and drove past the gloomy spires, squealing to a stop outside the Ashmolean, charging through its doors and running down the dark avenue of slurring longcase clocks.

4. TIP FOR THE TOP

The morgue was colder than ever.

He opened the drawer and saw that a thin veil of ice had formed over Catherine's body.

He pressed his hands to her breasts and forced his heat into her.

This time she did not stir, but the ice gradually evaporated, then reformed on his body. Feebly he brushed at it, leaned on the drawer until it was closed, stumbled from the morgue to the room where the red, gold and silver machine took him into its webs.

The machine's voice was faint, its rustling sluggish, and it was a very long time before Jerry revived enough to hear the clock within him begin to move again.

Jerry Cornelius ran across the hall and into another steel room that contained nothing but a huge tape deck. He activated the deck and the twenty inch spools slowly started to revolve.

He twisted the volume control up to full; gave it maximum bass and treble response.

The Deep Fix began to play *That's My Baby*. The old strobes went bravely at it. The wall drifted apart.

Jerry entered the Shifter, nervous as a cat.

5. THAT'S NO WAY TO SAY GOODBYE

Sweet Orb Mace appeared for a moment. She looked sad.

Jerry dashed through the Shifter.

Scenes took a long time and a long time to go. The jewelled air was pretty dull breathing.

Jerry saw himself sixteen times—black, white, male, female—and he was dead.

He raced across the flat, grey, infinite plain, his gun in his hand, sniffing the frigid wind.

There was no doubt that Beesley was operating the machine, had somehow managed to put it into reverse. Though it would mean the same thing in the end, Ragnarok Day was being put back and it didn't suit him. It had to be this Cycle or nothing.

He wheeled and the air was cold brass.

Bishop Beesley stood beside a contraption. At its centre were the belching boiler and the frantically moving pistons and cogs of an ancient red and black steam engine. A system of clockworks had been erected on top of the engine and from a large axle at the top ran a series of iron rods of different lengths and at different angles. At the ends of the rods were pewter balls of different sizes painted in bright primary colours. Jangling calliope music came from the box that had been geared up at the side of the steam engine. It hurt Jerry's ears as the rods turned, creaked and jerked to the calliope's rhythm.

Bishop Beesley beamed.

"My own invention, Mr. Cornelius! You see, you

are not the only one capable of building a sophisticated machine. This is the Beesley Steam Driven Cal-
liopic Orrey! BEHOLD—THE RHYTHM OF THE
SPHERES!"

Jerry ran at the machine and was hurled back by Pluto
striking him on the side of the jaw. He raised his gun.

But the balls whirled faster and faster and the music
shrilled and the steam engine bounced and bellowed.
Bishop Beesley waved his pale hands.

"You've thrown it out of control, you assassin!"

Beesley tried to crawl under the whizzing balls to reach
the controls. Jerry lowered his gun.

The balls began to shoot off in all directions. The
steam engine screamed. Neptune narrowly missed Jerry's
head.

"You have thrown it into chaos!" wailed Beesley.

The steam engine exploded.

Jerry was hurled into a field of lilies where a herd of giant antelopes grazed. He got up and kept on running, dodging into Fleet Street's horse-drawn traffic, weaving through the shallows of a tropical river and avoiding mangrove roots and alligators, loping into Wencslaslas Square as Russian tanks burned, and side-stepping into Regents Park Zoo by the Elephant Enclosure.

The elephants were dead, their skins blistered by napalm.

Jerry knew he was home.

The risk was paid off.

6. BRIGHTEN YOUR NIGHT WITH MY DAY

Some sectors had been overlooked.

Little monuments of trees, grass and buildings, undamaged by the bombing, stood out against the ash-covered rubble of London.

Jerry recognised a block of flats at Bow, several streets near Hampstead Heath, the public baths and the ABC Cinema at Bayswater, some half-timbered shops where Holborn had run, the British Museum, the Hilton Hotel in Park Lane.

At least a few tourist attractions remained.

Over near the canal eight gulls wheeled in the white sky. Jerry left the zoo and began to tramp across the park, his boots sinking several inches in the fine ash.

Beesley had almost certainly returned to London, but it was anyone's guess where he had set up his headquarters.

Time (in the local sense) was running down at an alarming rate. Beesley was obviously trying to slow the Cycle in order to preserve the present situation and, if possible, return to an earlier phase.

It was so bloody short-sighted.

Also it would be disastrous so far as Catherine were concerned. At least his identity was preserved, up to a point. It was his only advantage.

On the other side of a hedge which had been completely stripped of foliage was a neatly parked mini-hover with British markings.

He resheathed his gun to protect it from the ash and vaulted the hedge.

He opened the minihover's cabin door and climbed

in. The thing shifted under his weight. It was armed with two eight inch Banning cannon in Hamilton brackets. The cannon seemed to be low on charges.

The motor started slowly. Jerry rose a few inches in a huge cloud of ash and tilted the joystick forward, heading to where Edgware Road used to be.

Check Temperature

1. WHAT'S WRONG WITH U.S. MEDICINE

The armoured minihover coughed out of the ash and rode smoothly across the stretch of smooth green crystal. The crystal was what the West End had come to. It wasn't the sort of fusion Jerry liked to see.

As he reached the site of Regent Street, he saw an ash-cloud approaching on his left. He guided the minihover into a shallow basin in the crystal and watched. He recognised the jeeps and armoured cars. The Americans were coming back at a lick.

Jerry put the hover's periscope up and adjusted the magnification.

General Ulysses Washington Cumberland stood in the lead jeep, a flame-thrower pack on his back, the nozzle in his right hand. His left hand clutched the windshield, he wore dark combat goggles and his clothes were whipped by the wind. The cap on the general's head bore the legend *C-in-C Europe* and he wore a green, fringed shawl around his shoulders, a long yellow dress with a tight bodice and red buttons, a huge green sash, puffed sleeves, gored skirts and flounces everywhere. The skirt was flared by at least six starched white petticoats and there was a pair of blue tennis shoes on his feet.

Behind General Cumberland the jeeps and cars were filled with fine-featured marines in full battle-kit, here to seek and destroy resistance not cleared out by the bombing.

General Cumberland set an example with his flame thrower.

It flared at every possible hiding place.

Jerry shivered. There were signs of snow in the sky. He decided to move on.

As he started the motor he heard Cumberland's voice through his amplifiers.

"They're all queer! Queer! Queer! Queer! Burn 'em out! Out! Out! Out!"

When Jerry reached a higher point on the crystal plain he saw Cumberland leap from his jeep and lead the marines after him.

The flame thrower shrieked again, but Jerry was out of range.

Hesitantly some of the marines raised their weapons.

"Sissies! Pansies! Asslickers!" roared the general. He turned, spraying the soldiers with his flame thrower.

"Mother lovers! Mother lovers! You sons of bitches!" he sobbed. In a flurry of frilly underclothes he collapsed on a slab of concrete. There was a WHOOMF, a scream of pure ecstasy, and he went up in a roaring fireball.

At least he died happy, thought Jerry.

The smoke cleared behind him and he saw that the majority of the marines had fried. The rest were trying to put out their burning clothes or their burning vehicles, but then there were a few more explosions and they were finished off.

Jerry admired their energy.

2. DAMNED VIRGINS IN THE DEVIL'S LAIR

The minihover ran out of power sooner than Jerry had expected.

Near the ABC Cinema, Bayswater, he tramped to where an old Riley was parked. As he opened the door a woman with a pale, haggard face looked up at him from the driving seat.

"Can I drop you anywhere, Herr Cornelius?"

"You're still fond of green and purple, I see."

"It's really all I have left."

Jerry put his right boot on the nearside wing and began to brush off what remained of the ash. "Did Beesley send you?"

"I escaped from Beesley."

"How did you come to leave Amerika?"

"I couldn't stay on top of the job. A general lassitude, I suppose. Maybe I needed you, Jerry. So little new blood. I've become extraordinarily anaemic in recent months. Beesley found me and we flew back to England a few—a few . . ."

"Days?"

"Ago."

"You've changed."

"You haven't."

"I should hope not. It's been tough, though. Did Beesley set you up from the beginning?"

"Yes. But I fell in love . . ."

"Like a junkie with his dope."

"You weren't the dope I took you for."

"It's a shame, I know."

She licked her lips. "Can I drop you anywhere?" There was a smell about her and it reminded Jerry of Frank.

"I don't think so."

"Jerry—I need you more than you need me."

"I know that."

"I haven't been happy."

"I can believe that."

"Just a little, Jerry, understanding . . ."

"Too late."

"Mercy."

"Sorry, belle . . ."

She started the engine of the Riley. "What were you trying to do with the stars?"

"Just hoping to get everything over with quickly. Ragnarok, of sorts."

"You are fond of Wagner? I, too, am . . . Well, maybe not so fond. The end of the world. Is that why you were making all those converts? To take them over with you?"

"Something like that."

"But the world isn't going to end. My husband's seen to that, hasn't he?"

"He's making a good try."

"Why do you want the world to end?"

"It's not as simple as that. I've got a kid sister, you see. I want to give her a better break than I had. A niece, I mean."

"You're mixed up."

"Not as much as you, Karen."

He drew his vibragun. She put her foot on the accelerator. "Your brake's still on." The car bounced. Jerry pointed the gun and she shook so much she was soon indistinguishable from the ash. He hooked the green and purple clothes out of the seat with his boot. Poor woman. He didn't know where she'd found the energy in the first place.

In the end he had, after all, been merciful. He holstered the vibragun and got into her seat. It was very cold.

He didn't feel much warmer himself. The engine was hard to get started again. The motor wouldn't turn. He pumped in more fuel, and it sparked at last.

Through the grey day, through the ruins, he let the car roll straight down the obsidian length of Westbourne Grove.

He had a feeling Beesley was in this area. The bishop had probably sent Karen von Krupp to find him.

He reached the rubble of Ladbroke Grove and the car could move no further. He got out and began to climb over the concrete, between the fronds of twisted wire that had once reinforced it.

He reached the place where the convent had stood and clambered to the highest slab to sniff the scene.

Holland Park was visible. It stood intact on a rise to the south west, its trees ghostly gold and green. Jerry considered it.

A few minutes later, he unsheathed his vibragun from its chamois holster, turned, and, resting the gun on his bent left arm, sighted on a patch of rubble close to the centre of the demolished convent.

The rubble began to quiver and shiver. Then there was nothing left at all but a cloud of dust. Jerry stepped forward and looked into the smooth clearing.

The steel trapdoor was still there. It shone as if burnished. He kneeled on it, pressed his palm against it and murmured a couple of words. The door hissed and took him down twenty feet. He got off and looked up the shaft at the sky. He could see the sun. It had hardly moved.

The steel door ascended and shut off the light.

Jerry depressed a switch. A little illumination flickered for an instant around the room and then died. He moved cautiously through the darkness towards one wall, felt for a shelf above his head and found what he was hoping to find, took out his lighter and by its flame managed to ignite the wick.

He saw that the paraffin was low. He hoped it would last.

The lamp was of blue glass, decorated with gold and scarlet flowers. It cast shadows around a room full of dusty, alchemical equipment; part of an earlier era. Jerry crossed to a wooden door and pulled it open.

It creaked.

He entered a tunnel and the light shone on the semi-luminous white coats of half-dead rats. As he pushed his feet through them, they barely moved.

The tunnel was damp and cold and still. By the light of the lamp he saw that his own hands had gone a pale golden colour. He needed sustenance. Beesley must have increased the machine's power. He trod on a rat and it squeaked faintly.

After half a mile the tunnel began to slope upwards until it ended at another steel door. He pressed his hand on it. It didn't move. He murmured the words. The door stayed shut.

With a sigh, Jerry took out his vibragun. His bones ached.

It took much longer than usual for the gun to disintegrate the steel. Gradually daylight filtered in and there was a hole large enough for Jerry to crawl through. He was in Holland Park, close to the Belvedere Restaurant which had once been part of Holland House and had included the orangery.

He had left in the afternoon. Now it was morning. Did Beesley realise how senseless his plan was? A big waste of power.

He thought of Catherine and began to run.

3. SO YOU WANT TO BE A ROCK AND ROLL STAR?

As he reached the Elizabethan façade of Holland House, Jerry paused and looked up.

The American jets were dancing in the frozen sky. For several minutes they performed complicated formations then regrouped into conventional flights and flew away from London towards the Atlantic. Either they had been recalled or events had got on top of them.

With mixed feelings Jerry watched them leave.

He was on his own now.

Pushing open the mansion's heavy doors he entered a large, gloomy hall. A Shifter gateway had once been here, but he knew it must have dispersed by now. Beesley had buggered the phasing completely.

He drew his gun and started up the Tudor staircase.

Mitzi was waiting, unarmed, at the top. She wore an ankle-length dress in Regency stripes of dark and light pink. There were pink slippers on her feet and her blonde hair was combed to frame her face. Her large blue eyes regarded him.

"Herr Cornelius. You are not looking well."

"I'm as well as could be expected." He motioned with the vibragun. "Is Beesley here?"

"My father? Yes. He's waiting for you. He thinks you're probably ready to join us at last."

She smiled and Jerry saw that her teeth seemed to have grown to points, like a fox's. "It will soon be summer again, and we can be together . . ." She turned, walking back along the landing. "This way."

Jerry hesitated.

"What's the matter?" She paused by the door of the main bedroom.

"Death." His nostrils quivered. "A lot of death."

"There's nothing wrong with death. Nothing to be afraid of. A sleep . . ."

"It depends on the kind." He gripped the gun desperately.

"Don't you like the idea of life after death?"

"It depends on the kind."

"Herr Cornelius, you have no *trust*." Her eyes widened with sympathy. "You are so wild."

"I . . ." He felt very tired.

"You are a fierce beast."

"No . . ."

"You must be more tame. In time."

"I want . . ." He gasped as the tears flooded from his face. "I want . . ."

"Peace. We want nothing more."

"Peace?"

He rocked on his heels. His grip was still tight on his gun, though all his energy seemed concentrated in his right hand.

She came towards him. He tried to raise his gun. She stretched out her palm. He shook his head.

"Don't you want to rest? We can help you rest."

"Not that kind."

She frowned, her eyes concerned. "Why do you split hairs so? Does it matter about the kind?"

"Yes."

"We all grow older, you know. More mature."

"No."

"Love," said Mitzi. "Do you love nothing but your Cause? It is hopeless, you know."

"Love." The tears chilled his cheeks. He trembled as he thought of Oxford and Catherine and the Science of Innocence.

"You know," Mitzi murmured, "that what you have done is wrong. But we forgive you."

He snarled and laughed through his teeth. The energy left his right hand and blazed from his eyes. "I am Jerry Cornelius." The gun dropped. He bent but she swept forward and kicked the gun through the banisters and he watched it fall slowly to the floor of the hall below.

"It's a turning world, darling." Mitzi helped him straighten up, wincing as she saw his eyes. "There are many kinds of beauty."

Jerry staggered back from her with a growl.

The cardinal came out of the master bedroom. "Misericordia! The poor chap looks completely beaten. He needs help."

Jerry tried to descend the stairs. It was dawn outside. He gasped as the cardinal seized him around the waist.

"Could you bring him in here, please, Cardinal Orelli." Mitzi's voice was vibrant with sympathy. "He'll soon feel a new man."

Jerry shut everything down.

He let them get on with it.

Pulse Check

1. ONE TOO MANY MORNINGS

He was awakened by a cold caress.

Mitzi's waxen hand was on his brow. He felt the heat leave his head and he tried to jerk away.

She removed her hand.

He lay on a hard mattress in a wide four-poster with grey curtains that were drawn back so that he could see Bishop Beesley standing by the Jacobean dresser and bending over the box which stored Jerry's machine.

Ash-coloured light came through the window. Jerry took stock of his reserves. They were low.

"Good—um—hello, there, Mr. Cornelius. I see my daughter's been looking after you. She's an angel. A ministering angel."

Jerry sat up. He was still dressed in his red suit and he was unbound. He frowned suspiciously at Mitzi.

"I'm sick," he said, "of . . ."

"Cancer?" said Mitzi.

"Crabs."

"It's a complicated state of affairs, I'm afraid," said the bishop, chewing a Crunchie bar. The artificial honeycomb coursed down his chins. "I've got so far, but I now need your help. I want to find out where the rest of your 'converts' are, for a start. Some are hanging on, you know, against all common sense."

"I promised them nothing less than the Millennium." Jerry drew a sluggish breath. "What do you expect?"

"I'm afraid we'll have to put back the Millennium for a while." Beesley smacked his lips. "I know it's disappointing. They were all prepared for it, weren't they? Well, that's over. If you can help me locate them, I'll

get in touch with them and arrange a deconversion. Could
I say fairer?"

Jerry took a lock of his hair in his hand. It was stringy
and off-white. He sniffed.

"You knew the apolcalypse wasn't due for several million years yet, Mr. Cornelius," Bishop Beesley continued,
"and yet you wished to bring it about for purely selfish
reasons. Reasons, I regret, that I simply fail to understand. It may be all right for you—but consider your
dupes!"

"What do you think my crash programme was for?"
Jerry glanced out of the window. A wind was blowing
the ash northward.

"You can't save the whole human race, Mr. Cornelius. Besides, I insist that your motives were still suspect,
let alone your goals!"

Jerry got off the bed and walked weakly to the box
but Mitzi barred his way, looking questioningly at her
father. Bishop Beesley shrugged. "We've reached something of an impasse, I'm afraid. The power seems to be
weakening."

"You can say that again." Jerry smiled. "What else
did you expect?"

Bishop Beesley cast down his eyes in embarrassment
and unwrapped a toffee. "I never claimed to be a scientist, Mr. Cornelius."

"Naturally." Jerry stroked the box. "You'll have to
find a power source, won't you? Whether transmission of
any kind's possible now, I just don't know. Things are
fixed, Bishop Beesley. They are solid."

"The sun hasn't moved for an—for some t—" Mitzi
gave up. "It isn't moving."

"That's merely an indication," Jerry said. "An image,
if you like."

"What sort of power does the machine take?" Beesley
asked, chewing. "Electricity?"

Jerry laughed as best he could. "I'm afraid not. It
runs on primitive energy. It's all very basic, when you
get down to it."

"Where do we get this energy?"

"Is Cardinal Orelli still on the premises?"

"I think he went to the lavatory."

"Never mind. Ask him in when he's finished, will you?"

"Herr Cornelius," Mitzi whispered, "you must explain to us everything. You must not make mysteries. It is a time for frankness. You will admit that you have no choice now."

"Frankness." Jerry drew a deep breath. "You said it. Bring Cardinal Orelli in as soon as you can. I'm very tired. Time's slipping by."

"I think I heard him on the landing." Bishop Beesley opened the door. "Ah, cardinal. Would you step in here a moment, please?"

Cardinal Orelli smiled at Jerry. "How are you, my son?"

"How do you feel, cardinal?" Jerry asked.

"Very well."

"Good." Jerry opened the lid of the box and moved a plate set in the bottom left corner. It was about four inches wide and six inches long and eight inches deep, lined with a rubbery substance. "Would you place your hands together, cardinal? Palm against palm."

The cardinal smiled and assumed a praying position.

"That's fine. Now put the hands into the slot there. Don't worry, it won't hurt you."

The cardinal glanced at the bishop who nodded. Mitzi's lips parted, her eyes shone. The cardinal dipped his hands into the slot up to the wrists, the box hummed briefly, the cardinal's lifeless body crumpled to the floor.

"It's fueled again," said Beesley, bending over the gauge. "Good heavens!"

"It won't last long," said Jerry. He turned a knob and gripped a metal bar positioned in the centre.

A shock raced through him and he felt a little sick, but he kicked Beesley in the crutch so that he fell back into Mitzi's arms, picked up the box and made for the door.

They yelled at him as he raced down the stairs, paused in the hall to recover his vibragun and dashed out into the grey day.

He was using up energy very quickly, in spite of everything. He stumbled down the steps, through the gates, out over the cricket pitch, his boots sinking in ash, and behind him came Bishop Beesley and Mitzi who had paused only to get their Remingtons.

In the middle of the cricket pitch he fell and the box flew from his arms. He choked on the ash.

He tried to get up but collapsed, rolled over on his back to get his vibragun out, but already Mitzi and Bishop Beesley were standing over him, their rifles pointing at his heart.

"We'll have to try to manage on our own now that we know how to keep the machine's strength up."

Apologetically, Bishop Beesley squeezed the trigger.

There was a pop and a slithering noise and a bullet fell out of the barrel. Mitzi pulled her trigger and the same thing happened. Her bullet fell in Jerry's lap. He felt a mild shock in his right ball.

Mitzi raised her head at the sound of barking. Bishop Beesley followed her gaze.

Coming across the ash, his head and body swathed in white furs, driving a sled pulled by a team of a dozen dogs, including two St. Bernards, a borzoi and three salukis, was a tall man armed with a steel bow and a quiver of alloy arrows. Close by he stopped the dogs and they flung themselves down panting. He fitted an arrow to his bow.

"I wonder if you'd let Mr. Cornelius rise?" said the man in the white fur.

They stepped back and Jerry got up, dusting ash off his suit.

The new arrival motioned with his bow. "What I'd like to know, bishop—I take it you are a bishop—is what you think you're accomplishing, fucking about with the sun and so forth," said the tall figure.

"I'm trying to put things right," Beesley said sullenly. "I'm a journalist by trade." He studied the other man's weapons, obviously attempting to decide if the bow and arrow were as ineffective as his rifle.

"A bow has more power, at short range, than an ordinary rifle," said the tall figure.

"How much more power?" asked Mitzi.

"Quite a bit."

Mitzi sucked at her lower lip.

Jerry went down on his knees beside the box and began to drag it through the grey dust towards the sled. It took him a while to load it aboard. "I hope I'm not overburdening you," he said to the newcomer.

"I'd allowed for the extra. They're good dogs."

"I suppose you haven't . . ."

"Do you want it now?"

"I think I'd better."

"Look under the skin nearest you."

Jerry pulled back the wolfskin and there was a little replica of one of his webs. He switched it on and it began to pipe. He buried his head in it. "That's more like it."

"It was the best I could do," said the man in the white furs.

Jerry straightened up.

The sun had started to move again.

2. I'M SO GLAD

The sled slid away across the cricket pitch.

Behind it Mitzi and Bishop Beesley sat slumped in the ash. Mitzi had pulled up her skirt and seemed to be inspecting her inner thigh. Her father was unwrapping a Milky Way.

"You seem very fit," Jerry said to his companion as the man whipped up the dogs.

"Fitter than ever." They gathered speed. "I took the opportunity of diverting some of the energy to myself while that chap was trying to do whatever it was he was trying to do."

"So that's what happened to it. I couldn't understand . . ."

"It turned out for the best, I think you'll agree."

"You can say that again."

"Where to now?"

"Oxford, I think."

"Okay. I suppose it was wise, was it, to leave that pair where they are?"

"Oh, I don't think they'll be much trouble now. Poor things—if we succeed, they'll hardly survive the transformation."

"Quite."

The runners scraped the ash and they rode in silence for a few miles until they reached the outskirts of London and the ash gave way to the asphalt of the M.40. The dogs were cut from their traces and lay down panting.

Captain Brunner pushed back his hood and pointed to an intersection and a hotel called *The Jolly Englishman* which stood beside a garage. "That's where I left the car."

Pulling the sled behind them, they made for *The Jolly Englishman,* followed by the pack of dogs.

Jerry checked his watches. They were ticking perfectly. He was relieved, though there were still a great many uncertainties. It was difficult to work out in his head just what side-effects Beesley's attempts had initiated.

A counter-revolution, after all, was a counter-revolution.

They carried the equipment to the big Duesenberg and stowed it down by the back seats. Captain Brunner got into the car and started the engine. Jerry sat beside him and slammed the door.

The dogs began to howl.

"Faithful buggers," said Captain Brunner. "But there's nothing else for it, I'm afraid." He turned the car onto the M.40 and drove towards Oxford.

"It does you good to get out of London occasionally," said Jerry as the evening sunlight touched the red leaves of the elms lining the road.

"Especially at this time of the year," agreed Captain Brunner.

"Have all the Americans gone home now?"

"I think so. Beesley's messing about didn't help matters, of course. A general panic over there, by the sound of it. Just as things were settling down nicely, too." Captain Brunner turned on the tape machine and got John, George, Paul and Ringo doing *She's Leaving Home.*

Jerry relaxed.

3. I DON'T LIVE TODAY

Captain Brunner pulled off his furs and stretched himself out on the yellow silks of the bed in the Oxford underground pied-à-terre.

"This is a bit more like it. Hasn't changed much, has it?"

"Some things don't. Not very often, at any rate." Jerry poured two glasses of Pernod. "You're still fond of this, I hope."

Captain Brunner extended an arm that glowed with energy. "You can bet your life. Thanks." He sipped the Pernod. "I'm not particularly thirsty, of course, but it's nice just to taste."

"I know what you mean."

"Could I have a last look at Catherine, Jerry? Would you mind?"

Jerry felt a pang of jealousy. "Of course not."

They walked down the corridor together, entered the morgue, opened Catherine's drawer and looked down at her lovely face. "As beautiful as ever," murmured Captain Brunner. "It's been a long time."

Jerry patted his shoulder.

"I wish . . ." Captain Brunner turned away. "Still, I shouldn't be here at all. Maybe it wasn't wise . . ." He walked swiftly from the morgue, leaving Jerry to put the drawer back and close the door.

When Jerry returned to the room, Captain Brunner had taken off all his clothes and was sitting on the edge of the bed staring at the console and tapping his knees.

"Can we get it over with now?" said Captain Brunner.

Jerry lifted the box and put it between them. He slid

back the slot covering and with his red silk handkerchief he wiped it carefully. Then he stared straight into Captain Brunner's crimson eyes. "Cheerio. Thanks for everything."

"Cheerio, Jerry."

Brunner put his hands together and shoved them quickly into the slot. His lips parted over clenched teeth, his body began to sag, his complexion to dull, his hair to lose its lustre. He breathed more and more slowly until he stopped, but his hands still remained in the slot until his flesh shrank and his skin turned yellow and there was little more than a skeleton lying beside the machine.

Jerry picked the corpse up and carried it in one hand to the morgue, filing it in the spare drawer furthest from Catherine's. Then he went back and inspected the machine.

Brunner had been carrying a huge supply of energy

and the machine was charged to capacity, but the energy in itself wouldn't be enough to bring Catherine back for more than a few minutes. Much more energy had to be released and then channeled to give Catherine the few days of life Jerry wanted her to have.

It would require a massive build up and release of energy and this meant speeding up the time cycle (or what was left of it). Only those with their identities firmly established would survive the spin.

He felt lonely as he prepared the machine. But then he forgot his loneliness in his anticipation.

He brought Catherine in and laid her on the bed. He bolted the box to the bench he had assembled. He ran a thin pipe from the box to Catherine's throat and secured it with a piece of surgical tape.

He checked his instruments carefully.

Then he turned on.

Respiration Check

"Mind you, this is in Brisbane, well south in Queensland. Melbourne, 1200 miles further down, gets very variable weather and can get nippy days even in the middle of summer. Shocking place. Unreliable. But 1200 miles to the north, up past the Tropic of Capricorn, lies Cairns—beaches, palm trees, Great Barrier Reef, free coconuts, tropical paradise, the coming tourist Mecca of the Pacific. And still in Queensland, which is over 2½ times as big as Texas. How about that? And contains perhaps two million people—how about *that?* Away from the cities a man can often drive for miles and miles without sighting another human being. Smog? What smog? Color problem? What color problem? Population explosion? Jesus, you have to be kidding!"

Jack Wodhams, letter to *SFWA Bulletin*

1. THE STRANGER ON THE WHOLE ROAD

Jerry increased the power and checked that all dimensions could be phased in at the right moment. He synched Jimi Hendrix in. He began to sing *Third Stone from the Sun* very loudly. It was all part of the ritual; all part of the spell.

And it was a tense moment.

He twisted his head to look at Catherine, and set the pointer to Automatic.

Things began to hum.

Swiftly Jerry increased the entropy rate to maximum, preparing himself for the ensuing dissipation.

He began to feel dizzy as he gave the universe a whirl. For all the shielding in his lab, he wondered if he were safe after all. He blinked and could see the leaping cord that led to Catherine's throat, saw Catherine's body tremble.

He adjusted the identity stabilisers and locked in the coordinates. There was now a golden mist swirling everywhere and the box had become very hot.

When everything was on Full he fell backwards and onto and then through the bed and continued to fall.

He pulled himself together as best he could. It didn't matter about the extent of the dispersal so long as he kept everything in the right order. He began to flood through the universe and then through the multiverse, to the sounds of the Beatles singing *A Day in the Life*, throbbing in time to the cosmic pulse. Universe upon universe; dimension upon dimension; they spread out together and the extraneous energy released in the explosion poured into the box and into Catherine's body.

Faster and faster flew the particles and Jerry hung on. Framed against the spreading gases he saw other human shapes and he knew that some of the transmogs were managing to resist the conversion of the universe.

He looked about him and waited as *Helter Skelter* echoed through the infinite. It was quite a nice trip.

At last maximum diffusion was reached and everything became a little unreal. He felt a moment's concern before the switch clicked over, Jimi Hendrix started to play *Are You Experienced?*, and things began to come together again.

Soon he would know if the experiment had paid off.

2. A SWEET LITTLE SCHOONER

Jerry took a deep breath, opened his eyes and saw springs moving. He was under the bed. He rolled out and there was his machine steaming on the bench. Its circuits appeared to have fused. He activated the tv monitors and got the surface.

The towers of the Cathedral were white against the white sky. It was snowing. It was only to be expected. Otherwise Oxford looked pretty much as it had always looked.

With a sigh, he looked down at the bed. Catherine turned uncomfortably in her sleep, her long-fingered hands at her throat.

Jerry ripped off the surgical tape and threw the cord aside. "Catherine?"

She sniffed and moistened her lips. Then she woke up. "Jerry? Are you all right?"

"I think so. I had a bit of a turn a moment ago, but I'm fine now. How about you?"

"I thought I was dead."

"Strictly speaking you are. I managed to work out a way of getting you a few extra days—maybe a week or more—before you finally popped off. I've been experimenting for months."

"It was nice of you, Jerry."

"Frank's dead, by the way. He won't be bothering us."

"Oh, good. I was wondering about that." She got up. They were very much alike. "You've turned quite pale, Jerry."

"It's for the best, I suppose."

Operation Successful

Infant Stars

Each year two or three new stars are born within the Milky Way. They appear to condense out of dark globules of dust. Knowledge of how this happens would reveal much about the way galaxies—and the universe itself—were formed.

Science Journal, July 1968

1. THE OLFACTORY CODE

Apart from a tendency from time to time to imagine he heard various forms of audiosignals together with the voices of Karen von Krupp, of Bishop and Mitzi Beesley and of Frank, Jerry felt no ill effects. There was a touch of his old paramnesia, too, but, if anything, that was reassuring.

He and Catherine wandered hand in hand through Holland Park.

It was their last day together.

Jerry was wearing his green silk suit, red silk shirt and red boots. Catherine's outfit, with its full length skirt, matched his.

Holland Park was covered in snow. Long, glassy white icicles hung on the columns of the fountain and there was thick ice on the pond. The tropical evergreens sheltered the peacocks and guinea fowl while pigeons, sparrows, robins and blackbirds flew about looking for food. It was a peaceful day.

Over on the cricket pitch Catherine noticed two new statues. "I haven't seen those before."

As she led Jerry across the pitch they left black footprints in their wake.

They reached the statues.

Mitzi and Bishop Beesley had been transformed into the purest grey marble.

"Who are they, Jerry? There isn't a plaque."

"I'll get one fixed up. They're two people who achieved their hearts' desires. There's no looking back for them now. They look pretty permanent don't they?"

"They do indeed. So natural."

Jerry ran his hand over Bishop Beesley's marble paunch and stroked his marble Mars Bar. Affectionately he patted Mitzi's cool brow. "It's what they would have wanted."

In the middle-distance they saw the sharp outlines of Holland House. The light was very clear; the sky pure blue and the trees cast clean, black shadows on the white ground. They began to walk back, strolling past wooden benches piled high with snow, through the orangery, down the covered walk and stopping to look at the clock-tower that stood among the chimneys and the spires of the house.

"I feel very warm," said Catherine.

"You *are* very warm," said Jerry.

She lay down in the snowdrops and Jerry slowly took off her clothes and then his own. They made love for a long time until the snow had melted for several yards in all directions and the grass beneath was fresh and bright.

The sun got low and Catherine died again.

Jerry stood up shivering. He looked down at her with affection but without sorrow. He climbed into his own clothes and folded hers up and put them beside her.

Then he walked away from there, leaving her lying there, surrounded by the snow. It had all been worthwhile. He felt a new person.

There was still work to be done. He had to find the converts, set up a new organization, get back on the job.

And then there was the baby to consider. He could feel it stirring already.

Jerry left the park. He stood by the gates and looked across the vast plain of ice to where he could see his sled. He trudged towards it, breathing in the crisp air.

At his approach the eager dogs scrambled up panting. He assembled them in their positions, patted the head of the leader, a Great Dane, and shoved the sled so that its runners broke from the ice and it slid easily away, gathering speed.

He jumped in, cracked his whip, grinned at the sun as the wind rushed past. The dogs leaned in their traces.

"Mush," he said.

The English Assassin

A Romance of Entropy

Illustrated by Richard Glyn Jones
title page by Malcolm Dean

For Arthur and Max Moorcock

DEDICATED to the memories of Peregrine Worsthorne, Malcolm Muggeridge, Dennis Hopper, Shirley Temple, George Steiner, Angus Maude, Robert Conquest, Bernard Braden, Spiro Agnew, Christiaan Barnard, Norman St. John Stevas, Colin Wilson, Lord Longford, Rap Brown, John Wayne, Jerry Rubin, Chris Booker, Robert Heinlein, Sam Peckinpah, Miroslav Moc, Kingsley Amis, Sir Arthur Bryant, Richard Neville and all men of conscience and Jolly Englishmen everywhere.

The English Assassin is the third novel in a tetralogy about Jerry Cornelius and his times. The two previous books are *The Final Programme* and *A Cure for Cancer*. The last book will be called *The Condition of Muzak*.

Many of the newspaper quotations used here might cause further distress to parents and relatives of the deceased if they read them. Therefore I have in some cases changed the names. No other part of the quotation has been altered.

MICHAEL MOORCOCK

PROLOGUE (commencement)

As a child I lived in that well-kept back garden of London, the county of Surrey. In this century, at least, Surrey achieved vitality only once. That was during the World War when the incendiaries fell, and the Messerschmidts blew up, and the V-bombs dropped suddenly from the silent sky. Night flames, droning planes, banging ack-ack, shrapnel and bombed buildings are the happiest impressions from my childhood. I long to find them again. The pylon, the hoarding, the ruined street and the factory are images which to this day most satisfy and pacify my psyche. I was very happy then, while the world fought its war and my own parents quarrelled, suppressed quarrels and finally parted. The War was won, the Family lost, and I remained, as far as I knew, content. But now, with great effort, I recall the nightmares, rages, weeping fits and traumas, the schools which came and went, and I know that, after the war, I was only happy when alone and then chiefly when I was able to create a complicated fantasy or, in a book, enter someone else's. I was happy but, I suppose, I was not healthy. Few of my illnesses were not psychosomatic and I became fat. Poor child.

. . . I suspect that many people experience this nostalgia and would dearly love to recreate the horrifying circumstances of their own childhood. But this is not possible. At best they produce reasonable alternatives.

MAURICE LESCOQ. Leavetaking 1961

CONTENTS

**SHOT
ONE**

Addict Was Dead with Syringe in His Arm

A young North Kensington addict who had made an attempt to give up drugs was killed by his addiction, the Westminister Coroner decided last week. Anthony William Leroy (sometimes known as Anthony Gray) died at St. Charles Hospital in the early hours of August 29, after taking two shots of heroin in his arm when he was found, the coroner was told. Leroy was a boutique manager . . . Professor Donald Teare, pathologist, said that there were two recent injection marks on Leroy's right arm. Cause of death was inhalation of vomit due to drug addiction.

KENSINGTON POST, September 26 1969

A BUNDLE

South of Bude and its neighbour, Widemouth Bay, you come to the quaint little harbour of Boscastle, with its grey stone, slate roofed cottages and background of sheltering hills, and thence to Tintagel, home of the legendary King Arthur and the famous cliff-top ruins of his mediaeval castle. Although other counties in the West may dispute Cornwall's claim to be the sole possessor of the original authentic stronghold of the Knights of the Round Table, Cornishmen stick as closely to their time-honoured contention as the limpets to the rocky, sea-washed walls of Merlin's mysterious cave at the foot of the great granite cliff. It is the blood spilt by the magic sword Excalibur, they insist, that keeps a small lawn of turf within the precincts of the castle forever emerald green, as if constantly fed by spring water where none exists. And what else, they ask, was Camelot if it were not the old name for Camelford, the little inland town on the River Camel not half a day's horse-trot away?. .

CORNWALL: A TOURIST'S GUIDE

Some time ago, possibly in the winter of 1975, the following events took place at Tintagel Bay on the north coast of Cornwall:

Tintagel's bay is small and walled by high, bleak cliffs, a natural subject for romantic painters and poets of the past two centuries. Most of the castle ruins stand on the inland cliff, but some are on the west cliff, which is a narrow promontory now crumbling dramatically into the sea and carrying the ruins with it.

Though, in the summer, Tintagel is a great tourist

attraction, at other seasons it is virtually deserted, save for a few local inhabitants who remain in the village some distance inland. One dull December morning two of these residents, a butcher and a retired chemist, who had been born and brought up in the area, were taking their regular stroll along the cliffs when they paused, as usual, among the ruins and rested on a wooden bench provided for people like themselves who wished to enjoy the view of the bay in comfort.

The view on this particular day was not really up to much. The water in the bay was flat, sluggish and black. On its surface drifted grey scum and dark green weed. The sea resembled a worn-out blackboard upon which an inspired idiot had scrawled equations and then tried to erase them. The sky was clammy and the air was thick with too much brine. From the small patch of shingle on the beach below there came a strong and unpleasant odour of rotting seaweed. It was as if the whole place—castle, cliffs, sea and beach—were in a process of sudden decay. The butcher and the chemist were both old men, bearded and grey, but the butcher was tall and straight, while the chemist was small and bent. The wind tugged at their beards and hair as they huddled on the bench and massaged their legs and hands. Their skins were cracked, wrinkled, weather-beaten and, in colour and condition, very little different from the leather jerkins they wore to protect themselves against the weather. They chatted for about ten minutes and were ready to continue their walk when the tall butcher narrowed his eyes and pointed at the gap between the cliffs where the sea entered the bay.

"What d'you make of that, then?" he asked. He had one of those unfortunate voices which is naturally aggressive in tone and liable to misinterpretation by those who did not know him well.

The chemist frowned. He reached into his jerkin and found his spectacle case. He put the spectacles on and peered out over the water. A large, shapeless object floated in the bay. It was drifting with the tide towards the shore. It might have been the remains of a shark, covered in rotting algae; a tangle of dead eels, or just a mass of seaweed.

"It could be anything, really," said the chemist mildly.

They watched as the bundle drifted closer. It came to rest on the shingle below. It was vaguely cylindrical in shape but just a little too small to be any kind of wrecked boat. The weed which wrapped it seemed to have decayed.

"Bloody unsanitary looking, whatever it is," said the chemist. "The council should do something about this beach."

But the beach itself was unwilling to accept the bundle. The next wave that came in was forced to withdraw it. The bundle bobbed about twenty yards offshore: the sea wished to be rid of it, could think of nowhere else to deposit it, but refused to swallow it.

The chemist, a morbid man by nature, suggested that the object might be a corpse. It was the right size.

"What? You mean a drowned man?" The butcher smiled.

The chemist understood that his suggestion had been too sensational. "Or a seal, I thought," he said. "You don't know, do you? I've seen nothing like it before. Have you?"

The tall butcher hadn't any inclination to follow this line of thought. He got up; he rubbed his beard. "Well, she'll probably be gone by tomorrow. It's getting a bit nippy. Shall we—?"

The chemist took one last, frowning look at the bundle before he nodded agreement. They walked slowly inland, towards the almost deserted village.

After they had vanished, the tide began to turn. It hissed. It whispered. It sighed. As it receded, a lip of a cave was revealed in the west headland, a black gap flaked with foam. The sea pushed the bundle towards the cave; it forced the thing into the mouth which gurgled reluctantly, but swallowed. The tide fled, leaving behind it the weed-smothered beach, the salty stink, the foam-flecked entrance to the cave. The wind blew stronger, whining and moaning about the castle ruins like a dog at its master's grave, pawing a tuft of coarse grass here, sniffing a clump of shrubs there. And then the wind went away, too.

By now completely exposed to the air, the gloomy cavern contained a comprehensive collection of debris: rusty cans, pieces of drowned wood, glass shards worn smooth by the action of the ocean, plastic bottles, the torso of a child's doll, and the twisted corpses of about twenty deformed, oversized crabs; the creations of an effluent only recently introduced to this coast. On a shelf of rock about half-way up the slimy far wall, well out of the faint light from the entrance, lay the bundle where the sea had lodged it.

A gull flew in from the grey outside and perched on the bundle before fluttering down to peck at the soft shells and the hard flesh of the mutant crabs.

When the texture of the day had grown a little less disgusting, a cumbersome skiff, powered by an outboard motor imperfectly mounted in the stern so that its screw often lifted completely clear of the water and caused it to progress in a series of spluttering jolts, rounded Tintagel Head and made for the small patch of shingle leading up to the cave. There was only one person in the skiff. She wore yellow PVC oilskins, a yellow sou'wester and white plastic trousers tucked into red rubber seaboots. The sou'wester shaded her face. The tiller was tucked firmly under one arm as she directed the skiff at the beach. The engine coughed, screeched and spat. The bottom of the skiff rasped on the pebbles and the motor cut out. Awkwardly, the girl clambered from the stationary boat and pulled it completely clear of the sea; she sniffed the wind, then she reached over the side to remove a big blue Eveready flashlight, an old-fashioned gasmask and a coil of white nylon rope. She sniffed again, by way of confirmation, and seemed satisfied. She looped the rope over her shoulder and trudged in the direction of the cave. When she reached the entrance she hesitated, switching on her electric torch before going in. Her clean, protective clothing gleamed in the reflected glare. Her booted feet crunched on the corpses of the crabs; a beam of light illuminated the awful walls, disturbed the carrion gulls. They squawked and flapped nervously past her head to the open air. She directed the beam over all the filthy flotsam before focussing on the shelf of rock from which came a smell partly of brine and partly like cat's urine. She put the torch in her pocket and used both hands to ease the gasmask under her sou'wester and over her hair and face. Her breathing became a loud, rhythmic hiss. Adjusting the rope on her shoulder she again took out the flashlight and looked the bundle over. The thing was predominantly black and green and had resumed its earlier, roughly cylindrical, shape. There were small grey rocks imbedded in it, some yellow grit, a few supine starfish, seahorses and shrimps, a fair number of mussels and limpets and pieces of what looked like tropical coral. The black and green areas were unidentifiable; they were possibly organic; they might have been made of mud which had started to solidify. It was as if the bundle had been rolled along the bottoms of the deepest oceans, gathering to it a detritus which was completely alien to the surface.

The girl bent down and wedged the flashlight between two large stones so that the beam stayed on the shelf. Then she crossed to the wall and began to climb skillfully and rapidly until she stood with her legs spread wide, balancing carefully on the ledge beside the bundle while she pulled on a pair of rubber gloves. Steadying herself with her left hand against an outcrop of granite, she bent and felt over the bundle with her right hand. At last she found what she was looking for and withdrew it with a squelch from a tangle of weed.

It was a transparent polythene bag dripping with green algae. She wiped the plastic against her thigh until it was as clean as she could get it, then she held it in the torch's beam so that she could see the contents. There was a single sheet of white paper inside, covered with doodles in black ink:

She was satisfied. She stuffed the message into an inside pocket and unslung the rope from her shoulder, winding it round and round the slippery bundle until it was thoroughly tied up. With considerable difficulty she managed to brace her back against the wall and with her booted feet shove the bundle to the edge of the shelf. Taking a coil or two of rope around her right arm she was able to lower the bundle to the cavern floor. Then she let the end of the rope drop and climbed down after it. She rested for a moment, retrieved her torch, switched it off and put it away. Working in the faint light from the entrance, she picked up the rope and wound it twice on each hand. She turned so that the rope was now braced on her shoulder. She strained forward, hauling the bundle after her. Broken corpses of crabs scattered in its path as the girl slowly pulled it from the cave and dragged it bumping down the beach to the waiting skiff. Panting painfully into her gasmask she heaved with the last of her strength and got the thing into the boat, putting her whole weight against the bow so that the skiff slid back into the sea. Standing knee-deep in the seedy water she pulled the painter until the bow was pointing away from the beach, then she carefully got in and resumed her place at the tiller, lowering the screw into the sea and tugging at the motor's cord.

After a number of false starts she brought the outboard to life and the screw began to turn. The boat moved into deeper water, going back the way it had come. It still made jerky progress, so that at times the girl in the yellow sou'wester, gasmask and oil-skins was lifted completely from her seat. At last she disappeared round Tintagel Head, bouncing out to sea.

As if commissioned to wash away from the bay all traces of these events, the sky let loose its rain.

MAJOR NYE

"Another age will see all this in quite a different perspective."

It was not certain what he meant as he stared about him at the little white laboratory, at the formica-topped benches, the racks of test-tubes, the specimen jars and the aquarium which occupied one whole wall.

"So you say, general." The young Japanese marine biologist sounded sceptical as he held a bottle of sea-water up to the light from the plate glass window which offered a view of the Atlantic.

"M . . ." Major Nye put his hands in the pockets of his threadbare blazer and drew out a crushed wooden matchbox. He held it with the tips of his fingers, in both hands, as if afraid to damage it further. Part of the tray was still inside the box, but all the matches were gone. The label was predominantly blue, white and brown and the picture showed three dark skinned men in blue loincloths and red caps trying to launch a sampan into the sea. Along the right edge the label was torn a little but most of the trademark was visible: a diamond with the word *WIMCO* printed inside it. In the top left quarter of the box was the slogan: **SEA-FISHER.** At the bottom centre: "SAFETY MATCHES Made in India." On the reverse side of the box it said: *These matches are made in India by the celebrated WIMCO works at Bombay. They are specially imported by* THE CORNISH MATCH COMPANY *Av. contents 45*.

Major Nye was a stringy man in his late sixties with a scrubby grey moustache and pale, introspective blue eyes. He was just above average height. The veins in his hands

and wrists were prominent and purple and matched the
ink-stains on his finger-tips. The badge of his old regiment was stitched onto the breast pocket of his blazer and
the badge was as faded and frayed as the blazer itself.
He put the matchbox carefully back in his pocket. He
cleared his throat and went to his seat behind the green
steel desk which had been erected for him at the far end of
the lab. There was nothing on the desk. He opened
a drawer and took out a Rizla tin. He began to roll himself a thin cigarette.

"I only agreed to do all this because my daughter was
keen on it." He seemed to be trying to explain his embarrassment and apologise for it. Not so long ago he
had loved India and sworn loyalty to the Empire. Now he
had only his children to love and only his wife demanded
his loyalty. This was something of a come-down after a
sub-continent.

He lit his cigarette with a Swan Vesta, cupping his hand
against a non-existent wind. He puffed hard and began to
hum a tune—always his unconscious response to small
pleasures like smoking. Through the window of the little
square marine biology lab Major Nye could see the rocks
and the grey, roaring sea. He was puzzled by this coast.
Cornwall was alien to him; it depressed him. He could not
understand the Celtic point of view. These people seemed
to enjoy burrowing into the ground for no particular reason. Why else had they built their fougous? He had noticed, too, how they had turned quite naturally from wreck-
ing to tourism without, apparently, any change of spirit.
His right hand went to his thinning grey hair and smoothed
it, descended to the grey eyebrows and smoothed them,
came finally to the grey moustache and smoothed that.
With both hands he tightened the small knot of his regimental tie and tugged at the frayed collar of his shirt,
which was white with thin blue and red stripes which had
almost faded to invisibility. There was a khaki handkerchief protruding from his left sleeve. The cigarette was now
unnoticed and unappreciated in the corner of his grey
mouth.

A surly looking laboratory technician, with long, black
hair falling over the shoulders of his white coat, came
in, hovered over a bench, picked up a rack of test-tubes,

nodded moodily at the Japanese and the Englishman. Then he left.

Major Nye got up and went to look at the bound and spread-eagled assassin who lay on the slab just under the window-sill. The wrists and ankles were in steel clamps.

"How are you feeling, old son?"

He had spoken awkwardly and gruffly. He cleared his throat again as if he wished he had been able to use a more natural tone.

Jerry Cornelius snarled. A high-pitched screech broke from his writhing lips. He began, pathetically, to struggle on the slab.

"Eeeeeeeeee! Eeeeeeeeee!"

Gently, Major Nye frowned. "Damned shame. Poor old chap." He turned his pale eyes upon the Japanese biologist who had been attracted by the screech and now stood beside him. "How long was he down there?"

The biologist shrugged and scratched behind his left ear with his right hand. "A year? The brain has been flushed. The flesh, however, is surprisingly fresh. Like a baby's, general."

Major Nye plucked at his heavily veined nose and rubbed the under edge of it with his right forefinger. "Poor old chap. Young, too, eh?"

"Who can say? It is a strange physiology. Hard to guess the age without the proper instruments. We should have been warned. Then maybe we could have had some equipment sent down from London. As it was, he was just dumped on us. Like a baby on a doorstep."

Major Nye's ulcer bit suddenly and he straightened his shoulders and firmed his jaw to take the pain. "Sorry about that," he said. He removed the cigarette from his lips and dropped it to the floor. "There wasn't very much time, as I understand it. It was 'goodbye Dolly I must leave you' and then 'tramp, tramp, tramp the boys are marching'."

"I realise that. I was not complaining about your organisation, general. I was merely explaining our inability to do more than superficial tests."

"Naturally. You've done jolly well, anyway. Splendid show." The major looked at his watch. It seemed to be losing again. "First class," he muttered absently. "Not my organisation though, you know. Nothing to do with me. Friend of my daughter's . . . Well, we'd better get off before dark. It's a goodish run from here up to Sussex."

"You're taking the truck?"

"The old lorry. Yes, I thought so, unless—?"

"No. No. By all means take it."

"Splendid. Good, well, shall we um?"

Jerry Cornelius was all but insensate. His eyes glowed, his lips curled back from his stained teeth, his fingers curved like claws and he still stank of brine and tar. Even after they had cleaned him up (using for the most part methylated spirits and linseed oil) he had continued to glare at them silently, like a mad gull.

Major Nye and the Japanese biologist wheeled the slab from the lab and out onto the concrete which had replaced the turf. Parked close to the cliff was a run-down 1947 Bedford two-ton military lorry with a khaki canvas canopy. Major Nye untied the canopy flaps, got into the back and let down the tailboard. He pushed two planks from the lorry to the ground so that they made a ramp up which they could roll the slab with Cornelius on it. They wheeled the slab to the far end of the lorry, nearest the cab, and secured it there using chains. Major Nye turned the key in the padlock and put it in his pocket. He straightened up and crossed back towards the tailboard. As he did so his foot struck a rusty spanner on the floor of the lorry. The spanner skidded and clanged against a greasy jack pedestal. Major Nye winced. He jumped down, slid the planks into the lorry, bolted the flap up and fastened the canvas. He shook hands with the Japanese, walked round to the cab, opened the door and climbed onto the tattered bench seat. He rolled himself another smoke in his Rizla machine before giving his attention to the controls. He had some difficulty starting the engine and getting into gear but at last with a wave he drove off down the bumpy mud track towards the tarmac road which led to the A30 and thence to the M.5.

The sky changed from cold white to cold, dark grey and a cold rain was falling by the time Major Nye left the lane and headed north between flat, grey fields.

He shivered. Keeping his left hand on the steering wheel, he buttoned up his threadbare blazer.

The lorry rattled and whined. It snarled with every gear shift. The noise did much to drown the occasional screech from the back. The fumes from the engine helped cover the smell of brine.

It was nearly dark when they reached the A30. Major Nye rolled himself another cigarette as he waited to get onto the road. The rain was beating down on the black tarmac. The Bedford's single windscreen wiper clacked erratically. Moving out, Major Nye began to sing to keep himself awake. He sang *Hold Your Hand Out (Naughty Boy), My Old Dutch, I Love a Lassie, It's a Long Way to Tipperary, Pack Up Your Troubles, The Army of Today's All Right, Burlington Bertie from Bow, If It Wasn't For the Houses in Between, Are We to Part Like This, Bill?, The Honeysuckle and the Bee, You're the Cream in My Coffee, Dolly Gray, On the Road to Mandalay, Rio Rita, Maxim's, Only a Rose, Moonlight Becomes You, Jolly Good Luck to the Girl who Loves a Sailor, Am I Blue?, Change Partners, Fanlight Fannie, Auld Lang Syne, White Christmas, The Riff Song, My Little Wooden Hut, We're Here Because We're Here, The Cornish Floral Dance, Maggie's Wedding, Phil the Fluter's Ball, My Old Man, Mammy, The Eton Boating Song, Yesterday* (half), *A Whiter Shade of Pale* (part), *What Shall We Do With the Drunken Sailor?, The Dying Aviator, When This Bloody War is Over, Sonny Boy, Sally, Maybe It's Because I'm a Londoner, I Belong to Glasgow, Molly Malone, Land of My Fathers, Underneath the Arches, Run, Rabbit, Run, Rose O'Day, I'll Be Seeing You, Coming in on a Wing and a Prayer, That Lovely Weekend, Lucky Jim, September Song, The Man Who Broke the Bank at Monte Carlo, Mr. Tambourine Man* (part), *The Physician*, until at last he reached Ironmaster House in Sussex croaking the last few bars of *Has Anybody Here Seen Kelly?* and stopped the lorry by the brook.

UNA PERSSON

"The peak was reached in 1808 and civilisation has been in decline ever since, thanks, in particular, to the Saxon race—many of whom happened to share my view. Here's to Beethoven!"

Prinz Lobkowitz saluted with his stein, lowered it to his lips, tilted his leonine head and swallowed a litre of Bil beer. His voice had been drowned almost entirely by the first movement of the "Pastoral" played by the Berlin Philharmonic Orchestra conducted by Eugene Jochum which came from the two great Vox speakers on either side of the bay window. Wiping the foam from his moustache he went to the ornate Victorian mantelpiece on which stood the newish Garrard deck with its Sony amplifier and turned a knob to reduce the volume slightly, adding: "Open the window. It stinks of disinfectant in here." The first movement ended and the second began.

From a gilded chair upholstered in stained red and white Regency stripe, his mistress Eva Knecht efficiently rose and with long strides crossed the wide eighteenth century room which was full of half-emptied packing cases, a grand piano with roses painted on its light walnut wood, scattered dust-sheets and piles of objets trouvées. Reaching the diamond-paned windows she raised her hands to the catch but paused as the huge bulk of a Zeppelin filled her entire field of vision; it was flying low over the ruins to the South East of the city. It coursed towards the sunset. She smiled quietly and pushed open the double windows. The distant mumble of the Zeppelin's engines reached her. She took a deep breath as if to inhale the sound rather than the stink which blew from the Koenigstrasse gravepit. She looked back enquiringly at the Prinz who waved his hand. "I suppose so. Though I don't know which I prefer—that or the DDT. It's about time something was done for Berlin."

There came a faint vibration and a faraway thump as the Zeppelin began to distribute its first incendiaries of the evening. Prinz Lobkowitz lit a Jamaican corona and burnt his thumbnail with the match when the beginning of the third movement (Merry Gathering of Peasants) struck up. "Fuck," he said, and then: "What's German for fuck?"

"I haven't got that far yet." She started towards the shelf of dictionaries in the far alcove.

"Don't bother, Nobody else does. What's the point of trying to revive a dead language? Who wants a 'national identity' any longer? Politics has come down to rather more fundamental issues."

"Who wants to *talk* about it?" Eva smoothed her skirt. "That newspaper soon went back to English."

"The bloody language is always at the root of it." He coughed and put the cigar in the Directoire chafing dish he used as an ashtray. "Do you still want to go to the waxworks tonight?"

"Suits me."

"I bet it does!"

He roared with laughter, frowned, and turned off the stereo.

The house, most of which was still intact, had been restored in 1850 and was huge with lavish appointments. It had all the tatty grandeur of a Versailles, with the same fading gilt, fly-specked mirrors and chipped, painted terra cotta.

A gentle knock on the great oaken double door.

"Come," said Lobkowitz.

The doors opened and a small black and white cat walked in, its tail erect. It stopped in the middle of the dusty Persian carpet. It sat down and looked up at them.

It was followed by a beautiful girl in a black military topcoat and patent leather boots with gold buckles (from *Elliotts*). Her brown hair was cut relatively short and her face was heart-shaped, amused, controlled. She held a heavy Smith and Wesson .45 revolver in her right hand

and her left hand was still resting on the door knob as she paused and surveyed the room.

Eva Knecht scowled. "Sebastian Auchinek's side-kick," she muttered. "Una Persson. What an actress!"

Eva, only slightly beautiful, with the same kind of brown hair, felt herself fade. She wished that she were wearing something other than the fawn Jaeger twinset and green spikeheels as she hissed: "Proper little heroine of the revolution, isn't she."

Prinz Lobkowitz ignored his mistress. He flattened one palm against his waistcoated diaphragm and made his dignified way towards the door, the other palm extended. He was wearing a black frock coat and pinstripe trousers. In the lapel of his coat was the tiny button of the Legion de Liberté. Under the trousers were the outlines of his brown riding boots. He had forgotten to take off the silver spur attached to his right heel. He smirked (though he thought the expression one of friendly dignity) and as a consequence ruined the handsome lines of his face. He rumbled some pleasantry, of which his smirk made ingratiating nonsense, and introduced himself to the new-comer. "Prinz Lobkowitz."

"Una Persson," she replied contemptuously. "Auchinek said you would take delivery."

"I thought it was tomorrow." Lobkowitz looked vaguely about him. "Tomorrow." Slowly the smirk dissolved.

"I saved time by coming through Czechoslovakia." Una Persson put the gun into her deep pocket. She turned and snapped her fingers. Four unhealthy Slavs stumbled in. There was a pine coffin on their shoulders. The coffin was stamped *VAKUUM REINIGER (ENGLISCH-PRODUKT)*. The Slavs put it down on the Persian carpet. They trotted off.

Una Persson reached inside her maxicoat and withdrew a document and a blue ballpoint. "Sign both copies, please," she said. Lobkowitz put the papers on the lid of the walnut grand piano and signed without reading. He handed them back to her. "And how is Auchinek?"

"Very well. Shall I open the box for you?"

"If you would."

She slipped out her Smith and Wesson and accurately shot off the bolts on the coffin's four corners. One of the spent bullets narrowly missed Eva Knecht. With the barrel of the gun Una Persson plucked away a blanket, revealing the glaring countenance of Jerry Cornelius, still stinking of the sea.

Lobkowitz backed off and went to put the Mozart Clarinet Quintet in A on the deck.

"Mein Gott!" said Eva Knecht self-consciously. "What caused that?"

Una Persson shrugged. "Some form of hydrophilia, I gather. A disease with symptoms similar to enteritis in cats."

'I mourn the Age of Steam," said Lobkowitz returning with a box of *Rising Sun* matches. They were made by the Western India Match Co. Ltd.

"A peculiar diagnosis." Eva Knecht bent to look more closely at the creature. "Where was it found?"

"On the coast of North Cornwall, eventually, but he'd been seen once or twice earlier. They think he went in somewhere around the Bay of Bengal. I was to take delivery of five cases of M16s?"

"Yes, yes, of course." Lobkowitz indicated the crates laid out under the grand piano. "With ammunition. Shall I get someone to load them for you, or . . . ?"

"Thank you very much."

Lobkowitz pulled a frayed velvet bell-rope near the mantelpiece. "This is the old Bismarck mansion," he told her.

"I gathered." With a battered brass Dunhill Una Persson lit a long brown Sherman cigarettello. "I should like to wash my hair before I leave."

As best she could, Eva Knecht flounced from the room. "I'll check if the water's on."

Four ex-POWs with shaven heads and wearing stained blue dungarees, came in and began to take the crates of M16s outside to Una Persson's SD Kfz 233 armoured truck. The ornate ormolu 'Empire' style telephone commenced to ring. Lobkowitz ignored it. "They all do that. It means nothing."

"Well, I think I'll just . . ." Una Persson strode across and lifted the receiver to her head. "Hello."

She listened for a moment and then replaced the receiver. "A sort of rushing noise."

"That's right." Lobkowitz moved rapidly towards her, his spur jingling. "Jesus Christ, I'd like to . . ."

She placed a small hand against his chest and kissed him on the chin.

Eva Knecht stood in the doorway, one hand clutching her Jaeger cardigan round her shoulders. "I'm afraid there'll be no more water today."

Una Persson stepped away from Prinz Lobkowitz and nodded gravely at Eva. "I'll be off, then."

Lobkowitz coughed behind his hand. His eyes fell on his right boot and for the first time he noticed that he was still wearing one spur. He bent to unstrap it. "Don't leave, yet . . ." He glanced up at Eva and added briskly: "Well, cheerio, my dear."

"Cheerio," said Una Persson. Decisively, she left the room.

Eva Knecht glared at Lobkowitz as he straightened to his feet, holding the spur in his hand. "Mozart!" she said. "I should have . . ."

"Don't be corny, sweet." Lobkowitz put the spur on a pearl inlay table.

"Corny!"

Picking up an Erma 9mm machine pistol from the Jacobean sideboard, she offered him a round in the hip. He pursed his lips as if objecting to the noise rather than the pain, and went down on one knee as the dark stains dilated on his jacket and pin-stripes. He clutched the ruined hip.

She spent the rest of the clip on his face. He fell. Smashed.

Una Persson came back at the sound. She raised her S & W and shot Eva Knecht once below the left shoulder blade. The bullet entered Eva's jealous heart and she toppled forward. Murdered.

Eva Knecht's murderess took a black beret from the pocket of her maxicoat and adjusted it on her head, glancing once into the mirror above the mantel. For a moment she looked thoughtfully from the coffin to the corpses. She replaced the S & W in her other pocket. She opened her mouth a quarter of an inch and then closed it. She took off the Mozart and flicked through the pile of albums on the floor until she found a Bach Brandenburg Concerto. She put the record on the deck, glanced down at the contents of the coffin, hovered undecidedly by the door, and then she left as quickly as her coat would let her.

The Brandenburg was an inferior performance, spoiled further by a persistent screeching from the box.

From below there came the noise of an Sd Kfz 233 starting up, backing out and roaring off down the emergency track through the rubble.

The screeching assumed a melancholy note and then ceased. Night fell. From time to time the room was illuminated by incendiary explosions from the East. Later there was darkness relieved by a little moonlight and the sound of the Zeppelin returning to its shed. Then there remained only a rustle of atmospherics from the speakers.

The small black and white cat, forgotten by Una Persson, woke up. It stretched and began to walk towards Lobkowitz. It lapped at the congealed blood on the face, then moved off in disgust. It washed itself beside Eva's corpse and then sprang into the coffin to curl on Jerry's chest, heedless of the insensate, agonised eyes which, wide open, continued to stare at the terra cotta ceiling, before slowly filling with tears.

SEBASTIAN AUCHINEK

The long, gentle hands came down to reveal a sensitive
Jewish face. The large, red lips moved, emitting softly-
accented English: "Perhaps you should have brought him
back, Una?" He was a thin, pale intellectual. He sat on
a camp chair with its back against the far wall of a dry,
limestone cave. He was dressed in standard guerilla gear;
it hung on his thin body like a wet flag.

The cave was full of crates; it was lit by a tin oil-lamp
which cast black shadows. On one of the crates stood a
half-eaten Stilton cheese, an almost full bottle of Vichy
water and a number of East German and Polish military
maps in leather cases.

She was undoing the top button of her black maxicoat.
"That would have been theft, Sebastian."

"True. But these are pragmatic times."

"And we agreed we wanted no part of them."

"True." He sucked his upper lip into his mouth, his
large lids slowly falling to cover his eyes.

She said defiantly: "The M16s are as good as new.
There's plenty of ammunition. He kept his side of it. Many
new Germans are very straight in that respect." She
shrugged. "But her violence upset me." She lit another
Sherman's with a match from a box on the nearby crate.
"I've still got a feeling I've forgotten something." She
reached into her pocket and pulled out her gun, turning
it this way and that. "What else could I do? If saving her
would have brought him back to life . . ."

"True."

"Well, I know if I'd thought about it for a moment I
might not have done it. But so many people waste time

thinking about things and when they act it's too late. I didn't want to hurt anybody."

Sebastian Auchinek got up from the camp chair and walked to the cave entrance, drawing back the camouflage net. Outside, the drizzle fluttered like a tattered curtain in the wind and Auchinek peered through it, hoping to get a sight of the tiny Macedonian village in the rocky valley below. A herd of goats emerged from the thin rain. They bleated their discomfort as they trotted down the mountainside and disappeared. The water swished on the rocks and it smelled faintly of benzine. At least the air was reasonably warm.

"Sebastian."

His inclination was to leave the cave, for he hated any form of homecoming ceremony, but he turned.

She was kneeling by the chair wearing a gold and brown puff-sleeved shirt with a long black waistcoat and matching black trousers. Her coat was folded neatly beside her.

With a sigh he returned to his place and spread his spider legs. She reached forward and undid his fly. He gritted his teeth and his hand stroked her head once or twice before falling back at his side. He squeezed his eyes shut. Her face was grave as she moved it towards his crotch, as if she were considering different and more pleasant things while conscientiously performing a distasteful but necessary task.

Auchinek wondered if she did it because she thought he liked it. She had done it regularly for the past few months; at first he had pretended to be pleased and now he could never tell her the truth.

When she had finished, the fellatrix looked up at him, smiled, wiped her lips, swiftly closed his zip. He gave her a strained, bewildered smile in return, then he began to cough. She offered him one of her cigarettellos but he waved his hand towards the bottle on the upturned crate. She did not notice the gesture as she lit and then drew upon the long, brown Sherman's staring pensively at her own shifting shadow on the floor. Her eyes were blue and private.

"Perhaps I should go back for Cornelius. We might need him if things get any tougher. On the other hand he might be dead by the time I got there. Is that my fault,

I wonder? And the Cossacks are supposed to be moving in, too. Did you say you wanted a cigarette?"

His pale face was puzzled, his gesture nervous as he lifted an exhausted hand to point again at the bottle.

"No," he said. "Water."

Mrs. C. and Colonel P.

"Yerst." Folding her hands together on her great stomach, the fat old bag got her forearms under her unruly breasts and jostled them in her dress until they were hanging more comfortably. "'S'im, orl right." Her three sly chins shivered. Her round, red stupid head cocked itself on one side. Her tiny eyes narrowed and her thick mouth opened. "Pore littel bleeder. Wot they dun to 'im?"

"We do not know, Mrs. Cornelius." Colonel Pyat stepped away from the coffin which lay where Una Persson's Slavs had left it. The other bodies were no longer visible, though the small black and white cat was still hanging around. "But now that you have positively identified him . . ." He drew off his white kid gauntlets. They were a perfect match to his well-cut, gold-trimmed uniform, to his kid boots, his dashing cap. ". . . we can try to find out. I almost caught up with him in Afghanistan. But the express was delayed as usual. This could have been avoided."

" 'E always wos a bit've a pansy, I s'pose," Mrs. C. said reflectively.

Colonel Pyat went to the grand piano where his vodka things had been arranged by an orderly. "May I offer you a drink, madame?"

"Where's all them balloons gorn? I 'eard . . ."

"The Zeppelins have left the city. They belonged to the Nieu Deutchlanders whom we routed yesterday."

"Well, I'll 'ave a small one. Did anyone ever tell yer— yer look jest like Ronal' Colman."

"But I feel just like Jesse James." Colonel Pyat smiled and gestured towards the record player on the mantelpiece.

Faintly, from the Vox speakers, came the muffled sounds of a Bob Dylan record. The colonel poured an ounce of Petersburg vodka into a long-stemmed Bohemian glass, poured the same amount for himself, crossed back and handed Mrs. C. her drink.

She drained it. "Ta." Then, with a fat, knowing chuckle, she flung back her monstrous arm and hurled the glass at the mantelpiece. "Sköl! Eh? Har, har!"

Colonel Pyat took an interest in his white knuckles. Then he straightened his shoulders and quietly sipped his drink.

Mrs. C. ran a grimy finger round the neck of her cheap, red and white print dress. "'Ot enough fer yer?"

"Indeed?" Pyat put a finger to his lips and raised his eyebrows intelligently. "Aha."

"Wouldna thort it. Not in bleedin' *Germany*—innit?" "No?"

She turned, digging at a rotting back tooth with her thumbnail so that her voice was strangled. "Will 'e get better, Kernewl?"

"That's up to the boffins, madame."

"Courst, 'is *bruvver*—Frankie—was allus th' nicest of 'em. I did me best after 'is dad run orft, but . . ."

"These are unsettled times, Mrs. Cornelius."

Mrs. C. looked at him with mock gravity for a moment, a little smile turning up the corners of her crimson mouth. She opened the lips. She belched. Then she burst into laughter. "Yer not kiddin'—ter-her-ka-ka—ooh—give us anovver, there's a pet . . . nkk-nkk."

"I beg your pardon?"

"Nar—sawright—I'll 'elp meself, won' I?" She waddled to the grand piano. Grunting contentedly, she poured half the remaining contents of the bottle into another long-stemmed glass. She rounded on him, raising her glass with a leer and tossing off the best part of the contents. "'Ere's ter yer!" The drink warmed her further and large beads of sweat sprang out on her happy face. She sidled up to Colonel Pyat, nudging him with her lumpy elbow. She winked and nodded a streaky orange head at the vodka. "Not bad." She belched again. "Not 'alf! He, he he!"

Colonel Pyat clicked his heels and saluted. "I thank—"

A piercing screech came from the coffin. They both turned their heads. "Gawd," said Mrs. C.

Cautiously, Colonel Pyat went to peer in. "I wonder if they've been feeding him."

" 'E never wos much of an eater." Mrs. C.'s bosom heaved as she joined the colonel and stared sentimentally down at her son. "I never knew where 'e got 'is energy from. Proper little fucker you wos, woncha, Jer?"

The head rolled. The stink of brine was nauseating. The screech came again. The hands, thin and knotted, with broken nails and bruised knuckles, were rubbed raw at the wrists by the twisted nylon cords holding them in the coffin. The mouth opened and closed, opened and closed; only the whites of the eyes were visible.

With a decisive and slightly censorious gesture Mrs. C. looked away from her child, finishing her vodka. She glanced almost thoughtfully at the colonel before putting her glass on the Jacobean sideboard. She wriggled her massive shoulders, rubbed her left eye with the index finger of her left hand, gave the colonel a quick smirk of encouragement and said: "Well . . ."

Colonel Pyat bowed. "Some of my men will escort you back to London."

"Ah," she said. "That wos it . . ."

"Madame?"

"I wos thinkin'v seein' some o' th' sights whilst I wos 'ere. Y'know." Another wink.

"I will instruct my men to make a tour of the city. Though there are very few sights left."

"Oo! All them soljers all to meself! Oo-er!"

"And thank you so much for your help, Mrs. Cornelius. We'll get your boy back to normal. Never fear."

"Normal! That'sa good 'un!" Her entire body quivered with laughter. "You'll do, Kernewl! Eh? Har, har, har!"

She shambled cheerfully from the room. "You'll do!"

The Bohemian glass fell off the Jacobean sideboard and landed unbroken on the Persian carpet.

The sounds from the coffin became pensive. Colonel Pyat was filled with sadness. He picked up the fallen glass and took it to the grand piano where he poured himself the last of his vodka.

REMINISCENCE (A)

Beautiful love.

Beautiful love.

Late News

Terence Green, 9, and Martin Harper, 8, died last night when overcome by fumes from water heater while having bath in house in Estagon Road, Norwich.

SUNDAY TIMES, April 5 1970

At least 90 Vietnamese men, women and children, held behind barbed wire in a compound at the Cambodian town of Prasot, were killed by machine gun and automatic rifle fire early yesterday, as a Vietcong force launched an attack in the area.

The events surrounding the killings were not clear.

THE TIMES, April 11 1970

A French woman, aged 37, stabbed three of her children, killing one of them, before committing suicide in Luneville yesterday, police said. Mme. Marie-Madeleine Amet stabbed Joanne, aged 14, and Philippe, aged 11, who managed to escape. But Catherine, aged 10, was killed.

GUARDIAN, April 14 1970

The Alternative Apocalypse 1

It's a shame, really, said Major Nye as they stood on the
flat roof of the looted dispensary and watched the barbarian migration cross the swaying remains of Tower Bridge.
The sky began to lighten and to some degree improve the
appearance of the horde's filthy silks, satins and velvets. A
few were mounted on horses, motorbikes and bicycles, but
the majority trudged along with their bundles on their
backs. Some were playing loud, primitive music on stolen
Gibsons, Yamahas, Framus twelve-strings, Martins and
even Hofners. It's a shame, really. Who can blame them?

Jerry fingered his new gloves.

You and they have more in common than I, major.

Major Nye gave him a sympathetic glance. Aren't you
lonely, Mr. Cornelius?

For a moment self-pity flooded all Jerry's systems. His
eyes gleamed with water. Oh, fuck.

Major Nye knew how to get through.

When half the barbarians were on the South Bank, the
bridge, shaken by a hundred different twelve-bar blues and
a thousand moccasins and calf-length suede boots, fell
slowly over into the grease of the Thames. Large stones
broke away from the main towers as they toppled; pieces of
asphalt cracked like toffee struck by a hammer. The whole
mock-Gothic edifice, every inch of grimy granite, was falling down.

Their long hair fluttering behind them, those babies not in
slings and packs falling from their arms, their guitars and
bundles scattering around them, their beads and furs and
laces flapping, the barbarians sank through the air, struck,

458

and were absorbed by, the river. For a moment a cassette tape recorder could be heard playing *You can't always get what you want* by the Rolling Stones and then that, too, was logged by the water.

Arriving too late, a Panther patrol lowered its .280 EM1s as if in salute to the dying. Standing in single file along the North Bank they watched the children drown.

The Panthers were led by a tall aristocrat in a finely tailored white suit, a neatly trimmed Imperial beard and moustache and short hair cut close to the nape of his black neck. He carried an elegant single-shot Remington XP-100. The bolt-action pistol was borne more for aesthetic effect than anything else. He held it in his right hand and his arms were folded across his chest so that the long barrel rested in the crook of his left elbow. The Panthers in their own well-cut cream uniforms, looked inquiringly at their Head. It was unquestionably a problem of taste. The Panthers lived for taste and beauty, which was why they had been the most virulent force against the barbarians. The war between the two had been a war of styles and the Panthers, under their American leaders, had won all the way down the line.

At last the Panthers on the North Bank reached a decision. Lining the embankment, they turned their tall backs, dropped their chins to their chests and lounged against the balustrade, listening to the fading cries of the dying until there was silence in the river again. Then they climbed back into their open Mercedes and Bentley tourers and rolled away from there.

A few barbarians stood on the far bank, twisting themselves joints, hesitating before rejoining the exodus as it ploughed on towards the Borough High Street, heading for the suburbs of Surrey and Kent and what was left of the pickings.

And those, said the major, indicating the disappearing Panthers, do you identify, perhaps, with them?

Jerry shrugged. Maybe a little more. No—no, there's nobody left at all, major, let's face it. I'm on my own in this one and I can't say I like it. My fault, perhaps.

Possibly you lost sight of your targets, Mr. Cornelius.

I've hit all the targets, Major Nye. That's the trouble. He took out his needler and turned it this way and that to catch the light on its polished chrome. Is there anything sadder, I wonder, than an assassin with nobody left to kill?

I shouldn't think so. Major Nye's voice was now more than sympathetic. I know exactly what you mean, my dear chap. And I suppose that's why we're both standing here watching. Our sun has set, I'm afraid.

Keep moving towards the sun and it will never set, said Jerry. That's positive thinking major. It will never happen. It's a matter of finding the right place. The correct speed for forward momentum.

Major Nye said nothing as he shook his grey head.

It will never fucking happen! Jerry shouted.

The masonry had blocked the flow of the river and was making it flood over the embankment. A few corpses were washed up and there was other, fouler, flotsam, too.

Jerry went back to the skylight and put his feet on the scarred wooden steps. He was going inside. Coming, major?

No, I'll stop here for a while, old son. And keep your chin up, eh?

Thanks, major, Same to you.

Jerry climbed down into the ruined bedroom and stood staring at the dreadful corpse of the girl in the fourposter. The rats ignored him and went on eating. He aimed the gun but, after a minute or two, replaced it in his holster without shooting. Even the rats couldn't last much longer.

The Alternative Apocalypse 2

Smoothly, with mock-apologetic smiles, they nailed him to the lowest yard of the mizzen. They were standing off the Kent coast, near Rommey, out of sight of land. The three-masted schooner-rigged yacht rocked in the heavy sea. The sea tugged at the anchors, hurled its weight against the white sides. Waiting for the waters to subside, they paused in the hammering. Almost expectantly they looked up at him. The two women, who had nailed his hands, were Karen von Krupp and Mitzi Beesley. They were dressed in deck pyjamas and chic little sailormen's hats. The man who had nailed his feet was his brother Frank. Frank wore grey flannels, a white open-necked shirt and a fairisle pullover. He was kneeling beside the mizzen, the hammer in both hands.

Jerry spoke with great control. I made no claims.

But many were made *for* you, said Bishop Beesley through a mouthful of beige fudge. He stood by the rail, his bottom wedged against it. You didn't deny them.

I deny nothing. Have I disagreed with your opinion?

No. But, then, I'm not sure . . .

We have that in common, at least.

The sea grew calm. Bishop Beesley made an impatient gesture, withdrawing a Mars Bar from under his surplice. The three resumed their hammering.

Together with the nails in his palms there were ropes supporting his wrists so that the weight of his hanging body would not rip the impaled flesh too quickly, for they wanted him to die of asphyxiation, not of pain or loss of blood alone. He breathed hard. The sharp pressure increased in his chest. The last blows fell. The three stood back to inspect their work. The corpulent Bishop Beesley licked his lips, sniffed the odour of the stale sea.

Dead fish, said the bishop. Dead fish.

Late News

Alan Stuart, aged four, who sprayed his mouth with what is believed to have been a pressurised oven cleaner at his home in Benhillwood Road, Sutton, Surrey, has died in hospital.

THE SUN, September 28 1971

A boy aged 14 died after being stabbed in the chest in the playground of Wandsworth School, South London, yesterday. He died in Queen Mary's Hospital, Roehampton, soon after the stabbing, which happened during the morning break at the boys' comprehensive school. Last night another boy, also aged 14, was accused of the murder. He will appear at Southwark North juvenile court today.

GUARDIAN, November 19 1971

Shirley Wilkinson, aged 16, daughter of the train robber Jack Wilkinson, died last night in the South London hospital where she had been detained after being injured in a car crash.

GUARDIAN, November 20 1971

Scores of rush-hour cars flashed by as a 10-year-old girl fled naked and terrified from a sex maniac. But not one driver stopped. And motorists took no notice of the girl's frantic cries for help as the man dragged her into his car. Later the man raped and strangled her. The body of little Jane Hanley was found at the weekend in a field outside Rochester, New York. "At least 100 people must have seen her," said a policeman. "She had apparently been kidnapped but jumped from the man's car and pleaded with passing motorists to help. The kidnapper grabbed her and drove off again." Now rewards totalling £2,500 have been offered by newspapers and citizens' organisations for information leading to the killer. Three drivers have now admitted they saw the drama on Highway 400—10 miles from where Jane disappeared while on a shopping errand. One said: "I went by so fast I couldn't believe what I saw."

THE SUN, November 22 1971

REMINISCENCE (B)

Save us.

From the basement in Talbot Road. From mother's breath and mother's saliva. From cold chips. From dirty hand-me-downs. From stained mattresses. From old beer bottles. From the smell of urine. From damp squalor.

From the poverty trance.

Mrs. C. and Frankie C.

"So we fetched up 'ere again 'ave we?" Mrs. Cornelius said sullenly as her lean son guided her off the decrepit street and down the foul basement steps. "Yore doin' okay fer yerself, incha? Yer ole mum'd never know it."

"You prefer it here, mother," said Frank patiently. "When we got you that council flat you complained."

"It wasn't the bleedin' flat it was the arrangements. Orl them stairs. I can't get inter a lift it makes me sick. And them neighbours reckonin' theirselves . . ."

"Well. There it is." Frank took the door handle in both hands and lifted it so that the damp wood just cleared the step. "I'll get you some more batteries for your wireless."

They entered the stinking gloom.

"I could do wiv a drink."

Frank took a half-bottle of Gordon's gin from the pocket of his sheepskin coat. She accepted it with dignity and placed it on the warped and littered sideboard, near the primitive television which had stopped working, well before the electricity had been cut off. "I'd make yer a cuppa tea," she said, "but . . ."

"I've paid the gas bill. They're coming round to turn you on tomorrow."

She waded through the litter of old newspapers and broken furniture. She lit the two stumps of candles on the rotting draining board. She moved a pile of old, damp Christmas cards. "Wot yer fink Jerry's chancest are, Frankie?"

"Ask the experts." Frank shrugged and rubbed at his pale face. "It's probably nothing more than exhaustion. He's been overdoing it recently."

"Workin'!" said Mrs. Cornelius derisively.

"Even Jerry has to graft sometimes, mum."

"Lazy sod. 'Ow's yer antique business doin'?"

Frank became wary. "So so."

"Well, at least yer 'elp out sometimes. I don't see *'im* one year ter the next." She sighed and lowered herself into the discoloured armchair. "Ooooh! Them fuckin' springs. Damp as Brighton Beach, too." The complaints were uttered in a tone of comfortable approval. She had been too long out of her natural environment. She reached up for the gin and began to unscrew the cap. Frank handed her a dirty glass from the sink.

"I must be off," he said. "Got everything you need?"

"Couldn't lend us a coupla quid couldya, Frankie?"

Frank reached into the right pocket of his cavalry twill trousers and removed a mixed handful of notes. He hesitated, then extracted a fiver. He showed it to her and put it on the sideboard. "You'll have to go down to the assistance on Monday. That should do you for the weekend. I won't be around for a while."

"Be up in yer flat in 'Olland Park wiv yer nobby mates, eh?"

"No. Out of town."

"Wot abart the shop?"

"Mo's looking after that. I'm off to Scotland to see what's still going in the big houses there. Everybody's running out of antiques. There's nothing left in England —even the sixties have gone dry. We're catching up on ourselves. It's funny." He smiled as she stared uncomprehendingly at him. "Don't worry, mum. You enjoy your drink."

Her features flowed back into their normal lines of stupid complacency. "Thanks, Frankie."

"And give Cathie my love if you see her."

"That slut! Wors'n Jerry if yer ask me! I 'eard she was on the game. Shacked up wiv a black feller."

"I doubt if she's on the game."

"I disown 'er." Mrs. Cornelius said grandly, raising the bottle to her lips, "as any daughter o' mine."

Frank buttoned up his suède car coat and pulled the lambs-wool collar around his dark face. He smoothed his Brylcreemed hair with the palm of his hand then slipped the hand into a suède-backed motoring glove.

"Mo said he'd come and clean this place out—give you some better furniture."

"Yeah?"

"When shall I tell him to come?"

She looked nervously around her. "Later," she said. "I'll 'ave ter fink abart wot I do and don' wanna keep. We'll discuss it later, eh?" She hadn't thrown a thing out since well before the war.

"You'll have that bloke from the council round again," he warned.

"Don't worry abart *that!* I can deal with the fuckin' council!"

"They might find you alternative accommodation."

Her heavy face was full of apprehension. "Abart time, too," she moaned.

He left, pulling the creaking door shut behind him.

She leaned the gin bottle on the arm of the mephitic chair and looked tenderly around at her home. It had been condemned in 1934, was scheduled for redevelopment by 1990, which meant any time after the turn of the century. It would last her out. The first candle guttered and threw peculiar shadows on the mildewed walls. The gin began to warm her chest and belly. She peered at the cracked mantelpiece on the far side of the room, locating the faded pictures of the fathers of her children. There was Frank's father in his GI uniform. There was Cathy's father in his best suit. There was the father of the dead twins, of the three abortions—the one who had married her. Only Jerry's father was missing. She didn't remember him, for all she'd borrowed his name. Through all her marriages she'd always been known as Mrs. Cornelius. She'd only been about sixteen, hadn't she? Or even younger? Or was that something else? Was he the Jewish feller? Her eyelids closed.

Soon she was dreaming her nice dream as opposed to her nasty dream. She was kneeling on a big white woolly carpet. She was completely naked and there was blood dripping from her mangled nipples as she was buggered by a huge, black, shapeless animal. In her sleep her hands fell to her lap and she dug at herself with her nails and stirred and snorted, waking herself up. She smiled and drank down the rest of the gin and was soon fast asleep again.

AUCHINEK

"Poverty," said Auchinek to Lyons, the Israeli colonel, "increased markedly in Europe last year. This, in itself, would not have threatened the status quo had not a group of liberal politicians persistently offered the people hope without, of course, any immediate prospect of improving their lot. Naturally they moved swiftly from apathy to anger. Without their anger I doubt if I should have been anything like as successful." He smiled. "I owe at least some of my success to the human condition."

"You're modest." The colonel stared approvingly at his troops as they joined with their Arab allies and began, systematically, to lay dynamite charges throughout what was left of the city of Athens. "Besides, wasn't the collapse to some extent cultural?"

"It was a culture without flexibility, I agree. I must admit I share the view that Western civilisation—European civilisation, if you like—was out of tempo with the rest of the world. It imposed itself for a short time—largely because of the vitality, stupidity and priggishness of those who supported it. We shall never be entirely cleansed of its influence, I'm afraid."

"You aren't suggesting that the only values worth keeping are those of the Orient?" Lyons' murmur was sardonic.

"Basically—emotionally—I do think that. I know the question's arguable."

"I detect a strong whiff of anti-aryanism. You support the pogroms?"

"Of course not. I am not a racialist. I speak only of education. I would like to see a vast re-education programme started throughout Europe. Within a couple of generations we could completely eradicate their portentous and witless philosophies."

"But haven't our own thoughts been irrevocably influenced by them? I can't echo your idealism, personally, General Auchinek. Moreover, I think our destiny is with Africa . . ."

"The chimera of vitality appears again," Auchinek sighed. "I wish we could stop moving altogether."

"And become like Cornelius? I saw him in Berlin, you know."

"There is a difference between tranquility and exhaustion. I had a guru, colonel, for some time, with whom I would correspond. He lived in Calcutta before the collapse. He convinced me of the need for meditation as the only solution to our ills."

"Is that why you became a guerilla?"

"There is no paradox. One must work in the world according to one's temperament."

The hillside, covered in tents, shook as the white ruins of Athens began to powder under the impact of the dynamite explosions.

Dust clouds rose slowly into the blue air and began to form peculiar configurations: ideograms from an alien alphabet. Auchinek studied them. They were vaguely familiar. If he studied them long enough, they might reveal their message. He changed the angle of his head, he narrowed his eyes. He folded his thin arms across his spare chest.

"How beautiful," said Colonel Lyons, and he seemed to be speaking of Auchinek rather than of the explosions. He placed his brawny hand on Auchinek's bony shoulder. His large digital wrist-watch shone beneath the tangle of black hairs, the coat of dust. "We must get . . ." He removed his hand. "How is Una?"

"In excellent health." Auchinek coughed on the dust. "She's leading our mission in Siberia at present."

"So you are serious about your loyalty to the Oriental idea. Have you forgotten the Chinese?"

"Far from it."

"Would they agree to an alliance? And what about the Japanese? How deep is their reverence for occidental thought?"

"A few generations deep in both cases. You've seen their comic books. All China wants, in international terms, is her old Empire restored."

"There could be complications."

"True. But not the confusion created artificially by western interference since the fifteenth century."

"*Their* fifteenth century," smiled Colonel Lyons.

Auchinek missed the reference.

PERSSON

Una Persson watched the military ambulance bouncing away over the yellow steppe towards the wooden bridge which spanned the Volga. The sky was large, livid, on the move, but it could not dwarf the Cossack sech with its ten thousand yurts of painted leather and its many corrals full of shaggy ponies. Compared with the sky's swift activity the sech was almost static.

The ambulance reached the bridge and shrieked across it, taking the Cossack wounded back to their special encampment. A dark eddy swept through the sky for a hundred miles. The Volga danced.

In the strange light, Una Persson left her Range Rover and strode towards the sech. Cool and just a trifle prim, with her big coat completely open to show her long, beautiful legs, the short multicoloured kaftan, the holstered S & W pistol on the ammunition belt around her small waist, the knee-length black boots, she paused again on the edge of the camp, allowing her blue-grey eyes to reveal the admiration she felt for the Cossack Host's picturesque style.

These were not the Westernised cossacks who had taken Berlin with their sophisticated artillery and mechanised transport. These were the atavists; they had resorted to the ancient ways of the Cossacks who had followed Stenka Razin in the people's revolt three hundred years before. They wore the topknots and long flowing moustachios copied from the Tartars who had been their ancient enemies but who now rode with them. All who presently dressed in Cossack silk and leather had been recruited east of the Volga and most of them looked Mongolian.

Their leader, wearing a heavy burka, blue silk trousers and yellow leather boots typical of the Zaporazhian cossack, rode to where she stood. A Russian SKS carbine jostled on his back as he dismounted from his pony and wiped a large hand over his huge, hard face.

His voice was deep, humorous and resonant. "I am Karinin, the Ataman of this Sech." His oval eyes were equally admiring as he studied her, putting one foot in his pony's stirrup, hooking his arm around his saddle pommel and lighting his curved, black pipe with a match which he struck on the sole of his boot. "You come from Auchinek, they tell me. You wish to make an alliance. Yet you know we are Christians, that we hate Jews worse than we hate Moslems and Muscovites." He removed his floppy grey and black sheepskin shako to expose his shaven head, the gold rings in his ears, to wipe his dark brow and thick moustache. A calculated set of gestures, thought Una Persson, but well accomplished.

"The alliance Auchinek suggests is an alliance of the Orient against the west." She spoke precisely, as if unimpressed by his style, his strength, his good looks.

"But you are—what?—a Russ? A Scandinavian, uh? A traitor? Or just a romantic like Cornelius?"

"What are you but that?"

He laughed. "All right."

The wind began to bluster, carrying with it the overriding smell of horse manure. The sky seemed to decide its direction and streamed rapidly eastward.

Karinin took his foot from the stirrup and slid the slim, scabbarded sabre around his waist until it rested on his left hip. He knocked out the pipe on his silver boot heel. "You had better come to my yurt," he said, "to tell me the details. There's no one much left for us to fight in these parts." He pointed into the centre of the sech, where the circles of yurts were tightest. His yurt was no larger than the others, for the Zaporozhians were touchily democratic, but a tall horsehair standard stood outside its flap.

Una Persson began to see the farcical side of her situation. She grinned. Then she noticed the gibbet which had been erected near Karinin's yurt. A group of old Kuban cossacks were methodically putting a noose about the neck of a young European dressed in a yellow frock coat, lilac cravat, yellow shirt and a blue, wide-brimmed

hat. The European's expression was amused as he let
them tie his hands behind him.

"What are they doing?" Una Persson asked.

The ataman spoke almost regretfully. "They are hanging a dandy. There aren't so many as there were."

"He seems brave."

"Surely courage is a characteristic of the dandy?"

"And yet those old men plainly hate him. I thought
cossacks admired courage?"

"They are also very prudish."

The tightening rope knocked the blue hat from the fair
hair; it covered the face for a moment before falling to the
the mud. The dandy gave his captors a chiding glance.
The Kubans slapped at the rumps of the two horses on
the other end of the rope. Slowly the dandy was raised into
the air, his body twisting, his legs kicking, his face turning
red, then blue, then black. Some noises came out of his
distorted mouth.

"Sartor Resartus." Karinin guided Una Persson past the
gallows and ducked to push back the flap of his yurt and
allow her to precede him. The yurt was illuminated by a
lamp on a chest—a bowl of fat with a wick burning in it.
The little round room was tidily furnished with a wooden
bed and a table, as well as the chest.

Karinin came in and began to lace up the flap from the
inside.

Una Persson removed her coat and put it on the chest.
She unbuckled her ammunition belt with its holstered
Smith and Wesson .45 and placed it on top of the coat.

Karinin's slanting eyes were tender and passionate. He
stepped forward and took her to him. His breath smelled
of fresh milk.

"We of the steppe have not lost the secret of affection,"
he told her. They lay down in the narrow bed. He began
to tug at his belt. "It comes between love and lust. We
believe in moderation, you see."

"It sounds attractive." Much against her better judgement she responded to his caress.

NYE

Ironmaster House was built of grey stones. It was Jacobean, with the conventional small square-leaded windows, three floors, five chimneys, a grey slate roof. Around its walls, particularly over the portico, climbed roses, wisteria and evergreens. Its gardens were divided by tall, ornamental privet hedges; there was a small lawn at the front and a larger lawn at the back. The back lawn ran down to a brook which fed a pool in which water-lilies were blooming. In the middle of the lawn, a water-spray swept back and forth like a metronome, for it was June and the temperature was 96°F.

From the open windows of the timbered sitting room it was possible to see both gardens, which were full of fuchsia, hydrangeas, gladioli and roses all sweetening the heavy air with their scent. And among these flowers, as if drugged, groggily flew some bees, butterflies, wasps and bluebottles.

Inside the shadowy house and seated on mock-Jacobean arm-chairs near a real Jacobean table, sat Major Nye in his shirt-sleeves; two girls, one fair and one dark; and Major Nye's wife, Mrs. Nye, a rather strong looking, weather-beaten woman with a contemptuous manner, a stoop and unpleasant hands.

Mrs. Nye was serving a sparse tea. She poured from a mock Georgian, mock silver teapot into real Japanese porcelain cups. She sliced up a seed cake and slid the slices onto matching plates.

Major Nye had not bought Ironmaster House. His wife had inherited it. He had, however, worked hard to support the place; it was expensive to run. Since leaving the army and becoming Company Secretary to the Mercantile Charitable Association, he had lost his sense of personal authority. Many of his anxieties were new; he had previously never experienced anything like them and consequently was at a loss to know how to cope with them. This had earned him the contempt of his wife, who no longer loved him, but continued to command his loyalty. One of the girls in the room was Elizabeth, his daughter. He had another daughter, Isobel, who was a dancer in a company which worked principally on ocean-going liners, and he had a small son who had won a chorister's scholarship to St. James' School, Southwark, a school reputed to be unnecessarily brutal but, as Major Nye would explain, it had been the only chance 'the poor little chap had to get into a public school', since the major could not afford to pay the kind of fees expected by Eton, Harrow or Winchester (his own school). In the army Major Nye had rarely had to make a choice; but in civilian life he had been given only a few choices and most of his decisions had been inevitable, for he had his duty to do to his wife, her house and his children. During the summer they usually took a couple of paying guests and they also sold some of the produce of their market garden at the roadside. Mrs. Nye was seriously considering selling teas on the lawn to passing motorists.

Major Nye had to work solidly from six in the morning until nine or ten o'clock at night all through the week and the weekend. His wife also worked like a martyr to help keep the garden and the house going. Her heart was weak and his ulcer problems were growing worse. He had sold all his shares and there was a double mortgage on the house. Because he was insured, he hoped that he would die as soon as his son went up to Oxford in ten years' time. There were no paying guests at the moment. Those who did turn up never came for a second year; the atmosphere of the big house was sad and tense and hopeless.

Elizabeth, the dark-haired girl, was large-boned and inclined to fatness. She had a loud, cheerful voice which was patronising when she addressed her father, accusing when she spoke to her mother and almost conciliatory when she talked to the fair-haired girl with whom, for the past nine months, she had been having a romantic love affair. This affair had never once faltered in its intensity. The fair-haired girl was being very polite to Elizabeth's parents whom she was meeting for the first time. She had a low, calm, unaffected voice. Her name was Catherine Cornelius and she had turned from incest to lesbianism with a certain sense of relief. Elizabeth Nye was the third girl she had seduced but the only one with whom she had been able to sustain a relationship for very long.

It was Catherine who had asked Elizabeth to get Major Nye to collect Jerry Cornelius from Cornwall and deliver him to Ironmaster House where her brother had been picked up by Sebastian Auchinek's agents and transported to Dubrovnik. Catherine had come to know Sebastian Auchinek through Una Persson who had introduced Catherine to her first lover, Mary Greasby. Una Persson had once possessed mesmeric power over Catherine similar to that which Catherine now possessed over Elizabeth. Una Persson had convinced Catherine that Prinz Lobkowitz in Berlin would be able to cure Jerry of his hydrophilia and so Catherine had been deceived into providing the collateral (her brother) for the guns which had helped reduce Athens. She had also been instrumental in delivering Jerry into the hands of his old regimental commander, Colonel Pyat of the 'Razin' 11th Don Cossack Cavalry, who, for some time, had been obsessed with discovering the reason for Cornelius's desertion. He desperately wanted, once he had proved Jerry authentic, to revive the assassin and question him.

Catherine was only gradually becoming aware of her mistake. She had still not voiced the suspicion, even to herself, that Una Persson might have deceived her.

"And how is the poor blighter?" asked Major Nye, dolefully watching the water fall through the overheated air and rolling himself a thin cigarette. "Hypothermia, wasn't it?"

"I'm not sure, Major. I haven't heard from Berlin yet. It's confused, as you know."

"It beats me," said Mrs. Nye harshly, rising to collect the tea paraphernalia, "how your brother managed to get himself into that state. But then I suppose I'm behind the times." Her wide, cruel mouth hardened. "Even the diseases have changed since I was a girl." She gave her husband a sharp, accusing glare. She hated him for his ulcers. "You haven't eaten your scone, dear."

"Old tummy . . ." he mumbled. "I'd better see to that weeding." His wife knew how to whip him on.

"The heat . . ." said Catherine Cornelius, and her bosom heaved. "Isn't it a bit . . .?"

"Used to the heat, my girl." He squared his shoulders. A funny little smile appeared beneath his grey moustache. There was considerable pride in his stance. "Drilled in full dress uniform. India. Much worse than this. Like the heat." He lit the cigarette he had rolled. "You're the cream in my coffee, I'm the milk in your tea, pom-te-pomm-pom-pom-pom." He smiled shyly and affectionately at her as he opened the door which led into the back garden. He gave her a comic, swaggering salute. "See you later, I hope."

Left alone, Elizabeth and Catherine looked longingly at each other across the real Jacobean table.

"We should be getting back to Ladbroke Grove soon if we're not to get caught in the traffic," said Catherine glancing at the door through which Mrs. Nye had passed with the tea things.

"Yes," said Elizabeth. "We shouldn't leave it too late, should we?"

J.C.

Jerry's coffin was being rocked about quite a lot. The train carrying it stopped suddenly once again. It was about a mile outside Coventry. The awful smell always increased when the train was stationary. Was it the steam?

Colonel Pyat got up from the dirty floor to peer through the little hole in the armour plating of his truck. The light was fading but he could see a grimy grey-green field and a pylon. On the horizon were rows of red brick houses. He looked at his watch. It was nine o'clock in the evening; it had been exactly three days since the train had left Edinburgh. Pyat brushed at his torn and grubby uniform. He had nothing else to wear, yet it was now far too dangerous to be seen in military uniform outside London. He munched the last half of his stale sandwich and sipped a drop of vodka from his hip flask. There had been no change in Cornelius and Pyat had had no time to revive and question him. The colonel had given up his original ambition, anyway; now he hoped he might use the contents of the coffin as his safe-conduct, his guarantee of asylum, when he reached Ladbroke Grove and contacted one of the Cornelius relatives. Matters had not gone well in Berlin after Auchinek and his Zaporozhian allies had arrived. Somebody had told Pyat that no one could hold Berlin for more than a month and he hadn't believed them. Now this knowledge was his consolation—even the Jew would not last long before someone else took over what was left of the city.

From within the coffin came a further succession of

479

muffled shrieks and cries. Pyat heard a querulous shout
from further up the train. Another voice replied in a
strong Wolverhampton accent.

"Electricity failure, they think. The two other trains
can't run. No signals, see."

Again the distant shout and the Wolverhampton voice
replying: "We'll be moving shortly. We can't go until
the signal says we can."

Pyat lit a cigarette. Sourly he paced the carriage,
wishing he had thought of a better plan. A week ago
England had seemed the safest state in Europe. Now it
was in chaos. He should have guessed what would happen. Everything broke down so rapidly nowadays. But
then, on the other hand, things came together quickly,
too. It was the price you paid for swift communications.

The light faded and the single electric bulb in the
roof glowed and then dimmed until only the element
shone with a dull orange colour. Pyat had become used
to this. He settled down to try to sleep, convinced that
the sharp pain which had returned to his chest could
only be lung cancer.

He began to nod off. But then the sounds from the
coffin filled his head. They had changed in tone so that
this time they seemed to be warning him of something.
They had become more urgent. He stretched out his
boot and kicked at the coffin. "Shut up. I don't need any
more of that."

But the urgency of the cries did not abate.

Pyat climbed to his feet and stumbled forward with
the intention of unstrapping the lid and putting a gag of
some kind into Cornelius's mouth. But then the truck
lurched. He fell. The big Pacific class loco was moving
again. He hugged his bruised body. His eyes were tightly
shut.

It was dawn.

A green Morgan of the decadent Plus 8 period droned
swiftly along the platform, passing the train as it pulled
at last into an almost deserted Kings Cross station. The
car followed the train for a moment, then turned off the
platform into the main ticket office and drove through the
outer doors and down the steps into the street. Through
his peephole Colonel Pyat watched blearily, certain that

the Morgan had some connection with himself. A strong smell, like that of a fair quantity of hard-boiled eggs, reached his nostrils. He spat on the boards and jammed his eyes once again to the spy-hole.

Expecting a large crowd at Kings Cross, he had planned to lose himself in it. But there were no crowds. There was no one. It was as if all the people had been cleared from the station. Could it be an ambush? Or merely an air-raid?

The locomotive released a huge sigh of hot steam and halted.

Pyat remembered that he was unarmed.

If he emerged from the carriage now, would he be shot down? Where were the marksmen hiding?

He unbolted the sliding doors of the wagon and slid them back. He waited for the other passengers to disembark. After a few seconds it became clear that there were no other passengers. A few small, innocent sounds came from various parts of the station. A clatter. A cheerful whistling. A thump. Then silence. He saw the fireman and the driver and the guard leave the train and swagger through the barrier towards the main exit, carrying their gear. They wore dirty BR uniforms; their caps were pushed back as far as possible on their heads. They were all three middle-aged, stocky and plain. They walked slowly, chatting easily to each other. They turned a corner and were gone. Pyat felt abandoned. Steam still clung to the lower parts of the train and drifted over the platform. Pyat sniffed the smoky air as a hound might sniff for a fox. The high, sooty arches of the station were silent and the glass dome admitted only a little dirty sunlight.

Because it was dawn, a bird or two began to twitter in the steel beams near the roof.

Pyat shivered and got down. Walking to the far side of the platform he took hold of a large porter's trolley. The wheels squeaked and grated. He dragged it alongside the armoured carriage. He felt faint. He looked warily about him. Silent, untended trains stood at every platform. Huge black and green steam engines with dirty brasswork faced worn steel bumpers and the blank brick walls beyond. They were like monsters shocked into catatonia by a sudden understanding: this had been their last journey. They had been lured into involuntary hibernation, perhaps to remain here until they rusted and rotted to dust.

Pyat manhandled the heavy coffin onto the trolley. It bumped down and a somewhat pettish mewling escaped from it. Pyat took the handles of the trolley with both hands. He strained backwards and got it moving. He hauled it with some difficulty along the asphalt. The wheels squeaked and groaned. In his filthy white uniform he might have been mistaken for a porter who had been mysteriously transferred from some more tropical station, perhaps in India. He was not really as conspicuous as he felt.

He trudged through the ticket barrier, crossed the grey expanse of the enclave and reached the pavement outside. The streets and buildings all seemed uninhabited. Wasn't this the heart of London? And a Thursday morning? Pyat looked up at the bland sky. There were no aircraft to be seen. No dirigibles. No flying bombs. The bright early sunshine was already quite warm. It dulled his shivers.

A tattered horse-drawn lavender cab stood untended by the kerb outside the main entrance. Now that the Morgan had disappeared, it was the only form of transport in sight. The driver, however, was nowhere to be seen. Pyat decided that he did not care about the driver. With almost the last of his strength, Pyat got the coffin into the hansom and climbed up to the box. He shook the reins and the bony mare raised her head. He flicked her rump with the frayed whip and shouted at her. She began to walk.

Slowly the hansom moved away, the horse refusing to go faster than a walk. It was as if the hansom were the only visible portion of an otherwise invisible funeral procession. The horse's feet clopped mournfully through the deserted street. It reached Euston Road and began to head due west for Ladbroke Grove.

PROLOGUE (continued)

. . . and perhaps the greatest loss I still feel is the loss of my unborn son. I was certain it would have been a son and I had even named it, my subconscious coming up with a name I would never have chosen otherwise: Andrew. I had not realized what would happen to me. The abortion seemed so necessary at the time if she were not to suffer in several ways. But it was an abortion of convenience, scarcely of desperation. For a long while I did not admit that it had affected me at all. If I had ever had a son after that, I feel it would have banished the sense of loss, but as it is it will go with me to my grave.

MAURICE LESCOQ, Leavetaking

SHOT
TWO

Thunder Brings Coma Boy Back to Life

Only a miracle could save nine-year-old Lawrence Mantle, said doctors. For four months he had been in a deep coma. Twice he 'died' when his heart stopped beating. There was no sign of life from his brain, surgeons told his parents. Then, in the middle of a thunderstorm, it happened. A flash of lightning and a loud thunderclap made nurses in the children's ward at Ashford hospital, Middlesex, jump . . . and Lawrence, still in a coma, screamed.

LONDON EVENING NEWS, December 3 1969

THE OBSERVERS

Colonel Pyat had first met Colonel Cornelius in Guatemala City, in the early days of the 1900-75 War, before the monorails, the electric carriages, the giant airships, the domed cities and the utopian republics had been smashed, never to be restored. They met at some time during what is now called the Phoney War period of 1901-13. They were both representing the military establishments of two great and mutually suspicious European governments. They had been sent to observe the trials of the Guatemalans' latest Land Ironclad (the invention of the Chilean wizard, O'Bean). Their two governments had been interested in purchasing a number of the machines should the trials prove successful. As it happened, both Pyat and Cornelius had decided that the 'clad was still too primitive to be of much practical use, though the French, German and Turkish governments, who also had observers at the trials, had each ordered a small quantity.

Their duty done, the two men relaxed together in the bar of the Conquistador Hotel, where they were both staying. Next day they would catch the aerial clipper *Light of Dresden* to Hamburg. Once there, they would go their separate ways, Cornelius to the West and Pyat to the East.

Through the tall, slightly frosted Charles Rennie Mackintosh windows they could see Guatemala City's bright marble streets and elegant mosaic towers with shopfronts by Mucha, Moulins and Marnez. Sometimes an ornate electric brougham would hum past, or there would be the somewhat anachronistic jingle of harness as a landau, drawn by high-stepping Arab stallions, rattled by; sometimes a steam car would come and go, the hiss from its engines barely audible, the sun catching its brasswork and making its stainless steel body shine like silver. The steam car was now in use all over the world. Like the mechanical farming equipment which had turned South and Central America into such a paradise, it was the creation of O'Bean.

Colonel Pyat, leaning back in his black plush chair, signalled for the waiter to bring fresh drinks. Jerry admired his grace. The Russian had been wearing his white uniform for the best part of the afternoon and there was not a smudge of dust to be seen on it. Even his belts, his holster and his boots were of white kid, the only colour being the gold insignia on his collar and a touch of gold on his epaulettes. Jerry's dark green uniform was fussy in comparison, with a smear of oil evident on the right cuff. Some of the gold braid frogging on his sleeves, shoulders and chest was badly snagged, too. His belts, holster and boots were black. They were not quite as brightly polished as they might have been. Like Pyat's, his was a cavalry uniform, that of some Indian regiment by the cut of the long-skirted coat, but worn without a sash. (Pyat, who had seen some service on the frontier—largely courier work of an unofficial nature—could not place the uniform at all. He wondered if Cornelius might be a civilian given military rank for the sake of this assignment. Cerainly Cornelius did not look much like an English cavalryman. The way he had undone his coat at the first opportunity suggested that Cornelius found military dress uncomfortable.)

The drinks were brought by a haughty waiter who refused to respond to Pyat's friendly and condescending smile and left the proffered tip on the Husson silver salver he placed on the table. "Democracy gone mad!" said Pyat with a movement of his eyebrows and leaned forward to see what they had. There were Tiffany glasses. A bottle of Malvern water. A Glen Grant malt whisky and a Polish vodka. Jerry looked at them all resting on the Dufrêne inlay.

"They think we are barbarians," said Pyat, filling Jerry's glass with whisky and letting Jerry add his own Malvern water, "but they do not mind selling us weapons and war machines. Where would their economy be without us?"

Jerry reached his hand halfway to his drink. "They'd like us to get it over with, though. We disturb them by our

continued existence. We've been staving off the apocalypse
for so long. Suppose we turned on them? They have no
army."

"Then they are fools. How long can this *traumrepublik*
last? A few more years?"

"Months, more likely. Keep your voice down. They don't
have to know . . ."

Pyat's ironic glance gave way to a look of introspection.
"You speak like a priest. Not a soldier." It was a statement
which hoped for a reply, but Jerry merely smiled and
picked up his glass.

"To which regiment do you belong, Colonel" Pyat decided on a direct approach.

Jerry looked curiously at his uniform as if he himself
hoped to find some clue to the answer there. "The 30th
Deccan Horse, I think."

"You have been seconded, then?"

"Quite likely. No."

"You are a civilian!"

Jerry laughed. "Well, I'm not sure, you know." He shook
his head. There were tears in his eyes now as his whole
body trembled with mirth. "I'm simply not sure."

Pyat laughed too, because he enjoyed laughing. "Let's
get a bottle each, shall we? I have a suite upstairs. And
perhaps someone can find us a couple of girls? Or perhaps
two girls will volunteer their services! Everyone is eman-
cipated in Guatemala City!"

"Fine!"

When they had risen, Pyat flung his arm around Jerry's
slender shoulders. "Do you feel like a girl, Colonel Cornelius?"

THE PERFORMERS

Dressed as a gentleman, Una Persson stalked the stage behind the green velvet curtain.

From the other side of the curtain came the noise of the crowd: shouts, laughter, screams, ironic cheers, groans, the clink of glasses and bottles, the rustle of heavy clothing. In the pit the orchestra was tuning up for the overture.

His paleness emphasised by the astrakhan collar of his chesterfield, Sebastian Auchinek raised a gold-tipped Unfiadis to his curved lips and coughed. He sat on a prop —an imitation rock—and looked through hooded eyes at the ballet girls in their frothy costumes as they took their places for the opening divertissement. Behind the girls was a backdrop showing Windsor Castle. The girls were dressed to represent *Rose, Shamrock, Thistle* and *Wales* (in a tall black hat and a pinafore because a Leek had been thought too indelicate a plant). The divertissement was entitled "Under One Flag." In the wings, waiting to go on, stood Sailors, Highlanders and Beefeaters. Una Persson was not appearing in the first of the two tableaux. She would feature in the second, "Honour to the Queen," and lead the chorus in the closing cantata.

"You will be a success, Una!" Auchinek got up and caught her by the arm. "You are bound to be! Come, the curtain!" The gas flared brightly above the stage, the electrical spotlights began to come on. "It is going up!"

She walked swiftly into the wings. Auchinek hurried behind her. She pushed her way nervously past Mr. Clement Scott, author of the opening Patriotic Ode. The orchestra began to play a rousing chorus of the satirical *Oh, What a Happy Land is England:*

We shall soon be buying Consols, at the rate of
                              Half-a-crown,
For like the Russian battleships, they're always
                              going down!
We have lately built an Airship and the only
                              thing it lacks
Is the power to go on rising like the British
                              Income Tax!

> *Hip-hip-hooray!*
> *Oh! what a happy land is England!*
> *Envied by all Nations near and far!*
> *Where the wretched Alien*
> *Robs the British working men!*
> *Oh! what a lucky race we are!*
> *Oh! what a happy land is England!*
> *Envied by all Nations near and far!*
> *All Foreigners have found*
> *This a happy dumping ground!*
> *Oh! what a lucky race we are!*

sang the audience and then began to cheer. The curtain rose.

Una reached the dressing room. Though she shared it with Marguerite Cornille, the comedienne, it was the best equipped dressing room she had ever used. This was her first time at the Empire, Leicester Square. It was one of the most respected of the newer, better class of music halls: a Theatre of Varieties. But it was the very reputation and respectability of the Empire which distressed Una so much. She was used to the friendlier, less ostentatious halls of Stepney, Brixton and Shepherds Bush.

"The atmosphere's a bit frosty." She entered the dressing room and nodded to Mlle. Cornille who was making up already, with one eye on the mirror and the other on a magazine she held in her left hand, even though she was tenth on the programme.

"You get used to it, love. The crowd's all right. Same as anywhere." The pert-faced girl was re-reading a short photographic feature about herself in *Nash's Magazine* which had just come out. "The rules and the snobs is the price you pay for regular work. It's my last week here. It'll be back to three different halls a night for me if I'm

lucky and no halls at all if it's really bad. So my two
weeks at the Alhambra over Christmas'll be like a holiday." She was boasting a bit, for a feature in *Nash's* usually meant a few good bookings at very least. Una wondered if *she* would ever go so far as showing her legs for
a *Nash's* photographer.

Auchinek came in, closing the door softly behind him.
"A good audience, by the sound of it."

"What I was saying," said Mlle. Cornille.

Auchinek offered them Unfiadis Egyptian cigarettes from
his gold Liberty's case. Mlle. Cornille shook her head, but
Una accepted one. As she lit it herself she looked closely
at Auchinek, wondering what his real thoughts were.

"It's a step up, Una." He was her agent and in love with
what he saw as her perfection, but he was embarrassed by
the fact that he found Mlle. Cornille's brown curls and
buxom charms more physically attractive. He was hoping
that Una had not noticed. That Mlle. Cornille had noticed
was evident in the attitude of friendly contempt she took
towards him.

Una picked up her music and read over the lines of her
songs as she finished the cigarette. There was a knock
on the door. "Overture and beginners second tab."

Una felt her stomach muscles tighten. She spread her
fingers wide as she ran her plams down the front of her
thighs, over her trousers. Auchinek stepped forward and
adjusted her bow tie. He handed her the cane and the silk
opera hat, he flicked a speck of glitter from her tailcoat.
"All right?"

She smiled. If she had had her own way she would have
remained out of the West End, but she knew that he desperately wanted her to get to the top; and that was what
performing at the Empire meant.

"Good luck, love," said Mlle. Cornille, both eyes now
on her article.

"Stay here," said Una to Auchinek.

"I'd rather . . ." He glanced guiltily away from the
comedienne. "Give you moral support."

"Stay here." She straightened her coat and put on her
silk hat. "You can come to the wings and watch as soon
as I'm on."

"Very well."

She walked down the corridor. Against a tide of

returning Highlanders, Sailors, Beefeaters, Roses, Shamrocks, Thistles and Welsh girls, she made her way towards the wings. In the wings she saw that the chorus was already arranging itself on stage. There were eight girls, each dressed as a colony. There was India, Canada, Australia, Cape Colony, the West Indies, Malta, Gibraltar and New Zealand, each with her own verse to sing. In the opposite wings waited Art, Science, Commerce, Industry and a splendid Britannia, whose carriage they were to draw on stage. That was when Una would come on.

The curtain rose and the orchestra began a rousing accompaniment as the chorus sang together:

We, the children of the Empire, pay homage to
our Queen!
And we know she can be counted on where e'er her
flag is seen!
She's good, she's just, she's mighty and we know
you will agree
She's loved, admired and envied through all the
seven seas!

Una felt calm now. The music was jolly enough and the audience applauded loudly at the end of every verse and joined in each chorus. They weren't anything like as stuffy as she'd thought they'd be.

Art, Science, Commerce and Industry began to pull at Britannia's carriage. The float moved forward with a slight lurch. India, Canada, Australia, Cape Colony, the West Indies, Malta, Gibraltar and New Zealand fell back on two sides of the stage. The orchestra struck up with the opening bars of Una's introduction. Una cleared her throat, took a deep breath and poised herself.

The gaslight dimmed.

At first Una thought it had been done for deliberate dramatic effect. But then the lights went out altogether, including the electrics, and the clapping faded, matches were struck, an anxious murmur began to fill the theatre.

Something exploded in the gallery. Someone shouted loudly. Women screamed. Una Persson was thrown backwards into the curtains and fell down. Feet struck her face and a body fell across her legs. The curtain collapsed over her. She heard muffled exclamations.

"Anarchists!"

"An air-raid!"

"Una? Una?" Auchinek's voice.

She tried to get up but could not fight free of the velvet folds.

"Sebastian!"

"Una!" His soft hands began to tear away the curtains. She saw his face. It was bright red. There were flames leaping in the stalls. The crowd was a confused mass of flapping coat-tails, bustles and feather hats. It was climbing onto the stage, unable to use the ordinary exits.

Auchinek helped her to her feet. The heat from the flames was horrible. They were almost pushed into the orchestra pit by the panic-stricken audience. He held her tightly.

"What happened?" She let him guide her back to the wings. They were carried with the crowd towards the stage door. The fire roared behind them. Smoke made their eyes water and stung their throats. Props crashed down. Individual voices blended into one terrified wail.

"Incendiary bomb. Dropped from the gallery, I think. Why did it have to be tonight, Una? Your most important chance. The theatre will be closed for a week at least."

They reached the alley which ran beside the theatre. It was clogged with bewildered entertainers in flimsy, polychrome costumes, the frightened audience in heavy serge and scarlet and green velvet. At the end of the alley stood a tall, bearded policeman trying to calm the crowd and stop it from rushing headlong over the edge of the street and into the forty-foot-deep crater which, until the air-raids had begun a month ago, had been Leicester Square.

By the time the fire engines arrived at the front of the theatre, many of the people had been allowed to pass through the police cordon and the press had thinned. It was cold and there was a trace of fog in the air. The gas must have been turned off at a main, for none of the nearby street lamps was alight. The only illumination came from the policemen's bullseyes and the fire itself. She felt full of relief. "Back to Brixton," she said. "What's bad luck for some is good luck for others, Seb, my boy."

He directed at her a mixed look of misery and malice. "Don't count on Brixton, Una. At this rate they'll be closing down all the halls." He regretted his spite. "I'm sorry." He took off his coat and placed it round her shoulders over the man's jacket she still wore.

More fire engines arrived—steamers this time—and the police let a substantial number of people through the cordon.

A sensation of being watched made her glance back at the theatre. She saw a young man leaning against the open stage door looking for all the world like a masher waiting casually for the appearance of his favourite chorus girl. He wore a dark yellow frock-coat with an exaggerated waist and flair, with brown braid at collar and cuff. He had a matching bowler with its brim tightly curled, a light brown cravat, and bell bottomed trousers cut very tight at the knee. The trousers were in a mustard check some would have considered vulgar. His gold-topped stick was in his left hand and an empty amber cigar-holder in his right. On the third finger of his right hand was a heavy gold signet ring. He seemed either unaware of the confusion around him or careless of it.

Una Persson regarded him with interest. His black, soft hair hung straight to his shoulders in the style of the aesthetes of some years earlier. His long, lean face bore an ambiguous expression which might have been amusement or satisfaction or surprise. His black eyes were large, deep-set, unreadable. Suddenly, with a nod to her, he stepped sideways and entered the burning theatre. Impulsively she made to follow him. Then she felt Auchinek's hand on her shoulder.

"Don't worry," he said. "This can't last forever."

She looked again at the stage door. The dark smoky interior of the theatre was now alive with red flame. She saw the young man's silhouette against the firelight before it disappeared, apparently marching without hesitation into the heart of the inferno.

"He'll die!" Una said softly. "The heat!"

Auchinek said anxiously: "Are you sure you're yourself, Una?"

THE SEDUCERS

Mrs. Cornelius settled her pink feather boa around her broad shoulders and patted it down over the green and white fabric flowers decorating her fine big bosom. She wasn't doing too badly for thirty, she thought, giving her image a wink and dabbing at the rouge on her right cheek with a damp finger which protruded from her *broderie anglaise* cuff.

"'And up me 'at, love."

The mean-faced boy of fifteen wiped his nose on the sleeve of his tattered Norfolk jacket and reached up to the mock Georgian mahogany chiffonier for the extravagant pile of artificial roses, peonies and sweet williams topped off by a yard or two of pink gauze, some wax grapes and a pair of pheasant's wings, which rested amongst her nicknacks. In both hands he carried the hat to where she stood before the full-length fly-specked wardrobe mirror in its gilded cast-iron frame.

"And the pins, love," she reproved, donning the hat as if it were the Crown of England.

He took the three long pins with their blue, red and gold enamelled butterfly wings and presented them in the flat of his unhealthy hand, his expression cool, like a nurse proffering a surgeon his instruments. One by one she picked them from his palm and slid them like a conjurer expertly into her hat, her hair and, apparently, her head.

"Cream!" She was satisfied. She tilted the brim just a fraction to the right. She flicked at a pheasant feather.

"Shall I be in this evening?" asked the boy. His accent while by no means educated was indefinably in contrast to the woman's. "Or not?"

"Better stay at Sammy's, love. I think I'll be entertaining tonight." She smiled comfortably at herself and admired her large, well-corsetted figure for a while, hands on hips. "You're looking prime, girlie." She gathered her pale green satin skirts and pirouetted on her matching patent leather boots. "You'll do, you will."

The boy put his hands in his pockets and swaggered about the untidy, over-furnished bedroom whistling, without irony, *I'm Gilbert, the Filbert, the Colonel of the Knuts*. He marched through the open door into the gaslit parlour. The parlour was a dark jungle of aspidistra and mahogany. Opening the front door of the flat he spread his arms, running and leaping down the lodging house's uncarpeted stairs and making a high-pitched whining sound as he pretended he was a fighting aeroplane making a death dive on its enemies. He rushed panting into Blenheim Crescent and was almost knocked over by the baker's motor van which hooted at him as it puffed past in the twilight. On the corner of the dowdy street, where it met Ladbroke Grove, under the unlit lamp and by the wall of the newly-built Convent of the Poor Clares, stood a group of younger urchins. They spotted him at once. They yelled at him, jeering insults which were more than familiar to him. He veered and began to walk in the opposite direction, pretending not to have noticed them, and went up towards Kensinton Park Road and Sammy's pie shop on the corner. Some people thought Sammy might be the boy's dad, the way he favoured him. The boy always got first chance at shooting the rats in the cellar. Sammy kept a .22 pistol for the purpose. But, when pressed, the boy's mother usually claimed the Prince of Wales for the honour.

A thick, tasty smell of grease billowed from the warm shop and steam boiled in the yellow light from the street door and from the grating in the pavement under the window where, on gas burners, sat enamel trays of pies, sausages, bacon, faggots, saveloys and baked potatoes, heavy with shining, dancing fat. At his stoves behind the wooden counter stood warm, greasy Sammy. With his thin assistant beside him he gave his attention to a score of long handled frying pans, each of which contained a different kind of food. The shop having just opened for the evening, the only customer was little frightened Mrs.

Fitzgerald, from round the corner in Portobello Road, getting her husband's dinner. Her shawl was drawn close to her face, but Sammy had noticed what she was hoping to hide. "That's a lovely shiner!" He grinned sympathetically as he wrapped the pies but Mrs. Fitzgerald looked as if he had caught her in the act of some mortal sin. Her right eye was swollen green, blue and purple. She gave a barely audible but evidently embarrassed cough. The boy stared neutrally at her bruise. Sammy saw the boy. "Hello, there, nipper!" The colour of his own sausages, his fat, Jewish face ran with sweat. His striped shirt sleeves were rolled to his elbows and he wore a big white grease-spotted apron. "You come to give me a hand have you?" The boy nodded, stepping aside from Mrs. Fitzgerald who seized her pies, left the correct number of pennies on the counter, and, like a mouse making for its hole, scuttled from the shop. "Mum says can I stay the night?"

Sammy's expression became serious and he said in a different tone, attending suddenly to his frying pans, "Yes, that's all right. But you gotta work for your keep. Get yourself an apron off the hook, son. We'll be busy in a minute."

The boy removed his threadbare Norfolk and hung it on the hook at the back of the shop. Taking down a sacking apron he pulled it over his head and tied the strings round his waist. He began to roll up his sleeves. Sammy's assistant was a young man of eighteen or so, his face gleaming with large, scarlet pimples. He said, "Go on up the other end. I'll do this end." The boy squeezed past Sammy's great bottom and went to stand near the window where the sizzling trays filled his nostrils full of the stink of frying onions. His eyes wandered past the trays and through the misted glass where they fixed on the street.

It was now dark and populated. Men, women, and children came from all sides, bearing down on the pie shop, because it was Friday. They all had the glazed look of the really poor—the poverty trance had overtaken them, robbed them of their wills and their intelligence, enabling them to continue life only in terms of a few simple rituals. There was little animation on even the faces of the children and their tired, heavy movements, their set expressions, their dull eyes made it seem that they all belonged to the same family, so strongly did they resemble one another. The boy felt a shudder of fear and for no reason that he could tell he suddenly thought, with some tenderness, of his mother. He turned to look at the pub on the opposite corner to Sammy's, the Blenheim Arms. The gas was being lit. The large crowd of out-of-work Irishmen and local loafers which had gathered outside its doors gave a ragged cheer. It was opening time.

Again the boy shivered.

"What's the matter, son," said Sammy noticing. "You catching something?"

THE INTERPRETERS

Captain Nye received an order to report to his barracks, the Royal Alberts in Southwark, where his C.O., Colonel Collier, informed him that the Black Flag had been raised in Argyll and that an anarchist army of some 8,000 men was camped in Glen Coe where it would shortly be joined by a force of French Zouaves (about a thousand) which had landed at Oban a week earlier, claiming to be independent volunteers. It was no secret that the French had territorial ambitions in Scotland, but this was the most blatant act of support to the rebel clans they had yet given. It was putting a distinct strain on the fiction of the Entente Cordiale.

"We do not want a direct confrontation with France for all sorts of reasons at the moment." Colonel Collier fingered his buttons and the cuffs of his tunic. "So this must be handled damned delicately, Nye. Neither, it seems, does the present government want any military action against the hill tribes if we can help it. You've had dealings with these people before, I gather?"

"I've some experience of the Highland clans, sir."

"I want you to go and talk to Gareth-mac Mahon, their chief. He's a sly old devil, by all accounts. Used to serve with one of our native regiments. Learned all our tricks, needless to say, and took 'em back to the hills with him. I'm sure he knows he can't beat us. Probably be satisfied with a few concessions. So find out what he wants and let us know as soon as possible. This is more in the nature of a diplomatic mission than a military one."

"I understand, sir."

"They're plucky blighters, but it looks as if their virtues

499

have turned into vices." Collier stood up behind his desk.
"It's the same with their pride. They're prepared to sacrifice all that they've gained under British rule in order to
chase this chimera of 'independence'. Even if they should
have some success, the French would move in at once. Mahon must realise this. They call him the Red Fox, I gather.
Because of his cunning. Well, he's certainly no fool. Try to
talk him round."

Captain Nye refused the offer of a squadron of motor
escorted cavalry and instead asked for a single small dirigible flying machine which might be loaned by the Royal
Airship Corps. "Let us impress them," he said, "with our
science rather than our sabres."

Glen Coe was glorious in her autumn colours. Her
bronze hills shivered with white streams which fell from
scores of sources high up near the crest of the range. The
dirigible hovered over the valley and Captain Nye peered
through the observation ports in the large aluminium gondola and noticed, with some satisfaction, the consternation
of the Zouaves in their blue tarbooshes, blue tunics and
baggy red trousers as they became aware of the green and
khaki camouflaged monster over their heads. The shadow
of the ship moved implacably across the camp, its steam
turbines purring as a hungry leopard might purr while
stalking a herd of unsuspecting and succulent antelope.
Down the glen sailed the aerial frigate, just a few feet
above the tops of the tallest hills, following the boisterous
river upstream to the falls at the far end of the valley. The
bravest of the French mercenaries (if mercenaries they
were) took a few pot-shots at the airship, but either they
missed, fell short, or their bullets failed to penetrate the
tough boron-fibre shell of the vessel.

Then the Zouaves were left behind and Captain Nye
signalled to the captain to cut his engines to half-speed, for
they were almost at their destination. The main camp lay
ahead, a collection of semi-ruined crofts, hide tents, and
peat or bracken shelters. They were clustered on the tawny
hillside which shone like beaten gold as the sunlight struck
it. Horses, tracked vehicles, Bofors guns and Banning cannon, as well as cooking and medical equipment, had been
scattered apparently at random amongst the other paraphernalia of the camp. Broadswords, dirks and lances glit-

tered beside pyramids of stacked rifles with fixed bayonets. Kilted clansmen sat talking in groups, passing bottles and cigarettes, or else wandered drunkenly about with no apparent purpose. Over this savage encampment fluttered the sinister black banner of Anarchy—Mahon's adopted standard. Gareth-mac Mahon's own tent was easily spotted. It was a huge expanse of intricately woven blue, yellow, green and scarlet plaid. The scarlet was predominant. The folds of this great pavilion undulated slightly in a wind which blew through the hills from the west.

"Break out the flag now, sir?" The smart young second officer saluted Nye and the airship's captain, a man named Bastable. Bastable looked enquiringly at Nye. Nye nodded. They watched as the white parley flag billowed over the side, suspended from a line attached to the stern of the control gondola.

"Take her down a couple of degrees height, coxswain," said Captain Bastable.

"Two degrees down, sir."

The ship dropped lower. Its engines reversed to keep it steady against the wind. As it fell, a number of the savages dived for cover while their braver (or drunker) comrades ran forward waving their broadswords and howling like devils. They calmed down when they recognised the white flag, but they did not sheath their swords. They watched with glowering suspicion as the ship steadied less than fifteen feet over the Mahon's own tent. Captain Nye brushed his fine brown moustache with the back of his hand, waited a few moments and then stepped onto the outer gallery and stood with one hand on the rail, the other in a dignified salute of peace, speaking clearly in their own language. "I come to offer peace to the Mahon. To you all." There was a pause while the savages continued to glower and then the flap of the pavilion was pushed back and a heavy Scotlander emerged. For all his barbaric finery, the Mahon was an impressive man. He was clad in the traditional costume of the hill chieftain: the philabeg kilt, the huge, hairy sporran; the elaborately worked (if rather grubby) lace shirt, the plentitude of little leather straps and buttons and buckles and pins of bronze and silver, the big woollen bonnet secured by a hawk-feather badge; the green coatee with silver epaulettes; the black, buckled shoes; the clan plaid flung over his shoulder—the regalia befitting a great clan leader. All the cloth he wore, save for the coat and shirt, including the decorative tops of his green cross-gartered stockings, was of the same tartan as the tent. Nye recognised it as the red Mahon Fighting sett. The Mahon himself was short and broad-shouldered, with a red, belligerent face. He had a hooked nose, pale, piercing blue eyes and a monstrous grey-streaked red beard. With one hand on the hilt of his heavy, basket-hilted broadsword and the other on his hip he raised his head slowly, calling out in a proud growl.

"The Mahon acknowledges your truce flag. Do you come to parley?"

Although the Red Fox revealed nothing by his expression, Captain Nye was sure he was properly impressed by the aerial frigate. "My government wants to preserve peace, O Mahon," he said in English. "May I descend to the ground?"

"If ye wish." Gareth-mac Mahon replied in the same language.

At Captain Nye's request, the rail was broken and a rope ladder rolled through the gap. Nye went down the ladder with as much dignity as was possible until he stood confronting the wily old hill fox. This was a man who had discovered the creed of anarchism while serving as a soldier in the capitals of the civilised world. He had brought the creed back to his native land, adapted it and turned it into a philosophy capable of bringing together all the previously disunited tribes. Nye was by no means deceived by the Mahon's appearance. He was well aware that he was not addressing a simple savage. If he had known nothing at all about the Mahon, he would still have recognised the look of profound cunning which glinted even now in those pale eyes.

"O Chieftain," began the captain in Scottish as soon as he had recovered his breath, "you have made the great Chief-of-us-All sad. I come to tell you this. He wonders why his children gather all these weapons to themselves." He spread his arms to indicate the camp. "And give hospitality to soldiers from other shores."

In the distance the autumn river roared down the narrow gorge, its flow altering constantly as it was fed by a thousand tiny streams which streaked the hills; white veins in yellow marble. Throughout the half mile radius of the camp the savage warriors stood and looked as their leader talked with the soldier who had come from the sky. Each of the men had a naked sword in his hand and Nye knew that if he made one mistake he would never be able to reach the airship before he was slaughtered beneath those shining blades.

The Red Fox's smile was grim and his eyes were like polished granite. "His Majesty will be sadder still, O Emissary, when he learns we intend to make war on those of our own folk who are foolish enough to side with the soldiers. We have already razed Fort William IV."

"The Chief-of-us-All should punish you for that," said the captain. "but he is slow to anger. He understands that his children have been misled by the honeyed tongues of men from across the seas. Men who would make his children fight their battles for them."

The Mahon rubbed his nose with a large hand and looked amused. "Tell His Majesty that we are not his children. We are mountain warriors. We shall preserve our ancient ways. We would rather die than become the subject race of any foreigner."

"But what of your women? Your sons and your daughters? Do they wish to see their menfolk die? Will they be happy if the schools, the doctors, the medicines— aye and the merchants who buy their wares—disappear from this land?"

"We'll provide our own schools and doctors—and we'll have no more merchants ever again in the mountains of Argyll!"

Captain Nye smiled at the idea and was about to reply when he noticed a movement of the tent flap behind the Mahon.

A tall figure emerged to stand at the chief's side. He wore a suit of heather-mixture tweeds. A shooting hat was pulled down to shade his face, a monocle gleamed in his right eye. From his mouth jutted a black cheroot. "I'm afraid you'll have no luck with that argument, captain. The chief here has already decided that the advantages of British rule are outweighed by the dis- advantages."

For all the evidence of his eyes and ears, Captain Nye could hardly believe that this was an Englishman. A renegade. He tried to hide his astonishment. "Who the devil are you, sir?"

"Just an observer, old chap. And an advisor, of sorts, I suppose." The man paused, his attention given to the faint humming which filled the air, drowning, eventually, the sound of the water. He smiled.

"This is Mr. Cornelius," said the Mahon. "He has helped us with our fleet. Here it comes now." The hill chieftain pointed behind Nye. The captain turned to look.

Over the brow of the farthest hills came swimming upwards of a hundred massive aerial men-o'-war. They were airships of a type far in advance of anything Nye had seen before. They bristled with artillery gondoli. Their slender cigar-shaped hulls were like the bodies of gigantic sharks. On each silver-grey side, on each elevator fin was painted a livery which combined the black flag of Anarchy and the blue cross of Scotland.

"Cornelius . . .?" Nye looked back towards the tent but the tall man had gone inside. The Red Fox chuckled. "An engineer, I believe," he said, "of some experience." He broke into English. "Perhaps we shall meet again in Whitehall, will we not, Master Emissary?"

"I'll be damned!"

Nye turned again to look at the massive battle fleet cramming the sky, to notice the power of the guns, to speculate upon the destruction they and the aerial torpedoes could accomplish. "I'm dreaming."

"D'ye think so?"

THE EXPLORERS

Catherine Cornelius left her brother's lodgings in Powys Square. She hurried back through the dark streets to her own house where she had heard Prinz Lobkowitz and his friends awaited her. One or two gaslamps glowed through the clinging fog but cast little light. There were a few muffled sounds, but she could identify none of them. It was with relief that she entered Elgin Crescent with its big overgrown trees and its tall comfortable houses; perhaps because the street was so familiar the fog did not seem so thick, though she still had to walk with some care until she reached Number 61. Shivering, she unlatched the gate and at last mounted her own steps, searching in her Dorothy bag for her key. She found it, unlocked the door and went inside. Fog drifted in with her. It filled the cold and gloomy hall like ectoplasm. Without taking off her coat she crossed the hall and opened the door to the drawing room. The drawing room was painted in a mixture of yellow and pale brown. She noticed that the fire was almost out. Removing her gloves she reached down and put several pieces of coal on top of the red cinders, then she turned and acknowledged the company. There were two others beside Prinz Lobkowitz; a man and a woman.

"These are the guests I mentioned," explained the Prinz softly. "I'm sorry about the fire." He indicated the woman. "Miss Brunner"—and the man—"Mr. Smiles" —and sat down in the horseshoe armchair nearest the grate, one booted foot on the brass rail.

Catherine Cornelius looked shyly at Miss Brunner and then became wary. Foxy, she thought. Miss Brunner had neat red hair and sharp, beautiful features. She wore a well-cut grey travelling cape and a small pill-box hat perched over her right eye, decorated with a green feather, a tiny veil. Her clothes were buttoned as tightly as the black boots she revealed when seating herself on the arm of Prinz Lobkowitz's chair. Mr. Smiles, bald-headed and large in a dark brown ulster, a long scarf wound several times round his neck, cleared his throat, fingered his mutton-chop whiskers as if they were not his own, unbuttoned the ulster and felt in the watch-pocket of his waistcoat, producing a gold half-hunter. He peered at it for a while before he began to wind it. "What's the time? My watch has stopped."

"Time?" Catherine Cornelius stared around the room in search of a clock that was going. There was a black marble one on the mantle, a grandfather in the corner.

"Nine twenty six," said Miss Brunner, referring to the plain silver pendant watch she wore about her neck. "Where are our rooms, my dear? And when shall we expect supper?"

Catherine passed her hand over her forehead and said vaguely, "Soon. I must apologise. My brother gave me very little warning, I'm afraid. The preparations. Excuse me. I'm sorry." And she left the room, hearing Miss Brunner say, "Well, it's a change from Calcutta."

Catherine found Mary Greasby, the maid-of-all work, in the kitchen enjoying a glass of madeira with cook. Catherine gave instructions for beds and supper to be prepared. These instructions were received with poor grace by the servants. She returned to the drawing room with a tray on which were glasses and decanters of whiskey, sherry and what remained of the madeira.

Mr. Smiles stood with his back to the grate. The fire now blazed merrily. "Ah, splendid," he said, stepping forward and taking the tray from her. "You must forgive our manners, dear lady. We have been travelling in a rough and ready way in some rather remote parts of the world. Just the thing. We were reluctant to impose, but —well, fugitives, you know, fugitives. Ha ha!" He poured whiskies for all save Catherine who raised her hand to decline.

"How is your dear brother, Miss Cornelius?" The

redheaded woman's tone was patronising. "We have missed him so much while we have been abroad."

"He is well, I think," replied Catherine. "I thank you."

"You are very alike. Are they not, Mr. Smiles?"

"Very."

"So I believe," said Catherine.

"Very alike." Reflectively Miss Brunner lowered her eyelids and sipped her drink. Catherine shivered and sat down on a hard chair near the piano.

"And how is old Frank," said Mr. Smiles. "Eh? We've had some exciting times together, he and I. How is he?"

"I am sorry to say I have not seen him recently, Mr. Smiles. He writes to Mother. The occasional postcard, you know."

"Like me, young Frank. Bit of a globe-trotter."

"Yes."

Prinz Lobkowitz rose. "I must be going, Catherine. It isn't very wise of me to stay here, considering the opinion the police hold of me at the moment. Perhaps we'll meet at the conference."

"Shall you find a cab at this time of night? If you would care to stay—"

"I dare say I'll find one. It's a long way back to Stepney. But I thank you for the offer." He bowed to Miss Brunner and kissed her hand. He shook hands with Mr. Smiles. "Goodbye. I hope your stay is peaceful." He laughed. "For you if not for them!" Catherine helped him on with his old-fashioned Armenian cloak and saw him to the front door. He bent down and kissed her on the cheek.

"Keep your spirits up, *petite Katerina*. We are sorry to make use of your house like this, but there wasn't much choice. Your brother—give him my regards. We'll probably meet soon, tell him. In Berlin, perhaps. Or at the conference?"

"I think not the conference." Catherine hugged him. "Be careful, my dear, my own dear Prinz Lobkowitz."

He opened the door and drew his muffler about his mouth and chin as the fog surged in. He fitted his tall hat on his head. There came the sound of horses' hoofs on the road outside. "A cab." Gently he squeezed her arm and then ran into the cold darkness. Catherine closed the door and started as the maid spoke from where she stood halfway up the stairs.

"Is it just the three of you now, mum?"

Miss Brunner appeared in the drawing room doorway. Her face seemed flushed, perhaps by the alcohol. She offered Catherine a look of considerable intimacy. "Oh, I think so," she said, "don't you?" She smoothed her red hair back, then she smoothed her straight flannel skirt over her thighs and pelvis. She stretched out and took Catherine's hand, leading her back into the room. Mr. Smiles stood by the piano glancing through a Mozart Sonata.

"Do you play, Miss Cornelius?"

REMINISCENCE (C)

Someone singing.

Late News

Two young boys who disappeared from Ballinkinrain approved school near Balfron, Stirlingshire, a month ago were found dead last night at the bottom of a gorge in the Frinty Hills, two miles from the school. The bodies of John Mulver, aged 10, of Balornock, Glasgow, and Ian Finlay, aged 9, of Raploch, Stirling, were found by a search party of police and civilians who have been combing the area for the past month.

GUARDIAN, April 13 1970

Two boys aged 15 and 9 were killed in Dacca today in the latest of a series of bombing incidents. A home-made bomb buried under rubbish in front of Pakistan's council building exploded. A man who was injured was seen riding frantically from the scene on his bicycle.

GUARDIAN, May 12 1970

A three-year-old boy found dead in a disused refrigerator in the garden of his home in Somerset was yesterday named as Peter Wilson, of Hillside Gardens, Yatton. It is understood the refrigerator was self-locking. Eight weeks ago three-year-old twins, Lynn and Caroline Woods, died of suffocation in a disused refrigerator in their home at Farley, near Thames Ditton.

GUARDIAN, June 2 1970

Paul Monks, aged 14, was found dead yesterday after an explosion in a wood near his home at High Street, Dawick, near Buckingham. The boy was seen on Sunday night with what appeared to be an unexploded mortar bomb.

GUARDIAN, June 2 1970

Four people were killed and six injured when a van and two
cars collided at Wroot, Lincolnshire, yesterday. Two of
the dead were children.

GUARDIAN, June 29 1970

An inquest was opened yesterday into the death at Eton
of Martin Earnshaw, aged 14, son of Lady Tyneford and
Mr. Christopher Earnshaw. The boy was found hanging
in his room at the school in the morning . . . Mr. Anthony
Chenevix-Trench, headmaster of Eton, had said earlier
that Martin was extremely popular. "During the last few
days he had been sent three times to me to be commended
for his good efforts. We cannot account for this tragedy."

GUARDIAN, December 6 1969

The Alternative Apocalypse 3

Jerry turned the corner from Elgin Crescent into Ladbroke Grove. He saw that the ragpickers were still out. They had been working through the night, using stolen hurricane lamps, shuffling in and out of the huge banks of garbage lining both sides of the street. Here and there among the plastic bags and the piles of cans a discreet fire was smoldering.

Jerry made his way down the centre of the road, listening to the sly sounds, the secret scufflings of the people of the heaps, until at last he reached the corner of Blenheim Crescent and realised with a shock that the Convent of the Poor Clares was down. His headquarters lay in ruins. The walls had been demolished, as had most of the buildings. Bricks and rubble had been cleared neatly into piles, but for some reason a few of the trees had been preserved, protected by new white fences—an oak and two black, twisted, stunted elms. The rest of the trees had been sawn down and stacked in a pile in the centre of the site. The best part of the original chapel and the administration wing attached to it, on the Westbourne Park Road side, were still standing. The machinery of demolition was parked here and there: trucks and earth-movers cloaked in dark canvas glistening with drizzle. Jerry climbed over the rubble and plodded through the thick mud until he stood under the nearest elm. He reached up and touched the lowest of the gnarled branches; he kicked at the stake fence. It quivered. He stumbled up a pile of bricks and masonry and got through a gap in the chapel wall. Fragments of stained glass clung to lead frames. The pews had been torn up and scattered, the altar had been ripped out, the electrical wiring had been pulled down and everything was covered with plaster and white dust. High up, the light fell through the ruined roof onto a crude painting of the resurrection, its lurid greens, yellows and reds already faded by the action of the rain and the wind. On all the walls were patches the size and shape of the devotional pictures which had hung there. He walked into the administration wing; the first two floors of this had hardly been touched as yet. He noticed small piles of human shit in some of the empty rooms. In the Mother Superior's office, which had been his office, too, he saw the white outline of the big cross which had hung there when he had last visited the convent. All furnishings, with the exception of two sodden mattresses in one room, had been carried off; his friends, his employees, his pets had gone.

As the light improved he moved through the wreckage, picking up small things. A triangle of green stained glass, a fragment of wood from a pew, the bulb holder from a light fixture, a hook on which the nuns had once hung their habits, a key from a cupboard, a 1959 penny left on the floor of the chapel, a nail which had secured part of the large cross to the wall. He put them in the pockets of his black car coat. A few relics.

Then he climbed out the way he had come, trudging back to the road and noticing that his heavy Frye boots were coated with mud and shit.

On the other side of the garbage heap he heard the note of a taxi's engine. He clambered quickly over the refuse, waving urgently at the cab. Rather reluctantly it stopped and let him get in.

"The airport," he said.

As he had often suspected, the end had come quietly and the breakdown had been by slow degrees. In fact the breakdown was still going on. Superficially there was nothing urgent about it. As the weeks passed and communications and services slowly worsened, there always seemed to be a chance that things might improve. He knew they could not improve.

He remembered his old friend Professor Hira (who now sometimes called himself Hythloday) escorting him through the chaos of Calcutta and saying "There *is* order in all this, though it's not as detailed as we're used to, I suppose. All human affairs can be seen as following certain basic patterns. The breakdown of a previous kind of social order does not mean that society itself has broken down—it is merely following different forms of order. The ritual remains."

The cab-driver glanced nervously at the rag-pickers. Some of them seemed to be eyeing the taxi as though it were an especially fine piece of carrion. The driver speeded up as much as he dared, for there was only room for a single line of traffic on what was still, officially, a two-way road.

Jerry stared reflectively at the shit on his boots.

The Alternative Apocalypse 4

You got to believe in something. You can't get excited about nothing, Colonel Cornelius, said Shakey Mo.

The four of them were squeezed into the cabin of a 1917 Austin-Putilov half-tracked armoured car. Beesley was driving while Cornelius, Shakey Mo Collier and Karen von Krupp manned the machine guns. The car was travelling slowly over the stony countryside of West Cornwall. In the distance a farmhouse was burning. They were trying to reach St. Michael's Mount, a fortified islet about ten miles down the South Coast, opposite the town of Marazion. Beesley believed he would find friends there.

Cornelius tried to make himself more comfortable on the pressed steel saddle seat, but failed. They went over a bump and everyone clung on to the hand-grips. It was very hot inside the half-track, even though they had lifted up the lid of the conning tower for ventilation. The original crews had worn gas-masks.

You're probably right, said Cornelius.

He saw a few figures, armed with rifles, move along the crest of the hill where the farmhouse burned. They didn't seem to offer a threat, but he kept his eye on them. His machine-gun was inclined to jam. He took out his Smith and Wesson .45 revolver, retrieved, like the rest of their equipment, from the Imperial War Museum, and checked it over. There was nothing wrong with that.

He was worrying about his wife and children. It was years since he had last remembered them: There was a list in his mind:

One Woman
One Boy

One Girl

A woman had recently slashed her wrists in Ladbroke Grove after gassing her little boy and girl. All were dead. There was no reason why it should be his particular relatives. But there had been something about a Nöel Coward and Gertrude Lawrence record on the gramophone and it seemed to him to be a clue to something even more familiar. He wiped the grime and the sweat from his face and glanced across the cabin to the opposite position. Karen von Krupp, her skirt hitched up, straddled her seat looking at him, her back to her gun. She was so old. He admired her stamina.

Whoever suggested the Highlands as a safe retreat was a fool, said Bishop Beesley, not for the first time. Those Scotchmen are barbarians. I said the Scilly Isles was a better bet and now we've wasted three months and nearly lost our lives a dozen times over.

The half-track droned on.

I think I can see the sea, said Karen von Krupp.

Jerry wondered how he had come to throw in with these three.

It's getting dark, said Mo Collier. He climbed out of his seat and stretched, making the stick-bombs at his belt rattle. What about making camp?

Let's wait until we reach the coast road, if it's still there, said Bishop Beesley. He looked over his shoulder, straight into Jerry's eyes. He smirked. Now what's wrong with you? Can guilt be anything more than a literary conceit, Mr. Cornelius? He uttered a suggestive chuckle. What truly evil person ever feels guilty? You might almost argue that evil-doing is an honest reaction against that sham we call 'guilt'. Repentance is, of course, a rather different kettle of fish. He returned his attention to his steering.

Jerry considered shooting him and then seeing what happened to the half-track without a driver. The bishop was always transferring his own problems onto others and Jerry seemed his favourite target.

Speak for yourself, he said. I've never understood you, Bishop Beesley.

Mo sniffed. You sound as bored as me, colonel. I could do with some action, I don't know about you.

It's freezing. Karen von Krupp drew up the collar of

her dirty sheepskin jacket. Could we have the tower closed now?

No, said Bishop Beesley. It would be suicide with our exhaust in the condition it is.

Karen von Krupp said sulkily: I'm not sure I believe you.

Anyway, it's still quite warm. Shakey Mo was conciliatory. Chin up, Frau Doktor. He grinned to himself and began to move his machine gun about in its slit. Brrrrr. Brrrrr. We might just as well've come on bikes, the chances we've had to use these.

Portsmouth wasn't enough for you, eh? said Karen von Krupp bitterly.

Mine was the only bloody gun working, Collier pointed out. I maintain my equipment. All the others jammed after a couple of bursts.

We were nearly killed, she said. She glanced accusingly at Jerry. I thought that Field-Marshal Nye was a friend of yours.

Jerry shrugged. He's got his duty to do just like me.

Law and Order freak, explained Collier, lighting a Players. Groovy. I wish we had some music.

An explosion rocked the car and the engine whined miserably.

Bloody hell! yelled Collier in relief. Mines!

Late News

A 14-year-old boy died after falling 60ft from the roof of a block of shops near his home in Liverpool on Saturday night. He was William Brown of Shamrock Road, Port Sunlight.

GUARDIAN, December 29 1969

A boy of 13 was remanded in custody until February 16 at Ormskirk, Lancashire, yesterday accused of the murder of Julie Mary Bradshaw, aged 10, of Skelmersdale. The girl's body was found on Monday night in the loft of a house.

GUARDIAN, February 11 1969

A boy aged 12 found murdered on a golf course at Bristol yesterday was killed by four or five savage blows on the head it was said after a post mortem last night. The blows could have been made with a tree branch, said police. Martin Thorpe, of Rye Road, Fulton, had gone to Shirehampton golf course to search for golf balls.

GUARDIAN, April 2 1970

A schoolgirl was killed and five other children and three adults wounded when Arab guerillas fired Russian-made Katyusha rockets into the Northern Israeli town of Beison yesterday. Three of the rockets fell in the playground of the school. Two of the injured children were in a serious condition.

GUARDIAN, April 2 1970

Schoolboy Michael Kenan, aged 12, was drowned in a

reservoir at Durford, near Chelmsford, Essex, yesterday while bird nesting with friends.

DAILY EXPRESS, June 8 1970

Police tightened security in Warsaw yesterday as a curfew was again clamped on the port of Szezecin, the scene of violent street fighting on Thursday . . . A Swedish radio reporter, Mr. Anders Tunborg, said, "The tanks repeatedly charged the crowds who sprang out of the way to avoid being run down. A mother and her young daughter did not get out of the way in time and an onrushing tank hit them both. A young soldier stood watching nearby and crying."

THE SCOTSMAN, December 19 1970

REMINISCENCE (D)

You are killing your children.

THE LOVERS

With her chemise pulled up to her navel, Una Persson pressed her slim self to Catherine Cornelius who lay beneath her. Catherine's clothes were neatly folded on the stool near the dressing table. Una Persson's summer shirt-waist frock, stockings, drawers and corsets were scattered on the carpet. The bedroom needed painting. It was a bright summer afternoon. Sunlight crept through the tattered net and the dusty glass of the windows.

With passion Una said:

"My own dear love. My darling sweet."

And Catherine replied:

"Dear, dear Una."

She arched her perfect back, quivering. Grasping her buttocks, Una kissed her roundly in the mouth.

"Love!"

Una gave a long, delicious grunt.

"Oh!"

Later the door rattled.

In stepped Miss Brunner, trim and prim.

"All girls together." She laughed harshly. She made no apology because it was obvious she relished interrupting and embarrassing them. "We must be about our business soon. This place needs a tidy."

Una rolled clear, directing a muted glare at Miss Brunner who was crisp in linen and lace, like an ultra-fashionable bicyclette.

"The new chambermaid's arrived," said Miss Brunner. She began to fold Una Persson's dress. "She wants to clean in here."

Catherine was puzzled. "There's no need . . ."

"Come now," said Miss Brunner, flinging open the door, "we mustn't let ourselves go." She revealed the maid, a huge, red figure in a green baize overall and a sloppy cap, a bucket in one hand, a mop in the other. Her hair hung down her face. "This is Mrs. 'Vaizey'."

Una pulled up the sheets.

"Oh, my gawd!" said the cleaner, recognising her daughter.

Catherine turned over.

Mrs. 'Vaizey' gestured with the mop and bucket. She was miserably upset. She looked ashamed of herself. "This is on'y temp'ry, Caff," she said. She looked wretchedly at Miss Brunner, who was smiling privately. "Could I—?" Then she realised that Miss Brunner had known all along that her name hadn't been Vaizey (one of her post-Cornelian husbands) and, moreover, that Miss Brunner had known Catherine was her daughter.

Mrs. Cornelius sighed. "You bloody cow," she said to Miss Brunner. She glanced at the pair in the bed. "Wot yer up ter?" She remembered how she had looked like Catherine once. She recalled the money she might have had if she had not been so generous, so soft. Her heart went out to her daughter then. She dumped the mop into the bucket of water, pointing the handle at Miss Brunner. "You watch this one, love," she said to Una Persson, since only Una Persson was now visible above the bed clothes. "She'll 'ave yer fer sure if she gets a chance."

"You're not being paid for cheek, you know," Miss Brunner replied somewhat feebly, striding towards the door, "but to clean the rooms. Your type, Mrs. 'Vaizey', are ten a penny, as I'm sure you know. If you're not happy with the position . . ."

"Don't come it wiv me, love." Mrs. Cornelius began to splash about the linoleum with her mop. "Not everybody'll work in a third-rate whorehouse, neither!" Her anger grew and she became proud. "Fuck it." She picked up the bucket and threw the contents over Miss Brunner. As the starch ran out, the linen and the lace sagged and the Lily Langtry wave fell apart over her forehead.

Una grinned, sitting up with interest.

Miss Brunner hissed, clenched her hands, began to move with staring eyes upon Mrs. Cornelius, who returned the stare with dignity so that Miss Brunner paused dripping.

"Yore nuffink, yer silly little tart. I've 'ad too much. Caff!"

Catherine peered out from the bed.

"You comin', Caff?"

Catherine shook her head. "I can't, mum."

"Jest as yer like."

Una Persson said: "I'll look after her, Mrs. Cornelius."

Mrs. Cornelius removed her cap and apron and threw them at Miss Brunner's feet. "I'm sure yer'll do yer best, love," she said softly. "Don't let Modom 'ere shove yer abaht!"

Miss Brunner seemed paralysed. Hands on fat hips, Mrs. Cornelius appeared to grow in stature as she waltzed around the drenched figure. "I know yer! I know yer!" she chanted. "I know yer! I know yer! Ya ya ya!"

"Everything all right at home, mum?" said Catherine desperately.

"Not bad." Mrs. Cornelius was pleased with herself, although later she might regret this action. She'd taken the job because of the boy, after she and Sammy had had words. But tonight it would be feathers and frills again and a trip to the Cremorne Gardens. Her right hand swept down on Miss Brunner's sodden and corsetted rump. There was a loud bang as flesh struck whalebone. Still Miss Brunner did not move. Mrs. Cornelius giggled. "Don't let 'er wear yer aht." She circled Miss Brunner once more and then waved at her from the door. "Ta, ta, Lady Muck."

In terror, Catherine murmured to her mother. "See you soon."

"Keep yourself clean and yer can't go wrong," advised Mrs. Cornelius as she closed the door. The last Catherine saw was her leering wink.

Miss Brunner came alive with a snort. "Dreadful woman. I was forced to sack her. I'll get changed. Can you two be ready by the time I've finished?"

Una was amused by Miss Brunner's attitude. "This is a farce. Whom are we to entertain this evening?"

"Prinz Lobkowitz and his friends will arrive at six."

"Oh," said Catherine, reminiscently.

"Silly creatures," said Miss Brunner.

Una Persson raised her lovely eyebrows. "Aha."

"Our success depends on tonight's meeting," Miss Brunner said as she left. The door slammed.

Una stroked Catherine's thigh beneath the sheet. "I wonder if this is the 'big meeting'?"

Catherine shook her golden head. "That isn't for a while."

"For all we know it's already happened. And what comes after the meeting? This identity's getting me down. Not enough information. Do you ever think about the nature of Time?"

"Of course." Catherine twisted so that she could place her decilate lips on Una Persson's flat stomach and at the same time her hand rose lightly to touch her friend's clitoris. Una sighed with pleasure. From where she lay she could see the abandoned mop, the fallen bucket, the apron and the cap. "Your mother has spirit. I hadn't expected that."

"Neither had I." Catherine's tongue fluttered like a trapped butterfly, the pressure of her hand increased. Una made a noise.

"I was terrified of them both," said Catherine. "I still am."

"Forget it."

Una gave a coarse, satisfied grunt.

"Good?" whispered Catherine Cornelius.

THE BUSINESSMEN

> "Molly O'Morgan with her little organ
>   Was dressed up in colours so gay,
> Out in the street every day,
>   Playing too-ra-la-oor-a-li-oor-a-li-ay.
> Fellows who met her will never forget her,
>   She set all their heads in a whirl.
> Molly O'Morgan with her little organ
>   The Irish-Aye-talian girl!"

sang Major Nye, twirling his splendid moustache and swirling his huge, tartan ulster as he strode over the moor with Sebastian Auchinek in tow. Auchinek was miserable and sought desperately about him for some sign of human habitation, preferably an inn. But there was none; just grass and gorse and boulders, the occasional bird and a few shy sheep. If Major Nye had not been the largest shareholder in a chain of well-appointed provincial halls. Auchinek would have complained. But he had to get Una a good year's bookings, at least thirty weeks, outside London (for as he predicted they had closed the London halls), if he was going to make it up to her for the disappointment she must feel at losing the Empire.

"One of Ella Retford's," explained Major Nye, pausing in his stride and looking with relish at the dark green Exmoor heather.

"Has your girlie got anything like that?"

"Better," said Auchinek automatically, staring at the vast moor with disgust and resignation. "She has the real quality, major." He whistled a complicated melody. "That's one of hers. *Waiters get me going.*"

"It will mean a trip to London for me," Major Nye said, stalking on. "And London's not the safest place in the world these days, is it?"

"No really exciting place is, major."

"I heartily dislike London, Mr. Auchinek."

"Oh, well—yes, I suppose so." Uncertainly, Auchinke watched a large bird flap in the sky. Major Nye lifted his ashplant and pretended to sight down it at the bird.

"Bang!" said the major.

"Well," he continued, "I have, as a matter of fact, got to be in London on some pretty important business fairly shortly. Not quite certain of the date, but ask my office. They'll keep you posted."

"And you'll give her an audition."

"That was the idea, old boy. If I've time. By the way, what is the time?"

Auchinek stared at him in surprise.

Major Nye shrugged. The sky was deep blue, bland and warm. "I'm kept pretty busy," he said. "What with one thing and another."

"You have many interests," Auchinek said admiringly.

"Oh, many. I play," the major laughed, "a wide variety of parts, you might say." He put a hand to the knot of his Ascot cravat. "But then we all do, really . . ." His moustache tilted upwards on the right side as he gave a mysterious smile. Auchinek determined to get himself a suit of solid tweed, like the major's, and a good ulster, and aim towards the acquisition of a small estate somewhere in Somerset or Devon. He hated the country, but these days there was hardly any choice. They came to a hill overlooking the winding white road to Porlock. Beyond the road lay the sparkling sea. On the dusty, unpaved road a carriage, drawn by two pairs of bays, was struggling, making poor time. The carriage was old and much in need of an overhaul.

Major Nye leaned on his ashplant and stared in amusement as the carriage slowly climbed the hill. "Could this be the vicar on his way to see me? He travels in style, our vicar. Used to ride. One of the best hunting men in these parts. He fell off his horse, though. Ha, ha."

A white head appeared at the window and a pale hand hailed the couple. "Major! Major!"

"Vicar! Top o' the morning to ye!"

"Your son, major, have you heard?"

"What about the young rip?" Major Nye smiled at Auchinek. "He's in the army, you know."

"Captured, major. A prisoner of war."

"What? The eldest boy?"

"Yes, major. I have the telegram here. I was in town when it arrived. I told them I'd deliver it."

Auchinek knew that his luck hadn't changed yet. He sighed. He had picked a bad time to see Major Nye.

"Armoured steamrollers of some kind," continued the vicar, growing hoarse, "broke their lines and cut them off. Almost all were killed. He fought bravely. It will be in tomorrow's press."

"The devil!"

"He's wound-ay-ed!" The vicar's voice cracked completely as the carriage hit a rock and bounced. His coachman shouted at the horses.

"You'll be returning to London on the seven-twenty, won't you, Mr. Auchinek?" said Major Nye.

"Well . . ." Auchinek had hoped to be invited for the night. "If that's the most convenient train."

"I'll come with you. Quickly, get a hold on those leading horses and make 'em move. We'll take the vicar's carriage back to the house and I'll just have time to pack a bag."

"In what engagement was your son captured?" Auchinek asked as they clambered down the hill towards the road.

"Damn!" said Major Nye, catching his sock on a piece of gorse and stopping to free himself. "Regiment? 18th Lancers, of course."

"Engagement?"

"What? My boy? Never!"

THE ENVOYS

Prinz Lobkowitz was almost sure that he had been followed all afternoon by a police agent. He hoped that he was wrong. He glanced at his watch, waiting outside the remaining gate to Buckingham Palace. He looked out of the corners of his eyes to see if he could recognise the agent; surreptitiously he inspected each of the passers by (there were few) but none was familiar. He turned to inspect the palace. It had been boarded up for a year now, but there were still redcoated and bearskinned Guardsmen standing in sentry boxes at various points. This had seemed as good a place as any to meet the other envoy. And surely it must be some of the most neutral soil in the world at the present moment. The watch, a Swiss hunter with an alpine scene decorating the inner case, was a gift from Miss Brunner. He had never been able to find the catch. As soon as the big meeting was over, he thought, he'd buy himself a twenty-four-hour digital wrist-watch of the kind the French were now making. He loved gadgets. It was what had led him into politics, after all.

The other envoy was late.

Prinz Lobkowitz took a rolled copy of *The Humorist* ('Typically British, but not old-fashioned') from his Prince Albert frockcoat pocket and began to study it intently, displaying the cover which sported a Bonzo dog cartoon. This had been arranged earlier and the specific issue of the specific magazine agreed upon. Prinz Lobkowitz was fond of *The Humorist*. Already he was becoming absorbed in it, smiling involuntarily at the jokes.

A few moments later a distinguished middle-aged man

of military bearing bumped into Lobkowitz and pretended to recognise him. In slightly accented English he cried with delight: "Good heavens! Why, it's old Henry, isn't it?"

For a second or two Lobkowitz feigned puzzlement. Then he said: "Could you be George?"

"That's right! Spiffin', seeing you again!"

Lobkowitz frowned as he tried to recall his lines. A little reluctantly he rolled up his magazine and replaced it in his pocket where it made a noticeable bulge in the line of the overcoat. "Come and have a drink, old boy." Lobkowitz clapped the man on the shoulder. "We've a lot to talk about."

"Yes, indeed!"

As they crossed the road and entered St. James's Park, which was filled with the noise of a dozen different calliopes from the nearby fairground, a man said softly: "I am Colonel Pyat, our Embassy sent me."

"And I'm Prinz Lobkowitz, representing the exiles. I hope this will be a fruitful meeting at long last."

"I think it might be."

They had reached the fairground which occupied both sides of the ornamental lake. Bunting and banners and candy-striped canvas, brass and steel and luridly painted wood, moved round and round and up and down as the people screamed or giggled or laughed aloud.

Pyat stopped at a stall on which sat a miserable monkey tended by an old Italian in a stovepipe hat. The Italian grinned and offered to sell Pyat an ice cream. Pyat reached out his hand and stroked the monkey as if looking for fleas, yet the touch was tender. He shook his head and moved on. Ice cream!" shouted the Italian, as if Pyat had forgotten something. 'Ice cream!"

In his frock coat and top hat, Pyat moved with dignity away.

"Ice cream?" said the Italian to Lobkowitz who was a few paces behind Pyat. Lobkowitz shook his head. Pyat spoke over his shoulder. "Any news of Cornelius?"

"Jeremiah, you mean?"

"Yes."

"None. He seems to have vanished completely."

"Perhaps it's for the best. Yes?"

"His insight's useful."

"But he could foul things up. And we don't need that at present, with the big meeting coming along."

"No."

Under the low-hanging willows, where young prostitutes showed off their soft, painted flesh, they went, through the happy crowds, between the merry-go-rounds, the swing-boats and the helter-skelters.

"How jolly the peasants are," said Pyat in an attempt at irony which somehow failed. "Alas! regardless of their doom, the little victims play."

"Were you at Eton? So was I," said Lobkowitz grinning back at a cheeky girl. "Don't you enjoy fairs?"

"I've hardly ever seen one of this kind. In Finland once. With the gypsies, you know. Yes. Near Rouveniemi, I think. In Spring. I didn't attend. But I remember seeing the gypsy women by the river, breaking the Spring ice to wash their clothes. The sideshows were very similar, though there was more wood and less metal. Bright colours." Colonel Pyat smiled.

"When were you last in Finland?" Lobkowitz avoided the guy rope of a sideshow tent. He took a deep breath of the air which was heavy with motor oil, candy floss and animal manure.

Colonel Pyat shrugged and waved his hands. "When there was last a Finland." He smiled again, more openly. "I used to like Finland. Such a simple nation."

An old woman selling lavender appeared. She wore a bright red shawl which clashed with her flowers. She whined pathetically at them, holding out her sprigs. "Please, sir. Please, sir." She nodded her head as if she hoped, by sympathetic magic, to make them nod back. "Lucky, sir. Sweet lavender, sir. Please buy some, sir."

Pyat was the first to reach into his trouser pocket and pull out a half-crown. He handed it to her, receiving the sprig in return. Its stem was wrapped in silver paper. Lobkowitz gave her two shillings and received a similar piece. The woman tucked the money away in the folds of her thick, dirty skirt. "Thank you, gentlemen."

The lavender forgotten in their right hands, they walked on.

"But you people had to take Finland out," said Lobkowitz.

"Yes." Pyat raised his hand to his face and noticed the

lavender there. He began to adjust it in his buttonhole. "It was a question of widening the available coasts."

"Expediency." Lobkowitz frowned.

"Does anyone act for another reason? Come now, Prinz Lobkowitz. Shall we confine ourselves to schoolboy moralising? Or shall we discuss the real business at hand?"

"Perhaps that, too, involves schoolboy morals?" Lobkowitz flung his lavender from him. It fell into the mud near the water's edge.

Colonel Pyat said sympathetically, "Forgive me. I know . . . I know—" He gave up.

A crowd of urchins ran past them shouting. One of the urchins gave Lobkowitz a brief, piercing glance before running on. Lobkowitz frowned and felt over his pockets to see if he had been robbed. But everything was there, including *The Humorist*.

They mounted a boardwalk which led through the mud to the jetty which stretched out into the lake. There were two couples on the jetty. They stopped.

"The sides change," said Prinz Lobkowitz. They stood side by side watching the ducks and flamingoes. On the opposite bank promenaded a score of belles in pretty dresses, arms linked with a score of beaux, dressed to the nines, their curly-brimmed bowlers tilted at exaggerated angles. A barrel organ played sentimental tunes. A bear danced. A punt passed.

They could see the shell of Buckingham Palace outlined against the evening sky in the west and, to the east, the shell of the Treasury Garrison, bristling with big naval guns.

"It's growing colder," said Colonel Pyat, adjusting the collar of his elegant coat. Prinz Lobkowitz saw that Pyat had a silk handkerchief tucked into his left sleeve. Clouds of red-tinged grey streaked the sky and streamed north.

"Everyone's leaving now." Pyat stopped and picked up a pebble. He threw it into the dank water. Sluggish ripples appeared for a few seconds. A fish put its lips to the surface and then submerged. "There are hardly any of our old friends left. Dead singers."

THE GATHERERS

"It's nice ter go away, but it's nicer ter come 'ome, innit?" said Mrs. Cornelius as she sharpened the carving knife against the steel and looked with loving pride upon her roast pork.

The table had been laid with a red plush cloth. There were big blue tassels on the cloth. Over this had been laid a white linen cloth, its edges stitched with *broderie anglaise*. On the linen rested the vegetables in their monstrous china serving dishes with roses painted on the sides. There were large knives with weathered bone handles, solid forks, big spoons, napkins in rings of yellowed ivory, a silver salt cellar, a silver mustard pot, a silver pepper pot. Around the table sat Mrs. Cornelius's children and their guests. They had all come for one of Mrs. Cornelius's 'special' Sunday luncheons. Sammy, who always stood in as 'man of the house' on these occasions, sat in his tight best black serge suit beside her, sweltering as ever, but this time the quality of his swelter was different; the swelter of fear had replaced the swelter of work. The boy, pinch-faced and hungry, sat next to Sammy, his mouth watering as he waited for his share. His mother's huge red lips rounded as she scraped metal against metal. She had had her hair done in a pompadour coiffure with a Marcel wave and she was wearing the purple princess gown with the yellow imitation Valenciennes lace on it. The padded shoulders added to her already impressive size.

"Pass yer plates along," she said, preparing to cut.

There was a clatter as the plates were picked up and passed. Catherine, seated on the other side of her mother, stacked her brother Frank's plate on top of her own. Frank took his friend Miss Brunner's plate and passed it to Catherine. Frank and Miss Brunner were dressed in rather similar suits of severe grey. Frank, however, wore a rose. His ravaged face was set in a smirk which showed he was on his best party manners. Miss Brunner, too, was doing her best to be affable.

"It's a loverly bit o' pork," said Mrs. Cornelius as she sliced.

"It looks nice and juicy," said Miss Brunner. She winked across the table at Mr. Smiles, who was dressed as the vicar he had once been.

"Shall I be barman?" asked Mr. Smiles, indicating the beer barrel on the side board and gesturing at the same time towards their glass mugs. He grinned nervously through a black beard.

"Good idear," said Mrs. C.

"Light?" said Mr. Smiles.

"Suits me," said Sammy.

Mr. Smiles got up and put the first mug under the spiggot.

For all that it was lunchtime, the heavy velvet curtains were drawn and the gas lamps were full on at either side of the littered mantelpiece. Mrs. Cornelius was suspicious of the neighbours who overlooked her rooms at the back. She suspected they might be burglars. If they saw a spread like this, they could easily guess there'd be money in the house. As there was, at this moment.

The air was close. The smell of the meat filled the room. The vegetable dishes steamed.

Slice by slice the pork and the crackling and the stuffing was heaped on the plates. Mrs. Cornelius was a generous hostess, if an indifferent cook.

The noise increased as vegetables were ladled out.

"Gravy?" Miss Brunner passed the gravy boat to Frank.

"Apple sauce?" Sammy passed the sauce dish to the boy who helped himself to a large portion. He loved apple sauce.

"There's more spuds in the oven," said Mrs. Cornelius as Mr. Smiles considered the almost empty bowl. "Go an' get 'em, love," she told the boy. He sprang up, anxious to get the job over with so that he could tuck in.

"Greens?" said Catherine to Frank.

"Swedes?" said Miss Brunner to Mr. Smiles.

"Parsnips?" Sammy held the bowl inquiringly.

"Marrer?" Mrs. C. asked, looking for it.

"All the marrow's gone, mum," said Catherine in a small voice.

Mrs. Cornelius loved marrow. But she contained her fury and lifted her glass of light ale, toasting them all. " 'Ere's ter the lot o' yer, then!" She drained the glass. spluttered thickly behind her red hand, and delicately picked up her knife and fork. "Ah, this is ther life!"

Her son came back with the extra potatoes and put them on the table. Hurriedly he clambered into his place and began to wolf the food. Miss Brunner, eating rapidly but discreetly, eyed him as he ate. She dabbed at her thin mouth with a napkin. He did not notice her.

"It's a pity your friend couldn't come," said Mrs. Cornelius to her daughter, "Ill, wos she?"

"Yes, mum."

"Shame."

Save for the noise of the cutlery, they ate in silence for a while until Frank said, "I heard there were some people looking for Jerry, mum."

"Don't talk ter me about 'im!" she said.

The boy, who had almost devoured his whole meal, looked up in interest. "What's 'e done, then?"

"We won't go into that, will we?" said Mr. Smiles laughing. He glanced at Mrs. Cornelius. "No offence."

"None taken," said Mrs. Cornelius grimly. "Yore quite right. We won't go inter it."

"They'll never find 'im," said the boy.

"It's unlikely." Catherine looked tenderly and with some admiration at her little brother.

"Who were they?" said the boy. "These people that was looking for 'im."

"Foreigners," said Frank, "mainly."

Miss Brunner tapped his sleeve with her fork and left four tiny points of grease there, like little teeth-marks. "Maybe they want to give him a job?"

"And maybe they don't," said Frank.

"Seconds?" said Mrs. Cornelius.

Everyone, except the boy and Miss Brunner, refused.

"Yer get ter miss good 'ome cookin', I shouldn't wonder," said Mrs. C. to Miss Brunner. She laid two small slices of meat on Miss Brunner's plate.

"Tasty," said Miss Brunner. She offered Mrs. Cornelius a secretive smile, as if she referred to some shared experience about which only they knew.

Mrs. Cornelius gave the boy what was left of the joint and then, without reference to him, piled the cooled vegetables onto his plate.

Miss Brunner quickly finished and leaned back with a contented grunt.

Catherine began to take the dirty plates into the kitchen.

"See 'ow the duff's doin', luv, will yer?" requested her mother. She confided to Miss Brunner: "It's a loverly duff."

"I'm certain of that."

After the plum duff and the cheese and the port, the family and its friends, with the exception of the boy, who had gone to sleep, smoked their cigarettes, pipes and cigars.

"Well, that was a bit of all right," said Sammy. "Makes a change from meat pies, I can tell you."

Mrs. Cornelius smiled complacently. "Not arf, yer cuddly ole fat pig." She bent from where she was helping herself to a pint from the barrel on the sideboard. She kissed his bald head. He snorted and blushed.

Mr. Smiles, who had hated the meal, stroked his gravy-stained beard and said, with some strain, "You are a splendid cook, dear lady."

"A plain cook," Mrs. Cornelius replied, by way of confirmation and amplification of the compliment. "Oh fuck." The beer mug had overfilled. She dabbed at the sides with her fingers, raising the finger to her mouth and sucking it. "Sorry, vicar."

Sammy had taken out his spectacles and was polishing them. He inspected one side carefully.

"Lens," he said. "Cracked."

"'Ave yer seen the rest o' the 'ahse?" Mrs. Cornelius inquired of Miss Brunner. "Not," she laughed raucously, "that there's a lot ter show."

"I'd love to see it."

"Come on, then." The two women left the room.

"Any news from America at all?" Mr. Smiles packed tobacco into his pipe.

Frank was staring at the door through which Miss Brunner and his mother had passed. He looked worried. "Do what?" he said.

"America? What's going on over there? Much doing?"

"No, nothing much." Frank got up, glancing absently at Mr. Smiles. He leant against the mantelpiece. "How's business?"

"Which business?" Mr. Smiles winked at him. It was a sad old wink. Frank, staring again at the brown door, didn't notice. He began to move towards the door.

Catherine put her hand on his arm. "Cheer up, Frank. It's not the end of the world."

This idea seemed to frighten him. She said quickly. "A shilling for your thoughts."

"Cheap at arf the price!" desperately guffawed Sammy from the easy chair in which he now sat. He was feeling very lonely. As he had expected, nobody responded.

Mr. Smiles felt sick. "Ah, where's the you-know-what?" he asked Sammy.

Sammy pointed at the brown door. "Through there and on yer left," he said. He picked up an old copy of *The Illustrated London News* which had a coloured supplement on the Jubilee headed *The Glory that is England*. Sammy smiled. It was such a short time ago. He wondered what would have happened if the old queen had lived on.

On the landing Mr. Smiles turned right by mistake and found himself outside the bedroom door. There were peculiar sounds coming from inside. He stopped to listen.

"At least yer don't run ther risk o' 'avin' babies," he heard Mrs. Cornelius say.

"Don't count on it, dearie," said Miss Brunner.

Mr. Smiles remembered about the bathroom.

In the dining room Frank was saying, "If she doesn't hurry up soon, I'm off without her."

"Calm down, Frank," said Catherine.

But Frank was glaring now. "Why does she always have to spoil everything? The fat old bag."

"Oh, don't Frank."

His head among the used dishes on the table, the boy stirred. He groaned.

They all looked at him.

"Poor little sod," said Sammy. "Let's not have a row, eh?"

"Well . . ." said Frank, reluctant to stop before his climax. "I mean . . ." He felt nothing for the boy, but he did not wish to offend his sister at that moment, particularly since there was a likelihood that she knew where Jerry was.

Catherine's perfect features bore an expression of infinite sympathy as she went to stroke the sleeping child's hair. "He's having a nightmare, I expect."

THE ROWERS

Considering that he was a prisoner of war, Captain Nye was having quite a good time. It was almost like a holiday. His captors had proved to be courteous and allowed him considerable freedom within the reservation. Even now he was boating on Grasmere Lake with a very pretty girl. Save for the basic facts of his circumstances, he couldn't have imagined a more perfect situation. The sky was a beautiful deep blue and the surrounding hills were a rich, varied green. The lake was absolutely still, reflecting in impressive detail the oaks and willows on its banks.

Captain Nye pulled vigorously on the oars and the boat shot away from the little landing stage at the end of the tea-gardens with their comforting wrought-iron balconies overlooking the water. All the iron was painted green, to blend in with the hills and trees.

The girl was called Catherine. She made a lovely picture as she sat in the stern with a Japanese silk parasol over her shoulder, a wide-brimmed Gainsborough straw hat on her golden curls, her filmy summer frock cut low at the neck and high on the ankle. With touching lack of expertise she gingerly held the rudder rope and pulled it to left or right when Captain Nye directed.

Soon they were alone in the middle of the lake. Far away on the other side there were one or two more boats. Captain Nye rowed towards a little island, eager to get a better look at the rather picturesque ruined bell-tower which stood on it. A system of these towers had once covered the area, the work of an eccentric clergyman who had erected them so that travellers or boatmen would hear them through the fog and thus be able to find their bearings. Unfortunately there were a number of tragic accidents and the flaws in the system became more than obvious when the clergyman had himself drowned on Derwent Water under the impression he had reached the sanctuary of his own churchyard. Now the towers were merely romantic and a source of speculation amongst those who knew little of the local history of the Fell country.

"What mysteries shall we discover, I wonder, in Merlin's castle?" asked Catherine, in a fanciful mood.

Captain Nye looked back over his shoulder at the remains of the building. "Perhaps we'll find Arthur's sword and with it bring peace where today there is nought but strife." She alone could elicit these fantasies from him. He wished very much that they were on the same side. He knew that essentially Catherine was his gaoler and that therefore she must be highly trusted by his enemies. It was a damned shame.

"Nearly there," he said. "Standby for landing!" He shipped the oars as the bottom scraped on the tiny beach. Leaping into the shallow water, careless of wetting his white flannels, he took the painter and hauled the boat up to the point where Catherine, gathering her skirts about her, could reach the prow and take his hand, descending prettily to the land. She twirled her parasol and smiled at him.

"But if we find the sword," she said, "will you be able to pull it from the stone?"

"And if I could, what would you think then?"

She frowned. "I don't know. People play such awful tricks on one, these days."

He laughed. "I know that." He held out his hand. "Come. To the castle!"

They climbed the grassy slope to the tower but were less than halfway there before the smell struck them.

"Ugh!" Captain Nye wrinkled his nose.

"What could it be?" she asked. "Sheep droppings?"

He was a little shocked by her outspokenness. "Maybe. Or a dead animal, even?"

"Shall we look?" Her face became concerned. "In case it isn't a sheep or something?"

"What . . .?"

"I mean—"

He understood what she meant now. Reluctantly he said, "You stay. I'll go."

She stood, heels together, holding her parasol, while he forced himself to the top of the hill and disappeared behind the wall of the ruin. She was puzzled by the peculiar briny aspect of the smell. They were a good forty miles from the coast, surely?

She knew that she should have stayed with the captain. It was her job. But the smell disturbed her more than physically. She felt extremely nervous and depression was swiftly creeping in. The perfect day was over.

When Captain Nye returned he was pale and he could hardly look at her. He had a handkerchief over his mouth. Wordlessly, he took her arm and guided her back to the boat.

She climbed in and he shoved off. All his movements were disorganised, hasty. The boat almost turned over as he got aboard and swung the oars into the water, rowing back towards the tea-gardens. But he had only gone a few strokes when he was forced to abandon the oars and lean over the side, vomiting, as discreetly as he could, into the water.

Catherine came forward and took the oars before they could slip from the rowlocks. She did her best to keep the boat on course.

Captain Nye wiped his lips, then dipped his handkerchief into the water, wiping his whole face. "I must apologise."

"Good heavens! Why? What was it you saw?" With a steady, accomplished stroke, she began to row for the shore.

"I must report it to the pol—to your authorities. A man, I think. Or something that had been a man. Or—I'm not sure . . ."

"Murdered?"

"I don't know."

The really awful thing about the dead creature was that it had had a certain ape-like cast of features and yet at the same time the remains of the face had reminded him unmistakeably of the girl who now rowed so smoothly away from the island. Every time he looked at her frank, blue eyes, her full, pink lips, her well-shaped nose, he saw the ape face of the rotting creature which had lain amongst the debris and sheep-dung in the gloomy interior of the tower.

He began to wonder if the whole thing had been deliberately arranged for him. Perhaps his captors had other reasons than kindness for allowing him so much freedom. But what could they possibly want from him, anyway? He knew no secrets.

"Do you—? Did you expect to find anything like that in the tower?" he asked her.

Her body moved rhythmically back and forth as she rowed. She shook her head.

"Intimations," she said. "I couldn't explain."

THE PEACE TALKS

Preliminary Speech

In his speech to the Court of Appeal, shortly before his exile, Prinz Lobkowitz said:

"In our houses, our villages, our towns, our cities, our nations, time passes. Each individual will be involved, directly or indirectly, in some 150 years of history— before birth, during life, and after his death. Part of this experience will be received from parents or other adults, from old men; part will be received from his own life, and his experience will, in time, become part of his children's experience. Thus a generation is 150 years. That is how long we live. Our behaviour, our prejudices, our opinions, our preferences are the produce of the fifty or sixty years before we were born and in the same way do we influence the fifty following our deaths. Such knowledge is apt to make a man like me feel that it is useless to try to alter the nature of his society. It would be pleasant, I think, if we could somehow produce a completely blank generation—a generation which has not acquired the habits of the previous generation and will pass no habits on to the next. Ah, well, I thank you, gentlemen, for listening to this nonsense with patience. I bid you Au Revoir."

AT THE PEACE TALKS

The Ball

The major social event during the Peace Talks was the Gala Ball at San Simeon. Hearst's monstrous white castle had been bought for the nation by an unknown benefactor some years before and re-erected on the site of the old Convent of the Poor Clares at Ladbroke Grove, where it was now a familiar local landmark and a favourite tourist attraction, more impressive, in the opinion of many, than the buildings of Versailles, Canberra or Washington.

Everyone had been invited. Commentators said that it was equal in magnificence to the Great Exhibition, the Diamond Jubilee, the New York World's Fair or the Berlin Olympics. In a mood of immense optimism (the Peace Talks could be said to be going splendidly) the castle was prepared for the Ball. Illumination of every sort was used. There were tall Berlage candelabra of silver and gold in which were fitted slender white and yellow candles; Schellenbühel crystal chandliers holding thousands of red candles; Horta flambeaux in brackets along the walls; huge globular gas mantels, electric lights of a hundred different shades of colour, neon of the subtlest and brightest, antique oil lamps the height of a man, and little faceted glass globes containing fireflies and glow-worms, strung on threads through the grounds of the various 'cases' which made up the whole of the original Hearst complex. Hearst himself had always called his castle The Enchanted Hill. Now, of course, it was, if anything an Enchanted Dale. The Casa Grande, with its twin Hispano-moresque towers containing thirty-six carillon bells, its hundred rooms and its ornate bas-

reliefs carved from white Utah limestone, dominated the
other three 'guest castles' arranged before it, north, south
and west—Casa del Monte, Casa del Sol and Casa del
Mar. Tall cypresses, willows, poplars and firs had been
planted thickly among the buildings, replacing the Californian palms which had once grown there. Within
the branches of the trees and the privet hedges had been
buried more tiny lights to make the gardens sparkle like
fairyland. Rhododendrons, poinsettias, orchids, chrysanthemums, roses and azaleas grew in well-ordered profusion and the overall appearance reminded at least one
visitor of the old roof garden at Derry and Toms blown
up to an enormous scale ('and none the worse for that').
Bas-reliefs decorated the Spanish walls of the gardens
and there were copies of famous statues from all over
the world, in marble and granite or cast in terra cotta or
bronze, one of the grandest being Boyar's copy of
Canova's 'The Graces' in St. Petersburg. This statue,
in the classical manner, was permanently illuminated and
showed Joy, Brilliance and Bloom, representing, in the
words of the guide book, "all that was beautiful in Nature and that which was gracious and charming in
Mankind." *The Times,* in its leader for the day of the
ball, had written: "It is to be hoped that this lovely
statue will symbolise to the guests the rewards whch they
can win if their talents are devoted to the pursuit of
peaceful endeavour, rather than to Strife and her attendants, Greed and Envy." Many newspapers had
echoed these sentiments in one form and another and
even the weather, which had been singularly delightful
for several weeks, seemed to make a special effort
for the occasion. All through that day hundreds of footmen, housemaids, cooks, butlers, kitchen-maids and
pages had hurried to and from among the lavish rooms
preparing them for the ball. There was to be available
every kind of culinary delight. In the ballrooms (or
those rooms which had been turned into ballrooms for
the occasion) musicians, practised many styles of music. The flags of all nations, embroidered in threads of
precious metal on the finest silks, glittered from the walls.
Tapestries in rich brocades proclaimed the glories of
those nations' histories and the set pieces of the buffet
tables were the great national dishes of the world. In

the grounds were mixed forces of soldiers, arranged there
both for ceremonial and for security reasons, their dress
uniforms dazzling in the variety of their colourings, their
swords, pikes and lances shining like silver. Through
rooms lush with mosaics, murals, carvings and bas-reliefs, with gilt and silver and enamelling with paintings
and sculpture from Egypt, Greece, Rome, Byzantium,
China and India, from Renaissance Spain, Italy and Holland, from eighteenth century France and Russia from
nineteenth century England and America, with tiled floors
and inlaid floors set with mother-of-pearl and plantinum,
with wall-hangings and curtains from Persia, with carpets
from Afghanistan, with carved wooden ceilings from sixteenth century Italy and seventeenth century Portugal, all
polished so that they shone with a deep, warm glow, crept
the smells of roasting ox and sheep and pigs and claves, of
delicious curries and dhansaks of Chinese soups and fowl,
of paellas, strudels and bouillabaises, of succulent vegetables and subtly spiced salad dressings, of pies and
cakes and patés, of glazes and sauces and gravies, of
bombes surprises, of lemon, orange, pineapple and
strawberry water-ices, of peacocks and quails, grouse,
pigeons, ortalons, chickens, turkeys, wild ducks, turning
on spits or stewing in pots, of rottkraut and kalter fisch,
of syllabubs, of sausages and baked ham, of tongue and
salt beef, of fruits and savoury roots, of carp and had-
dock and halibut and sole, of mushrooms and cucumbers,
of peppers and bamboo shoots, of syrups, creams and
crêpes, soups and consommes, of herbs and fats, of veni-
son and haggis, of whitebait, mussels and shrimps, of
hares and rabbits and caviar, of livers and tripes and
kidneys. There were wines and spirits and beers from
every province of the world. There were glasses and
steins and goblets of the clearest crystal and the most exquisite china. Cups and plates and dishes of gold, pewter,
silver and porcelain stood ready to receive the food;
pretty girls and handsome men in national costumes
stood ready to serve it. Only one tradition would not be
kept tonight: there would be no host or hostess to receive
the guests. The first guests to arrive would make it their
business to receive the others and introduce them after
the Master of Ceremonies had announced them in the
main ballroom. This peculiar arrangement had been con-

sidered the most diplomatic. And now the sun was setting. The ball was about to begin.

"I do hope," said Miss Brunner, curling her ermine robe over her arm as Prinz Lobkowitz helped her from the carriage, "that we are not the *first*." Up the marble staircase they went, between rows of rigid soldiers, holding flickering candelabra, to where, from behind colonnades, two footmen appeared and took their invitations, bearing them through the great gold doors into the anteroom of lapis lazuli where they were handed to a head footman, in scarlet and white with a tall, many-waved white wig which curved outwards over his head, who gave them to the Master of Ceremonies who bowed, read the cards, bowed again and ushered them through doors of crystal and filigree into the blazing splendour of the great ballroom.

"Prinz Lobkowitz and Miss Brunner!"

"But we *are*." Miss Brunner glowered furiously as her name and his echoed through the empty expanse. She smoothed her green velvet gown and fingered the pearl collar at her throat.

"Is it my fault, dear lady," Prinz Lobkowitz was equally put out, "if you are obsessed with time? We are always too early."

"And, consequently, always too late," she sighed, making the best of it. They walked slowly towards the far end of the hall. They inspected the servants; they went to the sideboards and tasted a morsel or two while glancing rather disdainfully about them at all the opulence. "What a lot of gilt."

He turned solicitously to listen, his many orders dazzling her for a moment. "Mm?"

"Gilt."

"Ah." He nodded thoughtfully, his patent leather toe tracing whorls of mother of pearl on the floor. "Quite so. A great deal of it. Still, perhaps we'll be able to do something about that now. We mustn't quarrel. That would not be in the spirit of the occasion."

"I'm reconciled to that," she said.

Footsteps sounded in the distance. They looked towards the doors. They saw the Master of Ceremonies raise a scarlet sleeve and read the card before him:

"The Right Reverend, Father in God, Denis, by Divine permission Lord Bishop of North Kensington!" intoned the M.C.

"He's overdoing it a bit, isn't he?" Miss Brunner prepared to receive Bishop Beesley. The corpulent priest had dressed himself in his cloth-of-gold cloak, his most ornate mitre and held a crook so rich in engravings and curlicues that it outdid anything San Simeon could offer. The bishop's pale face broke into a smile as he saw his old friends. He waddled slowly forward, his eyes wandering over the cakes and trifles on the buffet tables. At last he reached the pair and, with his attention still on the food, held out a beringed hand, either to be kissed or to be shaken. He did not seem offended when they did neither. "My dear Miss Brunner. My dear Prinz Lobkowitz. What a scrumptious feed they've laid on for us! Oh!"

From the gallery, musicians began to play selections from Coward's *Private Lives*.

"How charming," said Bishop Beesley, leaning forward and scooping up a handful of syllabub in his palm and sliding it gracefully into his maw, licking each of his little fat fingers and then both his little fat lips. "How nice."

Again the great voice echoed:

"My Lady Susan Sunday and the Honourable Miss Helen Sweet!"

"Well!" whispered Miss Brunner. "The S.S. I hadn't expected *her*. Her friend looks worn out."

"Captain Bruce Maxwell!"

"And I thought he was dead," said Bishop Beesley.

"His Excellency the President of the United States."

"And he looks it," said Miss Brunner. She smiled as Lady Sue and Helen approached. "How delightful."

Prince Lobkowitz noticed how alike the two older women were. Miss Brunner had been right about Helen Sweet. The girl had faded. Even her ball gown was a faded blue in comparison with the royal blue of Lady Sue's.

"My dear!" Lady Sue was saying. She embraced Miss Brunner. A slim, well-corsetted woman in a dress by Balenciaga, she wore six strands of blue diamonds at her powdered throat, with matching pendant earrings

and tiara. It was to be an evening of ostentation, it
seemed. "Good evening," said Helen Sweet mildly.

The band was now playing an instrumental version of
Little Red Rooster.

Captain Maxwell was shaking hands with Prinz
Lobkowitz. The captain's hands were cool and damp.
There was sweat on his brutish forehead. His great back-
side, much heavier than any other part of him, seemed
to waggle in sympathy. "Good to see you, old boy,"
he said in a military accent (though in fact he was a
Salvationist).

"Professor Hira!"

In impeccable Indian dress the small professor crossed
the floor, nervously fingering his white turban. His coat
was of deep pink silk with little round panels of a lighter
pink stitched into it. The trousers matched the panels.
The buttons were perfect pearls.

"Professor Hira!" Miss Brunner was genuinely pleased
to see the physicist. "How long has it been?" She
scowled. "Will it be?" She smiled. "Well, how are you,
anyway?"

"So so, thank you." He did not seem to share her
pleasure at the meeting.

"Mr. Cyril Tome." Thin, pale, with white hair but
with lips so red they seemed rouged, his hornrims glittering, the critic and would-be politician stood in his
monkish evening dress for a second or two beside the
Master of Ceremonies before braving the floor. Nobody greeted him.

"Mrs. Honoria Cornelius and Miss Catherine Cornelius."

"Good God!" said Captain Maxwell, chewing a stick
of celery. "Who d'you think put her on the list?" Largely
because it was what they had all been wondering about
him, nobody answered. "Honoria, eh? I bet!"

"Major Nye and Captain Nye."

"They do look alike, don't they?" murmured Lady
Sue to Miss Brunner. It was true. Save for the obvious
difference in ages, father and son might have been the
same man. The impression was sharpened by the fact
that they wore the uniform of the same regiment.

The guests began to spread themselves a little more
evenly around the perimeters of the room.

"The Right Honourable Mr. M. Hope-Dempsey."

"He's drunk!" murmured Prinz Lobkowitz as the young Prime Minister looked vaguely around him, then weaved genially in the general direction of the others, his long hair waving behind him. He seemed to have a live animal of some sort hidden under his coat.

"It's a cat," said Miss Brunner. "Where on earth did he get hold of it?"

The guests were now arriving thick and fast. Vladimir Ilyitch Ulianov, resident in China and extremely old and bad-tempered now, wearing a baggy black suit, hobbled in. Following him was his friend and protector the Eurasian warlord General O. T. Shaw, ruler of North China. Beside Shaw was Marshal Oswald Bastable, renegade Englishman and chief of Shaw's airforce. After them came Karl Glogauer the Revivalist, small, shifty, intense; a tall, moody albino, whose name nobody caught; the ex-Literary Editor of the Oxford Mail; a score or so of assorted conference delegates; Hans Smith of Hampstead, Last of the Left Wing Intellecutals; the Governor-General of Scotland; the Viceroy of India, the King of North Ireland, the recently abdicated Queen of England; Mr. Roy Hudd, the entertainer; Mr. Frank Cornelius and his companion Mr. Gordon 'Flash' Gavin; Mr. Lionel Himmler, the theatre impresario; Mr. S. M. Collier, the demolition expert; Mr. John Truck, the transport expert and Minister of Controls; the Israeli Governor of Central Europe; Admiral Korzeniowski, President of Poland; General Crossman (Crossman of Moscow) and Lady Crossman; Miss Mitzi Beesley and Dr. Karen von Krupp; Miss Joyce Churchill, the romantic novelist; the cathedral correspondent of *Bible Story Weekly* and his son and daughters; the Paris correspondent of *Gentleman's Quarterly* and his friend Sneaky John Slade, the blues singer; Miss Una Persson and Mr. Sebastian Auchinek, her agent; a Lapp parson called Herr Marek; Colonel Pyat with Miss Sylvia Landon, Presidente of the Académie Française; more than a hundred of the finest male and female film stars; a round thousand politicians from all over the world; thirty American deserters; five fat field-marshals; eighty-six ex-nuns from the original Convent of the Poor Clares; some Arabs and a German; Spiro Koutrouboussis, the Greek tycoon, with a group of other Greek millionaries; a bank manager and a television script writer; a Dutch soldier, the King of Denmark and the King of Sweden; the Royal Canadian Mounted Police rugby team; Mr. Jack Trevor Story, the jazz band leader, and Miss Maggie Macdonald, his star singer; the Queen of Norway and the ex-Emperor of Japan; the Governor of England and his chief advisor General K. G. Westmoreland; Mr. Francis Howerd, the comedian; a number of dons who wrote children's novels at Oxford; the most corrupt and feeble-minded paperback published in America; Mr. Max Miller, the comedian; a number of television producers; Nik Turner, Dave Brock, Del Dettmar, Robert Calvert, Dik Mik, Terry Ollis: members of the Hawkwind orchestra; some advertising executives, pop music critics, newspaper correspondents, art critics, editors and recording artistes and show biz personalities including Mr. Cliff Richard, Mr. Kingsley Amis, Mr. Engelbert Humperdinck and Mr. Peter O'Toole; the Dalai Lhama, some Trades Union officials; thirteen schoolmasters; Mr. Robert D. Feet, the pedant (who had thought it was a Fancy Dress Ball and had come as G. K. Chesterton); Miss Mai Zetterling and Mr. David Hughes; Mr. Simon Vaizey, the society wit, and a host of others. They ate, they conversed, they danced. The mood became gay and the worst of enemies became conciliatory, claiming with sincerity and passion that they had never really disliked one another. Peace was just around the corner.

"We could all be said to be prisoners, Mr. Cornelius," Bishop Beesley was saying as he munched a piece of short-bread, "and these revolutionists are perhaps the most hopeless of all prisoners. They're prisoners of their own ideas."

"I'll drink to that, bishop." Frank Cornelius raised his champagne glass. "Still, abolish war and you abolish revolution, eh?"

"Quite so."

"I'm all for the good old status quo."

Miss Brunner was laughing. Gordon Gavin, for all he was dressed in evening clothes, still managed to give the impression that he was clad from neck to knee in an old gaberdine raincoat. The seamed and seedy face, the hot, guilty eyes, the hands that rarely left the pockets of his trousers or else hovered helplessly near his flies, all contributed to the impression. "I'm flattered," said Miss Brunner. "but I'm afraid all my dances are spoken for." Flash looked relieved.

The musicians were playing Alkan's *Symphony for the Piano on the theme "Five"* to waltz-time. Mrs. Cornelius was having marvellous fun. All the boys were after her! She clutched the little Lapp parson, Herr Marek, to her and raced him round the floor. He was scarcely visible, buried, as he was, in her bulk, but he seemed to be enjoying himself. He had an evil glint in his eye as his muffled, heavily accented English came from the region of Mrs. Cornelius's bosom. "Morality, my dear lady, what is that? If it feels good, do it. That's my philosophy. What do you say?"

"Yore naughty, that's wot I say!" She laughed comfortably, completing a pirouette which took him off his feet. He giggled. They just missed colliding with Colonel Pyat and one of the most beautiful of the ex-nuns, Sister Sheila.

The dance ended and the laughter and the conversation swelled. Not only the main ballroom was packed, now. All the subsidiary ballrooms and many of the guest rooms were crowded. As Dick Lupoff was to report to the *L.A. Free Press* 'the world's finest were letting their hair down that night'.

The bank struck up with *A Bird in a Gilded Cage* and many of the guests began to sing the words as they took their partners for the dance. The babble of voices grew gayer and gayer. Champagne corks popped and glasses clinked.

Prinz Lobkowitz was commiserating with the ex-Queen of England as they waltzed discreetly in the shadows beneath the musicians' gallery. "My dear Eva, it is a situation one can never really get used to. Training, you know, and background. Not, of course, that you were expecting anything, I suppose, at the beginning."

"The epidemic . . ."

"Exactly. At least Lady Jane was executed. Poor girl."

"It's a bit warm in here, isn't it?" Frank Cornelius was saying on the other side of the ballroom as he danced expertly with Helen Sweet. "You look thoroughly washed out."

"Oh, it's all right." Helen Sweet glanced timidly into the gap between his chest and her breasts.

Lady Sue swept past in a flash of crystalline blue. "Don't overdo it, Helen!" Lady Sue was dancing with her friend the ex-emperor of Japan. Dressed in traditional Japanese costume, the old man was finding the waltz steps a bit difficult.

Catherine Cornelius, feeling a trifle dizzy, leaned against a buffet table. She was a picture of beauty and well-supplied with beaux. They crowded round her. She brushed a lock of fair hair from her forehead, laughing as Captain Nye, who had brought her another drink, said: "I'm afraid they've nothing non-alcoholic left. Will champagne do?" She accepted the glass, but put it down on the table. All of a sudden she began to shiver. "Are you cold?" asked three Austrian hussars solicitously and simultaneously.

"I shouldn't," she said. "Is anything speeding up?"

Captain Nye was filled with foreboding.

They started to play *The Wind Cries Mary* as a foxtrot. Captain Nye held out his hand to her and smiled kindly. "This must surely be mine." She gave him her hand. It was ice cold. He could barely hold on to it. With an enormous effort of self-discipline he drew her freezing body close to his. She had turned very pale.

"If you are not well," he said, "perhaps I might have the honour of escorting you to your door."

"You're kind," she said. Then she almost whispered: "But it is not kindness I need."

Major Nye had already had three dances with Miss Brunner. This was the fourth. Major Nye asked Miss Brunner if she knew anything of the theatre.

"Only what I see," she said.

"You must let me take you backstage sometime, at one of my theatres. You'll like it."

"I'm sure."

"You're a very lovely woman."

"And you're a very handsome man."

They stared into each other's eyes as they danced.

In the third bedroom of the Casa del Monte, seated on a black walnut panelled Lombardy bed, covered in seventeenth century carvings, the most corrupt and feeble-minded paperback publisher in America sipped his vodka and tonic and stared sourly at his tennis shoes while one of the Oxford dons bored him with a long and enthusiastic description of the joys and difficulties involved in doing *Now*

We Are Six into Assyrian. It was what they both deserved. Of all those at the ball, only the publisher was not enjoying himself.

Colonel Pyat and Prinz Lobkowitz smoked their cigars and strolled in the gardens, stopping on the terrace of the Casa del Monte. "Peace at last," said Colonel Pyat, breathing in the richly-scented air. "Peace. It will be such a relief, don't you think?"

"I, for one, will be happy," the Prinz agreed.

"It will give us so much more time to enjoy our lives."

"Quite."

Miss Brunner and Major Nye found themselves by the Venetian fountain outside the Casa del Sol. Most of the security guards had gone, withdrawn discreetly as the ball progressed. The house itself glowed with light and the waters of the fountain, topped by a copy of Donatello's David, were illuminated with a dozen different soft colours. Miss Brunner put her hand into the water and watched it run up her threequarter length evening glove and drip from her elbow. Major Nye gently stroked his moustache. "Lovely," he said.

"But imagine the expenditure." Miss Brunner smiled to show that she was not being vulgar. "And no one knows who paid for it. What a splendid piece of tact. Who do you think it is?"

"It's hard to guess who's got that kind of money in England today," he said without much interest.

Miss Brunner's eyes became alert. "That's true," she said. And she was thoughtful. "Oh, dear." She removed her hand from the fountain and placed it lightly against Major Nye's hip. "What a kind man you are."

"What kind? Oh, I don't know?"

The night was full of music, laughter, witty conversation. It came at her from all sides. "It's a magic night! I need someone, I think," she murmured to herself. She decided she would be wise to stick with the material at hand. "I want you so much," she breathed, propelling herself into the major's arms. He was astonished and took a little while responding.

"By God! By God! You beauty!"

The German band on the nearby terrace struck up with a selection of Buddy Holly favourites.

Miss Brunner looked round Major Nye's shoulder,

scanning suspiciously the privet hedges. It was just a feeling, but it was getting stronger all the time.

"My dear!" Bishop Beesley lay on a yellow bedspread in the yellow-draped Yellow Room of the Casa del Sol. The room was furnished largely in early Jacobean style and the bed-posts were topped by carved eagle finials. On the Bishop's right was a Giovanni Salvi *Madonna and Child*. Lying on the Bishop's left, and facing him, was the beautiful ex-nun with whom Colonel Pyat had lately been dancing. She had turned out to be an Australian. Now she had no clothes on. Bishop Beesley's mitre had fallen to the pillow and his hands were completely covered in chocolate. He had brought the girl and the chocolate mousse up here together and was intently covering her body with the stuff. "Oh, delicious!" The girl seemed uncomfortable. She put her hand between her legs, frowning. "I think I'm feeling a little crook."

Dr. Karen von Krupp was dancing in the main ballroom with Professor Hira. Professor Hira had an erection because he could feel Dr. Karen von Krupp's girdle and garter-belt through her gown. He hadn't had an erection since Sweden (and then it had proved his downfall). "The rhythm of the quasars, doctor," he said, "is, essentially, a lack of rhythm." He pressed his erection tentatively against her thigh. Her hand slipped from around his waist and patted him tenderly. His breathing grew more rapid.

"Quasars," said Dr. von Krupp romantically, closing her eyes, "what are they, compared with the texture of human passion?"

"They are the same! That is it! The same! Everything is the same. My argument exactly."

"The same? Are we the same?"

"Essentially, yes."

The music finished and they wandered out into the garden.

Everyone was smiling, shaking hands, patting one another on the back exchanging addresses, laughing uproariously at one another's jokes, making love, resolving to be more generous, more tolerant and to learn humility. The Peace Talks and the Gala Ball would not be forgotten by most of them for a long time. The whole spirit of the talks had been crystallised here. Nothing but improvement lay ahead. Strife would be abolished and heaven on earth would be established.

Only Miss Brunner, Catherine Cornelius and Captain Nye were beginning to wonder if there wasn't a snag. Bishop Beesley and Frank Cornelius, who would normally have been swift to spot the signs, were both too absorbed in their own activities to notice anything.

Frank Cornelius had locked the door of the movie theater (done in gold and crimson, with silk damask wall hangings and copies of Babylonian statues holding electric lights made to look like lilies) and sat in the back row with Helen Sweet with his hand up her skirt as they watched one of the prints of *Yankee Doodle Dandy* with James Cagney as George M. Cohan and Walter Huston as his father Jerry Cohan. Frank loved the feel of Helen's lukewarm, clammy thigh; it made him nostalgic for the childhood he'd never had. Shakey Mo Collier, operating the projectors, tried to peer through his little window and get a good look at what Frank was doing.

Bishop Beesley and his ex-nun were now completely covered in chocolate and were prancing around the Yellow Room in an obscene version of the Cake Walk.

Lady Sue Sunday, still in the ballroom, was doing the tango with Cyril Tome who had just proposed marriage to her. She was considering his offer seriously, particularly since he showed an unexpected aptitude for the tango. "We could probably both live on Sunday's money, I suppose," mused Lady Sue. "I have a certain income from my writing, moreover," said Cyril Tome. "And there would be so much we could clean up together."

'Flash' Gordon was in the garden taking a happy interest in the azaleas. Nearby, Mrs. Cornelius was wandering hand in hand with Professor Hira while Herr Marek hovered jealously in the background, planning to murder the Indian. In the Games Room, where billiard and pool tables rested on travertine floors and where the walls were decorated with rare Gothic tapestries and antique Persian tiles, with its sixteenth century Spanish ceiling showing scenes of bullfights, Dr. von Krupp and Una Persson were playing billiards while Sebastian Auchinek and Simon Vaizey looked on. "I used to be rather good at this," said Dr. von Krupp, making an awkward shot awkwardly. The spot ball struck the red with a click. "Isn't that a foul?"

asked Una Persson politely. "I mean, I thought I had the spot." Dr. von Krupp smiled kindly at her. "No you didn't, dear." Simon Vaizey was seized by a fit of hysterical giggling. "I shouldn't really be here, you know. I think I'm a gatecrasher."

The President of the United States and the Prime Minister of England were completely and happily drunk and were dancing round and round the otherwise deserted marble Morning Room together, making the huge silver sanctuary lamps on the ceiling jingle and shake with their merriment. A small black and white cat sat on the window sill, licking its paws.

"You look much nicer without your make-up," said the President. "I'm glad it's you who's the Prime Minister now."

Holding a rather grotesque Tiffany lamp above her head Mitzi Beesley, the bishop's daughter, was trying to limbo with Lionel Himmler, who had learned the dance in Nassau during his brief stay there. They were getting on well together. "I've never enjoyed myself so much," Mitzi told him. "I love you."

"And I love you," he said. His normally morose features were beaming. "I love *love!*"

Spiro Koutrouboussis had just shaken hands on a satisfactory business deal with his fellow Greek millionaires when he saw Catherine Cornelius standing in a dark corner of the Main Library, looking through a rare copy of *Paradise Lost*. He crossed the huge Meshed carpet and presented himself. "Are you free for the next dance, Mademoiselle Cornelius?" he asked in careful French.

"I'm afraid I'm feeling a trifle unwell, m'sieu." She tried to smile. "My escort has gone to find my cloak."

"May I put my landau at your disposal?"

"Thank you. You are very kind, M. Koutrouboussis. I was sorry to hear of the unfortunate collapse of your—" she shivered uncontrollably—"project."

"No matter. A new one is developing. That's business. *On mourra seul,* after all." His own smile was full and charming.

"*Il n'y a pas de morts, M. Koutrouboussis!*" She closed her eyes.

"Could I offer you my coat?"

"I—thank you." Gratefully Catherine accepted his heavy jacket, pulling it around her. "I'm sorry to . . ."

"Please." He raised a gentle hand.

One of the carved cabinets swung out from the wall and nearly struck Spiro Koutrouboussis on the shoulder. He leapt back.

From the space behind the bookcase emerged a tall figure with long, straight black hair, a pale, voluptuous face. He was wearing a short black overcoat with wide military lapels. His black trousers had a slight flare. His shirt was of the purest white silk and there was a broad, crimson tie at his throat. One long-fingered hand held an oddly shaped gun. "Hello, Cathy. I see you were expecting me."

"Oh, Jerry! I'm cold."

"Don't worry. I'll deal with all that. What are these people doing in my house?"

"Dancing."

"You might have dressed for the occasion," said Koutrouboussis, eyeing the gun. Jerry put the gun in his big pocket.

"It took some time getting warm, myself," he said, by way of apology. "How's tricks, Koutrouboussis?"

"The tricks are over. I am back in legitimate business now."

"Just as well. God, you go away for a little while and you come back to find the place crammed with guests. Is this my party, then?"

"I suspect so."

Jerry laughed. "Oho! You know me of old, don't you? But this isn't Holland Park. It's Ladbroke Grove. I'm reformed. I lead a very quiet life, these days."

"Jerry!" Catherine had turned quite blue and seemed on the point of collapse. "Jerry!"

He wrapped his arms around her. "There. Is that better?"

"A bit."

"I can see I'm going to have to take steps." Jerry poured himself a large whiskey from the decanter on the ebony and marble table. "I suppose Frank's about?"

"And mum."

"Fuck."

"She's all right, Jerry. Tonight."

"I haven't got a lot of time, either," said Jerry to himself. "Still . . ."

"How long are you staying for, Jerry?"

"Not long. Don't worry." He smiled at her, full of misery. "This is like the old days. I'm sorry."

"It's not your fault."

Miss Brunner came into the Games Room. "I knew it. You'd better not try anything, Mr. Cornelius."

"Oh, I don't know. This is my place, after all."

"Sod you, You set it up."

Jerry shrugged.

"Christ!" She spat on the rug.

In the Morning Room, the Prime Minister of England and the President of the United States were sitting side by side in the same big chair. "Culturally, of course," said the President, "we have always been exceptionally close. That must stand for something."

The Prime Minister laughed happily. "Me? I'll stand for anything. What's the score?"

The lights went out. The President giggled.

In the main ballroom the music went on for some time, until the candles and the flambeaux began to dim, to gutter and finally extinguish themselves. Everyone murmured with delight, expecting a surprise. Laughter filled the great hall as men and women speculated on the nature of the treat.

At the entrance, the gold doors swung back; the glass doors swung back. A cold wind blew.

In the gardens the glow-worms and the fireflies were still, but there was one light, from the beam of a large flashlight held in the hand of a shadowy figure who swung up the steps into the Casa Grande. The figure wore a short top-coat with its wide lapels turned up to frame a long, pale face. The eyes gleamed in the reflected glare from the flashlight. The figure entered the ballroom and pushed its way through the silent throng until it stood beneath the musicians' gallery.

The voice was cool: "There's been a mistake. It's time to call it a day, I'm afraid. You are all on private property and I advise you to leave at once. Anyone still here in half-an-hour will be shot!"

"Good God!" Prinz Lobkowitz stepped forward. "Who on earth?"

"This is difficult for me," said the figure. It directed the flashlight upwards. "It's to do with the third law of thermodynamics, I suppose." The musicians had replaced their instruments with a variety of sub-machine-guns and automatic pistols. "But I won't bore you with a speech."

"Do you realise what you are doing?" Prinz Lobkowitz swept his hands to indicate the crowd. "You could wreck everything."

"Perhaps. But things have to keep moving, don't they? Now you must leave."

A machine gun sounded. Bullets struck the chandeliers and glass flew. The guests began to scream and mill about. The ex-Queen of England went down, her shoulders cut by several shards. Mr. Robert D. Feet, the pedant, clutched a bleeding eye. Others sustained less important injuries. The scramble for the exit began. It was almost dignified.

As the guests flooded from the Casa Grande, others began to arrive from the various guest castles. They wanted to know why the lights had gone out. Car engines started up. Horses stamped and snorted. Wheels churned in gravel. There was a smell of May.

In the cinema, Frank Cornelius began to guess that something was up. Abandoning Helen Sweet, he crept to the doors and gingerly unlocked them. "Jerry?"

In the Yellow Room Bishop Beesley was struggling to get his surplice on over the hardening chocolate, leaving the half-eaten ex-nun on the floor where she lay. He adjusted his mitre, picked up his crook, stooped for one last lick and then hurried out.

In the Morning Room the President of the United States and the Prime Minister of England had already left. Only the cat remained, sleeping peacefully in a warm chair.

Captain Nye found the library and opened the door. "Are you there, Miss Cornelius?"

"Yes, thank you. I'm feeling awfully better."

"We must go."

"I'm afraid we must."

"This will be the ruin of the talks."

"Quite a good ruin, though."

Laughing, they left the library.

Mrs. Cornelius, Professor Hira and Herr Marek were already in Ladbroke Grove. "It'll be nice to get back." Mrs. C. felt in her reticule for her key. "It's only round the corner, luckily." The three of them were unaware that anything had happened to mar the ball.

"Can you smell velerian?" asked Flash Gordon as Helen Sweet, weeping, stumbled into his hedge. "You're a little darling, aren't you?" He gathered her up. "Come and see Holland Park with me."

She sniffed. "All right."

"What's bad news for some is good news for others," said Lady Sue as her carriage raced past the couple. She had lost her tiara but had gained Bishop Beesley. She didn't know at that point that he wasn't a negro.

Slumped in the far corner of the brougham, the bishop groaned. He had horrible indigestion.

Cars and carriages erupted into Ladbroke Grove, scattering in all directions, some colliding in the gloom (for the gas lamps had also been extinguished). A small boy was run over by Colonel Pyat's Lamborgini.

In the third bedroom of the Casa del Monte, several Oxford dons and the most corrupt and feeble-minded paperback publisher in America were blown to bits by explosive shells from the big Schmeisser in the hands of the second cellist. The publisher, for one, was almost grateful for this change of pace.

Some, mostly those who had walked to the gates and were now strolling up Westbourne Park Road towards the Portobello Road looking for taxis, had taken the events with a certain amount of amused relish. They chattered and laughed as they walked along, listening to the distant sounds of machine-gun fire.

"Well," said Dr. von Krupp, who was of this party, "it's back to square one, I suppose."

"Do you live in London?" asked Una Persson, her arm around Sebastian Auchinek's neck.

"Oh, I think I'll want to now," grinned the doctor.

In Spiro Koutrouboussis' landau, which had been the first carriage to get away, Captain Nye and Catherine Cornelius embraced in a long and tender kiss. They were already halfway to the Surrey border, heading for Iron-master House.

Spiro Koutrouboussis was still in the Casa, having survived the massacre of his colleagues. He had a gun and was looking for his host. He bumped into Frank on the stairs, mistook him for Jerry, and shot him. Frank, thinking that he had been shot by Jerry, returned the fire. The two bodies tumbled down the stairs together.

Miss Brunner and Major Nye gave up any thoughts of revenge and clambered into the major's camouflaged Humber Snipe. As they roared away, one of the violinists emerged on the steps and lifted his Tommy gun to his shoulder, firing after them, but the bullets bounced off the car's armour and then they had turned a corner and were safe.

Easing the car into Ladbroke Grove, Major Nye asked Miss Brunner: "Well, what did you make of all that?"

"Now that I look back," she said, "I suppose it seems inevitable. But not to worry."

"I must say you know how to make the best of things," he said admiringly.

Slowly the great house grew still until the only sound that could be heard anywhere was the purring of the small black and white cat as it stretched itself, licked its whiskers, then settled back to sleep again.

THE PEACE TALKS

Concluding Remarks

Upon his return from exile at the request of the new revolutionary junta, Prinz Lobkowitz made a short speech as he stepped off the airship. The speech was addressed to Colonel Pyat and an ecstatic crowd. He said:

"The war, my friends, is ceaseless. The most we can expect in our lives are a few pauses in the struggle, a few moments of tranquility. We must appreciate those moments while we have them."

PROLOGUE (continued)

. . . the ghosts of the unborn. And the ghosts of the unknown: the wardead and those who died in the concentration camps. Dying in anonymity, without witnesses,
they are never decently brought to rest. It's hard to
explain. And yet the birth of every new child is a kind of
resurrection. Every child welcomed into the world helps
to lay a ghost to rest. But it takes so long. And these days,
it's hardly a lasting solution. Perhaps we should simply
stop killing people.

MAURICE LESCOQ, Leavetaking

**SHOT
THREE**

"Miracle Cure" of Frances, 6

The Pope has been asked to declare that six-year-old
Frances Burns is a miracle girl. Three years ago, she was
dying of cancer. Surgeons who had been fighting for her
life gave her only a few days to live. Now she is a happy,
laughing tomboy of a girl. And the consultant who treated
her admits: "A miracle is not too strong a term for her
recovery." The astonishing cure of Frances Burns began
when her mother, Mrs. Deirdre Burns, took her pain-
racked daughter from Dennistoun, Glasgow, to the
Roman Catholic shrine of Lourdes in Southern France.
Frances was bathed in the waters of the mountain spring
where thousands of invalids have sought a cure. Back in
Glasgow, after two days in the Sick Children's Hospital,
Frances sat up and asked for food. A week later the
tumours on her face had disappeared. She was on the
road to an amazing recovery. The panel of 31 specialists
who make up the Lourdes Medical Bureau have asked the
Pope to consider pronouncing Frances's cure a miracle.

THE SUN, August 23 1971

THE THEATRE

Una Persson was on stage. She was playing Sue Orph, latest of Simon Vaizey's sophisticated heroines, in Vaizey's most successful musical comedy to date—*Bright Autumn*—at the Prince of Wales' Theatre. The house was full and Una noticed her old agent, Sebastian Auchinek, in the front stalls. Auchinek was in politics now and writing thousands of articles and pamphlets. His latest production was called "A New Deal for Britain's Jews."

Draped in a light pink silk Chanel pyjama suit, Una leaned against a grand piano and confronted her leading man, Douglas Crawford, as he said:

"I never guessed you kept a diary, darling."

Una held the book insouciantly in one long hand and said lightly: "Oh, darling, it's hardly a *real* diary."

The line had become a catch-phrase everywhere now. Comedians imitated it on the wireless. It might have been written especially for her rich Rs.

"But it *is* secret, I suppose," Douglas continued. "Is it awfully secret?"

"It is rather."

"I thought we weren't to have secrets, you and I. I thought we had agreed it wouldn't be that kind of marriage." He was offended.

She was eager to reassure him. "Darling, it *isn't*—it's just that—"

Icily remote, he said: "Yes?"

"Oh, darling don't be a *bear*!" She turned away from him, looking down at the keys of the piano.

"A prig, you mean, don't you?" He folded his arms and stalked to the cocktail cabinet at the far end of the stage. "Well, what if I am a prig? What if I love you so horribly I can't stand to think of you keeping secrets from me? You know, people who keep diaries are usually afraid of something. Isn't that what they say? What are *you* frightened of, Susan? What have you written about that man you saw last night—you know—that man? What's his name?" He pretended he didn't care, but it was obvious to the audience that he was barely in control of his passions.

Una replied in a high, offended tone, speaking rapidly: "You know perfectly *well* what his name is. It's Vivian Gantry." She paused, becoming reminiscent. "We were lovers—years ago . . ."

"And you still love him? Is that what you're frightened to tell me? Is that what you've written in your damned diary?" Douglas wheeled round, his face tortured with emotion.

Una dropped the diary and swept towards him. "Oh, you fool, you fool, you sweet, precious fool! How could I love anybody but *you?*"

"Tell me?"

She stopped suddenly, lowering her head. Then she turned to point at the fallen diary. "Very well, read it if you like."

He hesitated. He started to mix himself a drink at the cabinet. "What does it say?"

"That I love you in so many ways I can't even say it to your face."

"Oh?" It was possible to see now that he wanted to believe her but was still cautious.

Her voice was almost a whisper and yet it reached the back of the theatre. "Yes, Charles. I suppose I'm too much in love with you, really . . ."

He put the drink down and seized her shoulders. Her face remained averted. "Swear it?" he said, almost savagely. "Do you swear it, Sue?"

She recovered her composure and stared him directly in the eyes. Mockingly, spreading her fingers over her heart, she said lightly, but with something of an edge to her voice. "Very well, if you think it necessary. There! I swear it." Her tone softened. She took his hand. "Now stop all this—this *silly* jealousy."

By now he was completely miserable for having

doubted her. "Oh, darling I'm sorry." He folded her in his arms. Softly the orchestra started the introduction to the most popular song of the show. "I *am* a bear! An utterly boorish bear! And a prig! How could I possibly, possibly doubt you. Forgive me?"

Her voice was warm and soft when she breathed:

"Forgive you."

"Oh, darling!"

He began to sing:

> *"You know I'd be blue, dear,*
> *With someone new, dear.*
> *I'll never weary—of you.*
> *Heartbreak and sorrow,*
> *Will never spoil tomorrow,*
> *And I'll never be blue, dear, again . . ."*

As the curtain fell on the act, Sebastian Auchinek, his eyes full of tears, clapped and clapped until a hand fell on his shoulder and he looked into the grave, polite faces of two plain-clothes policemen. "Sorry to interrupt your evening out, sir. But we wonder if you wouldn't mind coming with us to answer one or two questions."

It was like a bad detective story compared with the fantasy he had just been watching. He said almost pathetically and with an attempt at levity:

"Can't I answer them here?"

"I'm afraid not, sir. We've a warrant, you see."

"What are you arresting me for?"

"Wouldn't it be less embarrassing if we answered that when we're in the street, sir?"

"I suppose so. Can I get my coat?"

"That's waiting for you in the lobby, sir." The policeman scratched his little moustache. "We took the liberty."

Sebastian Auchinek looked around at the other people in the stalls, but they were all involved in getting to the bar, studying their programmes or chatting amongst themselves.

"I see," he said. "Well . . ." He got up, shrugging. "I am Miss Persson's manager, you know. The papers will know you've arrested me."

"Not an arrest, as such, sir. A request for help. That's all."

"Then surely I can see the play through?"

"It's urgent, sir."

Auchinek sighed. He darted one last look at the curtain, drew one last breath of the atmosphere, and then left by a side exit.

THE FLYING BOAT

The great grey flying boat manoeuvred on her two outer
forward-facing propellers, slewing round in the shallows
until she faced the main expanse of the blue lake. Save for
the ripples which spread from the flying boat's massive
angular floats, the lake was flat, shining and still. In the
early morning air the growling Curtiss Conqueror
engines drowned every other sound. The boat was a
Dornier DoX with twelve 600 hp liquid-cooled back-to-
back engines mounted on her 160ft wing.

There was space on the ship for a hundred and fifty,
but, with the exception of Captain Nye, who was piloting
the plane, there were only three people aboard.

Even the snow-capped grandeur of the Swiss Alps failed
to dwarf the monoplane as she coursed over tranquil Lake
Geneva, all twelve props twirling when Captain Nye flicked
the toggle-switches which brought them to life.

"We're flying light. We'll make time, everything else being equal." He chatted casually to Frank Cornelius who
lounged seedily in the roomy co-pilot's chair and stared
through the glass at the glare from the rising sun, a ball
of pulsing brass whose rays pierced the morning mist.

The boat surged across the deserted lake and headed towards the ruins of the city on the far shore. Captain Nye
waited until the very last minute before taking her up,
flying playfully low over the collection of shanties near the
lakeside. A few children scattered in fright; then the
Dornier was climbing steeply, banking into the sun, going
East.

"She's an ugly bitch, but she's fast." Captain Nye levelled out. They were doing at least 130 mph. "Go and check

if the ladies are all right, would you, old man?" They were now well clear of all but the highest mountains.

Frank unstrapped himself and slid the cabin door open. He crossed Joubert and Petit's 60ft Art Deco ballroom and descended the angular staircase to the first class deck where Miss Brunner and his sister Catherine were already seated on high bar-stools having Pimms Number Ones prepared for them by Professor Hira. The physicist was to be their guide on this expedition.

"Everything okay?" said Frank. "Isn't it smooth?"

"Beautiful," said Miss Brunner, dabbing at her Eton crop and winking. Catherine looked away. Through the observation ports she could see the clean, shimmering peaks. "It's a lovely day," she said.

"We'll make Rowe Island by Monday easily," said Frank. "Six thousand miles, just like that. It's incredible!"

"Aren't you flinging yourself rather too hard into the part, Frankie, dear?" Miss Brunner fingered her lip-rouge.

"Dear Miss B. You've no enthusiasm left at all. I think I'll stroll back to the pilot's cabin." Frank blew a kiss to his sister and another to Professor Hira. Pointedly he ignored Miss Brunner. They were always quarrelling; even the Indian physicist paid no attention, placing the tall slab-side Vuitton glasses with a click on the zig-zag black and white inlay of the Kroll bar. He didn't drink himself, but he was a wizard at mixing things up.

"It'll be nice to visit the island again," said Catherine. "So warm. People go there for their health, I hear."

"Just as we are, dear, really." Miss Brunner adjusted her white cardigan over the blue and black silk day dress, offering Catherine a Gold Flake from her thin silver cigarette case. Catherine accepted. Professor Hira leaned over the bar and lit the cigarettes with the big table lighter which had been built to resemble a heavy Egyptian sarcophagus, but which was really made of aluminium and, like to much of the flying boat's equipment, a spin-off from the airship industry. Miss Brunner found airships not sufficiently *chic* for her taste; indeed, even Catherine thought them a trifle gross. Still, they did enable ordinary members of the public to travel from country to country for comparatively little money, if that was a good idea. She was disturbed, however, by the prediction that they would one day take the place of the flying boat. Progress was progress, but she was sure that people of taste would always prefer the elegance of an aircraft like the Dornier, with her lovely Joubert and Petit and Josef Hoffman interiors. Catherine leaned her elbow on the bar, her hand curving back at the wrist, the jade cigarette holder gripped loosely between her forefinger and middle finger perfectly matching the plain jade bangle on her slim arm. She wore the minimum of make-up, the minimum of clothing on her torso. Miss Brunner gave her an admiring once-over. "Frank is vulgar, but you dear, are more than perfect."

Catherine smiled a private smile, her foot tapping to the rhythm of the Ipana Troubadours record Professor Hira had just placed on the Victorphone. The muffled sound of the Curtiss Conquerors seemed to be beating to the same time. "I'll get by—as long as I have you," sang Catherine with the record.

"But Frank, I think, is more in tune, eh?" said Professor Hira, breaking both their moods.

Miss Brunner was frosty. "Should that be a compliment, I wonder?" She slid from her stool. "I'm going to the powder room. I feel a mess."

Catherine watched her go through the door marked *Damen*. Sometimes Miss Brunner could be a real stickler for form.

Left alone with Catherine, Professor Hira was ill at ease. He cleared his throat, he beamed, he played with the cocktail shakers, he looked vaguely up at the roof. Once, when they struck some mild disturbance, he made a move to help her steady herself, then became embarrassed, changing his mind half-way through the motion.

Catherine decided to check the cargo. With a pleasant nod to the professor, she gathered up her Worth skirts and walked aft. The companionway led down to the second-class lower deck, which Hoffman had redesigned as a galley and dining cabin. She went through the galley and into the cool forward cargo hold. Aside from their yellow and black pigskin luggage, there was only one piece of cargo, a cream-coloured box about five feet long, three feet wide and three feet deep. The lid of the box was padlocked. Catherine took a key from the side pocket of the little gold Delaunay bag and inserted it into the lock, turning it twice. Then she opened the lid. Inside was the shiny white skeleton of a child, aged between ten and twelve. The skull was damaged. In the bone of the fore-head, just above and between the eye sockets, was a large, regularly-shaped hole.

As a mother might move a sleeping child before draw-ing the covers over it for the night, Catherine rearranged the skeleton on its red and white leather cushions. She leant with a fond smile into the box, kissing the skull just above its injury; then tenderly she closed the lid and pad-locked it up, murmuring: "Don't worry."

She sighed, pressing her palms together in front of her lips. "The Indian Ocean is the friendliest in the world, Professor Hira says. And Rowe Island is the friendliest island in the Indian Ocean. We'll all be able to rest there." She staggered as the plane hit more turbulence, banking steeply. She managed to grasp the yellow and green silk safety rope secured to the bulkhead. The Dornier righted herself almost immediately. Catherine checked that the box hadn't shifted in its moorings and then carefully she began to make her way back to the bar.

THE PIER

"It's the 'ottest summer in years," Mrs. Cornelius was saying as she waded back to the shore, her jazzy print dress hitched above her red, dumpy knees. She was sweating like a sow, but she was happy, out of breath, having a high old time at Brighton. She'd been to the races, been on the sea-front miniature railway, had two sticks of rock, some winkles, five pints of Guinness, a bit of skate and chips and a sing-song in the pub just before she'd been sick. Being sick had cleared her system and now she felt like a million dollars. It did you good. Colonel Pyat, in perfect civilian summer dress, a white linen suit, a panama hat, two-tone shoes and a malacca cane over his arm, stood on the pebbles holding Tiddles, Mrs. Cornelius's small black and white cat, which, of late, she had taken to carrying everywhere she went, even to the shops, the pictures or, like today, on their honeymoon day excursion to the seaside.

"Wot abart th' pier?" Mrs. Cornelius panted. She cocked her thumb over her damp shoulder at the East Pier, an affair of rusty scaffolding holding a dance hall, a theatre, a penny arcade and a fun fair. From where she stood on the bank she could hear the dodgems clattering and crashing. Every so often, there came a high-pitched giggle, an excited yell.

Colonel Pyat shrugged his acquiescence. It was his duty. He would do it.

" 'Ere, give us th' cat." She seized the limp beast from his arms. "Looks daft, a man carrying a cat. They'll reckon yore a fairy or somefink if you ain't careful!" She laughed raucously, nudging him playfully in the ribs. "Not

that there aren't a few o' *them* darn 'ere. Brighton! I
should think so!" She cast an eye over the jolly crowd
which covered the beach, as if vetting them for signs of
sexual deviation. Deckchairs, newspapers, raincoats, fairisle pullovers, jackets, towels, were scattered everywhere
and on them lay or squatted mums and dads and adoles-
cent boys and girls, the sun shining on their Brylcreemed
crops and their permanent waves. The younger kids
wandered around eating ice-cream bricks from the Walls
Stop-me-and-buy-one man who pedalled his refrigerated
bin up and down the front. Other children, clutching their
scratched metal buckets and chipped wooden spades,
sought wistfully for some sand. The noise of a barrel-
organ came closer. Far away, on the promenade overlooking the beach, open top double-decker buses sailed
slowly along, crammed with men in white Oxford
bags and open-neck shirts, or girls in snazzy summer
frocks, their hair tightly curled or waved, their lips blossoming with scarlet and cerise. The smell of brine, of
grease, of chips and jellied eels drifted languidly on the
still air.

"Phew!" She wriggled her toes into her emerald-green
sling-back sandals and led the way through her fellow holidaymakers and up the shingle towards the pier. "It could
get yer darn, too much o' this, eh? The 'eat, I mean."

On the pier, having paid twopence each to go through
the turnstile, Colonel Pyat found to his relief that the wind
had changed direction and was blowing all the smells, save
that of the sea, back towards the town where the
Chinoiserie Pavilion's green domes could be seen among
the more down to earth Regency terraces. It certainly was
hot and the sun hurt his eyes, making him wish he had
brought his tinted spectacles. The cat struggled for a moment in his coat and then was still again.

"Wot a marf, wot a marf, wot a norf, an' sarf," sang
Mrs. Cornelius. "Lumme, wot a marf 'e's got. When 'e
was a nipper, Cor Lord Lovel, 'is pore ol' muvver use ter
feed 'im wiv a shovel! Wot a gap (pore chap), 'e's never
bin known to larf—'cos if 'e did it's a penny ter a quid, 'is
face ud fall in arf!"

Colonel Pyat looked apprehensively at Mrs. C. The last
time she'd sung that particular song, it was just before
she'd been violently sick in the gutter outside The Ship.

"This is wot I *corl* a Bank 'Oliday Mondy," continued Mrs. Cornelius, taking the cat from him, raising it close to her face and stroking it. "Let's go on the ghost train now, eh?"

"You don't want to overdo it, you know," said Colonel Pyat.

"Wot? Me?" She shook with mirth. "You must be joking!"

They went on the ghost train. Colonel Pyat was frightened by the monsters and witches and skeletons which sprang at him from all sides, the screechings, the howls, the cackling laughter, the clammy stuff that touched his smooth-shaven cheeks, the spider-webs, the flashing lights, the rush of cold air, the mirrors, the awful darkness through which they passed, but Mrs. Cornelius—although she yelled and shrieked incessantly—had a lovely time.

They took a cup of tea and a bun each in the pier cafeteria, looking out over the sparkling sea. All the waitresses gathered round to stroke Mrs. Cornelius's cat. "Innit *tame?*" said one. Another offered it a bit of biscuit, which it refused. Another girl, with a scrawny face and a wretched body, brought it a saucer of milk. " 'Ere, pussy. Pussy? Pussy?" The cat lapped the milk and the girl felt grateful all day.

They got on the dodgems. Mrs. C. went in one car, with the cat stuffed down her bosom with only its little head sticking out, looking really comical, and Colonel Pyat went in another. Mrs. Cornelius's car was bright red and gold with a number 77 on it. Colonel Pyat's car was green and white with a number 55 on it. The power arms cracked and flashed and sparks flew as the cars started up. Mrs. C. leaned forward, driving her car head-on at Colonel P. who resigned himself to the thump which shook his bones and grazed his knee. Through the loudspeakers came the distorted voice of Nat Gonella singing *If I had a talking picture of you.* "Yer too effin' slow!" screamed Mrs. C. delightedly, and off she went to deal damage to other unsuspecting drivers. Even the cat seemed to be enjoying himself on the dodgems. "Oo! Muvver!" shouted Mrs. Cornelius as she flung back her turbanned head and took another victim.

Colonel Pyat began to feel queasy. As soon as the cars stopped moving, he got out and stood on the side while

Mrs. Cornelius had another turn. He was amazed that so much violent activity could take place on such an apparently flimsy structure as the pier. It must be considerably stronger than he thought. He lit a cigarette and strolled towards the rail, looking down through the gaps in the planks at the sea swishing below, listening to the distinctive noises of the woman he had married, wondering if, after the destruction of the town, this pier would still survive.

The cars had stopped again and Mrs. Cornelius was clambering out and waddling across the floor to the boardwalk which ran round the outside of the dodgem arena. She was sweating and grinning when she joined him and she had picked up some of the oily aroma of the cars.

"Come on," she said, seizing him by the arm and leading him further up the pier, "we still got time fer a dance."

THE HILLS

A smoky Indian rain fell through the hills and woods outside Simla and the high roads were slippery. Major Nye drove his Phantom V down twisting lanes flanked by white fences. The car's violet body was splashed with mud and it was difficult to see through the haze that softened the landscape. In rain, thought the major, the world became timeless.

Turning into the drive outside his big wooden bungalow, he brought the limousine to a stop. A Sikh servant gave him an umbrella before taking over the car.

Major Nye walked through the rain to the veranda, folding the umbrella and listening to the sound of water on the leaves of the trees. It was like the ticking of a thousand watches. It smelled so fresh. Simla hadn't changed much. That was something.

His wife and two little girls were still in Delhi. They had been reluctant to make this journey of return with him. But there had been people he wanted to see. He had felt the need to reassure the servants that he was still in the land of the living.

Inside, the house was cold; all the furniture was draped in white dust-covers. There were no smells and, save for the rain, no sounds. The place was dead. He felt tired, borne down by responsibility, by the sudden understanding that all his dedication had been pointless. How much longer could the Raj last, with the Chinese, the Russians and the Americans hammering at the gates?

He saw that a fire had been lit in the grate. Someone had been burning books. He picked up the poker and turned over the covers, which were only partially burned.

How Michael Found Jesus was one title, and there were others: *Ragnarok and the Third Law of Thermodynamics, Time Search Through the Declining West, Bible Stories for Little Folk, A Cure for Cancer, How to Avoid Heat Death.* All religious and medical stuff, plainly. Who on earth could have bothered to set fire to them? He was crossing to the bell-pull when he was distracted by a sound from outside. On the veranda servants were shouting. He went to the window and opened it.

"What is it, Jenab Shah?" he asked the big Afghan butler.

The man shrugged and grinned in his thick beard. "Nothing, sahib. A mongoose killing a cobra. See." He held up the limp body of the snake.

Major Nye nodded and closed the window. He went to the door and into the shady hallway. He walked up the uncarpeted stairs. He entered the bedroom which he and his wife had once shared. The bed and the rest of the furniture was also draped in white sheets. He grabbed the edge of a sheet covering a massive teak wardrobe and yanked it down. Dust filled the room. He coughed. He pulled a bunch of keys from his pocket and selected one, putting it into the lock of the wardrobe. The door creaked open, revealing a mirror in which, for a second, he regarded himself with surprise. He had aged. There was no doubt of it. But he had kept his figure. He reached into the wardrobe and selected an Indian coat of silk brocade. It was blue, with circular panels of slightly lighter blue stitched at intervals all over it. The buttons were diamonds and the cloth was lined with buckram. The high, stiff collar was fixed at the throat by two hidden brass buckles. There was also a scarlet sash. Major Nye took off his own jacket and drew the Indian coat over his white silk shirt. Carefully he did up all the buttons and then clipped the collar together. Finally he tied the sash about his waist. With his greying hair and white moustache, his clear blue eyes and his tan he could still look impressive; as impressive as when he had received the coat. It had been a present from his defeated enemy Sharan Khang, the old hill fox. Was Sharan Khang still perpetuating the fiction that his Himalayan Kingdom was independent? Major Nye smiled.

Wearing the coat, he went downstairs to the gunroom.

With another key he unlocked the door. Lying on the table was the Mauser FG42 where he had left it last. Closing the door behind him, he went over to the gun and picked it up, brushing away the dust which had settled on the barrel. He slotted the telescopic sight into its mount, checked the magazine and cradled the gun in his left arm. A small drop of oil now stained his silken sleeve. He opened a drawer and found a box of cartridges. He put these into his left hand and then went out, locking the door again.

He looked at his wrist-watch, checking the time. The rain had stopped for a moment. He began to smell the grass, the rhododendrons, the trees. He went outside and walked across the lawn which still had croquet hoops sticking in it from the last game, years before. On the far side of the lawn and partly obscured by foliage was the white ruin of the mansion he had built when he had first come to Simla.

Major Nye had always had a superstitious reluctance to visit the ruin, the result of a single Tibetan bomb dropped from a Caproni Ca 90 B.B. during the brief Italian crisis some years earlier. It had been the only plane ever to get as far as Simla.

The mansion's roof had collapsed completely now and part of the front wall bulged outwards. All the windows were smashed and the double door at the front had been thrust out by the force of the blast. The only occupants of the house had been an aya and Major Nye's small son. They had both been killed

Major Nye took a firmer grip on his rifle. He fitted shells into the magazine and then continued to stalk forward, but it was becoming harder to move at all. He mounted the first two broken steps, making himself look at the door. He was sweating.

Until this moment, he had never considered himself a coward, but he stopped dead before he reached the last step to the doorway. He shuddered at what his imagination made him see behind the doors. Trembling, he lifted the Mauser to his shoulder and, without bothering to sight, fired the whole magazine into the timber. Then he dropped the gun and ran, his face twisting in terror.

He shouted for his car. The Phantom V was ready. He

got into it and drove away from Simla, his eyes wide with self-hatred.

In Delhi he booked a passage on a ship leaving Bombay a few days later. He didn't see his wife or children, but stayed at his club. Next morning he took the train to Bombay and, even when his ship, the SS *Kao An*, was well out into the Arabian Sea, he was still weeping.

THE STATUE

Prinz Lobkowitz straightened his uniform and stood shakily up in the open staffcar as it rolled into Wenzslaslas Square in the early afternoon. The troops, in smart black and gold uniforms, stood in their ranks, straight and tall and ready for review. On all sides of the square the watching crowd was eight and ten people deep. The Mercedes reached the rostrum erected below the statue of the martyr-king. The crowd cheered, the soldiers presented arms. A whistle sounded and the statue blew up. A chunk of stone rushed past Prinz Lobkowitz's head and he flung himself down into the car. General Josef, his aide, seated opposite the Prinz, drew his revolver and shouted for the driver to accelerate quickly, but the driver's nerve was gone and he was having trouble getting the Mercedes back into gear.

Save for the dead and wounded, the troops remained in reasonably good order, but the crowd had panicked. The air was filled with its screams as it tried to escape from the square. Two or three shots sounded. This increased the tension. People ran in all directions.

The smoke and dust was clearing now. Lobkowitz saw that the entire statue had been destroyed. Hardly a stump of the pedestal had survived the blast. The temporary rostrum had become a heap of shattered wood and twisted metal. Prinz Lobkowitz's standard lay half-buried in the rubble near a smashed, bloody corpse which he couldn't identify.

General Josef, the aide, began shouting hoarse orders to his troops. Rifles ready, squads of soldiers broke from the square and drove their way through the terrified

civilians, pouring into the surrounding buildings, occupying them and searching for the assassins. Suddenly something cracked above Lobkowitz's head. A banner had
unfurled itself from a bouncing telephone wire. The banner bore a single word:

FREIHEIT

Lobkowitz pursed his lips. Terrorists. And it wasn't as
if he'd taken the country by force. He felt let down.

The Mercedes was in gear now, reversing towards the
street by which it had entered the square. Lobkowitz tried
to straighten up and see what was happening. Old General Josef pushed him down again. On the roof of a house
on the far side of the square some figures appeared. They
wore civilian dress but they had bandoliers of cartridges
criss-crossed on their chests and there were rifles in their
hands. They looked a bit like Slovak brigands. The men
and women on the roof began to fire indiscriminately into
the square. Some soldiers fell; some ran for cover.

"There'll be hell to pay," General Josef kept muttering. Lobkowitz wasn't sure whether his aide was frightened of losing his job; whether Josef intended to sack his
security officers; or whether he was vowing to take reprisals on the terrorists, whoever they were. Lobkowitz
knew the terrorists could be anyone. They could be the
disguised 'volunteer' soldiers of half-a-dozen different
foreign armies; they could be anarchists; or mercenaries
in the pay of some extreme right-wing group; they might
be communards; they could even be Czech nationals.
Time would tell.

Now the driver had swung the Mercedes round in a
circle and headed down the broad, treelined Avenue
Mozart, making for the Presidential Palace where they
might still find safety. General Josef let the Prinz sit up.
Josef put his revolver away, buttoning the holster.

"That's the last time we use an open car," he growled
as he tidied his white hair and re-adjusted his cap. "It'll
be an armoured half-track next. The devil with public
relations!"

"They didn't do much damage." Lobkowitz spoke
mildly. He was unhappy in his uniform. It was too severe.
He preferred the more comfortable and colourful uni-

forms of his native land. How much longer should he go on listening to these advisors?

"Freiheit!" muttered the aide bitterly. "What do they know of freedom? They think it means license—self-expression. A little freedom is bought at great cost. I know. I was in the original Corps which made this damned city safe. You should have been here, Prinz, before we sent for you. The stink alone would have knocked you out. It wasn't a city of liberty: it was a city of libertines."

A feeling of intense boredom swept over Lobkowitz. He had heard this remark made by a score of men in a score of different cities.

"That's finished, at least," Josef went on. "But it could all be ruined again. We must work fast."

"Do you know what the terrorists are?" Lobkowitz asked. "Do you know what movement they support?"

"Not yet. That's the least of our worries." The aide tapped his teeth with his cane and became reflective. Prinz Lobkowitz asked him no further questions.

Back at the Presidential Palace, Prinz Lobkowitz felt lonely. He sat in his huge, impressive office and looked at no one and nothing. At his back were the crossed flags of both their nations, hanging over the eighteenth century fireplace. From a window which opened onto the balcony he contemplated the street. In the middle of the avenue, waving a sword and mounted on a horse, stood a granite statue of some other antique hero. Even as Lobkowitz looked, it blew up. It was as if every statue he glanced at immediately burst into fragments. The noble stone head rose towards him and then, as he covered his eyes, burst through the window, taking both glass and frame into the room and bouncing, chipped but unbroken, into the empty fireplace.

For a second Prinz Lobkowitz thought it was his own head. Then he smiled. He crouched down behind his massive desk, keeping it between him and the window in case there were further explosions. After all, he thought, he had no axe to grind. If they didn't want him, fair enough. He'd be glad to get home.

The telephone began to ring. Lobkowitz felt for it on top of the desk and found it. "Lobkowitz."

"Are you hurt, sir?" It was General Josef's voice.

"No, not at all, but the firedog's a bit bent."

"I'll be up right away."

As he waited for Josef's arrival, Lobkowitz sat on the edge of the desk and lit the last of his Black Cat cigarettes. Before he crumpled the packet and threw it into his wastepaper bin, he took the brightly coloured card (one of a series of 50 given away free with the cigarettes) and tucked it into the top breast pocket of the civilian waistcoat he had always worn under his uniform. It was a picture of a triceratops, number eighteen in a series of dinosaurs.

The red and black packet was the only piece of scrap in the otherwise clean steel wastepaper basket. He felt for it.

The gilded doors swung open. Una Persson stood there, dressed all in black, a rifle slung over her back, a beret on her shining curls. She opened her arms to him, smiling.

"Darling! I have defeated you again!"

REMINISCENCE (E)

In the early hours of a summer morning a cat kills a mouse in the kitchen, letting it run a little way and then stopping it again. Outside in the garden large black slugs crawl over the iron furniture. There is movement in the toolshed. There is a whisper from beyond the trees.

Late News

A crowd of about 200 attacked two Army scout cars and a Land Rover in Belfast last night after one of them ran over and killed a five-year-old girl. Cars, vans and lorries were set on fire and there were bursts of machine-gun fire which injured four young children. The girl was one of a crowd of children playing on the street corner. An Army spokesman said she jumped under the wheels of the leading scout car.

MORNING STAR, February 9 1971

A widow, her five children and an uncle died in a fire at a cottage in Pontypool yesterday. Firemen found the bodies of Mrs. Patricia Evans, aged 34, Jacqueline, 13, Garry, 11, Joanne, eight, Martin, six, and Catherine, two, in a bedroom. On the stairs was the body of Mr. John Edwards, aged 63, the uncle who came to rescue them.

GUARDIAN, February 9 1971

George Lasky, aged four, was drowned when he fell into an ice-covered pond in a field at Slough yesterday. He had gone on the ice to pick up a ball.

GUARDIAN, March 2 1971

Murder squad detectives set up headquarters in a holiday beach café in Cornwall yesterday after the badly-battered body of a 17-year-old high school girl had been found near the entrance to a cliff-top camp site.

GUARDIAN, March 15 1971

591

A three-year-old boy was found dead in a disused refrigerator last night.

GUARDIAN, June 29 1971

Lynn Andrews, aged 10, was stripped almost naked and punched and kicked to death while her mother looked on helpless, it was said in court at Woolwich yesterday. Raymond John Day (31), unemployed, was sent for trial charged with murdering the girl.

GUARDIAN, June 30 1971

The Alternative Apocalypse 5

Jerry Cornelius was in Sandakan when the news came of the resumption of hostilities. The news was brought by Dassim Shan, Jerry's major domo, while Jerry swam in the cool waters of the palace pool, all pink and blue marble and tinkling fountains.

Rajah? Dassim, feet together, stood uncertainly on the edge of the pool, one hand against a jade pillar. Jerry was some distance out in the middle of the pool, hidden in the shade. Milky light filtered down from the semi-transparent dome in the roof. Dassim's voice echoed a little.

They are fighting again, rajah.

Oh? A splash.

Does it not concern you, rajah?

Dassim peered into the water, searching every inch of it for his master, but he could see only goldfish.

The Alternative Apocalypse 6

Bishop Beesley, Mitzi Beesley, Shakey Mo Collier and Jerry Cornelius stood on the footbridge staring down at the railway as the train passed beneath their feet. Through the steam they could see the open trucks piled high with stiffening corpses. Dead troops.

Jerry pushed his helmet back from his forehead and eased the strap of his pack. Well, he said, our luck's still holding.

The smell! Mitzi Beesley, dressed in a complete ARP uniform, circa 1943, held her nose.

Her father sorted through his tin of emergency rations to see if there was any chocolate he'd overlooked. That's not the half of it, he said. He wore khaki battledress with his dog-collar rather ostentatiously displayed at the throat.

I remember a train like that when I was a kid, said Mo Collier nostalgically. On'y in that case the soldiers on it was alive.

Same difference, said Mitzi with a wink. She rubbed busily at her blue flannel thigh as the last truck went under the bridge.

Jerry looked at his left watch. Well, back to work. Not far to Grasmere now.

They all climbed on to the lightweight Jungle Bug, with its motorbike saddle seats and its canvas wind-shield. Jerry settled himself in front of the driving gear and started the engine. For a moment the machine reared, its front wheels spinning, and then they were off down the narrow lane as a thin cloud of rain drifted from the fells to the west and the green hills turned suddenly black.

We've never fully been able to reproduce World War Two conditions, Bishop Beesley yelled over the screech of the engine and the slap of the wind. I sometimes consider it a personal failure.

Your moral dilemmas always resolve themselves sooner or later, dad, Mitzi comforted. She reached over from where she sat alongside him on the pillion behind Jerry and straightened his M60 on his shoulder for him. Is that better?

He nodded gratefully, munching a piece of Nut Crunch he had found in the breast-pocket of his battledress. They bounced on towards Grasmere and, as the rain passed, glimpsed the lake on the far side of a hill lying almost directly ahead of them. They had heard that what was left of an enemy division was hiding out in Wordsworth's cottage. It was a long shot, but it was something to do.

The road went through a pine wood and then bent along the eastern shore of the lake, leading directly into the town of Grasmere. The town was a ruin of looted gift shops and tea rooms. In one or two places they were forced to steer round small craters in the road. Elsewhere a sack had burst and been abandoned, leaving a litter of plaster Wordsworth busts, oven gloves and daffodil vases.

They headed for the main road with its cracked and weedgrown concrete and at last sighted Dove Cottage and, a few doors away, another cottage that was the Wordsworth Museum. There were signs of fighting in the stone, half-timbered buildings. One or two cottages had been destroyed completely, but Dove Cottage, with its roses round the door, was intact. They climbed off the Jungle Bug and readied their weapons, approaching cautiously.

Dove Cottage seemed deserted, but Jerry didn't take any chances. He ordered Bishop Beesley forward. The bishop lay down behind a hedge and raked the windows. There was a musical tinkle as the glass broke. Bishop Beesley waited for a while and then stood up, munching a Mars Bar.

A Webley .45 sounded from an upstairs window and the bullet went past him, hitting the ground. He turned,

his Mars Bar half-raised, and darted an enquiring glance
at Jerry, who shrugged.

There was another shot. Bishop Beesley eased his bulk
to the ground again, put a new clip in his M60 and fired
at the window.

When there was no further answering fire, the four of
them spread out and approached the cottage. Jerry noticed that the plaque on the door reading 'Wordsworth's
Cottage' had been holed a few times by shells larger than
Bishop Beesley's. The door opened easily for the lock had
already been blown off. They went in. An American teenage girl, with long black hair and a red mou-mou pulled
up around her waist, lay on the polished timber floor.
Her blood had dried on her face and her left hand was
missing. Apart from the girl, the downstairs rooms, with
their glass cabinets of Wordsworth and Lake Poets trophies, were empty. Pictures of Southey, Coleridge, De
Quincy and the Lambs smiled down at them. Shakey Mo
broke one of the cabinets with the butt of his Sten and
lifted out an oddly shaped object of carved ivory. He
squinted at the label. Look at this! De Quincy's drug balance. Look at the size! What a head! He put the balance
into the gamebag he had slung over one shoulder and
rummaged through the rest of the cabinet's contents. He
found nothing else of interest. More glass broke in the next
room and the three of them trooped in to see what Mitzi
was doing. She had smashed the glass partition behind
which had been arranged a typical sitting room of Wordsworth's time. She had stripped off her ARP uniform and
was draping herself in the dead poet's clothes, his hat,
his jacket, his shawl and one of his waistcoats. She held
his umbrella in one hand. With her Remington tucked
under her arm, she tried to open the umbrella. They all
laughed as she paraded round the room pretending to
read from one of Dorothy Wordsworth's diaries.

Jerry heard a footfall upstairs and raised his Schmidt
Rubin 5.56 to rake the ceiling. The footfall stopped.

I suppose we'd better get upstairs, said Shakey Mo.

Jerry led the way.

The upstairs rooms were much the same as the downstairs rooms, with more cabinets and more trophies, some
of which had been smashed by Bishop Beesley's M60
bullets coming through the windows. In the front room

sat a woman of about sixty. She was tall, dressed in a plain blue dress and her hair was grey. The empty Webley was still in her hand. She was evidently upset. There are guided tours, you know, she said. You only had to ask.

Bishop Beesley grinned with relish as he advanced on her. I'm going to fuck the life out of you, he said.

Jerry and the rest made a tactful retreat.

Bishop Beesley joined them later in the Wordworth Museum where Shakey Mo was inspecting an old shot-gun labelled 'Wordsworth's Gun'.

My God, said Beesley in disgust, even this place has a tinge of vitality. Bishop Beesley argued that since too much life had led to their present difficulties (overcrowding and so forth), then life meant death and was therefore evil. Therefore it was his duty to wipe out the evil by destroying life wherever he found it. He was a wizard at that sort of thing. Jerry had his eye on him.

Are we all finished here? Jerry asked.

They padded away, turning only to watch when Shakey Mo lobbed a couple of Mills bombs into the cottage and the museum.

Damn! said Mitzi as the buildings went up. I left my uniform behind.

She wrapped Wordworth's shawl more tightly around her, pursing her lips in rage as she tripped, on Cuban heels, back to the Jungle Bug. Bishop Beesley, Shakey Mo and Jerry Cornelius took the opportunity to piss against a hedge; then the rain came on again.

In improved spirits, they mounted the Bug and headed towards Rydal and the big green hills beyond.

Late News

Lt. William Calley, charged with massacring 102 South Vietnamese men, women and children at My Lai hamlet, testified at his court-martial at Fort Benning, California, yesterday, that the army taught him children were even more dangerous than adults. He was taught that 'men and women were equally dangerous, and children, because of their unsuspectingness were even more dangerous'. The army also taught him that men and women fought side by side and women for some reason were better shots. He was told that 'children can be used in a multiple of facets. For example, give a child a hand grenade and he can throw it at an American unit. They were used for planting mines. Basically they were very dangerous.'

MORNING STAR, February 23 1971

Three boys died when a house caught fire in Cemetery Road, Telford, Salop. They were Keith William Troop, aged five, Peter John Green, aged three, and Matthew Percival Green, aged two. They were the sons of Mrs. Joan Green, aged 22.

GUARDIAN, May 3 1971

Mrs. Valerie Ridyard, aged 25, pleaded guilty to the manslaughter of Darren, aged five months, Michael, aged three, and Barbara, aged four, on the grounds of diminished responsibility. Her pleas of not guilty to murder were accepted. The children died in separate incidents between October 1970 and January 1971. Mr. Arthur Prescott, QC, prosecuting, said the facts were short and tragic. There had been a history of conduct by Mrs.

598

Ridyard resulting in illness to the children through partial suffocation and poisoning.

GUARDIAN, June 10 1971

The West Indian immigrant parents of seven children admitted at Berkshire assizes, Reading, yesterday to killing one of their sons in a ritual sacrifice. Olton Goring (40), of Waylen Street, Reading, was committed to Broadmoor after the prosecution accepted his plea of not guilty to murdering the boy, Keith, aged 16, but guilty to manslaughter on grounds of diminished responsibility. Goring's wife, Eileen (44), pleaded guilty to manslaughter and was ordered to be sent for treatment in a mental hospital. It was said the Gorings were members of a Pentecostal mission in Reading—a revival sect widely supported in the West Indies. Followers believed themselves possessed by the Holy Spirit while in a trance and felt they were in direct communication with God.

GUARDIAN, August 23 1971

A boy aged 14 will appear in court at Tamworth, Staffordshire, today in connection with the death of a man aged 19 whose body was found in a house on Saturday.

GUARDIAN, August 23 1971

A girl aged 14 was charged on Saturday with the murder of Roisin McIlone, aged five, whose body was found beside an overgrown bridle path near her home in Brook Farm Walk, Celmsley Wood, near Birmingham. A blood-stained stick was found nearby.

GUARDIAN, August 23 1971

REMINISCENCE (F)

The black, burning warehouses of Newcastle.

THE AIRSHIP

During the First Night Dance on board the L.S. *Light of Dresden,* bound for India via Aden, Mrs. Cornelius went out onto the semi-open observation deck to get some air. She felt a little queasy; it was her maiden trip on a zeppelin, but she was determined to enjoy herself, come what may. All she had to do was clear her head and let herself get used to a feeling that was like being permanently in a slightly swaying descending lift that was also moving horizontally. She stood outside the big hall where the spotlights played beams of red, blue, yellow and green on the dancers. The band was called The Little Chocolate Dandies. Their saxophones wailing, they launched themselves into their next number, *Royal Garden Blues.* Mrs. Cornelius wasn't too sure she was that keen on jazz, after all. At present she felt like hearing something just a teeny bit more restful. But the only thing she could think of was *Rock-a-by-baby:* in fact, she couldn't get it out of her head. She looked down at the lights of Paris (she thought it was Paris) and imagined the drop. Though she had been assured that it was completely rigid and part of the main frame containing the helium bags, she was sure she could feel the catwalk swaying below her. The music from the dance floor now seemed much more friendly. She reeled back in again.

Everyone was really jazzing it up tonight. She was nearly knocked down twice by couples as she moved towards the bar. She grinned. Ah, well! She felt a hand on her shoulder.

"Are you perfectly well, dear lady?"

It was that bishop she'd met earlier. She'd liked him

from the start, with his nice, jolly fat face, though she hadn't taken to his wife in the baggy pink evening dress, frizzy hair, with her thin, pale, nervous head constantly grinning in a way Mrs. C. personally found offensive. If you asked Mrs. C., the bishop's wife fancied herself a bit. Lady Muck. The bishop, on the other hand, was a real gentleman, he could mix with anyone at any level. Mrs. C. could go for him in a big way. She smiled to herself at the thought, wondering what it would be like with a bishop.

"Quaite well, thank yew, bishop, love," she said. "Jist gittin' me air-legs, thet's hall."

"Would you care to dance?"

"Oh, charmed Ai'm shewer!" She put her left arm round his ample, black clad waist and folded her dumpy right hand in his. They began to fox-trot. "Yore a lovely dancer, bishop." She giggled. Over the bishop's shoulder she saw his wife looking on, nodding to her with that same set, patronising smile, though you could tell she wasn't pleased. Mrs. C. defiantly pushed her bosom against the bishop's chest. The bishop's red lips smiled slightly and his little eyes twinkled. She knew he fancied her. She went all warm and funny inside as his hand tightened on her corset. What a turn up.

"Are you travelling alone, Mrs. Cornelius?"

"Well, Ai've got me littel boy wiv me, but 'e's no trouble. Got a cabin to 'imself."

"And—Mr. Cornelius?"

"Gorn, unforchunatly."

"You mean?"

"Quaite. R.I.P."

"I'm sorry to hear it."

"Well, it was a long time ago, you see."

"Aha." The bishop looked upwards, toward the gigantic gas-bags hidden behind the dance hall's aluminium ceiling. "He's in a happier state than we, all in all."

"Quaite."

Well, thought Mrs. C., he's not slow. Maybe he was the original bishop in the jokes, eh? Again she couldn't stop herself from smiling. Her queasiness had completely disappeared, to be replaced by that old feeling.

"And how are you travelling? First class, I assume?"

"Ai should fink so!" She roared with laughter. "No

such luck, Ai'm afraid. It's second class for me. It's not cheap, the fare to Calcutta."

"I agree. I, too—that is to say my wife and I—am forced to travel second. But I must say I've no complaints, as yet, though it is only our first night aloft. We are in cabin 46 . . ."

"Oh, reahlly? Wot a coincidence. Ai'm in number 38. Just deown the passage from you. Mai littel boy's in 30, sharin' wiv a couple of other littel boys."

"You have a good relationship with your son?"

"Oh, yes! 'E's devoted!"

"I envy you."

"Wot, me?"

"I wish I had a good relationship with my—my sole relative. Mrs. Beesley, I regret, is not the easiest woman with whom to be joined in holy matrimony."

"She seems a naice sort o' woman, if a bit, you know, out of things, as you might say."

"She does not take pleasure, as I do, in making new friends. Normally I travel alone, and Mrs. Beesley remains at the rectory, but she has a sister in Delhi and so she decided, this time, to accompany me." Now the bishop's stomach pressed against her stomach. It was so cosy, it made her legs feel like jelly.

"P'raps she should rest more," said Mrs. C. "Ai mean she could take the chance to relax before we get to India, couldn't she? It would probably do 'er good." She hoped the biship hadn't noticed the rather savage delivery of that last sentence. He certainly seemed unaware of the change in her tone and only smiled vaguely. The music stopped and, reluctantly, they broke their embrace and clapped politely at the coloured men in tuxedos on the bandstand. One of the musicians stepped forward, his black hands running up and down the keys of his saxophone as he spoke.

"And now, ladies and gentlemen, we'd like to give you my own *That's How I Feel Today*. Thank you."

Tuba, banjo, three saxophones, drums, piano, trumpet and trombone all started up at once and, oblivious to the other dancers, Mrs. Cornelius and Bishop Beesley began to Charleston, still holding each other very close. When Mrs. Cornelius next noticed Mrs. Beesley, the bishop's wife was quietly leaving through the exit onto the main corridor. Mrs. C. felt triumphant. Po-faced bitch! Didn't she believe in a feller enjoying himself?

"Ai'm afraid yore waife 'as decided to leave us," she said into his plump, red ear.

"Oh dear. Perhaps she's gone to lie down. I wonder if I shouldn't . . .?"

"Oh, come on, bishop! Finish the dance!"

"Yes, indeed. Why not?"

The lights dimmed, the tone of the music sweetened and Mrs. C. and Bishop B. began to fox-trot again. It was very romantic. Everyone on the floor sensed the mood and got smoochy. Mrs. Cornelius's bosom began to heave and she wriggled her bulk against Bishop Beesley's, who responded by moving his hand over her bottom.

She murmured, as the music subsided, "You feel like it, don't you?"

He nodded eagerly, smiling and clapping. "I do, dear lady. I do, indeed."

"Would you like to escort me to mai cabin door?"

"I should like nothing better." The old dog was almost panting with lust. She winked at him and put her arm in his.

"Come on, then."

This was what she called a ship-board romance.

They went into the passage and turned left, searching for the right cabin number in the dim, blue light.

They slipped surreptitiously past number 46 and Mrs. Cornelius searched hastily for her key as they approached number 38. She produced it with a flourish and inserted it delicately into the lock, turning the levers with a soft double click. She stood there coquettishly, a hand on her hip. "Would you care for a nip of something to keep out the cold?"

He snorted.

He darted a quick look up and down the corridor, and dived into the cabin, his mouth closing on hers, his hands caressing her huge breasts. His breath was oddly sweet, almost sickly, but she quite liked it.

She hitched up her skirt and lay down on the bunk. He pulled down his gaiters and flung his sticky body on top of her. Soon they were bouncing up and down in the narrow bunk, all the aluminium work creaking. They were shouting and grunting in unison as orgasms shook their combined thirty-eight stones of flesh when the door opened and blue light filtered in from the corridor. A spotty youth stood there, peering in. Evidently he couldn't see clearly. "Mum?"

"Oh, fuck me! It's orlright, son. Git along will yer? I'm busy at the minute."

The boy, who was probably in his mid-teens, continued to stand there, his mean, ratlike features those of an idiot, his large eyes dull and uncomprehending.

"Mum?"

"Bugger off!"

"Oh," he said, as his eyes got used to the dark, "sorry." The door closed.

Mrs. Cornelius clambered from the bunk, scratching her pelvis. "Sorry abart that, bishop. Fergot ter lock it." She pulled the bolt into its socket, then stumbled back, her knickers still around one ankle. She unbuckled her corsets and let them drop and was about to remove her dress when the bishop seized her by the hair and pulled her head down towards his penis which rolled back and forth like the mast of a storm-tossed ship. His eyes continued to stare thoughtfully at the door.

In the passage the boy grinned at his mum's antics and, dressed only in his raincoat, boots and socks, continued to search for a vacant lavatory. He listened to the vibrations from the vessel's great engines, listened to the faint sound of the wind as it slid over the monstrous silver hull, listened to the distant music of the jazz band. He ran his hand through his long, greasy hair and wished that he had a monkey suit he could wear. Then *he'd* go to the dance and the janeys had better look out for their virginity! He shuffed down a side-passage and then slid open the door onto the observation deck. The lights of the city were past now and the airship seemed to be flying over open countryside. Here and there were a few flickering lights from small villages or farmhouses. Even from this height he didn't much fancy the country. It made him nervous.

He looked up at the blackness above. There were hardly any stars out at all and a thin rain seemed to be falling. Well, at least the weather would be better in Calcutta.

The ship shivered as it turned a degree or two, correcting its course. The distant music wavered and then altered. There was something almost hesitant about the way the ship moved. The youth stared forward and thought he saw in the distance the white-topped waves of the Mediterranean. Or was it the Bay of Biscay? Whatever the name of the sea, the sight of it meant something to him. For no reason he could understand, the sight filled him with a sense of relief. They were leaving Europe behind.

The youth watched eagerly as they began to move out above the water. He grinned as he saw the land fall away. Apart from the crew, he was the only one to notice this change.

THE LOCOMOTIVE

Wondering how he had come to be involved in this revolution in the first place, Colonel Pyat swayed forward to have a word with the driver of the armoured train. Dirty steam struck his face and he coughed painfully, his eyes watering. He tried to rub at his eyes with his free hand, but the train snaked round a bend and forced him to reach out and grab the other steel hand-rail on the observation platform. The train travelled over a vast plain of burned wheat. In all directions the landscape was flat and black, with the occasional patch of green, white or yellow which had somehow escaped the flames. Colonel Pyat would be glad to get into the hills which he could just see on the horizon ahead. He opened the plate-armoured door of the next compartment and found that it was deserted of soldiers. Here there were only boxes of ammunition and light machine guns. He made his way cautiously between the stacks. Perhaps military responsibilities were the simplest a right-thinking man could shoulder without feeling feeble. Certainly, the responsibility of commanding an armoured train was preferable to the responsibility he had left at home. On the other hand, he could have been helping the sick in some relatively safe hospital behind the lines, not heading willy-nilly towards the Ukraine and the worst fighting of the whole damned civil war. 193– had not been a good year for Colonel Pyat.

He tried to brush the soot off his uniform and succeeded only in smearing more of the stuff over the white buckskin. He sat down with a thump on an ammunition box and, scraping his match on the barrel of a machine gun,

lit a small cheroot. He could do with a drink. He felt for
the flask in his hip-pocket. It was there, all slim brass and
silver. He unscrewed the top and raised the lip to his
mouth. A single drop of brandy fell onto his tongue. He
sighed and put the flask back. If they ever got to Kiev,
the first thing he would do would be to requisition a
bottle of Cognac. If such a thing still existed.

The thin strains of a piano accordion drifted down the
length of the train from behind him. The vibrant, gloomy
voices of his troops began to sing. He got up, the cheroot
held tightly in his teeth, and continued on his way.

'I should have stayed in the diplomatic corps,' he was
thinking as he opened a door and saw the huge log tender
looming over him, its chipped black enamel smeared with
streaks of green and yellow paint where someone had tried
to obscure the previous owner's insignia. There was a
door in the tender, leading to a low passage through
which he had to pass to get to the engine footplate itself.
He heard the logs thumping and rattling over his head and
then he had emerged to find the fireman hurling half a
tree into the yellow, roaring furnace. The driver, his hand
on the acceleration wheel, had his head sticking out of
the observation port on the left of the loco. Two guards
sat behind him, their rifles crooked in their arms, their
legs dangling over the edge of the footplate. They
were half asleep, their fur shakos tipped down over their
foreheads, and they didn't notice Colonel Pyat's arrival.
The footplate smelled strongly of the cedar wood which
was now their main fuel. Overlaying this was the well-
defined odour of human sweat. Colonel Pyat leant against
the tender and finished his cheroot. Only the fireman knew
he was there and the fireman was too busy to acknowledge
his presence.

Throwing the butt of his cheroot at the blasted fields,
he stepped forward and tapped the driver on his naked
shoulder. The thickset man turned reluctantly, showing a
face covered in dirty fair hair; his red-rimmed eyes glared
through the black mask of soot. He grunted when he saw
that it was Pyat and tried to look respectful. "Sir?"

"What sort of time are we making?"

"Not bad, sir, considering everything."

"And Kiev? When should we get there now?"

"Less than another eight hours, all things being equal."

"So we're not much more than half a day behind schedule. Splendid. You and your crew are working wonders. I'm very pleased."

The driver was wondering why they were bothering to go to Kiev in the first place, but wearily he responded to his commander's attempt at morale-building. "Thank you, sir."

Colonel Pyat noticed that, having tried for a second to look alert after they had noticed him, the guards had resumed their earlier slumped postures. "Mind if I stay on the footplate for a little while?" he asked the driver.

"You're the commander, sir." This time the driver couldn't stop the sardonic, edgy note in his voice.

"Ah, well." Pyat turned. "I won't bother you, then."

He ducked into the passage under the tender and stumbled through to the other side. As he tried to get the door open, he heard a faint cry from behind him. A rifle shot sounded. He went back through the passage. Now both guards were on their feet, shooting into the air.

"Look, sir!" One of them pointed ahead.

They were almost upon the lowest of the foothills and something was moving just behind the nearest ridge.

"Better take it easy, driver." Pyat grabbed for the cord to ring the alarm bell through the rest of the train. "What do you think they are?"

The soldier answered. "Land 'clads, sir. At least a score of them. I saw them better a moment ago."

Pyat tugged the alarm cord. The driver began to slow the train which was now about half-a-mile from a tunnel running under a high, green hill. Even as they watched, a pair of racing metal caterpillar tracks appeared on the roof of the tunnel, pointing directly at them. Then they saw a gun-turret above the tracks as they descended. The long 85mm cannon swung round until it pointed directly at the engine. Pyat and the rest threw themselves flat as the gun flashed. There was an explosion nearby, but the locomotive was undamaged. The driver looked to Pyat for his orders. Pyat was inclined to stop, but then he decided to risk a race for what might be the safety of the tunnel (if it hadn't been mined). There was a chance. The tank barbarians rarely left their vessels. Some hadn't seen direct sunlight for months. "Maximum speed," he said. The fireman stood up and dragged more logs off the

tender. Pyat yanked open the firedoor. The driver pulled
his acceleration wheel all the way round. The train hissed
and bucked and lurched forward. Another 85mm explosive shell hit the ground, this time on the other side of
the train. The tunnel was very close now. On either side
of it there emerged a motley collection of land ironclads,
half-tracks and armoured cars, mobile guns, all armed to
the teeth. The vehicles were painted with streaks of
bright, primitive colour and decorated with shells, bits of
silk and velvet. Strings of beads, strips of ermine and
mink, bones and severed human heads. Pyat's suspicions
were confirmed. This was the roving Makhnoite horde
which, months before, had swept down from beyond the
Volga, bringing terror and nihilism. The horde was virtually invulnerable. It would be pointless, now, to stop.

The train entered the darkness of the tunnel. Already
Pyat could see daylight at the other end. Then, from behind, came a massive explosion and the locomotive was
hurled forward at an incredible speed. They came out of
the tunnel with wheels squealing, with the whole loco
rocking, and in a few seconds had left the tank barbarians
far behind.

It was only later, as the driver began to slow the locomotive, that they realised they had also left the greater
part of the train behind at the tunnel. Evidently a shell
had broken the coupling between the first carriage and
the tender.

Pyat, the driver, the fireman and the two guards
laughed in relief. The train sped on towards Kiev. Now
there was a very good chance that they would not be off
schedule at all.

Pyat congratulated himself on the democratic impulse
which, originally, had led him to join the men on the
footplate. There were some advantages, it seemed, to
democracy.

THE STEAM YACHT

Una Persson shivered. She wrapped her heavy black mink more tightly around her slim body. The silk Erté tea gown beneath the coat was cold and unpleasant against her flesh. She was feeling old. It was as much as she could do to stay awake. She smiled to herself and made a few long strides through the clinging fog, over the deck to the rail of the yacht.

She could see nothing at all of Lake Erie and she could hear nothing but the dull flap of the waves against the *Teddy Bear*'s white sides.

They were fogbound. They had been lying at anchor for days. The wireless had broken and there had been no reply to signal rockets, sirens or shouts. Yet Una was sure that a dark launch had passed close to the yacht at least twice in the last twenty-four hours. She had heard the purr of its engine several times during the previous night.

The yellow-white fog shifted and swirled like something sentient and malevolent. It was as if she were trapped in some dreadful Munch lithograph. She hated it and wished bitterly that she had not accepted the owner's offer of this cruise. It had been so boring in New York, though. She really disliked Broadway much more than she disliked the West End.

She drew the red and black silk scarf off her tightly-waved, short-cropped hair and wiped the moisture from her hands and face. Why was everything so frightfully bloody?

She went back to the companionway behind the wheelhouse, paused, shivered and then daintily began to descend on high-heeled slippers, trying to make as much noise as possible on the iron steps.

Arriving in the corridor leading to the guest cabins, she noticed that some wisps of fog had at last managed to creep in. Now it was scarcely warmer here than it had been on deck. A 'brooding' silence. Were they to die here, then? It began to seem likely.

She tried to pull herself together, straightening her shoulders, putting a bit of bounce into her long step, bearing up manfully.

She went into the owner's large cabin, remarking, not for the first time, the incredible American vulgarity of it. It had been designed to look like a Tudor hall, with oak beams on the roof and pewter plates on the walls, claymores and tapestries. An electric Belling heater, built to resemble a log fire, only barely managed to take the chill off the cabin. The cabin had looked like this when the yacht had been purchased from its previous owner, but no attempt had been made to change it. It made her feel ill. It made her nervy.

The owner stood with his back to the cabin, staring out of the square, diamond-leaded porthole, into the fog. Once he leaned forward and, with his handkerchief, wiped condensation from the glass.

"Do you see any faces you recognise?" asked Una, attempting to sound friendly.

"Faces in the fog?" He glanced back at her and smiled. "All faces are foggy to me, my dear. It's my loss, I suppose."

Una gave vent to a dramatic sigh. "You and your old angst, darling! What would you do without it, I wonder?" She bent forward and pecked him on the cheek with her carmine lips. "Oh, it's so *cold*." She crossed to the genuine Tudor sideboard and picked at a dish of mixed nuts. "When *will* this boring fog lift?"

"Why don't you make the most of it? Relax. Pour yourself a drink."

"A tot of rum? I can't relax. The fog's so *sinister*." She ended this sentence on her famous falling note but then she let it rise again, almost without pause. "I like to *do* things, Lob." The pathos and the warmth in her voice was so strong that Prinz Lobkowitz was quite startled, as if he had found himself once again at the theatre where he had first seen her act. "I don't mean silly things," she continued. "Worthwhile things."

"Good causes?" He was ironic.

"If there's nothing else."

There was a sound on the water. The faint putter of a motor.

She crossed eagerly to the window and, standing beside him, peered out. She moved her head this way and that as if there was a particular angle at which she would be able to see through the fog. She saw a gleam of water, a shadow.

He put his arm around her shoulders. She was so womanly at that moment. But she shrugged him away. "Can you hear it? A motor-boat?"

"I've heard it frequently. It never comes very close."

"Have you tried shouting to it? Using your loud-hailer, or whatever it's called?"

"Yes. It never answers."

"Who can it be?"

"I don't know." He spoke almost in a whisper.

She looked searchingly up into his face. "You sound as if you have a good idea, though."

"No."

It was a lie.

"Oh, be as mysterious as you like. But you're rather overdoing the atmosphere, don't you think?"

"Not deliberately."

She went back to the sideboard and helped herself to a Balkan Sobranie cigarette from the silver box, lighting it with a flourish at the flamingo-shaped table lighter. Puffing pettishly, she began to pace.

He watched her. He loved to see her act. She was so talented. He was glad they were marooned, for it meant he could watch her almost all the time.

"You're wonderfully selfish," he said. "I love you. I admire you."

"I love you, too, Lob, darling, but couldn't we go and love each other somewhere warmer? Couldn't we go back to one of those cities? Chicago or somewhere? Couldn't we risk the fog?"

"There's a lot of hungry people waiting on the docks for unwary yachts. I'm afraid it wouldn't be wise."

The motor-boat started up again and went away.

"If he can move, why can't we?"

"He's smaller. He's got less to lose. I mean, there's less

risk for him." From the pocket of his white silk dressing gown he took a white box. He opened the box and took a pinch of white powder from it, sniffing it vigorously first into one nostril and then into the other. He put the box back and continued to stare out of the porthole.

She went to the big radiogram and picked up a record. It was her own, from last year's hit *Only You*. She put it on and listened to herself singing the blues number which came in the middle of the show, *Gonna Kill That Man*.

She smiled wistfully.

> *"Gonna kill that man, if I can.*
> *You have to be cruel to be kind.*
> *I can't get him out of my mind.*
> *He's the worst sort of guy you could possibly find*
> *To his vices, I guess, I am utterly blind.*
> *But if he should try to two-time me*
> *He'll discover that I won't sublime be.*
> *I'll take out my gun*
> *And I'll stop all his fun.*
> *I'm gonna kill that man—*
> *If he loves a she who ain't me."*

It was not her usual sort of material, yet it had been the number they'd all liked best, especially in London. She'd used a sort of Hoagy Carmichael technique for it. But she still didn't think much of it herself. She stopped the record and turned it over to *Dancing on the Clouds* which was much more *her*: bitter-sweet but essentially gay. Yet even this reminded her of the fog outside and she turned the bakelite volume knob off with a snap, though she could still hear her voice, very, very faintly from the turntable. It was like a ghost. It made her shiver.

Her lover came towards her.

Was it all over? she wondered. The whole thing? Was she finished?

He was handsome in his white sweater, his white gown and white flannels, but he was pale. Another ghost in this foggy purgatory.

He embraced her.

"Una."

THE FLYING BOAT

They were going back.

Captain Nye steered the DoX over the choppy waters of the harbour. Behind them, Rowe Island lay in ruins, her airship masts buckled, her hotels blasted, her streets wasted, her mines and mine-workers buried under the tumbled granite of the great volcanic hill. The placid Indian Ocean, a sheet of burnished blue steel reflecting a brazen sun, remained.

"Well, that's bloody that, then," said Frank Cornelius, stripping off his coolie blouse to reveal a loud, orange pullover. He wiped the best part of the make-up from his corrupt features. "And that's Jerry down the drain, if he isn't very careful indeed."

"I hope not." Catherine stood behind the two men who had already taken their seats. She dried her face with a Rodier towel. "It's such a beautiful day, isn't it?" She wore an open-necked white shirt and white jodhpurs. Her calf-length riding boots were light tan. Her longish hair fell in two tight waves to her shoulders. She wore little make-up. She looked wonderful.

"Best weather in the world on Rowe Island," said Captain Nye. "A great pity."

Miss Brunner was absent, as was the skeleton of the child. Nothing had gone right, really.

Captain Nye switched on all the engines and opened up the throttle, roaring out to sea. The floats began to rear beneath them, the wing-flaps whistled, and up they went into the clear, blue yonder.

Catherine wandered into the ballroom which had been refitted as a spacious lounge. Nobody felt like dancing at the moment. There were violently coloured Bakst murals on the walls. She looked enviously at the rich, fantastic scenes of fairyland forests and exotic Oriental princesses and Nubian slaves. It was a world she would feel happy in at the present moment. She was exhausted. She needed a rest, but she wanted a voluptuous rest. Hashish, honey and a handsome Hindu lover.

Professor Hira appeared, climbing the steps into the lounge and yawning. "I was asleep. I hadn't realised we were taking off so soon." His round, genial face held a faintly puzzled look. "How long have we been up?"

She nodded out of the nearest window. "Not long. You can still see the island. Look."

"I won't, thanks. I've seen quite enough of Rowe Island now. A terrible fiasco. I feel so guilty."

"Guilty? You shouldn't feel guilty." She closed her eyes, leaning back on the Beaumont tapestry cushions. She wished he hadn't come to interrupt what had promised to be quite a thrilling reverie. He was always too talkative when he got up. She pretended to doze.

"Yes," he said soberly. "It was all my fault. The ritual was infallible, in itself, and with the right *sort* of cosmic energy, we should have succeeded. But how was I to know that the majority of the coolies had been replaced by Malays? Those Muslims, they're the next best thing to an atheist. And then there was all the trouble with the time-concept, nobody quite agreeing on that. Again, the Malays . . ."

"Well, then—" She took a deep, lazy breath and drew her legs up on the couch. "It was their fault. It doesn't matter now. Though it's a pity about the Governor's residence. Wasn't that a charming building?"

"Did you like it? I've had to look at a spot too much of that type of thing in Calcutta, I'm afraid."

Catherine caught only the last words. "Afraid? It's a relief to know someone else is."

"Afraid? What of? I've never seen you looking better."

"The future, I suppose. And yet I hate the past. Don't you?"

"I've never quite understood the difference. I don't see it like that."

"A woman—well—I'm forced to. In some ways, at least. I know it would be better for me if I didn't."

"If time could stand still," said Hira reflectively. "I suppose we should all be as good as dead. The whole business of entropy so accurately reflects the human condition. To remain alive one must burn fuel, use up heat, squander resources, and yet that very action contributes to the end of the universe—the heat death of everything! But to become still, to use the minimum of energy—that's pointless. It is to die, effectively. What a dreadful dilemma."

Captain Nye stepped from the pilot's cabin into the lounge. "Your brother's steering. He picks things up fast, doesn't he?"

"Anything he can get." Catherine regretted her waspish tone and added: "He's very intelligent, Frank." She looked into Nye's blue-grey eyes and smiled.

"Well," he said. "I'm going to get some sleep."

"Yes," she said. "I think it's time I hit the hay. It's been a long—long . . ." She yawned.

She nodded to Hira and followed Captain Nye to the stairs, down past the cocktail bar, the cabin area and into the cabin. As he kissed her she held him tightly, saying: "I'd better warn you. I'm very tired."

"Don't worry." He unbuttoned his jacket. "So am I."

She saw him shiver slightly. "Are you cold?"

"A tiny touch of malaria, I shouldn't wonder," he said. "Nothing to worry about."

"I'll cuddle up to you and keep you warm," she said.

Professor Hira, feeling both lonely and jealous, joined Frank in the control cabin. Frank was wearing his fur-trimmed tinted flying goggles and looked a bit like a depraved lemur. He patted Hira's knee as the Indian physicist sat down. " 'Ello, 'ello, old son! How goes it?"

"Not so dusty," said Hira. "Are you sure that chap Nye's all right?"

"What? Nye? One of the best. Why?"

"Well—going with your sister . . ."

"He's been sweet on her for years. Cathy knows what she's doing."

"She's such a lovely girl. A generous girl."

"Yes," said Frank vaguely. "She is." He laughed. "I quite fancy her myself. Still, I'm not the only one, eh?"

He nudged Hira in the ribs. Hira blushed. The plane veered and started to dive, banking to starboard with the engines screaming. Frank inexpertly righted her, but didn't seem worried by the near-miss; he continued to chat cheerfully, telling Hira a succession of bad dirty jokes (mostly about incest, bestiality and Jews) until Hira thought he would cry.

He changed the subject as soon as he could. "I wonder what the political climate's like, back there." He motioned towards the west.

"Bloody hell! Not worth thinking about. That's as good as finished, anyway, nowadays, isn't it?"

"Does it 'finish'?"

"Well, you know what I mean. We've got our plane, we've got our health, we've got the Cornelius millions—or will have soon. We've got each other. Why should we worry?" Frank moved the joy stick from his left to his right hand and stretched his hand out towards Hira.

"I was thinking of the moral question," said Professor Hira.

"Oh, fuck that!"

Frank's hand dived into Hira's lap and squeezed.

The Indian physicist shrieked and was his.

The plane flew perilously close to the water and then began to climb as Frank took it up towards a cloud.

THE RAFT

Sun-baked, salt-caked, it lay in the middle of the Arabian Sea on a waterlogged raft made of oil-drums, ropes and rush matting. The raft had no mast, held nothing but the shapeless heap of flesh and rags which might have been dead save for the spasm which occasionally ran through it when a small wave lifted the raft or swept over it, so that it sank a little further into the warm sea. One of the drums had been holed by what looked like a series of machine-gun bullets; it was this which had helped to deprive the raft of its buoyancy.

The flesh was blistered as if it had been exposed to fire; it was blackened in places. In other places bones stuck through at odd angles. There was a flake or two of dried blood. From time to time there were sounds: a grunt, a moan, a few babbled words.

The raft was drifting out to sea. The nearest land was now Bombay, 400 miles away, where a great sitar master, dying of cholera, was the only man with any notion of the raft's whereabouts. There was not much chance of rescue, even if rescue had been desired.

Jerry felt nothing. He was one with the flotsam of the great sea; almost one with the sea itself. He was content, listening absently to the odd voice; remembering the odd image. If this were dying, it was a relaxing experience, to say the least.

"Remember the old days?" said Miss Brunner's voice. "Or were they the new days? I forget. The usual tense trouble." She laughed gently. "Echoes."

"Nothing but," murmured Jerry.

"But echoes from where?"

"Everywhere?"

"They would be, I suppose. Lapland won't be the same. Caves. Large bodies of water. The sky. The pleasures are constant, even if the problems change."

"Yes."

"Are the simple pleasures the *only* realities?"

Jerry couldn't reply.

"Oh, what a lovely, drifting sea this is." The voice faded away. "Who are we, I wonder?"

"Resistance," said a child, "is useless."

"Absolutely," Jerry agreed.

"The schizophrenic condition finds its most glorious expression in Hinduism," remarked Professor Hira. "Whereas Christianity is an expression of the much less interesting paranoid frame of reference. Paranoia is rarely heroic, in the mythical sense, at least."

But Jerry found this argument barren. He didn't encourage a discussion. Instead, he remembered a kiss.

"Feeling seedy? I know I am." Karl Glogauer came and went. Jerry had confused him with Flash Gordon.

"Time," said the sad voice of Captain Cornelius Brunner, "ruins everything." They would not be meeting again for another thirty-five years. "So long, Jerry."

"I love you," said Jerry.

With an effort he raised himself on his wounded hands. "I love all of you."

He looked at the sea. The sun was setting and the water was the burning colour of blood.

"Oh!"

A few tears dripped from his awful eyes. Then the head sank back. The night came and the raft dropped lower in the water until an observer might have thought that the body floated unsupported on the surface. The sun rose, pink and mighty on the western horizon, and Jerry raised his head for one swift glimpse. The sea ran through his burnt hair and made it float like weed; it washed his torn flesh and moved the rags of his black car coat; it ran into his reddened mouth and the sockets of his eyes, and Jerry, at peace, hardly noticed.

A little later, lizard-like, he crawled to the edge of the raft and slid quietly into the water, disappearing at once.

It was going to be a long century.

PROLOGUE (concluded)

. . . and in spite of their maudlin sympathy, self-interest finally dominated everything else and so I was betrayed again, left alone. I think it must have been the final straw. Certainly, I ceased to trust anyone else for several years, then when Monica came along I forgot all that. I trusted her absolutely. And, of course, she let me down. Perhaps she didn't mean to. Perhaps it was too much of a strain. She should have kept the baby. I don't know how long I stayed in the kitchen with her after I'd done it. You could say that the balance of my mind was disturbed. I mean, what's a country for? What do you pay taxes for? What do you give your patriotism to? You expect something from your own country, your parents, your relatives. And then they don't deliver. Nobody cares. Every promise society makes to you, it doesn't keep. They kill babies before they're born, after they're born, or they do it the slow way, prolonging the moment of death for scores of years. I am not pleading guilty. By pleading insane, I am pleading innocent. Surely, I'm the victim. What does it mean? But I want to die. It's the only solution. And yet I love life. I know that seems strange. I love the lakes and the forests and all that. But it seems unnatural now. We've got to go, haven't we? I never asked to be born. I tried to enjoy it, I tried to be positive and optimistic. I'm well-educated, you know. It was mercy-killing. And killing is, if you look at it one way. I am trying to control myself. I'm sorry I'm sorry.

MAURICE LESCOQ, Leavetaking

SHOT FOUR

Police Dig Up More Human Remains

Police digging at Leatherhead (Surrey) where a woman's hand was found on Thursday found more remains yesterday in a navy blue zip bag at a shallow depth.

Wrapped separately in polythene were two portions of thigh, a left leg and a foot with a blue slipper on it. Police said they thought other parts of the body were 'somewhere else'.

MORNING STAR, September 4 1971

OBSERVATIONS

"There's a future in chemicals, if you ask me," said Lieutenant Cornelius. He lifted binoculars to his bleak eyes and stared without interest at the Indian aircraft carrier his CA class destroyer *Cassandra* had been tracking for two days.

Overhead flew five or six small helicopters of different nationalities, including a British *Wasp;* below floated three or four of the latest nuclear submarines, among them the *Remorseless,* the *Concorde* and the *Vorster.* The Mediterranean fairly swarmed with busy bits of metal. Not too far off, a frigate of the Imperial South Russian Navy was keeping its eye on Lt. Cornelius's ship and a Chinese 'flying ironclad'—an armoured airship of obscure origin—observed the Russian.

"Chemicals and plastics," Cornelius's No. 2, Collier, agreed, leaning over the rail of the bridge and looking down at the rather dirty decks where bored seamen lounged in each other's arms. Under the barrel of the forward 4.5 gun, the deck cargo creaked in its ropes. It was a single box, marked AMMUNITION/DANGER. "That's what I'd put my money in. If I had any."

"Buy the plants," said Frank Cornelius. "Take over. Go for the durables. Oil. Water. Steel. Air. Chemicals. Plastics. Electronics. That's survival. My brother's got the right idea—or had—or will have . . ." He frowned and changed the subject, handing the glasses to Collier. "See if you can spot any change."

Collier was happy to get a turn with the binoculars. He straightened his shoulders and peered self-importantly

through the eyepieces. "Are they having a party or something on deck?"

"They've been up to that since this morning. It's disgusting. I think it's meant to distract us from whatever they
don't want us to know about."

"Big girls, ain't they?" said Shaky Mo.

"Hermaphrodites."

"I thought they were on our side."

Frank went down into the Operations Room and consulted his grubby charts. He could have done with something a bit more up to date. He'd inherited the charts from
his father and the political boundaries shown were nothing
less than ludicrous. He moved a couple of counters to
cope with the recently arrived South Russians. There was
hardly space on the chart for another marker. Fragment
split into fragment. Was it society or himself that was
breaking up?

He was getting tired of the whole thing. A bloody great
Prussian dreadnought had been after them for a week,
taking a particular interest in their deck cargo. That meant
a leak. Frank wondered if it wouldn't be wiser to turn
round and go back to their Marseilles base or, failing that,
make straight for Aden. With radio silence, there was no
chance of getting his orders changed until he reached a
port. He wished he hadn't taken on the responsibility of
the cargo, now. If he could have been somewhere suitable
when word came, he might have been able to turn a profit,
given a slight shift in the balance of power at home. That
was why he'd volunteered. Now he realised what a stupid
idea it had been. He was never any good at the big deals.
At little deals, he was great. He should have stuck at
what he knew he could do well. Here he was, in the middle
of the bleeding Med, while his nearest customers were
at the other end of the North Sea. Fuck a duck, it was just
his luck. He rubbed his greasy chin, flipping through his
Boatswain's Manual for the right order to give the coxswain and the engineers. He'd make for Hamburg and
hope for the best.

Idly turning the binoculars onto his own ship and its
crew, Mo Collier focussed on the big box and noticed for
the first time that it seemed to be moving to a different
rhythm from that of the waves. It was pulsing, like a rapid

heart beat, as if, Mo Collier grinned at the thought, two people were fucking in there. Well, that was impossible. On the other hand if the contents of the box were about to go critical, he'd better warn his captain. He let the glasses fall on their string and knock against his pelvis. He took the lift down to the Operations Room. "Sir? Sir?"

Frank looked up from his manual. "What?"

"The deck cargo. It's sort of bouncing. It might be going to blow up."

"Oh, shit," Frank put the book down and followed Mo up to the deck. He took the glasses and looked. "Oh, shit. I should have shifted it right at the beginning. He who hesitates is lost, Collier."

"Fire drill, sir?"

"Bloody hell. What's the point?" They went slowly back to the Operations Room. "Let's have a look at a map," said Frank when they got there. "No. We'll make for Sardinia and dump it. Break radio silence. Tell them our deck cargo hasn't been picked up on schedule and we're abandoning it on the nearest dry land."

"Can't we just dump it in the sea, sir?"

"Are you out of your mind? We don't want more trouble than we've got already. Oh, shit." Frank slumped down in a chair. "Oh, fuck it to buggery." He was the picture of whining impotence. Feeling this made his whine louder. At a certain pitch, his whine was echoed by a sound from the deck; the sound was almost in perfect tune, but constant, where Frank's was punctuated by his need to draw breath.

Soon the two brothers were howling in unison as night fell and the destroyer steamed for Sardinia.

GUARANTEES

Major Nye had his trousers off. He sat on a canvas stool with an old towel round him. Mrs. Nye spoke through clenched teeth as she stitched at the patched trouser leg. "It's not as if we could afford it," she said. "All I seem to do is *mend*. And you're so clumsy. You must have known about the barbed wire on the beach."

"Supervised its installation, I'm afraid," admitted Major Nye. "All my fault. Sorry, lovey."

It was late in the afternoon and they were outside the beach-hut where they had been billeted. After being turned down by his old regiment (now an armoured vehicle corps), Major Nye had volunteered to help with the Brighton coastal defences. Then Ironmaster House, some twelve miles inland, had been requisitioned as the head-quarters of the local territorials, so he and Mrs. Nye had had to move into the beach hut. Major Nye was not particularly upset by the takeover. The beach hut was not nearly so much of a burden and it was less effort tending the barbed wire than it had been looking after the market garden. Major Nye felt a bit ashamed. The war was proving something of a holiday for him. For all she would never admit it, even Mrs. Nye semed relieved. Her wind-reddened face had taken on something of a bloom, though this might have been the result of the cold. It was winter and the beach hut was heated only by a malfunctioning oil-stove. Their daughters had not joined them; both girls had volunteered for work in London. Isobel, the ex-dancer, was looking after her brother, who was still at school. Sometimes, at weekends, one or both of the girls would bring the little boy down to see his parents.

"Nearly Christmas," Mrs. Nye finished the darn with a sigh. "Is it worth doing anything at all about it this year?"

"Maybe the girls will have an idea." Major Nye went into the beach hut and drew on his trousers. He folded the tattered towel and hung it neatly over the back of the deckchair. The trousers, like his jacket, were khaki, or had been before the elements and all the patching had turned them into a garment of many indistinguishable colours. He lit the remaining third of his thin cigarette. "Tum-te-tum. God rest ye merry gentlemen, let nothing ye dismay, et cetera, et cetera, pom-pom." He put the tin kettle on top of the oil-stove, realised it was dry, and came outside to fill it at the tap which served his and two other huts. All these huts were now occupied by coastal defence volunteers. Many volunteers were older than Major Nye. With a loud, rasping sound, the kettle filled. The tap squeaked as he turned it off. Mrs. Nye shivered in his greatcoat and, stamping with cold, got up, collapsing both their canvas stools and hurrying inside.

"A strong cuppa's what you need after that, m'dear," he said.

"Don't throw away the old leaves this time," she said. "They'll last for another brew."

He nodded.

They watched the kettle boil and when it was ready he flipped the lid off the mock-Georgian, mock-silver teapot and filled it half-full. "Just give that a minute or two to stew," he said. He made a corned beef sandwich for her, using thin sliced bread and even thinner slices of meat. He put the sandwich on one of their plates, taken from the tiny rack above the tiny card table on which their provisions were laid. He handed her the plate.

"Thank you very much," said his wife. She nibbled at the sandwich. It was her tea. They were going to have a full tin of pilchards for supper.

"Well, I'd better go and check the searchlights before nightfall," he said.

"Very well." She looked up. "See if you can get a paper."

"Rightho!"

Whistling the half-remembered tune of *The Bore o' Bethnal Green,* he ambled down the stony beach, following the course of his barbed wire, stopping at intervals to inspect the searchlights set on small pedestals every thirty feet. The lights had originally been used to illuminate the Pavilion during the summer months.

The sky was grey and promised rain. The sea was also grey and even the beach had a greyish tinge to it. That always seemed to happen in wartime, thought Major Nye. Above, on the promenade, he noticed that the odd fish-and-chip shop and coffee-stall hadn't yet closed. The shops were illuminated by oil-lamps and candles. All electricity was being saved for the defense effort. The places looked cosy. After making sure that all his lights were in good order, he left the beach and tramped up a ramp to the pavement, crossing the street to the shops. One of the ice-cream parlours was still open. These days, in spite of the plastic sundaes and knickerbocker glories in the window, it sold only tea and soup. The parlour also sold *The Weekly Defender*, the only newspaper generally available. A new issue was in. Large piles were stacked outside the shop. The paper's circulation was not very good. Those piles would remain virtually untouched and would be taken away when the new issue arrived. Major Nye was one of the few regular customers for *The Defender*. He picked up a copy from a pile and read the headline as he ambled into the shop, his sixty-pence piece in his hand. "Evening, squire," said the shopkeeper.

"Good evening." Major Nye couldn't remember the man's name and he was embarrassed. "The paper."

"Sixty, please. Doesn't look too good, does it?"

The headlines read: *NEW GAINS FOR BRITAIN! SPIRITS RISE AS MINISTER ANNOUNCES PLANS. 'MORALE NEVER HIGHER' SAYS KING.*

Major Nye smiled shyly. "I must admit . . ."

"Still, it can't last forever."

To Major Nye it seemed it had already lasted forever, but he was, as usual, completely reconciled. You couldn't change human nature. You couldn't change the world. He smiled again. "I suppose not."

"Night, night, squire."

"Goodnight to you."

It was almost dark now. He decided to walk back along the promenade, rather than along the beach. The smell of fish-and-chips made his mouth water, but he resisted temptation, knowing what Mrs. Nye would say if he brought back even a few chips. It was an unnecessary expense on food which was not nourishing; also it was 'not quite the thing' to buy hot food from a shop. They had to keep their standards up. Major Nye had always been fond of fish-and-chips. When he had worked in London, he had had them once a week. Of course, the fish was terrible now, and the chips weren't proper potato at all. And that was a consolation of sorts.

He began to go down the ramp which led to their stretch of gloomy beach. He paused and looked out at the black, gleaming water. The sea was so large. Sometimes it seemed foolish, trying to defend the coast against it. He wondered what would happen if the big anti-aircraft gun on the end of the pier ever had to fire. Probably shake the whole bally thing to bits. He smiled.

He thought he saw something bobbing on the water, quite close to the shore, about twenty yards from the pier's girders. He peered hard, wondering if it were a stray mine, but the object had passed out of sight. He shrugged and stepped onto the beach. The shingle rattled and grated as he crossed it. Further out to sea a steamer's siren moaned and the moan was echoed by the rooftops of the town so that it seemed for a little while that the whole of Brighton was expressing its misery.

ESTIMATES

Una Persson made the plane just as it was about to leave Dubrovnik. She clambered up over the coffin-shaped flats and through the passenger doors. Inside, the plane was dark and crowded; people sat on the floor or, where there wasn't room to sit, clung to pieces of frayed rope fixed to the sides and roof. Refugees, like herself; though these were thin-faced civilians. She pushed through them, noticing the number of black-robed priests aboard, and found the companionways to the upper decks. There were people sitting on these, too, and she had to go up both flights of stairs on the tips of her battered boots. At last she reached the pilot's cabin. By that time they were already airborne, though two of the big wing-mounted engines were coughing on the starboard side. She wondered from what museum the plane had been resurrected. It was German, judging by its instrument panels. There was a lot of German junk around, these days. It wasn't surprising. Over the radio and heavily distorted came sounds she recognised as the Rolling Stones singing *Mother's Little Helper*.

The flying boat circled Dubrovnik once, dipping in and out of the thick, oily smoke from the burning city. "We shan't be seeing that again," said the Polish pilot. Colonel Pyat, who was seated in the co-pilot's chair, sighed. "It'll be good to get home again. We are all ideas in the mind of Mars."

Una gave him a puzzled look. "So you say, general."

"C—" Colonel Pyat mopped his heated forehead. "My dear Una, I thought you had taken the train."

"Changed my mind. Back to Blighty, after all."

"Just as well. Maybe our luck will change with you aboard." He raised an imaginary glass. "I salute Our Lady of Liberty." He was eager to please, not sardonic.

"You're tired," she said.

"Sing a song, Una dear. An old sweet song." He was drunk, but his white uniform was neat as ever. "If those lips could only speak, if those eyes could only see, if those . . ."

"The European campaigns were wholly disastrous," said the Pole, who was also a bit drunk. She could hardly hear him over the erratic roaring of the aircraft's engines.

"Why all the refugees?" she said. "Where are the troops?"

"That's what the refugees wanted to know." The Pole laughed. They weren't making much altitude as they flew out to sea. "We *are* the troops."

"*C'est la vie,*" said Colonel Pyat. "My dear ones will have missed me." He drew a flask from his hip pocket and tipped it up. It was empty. "Thank God," he said. "You're right, Una. I am tired. I thought England would be the answer. A triumph of imagination over inspiration. Ha, ha!"

"He lost the box," explained the Pole.

"In Ladbroke Grove," said Pyat. "It's been around a bit since then."

Una sighed. "So I gather. Well, it was just another straw, I suppose. Something to keep the fire going."

"Feeling the draught?" said the Pole.

"I've been feeling it all century," said Una.

From beyond the door came the sound of people at prayer, led by the droning voices of the priests. Even the plane seemed to be praying. Una went to find a parachute before they reached Windermere.

APPLICATIONS

There seemed to be gratitude in Sebastian Auchinek's large brown eyes. He looked up as the security policeman entered his cell.

"Of course I understand that you have to do this job," said Auchinek. "And rest assured, Constable Wallace, I shan't make it difficult for you. Please sit down or—" he paused "—whatever you wish."

Constable Wallace was a brute.

"I don't like spies, Mr. Auchinek." His skin was coarse, his eyes were stupid and there was a sense of pent-up violence about him. "And should we prove that you're one . . ."

"I'm a loyal citizen, I assure you. I love England as much as anyone, for all that I was not born here. Your countryside, your democracy, your justice . . ."

"You're a Jew."

"Yes."

"There's been a lot of Jewish spies."

"I know."

"So . . ."

"I'm not one. I'm a businessman."

"A poof?"

"No . . ."

"You go abroad a great deal. Macedonia?"

"Macedonia, yes. And to—well, to Belgium, Holland, Assyria . . ."

"Where?"

"Abyssinia, isn't it?"

"You've got *something* to hide," said the red face, sweating.

"A poor memory." Auchinek whimpered in anticipation.

"And I'm going to get it out of you."

"Of course. Of course."

"By force, if necessary."

"I'm not a traitor."

"I hope not."

Constable Wallace had completed the necessary rough and ready warming up ritual and he grabbed Auchinek by his grey prison jacket and pulled him to his feet. He balled his red fist and punched Auchinek in the stomach. Auchinek vomited at once, all over Constable Wallace's uniform.

"Oh, you filthy little animal." Wallace left the cell.

Auchinek had had enough. He sat back on his bed, careless of the vomit on his lips, chin and clothing. He gasped and cried and wished he hadn't had his breakfast. He should have known better. Or had he planned it? He had never been clear about his identity, his own motives, at the best of times, and now he was completely at sea. For all he knew, he might be a traitor. He should have retained his military role. It was easier.

The sound of rifle fire in the passage outside. Shouts. Running, booted feet. A clang. More shots. The bolt was withdrawn outside. Auchinek cringed as the door opened.

Catherine Cornelius, looking like a young Una Persson, stood in the doorway, an M16 over the shoulder of her brown trenchcoat, a green tam-o'-shanter on her golden curls.

"Are you the chap we're to rescue?" said Catherine. "Mr. A?"

"Auchinek."

"Shall we release the lot?" She indicated the other cells in the corridor.

"I don't know," he said, watching out for Wallace, who was sure to appear in a minute.

"This isn't my normal job, you see," explained Catherine pleasantly as she coaxed him from the cell and into the corridor of twisted iron and broken corpses. He saw Wallace. His red throat was cut by rifle bullets. He was dead. Auchinek gazed at him in wonder.

She led him past the corpse towards the outer door,

which was off its hinges. "I normally get the nursing jobs, but we're short-staffed, at present."

"Who are you?"

"Catherine Cornelius."

"No—your—outfit?"

"Biba's."

"Who do you work for?"

"I work for England, Mr. Auchinek, and freedom." Self-consciously, she put the M16 on automatic and rested it on her hip as they crossed the quadrangle of Brixton Prison and reached the main gate. "There's a car waiting. Perhaps you could direct me? It's been a long time since I've been in South London."

They stepped through the blasted gate and stood in a narrow street. A Delage Diane was waiting for them, its engine running.

"It's a bit of a waste of power," she said apologetically, opening a passenger door for him, "but I find the bugger rather hard to start."

"Miss Cornelius . . ."

"Mr. Auchinek?"

"I don't understand."

"I'm afraid I can't help you there. The ins and outs of the revolution—if it *is* a revolution—are a bit beyond me. I just work for the cause."

"But I'm not a revolutionary. I'm a businessman. I think you know more . . ."

"Honestly, no . . ."

"Perhaps I should go back? A mistake." He hesitated beside the car.

"Don't you remember Macedonia?"

"Were you there?"

"You were an idealist. A guerilla."

"I've always been in show business. All my life. Promotions. Management."

"Well, there you are, then." She opened the door of the car for him. "Nobody's going to beat you up any more."

"I'm tired."

"I know how you feel." She got into the driving seat and fiddled with the gears. The car seemed unfamiliar to her. "We've still got a long journey ahead of us." They began to move slowly forward. "Modification of species and so on. Perhaps it isn't really a revolution at all."

Auchinek saw misery in Catherine's mouth. He began to cry. She reached the main road, crashing the gears as she turned the Delage towards the Thames.

SECURITIES

"Good ole England!" said Mrs. Cornelius, raising her pint of ale and saluting a picture of a bulldog painted on the glass behind the bar.

"Oh, yore 'opeless, Mrs. C.!" Old Sammy in the corner guffawed, opening wide the black, wet circle of his toothless mouth and shaking all over. He lifted his own pint and poured its contents into his wasted, cancerous body.

" 'Ere, come on, I mean it," she said. "There'll orlways be an England. We've 'ad our ups an' darns, but we'll pull through."

"Well, *you* might," said Old Sammy bitterly, losing his good humour as the beer in his glass disappeared.

" 'Ave anovver," she said, by way of rewarding him for the compliment.

He brought his glass over to the bar where she sat on a high, saddle-shaped stool, her massive behind spilling over, so that the dark wood was all but hidden. " 'Aven't seen too much of you, lately," he said.

"Nar," she said. "Bin away. Visitin' an 'at, in I?"

"Go somewhere nice?"

"Abroad. Went ter see me son."

"Wot, Frank?"

"Nar! Jerry. 'E's ill."

"Anything bad?"

She snorted. 'Iber-bleedin'-natin' 'e corls it! Mastur-fuckin'-batin', *I* corl it!" She turned as a third customer entered *The Portobello Star*. "Oh, it's you. Yore late, incha?"

"Sorry, my dear. Delays at immigration." Colonel Pyat wore a cream-coloured suit, lavender gloves and white spats over tan shoes. He had a pale blue shirt and a regi-

mental tie. His light grey homburg was in the same hand
that carried his stick. His manner was hesitant.

"Sammy, this is ther Kernewl—my hubby."

"How do you do?" said Pyat.

"How do? Jerry's dad, eh?"

Mrs. Cornelius shook with laughter again. "Well, 'e
might 'ave bin once! Gar-har-har!"

Colonel Pyat smiled weakly and cleared his throat.
"What will you have, sir?"

"Same agin."

Pyat signed to the wizened old bat behind the bar.
"Same again in these glasses, please. And I'll have a
double vodka. Nice morning."

"Nice for some," said the old bat.

Mrs. Cornelius stopped laughing and patted the colonel
affectionately on the shoulder. "Cheer up, lovie. Yer *do*
look as if yer've bin in ther wars!" She opened her
shapeless handbag. "I'll git these. Pore ole sod." She cast
her eye about the gloomy bar. "Where's yer bags?"

"I left them at the hotel."

"Hotel!"

"The Venue Hotel, in Westbourne Grove. A nice little
place. Very comfortable."

"Oh, well, orl right!"

"I didn't want to put you out."

"Well, you *ain't!*" She paid for the drinks and handed
him his vodka. "But I woulda thort . . . First day 'ome . . .
Well . . ."

"I didn't mean to upset you, my dear." He rallied himself. "I thought I'd take you out somewhere tonight. Where
do you suggest? And then, later, perhaps, we could go on
a family holiday. The coast or somewhere."

She was mollified. "Crystal Palace," she said. "I ain't
bin there fer a donkey's."

"Excellent." He swallowed his drink and ordered
another. "Welcome austerity. Farewell authority!" He
saluted himself in the mirror.

She looked critically at his clothes. " 'Ad a run o'luck,
'ave yer?"

"Well, yes and no."

" 'E orlways wos a very smart dresser," said Mrs. C. to
Sammy. "No matter 'ow much 'e 'ad in 'is pocket, 'e'd
orlways be dressed just so."

Sammy sniffed.

Colonel Pyat blushed.

Mrs. Cornelius yawned. "It's better ter go away in the autumn. If the wevver 'olds."

"Yes," said Colonel Pyat.

"I've never 'ad an 'oliday in me life.", said Sammy proudly. "Never even let 'em evacuate me!"

"That's 'cause yer never worked in yer life!" Mrs. Cornelius nudged him. "Eh?"

Sammy bridled. But she put her fat hand round the back of his neck and kissed him on his wrinkled forehead. "Come on, don't take offence. Yer know I never mean it."

Sammy pulled away and took his glass back to his table in the corner.

Colonel Pyat climbed on to the next stool but one. His eyes kept closing and he jerked his head up from time to time as if afraid to go to sleep. He didn't seem to have the energy, these days.

"I 'ope yer brought somefink ter eat over wiv yer?" said Mrs. C. "Everyfink's running' art 'ere. Food. Fuel. Fun." She bellowed. "Everyfink that begins wiv 'F', eh?"

"Ha, ha, ha," he said distantly.

"One more for the road an' then we'll be off," said his wife. "Yer never reely liked pubs, did yer?"

"Excellent."

"Cheer up. It can't be as bad as orl that!"

"Europe's in a mess," he said. "Everywhere is."

"Well, we're not exactly at the 'eight of our prosperity," she told him. 'Still, fings blow over."

"But the squalor!"

"Ferget it!" She guzzled her light.

"I wish I could, my dear."

"I'll 'elp yer." She leant across the empty stool between them and tickled his genitals. "Tonight."

Colonel Pyat made a peculiar giggling noise. She took him by the arm and led him through the door and into the stinking streets. "Yer'll like the Crystal Palace. It's *orl* crystal. Well, glass, reely. All different sides. Made o' glass. An' there's monsters. It's a wonder o' the world, the Crystal Palace. Like me, eh?"

Mrs. Cornelius roared.

REMINISCENCE (G)

Children are stoning a tortoise. Its shell is already cracking open. It moves feebly, leaving a trail of blood and entrails across a white rock.

Late News

A 17-month-old baby girl was shot dead in Belfast to-night, Army sources said, by an IRA gunman's bullet meant for an Army patrol. A seven-year-old girl who was with her escaped injury although another bullet tore through her skirt.

MORNING STAR, September 24 1971

A drug given to women during pregnancy may cause a rare type of cancer in their daughters many years later, the British Medical Journal warned yesterday. The cancer has been found among girls aged 15 to 22 in New England and has been linked to the drug stilboestrol, which was given to their mothers for threatened miscarriages . . . Treatment has proved successful so far in the majority of cases, but one girl has died.

GUARDIAN, September 10 1971

A boy aged three was knocked down and killed by an army vehicle near the Bogside district last night. As the news spread, crowds began to stone army units in the area. Several shots were fired at the troops and petrol bombs were reported to be thrown. The army did not return the fire.

GUARDIAN, September 10 1971

The Alternative Apocalypse 7

Nothing survives, said Una Persson, who was older, more battered and wiser than Jerry had ever seen her, nothing endures.

While there's lives there's hopes. Jerry finished stripping the Banning cannon and immediately began re-assembling it. The ruby had not, after all, been faulty. It was just wearing out. The gun wouldn't last much longer. Still, it wasn't needed for much longer. He was more worried about his power armour. Some of the circuits, particularly those on his chest, were looking a bit frayed. They were holed up in the basement of a deserted old people's home in Ladbroke Grove. They listened to the scuffling of the rats with intense interest, expecting an attack.

It's almost over now, isn't it? she said without regret. Civilisation's had it. The human race has had it. And we've bloody had it. Are these all you've got? She held up a cerise Sobranie cocktail cigarette with a gold tip.

He opened a drawer in the plain deal table on which his cannon was spread. Looks like it. He rummaged through a jumble of string, coins and postcards. Yes.

Oh, well.

You might as well enjoy what's left, he said. Take it easy.

It isn't easy to take. What with everything speeding up so fast. It's all burning too quickly. Like a rocket that's out of control, with the fuel regulator jammed.

Could be. He slotted one piece of scratched black metal into another. He fitted the cumbersome ammunition feed and worked a couple of slides. He didn't

642

bother to put the safety catch on as he turned the cannon on its swivel mount so that it pointed towards the barred window. I don't know. He sighted along the gun; he stroked back his long, straight hair. Times come and go. Things re-cycle. The Jesuits . . .

Did you hear something?

Yes.

She went to the corner where her Bren lay on their mattress. She picked the Bren up and drew the strap over her leather-clad shoulder. She flipped a switch at her belt. It even took her power armour a few seconds to warm up now. After the village . . . she began.

You survive, Una. It wasn't something he wanted to hear about again. It disturbed him.

She looked at him suspiciously, searching his face for a sardonic meaning. There was none.

Alive or dead, he said and fired an explosive shell through the window and into the shadowy area. Magnesium blazed for a moment. Cold air came in. A shape darted away. Jerry flipped his own switch.

Beesley, Brunner, Frank and the rest, Una said, peering cautiously upwards. All the other survivors. I think some are trying to get into the house.

It had to come. In the long term there's never much safety in numbers.

I'd always believed you worked alone. A bit of a bourgeois individualist on the quiet.

Assassination's one thing, Jerry said primly. Murder's quite another. Murder involves more people and a different moral approach and that, of course, ultimately involves more murders. A reflex. People get carried away. But assassination is just the initial preparation. The ground work. Like it or not, of course, everything boils down to murder in the end. A grenade burst in the basement and the rest of the glass flew into the room, rattling against their power armour.

There's self-defense.

I've never been able to work that one out.

Jerry pulled the table nearer to the window, then angled the Banning upwards through the bars, firing a steady, tight sweep of shells. Two of the attackers flared up and fell. Karen and Mo, said Jerry. Not for the first time. They heard footsteps over their heads and then a few creaks on the cellar stairs outside their inside door. Una opened the door and, with her Bren, took two more lives. Mitzi Beesley and Frank Cornelius. Frank, as usual, made a lot of noise, but Mitzi died quietly, sitting upright with her back against the wall, her hands in her blood-stained lap, while Frank rolled and writhed and gasped and cursed.

Two more grenades came into the room and exploded, temporarily blinding them, but hardly denting their power armour.

This is almost the end, said Jerry. I think it's down to Miss Brunner and Bishop Beesley. It had better be. Energy's getting low.

Miss Brunner rushed down the stairs, her face twisted with rage, her red eyes blazing, her sharp fangs bared. She was awkward in her tight St. Laurent skirt. She tried to get her Sten to fire. Una killed her, shooting her in the forehead with a single bullet. Miss Brunner staggered back without grace.

Bishop Beesley appeared in the area outside the window. He was holding a white flag in one hand, a Twix bar in the other. Even from here Jerry could see that the chocolate was mouldy.

I give up, said the Bishop. I now admit I was ill-advised to quarrel with you, Cornelius. He crammed the Twix bar into his mouth and then reached towards his breast pocket. May I? He took out a delicate box of Chinese jade and opened it. From the box he removed a couple of pinches of sugar which he snorted into his nostrils. That's better.

Okay. Jerry nodded tiredly and pulled the Banning's trigger, plugging Beesley in the mouth. The face flared in a halo of flame and then disappeared. Jerry abandoned the gun and went to Una, who was pale and exhausted. He kissed her gently on the cheek. It's all over, at last.

They switched off their armour and lay down on the damp mattress, fucking as if their lives depended on it.

The Alternative Apocalypse 8

The ruins were pretty now that the fronds and lichen covered them. Birds sang. Jerry and Catherine Cornelius walked hand in hand to their favorite spot and sat down on a slab, looking out over the fused obsidian that had been the Thames. It was spring. The world was at peace.

Moments like these, said Catherine tenderly, make you feel glad to be alive.

Well, he smiled, you are, aren't you?

She stroked his knee as she lay stretched beside him, supported by one of his strong arms. It's so relaxing to be with you.

Well, familiarity, I suppose, is a lot to do with it. He, in turn, stroked her golden hair. I love you, Cathy.

You're good, Jerry, I love you, too.

They watched a spider cross the broken concrete and disappear into a black crack. They stared out over miles and miles of sun-drenched ruins.

London looks at her best on a day like this, Cathy said. I'm glad the winter's over. Now the whole world is ours. The whole new century, for that matter! She laughed. Isn't it paradise?

If it isn't, it'll do.

A light wind ruffled their hair. They got up and began to wander towards Ladbroke Grove, guided by the outline of the one complete building still standing, the Hilton tower. Black and white monkeys floated from broken wall to broken wall, calling to each other as the two people approached.

Jerry reached into his pocket. He turned on his miniature stereo taper. Hawkwind was half-way through *Captain Justice;* a VC3's synthetic sounds shuddered, roared and decayed. He put his arm round her slender shoulders. Let's take a holiday, he said, and go somewhere nice. Liverpool, maybe?

Or Florence. Those twisted girders!

Why not?

Humming, they made their way home.

Late News

Five teenage pupils from Ainslie Park School, Edinburgh, and a trainee instructor of outdoor pursuits, died near Lochan Buidhe in the Cairngorms yesterday in the worst Scottish mountain accident in memory. The tragedy was heightened by the fact that the party was found within 200 yards of a climbers' hut which could have ensured their survival.

GUARDIAN, November 23 1971

A schoolboy in a party of 21 teenagers is believed to have died on a mountain in central Tasmania. A police and helicopter search is to resume at first light for the boys who are thought to be huddled together as blizzards break over the mountain.

GUARDIAN, November 24 1971

Two babies died today in a fire at a tented tinker's camp —hours after their grandfather died in a road accident. Peter Smith (2) and his ten-month-old baby sister Irene, died as fire ripped through their makeshift canvas home at Ferebridge Camp, near Barnbroe, Lanarkshire. Earlier, their grandfather, farm labourer Mr. Ian Brown (54) was killed when he was involved in an accident with a car as he was walking near the camp.

SHROPSHIRE STAR, December 18 1971

Farm worker Alan Stewart, who had a lung transplant at

Edinburgh Royal Infirmary on Thursday—his 19th
birthday—died last night. Alan, of Kirkaldy, drank weed-
killer from a lemonade bottle a week ago.

SHROPSHIRE STAR, December 18 1971

REMINISCENCE (H)

A man wearing a papier mâché mask in the form of a skull enters the doors of a pub.

A drunk screams and attacks the wearer.

Mother's eyes.

THE FOREST

"It's like a magic wood," Cathy's voice was hushed and delighted. "So many soft greens. And, look, a squirrel! A red one!"

Frank Cornelius sniffed the air. "Lush," he said. He tested the ground with his patent-leather foot. "Springy. Give me the good old English broad-leafed tree any day of the week."

"Oo, wot luverly flars!" said Mrs. Cornelius, ripping some wild orchids from the moss and holding them to her face. "Thus is wot I *corl* a wood, Kernew!"

Colonel Pyat gave a modest, proprietorial, smile and wiped his forehead with a large handkerchief of coarse linen. "This is the English forest at her best. The oak. The ash. The elm. And so forth." He was pleased to see her happy.

"I 'ope yer remember where we left ther motor," said Mrs. C. fiddling with the controls of her little tranny and failing to find a station. She gave up. She put the radio back in her bag. She cackled. "We don't wanna be like ther fuckin' babes in ther wood!"

Mellow sunshine filtered through the leaves of the tall elms, the strong oaks, the aristocratic poplars and the languid willows, filling the flowery glades with golden beams in which butterflies, mayflies and dragonflies sauntered.

They wandered on over sweet-smelling moss and grass and feathery ferns, sometimes in silence, sometimes in a babble of joy when they saw a pretty animal or a bank of beautiful flowers or a little, shining brook rushing between mossy rocks.

"Something like this restores your faith," said Frank as they paused to watch a large-eyed doe and her faun nibbling delicately at some low-hanging leaves. He took out his rolled gold cigarette case and offered it round, quoting: " 'It is from the voice of created things that we discover the Voice of God never ceasing to woo our love. Gaudefroy.' " It was a quotation to which he would become particularly attached in the coming years, especially over the Christmas period of 1999, shortly before he and Bishop Beesley would pay the final reckoning in the Ladbroke Grove Raid, at a time when their theological disputes would have brought them close to blows. "Time stands still. Man is at peace. God speaks."

"I orlways said you wos the one should've gorn inter ther church," said his mother sentimentally. She took a cigarette, a Sullivans, and waved it in a vague, all-encompassing gesture. "And wot would our friend Jerry make of all this, I wonder. Turn up 'is nose? Nar! Even 'e couldn't knock this."

"Jerry . . ." said Catherine defensively, and then could think of nothing more.

"Jerry's far too involved in the affairs of the world to spare time for the simple things of life," said Frank piously.

"You'd fink 'e'd write a p.c." Mrs. C. puffed at her fag. "Oh, look over there !"

It was a pool overhung by willows and sapling silver birches with big white boulders all around it. A tiny waterfall cascaded into the pool from high above. They all walked towards it, listening to the water. Colonel Pyat followed behind. He didn't have the energy any more. He, too, was wondering what had become of the missing member of the Cornelius family. There had been conflicting rumours. One rumour had it that he had been resurrected. Another said he had been returned to the sea. They had all relied too heavily on him, as it turned out. So much for the optimistic slogans. Messiah to the Age of Science, indeed! Now it was plainly too late for action. The opportunities had passed. It was all fragmenting. Even this silly attempt of his to keep the family together was a reaction to the real situation which he could no longer hope to control. Messiah to the Age of Science! A bloody Teddy boy, more like. But Colonel

Pyat was reconciled, really. This holiday might be the
last of his life and he wished to make the most of it. He
only regretted that he could not go back to die in the
Ukraine. The Ukraine no longer existed. With his home-
land destroyed, there was little to live for, his love for
England being entirely intellectual.

Frank turned back to see what had happened to Pyat.
"Come on, old boy." Frank's holiday seemed to be doing
him good. His face glowed with a vitality that was almost
healthy. "Don't want to miss the beauty spots now we're
here, do you? Where on earth did you find this little corner of England? I didn't think places like it still existed.
If they ever did."

"Oh," Pyat shrugged. "You know how it is. Strangers
sometimes discover things in a place where the people
who've lived there all their lives have never looked."

"Well, you've turned up trumps with this one, I must
say. It's like bloody fairyland. Titania's wood." Frank was
in a literary as well as a religious mood today. "I'm expecting a visit from Puck at any moment. Can you lay that
on, too?"

Pyat smiled. "It isn't the wood that's enchanted." But
Frank hadn't heard him; he joined his mother and sister.
The two women were unrolling plastic raincoats and
spreading them on the rocks. Mrs. Cornelius began to un-
load her string bag, taking out a vacuum flask and two
packets of sandwiches.

" 'Ere we are. Git stuck inter these, you lot," said Mrs. C.

No wasps or ants came to disturb them as they ate their
picnic beside the shady pool. Catherine was fascinated by
the water. It was so dark and deep, but there was nothing
sinister about it. It was tranquil and seemed to offer peace
to anyone who considered entering its still waters. Because she didn't much care for these cheese and pickle
sandwiches anyway, she left the other picnickers and
climbed down to stand on a rock beside the pool. The
conversation above sounded a long way away. She stared
at her reflection for some moments until she realised with
a shock that it was not quite her face which looked at her.
There were strong resemblances, certainly, but this was a
man's face and its hair was black. It smiled. She smiled
back. She turned to remark on the phenomenon to her
relatives but they had disappeared out of sight on the

other side of the rocks. She felt, then, that she had been standing here much longer than she had realised. She started to climb back. There was a slight afternoon chill in the air.

"Catherine!"

The voice came from above. She looked up and was surprised when she recognised the man who had called her name. He was clad in rather tattered evening dress. He stood offering his free hand to her. His other hand held a Smith and Wesson .45, rather loosely, as if he really didn't mind if he dropped it.

"What a strange coincidence." Cathy smiled as she put her palm into Prinz Lobkowitz's. "How are you? It's been an age."

"How are you, dear?" His voice was low and intense, his expression melancholy and affectionate. "I hope you are well."

"Very well. But you, my dear, you look so tired. Are you running away from someone?" She reached up and brushed his hair back from his wrinkled forehead.

He held her to him. "Oh, Catherine." He was crying. "Oh, my dearest. It is all over. This is defeat on every level."

"We must get you something to eat," she said.

"No. I haven't much time. I came here for a reason. Colonel Pyat is here?"

"Yes—and mother, and Frank."

"I'm sorry," he said "but . . ."

"Well, look who it isn't!" Frank Cornelius emerged from around a rock, his mother and step-father in tow. "So you know about this place, too. What a sell! It's getting like Piccadilly. Perhaps this is the real heart of the Empire, eh? We went for a little walk. Hello, Prinz L."

"Good evening." Lobkowitz was embarrassed. "I'm sorry to interrupt." Birds began to sing everywhere and red-gold sunlight flooded the scene. Prinz Lobkowitz cast a startled glance over his shoulder. "I wanted a word with Colonel Pyat."

Pyat stepped forward. Then he changed his mind and began to retreat, climbing up the white boulders until he stood looking straight down at the pool.

"Wotcher doin' up there?" said Mrs. Cornelius loudly. And then she fell silent.

There was a smear of dark green on the elbow of Colonel Pyat's suit. Catherine was glad that Pyat himself didn't know about it. Or did he?

Colonel Pyat sighed and turned to look down at them all.

"Prinz?" he said.

Lobkowitz reluctantly raised the heavy gun with both hands, drawing in a deep breath before pulling the trigger. Pyat seemed to bow in acknowledgement, receiving the shot courteously in the heart. Then he fell backwards and dropped into the pool. The waters closed over him.

"Oh, blimey!" said Mrs. Cornelius, looking with nervous disapproval at the gun. "Oh, Gawd!"

Frank stepped prudently back into the shade of an oak.

Prinz Lobkowitz looked miserably at his old sweetheart. Then he began to climb up the rock on which Pyat had stood. Catherine watched, feeling only sympathy for both the murderer and his victim. Lobkowitz reached the top, turned, raised the revolver to his lips, kissed it and tossed it to Catherine. She caught it with instinctive deftness. At long last Lobkowitz had learned a style.

He jumped into the pool. There was a splash and a silence.

Catherine tucked the Smith and Wesson into the waist band of her skirt and walked past her mother and brother. She entered the cold wood.

"Where's she off ter?" said Mrs. C. "In one of her bloody moods agin, is she?"

"Let's see if we can find the motor," said Frank, frowning. "She'll turn up again when she's ready."

"And wot are we gonna do abart cash, I'd like ter know." said his mother, practically. "Talk abart ther end o' a perfict day!" She snorted. "An' I'm a bleedin' widder agin," she said, as if suddenly realising the essence of what had happened beside the pool.

She cheered up, nudging Frank in the side.

"Still, yer've got ter larf, incha?"

He looked at her in horror.

THE FARM

Sebastian Auchinek, bringing home the cows for their evening milking, heard the shot quite clearly and looked out across the fields to see where it came from. Hereabouts, people rarely hunted at this time of the year, though possibly someone was potting a rabbit or two for his dinner. Beyond the fields, where the wheat sheaves stood waiting for the next day's attention, he could see the great, green wood, almost a silhouette now in the late afternoon sun. The shot had probably come from there. Auchinek shrugged and trudged on. He flicked at the rumps of his cows with a light willow stick. "C'mon Bessy. Git a move on there, Peg." The phrases were mumbled automatically, for the cows had trodden this path more often than had he and they needed little encouragement. They plodded up the rutted track of red earth between sweet-smelling hedgerows full of briar roses and honeysuckle, towards the stone milking sheds which lay beside the farmhouse with its warm cobblestone walls and its thick, thatched roof.

When Auchinek had first gone to earth, he would not have believed that he could have taken so easily to farming. In his old corduroy trousers, his rubber boots, his pullover, leather jerkin and flat, dirty cap, a quarter of an inch of stubble on his tanned, ruddy face, he looked as if he had farmed these parts all his life; and he felt it, too. The shot didn't bother him. Poacher or gamekeeper, human or animal, what happened beyond the confines of his farm was none of his concern. He had a lot to do before dark.

It was almost dusk by the time he had milked the cows

655

and poured the milk into his electric separator. He drove the cows back into the nearest field and returned to manhandle the milk churns onto his cart. He harnessed up Mary, his old shire horse, and started off along the track towards the railway.

When he got to the railway, he lit the oil lamp which hung on its usual post. He had to see to get his milk onto the little wooden platform. In about an hour's time the train would stop here and pick the milk up, delivering it at the local village station for the dairyman.

Night sounds had replaced the sounds of day. A few grasshoppers chirped in the long grass of the railway embankment. An owl hooted. Some bats flapped past. Now that his work was over Auchinek felt pleasantly tired. He sat on his cart and lit a pipe, enjoying a smoke before returning to the farm. It was a warm, clean night, with a good moon rising. Auchinek leaned back in the seat and breathed in deeply. The old shire twitched her huge flanks and flicked her tail but was content to wait until he was ready to go. She leaned down in her yoke and began to tug at the grass with her large yellow teeth.

Auchinek heard a noise in the neighbouring field and identified it as a fox. He'd have to be careful tonight if a fox was on the prowl, though he hadn't really had much trouble from predators since he'd taken over the farm. Then the rustling grew louder and more energetic. Had the fox already found its night's meat? There came a peculiar, strangled whimper—perhaps a rabbit. Auchinek peered over the hedge, but the light from the lamp cast only shadows into the field. For a moment, though, he thought he saw an animal of some kind—a savage face that might have belonged to an ape rather than to a fox. But then it was gone. He picked up the reins. He had grown eager to get home to his supper.

"All right, Mary. Come on now, girl." The country accent came naturally to him. "Come on, old girl. Gee up, there . . ."

When he had turned a corner of the track and could see the yellow warmth glowing from his own windows he felt completely at ease again. It was funny what you sometimes thought you glimpsed at night. All that was over now. He'd never be involved again. And the war couldn't touch him. The countryside was eternal. It was a good job, however, that he wasn't superstitious. He might start to have silly fantasies about his past catching up with him. He smiled. He'd boil some eggs for his supper and have them with some of that new bread, then he'd go to bed and finish Surtees' *Hillingdon Hall*. Of late, his whole reading has been devoted to eighteenth and nineteenth century novels of rustic life, as if he were subconsciously determined to steep himself in even the metaphysical aspects of country lore. He had already read *The Vicar of Wakefield, Romany Rye, The Mill on the Floss, Clara Vaughn* and *Tess of the D'Urbervilles,* as well as other, more obscure titles. He didn't seem to enjoy anything else. Sometimes he would sample a more modern work by Mary Webb or R. F. Delderfield and he found them enjoyable, too. He was going off George Eliot and Thomas Hardy, though. He didn't think he would read anything more by them.

He drove into the farmyard and got off the cart, unharnessing the mare. As he led her past the milking shed towards her stable, he heard the milk separator going, the big blades swishing and clacking. He smiled to himself; he was more tired than he had realised. As it sometimes happened when you were feeling a bit worn out, the sound seemed to form a word.

He remembered Una Persson. What ever happened to her? It had been a dream, that period in Macedonia and Greece. A nightmare. He'd done some funny jobs in his life before finding the one which suited him.

Ch-ch-char, went the blades. *Traitor—traitor—traitor.*

He closed the stable door, stretching and yawning. The air had turned very cold. They could be deceptive, these autumn nights.

Traitor—traitor.

He went inside. It wasn't very warm in the house, even though the range had been lit in the kitchen. He flicked open the doors of the stove to let more heat out. He could still hear that damned separator going. He shivered. He'd be glad to get under the blankets tonight.

THE VILLAGE

The train picked up the churns and took them to the village station where they were unloaded by the dairyman who put them in his van.

The van rattled happily as it drove down the peaceful street from the station, past the cheerful windows of the two pubs, *The Jolly Englishman* and *The Green Man,* past the village hall, where music was playing, past the church, down the alley and round the back of the little bottling plant where the milk would be readied for the morning's deliveries. Thank God the monopolies didn't control the farm produce in this part of the world, thought the dairyman. There were still a few corners of old England which hadn't yet been overrun by so-called progress. The dairyman left his van in the yard and strolled back towards the village hall. There was something special on tonight—a break in an otherwise acceptable routine.

He pushed open the doors and saw with some pleasure that they had already got the parachutist to start to strip. She was quite a good-looking woman, if a bit on the slim side for his taste. A cut over her left eye didn't improve her appearance, either. Had that been necessary? He nodded to the other village men and smiled at Bert and John, his brothers, as he took his place near the front of the stage. He licked his lips as he settled back in his chair.

Una Persson had been captured two days earlier but had had to wait, a prisoner in George Greasby's barn, while the village decided how best to use her. She was the first parachutist they had ever caught and they understood the conventions involved: a captured parachutist became a sort of slave, the property of whoever could find and hold one. Nearby villages had several male parachutists working their fields, but this was the first woman.

Conscious of George Greasby in the wings with his brazier and red-hot poker, Una had already unbuttoned her long flying coat and dropped it to the floor. She didn't much care if he burned her; all she really wanted to do was take the easiest way out and get the whole business over with as soon as possible. It was their idea of dignity and individualism that was central here, not hers. Stripping to *King Creole,* the tinny single on the cheap record player, seemed the easiest thing to do. Not that she'd ever cared much for Elvis Presley. She took off her shirt, staring into the middle-distance to avoid looking at all the fat, red heads with their bristly haircuts who made up her audience. She'd had worse. She didn't waste time: off came her boots, her trousers and her pants until she stood passive and naked, showing the few yellow bruises on her left breast, her right thigh and her stomach. It was a bit chilly in the hall. There was a slight smell of damp.

"All right, now give us a song," said George Greasby in his high-pitched voice. He waved the poker, holding it in a big, asbestos mitten.

Fred Rydd settled himself at the piano, running his stubby fingers over the keys and then thumping out a series of discords with his left hand while he struck up a rousing chorus of *A Little of What You Fancy Does You Good.*

Una had played the provinces often enough before. This wasn't very much different. She tried to remember the words. Charley Greasby, the old man's son, jumped up on the stage and slapped her bottom. "Come on, lovey, let's 'ear yer!" With lewd winks at the others, he cupped her breasts in his hard hands and pinched her nipples and yelled in her ear while performing a sort of obscene Morris dance: "I never was a one to go and stint meself. If I like a thing, I like it, that's enough. But there's lots of people say, if you like a thing a lot, it'll grow on you—and all that stuff." His breath smelled of onions.

"I like my drop of stout as well as anyone," sang Una, now that he had started her off. She felt faint. All the villagers were on their feet now, laughing and stamping and clapping. "But a drop of stout's supposed to make you fat." The whole hall seemed to be shaking. More of the thickset countrymen were clambering onto the stage. Her vision was full of corduroy, leather and woollen pullovers. The piano played maniacally on. "And there's many a lah-di-dah-di madam doesn't dare to touch it, 'cause she mustn't spoil her figure, silly cat!"

They all joined in the chorus. "I always hold in having it, if you fancy it. If you fancy it, that's understood. And suppose it makes you fat—well, don't worry over that. 'Cause a little of what you fancy does you good!"

"Come on," said Tom Greasby, who was still wearing his police constable's trousers, "let's have all the verses, my pretty. I haven't heard that one in years. The old ones are the best. Haw, haw!" He put a horny finger into her vagina. She knew it was there but she didn't feel it much as she went into the next verse.

She finished the song and was half-way through *Someday I'll Find You* when they lost control of themselves and got their corduroys and flannels down, pushing her on her back as they began, in hasty turns, to rape her.

The greatest discomfort she felt was in trying to breathe beneath the weight of their heavy, sticky bodies. She had never cared for the country and now she knew why. From the distance came the sound of the record player starting up again with Cliff Richard's *Living Doll*. She realized that her eyes were still open. She closed them. She saw a pale face smiling at her. Relieved, she smiled back.

It was time to split.

As the fifteenth rural penis rammed its way home, she left them at it.

THE HILL

"There's lights on still in the village hall," said Mrs. Nye, closing the bay window. "Maybe they're having a dance down there. There's music."

"I'm glad they're enjoying themselves," said Major Nye from where he lay in crisp sheets in the topless Heal's four-poster. He had gone yellow and his lips were flaking. His pale eyes shone from deep cavities and his cheeks were hollow. "Say that for the English. They know how to make the best of things." He had just recovered from an attack of malaria. He was dying.

They had had to leave Brighton when the malaria got really bad. It had been disappointing, after building everything up there. They had moved further west, to his father's old place, a large Frank Lloyd Wright style house built on the hill. On one side the house overlooked the village, on the other, the sea. From its windows it was possible to view the valley, with its farm, forest, village and streams, and the little harbour town and the beach. There were very few fishing boats in the harbour, these days. But holidaymakers still came from time to time. It was all very picturesque. "The very best of England," as Major Nye's father had often said. But for some reason Major Nye was ill at ease here.

"I wonder where the doctor could have got to," said Mrs. Nye. "I sent Elizabeth in the Morgan. It was the last of the petrol, too." Her own complexion was beginning to match her husband's. Many of the village women were convinced that it would not be long before she 'followed him.' Once he had gone, she would be glad to follow. She had had quite enough. He, on the other hand, was uneasy about dying in his bed. He had never imagined that he would. It seemed wrong. He felt vaguely ashamed of himself, as if, in an obscure way, he had failed to do his duty. That was why, from time to time, he would try to get up. Then Mrs. Nye would have to call her daughter to help put him back in the four-poster.

A fat, jolly girl bustled into the room. "How's the patient?" demanded Elizabeth Nye. She had become very attached to her parents just lately. A month ago she had been kicked out of the girls' school where she had been teaching and it had given her the opportunity to come home and look after them. "Shall I take over now, mums?"

Her mother sighed. "What do you think?" she asked her husband. Major Nye nodded. "That would be nice. D'you feel up to reading a bit of the book, Bess?"

"Happy to oblige. Where is the damned *tome?*"

Her mother brought it from the dressing table and handed it to her. It was a large, red book called *With the Flag to Pretoria,* a contemporary account of the Boer Wars. Elizabeth settled herself in the bedside chair, found her place, cleared her throat, and began to read:

"Chapter Twenty Three. The March on Bloemfontain and opening of the railway to the south. With the capture of Cronje in the West, and the relief of Ladysmith in the east, the first stage of Lord Roberts' campaign may be said to have ended. The powerful reinforcements sent out from home, and the skilful strategy of the commander-in-chief had turned the scale."

She read for an hour before she was sure he was asleep. In a way she felt it was a pity to encourage him to sleep when he had so little time left. She wished he was just a bit stronger so that she could take him out for the day in his wheelchair, perhaps to the village, or to the seaside. There was no chance of using her car again. The trip to the doctor's had used up the last of the fuel. She no longer despised her father and had come to feel very close to him, for his weaknesses were her own in a different guise. Simple-minded loyalty was one of them. And he, too, she had discovered only yesterday, had been crossed in love as a young man.

As she was putting the book back on the dressing table he opened his eyes, smiling at her. "I wasn't asleep, you know. I was thinking about the little chap and what's going to become of him. You'll make sure he stays at school?"

"If there's a school to stay at." She felt sorry for her cynicism. "Yes, of course."

"And Oxford?"

"Oxford. Yes."

"He's a bright little chap. He was a cheerful lad. I wonder why he's so melancholy, these days."

"A stage," she said.

"No. I know it's the school. But what else could I do, Bess?"

"He'll be all right."

"But not the Army, eh? It's up to him to break the chain. Get a good civilian job."

"Yes."

"Could you get me a glass of water, do you think?"

Elizabeth poured him some water from the decanter on the bedside table. The room was so unfriendly. She tried to think of ways of making the atmosphere warmer.

"I heard on the wireless the other day that they can't find the ravens," he said.

"Ravens? Where?"

"Tower of London. All flown off. When the ravens go the White Tower will fall and when the White Tower falls, my dear, England will fall."

"There'll always be an England," she said.

"The chances are good, I admit that. Even Rome lasted in a way, and Greece and Persia before her. Even Egypt, really. But Babylon and Assyria. Well, well . . . I'm rambling." He sipped the water. "And America. So short-lived. But very powerful, Bess."

"It's all been fined down, I'll grant you," she said. "The barbarians don't come from outside the walls any more, do they?"

"We breed our own cancers," he said. "And never a cure. But perhaps that's always been the case." He let her take the glass. "Merry. Hectora. Garvey. Kalu. Grog. Brorai, I think. And Jet."

"What's that?"

"The names of the ravens."

She laughed. "Aha!"

His voice was tiring. It was little more than a croak as he continued. "I've led an ill-disciplined sort of life. No moral fibre. It's something about the army. There were thousands of people in my position. Perhaps it was just the standard of living, or something. My old colonel was a drunkard, you know, before he died, And penniless. I used to stand him the odd drink. Decent old boy." His head trembled and he shut his eyes tight. "All failures. To a man. He—" His pale lips tried to speak but could not. She bent over him.

"What was that?"

He whispered, "He committed suicide. Chucked himself out of a bally window at the Army and Navy Club."

"Maybe it was for the best."

"It's all gone, Bess." His face was horribly white, like a skull. His moustache looked incongruous, like a piece of weed which had caught on the skull. "I'm sorry."

She said awkwardly: "Nothing to be sorry about, I'd have thought. You've done your best for the family. For the country, too, if it comes to that. You've put more in than most. You deserve—"

She knew that the next sound was a death-rattle, but it didn't last long.

Her mother came in.

"He's dead," said Elizabeth. "I'll go into town tomorrow and make the arrangements."

Mrs. Nye looked down at the corpse as if she couldn't recognise it.

"It's all over," said Elizabeth. She patted her mother's shoulder. The action was mechanical and for a moment it seemed to both of them that Elizabeth was actually striking her mother. Elizabeth stopped and went to the window. The lights were off in the village hall. The village was silent.

Mrs. Nye cleared her throat.

"Well," she said. "Well."

THE SEASIDE

Next morning, Elizabeth cycled down to the harbour town to make the necessary arrangements. While she waited in the funeral parlour, she thought she saw Catherine Cornelius go past with two other people, a thin man and a fat woman. Elizabeth knew this was less than likely. It was just her mind playing her another morbid trick. Earlier she had had the impression that her father was still alive in the house. She would never see Catherine again. Everything was over now. Her sex-life was over. Having a sex-life involved too much responsibility and now she had her mother and her little brother to think about. She looked through the dark glass of the window at the gleaming sea; she listened to the children playing on the beach. And quite suddenly she felt full of strength; suddenly she was confident that she would have sufficient moral resolve to win through against all the difficulties which faced her. She prayed that the feeling would last.

"Clotted cream and strawberry jam and loverly choccie biscuits," said Mrs. C. "That's wot I feel like, kids. That bleedin' hotel thinks we're bloody budgies, if yer ask me. The size o' them meals! Fuck that!" She led them towards the beach, much relieved by her recent discovery that Colonel Pyat had left his wallet in the car and that the wallet had been stuffed with tenners. There would be no trouble about paying the bill or having a bloody good time while they were down here. They deserved it.

They stopped at the cafeteria near the beach while Mrs. Cornelius had her elevenses. The cafeteria smelled strongly of candy floss. Frank and Cathy shared a knickerbocker glory, looking rather wanly at the bright, yellow sand.

"It's a tidy sort of beach," said Frank. "Not like Margate, for instance. Very middle class, wouldn't you say?"

Catherine felt too warm, even in her light summer frock. She removed her blue cardigan and put it in her gay beach bag. She noticed that both Frank and Mum were sweating, too.

"'Urry up an' scoff that darn, you two," said their mother, who had finished three times as much in half the time. "Eat it all up. Don' wanna waste it. It's all paid for."

They crammed the rest of the tinned strawberries, the chocolate syrup, the nuts and the ice cream into their mouths and munched while their mother busied herself with her toilet, touching up her carmine lipstick, laying on a little more scarlet rouge, another coating of pink powder, and patting at her perm with a comb. Then she took each of her children by one of its hands and led the way from the cafeteria, down the asphalt slope to the beach.

"Deckchairs, Frank." She surveyed the beach, hands on hips, like Rommel planning a campaign. "The sea's lovely, innit?" Frank went to the neat stack in the little green shelter by the wall of the promenade and got three brand new candy-striped canvas chairs. "Right," she said. "This way." She led them towards a breakwater. Not far away from the breakwater were four little children, two boys and two girls, at work on an elaborate sand palace, with turrets and towers and minarets and everything. They were digging a moat round it. Elsewhere, in a rock pool, twin girls, aged about eight, with blonde page-boy haircuts, studied crabs and starfish and seaweed.

"It's like the bloody *Rainbow Annual*," said Frank with some approval. "Tiger Tim at the Seaside. It's almost too perfect." He set up the chairs and got them just so. Then he stripped off his jacket, his shirt, his vest and his flannels to reveal a pair of yellow and black silk boxer-style bathing trunks. He stretched his thin body in the chair and drew on a large pair of wrap-around mirror sunglasses. But he was still not ready. He got up again and found the Man-tan lotion in his jacket pocket. He began smearing the stuff on his pale, spotted flesh. Meanwhile Mrs. C. had applied all her various creams and had lifted her loud, print dress to reveal her pink satin directoire drawers and her huge, white thighs. She sat with her legs spread, as if to catch the sunbeams in her lap. Cathy was reading a copy of *The Rescue* by Joseph Conrad. "This'll do," said Frank, regarding the distant sea. "We can come here next year. Now we've discovered it." Merry laughter rippled from the throats of the children around the sand palace. They were digging a deeper and deeper trench. A few happy seabirds wheeled and screamed. A red-sailed boat drifted by on the horizon. A small black and white cat began to walk demurely along the breakwater. Frank picked up a pebble and chucked it at the cat. He missed.

"Are you going in, love?" said Mrs. C. "It must be loverly for swimmin'."

Frank shuddered. "I don't think so. Currents and that. Rip-tides. Undertows."

"But there's others bathing over there," Catherine pointed. "They seem to be okay. There'd be signs if it was dangerous."

"Maybe later, then," said Frank. "I might have a bit of a summer cold."

"Oh, all right."

Everything was so ideal that Frank almost expected to see a jolly face painted on the golden disc of the sun, or even on the buckets and spades. The sand might have been dyed that bright, clean yellow; the sea might have been stained that bright, clear blue. Well, there was no point in looking a gift-horse in the mouth, was there? He leaned back and began to study the pictures in his body-building magazine.

"We'll go ter that pub fer lunch," said Mrs. C. "The on'y complaint I got is there's no bleedin' Bingo. That's a issential part of an 'oliday, I reckon. An' bumper cars. I like 'em. An a bit o' fish-and-chips. Yum yum."

Cathy suddenly felt funny. "I just had one of those lurches," she said. "You know. Déjà vu."

Frank's mirror shades regarded her. "Reels within reels," he said with a thin smile. "Don't worry, love. It happens to me all the time." he sniggered.

"Frank."

"Yes, mum."

"Go an' git us an ice, there's a love."

Frank got up slowly. "I'll want some cash."

She handed him a tenner. "All the jack you need," she said. "I never bin a *rich* widder before. Git one fer yourself an' Caff."

But he returned quite quickly, empty-handed. "Sold out," he said. "They say they weren't expecting a heat-wave. Personally, I don't find it that hot."

"I'm boiling," said Cathy.

"Fuck," said their mother removing the tenner from Frank's fingers. "I don't call this much of an 'oliday resort. I mean, they don't seem ter want ter cater fer visiters. An' we 'ave got money ter spend. We're not paupers. I could git through this lot in a day at Brighton." She put the money back in her large red and yellow plastic bag. "I could do wiv a cuppa," she hinted. "Anyway, I don't like 'ome made ice cream."

Frank and Cathy were pretending to be asleep. They lay stretched in their deckchairs, facing out to sea.

Mrs. Cornelius shifted in her chair, wondering whether to get up or not. She looked with some admiration at the huge sandcastle the kids were building. It was going on five feet tall and was elaborately detailed. She could almost have believed it was a real castle if she'd seen it in the distance. And the moat would soon be the size of an army trench. The energy of these kids! Where did they get it all from? They were working like beavers. They were moving about so fast! The sand was fairly flying from the ditch. The castle grew and grew. Turrets and galleries and towers appeared. The children laughed and shouted, carrying their buckets of sand to key points, patting down a tesselation with their little wooden spades. It must be very good sand, thought Mrs. C. vaguely. It must be very easy to work with. Now two of the boys were actually burrowing into the castle, hollowing it out. A Union Jack flew proudly from the highest tower. She took a deep breath of ozone. She hadn't smelled sea like that since she was a kid herself. She reached for the radio in her bag, but changed her mind. It wasn't too bad, this beach. Her hunger and thirst diminished; she stopped fidgeting. It was peaceful. She closed her eyes, listening to the sound of the surf, the cries of the gulls, the distant chatter of the happy children. Poor old Pyat. She still wondered why he'd married her. He must have been after something. It wasn't the sex, more's the

pity. She hadn't done badly out of him. She'd got something out of all her husbands, really. Not to mention the
others.

Frank got up and pulled on his shirt. "Don't you feel
cold, Cath?"

"What? Sorry. I was miles away."

"Aren't you chilly?"

"I was thinking it was too warm."

"You must be running a temperature." He sniffed. "Or
I am. Maybe we're sickening for something."

She yawned. "It would be a shame to have our holiday
cut short. Still, in a way I wouldn't be sorry. I feel a bit
guilty, really. Poor Colonel Pyat."

"It was a private issue. Nothing we could do. An accident as far as we were concerned. Unavoidable. I expect he died for a cause or something. Is that a boat on
the horizon? A warship?"

"I'm not sure I believe in accidents, as such." She
looked to where he was pointing. "Could be. Oh, dear,
I feel so lazy. And yet, at the same time, I feel I should
be doing something. Aah!" She stretched. "Fancy a game
of cricket, eh, Frank?"

He sneered.

She glanced at the towering sandcastle. The children
had found the little cat and were pushing it into the
hollowed out main entrance. They didn't mean any harm
and, in fact, the cat seemed to be enjoying himself as
much as the children. Soon Cathy saw the amused black
and white face staring at her from one of the upper windows. She smiled back at it, remembering the pool in the
forest. She dug her bare feet into the sand and wiggled
her toes.

A huge, reverberating snort came from the other deck-
chair. With a great dopey grin on her face, Mrs. C. was
snoozing. She looked as if she were having a happy dream.

"Well, she's all right, anyway," said Frank. He held his
arms round his body, leaning forward in the deckchair
and shivering. "I'll have to split back to the hotel if this
goes on. What's got into those kids?"

There was a slight note of alarm in the children's voices.
Cathy rose from her chair and walked towards them.
"Anything the matter, boys and girls?" But now she could
see what was wrong; the roof of the castle had caved in

completely. They had got too ambitious and ruined their creation. Also the moat was beginning to fill with foaming water. The tide was coming in.

"That cat's in there," said one of the little girls in panic. She twisted at her hair with her fingers. "The roof's fallen on him, miss." The other children were all in tears, shocked by what they had done. It was plain that they thought they had killed the cat. Only one boy was trying to do something about it, digging frantically into the side of the castle with his small wooden spade. Cathy picked up the largest spade she could find and started to dig from the other side, listening for any sounds which the trapped animal might be making. She was afraid it was dead already. "Block that stream," she said, indicating the channel which fed the moat. "We don't want to be flooded any sooner than we have to." She dug and dug, getting her frock all smeared with wet sand, while the other children stood in a silent semi-circle watching her. "Come on," she cried. "Get your spades and help." Nervously, they came forward. Evidently they would much rather have gone away and forgotten the whole incident. They picked up spades or buckets and began to dig. Sand flew in all directions. Frank came up. He stood there with his hands on his hips, his mirror shades glinting. "What the hell are you doing, Cath?"

"Trying to get the cat. Can you give us a hand, Frank?"

"I would," he said. "But this cold's got worse."

She panted. Her dress, her arms, her legs, her face and hair were now all covered in sand. "Then go back to hotel and keep warm." Not for the first time she felt annoyed and let down by him.

But he just stood there, shivering and watching as they dug on. Soon the whole castle was down and there was no sign of the cat.

"Could it have escaped?" Cathy spoke to the boy who had first started digging. "Before the roof collapsed?"

"I don't think so, miss. He might be in the cellar."

"What?"

"We dug a cellar—underneath."

Catherine wiped her hot forehead. Her arms and back were aching terribly. She summoned more strength and began to dig below the surface of the beach. She was quite surprised how strong she was, considering how much energy she had already expended.

By the time they had dug a hole some six feet deep, it had become difficult to work, for water kept dripping in and sand would fall back into the pit. Cathy looked for Frank but he had retreated. Her dress and hair were soaked and gritty. She must look a mess. Then she felt her spade strike something solid; something hollow. She sank down and gasped. "Phew!" She looked up. The children were all peering over the edge at her. "Phew!" she said, "I think I've reached some sort of old breakwater. That was a waste of energy, eh? That cat *must* have run out of one of the doors or windows. What a lot of excitement for nothing." And then she heard a sound which was almost definitely a cat's mew. It came from under her feet. She scraped sand away from what she had thought was a breakwater, revealing pale polished timber. "We've found a treasure," she said with a grin. The children's eyes widened. "Really and truly, miss?" said one.

"I'm not sure." She dug away more wet sand and then felt a spasm of anxiety as she exposed the whole of the box's surface, including the blank, brass plate. "You kids had better find your mums and dads," she said. She ran her hand over the surface of the coffin, wondering how it could be so warm.

"Oh, miss! Please!"

She did her best to smile. "Go on," she said, "I'll let you know if it's a treasure chest. Don't worry."

Miserably, reluctantly, they fell back from the edge of the pit.

Catherine wondered if the coffin were really an unexploded bomb. A booby trap? She'd heard of such things. And it *was* warm and there was a regular, slow ticking sound coming from inside it.

"Frank," she called. "Mum?" But neither answered. A gull squawked. Or had the sound come from inside the box? She had the impression that the beach above was now deserted. She looked at the sides of the pit. "Oh, God!"

Water was seeping down. The sand under her feet had the consistency of a quagmire. She was sinking into it. "Frank? Mum?" Gulls replied. They were miles away. How had she got into this situation? It was ridiculous.

There was nothing for it, she decided, but to free the

box completely. If it floated, she might be able to climb on it and drift to the surface as the pit filled. If not, she could put it on its side and perhaps climb up over it. She dug as fast as she could, but wet sand kept falling back into the holes. At last she was able to grab one of the brass handles and heave it, with a disgusting, sucking sound, upwards. Something heavy bumped about inside. The ticking stopped. A muffled screech replaced it. A bird? Could the cat have got inside somehow? She looked at the four bolts securing the lid and she had an idea. The Smith and Wesson .45 was still in her waistband. She took it out and screwed up her eyes, aiming for the first bolt. She pulled the trigger. The bullet hit the bolt and knocked it out. She aimed and fired three more times and by what seemed sheer luck managed to shoot all the bolts free.

She put the gun down and then, on second thoughts, picked it up again.

She pulled away the lid of the coffin.

A dreadful stink of brine and human excrement flooded from the box. She covered her mouth, staring at the creature she had revealed. Its eyes glowed, its lips curled back from its stained teeth, its fingers were curved like claws as it wrenched at the bonds securing its wrists to the sides of the coffin. First one hand came free. Then the other. And Cathy, recognising her poor, mad brother, fainted.

"Cathy?"

She opened her eyes. She was lying on the edge of the pit. She could only have been insensible for a few seconds. She looked down and saw that the pit was full of bits of weed and pebbles and shells, as well as splintered pieces of wood which had comprised the coffin.

"Cathy?"

He was standing over her, on the other side. But he had changed completely. He was dressed in a white pierrot suit with big red bobbles on the front. He had a blue conical clown's hat on his head, a triumphant grin on his face. He looked down at his costume and brushed a speck or two of sand off the front. He was once again her favourite brother. "Gosh," he said, glancing up at the sun, "is that the time? I must have been dreaming. Hello, Cathy."

She was still a bit nervous.

"Sorry about the first sight," he said. "I didn't want to alarm you. But I had to have your help, you see."

Her alarm faded. She was suddenly delighted. She might have guessed he'd do something like this. "What a wonderful surprise!" She stood on tiptoe and kissed him warmly on his lips. "You are a one, Jerry."

"Mum and Frank about?"

She looked for them. "Somewhere. Frank got cold."

Her brother grinned. "I thought it was Frank. I had to get the fuel from somewhere. And Mum?"

Cathy laughed and clung to his arm. He was the best big brother in the world. "Look," she said, pointing. "There they are. Poor old Frank!"

Frank was virtually under their feet, but in a little dip in the sand and so out of sight. He was curled into a tight ball and his flesh was all blue. His mirror sunglasses stared sightlessly from the top of his head. Cathy couldn't help smiling. "It's time Frank had a turn," she said. "I shouldn't laugh, really."

Mrs. Cornelius was still sprawled in her deckchair, her legs wide, her arms folded under her breasts, her chins shaking with each mighty snore. "She's having one of her happy dreams," said Jerry. "Do you think the tide will come in this far?"

"Just," said Cathy, pointing at a mark on the breakwater.

"It'll wet her feet. Nothing more. Let's leave her there to enjoy herself."

"It does seem a shame to disturb her," said Jerry. He looked up at the sky. The gulls were still circling cheerfully overhead and the sea still sparkled, but the air was darkening a bit, though there wasn't a cloud to be seen. "We could be in for some rain."

"Leave her anyway," said Cathy.

"All right." He peered towards the horizon. "If you think it's a good idea." He frowned.

"There's that boat Frank saw," said Cathy. "It's getting closer."

"Ah, well, she'll have to take her chances," said Jerry. "Yes, I noticed that. It's a destroyer." He spoke absently, looking tenderly down at her. "Do you want to go for a sail, Cathy?"

"Lovely," she said. "Or a swim?"

"I think I'll hold off swimming for a while. I'm still a bit stiff." He brushed the sand from his costume and, with long, easy strides, led her up the asphalt ramp to the promenade. "This way," he said. "It's in the harbour."

It wasn't far to walk to the old stone harbour. There was only one ship moored there and Cathy recognized the white schooner at once.

"It's the good ole *Teddy Bear*!" she cried. She was delighted. All its brasswork shone and bright bunting danced in the rigging. "Oh, how wonderful!" They raced along the jetty and up the gangplank. The engines were already running. A small crowd of children stood on the quay, staring at the ship with mute curiosity. They cheered as Jerry picked Cathy up and carried her the last few paces onto the deck.

Almost as soon as they were aboard, the ship upped anchor, moved away from the jetty and out of the harbour, heading for the open sea. The children waved their pocket handkerchiefs and cheered again.

In her deckchair Mrs. Cornelius stirred. The tide had begun to lap at her toes. It had already covered Frank. Behind her, the shops were beginning to close up for the day and the main street was deserted, save for Elizabeth Nye, pedalling slowly up the hill towards her home. A woman, wrapped in an old sack, turned the corner and signalled to her, but Elizabeth Nye was intent on her cycling. She didn't notice Una Persson. Una looked out to sea and recognised the destroyer. She sat down on the pavement and waited.

On the sun-deck of the yacht, Jerry found a ukelele. He collapsed into a steel and canvas Bauhaus chair and began to strum the uke while Cathy swayed peacefully in a hammock under an awning and sipped her lemonade. The coast sank slowly behind them as the *Teddy Bear* steered a course for Normandy.

"I'm not stuck up or proud. I'm just one of the crowd. A good turn I'll do when I can!" Jerry sang his favourite George Formby medley. It had been a long time. "The local doctor one night needed something put right and he wanted a handy man . . ." Cathy winked at him and tapped her feet to the rhythm. Jerry rolled his eyes at her and wagged his clown's hat as he went into a fast ukelele break. She laughed and clapped.

A few moments later they were interrupted by a dull roar from behind them. "Sounds like thunder," said Cathy. "I hope we're not in for a storm."

Jerry put down the uke and pushed back the wide cuffs from both wrists, checking his watches. "No," he said. "We're all right." He yawned. "It's been a bloody long haul, all in all. You don't mind if I get half an hour's kip in, do you? Clausius summed it up in 1865. 'The entropy of the universe tends to a maximum.' I suppose that's when it all started. Did anyone celebrate his centenary? One idea leads to another. Ho hum." His feet up on a canvas footstool, his hands folded in his lap, his healthy face at peace, the light wind tugging at the ruffles, folds, pleats and pom poms of his red, white and blue pierrot suit, Jerry Cornelius fell asleep.

Catherine Cornelius got out of her hammock. She kissed her fingertips and put them on his smooth forehead. "Dear Jerry." She went to the rail and looked back towards the vanished coast. "Goodbye, England." The sound of thunder was fainter now. Perhaps the storm was moving away.

Dropping anchor a short distance offshore from the razed and smoking resort, the destroyer fired a few last rounds over the hill and got a direct hit on the village on the other side. A 4.5" shell took out the house. Four Sunstrike missiles turned the forest into an inferno. The farm, however, had been burning since the previous night.

The Condition of Muzak

A Jerry Cornelius novel

Illustrated by Richard Glyn Jones
Title page by Jill Riches

This book is dedicated with gratitude to the following people who, at different times, encouraged me through the eleven years this tetralogy took to complete:
Clive Allison, Hilary Bailey, Jimmy Ballard, Edward Blishen, Alan Brien, John Clute, Barry Cole, Mal Dean, Tom Disch, George Ernsberger, Giles Gordon, Mike Harrison, Doug Hill, Langdon Jones, Richard Glyn Jones, Philip Oakes, Keith Roberts, Jim Sallis, Norman Spinrad, Jack Trevor Story, Jon Trux, Angus Wilson.

CONTENTS

All art constantly aspires towards the condition of music. For while in all other works of art it is possible to distinguish the matter from the form, and the understanding can always make this distinction, yet it is the constant effort of art to obliterate it.

—Pater

What's more in HERCULES than HARLEQUIN.
One slew the Hydra, this can kill the Spleen;
In him Behold the Age's Genius bright;
A Patch-Coat Hero, this great Town's delight.
With Craft and Policy, his humour tends
To publick Mirth, and profitable ends.
Let Envy gnash her teeth, let Poets rail
Whilst PIERO is his Guide he cannot fail.

—Satirical print: The Stage's Glory, 1731

Each flower and fern in this enchanted wood
Leans to her fellow, and is understood;
The eglantine, in loftier station set,
Stoops down to woo the maidly violet.
In gracile pains the very lilies grow:
None is companionless except Pierrot.
Music, more music! how its echoes steal
Upon my senses with unlooked for weal.
Tired am I, tired, and far from this lone glade
Seems mine old joy in route and masquerade,
Sleep cometh over me, how will I prove,
By Cupid's grace, what is this thing called love.

[Sleeps]
—Dowson, Pierrot of the Minute

Hop! enlevons sur les horizons fades
Les menuets de nos pantalonnades!
Tiens! l'Univers
Est à l'envers. . . .

—Tout cela vous honore,
Lord Pierrot, mais encore?
—Laforgue, Complainte de Lord Pierrot

TUNING UP (1)

As Major Nye tried to brush some green and brown stains from the collar of his tropical combat jacket a little damp earth fell from his neck and struck the fused stone of the timeless causeway. Around him what remained of the ruins of Angkor merged with the blackened boles of a defoliated jungle; the area was at peace; it had ceased to be of strategic importance. About fifty feet away a huge stone head of Ganesh, elephant god of trade and good luck, lay on its side where a 105mm shell had shot it between the eyes, blasting a deep gash in the stone above the base of its trunk: the wound glinted white and crystalline against the surrounding mossy grey of the forehead; the god seemed to have acquired a disenchanted third orb. Though a few monkeys and parrots (no longer the rowdy insouciants of more glorious pre-war years) crept about in the higher terraces, pausing cautiously if they disturbed a fragment of plaster or dislodged a twig, there were few sounds of life in the city.

Major Nye had at first found the city peaceful but he was becoming increasingly uneasy with the tensions which had gone to produce that peace. He lifted his head towards his right as, from the twisted and fire-blasted turret of a wrecked tank, a poor copy of a Vickers Mark I Main Battle (the "Shiva"), emerged the chubby khaki bottom of a small Brahmin. Behind the tank the jungle brooded. "It's no go, I'm afraid, Major." The Brahmin wiped fat hands on his oily fatigues and wriggled round so that he could face Nye. "Not a scrap." He flourished an empty picnic hamper.

This was the Shiva which had scored the hit on Ganesh:

its occupant was the only survivor of retaliatory rocket fire which had, in turn, taken out the tank. He called himself "Hythloday" but Nye knew his real name. "Hythloday" had been a technical advisor with the Indian mercenary mechanised cavalry in its now famous sweep from Darjeeling to Saigon. Some months earlier, having no room for passengers, the cavalry had left him behind with his broken tank, and two days ago Major Nye, making a routine search and destroy operation in the area on behalf of his Khmer employers, had found him, recognising him as a former acquaintance. Major Nye had not reported his capture—there would have been little point, for yesterday he had intercepted a radio report: Phnôm Penh had sustained a tactical nuclear strike, possibly Tasmanian in origin. Without question it was curtains for the Khmers.

Unemployed again, bereft of the loyalties he needed so badly, Major Nye stroked his ancient tash and drew grey brows together. His pale hair, thin and sandy, his pale blue eyes, stood out in contrast to the heavy tan on his near fleshless face and neck. "Ah, well," he said in answer to Hythloday's statement, "there are always the emergency rations. I must say the world is not the one I knew as a boy." He lowered his Armbrust 300 anti-tank weapon to the ground and unpacked the box at his belt. "Still, peace has been restored and that's important. Though at a price, of course."

From behind a crackling mass of fried foliage a third figure climbed up the masonry and sat beside him on the slab: a young man in tatty out-of-date clothing, haunted and demoralised by something more than war. The major offered him a strip of pemmican. "You seem cold, old chap. Are you sure you haven't picked up a spot of fever?"

"It depends what you mean, Major." Jerry Cornelius turned the ragged collar of his black car coat so that it framed his face. He accepted the dehydrated meat and raised it reluctantly to his lips. His eyes were hot, his skin flushed. He was shivering.

Professor Hira joined them. "You've had the last of the medical kit, I regret to say, Mr. Cornelius."

Cornelius had revealed himself to them on the previous day. From what he had told them he seemed to have been hiding in the ruins for a long time, since well before the final battle. Today he was, physically, slightly better than when they had found him, though he continued to deny that there was anything wrong with him. He had accepted the morphine, he said, because he hated to look a gift horse in the mouth. Similarly the quinine, the penicillin and the Valium. There was at least a score of recent holes in his forearms.

"It's industrialisation I need." Jerry shifted himself so that he squatted at Major Nye's feet. "I've developed this horrible antipathy towards peasant communities. Particularly Slavs and South East Asians. What makes them so cruel?"

"It's hard to sympathise, isn't it?" Professor Hira nodded his head. "Original sin, I suspect. The devil come to Eden. It can't be the climate or the terrain." He had decided to skip the jerky and was gnawing, instead, on a root. "It can't be poverty."

"The very opposite, in my view, " said Major Nye. "The richest New Guinea tribes were always the nastiest. Don't Kiev and Bangkok have a great deal in common with Crawley or Brighton?"

"Or Skokie," said Professor Hira with a certain amount of feeling.

They looked at him in surprise. He shrugged. "It was a long time ago."

Major Nye carefully packed up the rest of the rations. "I wouldn't mind getting back to Blighty myself. Better the devil you know, eh? A return to reality."

"Oh, Christ." Jerry began to shiver again. He rose. "That's the last thing I need."

PRELUDE

As Errant Knight of Table Round,
In high resolve shall Harlequin fulfil his quest;
And thus his judges all confound.

    Harlequin Disguised as a Warrior (French print c.
1580)

Mother and Three Children Die from Asphyxia

No definite explanation for the cause of a fire which swept through two attic rooms in North Kensington on 14 January, killing a mother and her three young children, was forthcoming at the resumed inquest on Wednesday. Verdicts of "Accidental Death" were recorded. "I left the three children sleeping there when I went to work that morning," said Mr. Colum Cornelius who had been staying in the house at the time. Fire Officer Cyril Powell said after the fire had been put out the bodies of the mother and her three children were found in the front attic room. Pathologist Dr. R. D. Teare said that the cause of death was asphyxia due to the inhalation of fire fumes.

KENSINGTON POST, 12 February 1965

J.C.

*Affluence and poverty are here in their extremes. Bo-
hemians and traders, prostitutes, millionaires and famous actresses, writers, painters, street singers,
drug-pushers, pop-stars, rag-and-bone dealers and
antique dealers, immigrants from every part of the
world—West Indians, Greeks, Pakistanis, Irish, Ital-
ians, Americans—and rich women from South Kensington come to London's finest vegetable market
to shop cheaper. Just a few of the types in one of
the world's most exotic streets. . . .*

The Portobello Road, *Golden Nugget,*
September 1966

Some two miles north of the abandoned shell of Derry
and Toms Department Store (now, like the ruins of
Tintagel and Angkor, a mere relic) there once stood a
grey-brown collection of nineteenth-century brick buildings surrounded by a high wall, also of brick: the Monastery of the Poor Clares Colettines, Westbourne Park
Road, established in 1857 at the request of Dr. Henry
Manning, Superior of the Oblates of St. Charles. The buildings themselves were erected in 1860, modelled on those
of the Convent of the Poor Clares at Bruges which supplied the first nuns. Notting Hill, according to *The
Building News* of the period (quoted in the Greater London Council's Survey of North Kensington, 1973), was
nothing more than a dreary waste of mud and stunted
trees, where the convent shared "the sole interest" of this
desolate district with "Dr. Walker's melancholy church"
of All Saints', then still unfinished, and a lonely public

house, now called the Elgin, in Ladbroke Grove. A number of "low Irish" had settled in the vicinity, and already there had been "a plentiful crop of Romish conversions there." The convent looked East onto Ladbroke Grove, North onto Westbourne Park Road and South onto Blenheim Crescent, while to its West were rows of rundown Victorian terraces, separated, back-to-back, by tiny yards.

During the decade 1965-75 (the period during which the major part of our story probably took place) the convent was sold to the Greater London Council who subsequently built on the site a number of blocks of flats and a multi-storey car-park to serve the needs of their richer tenants. The nuns were moved to Barnes, across the river.

Before the convent was demolished it had been possible for people living on the upper floors of the surrounding houses to glimpse occasionally the activities of the nuns, members of an enclosed order, in the convent gardens, where vegetables and flowers were grown. In the summer the nuns would enjoy a game of rounders on the lawn or take picnics under the shade of the many elm trees whose old branches could be seen by those who passed by on the other side of the time-worn brick. The walls provided the nuns with a tangle of rambling roses and ivy and on their reverse offered the public slogans, some cryptic (VIETGROVE) and some relatively clear (QPR RULE OK), as well as the usual spray-painted selection of quotations from the works of Blake and Jarry. For those residents of Blenheim Crescent, Ladbroke Grove and Westbourne Park Road who found themselves with time on their hands the convent represented a regular diversion. At any one time during the height of the summer at least fifty pairs of eyes would be trained on the convent from a variety of angles, from windows, balconies and roofs, waiting for a glimpse of a figure at a window, the sight of a black habit crossing from a residential wing to the chapel or, more rarely, the spectacle of a cricket match. The convent proper, being, according to local legend, forbidden to any man (apart from the confessor, the electrician and the plumber who attended to the failing central heating) and most women, represented an ideal, a mystery, a goal, a challenge. Some doubtless hoped for a glance of flesh, a suggestion of illicit love between the nuns, while others were merely curious as to how the inhabitants spent their time. To certain ladies the convent represented a haven, a sanctuary from the complications of children, husbands, lovers, relatives and jobs.

On one particular summer afternoon, at the beginning of the decade already mentioned, a young man sat on the ledge of a window of a wretched tenement in Blenheim Crescent staring intently at the door of the chapel from which, in five minutes, almost all the Poor Clares would emerge together. The young man had lived most of his life in the three room apartment and had an intimate knowledge of the nuns' movements as well as an affectionate proprietorial attitude towards them: several had nicknames—Old Ratty, Sexy Sis, Bigbum, Pruneface—for he had grown up with them; they were his pets. Given the opportunity, he would probably have died to protect them. He did not, of course, regard them as human beings.

From behind the young man and in the next room came the sound of crockery being washed; a noise accompanied by a rhythmic almost sub-vocal litany which was familiar and restful to him, like the drone of insects in a country garden, the tinkle of water over rocks.

Jerry Cornelius yer kin jest git yer shitty littel finger art an' do and 'ands turn like ther rest'v us, yer bugger. Fuckin' 'ell, yer dad woz fuckin' lazy but yore ther fuckin' world champion you are. If it wosn't fer me eyes I'd be doin' a bleedin' job, I worked fer years fer you lot and where'd it fuckin' get me, look at this bloody place it's a pigsty, an' Frank keeps promisin' me 'e'll git us a noo flat an' thass bin four years NAR!

A totter's cart, piled with the discarded debris of a score of slum houses, turned into Blenheim Crescent. It was drawn by a brown and white pony. Jerry automatically found himself inspecting the junk from where he sat, high overhead: it was an inbred instinct of all children born in the district. There were two old gas-stoves, a wooden bedstead, a water-heater, a tin bath, some boxes of rusty cutlery. The pony's hooves clattered on the tarmac of the street. The driver, in a stained brown overcoat, his eyes owl's eyes behind thick lenses, had propped his main prize of the day, an old set of stag's antlers, behind him so that for an instant it seemed that he himself was horned. He gave a throaty instruction to the horse and it turned right, vanishing into a nearby mews.

Jerry yawned, stretched, and settled a thin shoulder against the window frame, swinging his legs above the tiny balcony formed by the house's front porch. The balcony had once been painted green but most of the paint had peeled. It contained dilapidated window boxes, some of which managed to sustain a few weeds in their sour earth; a collection of grimy plastic woodland animals and gnomes; part of a black Raleigh roadster bicycle which Jerry had begun reconstructing two years before; a deck-chair whose canvas had rotted and which had ripped when, with a yell, his mother had fallen through three days earlier. Sooner or later, Jerry had reassured her, she would not recognise the balcony. He planned, eventually, to turn it into an ornamental conservatory with semi-tropical plants.

The afternoon was very warm for early summer and was relatively still, for it was a Thursday, when almost all the local shops and stalls closed down. Jerry could turn his head to the right and see, at right angles to Blenheim Crescent, a tranquil, deserted Portobello Road, or to the left a Ladbroke Grove with about half its normal volume of traffic. It was almost as if, for a few hours, an aura spread from the convent and made the world outside as tranquil as the world within.

Before the nuns emerged, Jerry's attention was distracted to the street by the chuckling drums of some Pakistani love song which almost immediately stopped and became the last few bars of a Rolling Stones number. Three black youths, in jeans and jazzy jumpers, were springing down the steps of the house immediately opposite Jerry's, a house even more dilapidated than his own, of tired red brick. The tallest youth swaggered, holding in his hand a transistor radio which now played the Beatles' latest hit; the other two were jostling him, trying for possession of the radio. The tall boy pulled away from his companions. "Lay off me, man." He made loose, dancing movements. The volume rose and fell as he moved the radio. "Come on, man—let's have it." One of his companions grabbed and the station was lost. Jerry could hear the static. "You broken it, man!" They paused, seeking the correct wave-length. "No, I ain't!" They found the programme just as the song faded. They began to scuffle again. "Give us a go, man." The tall boy broke and ran with the radio, up towards Portobello Road. "Get your own. It's mine, ain't it?" The other two caught him almost immediately, tackling him around the legs, bringing him down.

As the fight became more serious a policeman turned the corner from Ladbroke Grove. He was young, pink and all the character seemed to have been scrubbed from his sober features. Without altering his pace he raised his voice:

"Oi!"

Unheeding the boys began, almost amiably, to kick and punch their companion, who lay on the ground, his knees drawn up, the tranny hugged to his chest. It was playing Jimi Hendrix now.

"Oi!"

The policeman loped towards them. They turned. The two shouted a warning and ran towards Kensington Park Road. The third picked himself up and followed them. The policeman stopped, drew a couple of breaths and wiped his forehead with a navy-blue handkerchief. Then he continued to pace in their wake, obviously not in pursuit.

"There's never a copper around when you need one!" Jerry found himself shouting into the silence of the street. Startled by the loudness of his own voice he turned his head in the opposite direction. When, after some seconds, he turned his head back he saw the policeman glaring up at him. Jerry winked.

"Wot's 'appenin'?" His mother entered her bedroom and saw her son on her ledge. "Git off a there! Yer'll fall!" She neared the window and saw the policeman. "Blimey! Wot's 'e want?"

"Dunno, Mum."

"Nosey bloody parkers ther lot of 'em."

Mother and son contemplated the policeman. Eventually he became self-conscious and resumed his beat.

Mrs. Cornelius cocked her head. "Someone comin' up. Are yer *sure*. . . . Oh, it's Frank." The door opened.

Frank came into her room. Frank wore a blazer with polished steel buttons, grey flannels, an open-neck white shirt, a yellow cravat with a horse-shoe motif. He stared in affected contempt at his brother whose own costume was a red satin shirt with the words *Gerry and the Pacemakers* imprinted in yellow on the back, skin-tight drainpipe jeans and suede desert boots. His black greasy hair had almost grown out, but was still streaked with blonde dye at the ends. "Bloody hell," Frank placed a large bar of Cadbury's Fruit and Nut on the confused dressing-table. "They should never have abolished National Service. Look at you!"

"Piss off." Amiably Jerry took in his brother's gear. "What was the regatta like? Just come up from Henley, have you?"

"I've been *working*." Frank ran a hand down his waist.

"Conning some poor ignorant foreigner, eh?" Jerry looked speculatively at the chocolate on the table.

"I've made an important sale this afternoon." Frank produced a huge roll of dollar bills from his trouser pocket. "Don't knock it, Jerry."

Noting the expressions on the faces of both his brother and his mother he quickly slipped the roll back where it had come from.

"Not a bad little bundle," said Jerry. "Did you sell some of them authentic Chippendale vases you antiqued up last week?"

Frank tapped his forehead. "Intelligence got me that." He preened himself. "Information. Property. That's my commission."

"You can be had up for playing Monopoly with real money." Jerry swung his legs into the room. "Say, lend us a couple a bucks, will ya, bud?"

"Oh, Christ!" Frank returned to the living-room/kitchen. He glared around him at the crowded, ruined furniture, the half-done washing up, the piles of magazines and broken china ornaments. "Don't let him talk in that fake Yank accent, Mum. He's so *common*."

"Make it ten bob, then," said Jerry reasonably, in his own voice.

"Piss off." Frank sniffed. "Get a bloody job."

"I'm organising this beat group," said Jerry. "It takes time."

"What is the time?" Frank glanced at his wrist. "My watch has stopped."

"Is that the bargain that fellah sold you in the pub?" Jerry was triumphant. "Solid gold wasn't it? Fifty jewels? Con men always make the best marks, don't they?"

"I didn't come to see you." Frank slid his white cuff over his malfunctioning watch. "I came to see Cathy—and mum, of course. Is she here?"

"That's Mum, by the sink."

"How childish," said Frank.

"What you doing then?" Jerry asked with genuine curiosity, ignoring his brother's last remark. "Following in Rachman's footsteps."

"Tenements?" Frank was shocked. "This is *property development*. Offices and that."

"Round here?"

"It's going up all the time. A rising residential area, this is. All the people from Chelsea and South Ken are moving in."

"Buying themselves nice little ragshops in Golborne Road, are they?"

"Multiple tenancies are giving way to one-family houses. It's council policy." Frank savoured the sound of the words.

Jerry looked out of the window over the sink. He had missed his nuns. "You know what I'd do, if I had the chance? I'd buy that bloody nunnery."

"I've got news for you," began Frank. "The GLC. . . ."

"Just to own it," said Jerry dreamily. "Not to do anything with it."

"Well, you'd better start saving up, hadn't you?"

Jerry shrugged. "Wait till our group gets to number one."

Frank laughed. "You'll be lucky if you're all awake at the same time."

Absently, Jerry popped a mandy into his mouth. "It's idealists like me the world needs. Not grafters like you."

This seemed to improve Frank's spirits. He put a condescending hand on Jerry's forearm. "But it's a grafter's world, my son."

"Yeah?"

"Most definitely, young Jerry."

Jerry sniffed. "I'll let you get on with it, then."

He turned to his window.

Frank wandered to his mother's side. "Hello, Mum. Any chance of a cup of tea?"

MAJOR NYE

"I'm afraid it's not quite the thing for our little theatre."
Major Nye tried to sit on one of the bar-stools and then
decided to remain at attention. Gingerly he sipped his
pint of shandy, revealing shiny cuffs. The suit was twenty
years old at least. "I really am sorry, old chap. What is it?
A pint?" His pale eyes were sympathetic.

"Thanks, major," said Jerry. "I'm sorry I can't get you
one." He was scarcely any more fashionably dressed than
Major Nye. He wore his black suit with the high, narrow
Edwardian lapels and the slight flare to the trousers,
which he had got Burton's to make up for him, albeit
reluctantly, when he had been flush. The only black shoes
he had were the elastic-sided cuban-heeled winkle-pickers
pre-dating the suit and he felt awkward in his rounded,
button-down-collar white shirt, with the black knitted tie.
"But you've only heard the cassette on a cheap player.
If you heard it over proper speakers you'd get our full
sound, you know."

"Surely you can get bookings in these pop clubs they
have everywhere these days?" He caught the attention of
the purple-cheeked barman. "Pint of best, please." He
leaned cautiously against the mahogany counter, looking
beyond Jerry at Hennekey's other customers crowding
round the pub's stained wooden benches and big tables.
It was evident that while he did not judge the shaggy young
bohemians he was mildly curious about them. He fingered
the ends of his cuff. "I thought they were mushrooming."

"They're not interested in us," Jerry told him. "You
see we're a bit more than an ordinary rock group—
we're trying for something that combines a story, a

light-show, spoken words and so on. That's why I guessed you might be interested, since you're local. The only local theatre. And it's more of a theatrical show, you see."

"I'm just the secretary, old chap. I'm probably the least powerful person in the whole outfit. And acting, unpaid, at that. It was my daughter got me involved, really. I'm retired, you see. I was adjutant of the—well, we got kicked out—the regiment was incorporated—no room for old fogies like me. Anyway, she's an actress. Well, of course, you must know that already, since it was through your sister. . . ."

"Yes," said Jerry. "I do know. But you're the only person connected with the Hermes Theatre who'd even bother to listen to me."

"They're a bit old-fashioned there, by and large, though I think they're going to do Pinter next year. Or is it Kafka? *A Night at the Music Hall's* about as far as they're prepared to go, eh? The boy I love is up in the gallery. . . ."

"I see," said Jerry. "I suppose you don't know anybody else I could approach?"

Major Nye was disappointed at not being allowed to finish the line. "Not really."

"Everybody's hopes are pinned on this, you see."

Major Nye said seriously, as a group of newcomers jostled him against Jerry's chest: "You shouldn't stop trying, old chap. If you've got something worthwhile it will be recognised eventually."

Jerry sighed and sipped his bitter.

UNA PERSSON

"Bloody hell," said Jerry miserably as he backed into the corner of the white room, his elbow almost dislodging a particularly ugly china dog on a shelf, "there must be every trendy in the King's Road here, Cath." The party bubbled about his ears. There was a great deal of blue and orange, of op and pop and pastel plastic, of the Tilsonesqueries loading the walls, of coloured stroboscopes and Warholian screenprints, light screens displaying shapes of an oddly Scandinavian neatness, hunt-ball whoops and giggles, stiff upper-class bodies in a terrifying parody of vitality. His sister shook her head. "You're such a snob, Jerry. They're nice people. A lot of them are friends of mine."

Jerry tasted his punch. He had got his new brown and white William Morris shirt sleeve wet ladling the stuff into his cup. He had only come because Catherine had told him he would be able to make the right sort of contacts. The trouble was that every time someone spoke to him in one of those high-pitched voices his throat tightened and he could only grunt at them. The strobes turned the whole scene into a silent movie—something about decadent modern times called *Despair*—as the hearty girls in their shorts and mini-skirts danced with pale young men in neat neckerchiefs and very clean jeans who puffed at machine-rolled joints and staggered against the chrome and leather furniture in an unaesthetic danse macabre.

The Rolling Stones record finished and was replaced on the deck by a fumbling drunkard who lurched against the amplifier and knocked it half off its shelf. The amplifier was saved by a tall girl with short hair and sardonic grey eyes. The girl wore a long calf-length skirt and a rust-coloured jumper to match; she had an assured elegance possessed by no one else in the room. She squeezed past the drunkard as he let the pick-up fall with a crunch on the record he had selected: *Elvis Presley's Golden Hits,* already much scored. "Oh, fab!" cried more than one melancholy soul.

Jerry watched the girl until she looked back at him and smiled. He turned his head to find himself face to face with the dark young man whom Catherine had introduced as Dimitri, doubtless one of her many Greeks. At least Dimitri wore a suit, albeit a "Regency" cut. Dimitri's eyes widened in panic at the prospect of a further exchange of grunts. The elegant girl entered Jerry's field of vision again. She was carrying a glass. "You seem as much out of place here as I am."

Jerry's being flooded with gratitude but he hoped it didn't show. "Chelsea wankers," he said, playing it cool. He tossed back his drink. "What's a nice girl like you doing here?"

"I came with a friend."

Jerry was disappointed. "One of these blokes?"

"One of these—chicks."

He wondered if she were foreign.

"Liz Nye," explained the girl.

"She's a friend of my sister's."

"Catherine's a great pal of mine."

"Who are you, then?"

"My name's Una."

Jerry smirked, in spite of himself. He knew all about Una Persson. "You're a legend in your own lifetime," he said. "You're not like I imagined."

Her smile was for herself but she replied quickly to save him embarrassment. "Catherine sees just one side of me."

"Have you got a lot?" Jerry asked. "Of sides."

"It depends what you mean."

Jerry's smile broadened and became a grin which she shared. She winked at him and stood beside him, shoulder to shoulder, so that they both faced the party. "They should be putting the Vivaldi on soon," she said. "And begin to 'smooch.' "

Somehow she had given him courage. "Do you want to split?" he asked.

She frowned. "You mean 'leave'?"

"Yes. Sorry."

"There are so many levels, aren't there? I'll have to find out what Liz wants to do. She's in the next room." Una Persson touched his arm. "But I'll be back."

Jerry began to come to life. Gracefully he reached towards his guffawing hostess and accepted another punch.

SEBASTIAN AUCHINEK

Fingering the hand-stitching on his blue velvet Beau Brummel jacket Sebastian Auchinek bent an ear towards the Dynatron cabinet stereo to which was attached, five pin DIN to five pin DIN, Jerry's little cassette tape recorder. "Well, it's certainly different, isn't it?" He added: "Man."

"It's underground music," Jerry explained.

"Yeah, ther bleedin' eight-forty-five ter Aldgate, by ther sarnd o' it!" Mrs. Cornelius laughed as she put two cups of cocoa on the surface of Jerry's battered amplifier. They were in Jerry's room at Blenheim Crescent. The untidy bed was littered with magazines, of a different kind from his mother's, and most of the rest of the space was given over to valves, wires and speakers, the majority of which didn't work. "Sorry, I'm shore!" said Mrs. Cornelius. She departed, closing his door in a pantomime of courtesy.

Luckily Sebastian Auchinek's sense of humour functioned only in direct relation to his own sense of despair. He puzzled over the music. He removed his little hat. He sucked at his huge lower lip. He rubbed his monstrous nose. "But will it catch on with the general public? That's what we have to think about—Jerry? You don't mind?"

"No, no. 'Course not." Jerry looked anxiously into the liquid eyes of the handsome promoter. "You've heard of The Pink Floyd, haven't you? They're getting quite popular."

"Oh, yes. I don't doubt it. But you know what public taste's like. Twinkle one week, Mojos the next. Whether this sort of music's got any future—I honestly don't know.

I can see you're serious. But are you commercial? I'm sorry." Sebastian Auchinek held up a shapely hand as if to ward off a light blow. He put his cap down. "It's what we have to think about, *if* we're going to back you. It still boils down to investments. You're a talented boy, I don't doubt it. I mean, what we have to say to our-selves is—How do we promote this kind of music? All right, we can get a minor record company to do one LP—but it's the singles market that's important. I can't see any of this as single material, quite frankly. Miss Persson led me to understand that you were more of an R&B group. Like Graham Bond and Brian Auger. We're considering them at the moment."

"We don't do that sort of thing any more," said Jerry with a certain disdain. "Una said you were into progres-sive stuff."

"We are. We are. But we have to *see* it. In context. We have to be able to feel we can do something positive for a group. It wouldn't be fair to you, would it, if we just took you on and then did nothing?"

"Yes, I can see that. . . ."

"Maybe if I came along and heard you at your next gig?"

"That's why I'm talking to you. We can't get any gigs."

"Not even locally?"

"There aren't any local venues, are there?"

"It's difficult, isn't it?"

Jerry turned the recorder off. The hissing had begun to irritate him. "Some people think we're ahead of our time."

"Could be. When's your next rehearsal?" Auchinek was eager to prove to Jerry that his mind was still open.

"I'm not sure. We have trouble finding places."

"Well, look, get in touch with me when you know what your plans are. Maybe I can fix up a rehearsal room for you."

"It'd be something, anyway. Thanks."

Sebastian Auchinek removed a leather-bound note-book from his inside pocket. He clicked a ballpoint with his thumb. "What's the name of the group?"

"The Deep Fix."

"You might have to change that a bit. It's not really—you know. . . . The BBC's still a power in the land, eh?

They don't like drugs. Have you thought of any other names?"

"Yes," said Jerry. "The Cocksuckers."

Sebastian Auchinek managed a small smile. "Well, we'll talk about that when the time comes." He tore a page from the book. "Here's my office number. Keep in touch. Leave a message with my secretary if I'm not there. Don't think I'm being negative. And remember—I'm not the only promoter on the beach."

He looked around for his corduroy Dylan cap. He had put it on top of his cocoa.

MRS. C. AND COLONEL P.

"Of course," said Colonal Pyat as he poured Mrs. Cornelius another gin, "we lost everything in the war, including our titles. My uncle had a very big estate not far from Lublin. And his father, you know, had an even bigger one in the Ukraine. He was shot by Makhno who in turn was shot by Trotsky who was killed by Stalin." He shrugged and his smile was crooked. "So it goes." He fell back into Mrs. C.'s best armchair, the white plastic one, his eyes fixing on the silent television screen. The warped monochrome picture displayed a nurse, a nun and a black man in a hospital bed.

"We're surpposed ter be related ter '*im*," said Mrs. Cornelius, brushing crisp crumbs from her pink cotton lap. "Shouldn't eat crisps. They make yer sweat."

"My uncle?"

"Nar! The ovver one. Trotsky, innit? Though I 'eard 'e corled 'isself somefink else. Brahn or somefink."

"Bronstein. His real name was Bronstein. Jewish, you see."

"Nar! It woz nuffink forin'." She raised her glass. "Darn the 'atch then."

Bemused, the drunken colonel imitated her action.

"It's more comfy 'ere, innit, than ther pub?" said Mrs. Cornelius. She could see that Colonel P was a gent (even though currently in need of a spot of luck) by the cut of his greasy tweed jacket, his shiny flannels: but his breeding was revealed by his bearing rather than his clothes, she supposed. And he hadn't hesitated to fork out for a half bottle of gin when she'd taken a fancy to him and suggested coming back here. Tonight wasn't the first time she had seen him in the Blenheim, of course, but it was the first time she'd had a chance to have a decent chat.

"Definitely Brahn," she said. Her expression softened. She moved closer to Colonel Pyat. He looked at her through wary, red-rimmed eyes. He stroked the stubble of his chin. "Is Pyat yore real name, then?"

"Well, it's my official name, you know. In the last war. . . ."

From the next room, Jerry's, there suddenly came the ear-splitting squawk of a feeding-back amplifier. She was shocked. It hadn't occurred to her to check if her son was in. Automatically she lifted her great red head and raised her voice:

"I thort yer said you woz garn art ternight! Turn that fuckin' thing darn!"

"Pardon?" thickly said Colonel Pyat.

"Not you, Kernewl. Sorry. Turn it darn, carn't ya!"

"I meant to go back after the war." Colonel Pyat raised a sorrowful glass to his lips. "I was in intelligence, you know. Liaison officer for your chaps. Stuck here when the war ended. But, naturally. . . ." He shrugged.

She was vaguely sympathetic. "The Russians, eh?"

"Worse than the Germans."

"But I thort you said you *woz* Russian."

"No, no—I was *with* the Russians."

"Oh really? Where woz that?"

A high-pitched shriek filled the flat.

"My God!" Colonel P. covered his ears. His eyes hunted about the room. He stared through the window as if he expected the sky to fill with planes.

" 'Ang on a sec." Carefully Mrs. Cornelius got to her broad feet. "Ooo." She coughed. "It's me kid," she said.

Before she could reach Jerry's door the sound from behind it had changed again, rising and falling, so that now it resembled the distant wailing of some demented creature of the sea.

EARLY REPORTS

Scotland Yard will keep up its drive to recruit black policemen despite the failure of the campaign so far. Revealing this yesterday Metropolitan Police Commissioner Sir Robert Mark said: "We won't take No for an answer. We shall keep at it."

Daily Mirror, 31 March 1976

The chances of our moderate climate changing soon to a prolonged cold spell, but not glacial, are high, Dr. E. J. Mason, FRS, director general of the Meteorological Office, suggested last night. With the caution of a man carrying ultimate responsibility for the precision of the official day-to-day weather forecasting methods, he added: "There is no real basis for the alarmist predictions of an imminent ice age, which have largely been based on extrapolation of the 30-year trend of falling temperatures in the northern hemisphere between 1940 and 1965. Apart from the strong dubiety of making a forecast from such a short-period trend, there is now evidence that the trend has been arrested."

Guardian, 18 March 1976

The annual meeting of the National Front voted in London at the weekend to expel all members who are of mixed race, non-European ancestry or coloured. About 20-25 members are affected. But yesterday, Mr. Eugene Pierce, an Anglo-Indian accountant who has been a member of the National Front and walked out of the meeting in protest at the vote said: "I was immediately assured by members of the directorate that the vote was only a recommendation. . . ." Mr. Pierce, 65, whose British grandfather married an Indian, earlier told the meeting: "I was a member of the British army, along with thousands of other Anglo-Indians." But the meeting became increasingly noisy and his words were drowned in the uproar. "'We have to be 100 percent racialist in the National Front," said the mover of the resolution, Mr. Bert Wilton, of Southwark, London, to loud applause: "If people who are half or quarter coloured are allowed in, it will kill everything."

Guardian, 6 January 1975

Police frogmen were hunting for more bodies yesterday after the cut-up remains of two teenage sisters were found in a lake in the Catskill Mountains, 110 miles north of New York. The self-styled "Bishop of Brooklyn," 51-year-old Vernon Legrand, leader of a bizarre religious cult, has been charged with the murders.

Daily Mirror, 15 March 1976

Two members of a British-based religious sect are believed to have been the victims of ritual killings. Police think that they were hypnotised—and then vital organs in their bodies were crushed. The probe began after the body of artist Michel Piersotte was found at the foot of the 250 ft Citadel in Namur, Belgium. Michel was a member of the Children of God sect, whose international headquarters is at Bromley in Kent. A post-mortem revealed that his liver and kidneys were crushed, as though in a vice. Police decided to re-open an inquiry into the death of another member of the sect. This was 20-year-old Jean Maurice, who was found dead at the foot of the Citadel in Dinant, Belgium, in December. Again police established that vital organs had been crushed. The men were close friends. They were believed to be trying to break away from the sect. A Belgian police spokesman said last night: "We're studying a Scotland Yard report about the sect." The report says that hypnotism is used at indoctrination ceremonies. Youngsters are encouraged to break off all ties with their parents.

Daily Mirror, 15 March 1976

TUNING UP (2)

Jerry hauled on the reins to bring the lead dog to a sudden stop. At once the other dogs lay down in their traces, the breath from their pink panting mouths melting the surrounding snow. The small red sun overhead was the only bright colour in the dark grey sky, the only light, yet it was possible to see for miles over the twilight landscape to a range of mountains in the north-west, to the black line of the horizon elsewhere. It had taken him months to reach Lappland, travelling mostly by sled. He hauled a sack from the wicker rack behind him and began to walk along the line, throwing the dogs chunks of skinned half-frozen wolf. As he reached the lead dog and produced a larger than average lump of meat from the sack he heard in the distance a bass drone, coming from the direction of the mountains. He recognised the motor of an old Westland Whirlwind and automatically looked about for cover. There was none, save the sled. He pulled his bow and his quiver of arrows from beneath the furs and bric-a-brac on the main section and prepared for the worst. Things were waking up a little sooner than he had anticipated. He supposed that, in spite of the immediate problems, he was relieved. At least the birth (or re-birth, depending how you look at it) had been relatively easy this time.

The big chopper appeared in the sky, black and glimmering, and the dogs looked up from their flesh, eyes bright, ears pointing. One of them snarled; Jerry was sure that they had not responded to any specific stimulus. They were a strange breed of huskies, with red eyes, white coats and red-tipped ears.

Snow began to fly. Clouds seemed to form just above
the surface. The helicopter came down heavily, still
only partially powered, bumping and groaning. The motor
was switched off. In the stillness the rotors clacked slowly
to a halt. Jerry saw muffled figures moving inside the
breath-clouded canopy. He fitted an arrow to his bow as
a door in the Whirlwind's body opened and a woman descended. She had a large 7.63 mm Borchardt automatic
pistol in her gloved right hand. Her face was hidden in
the hood of an ankle-length Panda-skin parka. Her breath
coiled from shrouded lips as she peered towards the sled.
She walked with a kind of Sarah Bernhardt limp.

"Mr. Cornelius?" The voice was sharp, demanding.

"Which Mr. Cornelius would that be?" Jerry recognised
her at once.

Miss Brunner was her usual petulant self. "Oh, don't be
silly. What have you got in your hands?"

"A bow and arrow."

She buried her pistol in her clothing. "I understand. Put
it away." She held up her heavy arms.

"Oh, sure." Jerry indicated the swivelling gun-turret in
the chopper.

She shrugged. "Merely a gesture. You know there's
little chance of a gun working in the current moral climate. What are you doing in Lappland? Looking for
someone?"

"Just trying to recapture the past."

"That's not like the old Jerry."

"I can't say the same for you. But then I always admired your consistency."

"There's a bit more mass than there used to be." It was
obvious that she had taken his remark for a compliment.
"You look like a mountie. Well, what do you want from
us?"

"Nothing," he said. "I didn't even know you were out,
did I?"

She became suspicious. "Aha." The snow crunched.
She moved tentatively forward. The dog snarled again,
pricking its peculiar ears. She stopped, glaring at it in considerable dislike. "You won't be able to get to the laboratory. Not for a while. It'll be frozen up. Is that where
you were thinking of going?"

"I haven't been thinking much at all. You don't in these

conditions. I suppose I was making for the lab. Instinct."

"Instinct!" She cackled. "You!"

She had hurt his feelings. "It's the only explanation I can think of. You were heading south. Does that mean you've been to the lab already?"

"That's how I know about it. We came via Russia. And before that Canada. We've been flying for ages."

Luxuriously Jerry inspected the vast sky, half expecting to see a formation of geese, but it was still empty. "It's probably the spring," he said.

INTRODUCTION

On New Year's Night, 1091, a certain priest called
Gauchelin was terrified by a procession of women, warriors, monks, etc. who swept past him, dressed in black,
half-hidden by flames, and wailing aloud. Astonished and
dismayed, the priest said to himself: "Doubtless this is the
Cornelius family. I have heard that it has formerly been
seen by many people, but I have mocked at such tales.
Now, indeed, I myself have truly seen the ghosts of the
dead." Gauchelin was, indeed, neither the first nor the last
to see the notorious "maisnie Cornelius" (Harlequin-
troupe), which appeared so frequently both in mediaeval
France and England. For Harlequin (Harlechin, Helle-
quin, etc., are all variations of the same word) appears
first in history or legend as an aerial spectre or demon,
leading that ghostly nocturnal cortège known as the Wild
Hunt.

Enid Welsford, *The Fool: His Social and Literary
History*, London, 1934

Prince Philip Opens Dream Flats in W.10

Trains roared behind a VIP canopy, the sun popped out suddenly and children whistled from the roof-tops when the Duke of Edinburgh arrived in dreary North Kensington on Tuesday afternoon (to open) Pepler House, the biggest project to date by the Kensington Housing Trust.

KENSINGTON POST, 12 November 1965

1. The dog-fight missile designed to dominate its decade

Jerry struggled into his pink tweed Cardin suit. The waistcoat was a little tight and he had to undo the shoulder holster by a notch but otherwise he looked as sharp as he had always done. He pulled his needler free and checked that the magazine was full, each hollow dart containing a neat 50ccs of Librium: a perfect hunting charge. He smoothed his long, fine hair about his face as he stood in front of the looking-glass, well-satisfied, in the circumstances, with his appearance. He checked his watches. Both waited at zero. He crossed his wrists and started the watches. The hands moved at a steady rate.

"Pretty," he said. He smirked. He faced the room, squinting in the glare from the white plastic furniture, the neon, the ivory walls. He took mirror shades from his top pocket and slid them over his eyes. He sighed. "Nifty."

He sailed out into the currents of the day, high on painkillers and a sense of his own immortality, swinging his hips to the sound of Eleanor Rigby from the receiver built into his unfashionably rigid collar, down Holland Park Avenue beneath the tall spring trees, stepping wide on two-inch Cuban heels. The bravest dandy of them all: he had a smile for everybody. Under his breath he sang along with John, George, Paul and Ringo and turned right into Campden Hill Square where his great big Duesenberg, chocolate and cream, waited for him alone. He unlocked the door, slid behind the wheel, started the perfect supercharged straight-8, let go the brakes and was on the move. A masterpiece to equal any one of its European contemporaries, the 1930 SJ Torpedo Phaeton was the most elegant car America had ever produced. Euphorically, both mind and body in ecstatic unity, he cruised between the labouring corpse-waggons which parted so that he could pass through them, as if by divine command. He offered a friendly wave to all he overtook, then he reached the top of Ladbroke Grove's hill and began the descent into the mythical netherworld of Notting Dale. The road was suddenly almost deserted; sounds were muffled; the sun was hotter.

Turning right into Westbourne Park Road he stopped outside the main gate of the Convent of the Poor Clares. He did not bother to lock the car. He knew he could rely on its aura to protect it.

Sister Eugenia, the Mother Superior, herself greeted Jerry as she opened the grilled steel door which led directly into the shadowy Visitors' Chapel with its hideous green, yellow and pink Crucifixion above the green marble tiles, the brass, the tasselled purple of the altar. She spoke in carefully modulated tones like a consultant psychiatrist and when she smiled it was sweet and good. Jerry admired her smile in particular, as he admired professionalism wherever he found it.

"Father Jeremiah." She gestured for him to precede her while she supervised the tender young novice locking the gate. They followed single file behind him as he headed through the side exit and onto a gravel path, making for the main building, smelling the air, admiring the blooms and the well-kept lawns, the peculiar, ingrown dwarf elms. He was not sure but he thought he heard, somewhere in the chapel on his left, the second part of Messiaen's *Turangalila Symphony*. He pressed his head against his collar and cut off the Beatles, looking enquiringly back at the Mother Superior. "A record?"

"Oh, no!" The Mother Superior was amused. Behind her the soft little novice giggled.

They reached the main building and climbed steps into quiet passages, arriving at last at the second floor and the Mother Superior's office which looked out onto the garden. It seemed to Jerry, surreptitiously sniffing the air, that the infirmary was nearby. At her desk the Mother Superior lowered herself into her high-backed Windsor chair, signing for Jerry to sit in the chair's twin facing her. "It is a very great pleasure to see you again, Father Jeremiah. You are looking well."

"And you, too, Sister Eugenia. Congratulations on your appointment. . . ."

"I pray that I will fulfill. . . ."

". . . there can be no question. . . ."

"You are kind. It seems such a short time since you took confession at Harrogate. How greatly our lives have changed. Your own responsibilities. . . ."

He dismissed them. "I'm very grateful for what you've been able to do."

"The poor child. I was glad to help. She's perfectly safe here and will be until—?"

"Eventually, of course, it will be possible for her to leave."

"How is Father—?"

"We no longer communicate, I fear. But I hear he is in good health. In France."

"He has similar duties to your own, then? There were rumours of dissolution. . . ."

"Nobody's perfect."

She was full of sympathy. It was almost as if she restrained herself from reaching across the desk and touching his hand. "The burden . . ." she murmured.

"It's born of joy."

Her eyes shone. "You have a vocation."

"I'm due for one. I hope so."

"Oh, you have!" Her smooth features were radiant. "You're an inspiration to us all."

He accepted this with modest dignity.

She reached into a desk drawer and produced a ledger. "I regret the formality." She found the appropriate page and offered him the book. He removed a large Mont Blanc fountain pen from his inside breast pocket and signed his name and title in full, giving his usual tasteless flourish to the initials S. and J. She looked with pleasure upon the signature for a moment before putting the book away. She took some keys from the desk. "These are such dangerous times. You risk so much in coming."

"I gain much." Once again he heard the sound of music. This time they were playing Schoenberg's *Pierrot Lunaire*.

"You're too kind."

They left the office, passed the infirmary, descended

three flights of steps. Jerry realised, by the artificial lighting, that they were underground. This passage, with its stout doors at regular intervals on both sides, all painted the same olive green, was much colder. The Mother Superior stopped at the end of the passage, the last door. She unlocked it. "I'll leave you with her. She needs your help. I am so glad. . . ."

"Thank you."

"When shall I . . .?"

"In two hours."

"Very well." Another admiring, insinuating smile and she had departed. Jerry pushed the door open.

His sister Catherine looked up from her iron-frame bed. A little daylight entered the cell from a small window near the roof, a single exquisite ray, but she had been reading with the help of an electric lamp, its 40 watt bulb shielded by a shade of green glass. She looked much better than when he had last seen her. Her hair was pure blonde again and her skin was rosy. She was wearing her shift and she automatically reached for her white habit, hanging over the chair beside the bed, before she grinned and dropped her hand. She spread her arms wide. He closed the door and bolted it. He stood over her, grinning down, all his lost innocence momentarily restored.

"You don't half look sinister," she said. "What are you playing at today?"

"I'm the tortured priest, aren't I?" With a flourish he removed his shades.

"Did you come to add another sin or two to your conscience?"

He sat down beside her. He hugged her warm, yielding body. "You've really improved."

"I couldn't have had a nicer rest. You told them I had amnesia?"

"To save explanations. Anyway, I was right, in some ways." He bent away from her, studying her face. "Not a bad resurrection job, though I say it myself."

She frowned. "I'm steering clear of hard drugs in the future. It's taught me a lesson. Nothing stronger than coke from now on."

"I think you're wise."

She stroked his hair. "No. You're the wise one. What a lovely pink suit. Omniscient old Jerry."

"Don't say that. You'll bring all my anxieties back." He removed his jacket and threw it on top of her habit, leaning across the bed so that he was resting against the wall. "I must say I envy you the peace and quiet."

"You've never liked peace and quiet."

"I envy it, all the same." He stroked her right breast through the coarse linen of her shift. She seemed unusually disturbed. "Is anything wrong?"

She held his hand against her breast. "I was wondering why you sent that other bloke along to see me. He didn't look like one of your usual friends."

"I didn't send another bloke."

Her lovely shoulders slumped. "The gaff's blown, then. Frank will know where I am now."

"Blokes aren't normally allowed in at all. What did he look like? How did he get in?"

"Fat and oily. Purple shirt. Gaiters. Dog-collar. Definitely clerical gear. Plummy voice. Apparently he was surveying the place for some reason. He knew me. So I realised. . . ."

"Beesley?"

"That's the name."

"Sod." Jerry sighed as he drew off his pink tweed trousers and folded them over the back of the chair. "You're right, Cath. He's Frank's mate. The Bishop of North Kensington. Though how he managed to get to see you is still a mystery."

"Pulled strings." She removed her shift and handed it to him as he unbuttoned his waistcoat. Absent-mindedly he held the shift in one hand and unstrapped his shoulder holster. He put everything in a bundle on the chair and began to remove his shirt and tie, then his socks and underpants. He drew trim brows together. "He's good at pulling strings."

Jerry paused, hands on hips, trying to order his thoughts. Then he glanced up, noticing that her expression had changed to one of open astonishment. Her wide blue eyes stared at his lower torso.

"What's the matter?" he asked her.

"When on earth did you get yourself circumcised?"

In puzzlement he fingered his penis. Vaguely he shook his head, grinning. He shrugged, dismissing the problem as he squeezed in beside her. She switched off the light. The ray of sunshine, like the light from some new-found grail, fell upon their heads. He took her bottom in both his large hands. "You're not the only one prone to amnesia, you know."

2. Matra ubiquity with 2nd and 3rd generation missiles

The gate of the convent closed behind him and Jerry adjusted his eyes to the light, resuming his shades, making for his Duesenberg. As he had half-expected Frank was sitting in the back seat. "Watcher, Jerry. Long time no see." He grinned through the wound-down window, his drug-ravaged lips twisting in peculiar directions. "Your education's certainly coming in useful, these days."

Jerry sighed. He looked down at Frank. "What are you doing here?"

"I was just passing, recognised the motor, thought I'd give you a surprise."

"It's no surprise. I already know your mucker's been in the convent."

"Oh, really? I haven't seen Dennis for ages."

"Get out of my car," said Jerry. "You're coming to bits all over the upholstery. You used to be such a nice young man, too."

"I'm a martyr to science, that's my trouble. I abandoned a lucrative profession in the property business in order to further my researches and thus become a slave to tempodex." Frank's skin twitched all over. Then, as Jerry watched, he changed to the colour of grey flannel. Frank had always had a penchant towards respectability. "I feel sick."

Jerry opened the door and bundled his brother to the pavement.

Frank went to lean with one hand against the convent wall. "Come on, Jerry. Blood's thicker than water."

"Not in your case. There's no need for you to be out on the street. You've got a home to go to. Several."

"I'm having an identity crisis. How's Catherine?"

"Much better."

"Better? That's funny." Frank pulled his cracked plastic flying jacket around his shivering chest. His horrid head lifted like a pointer on the scent. His eyes glazed but seemed to fix on an invisible target. He began, stiff-legged, to walk in the general direction of Lancaster Road. "Well, see you around, Jerry. Got to—um. . . ."

Jerry sank into his car and watched Frank march like a zombie across Ladbroke Grove and into the Kensington Park Hotel. The KPH had not been used as a hotel for some years and was now merely a large pub. Surely Frank hadn't come down to scoring from dealers in public houses? Jerry felt that his family pride was under attack but he resisted the urge to follow. Probably the KPH was no more than one of Frank's bolt-holes. Doubtless it led somewhere else.

At this, Jerry became suspicious. He recalled a rumour he had heard from a fourteen-year-old biker speed freak who had given him a lift when his Phantom had been shot up by local vigilantes just outside Birmingham. According to the biker there was at least one ancient tunnel running under Ladbroke Grove from the Convent of the Poor Clares. The tunnel, the speed freak had told him, led into all sorts of other dimensions. It was a familiar rumour. A family legend hinted at something similar. Jerry had paid the story very little attention; he had been only too glad that a little romance was coming back into the lives of the younger generation. But now he recalled Bishop Beesley's excuse for visiting the convent. Something about a survey. Perhaps Beesley had had a double purpose for going there.

Jerry stepped out of the Duesenberg with the intention of ringing the bell of the convent but then he changed his mind. He had already tipped off Catherine and there was not much else he could do until he found a new hideout for her, at least until her amnesia was completely cleared up.

He returned to the driving seat, started the car, reversed into Ladbroke Grove, drove as far as the KPH, stopped and got out. He entered the ill-lit pub. Frank was there, talking to a couple of undersized girls who, by the look of their skins and eyes, had been helping him in his experiments. Even as Jerry came in he saw Frank stoop and kiss one of the girls full on the mouth, seeming to suck the last of her substance from her. Now she was in pretty much the condition in which Frank had been a moment or two ago. She stumbled towards the door marked Toilets and disappeared. Frank wiped his mouth and grinned. "Hello Jerry. What are you having?" He put a seedy elbow on the damp bar and attracted the landlord. "Sid!" Through the gloom came service.

"I thought you might want a lift," said Jerry.

"I've just had one. Two pints, please, Sid," said Frank. "Could you manage to get these, Jerry?"

Jerry put a ten-pound note into the pool of alcohol on the greasy counter. "You know I don't drink beer."

"It's for Maureen." Frank winked at the remaining grey girl. The beer arrived and Frank handed over his brother's money. "You can have Barbara, if you like. When she comes back from the lavatory."

"Well," said Jerry. "Don't you want a lift, then?"

"How far would you be going?"

"How far do you want to go?"

"Get you!" said Frank. "France?"

"Don't be silly."

"I was thinking of taking up residence in the old place. The Le Corbusier chateau. There's a lot of ideas I've got. Following in father's footsteps, following the dear old dad. There again I could open it to the public."

Jerry shuddered. "It's not a real Le Corbusier chateau."

Frank shrugged. "There's no need to be so fucking literal minded, Jerry."

"I'll take you as far as Dover, if you like."

Frank's eyes narrowed. Mucus seemed to squeeze from the corners. Red irises shifted in decaying sockets. "I wasn't thinking of leaving for a day or so."

Jerry folded his arms. "It's now or never."

"You're right." Frank looked vaguely around for a clock. "It always bloody is."

3. Acquire targets simply, reliably and accurately with inland direct-drive tracking and guidance servo elements

They had reached a compromise. Dropping his brother off at the Army and Navy Club near Waterloo Station, wondering when Frank would try to get hold of Catherine, Jerry drove back to his house in Holland Park Avenue. Frank would almost certainly act in the next couple of days: he ran in old grooves; he would want to take Catherine with him to France. Jerry couldn't blame him. The weather was perfect. There was, in fact, something remarkable about the whole season. He had never known the world so fresh. Jerry smacked his lips.

London was alive with flowers; gigantic hydrangeas and chrysanthemums, monstrous carnations, vast tulips and looming daffodils; sweet williams, peonies, cornflowers, snapdragons, hollyhocks, foxgloves; their scent hung like vapour in the beautiful air. And people were wearing such pretty clothes, listening to such jolly music; the first ecstatic flush of a culture about to swoon, at last, into magnificent decadence, an orgy of mutual understanding, kindness, tolerance and a refusal to maim or kill. Jerry turned on the Duesenberg's stereo and got Jimi Hendrix singing *Waterfall*. He leaned back, a casual hand on the wheel. The Dubrovnik disease certainly had its compensations. It was all a matter of how you looked at things. As he entered Hyde Park he found other signs of the improving times as gangs of men and women in bright blue municipal uniforms dismantled the gallows on either side of the road. He reached towards the spring-clip on the dashboard and removed the half-full paper-cup, swallowing a snazzy fifth of Glen Nevis to unclog the jam of uppers and downers in his throat. For a moment he had an urge to turn back the way he had come and shoot a few pins in Emmett's but decided, after all, to go home. He had to do something about his head lice.

He had stashed the car at the side entrance of his fortress and had walked round the tall white walls and up the steps to the black front door before he saw a movement behind one of the pillars on his right. His hand swam for his needler but dropped. He smiled instead. "Afternoon, Mo."

" 'Ullo, Mr. C." By way of apology Shakey Mo Collier shrugged in his filthy denim suit. His bright, kitten's eyes, greedy for violence, shifted, and his scrubby moustache and beard twitched like the whiskers of a rogue beast. "Can I come in?"

Jerry put his hand against the print-plate and the door opened. He led the way into a wide, mosaic hall, turning off strobes and substituting limelight. Mo panted behind him muttering to himself. "Oh, fuck. Oh, fuck." He scuttled for a side door and entered Jerry's back parlour, a tangle of electronics and dirty, expensive upholstery. The room was dark, only a little light coming through the thickly curtained french windows. Mo crawled into the comfort of a huge mohair sofa, feeling down its sides for something to sustain him, slipping pills and capsules at random into his mouth. "What's it all about, I ask myself." Quickly he achieved a philosophical equilibrium. "Eh, Mr. C?"

Jerry pulled the curtains back a fraction. "You don't mind?" Light sidled into the room.

Mo nodded. "I came with a message, actually. Shades is on the dole and wondered if you had any ideas."

"I thought he was in the States."

"Things have dried up there, as well. You know how fashions change. Last year it was all assassinations, this year it's all sex scandals and religion. Could we have a little music?"

Jerry fiddled with an already glowing console. Faintly Zoot Money's band gave them *Big Time Operator*.

"That'll do," said Mo. "It doesn't need to be loud. Just there. Anyway, Shades thought you might be looking around."

Jerry smiled. "You have to, don't you, with Shades. Tell him I'll probably be in touch."

Mo nodded. "He says all he needs is a pair of kings."

"It's good news for everyone else." Absently Jerry toyed with a decaying packet of Chocolate Olivers. "Though his interpretations are all his own."

"And I saw Mr. Smiles. He says to get in touch sometime. It's about what Simons and Harvey are after, he says."

Jerry shrugged. "All that's in the past." He glanced through an electron microscope. "Or maybe the future."

Mo had lost interest in the conversation. He began to move slowly about the room, experimentally fingering any loose wires he discovered. "Oh, and I saw your mum in the pub. When was it? Tuesday?"

"Did you tell her I was back?"

"What do you think? But she'd heard you was living around here. She was more interested in knowing where Cathy was."

Jerry smiled at this. "They always were close."

"She said Frank was doing very well for himself but was looking a bit tired. What is he doing with himself, these days, anyway?"

"Services," said Jerry. "Power and communications."

"Only I heard he was dealing."

"It's the same thing, isn't it?"

"Everything is. . . ." Mo returned to the sofa and curled up. He went to sleep. Jerry pulled a huge silver metallic sheet over him to retain what heat was left in his body and headed for the kitchen. He searched amongst the collection of Coronation biscuit barrels and jugs and cottage-shaped tea-pots until he found the half-full bottle of Prioderm. He climbed the stained white carpet of the curving staircase and went into the bathroom, glad to find that the hot water was working in the shower. He stripped naked and, bottle in hand, stepped into the stall.

Soon his head was engulfed in hellfire.

4. Introducing a new dimension of realism in visual simulators, Vital III

Jerry rarely visited his father's fake Le Corbusier chateau and this was probably the first time he had used the front entrance, but he was in unusually high spirits as he eased his Phantom V up the weed-grown drive and depressed the horn button to let his father's faithful retainer know he had arrived. Beyond the broken outline of the house was the grey Normandy sea. Rain was coming in from England and with it waves of inspirational music interspersed with the babbling voices of that crazed brotherhood of the coast, the pirate deejays. Jerry stepped out of the car and took a deep breath of the cold, moody air. His father—or the man who had claimed to be his father —had died without leaving a will, so Frank (who was convinced that he was both the only legitimate and the true spiritual successor to the old man) had claimed the house and its contents as his inheritance; but John Gnatbeelson swore the dying scientist had bequeathed his roof and its secrets to his namesake Jeremiah (there was even a rumour that old Cornelius had changed his name to Jeremiah soon after his son had been born). The matter had been settled, in Jerry's view, by his letting Frank use the place whenever he wanted to. In spite of the complications, Jerry had been glad that his father had died. It removed an uncomfortable ambiguity. Jerry hated keeping things from his mother.

Before he could put his palm against the print-plate the grey steel door moved upwards and John Gnatbeelson, in tattered Norfolk jacket, grey moleskin britches and scarlet carpet slippers, greeted him awkwardly. He was thin, his cancerous skin given a semblance of life by the many broken blood-vessels spreading purple and red beneath it. His chin sprouted a few long, grey wisps of hair, perhaps the remains of a beard, and his cheek-bones were set so low as to give his head an oddly unbalanced look. A stooping six-foot-four, he looked fondly down on his young master who strode into the dark interior. Originally the house had possessed enormous windows, but these were now shielded with steel-plate. As old Cornelius's suspicion of the outside world had increased he had introduced more and more modifications of this sort.

"Have you come to stay, sir?" Gnatbeelson whispered habitually. His former employer had hated the sound of the human voice and had communicated almost entirely by a variety of mechanical means, never leaving his heavily guarded laboratories. Neither Jerry, Catherine or Frank had ever met their father personally, though they had all lived here from time to time. The house trembled with profound and unusual memories; it stank of the experiences of a hundred lifetimes, centuries of technomania tinged with the desperate eroticism of those who cast desperately about for their lost humanity and found only flesh.

"Just a flying visit," Jerry said. "I'd have phoned, but you've been cut off."

"The bill seemed unreasonable, sir. It was all Mr. Frank's reverse charge calls. I did write to you. . . ."

"As long as the generators are working."

"I tested them last week. They're just fine."

"I want you to activate the defences as soon as possible," Jerry told him. He walked rapidly through haunted galleries, Gnatbeelson, his limbs moving irregularly, lolloping in his wake. "Particularly those towers."

"The hypnomats, sir?"

"Set every one at go."

"Are you expecting trouble, Mr. Cornelius?"

"From Mr. Frank. He's on his way. I don't know what he's up to, but I know it involves this place. He mustn't get in."

"I thought you didn't mind, sir."

"I don't normally."

"Is anything up, sir? Some sort of situation?"

"It's all instinctive. I couldn't really pin it down."

"I've been reading about it in the book, sir. The millennium and so on."

Jerry stopped as the corridor opened onto another gallery. He looked down through filthy light at the scattered shells of computers, their innards spread at random over the large black and white tiles of the floor. "That wasn't here last time." He put his hand on the balustrade, close to a fragment of canvas on which had been painted a patchwork of red, yellow and blue diamond shapes, faintly bloodstained. His foot struck a gilt frame on the floor. "The sod's eaten it!" He was shocked. "Watteau!"

"What ho, sir. . . ." Gnatbeelson's face sagged a little lower. "Mr. Frank was looking for something, I think. He kept sucking at those vacuum tubes in the corner. He said the marrow was good for his piles. He's not himself, sir."

"Then who is?" Jerry put the scrap of canvas into his pocket and continued his inspection of the house.

"I'm glad you've decided on a firm line at last, sir." Gnatbeelson's legs bent and straightened, bent and straightened. "I took the liberty of saving one of those books you gave me to put in the furnace. *The Million Spears and the Coming Corruption*. Do you think—?"

"It's lies. It's your moral duty to burn it."

"Then of course I shall, sir. But are you sure this isn't to do with that?"

"It's all a question of how you look at it. What about the reactor?" Jerry peered over the rail of another gallery. Below was a swimming pool, the water stagnant, filled with every kind of rubbish. Something living seemed to move just below the surface. "I've changed my mind. Things are settling down. They've never been better."

"Then why are you so anxious?" The whisper came from miles away but when Jerry turned Gnatbeelson was at his shoulder.

"Because I want to maintain the balance. I've a right to take a few precautions." Jerry was defensive. "What's wrong with that?" He peered down at the far wall. Written in a substance resembling, in colour, the ichor of spent batteries, were the words:

Encore un de mes pierrots mort;
Morte d'un chronique orphelinisme;

*C'était un coeur plein de dandyisme
Lunaire, en un drôle de corps.*

Jerry became sentimental. "How we loved to luxuriate
in terror." There had been good times here, when the
three of them had spent their holidays, at play amongst
their father's discarded inventions, stretched upon heaps
of confused circuits, with a bag of apples and a
Wodehouse or a Sade. Simpler, if not sunnier, days.

"I'm in full agreement with you, sir." The old retainer's
voice seemed closer now, almost normal. "But why have
you rejected all those books out of hand?"

Desperately Jerry rounded on Gnatbeelson, displaying
glowing eyes. "Can't you see? It's my last bloody chance
to achieve a linear mode!"

5. Need actuators that won't freeze, burn, dry out, or boil?

It might be 196–, thought Jerry, but the countryside beyond Dover had returned with incredible speed to its mediaeval state. Kent was wild and beautiful again; so lush that few would have guessed it had sustained and recovered from a major nuclear bombardment during the "Proof of Good Faith" contests between the major powers. There were disadvantages: poor roads and slow progress; but his car wasn't badly affected, even when it was forced to inch through bramble thickets or cross small patches of ploughed land where angry peasants occasionally appeared, to pelt him with pieces of rock or crude spears. The people of Kent, happy at last in their proper primitive state, were much more at one with themselves.

A fairly unspoiled stretch of road took him close to the remains of Canterbury where skin-clad monks had erected a timber reproduction of the Cathedral, almost the same size as the original. The unseasoned scaffolding still surrounded it and more monks were at work with what was probably liquified chalk, painting the exterior in an effort to make it resemble stone. Elsewhere a project to restore the shopping precinct was in hand; soon Canterbury in facsimile would flourish again: triumph of Man's optimism, of his faith in the future. Jerry hooted his horn and waved, turning up the stereo, to give them a friendly blast of *Got To Get You Into My Life,* pursing his lips regretfully as one of the monks lost his footing on the scaffold and fell fifty feet to the ground.

Soon he was nearing London. In the evening light the city was phosphorescent, like a neon wound; it glowed beneath a great scarlet sun turning the clouds orange and purple. And Jerry was filled with a sudden deep love for his noble birthplace, the City of the Apocalypse, this Earthly Paradise, the oldest and greatest city of its Age, virgin and whore, mother, sister, mistress, sustainer of life, creator of nightmare, destroyer of dreams, harborer of twenty million chosen souls. Abruptly he left the middle ages and entered the future, the great grey road, a mile wide at this point, gradually narrowing to its apex at Piccadilly Circus. Now, as night drenched the tall buildings and their lights burst into shivering life, he could again relax in his natural environment.

Against all the available evidence he was betting everything on simple cyclic time, on cause and effect, on karma. He passed through the first toll-check; now the road was covered; its perspex roof reflected the myriad colours of the headlamps below. He took the first exit up to the fast tier and joined the hundred and seventy mph stream; within a minute or two he was leaving it again, spiralling down the Notting Hill exit and making for home through the crowded park. The booths and tents of the nightly fair were only, he noticed, doing moderate business. At his favourite roadside fish and chip bar he stopped and paid four pounds for a piece of warm carp and some fried reconstituted mashed potato. It had been days since he'd had any real food. He wasn't looking after himself properly. There were too many fresh shadows. He enjoyed the meal, eating it off the passenger seat as he drove, but felt sick afterwards and had to munch a couple of Milky Way bars to make himself better. He was already improving by the time he drove through the back gates of his house and garaged the Phantom beside the Duesenberg.

He went into the house and found his old black car coat, his black flared trousers, his high-heeled boots, his white linen and, as he dressed, he became depressed. It was probably association, he thought. Dark clothes often brought him down. He turned away from the wardrobe, seeking a stereo, and at last found a deck and amplifier where he must have shoved them under an old-fashioned bentwood and china washstand. He switched the kit on. From the ceiling came the miserable, neurotic drone of the Everly Brothers. He let it play, deepening his mood.

If a mood was worth having, he thought, it was worth having profoundly.

He went downstairs and turned up some mail which must have come with one of the last runners to get through. There was a letter from Mr. Harvey, one of Frank's wholesalers, saying that he had some information which might be useful to Jerry and Mr. Smiles, Jerry's sometime business partner. Although he had made at least a million in the last job he was disinclined to work with Mr. Smiles again. Smiles usually claimed to have a "purpose" to his ventures and thus tended to confuse Jerry. He crumpled the letter, wondering why Harvey should wish to double-cross Frank, an excellent customer for any new chemical to come in.

Jerry began to worry about Catherine again. She was his ideal, his goddess, his queen; he loved her and she represented everything else he loved, no matter how she changed, whereas Frank represented everything Jerry hated: greedy hypocrisy. If Frank got hold of Catherine again Jerry knew that he would have to risk repercussions and kill his brother. It would be a shame, since events were just beginning to stabilise into a fixed pattern, like a clockwork train on its little oval track. After a while one got to know the dodgy bits of line. Any deaths at this stage would produce a whole new train set, with all kinds of bends and twists, moebius strips and dead ends: exactly what he was hoping to escape. He gave into his instincts' demands. He must check to see if Catherine were all right, no matter how irrational the impulse was.

He left the house, taking the Duesenberg to Westbourne Park Road and stopping outside the convent. There was no other traffic. The walls of the convent seemed higher than usual in the darkness.

Against every desire his mind had filled up with prescience, with a knowledge of the futures he refused to accept.

With a groan he went straight over the wall, using the hooked nylon ladder from the back of the car. He dropped amongst runner-bean poles, scraping his shin, trod as lightly as possible through the flower-beds and vegetable patches, crossed the garden, hit his shoulder on the corner of the potting shed, and arrived at the main door. There was some sluggish movement from within, but not much. He got the door open and went inside; raced on tip-toe through the corridors until he came to the top of the flight of stairs leading underground. So far he had not been spotted by a single nun. He went down the stairs and reached the cold corridor. There were stirrings, now, behind many of the doors; they were conclusive. As he approached, lights went off one by one in the cells until only the light in Catherine's cell remained. Her door was open. He looked in on a discarded habit, an unmade bed, an empty lipstick case, an unread paperback with a cover reproducing an Adolphe Willette poster, the smell of Guerlain Mitsouko. He was too late. Frank had struck already. He would have reached the fake Le Corbusier chateau just after Jerry left. There would have been no time for John Gnatbeelson to activate the defences. Sister and house were now Frank's.

Jerry howled. His eyes blazed red in the gloom of the convent cell. His lips snarled back from wolfish teeth. An era had ended for him and he was never to know such innocence again.

Rebellion or insurrection, on the other hand, being guided by instinct rather than reason, being passionate and spontaneous rather than cool and calculated, do act like shock therapy on the body of society, and there is a chance that they may change the chemical composition of the societal crystal. In other words they may change human nature, in the sense of creating a new morality, or new metaphysical values.

Herbert Read, *Revolution and Reason*

It is essential to take the greatest pains to rouse the might of the German people by increasing its confidence in its own strength and thus also bringing a stability into the minds of our people to assist their appreciation of political problems. I have often, and I have to add this in speaking to you, felt doubts on one single matter, and that is the following: if I look at the intellectual elements of our society, I think what a pity, unfortunately they are needed; otherwise, one day one might, well, I don't know, exterminate them or something like that. But unfortunately one needs them. If now I take a good look at these intellectual elements and imagine, and check, their behaviour towards me, and towards our work, I feel almost afraid.

Adolf Hitler, private speech to German Press, Munich, 10 November 1938 (day after Kristellnacht).

S.A.B. Zeman, *Nazi Propaganda*

6. In the beginning was the flight—today it's security and security means chiefly electronics

Jerry clambered out of his stockings and suspenders and threw them on top of his Courreges suit. All he had left now was his perm; he wondered why he had ever thought red hair would suit him. He needed a complete change of identity. He searched through the heaps of clothes he had brought with him to the deserted convent but could find nothing he wanted to wear. He walked the length of the cool guest room, with its hard beds and green radiators, to the pine writing-table where he had placed his little Sony cassette player. He pressed the play button. Slow, heavy sounds crept from the speaker; the batteries were exhausted.

He switched off. For a second he thought he had heard foot-steps in the passage outside, but it was unlikely that anyone could have traced him here now that London was almost entirely depopulated. The exodus had been a huge success. He touched his forehead, glad to find that his temperature was dropping at last. Whistling, he stirred a skirt with his toe just as the door opened and Miss Brunner came in.

She glanced disapprovingly around at the mess. She wore some kind of standard Slavic peasant costume and had an MG42 tucked under her muscular right arm. Crossing to one of the beds she lowered the heavy machine gun onto the grey blanket which was as neat and clean as the last occupant had left it.

"There's evidently been some confusion," she said. She sat down beside her gun and began to stroke its stock. "What on earth are you doing?"

"I'd heard you were dead—or, at least, transferred."

He picked up the nearest pair of underpants—Daglo yellow—and put them on.

"You more than anyone should know about temporal shifts, Mr. Cornelius. Everything's well and truly up the spout." She drew in a sour breath. "I thought I had you under control this time. There's a rumour about your black box, that you've got it back. If that's true you haven't really used it to your advantage, have you, eh?"

"I've been resting." He began to sulk. He found two orange socks that almost matched. He sat opposite her and pulled them onto his grubby feet. "Anyway, if we're being accusatory, what happened to you? I thought we were going to be together always."

"It's your sentimentality I can't stand." She rose like a disturbed wasp, leaving her gun where it was. "It's your main drawback. You could have been a brilliant physicist. If you'd only had a better grip on the scientific method."

"My black box. . . ."

"Your father's invention, and you know it. You developed it, certainly, but to ends that were completely irresponsible. Think how much better things could be if you hadn't started experimenting for your own amusement rather than for the good of the world."

"People get what they want out of my box."

"What they think they want. And its power source is ludicrous. Utterly wasteful."

"It's not much different to yours."

She clicked her tongue.

"What they think they want is usually what they do want," he added. "Is there anything wrong—?"

"God almighty, you don't know what morality is, do you?"

"I tried to find out. I became a Jesuit. . . ."

She turned over his clothing with her pointed foot. "Is this junk all yours?"

"You can have it, if you like."

"What would I do with it? You've no ambitions, have you, Mr. Cornelius? No sense of purpose? No ideals?"

"Since Catherine was killed. . . ."

"I don't think necrophilia counts as an ideal."

"Standards change." Jerry was miserable. "And we're proof enough of that, aren't we? After all, we didn't need to become divided. . . ."

"We've discussed that already. The scheme didn't work out. Too many regressive genes—put us straight back to square one."

He shrugged and stooped to pick up a black T-shirt.

"Everything's fluxed up, thanks to you," she said. "I had this perfect programme all plotted and ready to go, then suddenly the co-ordinates are haywire. I didn't need to make too many enquiries to find out where the interference was coming from. I had to abandon the whole programme because you were playing games with your silly little box."

"Well, you needn't worry. I haven't got it any more."

"It's too bloody late now, isn't it! Where is it?"

"I lost it. Or lent it."

"You're lying."

"I had a touch of my old trouble. Didn't you have it, recently? Paramnesia? Paramnesia?"

"That wouldn't—"

"Then it developed into ordinary amnesia. I'm not even sure how I got here. There was a party at Holland Park. . . ."

"I don't know what you're talking about," she said.

"Then maybe it hasn't happened to you yet," he told her reasonably. He paused to think. "Or maybe it hasn't happened to any of us yet. Maybe it won't happen, after all."

"Oh, you shifty little sod."

"That's another thing I was wondering about. . . ."

"I came here to try to clear up the confusion." She found a wallet and began to search through it, emptying company credits and luncheon vouchers onto the floor. She turned a fifty million mark silk banknote in her fingers and absently touched it to her lips, licking it. "Why did you choose this mausoleum, anyway?"

"I forget."

"You usually stay with your mother in a crisis." She picked up another wallet. It contained nothing but a bundle of over-stamped Rhodesian guinea-notes.

"Is she around?"

"Apparently."

"I'm tired." He reached for her gun.

"Steady on, Mr. Cornelius." She became alarmed.

"I only wanted to look at it. I've hardly ever seen one. Are they still making them?"

"How should I know?" She shook out the pockets of a black velvet jacket and began carefully to inspect each worn piece of paper. "Where are your own weapons, by the way?"

"In store somewhere." He was vague. "Do you want to look at them?"

"Certainly not." She had discovered a huge perfectly cut diamond and was holding it up to the green-shaded light bulb. "This is real." She inspected the facets, one by one. "Where did you get it?"

"It's only a model." He put his legs into a pair of purple bells.

7. Optics for defence

Grass and moss were growing over the paving stones of Westbourne Park Road. Jerry saw Miss Brunner to the gate and took in the scenes of soft decline, much more congruent, at last, with the rural atmosphere of the convent's garden. Even the air was relatively fresh. "It's lovely now, isn't it?" He watched her walk to her Austin Princess. "It smells so rich."

"Stagnation's no substitute for stability." She wrenched open the car's door. "I hope you're pleased with yourself." From behind the façade of deserted houses on the opposite side of the street a few small dogs barked. "It's going to take England a long time to get back on her feet. And as for the rest of the world. . . ." She entered the car. He saw her through the clouded glass as, aggressively, she put the engine into gear. For someone who had so much to do with machines she displayed a stern hatred for most of them. He waved as she swerved into Ladbroke Grove, still puzzled as to why she had taken the laundry box with her; it had been full of his old junk—a broken watch, tickets, empty matchbooks, old calendars, torn note-books, catalogues, useless maps, out of date maintenance manuals; all had gone into her box. Perhaps she thought she could feed the information into a new computer and thus reproduce his lost memory. He was quite grateful to her; there was nothing, he felt, of his past he wished to retain. He had been glad to offer her his clothes and tapes, but she had declined most of them with the air of someone who had already researched them thoroughly. Deciding against returning to his room, he locked the gate behind him and walked round to Blenheim Crescent, peering up at his mother's flat as he passed but making no effort to see if she was still there. He was sure that Mrs. Cornelius, of all people, wouldn't have moved. He turned left at the antique shop with its smashed windows, its contents scattered on the pavement, where Sammy, his mother's lover, had once sold pies, into Kensington Park Road. Assegais, brass microscopes, elephants' feet, bits of sixteenth-century armour, the innards of clocks, broken writing chests, Afridi rifles inset with copper and mother-of-pearl, their stocks crumpled by woodworm, rotting books and fading photographs lay in heaps all across the street, exuding a sweet, musty smell that was not unpleasant. He entered Elgin Crescent, going towards Portobello Road, and found a shop that had once specialised in theatrical costumes and musical instruments. The door was ajar and the bell rang as he entered. Most of the costumes were still intact, in boxes or on hangers depending from racks on both sides of the showroom. He tried on the full dress uniform of a captain in the 30th Deccan Horse, discarded it. He dressed himself as Zorro, as Robin Hood, as Sam Spade. He tried the Buffalo Bill outfit and felt a little more at ease in it; he forced himself into a lurex Flash Gordon, a Sherlock Holmes deerstalker and ulster, a Zenith the Albino dress suit, a Doctor Nikola set, a Captain Marvel costume, even a Tarzan loincloth; a suit of motley, a Jester, seemed better, but he was seeking security at present, so he also discarded the Harlequin trickster set, but eventually decided upon an elaborate black and white satin pierrot suit, the main colour being black, the pom-poms, ruff and cuffs being white, the skull-cap being white also, a reverse of the usual arrangement. He was pleased with his appearance. He found a pure white wig, perhaps originally for an old lady character, and put this on under his skull-cap. As an afterthought he picked up some greasepaint and blacked his face and hands then, for an hour, he sat in front of the long mirror playing a Walker five-string banjo to himself, raising his spirits still further: *On the road to Mandalay-ee, Where the flying fishes play-ee.* . . . It was all so much more comfortable than the stockings, suspenders and girdle of his earlier disguise, so much more tasteful than the bright colours of a vanished youth. Indeed, it was the nicest of any of the disguises he had assumed since his boyhood. Nobody made any demands on a pierrot. All in all things weren't looking too bad, really.

"Hide your tears behind a smile." He sang blithely as he searched through the wicker baskets. "Hide your fears inside a file." He found two or three more pierrot costumes, two harlequins, a columbine and some masks, and bundled them all into a hessian sack.

He had decided, once his new equipment was installed, to open up the convent as a kind of health-farm. Sooner or later London would come back to a version, at least, of its old self, and this time he would be ready for it.

He paused once more beside the mirror. "I could be happy with you," he sang, "if you could be happy with me." He gave himself a big kiss and left a smear of black make-up on the glass.

8. The BL 755 cluster bomb is highly effective against tanks and other armoured vehicles, aircraft, transport, patrol boats, and personnel

The convent was coming along a treat. Jerry had signed a formal lease for the place and had been lucky enough to secure the services of some of the ex-nuns. He had left the outside pretty much as it had always looked, but the buildings inside had been thoroughly restructured. Now wide picture windows looked out into old English gardens where pious and apple-cheeked Poor Clares worked with hoe and rake as they had worked since time immemorial. Jerry expected his first customers soon. So far his only client had been his financial backer, his sister's friend Constantin Koutrouboussis, the young Greek millionaire who had inherited the family business on the death of his older brother Dimitri. Koutrouboussis hadn't been entirely satisfied with the cure. Koutrouboussis was rarely satisfied with anything but miracles and Jerry hadn't been in business long enough to gain experience enough to provide them. But when the Americans started arriving things should look up.

Koutrouboussis stopped off one day, on his way through to his Soho headquarters. He was carrying a new line in riding crops and was keen to show one to Jerry. "Look at that!" He swished it through the beam of dusty sunlight which entered Jerry's spacious office by way of the half-closed blind. "The secret's in the weight of the handle."

Jerry was searching white plastic drawers in his desk. Of late he had affected a great deal of white. He wore a surgeon's smock at this moment, and a chef's hat. It contrasted nicely with his freshly stained skin. "What?"

"The handle." Koutrouboussis put the crop back in his case. "How's your sister keeping, by the way?"

"Oh, all right. I checked this morning."

"Are you sure—?"

"There are no certainties in this business, Mr. K."

"I suppose there aren't. A science in its infancy."

"It'll stay that way, if I have anything to do with it," Jerry promised. "Adult science doesn't seem to produce a satisfactory variety of results."

Mr. Koutrouboussis fingered his new beard. His hands wandered down to his expensive collar, his neat lapels, his dapper buttons. "You won't tell the clients that?" He moved towards the wall and stared at the tastefully framed French prints showing characters from the Commedia dell'arte.

"There aren't any clients for our kind of science. You're too much of a cynic for this sort of clinic. . . ." Jerry stopped himself quickly and inspected his watches. "A drink? I've a wide selection of Scotches. . . ." He gave up.

"No time."

Jerry wondered why Koutrouboussis always made him feel aggressive. Maybe it was the tension the man carried with him; it could even be that Jerry resented his financial involvement, his power.

Mr. Koutrouboussis reached the door and lifted his gloved hand in a moody wave. "No time."

"I'll be seeing you," said Jerry.

Koutrouboussis chuckled to himself. "At this rate you'll be raising me, too. Cheerio for now, Mr. Cornelius." As an afterthought he said from the passage: "And if you should discover the identity. . . ."

"I'll let you know."

"I would be grateful."

Jerry put his elbows on his desk and rubbed at his face. One thing was certain: he was under an obligation and it was making him uncomfortable. Then he consoled himself with the knowledge that Koutrouboussis was no idealist. His interest in the whole affair was connected with Catherine alone and justified by a profit motive. If Jerry was going to make his clinic in any way successful he would have to forget both his sister and her admirer for a while. He was sure he was on the right track this time around. He had found hope again. If these new machines couldn't beat the human condition then nothing could.

A tasty young nun knocked and entered. "You're looking tired, sir. You've so much on your shoulders."

He straightened his back. Automatically he checked his lapels for nits. "Lice," he murmured, to explain.

"The world is full of them, sir. But the truth shines through."

He glanced at her faithful face. "The trouble is," he said, "that we're all at least a hundred and fifty years old. How many generations need to comply in a fallacy before it becomes accepted as truth?"

She was untroubled. "Can I bring you a nice cup of tea, doctor?"

"It would certainly help."

"Your machines. . . ."

"They're not oracles, you know. They just get rid of the demand for oracles. Abolish the future and you lose the need for faith. Familiarity, by and large, banishes fear. . . ." He clutched, again, at his head. "I wish I knew how the damned things worked."

"I was going to say. They're moaning again."

"They haven't got enough to do."

"Soon," she reassured him.

"The whole idea is that we should do away with 'Tomorrow'. . . ."

"I'll make the tea immediately." The door closed on her whispering gown.

He got up and drew the blind so that he could see into the quiet garden. "Heritage. Inheritance. The secret's in the genes. Chromosomes. Chronos zones. It always comes down to those fucking flat worms." He really needed a chemist at that moment, but he was buggered if he was going to bring his brother back. Frank would have a vested interest in the status quo; his whole identity depended on its preservation. The same could be said for Miss Brunner and the rest. He couldn't blame them. They thought they were fighting for their lives.

The phone began to ring.

He uttered a disbelieving laugh.

9. **The Strim antitank rocket launcher is light (4.5 Kg), accurate (very high single shot hit and kill probability), easy to use, low-cost instruction—no maintenance, no overhaul . . . complementary rockets, smoke/incendiary, 1,000 meters, illumination, 100 to 2,000 meters, antipersonnel, up to 2,000 meters**

With only a few reservations Jerry watched the new arrivals as they were herded from the big white bus through the narrow gates of the convent. There were only three men; all the others were women under thirty—or, at least, they resembled women. Some of the patients, he gathered, had already made a few faltering steps towards a crude form of self-inflicted transmogrification, some of it involving quite terrifying surgery.

He had decided not to present himself to his patients until the evening, during the Welcome Ceremony (which would be held in the ballroom, once the twin chapels) since, at this stage, he would be bound to make them feel self-conscious. Even as the white bus disappeared into the new underground garage a black Mercedes two-tonner took its place, unloading amplifiers and instruments, music for the ball. He stepped back from his window. As the population increased, so, in direct proportion, would his clients. He went over to his new console, turning the master switch to make every television monitor screen work at once, showing him a clinic now satisfyingly busy. He was particularly pleased with the way in which the nuns had adapted to their new nursing work. He looked for a moment at the reception desk where guests were cautiously signing their names (mostly fictitious) in the gold-embossed green leather register. Their faces, haunted by hope and anxiety, were familiar to him. For many of them the treatment, even if partially successful, could not come too soon.

The thing he was looking forward to, however, was the ball. It had been a long while since The Deep Fix had played together. As soon as he could he would go down for the sound check. It would be good if he could get some rehearsing in before the event.

His eye was drawn back to the screen. He was sure he had seen the old military-looking character quite recently. He recognised the frayed cuffs. "We are all offered a selection of traditional roles," he murmured. "The real problem lies in finding a different play. In the meantime we attempt to console as many of the actors as possible by finding them the parts in which they can be as happy as possible." His voice was carried over the PA to all parts of the building, interrupting the Muzak.

"You're becoming a regular telly freak, ain't ya, Mr. C."

Shakey Mo Collier now stood there, arms folded, most of his weight on one leg. He was wearing a yellow and red paisley shirt, a light suede waistcoat, filthy with the remains of a thousand fruitful meals, a tattered green and blue Indian silk scarf, patched and faded jeans and scuffed black cowboy boots with white decoration. His hair was longer than when Jerry had last seen it and he had grown a Mandarin moustache. Jerry was pleased to see him. "Where have you been, Mo? The first I heard you were around was when someone brought me your postcard."

"I've been asleep, haven't I?" said Mo. "Up in the Lake District mostly. It's nice up there. Good roads. Plenty of shale. All dead. Lovely. You want to go."

"I know it. Grasmere. Daffodils and dope. Or that's the way it used to be."

Mo was unusually astute. "That scene's shifted, hadn't you heard? To Rydal. But the best days are over."

"Well, a word's not worth much these days. I heard the town had gone all chintzy."

"Quincy?"

"Chintzy."

They giggled together. Mo sat down on the posh carpet, cross-legged, and began to roll himself a joint. "Anyway you seem to be doing all right with this lot."

"I can't complain. There's no profit in it, though."

"Aren't they paying?"

"All the takings go to my sleeping partner, Mr. Koutrouboussis."

"Well, well." Mo licked his papers. "So, really, you could leave here any time you liked?"

"I've got responsibilities, Mo."

Mo looked at him in some disappointment. "Blimey!"

"How long has the group been back together?"

"Not long. We all met up in Ambleside. Tried out a few things—acoustically, of course. You can get some of those old reed organs to sound just like electronics if you work at it. But we needed power, so we trucked back to London, hoping we'd find some. Of course we hadn't realised everything was coming alive again. We picked just the right time, for once. We must be the only beat group around. We're getting a lot of work. Too much, really. The tensions. . . ."

"It's done your ego a lot of good," said Jerry. "You're your old cocky self again."

"Thanks. I feel cocky. Yes." His grease-stained fingers explored a waistcoat pocket for a match. He lit his joint. "I just wish they'd bring back the money system. All this fucking bartering's getting beyond a joke. Half our wages rot before we can eat them and we can't trade them because nobody's got the kind of stuff we need."

"I don't know what you want."

"Cheap tat, of course. And weapons. Just like the old days. Colour tellies. But don't worry. This gig's free."

"We've got a few new drugs."

"Nar," said Mo. "We're not into drugs anymore. Well, not at the moment, anyway. We're into beer."

"You don't mind me . . . ?"

"Smashing. It'll be like the Friendly Bum days. You remember?"

"My memory isn't what it was."

"It's a fucking opium den now. For the tourists."

"I've been staying away from the centre. My work. . . ."

"Oh, sure." Mo was suddenly embarrassed. Hesitantly he offered Jerry the joint.

Jerry enjoyed a drag. He went to sit on the ledge of the open window, looking towards Blenheim Crescent then up into the sharp blue sky. "I think we should see an improvement, soon. It's a bit early, though." He cocked an ear to the East, detecting a whine. He smiled. "They're here, at last."

Mo joined him at the window as the first black wave of

Starlifters shrieked in at minimum altitude, banking slowly until they had located Heathrow.

"Far out!" said Mo in delight, as soon as his voice could be heard. "Those jobs carry over a hundred and fifty troops apiece. There are thousands coming in. Oh, it's all going to liven up! The Yanks are back!"

Jerry moved to the intercom. He must warn his staff to be ready for the extra volume.

10. Rapier, ultra low-level air defence system in service with the British Army and RAF Regiment, ordered by the Imperial Iranian Government, lightweight, direct-hitting missile, high kill-to-engagement ratio, optional "add-on" blindfire unit, outstanding cost-effectiveness

Jerry rubbed more of the dye into his skin, regretting once again that his machines simply weren't up to handling his own problem. It was high time that they were overhauled, anyway, since the convent had been placed off-limits to all advisory forces: though it had only been civilian auxiliaries who had been coming in the first place; patronising the clinic now counted, on General Cumberland's orders, as fraternisation with hostile personnel.

Jerry couldn't complain. It meant he could expand his own activities if he wished. In the meantime the money-system had been re-introduced, Koutrouboussis had been paid back and was receiving an excellent dividend; Jerry was no longer beholden to the Greek who had, on his own initiative, formed a consortium together with his younger brother Spiro, to exploit the Cornelius patents world-wide, offering Jerry a flat commission on every client, including those who wished to change nationalities as part of their transmogrification. Jerry intended to take more of an interest in this international aspect of the enterprise now that the original clinic was running so well. Spiro, by mutual consent, would act as chief liaison man.

When he had finished with his face he picked up a tangled sheaf of traumograph printouts, leaving black smudges on the semi-opaque paper, and crammed them into one of his desk drawers. He was wearing a white German suit, black shirt and no tie, as part of his current disguise. His hair was bleached bone white. For the moment, too, he had discarded his needlegun and wore the more comfortable vibragun which, he felt, was a trifle better in tune with the zeitgeist. Currently, he felt, the world could accept any ambiguities so long as he retained a certain dramatic resolution to events.

He left the office and strolled through his pale blue corridors, amiably greeting his nuns, nurses and doctors as he passed them. Most of them had already made preparations to leave for the country; only a skeleton staff was to be retained in London.

His Phantom VI was already at the gate, its motor running. He stepped into the driving seat and drove up Westbourne Park Road, turned right into Kensington Park Road, heading for Notting Hill and beyond.

He arrived in Church Street just in time to see a silver Cadillac disappearing into Holland Street. The area was otherwise deserted of cars, although a few M-75 armoured personnel carriers were parked here and there, their crews lazily giving his Phantom the once-over as it went by. He turned into Kensington High Street and parked outside Derry and Toms which he had acquired only recently in the deal granting Koutrouboussis full control of European exploitation rights on his father's original patents. Jerry disembarked and entered.

Within, the department store was hushed as usual: middle-aged women moved slowly from counter to counter; murmuring assistants in dove-grey uniforms addressed them respectfully. When re-opening the store Jerry had made it clear to his staff that only a certain sort of customer was to be encouraged. He had always been very strong on tradition.

He took the lift to the sunny tranquillity of the roof-garden and crossed a few feet of crazy-paving to enter the restaurant whose wall, facing the gardens, was completely of glass. He was keeping an illicit rendezvous with Captain Hargreaves. He sat at his usual table, completely alone, for the restaurant had not begun to serve lunch, watching the pink flamingoes wading about in the tiny rivers and fountains, listening to the whistlings and chirrupings of the less flamboyant birds in the foliage.

Any intimations of trouble which he might have had during his drive here were now dispersed. He relaxed and looked over his shoulder to see Captain Hargreaves, very smart in tailored olive fatigues, come through the plate-glass doors. He stood up, smiling. He pulled back a chair and Captain Hargreaves sat down.

"Thanks. I got that stuff for you. Gnatbeelson's alive and in London."

Jerry resumed his chair. He frowned. "What about his memory?"

"It's a typical case of amnesia—of the sort you described to me. He believes his name to be Beale. And, as you guessed, he's taken a job in a library."

"The books are there?"

"At least one copy of *Time Search*."

"Then it's conclusive." Jerry leaned forward and slid a friendly fingernail along the inside of Captain Hargreave's thigh. "Do you want lunch now?"

Captain Hargreave's hand fell on Jerry's. "Afterwards, I think."

"There might not be time. They know where I am—or should do."

"I'm not too hungry." The captain reached into a large satchel and drew out a piece of paper. "The address."

Jerry tucked the paper down inside his holster, rising slowly. "Give me a moment. I've got to change my clothes. I'll join you in the Dutch garden, if you like."

"Okay." Captain Hargreaves stood up, kissing him on the cheek. "You'll be quick?"

"Don't worry."

But he was frowning as he went through the back of the restaurant into the cloak room and began slipping into the costume he kept there.

There was no doubt about it, he thought. Things were looking black for the English assassin.

EARLY REPORTS

Editors: Hitler stopped too soon! He should have gotten rid of the Ginzburgs and the Borosons and a lot more like you. Indeed we should have a Hitler in America to rid the country of the merchants of filth, pervertors and corruptors of morals, and muckrakers!

Mrs. John W. Red, Memphis, Tennessee; letter to
Fact, Jan-Feb 1965

Contrary to the national trend, crime decreased in the Notting Hill area last year.

Kensington Post, 8 January 1965

The one thing you can say about Hilter is that he was a damned sight more pro-British than M. Pompidou.

Kingsley Amis, *Speakeasy* (BBC Radio) 18 July 1971

Even in these enlightened days cancer continues to be a disease evoking dread and horror in the general public. Perhaps because of this peculiar emotional response to cancer, quite unlike that seen with other diseases, there has always been a fringe of unorthodox practitioners specialising in unusual treatments to lead to dramatic "cures."

M.A. Epstein, *Times Literary Supplement,*
16 January 1976

Hammersmith Palais

242 SHEPHERDS BUSH ROAD W6   01 748 2812

World Premiere

FRIDAY 13 FEB   8pm–2am

Sex Equality Dancing

Where men dare not refuse
Ladies! Pick your man!
Don't miss this night
of Liberation

**THIS TICKET ADMITS TWO
FOR THE PRICE OF ONE**

TUNING UP (3)

"I feel like a right ponce." Jerry climbed gingerly into the large rowing boat, seating himself in the stern, glaring miserably at the misty lake. The boat's name was on the back-rest behind him: *Morgana le Fey*. He arranged the skirt of his lilac jacket around him; he plucked at the knees of his lilac flares to reveal daffodil socks, daffodil cuffs; he was cold.

"Well, I think you look lovely." Karen von Krupp unshipped the oars, handing one pair to Miss Brunner, one to Una Persson. "Doesn't he?" she asked the others.

"Lovely." Una Persson's back was to him but Jerry could imagine her expression. Miss Brunner, in russet Ossie Clarke battle-dress with matching boots and bush-hat, was silent. She seemed to think that Doktor von Krupp should be doing some of the rowing.

"I wish you'd all stop taking the piss out of me. I've had a hard time of it." Moodily, Jerry tugged at a tiller line. "Who's going to shove off?"

Karen von Krupp signed to Mitzi Beesley; Mitzi was to remain on the bank as look-out until they returned. She pouted and swung her customised Winchester .270 over her shoulder, lifting her white Dorothee Bis skirt to her thighs so that she could wade into the shallows, feet protected by Paulin espadrilles. The mother-of-pearl in the rifle's stock clashed a trifle with her skirt as the butt bounced against an angry bottom and Jerry felt her heavy breath on his head as she shoved. The boat shifted a little in the shingle. Mitzi pushed blonde Marcel-waved hair back from her face and tried again. Gradually her face grew almost scarlet to match her horrible Maple Red Max Factor mouth. Karen von Krupp rocked the boat at the other end. Suddenly they all slid out into the lake and Mitzi waved her arms, barely recovering her footing. Petulantly she waded back to the shore and swung the Winchester into both hands. She kept her spine displayed to them. She wasn't much for vocalising her displeasure. In reply to Mitzi's gesture Doktor von Krupp wrapped her dove-grey C&A trench-coat more firmly around her large body. "That way," she said, gesturing beyond the reeds in the direction of the island, a dim outline, already being obscured by the thickening mist, in the middle of the lake. "Are you sure you know how to steer, Jerry dear?"

Jerry dragged the line hard over so that the boat moved suddenly to starboard.

"We don't need demonstrations from anyone else to-day, Mr. Cornelius." Miss Brunner was panting. "I think we're sitting the wrong way round, by the way."

Una Persson had first pointed this out when they had entered. But she remained as patient as ever. Una wore her usual light-weight khaki under an open black maxi-coat; though the coat tended to hamper her movements, she was evidently reluctant to remove it. Crouching, she turned herself carefully so that she was looking up at Jerry. She winked grey eyes, first one, then the other, and sat down again, taking hold of the sweeps. Behind her, Miss Brunner swivelled, much more awkwardly, her legs held by her red-brown midi. Her long bottom struck the seat somewhat heavily and the boat responded dramatically, rocking from side to side, shipping a little water to port. "I don't think much of this thing's construction," she said. Then they were rowing again.

"Let's try to keep the same rhythm this time, shall we?" Miss Brunner hissed as one of her oars reared from the water, weed dripping from its blade.

The morning was very misty. They moved through a strip of clear water between thick reeds, not yet on the lake proper, but already the heavily wooded bank was invisible. Some ducks flapped low over the grey surface, as if trying to keep below the mist-line. A light drizzle formed rather than fell around them. They rowed into shrouded silence, their own sounds muffled.

"You're the only one of us familiar with the island, Mr. Cornelius," said Doktor von Krupp. "You'll have to keep us on course." She picked up the Remington 700 Mitzi Beesley had loaned her and placed it carefully across her knees. Both Miss Persson and Miss Brunner were armed with identical Smith and Wesson .45 revolvers. Jerry had a heater on one hip, his vibragun on the other hip and his needler under his arm-pit, but none of these gave him much sense of security.

"I hope we bloody find something after all this." Miss Brunner had caught another crab. Una Persson leaned on her oars as she waited for the woman to start rowing again. Jerry was glad of her friendly, resigned face, even though it had been Una who had tipped the others off about the island (but it had been Mitzi Beesley who had tracked him down to where he had hidden his naked body in Gaping Gill pot on Ingleborough in the West Yorkshire Pennines, and Miss Beesley and Karen von Krupp who had dressed him in this outfit before he had had a chance to revive; he was still not quite sure what was going on). Una seemed somewhat regretful. She wiped the clinging moisture from her cheeks with the back of her hand—a mixture of mist and sweat. It was playing hell with the others' make-up.

The boat began to move again. Jerry couldn't remember what they were looking for on the island. He knew that something important had happened there once, perhaps to him, perhaps in his childhood, and he could certainly remember the stone barn very well (he had always been curious about the function of the place), but the rest was mysterious. "There was a sun once," Miss Brunner had said, just as he had woken up. Or had she said "son"? He glanced into the water, seeking the source of the bad smell, like dead fish. Terror blossomed in the back of his brain. He tried to speak but could not. He searched the cold mist. There was no escape.

The three women were all staring directly at him, each lost in her own thoughts, as the boat moved on through the Grasmere clouds.

He looked down at his hands; he realised for the first

time that they had turned a funny colour. The pain in his spine made him want to bend double, to go on all fours. He grunted. His nostrils shivered. A small primitive noise formed in the back of his throat.

"Oh, god," said Miss Brunner. "It's starting again."

DEVELOPMENT

Poor Gauchelin was much alarmed by his experience, but as time went on—at any rate in France—the Hunt lost some of its terrors, and the wailing procession of lost souls turned into a troupe of comic demons who flew merrily through the air to the sound of song and of tinkling bells. Nor did it always remain a mere nebulous, ghostly phenomenon. I have suggested, elsewhere, that the mummery probably originated as a miming of a Wild Hunt led by a certain Mormo, a child-devouring ogress of Greek origin, not unlike Perchta, the mythical patroness of the Perchton. That the Harlequin-Cornelius troupe was also sometimes mimed is suggested by the fact that it makes a partial appearance in Adam de la Halle's *Jeu de la Feuillée*, which, as we have seen, had for its central theme the entertainment of fairies by the citizens of Arras. "Already I hear the Harlequin-troupe approaching," cries Croquesot (Biter-of-fools), "a little bearded man," who having cheerfully enquired of the audience whether his "hairy phiz" doesn't become him well, proceeds to woo the fairy Morque on behalf of his mighty master Cornelius, the Harlequin, who, though still supernatural, has obviously developed into a more substantial and more comic figure than his ancestor, the demonaic leader of lost and wandering souls.

Enid Welsford, The Fool, ibid

> The jingle-cap is such a great grinner,
> He will dance for you, not well, but with vigour,
> His jingle-head full of coloured beads.
>
> Maurice Lescoq, Posthumous Poems

Triomphe et que l'envie en crevie de depir,
Brave Arlequin queton nom plein de gloire
Soit, pour test faits, ton bel esprit,
A l'avenir en lettres d'or ecrit
Dans la temple de la memoire.

The Stage's Glory, ibid

Fairy Benigna: *Poor Afric's children sigh for liberty.*
Alas! That task was not reserved for me.
Furibond; or, Harlequin Negro, Drury Lane, 1807

Notting Hill Doomed to Be Racial Battlefield

The 1962 Commonwealth Immigrants Act came immediately after the racial troubles from campaigns against immigrants from the West Indies, Africa and Asia. One of the centres of racial violence then, and earlier, was Notting Hill; indeed this area's name is now almost synonymous with racial prejudice. . . . Notting Hill seems doomed to be the battlefield of racial discrimination: the Government's White Paper will not stop the battle. But sense and responsible reaction from the people against whom legislation is directed should at least let us know what the causes of the war really are.

KENSINGTON POST, 3 September 1965

1. Seven years for bank-raid vicar

From Sumatra it wasn't too hard to get back to Sandakan and something like sanity, though the sari could not safely be abandoned until he could look down on his yellow palace, last remnant of a great personal empire, his inheritance, in the dark green hills above the desert harbour. Quite a lot of jungle had grown around the building since he had last visited it; trees and architecture were rounded, their contours softened by the hazy light, seeming to merge, and in the distance were the great blue and purple mountains of the island's interior, the "real Borneo" as Major Nye had once termed it. To see if there were any signs of danger Jerry flew twice over the red and grey town. There were a few steamers at anchor against the broken concrete of the quays; some were already sinking into the emerald water, others were entirely discoloured by rust. On the quay he saw three isolated figures looking up at his giant Dornier DoX flying boats. Perhaps they recognised the sound of the twelve Curtiss Conqueror engines spluttering and misfiring around him as usual. He flew out to sea towards the Philippines, to make a wide turn so that he could begin his landing approach. He now wore a white one-piece flying suit, trimmed with ermine, gold-trimmed goggles and a white kid helmet. He had always been expected to show a little face in Sandakan.

The plane began to drop too steeply. Jerry pulled her up a bit; she responded as poorly as usual, but he managed to keep to his original path until he was almost on top of the broken mouth of the harbour. The Dornier's huge floats touched tranquil water, bounced, swerved; he was taxi-ing between sagging, extinguished light-towers, forcing his heavy craft away from the protecting walls which formed an almost perfect circle and towards the mass of rotting steamers and water-logged fishing sampans, the deserted house-boats and the junks. It began to occur to him that he had not been paying attention to his real responsibilities. He let the flying boat drift in crab-wise until it was bobbing against the side of a junk which seemed relatively intact. He shut off the engines and clambered from the door of the cockpit onto the forward floats, clutching a strut to keep his balance as the machine rocked badly, and from the floats boarded the junk, testing its timbers carefully as he crossed the deck to walk slowly down a bouncing, flaking gangplank still resting on the quay. Empty mouldering buildings presented themselves to him, a mixture of Victorian Gothic and Malaysian-Dutch stucco. Rats watched from ledges and windows. Sadly he walked up the hill, through ruined streets where timber-merchants' and rubber-planters' offices, shipping companies, importers, exporters, chandlers, money-lenders, insurance brokers, restaurants, bazaars, stall-holders, silk-sellers, paper mask sellers, puppet sellers, sellers of acrid pastries, savoury dumplings, sweetmeats, carved wooden boxes and bird-cages, had flourished in lazy competition.

Now a few starved Chinese and Dyak faces disappeared from doorways as he passed by. It was evident that nobody recognised him in his new costume and this saddened him.

The gates of the palace, which stood on its own hill outside the town, were slabs of grey marble on slender white tapering posts. They were exactly as he had left them, their pristine carvings and decoration reflecting a strong Islamic influence. He took a large key from his pocket and with considerable difficulty turned it in the great iron lock, pushing the gates open to find richer colours within. The gravel drive had been freshly raked and the lush shrubs had been trimmed and tended. Even the fountains of the ornamental lake were playing, perfectly orchestrated. Clear water rippled against a background of jade and lapis lazuli. Exotic birds looked carelessly at him as they dragged their glinting plumage about the perfect lawns where bowls, croquet and even cricket had been played in the old days. He reached the house, with

its three terraced verandahs, climbing quartz steps between monstrous tigers and dragons of coloured ceramic
and polished limestone, noting that the bronze doors, only
recently dosed with considerable quantities of Brasso so
that it hurt his eyes to look at them, were open, as if in
welcome. The doors were twice his height; he pushed
them back a fraction and squeezed through, entering the
cool shadows of his palace, pausing in the very centre of
the hall's bright mosaic floor, facing towards the main
staircase, of graduated shades of marble. There was no
dust. He cleared his throat. There was a discrete echo.

"Dassim Shan?"

His major domo·did not appear. The deities of a dozen
different faiths, bronze, ebony, porcelain, regarded him,
some glowering, some tranquil, from alcoves. Diffracted
light, entering through coloured patterned glass set close
to the ceiling, filled the hall with delicate shadows.

Jerry took a step or two towards the stairs, then paused,
hearing a movement overhead in the gallery behind him.
A light but perfectly pitched voice, a bitter-sweet voice
sang:

"Oh, Limehouse kid, oh, Limehouse kid, going the way
that the rest of them did. Poor broken blossom who's nobody's child. Haunted and taunted, you're just kind of
wild. Oh, Limehouse blues, I've the real Limehouse blues,
learnt from the Chinese those sad China blues. Rings on
my fingers and tears for a crown, that is the story of Old
China Town. . . ."

Languid as one of the peacocks outside, Una Persson
leaned against the carved marble balustrade. She wore a
long Molyneaux evening gown of the thinnest yellow silk
and her hair was cut short in a coolie crop with a fringe
at an angle on her forehead, framing her oval face, em-
phasising her ironic grey eyes. She began to move as he
looked up. She was smoking a cigarette without a holder.

Jerry had never seen her like this. "What?"

The gown caused her to stride in a peculiar swaying
gait. She walked round the gallery, her heels ticking, until
she came to the stairs. "Shall I come down?" she spoke
softly, laying a significant hand on the balustrade.

Jerry scratched his head under his helmet. He undid the
strap and removed it, shaking out his long hair. "Maybe
I'd better come up. I'm a bit more mobile."

"What's been going on in the big world?" she asked as she accompanied him to his study which lay almost at the end of the gallery. Some Guerlain perfume or other hung about her, making him uncertain of her identity as well as his own. He unlocked the door, intricately carved from local hardwood, and held it open for her. "It's delightful." She went directly to the french windows and opened them, admitting a certain amount of light and one or two insects which began enthusiastically to explore the large room. She swayed out into the sunshine, onto a balcony providing a view of the sea in one direction and the distant Iran Mountains in the other, all dark greens, blues and purples. The sky was perfect; blue with a touch or two of pink in it. "Oh, Jerry! This is the loveliest view!"

In the study there was a great deal of dust, as if it had all gathered in one place. Jerry wiped it from his desk with his white gauntlet, making long smears across the mother-of-pearl inlay. "Have you seen anything of Dassim Shan?"

"He's probably near the swimming pool. He spends most of his time there, I gather."

Jerry frowned. "Is he all right?"

"Well, he seems to have a rare form of hydrophilia which tends to make him a bit introspective. I shouldn't go to see him, if I were you, until I've had a chance to warn him. The shock could kill him."

"How long ago did this happen?"

"Soon after the resumption of hostilities."

"Sod," said Jerry. With a decisive gesture he threw off his flying helmet and reached to take a pre-wound ornamental turban, of red, green and yellow stripes, from the bottom drawer of his desk. He pinned up his hair. "It's my fault, as usual."

"You take too much on yourself," she said. She returned to the interior but then, when she saw that he intended to go onto the balcony, made a few backward steps so that she was outside again, her hands behind her, supporting her slim body as she rested against the racoco rail.

Adjusting the turban on his head he moved to join her. From where he stood he could see the lawns at the side of the palace, the cypresses which hid the servants' cottages, empty now. To his left he could make out the roofs of the deserted town. On his right loomed foothills, then mountains. "There are demands on one here," he told her. He tapped the turban. "There is more to this than a few privileges, Miss Persson. There is, perhaps, even a destiny."

He drew a deep breath of the sweet, heavy air.

"Duty?" She became immediately attentive.

2. Society hostess death riddle

"It's silly, I know," said Jerry as he and Una lay close together, knee to knee in the massive and uncomfortable bed, listening to the waves and the wild-life of the Sandakan dawn, "but I do miss America. I have ancestors there, you know."

"You're obsessed with your relatives." She reached for the silver filigree thermos jug and poured herself an inch or so of iced lime juice. She lifted the jade beaker to her lips. Already their affair had taken one or two turns for the worse.

He shrugged his blue silk shoulders. He flashed her a grin, his teeth unnaturally white against his unnaturally dark skin. "I have so many, Una."

The electrics were working unexpectedly well. As the dawn continued to bloom the four-bladed fan overhead hummed in sympathy with the voices of a thousand waking insects.

Jerry pulled back the netting and walked in bare feet to his dressing room next door and from there to the toilet. This suite was almost all polished mahogany, Victorian, designed, it appeared, to resist the Orient. He sat down on the elegant seat, at last able to relax. But within a moment or two she had joined him, quite naked apart from two ivory bangles on her left wrist, an Egyptian cigarette in one hand, the jade beaker in the other. She leaned against the door jamb, sipping from the glass. She studied his naked lower quarters. He regretted now that he had not locked himself in.

"I wish to god we could get some news, Jerry." She took a brief, nervous puff on her cigarette. "How's Dassim coming along with the radio?"

"He's had to cannibalise. From the plane. No luck so far."

"I'm frightfully bored, you see."

"I understand."

"I thought you'd be rounding up your faithful retainers, getting everybody back to work, clearing the harbour, sorting out the rubber and so on. There isn't one horse left in the stables. No ostlers or anything. You've done nothing except write in your notebooks."

"There's nobody to round up, you see," he explained. "They've either gone inland or else they're mentally deficient. The only people left in town are idiots."

"I quite agree. You couldn't give me a lift to the mainland, could you?"

"This is the mainland." He pointed through the door to the dark map on the wall behind her. He took a sheet of music manuscript from the floor and began to crumple it, to soften it. He stood up and wiped his black bottom.

"Of Borneo, though, darling."

He was still disorientated by the role she had adopted. He dropped the paper into the bowl and operated the lever to flush it away. "Where would you want to go?"

"What about—where is it?—Australia?"

"We'd have to stop for fuel before we reached Darwin. That DoX is a very greedy aeroplane, for all I've converted a lot of her passenger accommodation to fuel reserves. The only station I know of that's safe, because everyone's forgotten it, is Rowe Island. Moni?"

She sighed. "Too many skeletons."

"I must admit that's my feeling. One too many, at least."

"What about the other way?"

"We've only got a flying boat, don't forget."

"Singapore?"

"Singapore's out."

"Bangkok?"

"Bangkok's completely out."

"Anywhere else? Hong Kong? Formosa? Shanghai?"

"They're all out, too."

"Well, the Philippines, then."

"I told you what happened to the Philippines. Besides, I'd still have to come back and fuel would be a very serious problem."

"We'd be all right in the Philippines, wouldn't we? We could explain."

"I couldn't. I've had enough of that." He rolled his eyes and began to Charleston from the toilet. Gradually the Charleston turned into a cake-walk and from a cake-walk became a coon-dance. "I know where I'm well off." His arms flapped and jogged. "What do you think I was after in Sarawak? And I only left there in time!" He retreated into his netting again, peering at her through it. He stretched out on the bed. "I've no objection if you take the plane yourself."

"Oh, I'd never learn to fly."

"The last time I saw you—I think—you had a licence. Didn't you?"

"I may have told you something like that." She was vague, upset by the reference.

"It'll have to be Rowe Island, then. I've got to get back. I wouldn't be allowed into Australia under any circumstances."

"But your son . . . ?"

"I shouldn't have mentioned it."

"Ghosts," she said.

"You wouldn't recognise them now," he told her, parting the curtain and taking her hand. Tenderly he drew her back into the net.

3. An important message to every man and woman in America losing his or her hair

The lean steam yacht sailed fastidiously into Sandakan harbour, furled her white sails and dropped anchor. A little cream-coloured smoke drifted from her gleaming aristocratic funnels; her white sides were turned greenish blue, reflecting the water.

Watching from his balcony Jerry recognised the *Teddy Bear* and pursed his lips, in no doubt that his radio signals had been intercepted. She had hoisted a complicated collection of signals from her masthead, triatic stay, starboard yardarm and port yardarm, the simplest of which read *Coming to your assistance*. As Jerry looked, she ran the Red Ensign up her ensign staff. He made out the letters HBC in the fly and his suspicions were confirmed. There were few who would sail under the flag of the Hudson's Bay Company unless they had to.

He returned to his study to take from a table, on which there also rested a Harrison naval chronometer and a large globe of the world, his telescope. Once more on the balcony he focused the lens on the *Teddy Bear*. A number of sailors were at work on her decks; most of them wore uniforms closely resembling the tropical kit of the United States Navy. They were armed with Springfield rifles of an old-fashioned pattern; Jerry couldn't identify them. A moment later the flash of a maple-finished Remington stock confirmed everything he had suspected. He collapsed the telescope and went to find Una Persson.

She was in the swimming pool, bathing under the unseeing eyes of Dassim Shan. Her brown body flickered against shady jade, lapis lazuli and Tuscan marble.

Dassim Shan, in his elaborately embroidered coat of office, his small turban and his silk britches, sat where he always sat when not specifically employed, occasionally glancing up at the crystal dome of the roof, cocking an ear if he detected some slight difference in the sound of a fountain.

"It looks as if you'll soon be able to say goodbye to Borneo." Jerry squatted on the mosaic tiles at the edge of the pool. "Una. There's a ship turned up."

"British?"

"It might as well be. Beesley's tracked me down. I knew I hadn't really shaken him off in the States. He's been to Sumatra and picked up the steam yacht."

Her head came sliding over the surface to stare into his eyes. "Are you sure?"

"Quite sure. I recognised his daughter's butt."

"That he's come for you?"

"I suppose there's a slight chance he's run out of provisions and is hoping I've got the odd Tootsie Roll stashed away, but however you look at it the holiday's definitely coming to an end."

"I didn't want to go back to *work*." She pouted. "I'm far too tired. Besides, I'd do no good." She squeezed water from her eyes.

"You could always sing for the troops."

"Don't be vulgar, darling." Her head sought the depths.

"By and large," Jerry reflected, dabbling his fingers in the water, "I prefer a post-war situation to a pre-war one. But I was hoping to miss the current conflict altogether." He stared wistfully at Dassim Shan. The major domo seemed to have found a solution.

She was on the other side of the pool now, shaking liquid from her short hair. "What will you do?" she called.

"I'm a fatalist, these days. I'll play it by ear." He realised that his silk trousers were becoming damp. He rose. "What will you do?"

She wiped her mouth. "Look up Lobkowitz, I suppose. He usually has a fair idea of what's going on. This must mean the peace talks have broken down, eh?" Already she was beginning to sound like her old self.

"I don't think they've got to that stage yet." Jerry took a silver cigarette case from his jacket pocket, removed one of the last of his Shermans and hit it with a brass Dunhill lighter.

She clung to the side. "Beesley has some kind of official backing, you think?"

He drew on the brown cigarettello. "He's definitely not alone."

From far away there came the sound of a ship's siren.

Una pulled herself from the pool and wrapped a thick brocade robe about her. It was Chinese, in blue and gold. Dragons embraced her.

They waited for some time at the bronze doors of the palace before they saw Bishop Beesley marching through the gates towards them. He was at the head of a small party of marines in blancoed webbing, belts and puttees. Recognising Jerry and Una, Beesley stopped, signalling to his men who came immediately to attention, presenting arms. From behind them all Mitzi Beesley peeped out, waving the fingers of a malevolent imp.

Bishop Beesley was in full kit. His white and gold mitre, his bone and silver robes, were evidently fresh on, perhaps to impress any natives he might encounter. He held a rococo crook in one plump hand, a half-eaten bar of Zaanland Coffee Brandy Chocolate in the other.

"Still crawling away from the gibbering darkness are we, Mr. C? You should relax. Nothing's as bad as it seems." Bishop Beesley began a portly approach.

"Afternoon, Bishop," Jerry fell back on old dodges. "What brings you to the Islands?"

"Missionary work, my boy. We got your message and came as soon as we could. You wouldn't, by any chance, be able to offer us some refreshment?" He swallowed the remains of the Zaanland.

"We're a bit short-staffed, just now. More primitive than I care for myself." Jerry offered his arm to Una who took it. Together they led the way back into the palace.

"I thought you enjoyed living amongst the head-hunters, Mr Cornelius. After all, you and they have so much in common."

Jerry was genuinely puzzled. "There aren't any head-hunters in Sandakan. All that sort of thing's much further south. You're thinking of the Dyaks and their bloody oil-fields."

Bishop Beesley waddled in. "What a lovely home. I'll

just leave the boys outside, shall I? Mitzi! You don't mind if my daughter joins us?"

Mitzi Beesley was wearing a rather cheap rayon ensemble, loose sailor blouse and wide, baggy trousers, almost certainly a bad Schiaparelli copy of the sort obtainable from any second-rate tailor's shop in Bombay or Calcutta. Even the shade of pink was slightly off. Her golden hair was waved tightly against her mean little skull. She placed her small tongue on her thin lower lip and smiled at Una. "We've met before, haven't we?"

Una released Jerry's arm. "I don't think I'd be likely to remember," she said innocently. "How do you do, Miss Beesley?"

Mitzi sniffed. "Not bad. Not now. But times have been a bit chaotic until recently, when daddy got this new job." She removed her Remington from her shoulder and looked around for somewhere to put it.

"I'll take it," said Una hospitably.

Mitzi handed her the gun and Una crossed the mosaic to the large Ming ceramic umbrella stand, dropping the rifle, barrel first, among the walking sticks, sunshades and riding crops. "It'll be all right there, will it?"

"Fine," said Mitzi absently.

Bishop Beesley raised beringed fingers to his rosebud lips and uttered a little wind. "I hear they do a very pleasant dish in these parts. A local version of the baclava, eh?"

"I think there are a few cold ones in the storeroom," Jerry looked towards the door under the staircase. "Shall I show you where it is?"

"That's very kind of you, Mr. Cornelius. You seem, rather cleverly, to have adopted the manners as well as the style of a gentleman. Congratulations!"

"You're too kind."

"Standards are slipping everywhere. Credit where credit's due, sir. And, of course, I bear no grudges." His breathing became deeper. He was almost snoring by the time he had waddled to the door to the lower regions. "This is deliciously opulent, isn't it? The barbaric splendour of the East. You must feel much more at home."

"I can't complain, Bishop."

"Is Miss Brunner with you?" asked Una suddenly of Mitzi Beesley. It was as if she had remembered a name and nothing else.

"Not this trip." Mitzi moved closer to her. "That's a nice dressing-gown. Is it a man's?"

"I'm not sure." The two women followed Jerry and Bishop Beesley through the door and down stone steps cut from the living rock. It was suddenly much cooler.

"And as for Frank," continued Mitzi intimately, "Jerry's brother, you know—we couldn't get him to do a thing. It's as if there's a spell on everybody. Almost. You've met Doktor von Krupp, too, have you?"

"I think I might have. . . ."

"She's almost completely retired, now. Gave herself to the cause body and soul. Bishop Beesley has had to continue the work virtually single-handed. I help him as best I can, of course, but he complains that I don't really understand the importance of it all. He thinks my loyalties are sometimes divided." They were quite a long way behind the men. Mitzi smirked. "Of course, that's impossible. I haven't any loyalties at all."

"What a relief." Spasmodically, Una smiled down on the minx. She found that she was lying and enjoying the sensation. "How refreshing."

The minx began to stroke her exposed ribs.

The party descended still deeper into the darkness. From the gloom ahead Una could hear the sound of Bishop Beesley's awful breath.

"It's high time you were back in harness, Mr. C."

4. Cross country rape and slay spree of the frustrated bondage freak

"There's still a touch of vulgarity about you which I like," said Bishop Beesley. His marines had taken up permanent positions within the palace grounds and the bishop had almost completed his inventory of the building's contents. The two of them strolled between peacocks and birds of paradise and pedigree Sinhalese bantams, over the lawn towards the larger fountains which cast faint, flickering arabesques everywhere on grass and shrubs. The bishop was eating something sticky from one of Jerry's silver plates, holding the plate in his left hand while with his right he lifted the honey-flavoured food to his glistening lips. "What a riot of colour, those flowers and shrubs!" Flies were settling hopefully on his mitre. "America and Europe are getting along famously again. Say what you will about President Boyle, he's a dedicated international-ist. He's given the British authorities his whole support."

"It's the Islamic influence, I suppose," murmured Jerry. "I've always been a bit prone. . . ."

"Security is at a premium, Mr. Cornelius. Of course, it's given a tremendous boost to the navy. Britannia Resurgent!"

"We're a bit behind the times here." Jerry prised a determined mosquito from his cheek. "I'm afraid."

"How we'd all love to live in the past, particularly a past so splendid." Bishop Beesley expressed sympathy. He waved a cake. "No one understands all this better than I."

Jerry was doing his best to remember what had been going on. "I don't think I could go back to Britain," he said. "Not now."

"I would be the first to admit that there are, for certain people, difficulties. But with the proper papers you'd be quite safe. Restrictions aren't merely negative, you know. They work for you, too."

"They don't like me over there any more." He made a vague gesture towards the West. "Do they?"

"Nonsense. You can prove a change of heart!"

Jerry laughed. He put both his hands into a lattice of water, causing the fountain to alter its note. "That's the only thing that hasn't changed, Vicar."

"Come, come, come." Bishop Beesley clapped him on the back. For a few moments his fingers adhered to the silk of Jerry's pale blue kurta then came away with a small sucking sound. "You must be positive!"

Jerry said doubtfully: "I'll try. I have tried."

"I'll get my daughter to have a chat with you. She's helped you in the past, hasn't she?"

"I can't recall. . . ."

"It will come back." Bishop Beesley looked around for somewhere to put his empty plate. In the end he found a green soapstone sundial. "There isn't a great deal of time to spare. The box is still in England, I take it."

"Oh, yes," said Jerry dreamily, to be agreeable. He was incapable, just now, of thinking that far ahead.

"And with the box in the right hands, mankind will prosper again. A major war will be averted. The world will greet you as a saviour!"

"I thought I'd already turned the job down." Jerry found some seed in his pockets and began to throw it to the birds. From one of the upper floors of the palace came the strains of King Pleasure singing *Golden Days*. "That's a bit anachronistic, isn't it? Or is it me?"

For a moment Bishop Beesley's huge face became sober. "There is no need. . . ."

"Well, that's a relief, at any rate." Jerry rambled on. Ahead of him, on the other side of an ornamental hedge, two sailor hats drew down for cover. "What does Una say?" He sniffed a sweet magnolia blossom. "She's the brains of the outfit."

"I don't know how she feels but, as you say, she's an intelligent woman. My daughter's dealing with her. They are more sympatico."

"She'd feel all right about going back to Blighty. She wants to. Maybe you should just take her."

"Does she know where the box is?"

"I'm sure she does."

Bishop Beesley wiped his face with a red spotted handkerchief. He flicked at the flies and returned it to his back pocket. He inspected his left gaiter. "Is that a scorpion?" He pointed to the small insect crawling up his leg.

Gently, Jerry cupped his hand around the creature and held it on his palm, looking down at it. "It seems to be a wingless butterfly. Isn't that odd?"

Bishop Beesley glared around him. "Where's Mitzi?"

"Upstairs somewhere, with Una. Can't you hear the music?" King Pleasure was now singing his own *Little Boy, Don't Get Scared. Little fellow, don't get yellow and blue,* he sang.

Bishop Beesley smiled to himself. Jerry was still looking at the butterfly. "Hadn't you better kill it?" said the bishop. "I mean, it can't be happy."

"It doesn't look too unhappy, though." Jerry's hand shook a little. "I shouldn't worry." He placed the insect inside a scarlet rhododendron flower. "It might as well enjoy the time it's got."

Bishop Beesley evidently disapproved of these sentiments. He was about to speak when his small ears caught a sound from on high. Jerry heard it too and they both looked up.

Through the shimmering, heated sky there came a large, dark shape and, for some reason, Jerry became immediately more cheerful, even as he felt his last grip on consecutive thought slipping. "Well, well, well. An airship. From Rowe Island, I shouldn't wonder."

"Airships are—" Bishop Beesley clutched at his jowls. "Airships are—" His hand went to his back. His brow contorted. "Ah!"

Jerry began to jump about on the lawn, waving mindlessly to the massive black ship with its crimson markings. Disturbed, the peacocks and the bantams scattered screaming and clucking. Macaws filled the air, red, yellow, blue and green, shrieking.

"My back! Back!" moaned Bishop Beesley.

"It's tensions, I expect," suggested Jerry, turning for a

moment, but the bishop was already hobbling for the house. Jerry sat down on the lawn. There was a silly grin on his face. "Gosh! I never thought I'd be glad to see one of those buggers again!"

5. Spirit voices help me—Peter Sellers talks about the strange power that has entered his life

King Pleasure was doing *Tomorrow is another day* as, half his togs abandoned, his mitre over one sticky eye, Bishop Beesley rolled out of the palace, dragging Mitzi. His daughter was soft and naked, reluctant to leave, trying to work the bolt on her Remington, to remove a malacca cane from the barrel, slapping at his hands which seemed to be covered with feathers from a pillow. "Okay!" Her father shouted to the marines. "Okay!"

Bishop Beesley dragged Mitzi past Jerry. Her heels were making unsightly scars in the gravel. "I hope to god, Mr. Cornelius, none of this ever gets into the primary zone! I would like to remind you that this is the seventies."

"Almost a hundred, I'd have said. Phew, what a scorcher!" Jerry had begun to pick himself a bunch of flowers. "Blip," he added.

"It's all your fault," wailed Mitzi at him. "You and your rotten engines!"

"Blip."

The dark shadow of the circling airship passed over them for the fifth time. The birds of paradise were particularly disturbed by the commotion, running this way and that. The macaws and the bantams had completely disappeared. Only the peacocks had settled down and were screeching aggressively at the big vessel. For a moment or two Jerry imitated them, evidently for the fun of it, then he began to mumble, dropping his flowers. "Five. Birds. Water. Messiah. Ice."

Una emerged, in trench-coat and khaki, buckling on the heavy military holster containing her S&W .45. "That airship's come for us. Somebody's running a horrible risk.

We'd better bloody take advantage while we can. I'm
pissed off. What's Beesley got to do with me?"

"I'd thought airships were extinct," said Jerry. "Or not
invented yet. I'm slipping. Blip."

"We're all slipping. Everybody's slipping," screamed
Bishop Beesley, untangling his daughter from a jacaranda.
"Monstrous anachronisms! Come along Mitzi, please. The
co-ordinates haven't jelled yet, so there's a chance we can
escape before complete chaos results. Men! Men! Men!"
The marines began to emerge from peculiar hiding places,
like children interrupted in a game. "Deviants!"

"It's not my fault," said Jerry, "about Rowe Island. At
least, I don't think it is." His vacant eyes glanced questioningly at Una Persson. "Is it? It was dormant."

Her smile was brave and reassuring. "You'll be all
right, I expect."

*Tomorrow is the magic word. It's full of hopes and
dreams.* . . .

"Lovely." Jerry turned a seraphic face upwards. "I've
always thought they were, thought they were, thought they
were, thought they were, thought they were, thought they
were. . . ."

A long rope ladder fell from the centre section of the
gondola and almost hit him on his poor head. He continued
to stand there, mumbling, even as, from the other side of
the wall, rifles began to bark. "Get up it, you silly little
bugger!" shouted Una Persson. The Smith and Wesson
was now in her hand. For the moment the marines were
contenting themselves with pot-shots at the hull as they
retreated down the road and back through the town. "Get
up! Get up!"

"Yes, mum." He grinned a daft grin. He wondered why
he felt so happy. "What about you? Ladies first?"

"You've got a job to do, sunny jim," said Una grimly
and slapped him on the bottom. "Go on!"

He took hold of the rungs and began to climb the swaying ladder, chuckling childishly. The airship's engines
shouted and screamed as her crew manoeuvred her to
maintain her position in the air over the garden. Like the
Dornier, she had forward and backward facing engines,
the nacelles capable of turning through ninety degrees.
A late mark O'Bean, thought Jerry, as he lived and
breathed, but he did not know what he meant by the

thought. He was almost half-way up the ladder, giggling to himself, when he looked down. The golden dome, main roof of the palace, half-blinded him. "Get up!" cried a determined voice. With one arm hooked in the rungs, Una Persson was sighting along her revolver, picking off marines in the white, tree-lined road below. She called to the riggers peering at her from the open hatch through which the ladder had been lowered: "Take her up. Lift. Lift. I'll be fine." A winch creaked. The ladder rose a foot or two.

Jerry felt the wind in his hair. He had never had a better view of the island. "This is heavenly," he said. "What a smashing way to finish. Or begin." The rope swayed wildly. He almost fell off as he neared the top and the waiting gondola.

Hands found him: it was a disapproving Sebastian Auchinek, all scowls and moody, who hauled him in the last few feet. "You've got a long way to go yet, Mr. Cornelius." There were a number of dark figures in the bare aluminium interior, evidently a storage hatch. It reeked of high octane fuel. Through the gloom Jerry crawled towards the nearest bench, also of aluminium, bolted to the bulkhead. Out of the fresh air his high spirits had dropped away again and he was mumbling. "Airships. Human remains. Empires. War. Ideals. Science. . . ."

As Una Persson was dragged in, firing a last round or two at the marines, Prinz Lobkowitz sprang into the light from the entrance, reaching for the lever, closing the hatch-doors. "Thank god." He and Auchinek embraced the woman they loved. Lobkowitz wore riding britches, brown boots, spurs, a white roll-neck sweater, as if he had been taken away suddenly from a polo match. Auchinek wore a rather loud check suit that seemed to belong to the turn of the century.

Una frowned at them. "Should you be here, at all?"

There was a movement above and a pair of thin legs in dark green trousers with a red stripe climbed down the metal ladder into the hold. "We shouldn't." Major Nye was in the uniform of the 3rd Infantry, Punjab Irregular Force, rifle-green with black lace and red facings. "It's more comfortable above, by the way. This is just for stores, and we haven't any, of course." He looked over to Jerry, who drooled and simpered. "Poor old lad. We're dodging and weaving a bit, hoping for the best. He was due in England weeks before the *Teddy Bear*, you know. Everyone was contacted at very short notice, had to down tools and jump to it.—Shoulders to the wheel, lads, Shoulders to the wheel. . . ."

"What else could we do?" Gently Lobkowitz stroked Jerry's bewildered head. "Besides, he won't remember a lot. Neither shall we, for that matter. We'll drop him off in London and hope for the best."

Auchinek was sullen. Evidently he had taken part in the raid against his will.

"But California first stop. It's important that we all check our bearings again before we progress any further."

"Are you sure it's in California?" said Major Nye. "I thought it was in London, now."

"Not at the present," said Auchinek.

"Blip."

Tom McCarthy's patrol was supposed to round up a group of Rhodesian African guerrillas. Instead, he claims, it wiped out a village. There were about sixty victims—the entire population of a tiny village near the Mozambique border. McCarthy, a 22-year-old Londoner, who served in the Rhodesian Light Infantry, told the full story of the atrocity for the first time yesterday. McCarthy himself confessed that he shot a young terrorist as he lay wounded. He was ordered by an officer to shoot the boy. The death-mission began when the Rhodesian Special Branch was given a tip-off that the guerrillas would be slipping into the village to collect £1,000 towards their "funds." McCarthy and his patrol, including black scouts and members of the Rhodesian Special Air Service, were ordered from their base at Mount Darwin in the troubled border area north of Salisbury. They arrived at the village below the Mavura-donha mountain range, about 30 miles away, in darkness. Through their "night-sights" they saw 17 guerrillas arrive. But the Rhodesian soldiers did not move into the village to arrest them. Instead they illuminated the village with flares. Then they bombarded the huts with automatic fire and rockets. McCarthy maintained he could hear the screams of the villagers 300 yards away. Then he was called in to help with the "mopping-up operations." Thirteen of the terrorists died with the villagers. Four escaped but three were picked up later. McCarthy went into graphic detail of the alleged murder rampage by the Rhodesian troops. He said: "We were also told that the only prisoners we wanted were the terrorists. We were also told we were after the money. There was this boy of about seventeen. There was no doubt he was one of the guerrillas because I recognized him from the night-sight. He had been shot but he wasn't too bad and the medic was working on him. Someone must have decided that he knew nothing because the medic was told to move away." McCarthy was sending a radio message when an officer called him over and ordered him to shoot the youth. "I was frightened and asked if he wouldn't be any good. I was told: 'Certainly not.' I was shaking quite a bit and the officer said: 'Are you worried?' I knew that if I disobeyed a lawful command in an operational area I faced four years in the stockade. I remember putting the safety catch to 'rapid fire' and put my rifle to my shoulder. But I turned my face away before I fired. I missed by a foot—that will tell you how bad I was. He just lay there and put his arms up against his chest. I don't know why but he didn't say a word. He just looked at me and I'll always remember that as if it were just this morning." The officer then came behind McCarthy, grasped his head in both hands and said: "You useless —— bastard." McCarthy continued: "He forced my head down to look at the man on the ground and said: 'Now shoot the bastard.' This time I hit him between the nose and the mouth and his face just seemed to cave in."

Ellis Plaice, *Daily Mirror,* 27 February 1976

THE
REUNION
PARTY

William Randolph Hearst's monumental pile had first been displayed to the public on 2 June 1958 and since then had become one of California's greatest attractions, on a par with Hollywood and Disneyland, under the supervision of the California Department of Parks and Recreation, in accordance with Hearst's legacy after he had died, aged 88, on 13 August 1951; a mock Hispano-Moorish haven, crammed with the greatest collection of second rate art ever assembled in one private building, it lay on top of a hill once known as Camp Hill, now rechristened The Enchanted Hill and a visit to it was, according to the official guide book, "an experience unsurpassed by the other great dwellings built in a fabulous era when American tycoons were erecting imposing structures and importing art treasures found throughout the world. A walk through its grounds with terraced gardens, paths lined with camellia hedges, great banks of azaleas and rhododendron, more than 50 varieties of roses and the soft tinkling of water dripping from marble fountains, is a stroll through the epitome of beauty and grandeur. A great dream, never quite completed." The building began in 1919, nearly twenty years before the Derry and Toms Roof Garden, an echo, an exquisite miniature, had been opened in London. "There are," the guide book tells us, "100 rooms in the main building, including 38 bedrooms, 31 baths, 14 sitting rooms, 2 libraries, a theatre and an area that was meant to contain a complete bowling alley." Work on this building continued to 1947, when it was abandoned. There is no real evidence for the legend that in a year sometimes given as 1955, sometimes as 1985 and sometimes, obviously erroneously, as 1918, an important and secret meeting was held there of a number of men and women, representatives of most schools of thought and of many nations in the world. This has been variously described as the "Veteran's Meeting" or the "Reunion Party" and, of course, a number of books have been written in an effort to "explain" the legend. So far a satisfactory book has yet to appear, though all accounts are agreed on the authenticity of one piece of evidence, a guest list, giving the names of the guests in order of arrival, "with one notable absence, impossible to remedy at this stage" (as a pencilled note on the card points out). Accounts by local people concerning a huge concourse of ghosts on a day and a night in midsummer 1951, when shadowy figures were seen laughing and talking in the grounds, swimming in the Neptune pool, playing music of bizarre and unrecognisable origin, chiming the thirty-six carillon bells, housed in the twin Hispano-moresque towers of the Casa Grande; feasting in the huge refectory, with its silk banners representing the seventeen wards of Sienna, its Gothic tapestries and its fifteenth-century Spanish choir stalls, whilst seated at long tables of rich, old wood, burning oddly coloured lights, to ride off in a great flurry of hooves shortly before dawn, heading for the sea, have been independently confirmed and described, according to the taste of the teller, as a meeting of vampires, witches, devils or the Wild Hunt itself. Reports also agree that there was nothing sinister about the haunting, that, indeed, a great sense of peace and tranquillity pervaded the surrounding countryside on that Midsummer Night, a peace which those ancient Californian hills had not experienced for many a century, and the ghosts were generally thought to be "lucky" rather than "evil" (Butler, *Haunted California*, 1975). "Men and women from all sides of the conflict would meet on common ground and exchange information in the timeless halls and passages of the four castles, in the peaceful groves of this noble Tanelorn" (Butler, ibid). "Their voices were hushed and relaxed and there wasn't one who showed any animosity he or she might feel. . . ." (Hall, *The San Simeon Mystery Explained*, 1971). "The time of the final conflict was not yet. Their garments, their manners, their languages, their gestures represented the best that the twentieth century had been able to offer, the inheritance of Golden Age on Golden Age. Every enthusiasm was represented; every beast was in its prime. And, for a day and a night, there could be no question of invasion, even from within." (Morgan, *Law v. Chaos: The Last Great Meeting,* 1975). "Time travellers? Visitors from space? Ghosts? Or just a bunch of hoaxers—a gang of kids having fun? Then how to explain music that was years ahead of its time, fashions that were not seen until twenty years later, snatches of conversation referring to events occurring towards the end of this century?" (Fromental, *San Simeon, the Flying Saucers and Patty: Who is getting at who?* 1976).

The note of guests attending the "coven" or "sabbat," as others have called it, was found under the billiard table in the Game Room, written in longhand, not evidently American and probably English, headed "Manifestations" and, under that, "Arrivals in order of appearance." The names included the following:

Mr. J. Daker, Mr. J. Tallow, Mr. E. de Marylebone, Mr. Renark, Mr. E. Bloom, Mr. C. Marca, Mr. J. Cornelius. Prof. I. Hira, Mr. Smiles. Mr. Lucas. Mr. Powys. Miss C. Brunner, Mr. D. Koutrouboussis. Mr. Shades. Mrs. F. Cornelius. Mr. J. Tanglebones. Rev. Marek. Duge D. von Köln. Mr. K. Glogauer. Cpt. K. Arflane, Mrs. U. Rorsefne, Prof. Faustaff, Mr. U. Skarsol, Bishop D. and Miss M. Beesley, Dr. K. von Krupp, Captain C. Brunner, Mr. F. G. Gavin, Prince C. J. Irsei. Mr. E. P. Bradbury. Mr. J. Cornell. Mr. O. Bastable. Miss U. Persson. Cpt. J. Korzeniowsky. Mr. V. I. Ulyanov, Gen. O. T. Shaw, Major and Mrs. G. Nye. Captain and Mrs. G. Nye. Miss E. Nye. Miss H. Nye. Master P. Nye. Col. F. Pyat. Mr. S. M. Collier. Mr. M. Lescoq. Mr. M. Hope-Dempsey. Mr. C. Ryan. Prinz Lobkowitz. Mr. S. Koutrouboussis. Mr. C. Koutrouboussis. Mr. A. Koutrouboussis. Mr. R. Boyle, Mnr. P. Olmeijer. Mrs. H. Cornelius. Mrs. B. Beesley. Mr. S. Cohen. Miss H. Segal. Prof. M. O'Bèan. Mr. R. De Fete. Mr. C. Tome. Captain B. Maxwell. The Hon. Miss H. Sweet. Mr. S. Vaizey. Miss E. Knecht. Lady Sunday. Mrs. A. Underwood. Mr. J. Carnelian. Lady Charlotina Lake. Lord and

Lady Canaria. Miss Q. Gloriana. Miss M. Ming. Mrs. D. Armatuce. Gen. C. Hood. Lady Lyst. Mr. E. Wheldrake, Lord Rhoone. Lord Wynchett. Baroness Walewska. Sir. T. Fynes. Dr. J. Dee. Captain Quire, and a great number of other experienced people.

Notting Hill's annual Summer Carnival is unlikely to take place this year in its traditional form. The Royal Borough Council has told its organisers to find a fixed assembly point for this year's Carnival—preferably the White City Stadium in Shepherd's Bush. Alternative venues like Wembley Stadium and Wormwood Scrubs were also mentioned. But all the proposed sites are outside the Royal Borough, and the organisers have rejected these suggestions as boding "total destruction of the fundamental concept of what the Carnival should be." Their objections to deputy council leader Ald. Peter Methuen's "compromise" solution to the carnival problem were raised at a closed meeting between Royal Borough officials and various concerned parties at Kensington Town Hall last week. Cllr. Michael Cocks, who called the meeting, said it was vital to decide in good time how to avoid the controversy which followed last year's massive three-day celebrations. Nearly a quarter of a million people (mainly West Indian) flooded into the borough for last August's carnival —the tenth. But the aftermath of complaints from residents, the police and from certain councillors themselves, prompted the council to insist on a change of attitude to recognise that this once local event has now reached "national proportions." The objections of local residents, itemised in a 196-signature petition to the council, include noise (particularly from steel bands playing late into the night) and dirt and litter left after the weekend's festivities. Their petition called for "the immediate and effective prohibition of amplified music and vocal performances in the Westway and W.10 and W.11 areas and for the re-siting of the Notting Hill Carnival in 1976 and subsequent years."

The police added that the crime rate had increased seriously during Carnival time and that traffic congestion had blocked access for ambulances and fire engines. The council said that the event was now too large for them to provide adequate hygiene and litter amenities. . . . "To move to the White City would totally destroy the event as we know it," Mr. Palmer said. . . . "The festival is a street carnival and the whole atmosphere would be lost if it were moved out of the streets of North Kensington," said Labour leader Val Wallis. . . . But Mr. Anthony Perry, Director of the North Kensington Amenity Trust, warned that if the Carnival were to go ahead without approval, then the Trust, on whose land much of the festivity takes place, would not make the land available. "We are eager that it should be used by the community," Mr. Perry said, "but not against the wishes of the community."

Kensington News and Post, 6 February 1976

6. BAC cools hopes of airship boom

Jerry was still shivering as he waded out of the dirty
Cornish shallows onto Tintagel's ungenerous beach. A
careful search of all the caves in that half-eaten bay, of
the ruins of the castle, of the deserted town beyond, had
turned up nothing but debris, seaweed and dead fish.
Now his cold feet struck something white and mushy lying
on the shingle and, glancing hopefully down, he discovered only a bundle of quarto paper, secured by green
admiralty tags, typewritten. He went to turn the pages but
they disintegrated at once, like the flesh of a rotten sole.
He folded his arms for warmth, his ancient oilskins creaking and cracking at armpits and shoulders. He rid himself
of his stiff sou'wester, throwing it behind him, into the
Atlantic.

As he looked above the looming cliffs at the petulant
sky grey rain fell on his face. He tramped for the dangerous steps leading up the south face of the cove, beginning to regret overreacting and giving in to the impulse to
smash all his equipment, to rely entirely on metaphysical
methods for a final solution to his sister's malaise. Now his
foot slipped on a piece of rotten granite. He paused. A
darkness had entered the bay. His upward climb became
hastier. There was no use crying over diffused plasma (or
ectoplasm, for that matter): the world was splitting up,
like so many dividing cells, and the energy was unlikely to
be concentrated in any one place for much longer. He
had been foolish to believe that his remedy had been any
better than the others.

He reached the top of the cliff and made his way to the
old wooden cafe shack where he had left his camouflaged

jeep. It was still there, parked at an angle of forty degrees on the rutted path. He climbed in, thinking of Captain Brunner and wondering if the noble old anachronism's sacrifice had been worth anything in the long run. He took a yellowing packet of Black Cat cigarettes from the map compartment and lit one with the brass Dunhill he had found there; the lighter's flame was very low. He put the Black Cats in his pocket and abandoned the Dunhill. He turned the ignition key. The starting motor rolled sluggishly a few times but the engine failed to fire. Jerry had expected this. Even the American equipment wasn't what it had been; the mainland had sent no new supplies for months. In the back seats of the jeep he found his fur hat and mittens, his heavy P&O Norfolk jacket. He stripped off the oilskins and dressed himself more warmly, buckling the jacket's belt tightly around his waist.

He left the jeep behind, walking up the steep path towards the town. His search was proving entirely fruitless and he was tempted to give it up altogether, retiring from any kind of involvement, and yet his instincts had to be satisfied; he was resigned to continuing his quest. After all, most of his old enemies had themselves retired to safer zones. On the surface it seemed that the field was completely open.

The town had never been anything more than ramshackle, built primarily in response to the late 19th century tourist boom which had owed far less to Coleridge than to Tennyson and the Pre-Raphaelites. Even ruin could not make it picturesque. The streets were awash with weather-stained postcards, bedraggled and muddy King Arthur tea-towels, broken plastic Holy Grails, Excaliburs carved from chalk, tiny Round Tables to hang on the wall, and polystyrene crowns. In the reign of one Elizabeth the ideal had reached perfection and, in the reign of another, it had achieved its ultimate degradation. Jerry sniffed to himself. It had to happen sometime. Perhaps that was what he had failed to understand before.

He began to check the few parked cars, but all were in poor condition. The exodus had been made in less than a day, when the area had been, like so many, declared a non-civilian zone. Something to do with the Cornish Nationalist Movement. But the military had lost interest in the site almost immediately and had never established anything more than a few yards of barbed wire here and there.

Personally, Jerry thought the Americans had been a trifle naïve in thinking they had scored significant points in recruiting the CNM, a notoriously unreliable outfit whose members remained loyal only until they were trained and re-equipped when they deserted, returning to their rented farms and tithe-cottages to await the calling of their traditional landlord leaders. A few of them still worked freelance for the Americans but, Jerry had heard, the military advisers were reconsidering the system of paying scalp-bounty, since the scalps in question were always difficult to identify and, on more than one occasion, had proved to originate with their own personnel stationed in the remoter parts of West Penrith. Scalp-hunters had been reported in the area only a few days ago, so Jerry kept a wary hand on his vibragun and gave close attention to the shadows, though it was unlikely that any hunter would bother with Tintagel which was known to be abandoned.

Eventually Jerry gave up inspecting the cars and stepped through the smashed plate-glass window of a tea shop. From the counter a curious rat looked up and, for an instant, Jerry mistook him for the proprietor. Casting a prudent glance over its shoulder the rat beat a leisurely retreat. Jerry found himself a Coke in the powerless icebox and took it to a grimy table to consider his transport problems. The Coke tasted peculiar, having undergone some sort of transmutation, but he swallowed it anyway. It could always be that his own metabolism had changed, there had been so many fluctuations recently. At least the temporal shifts had become less crude, flowing smoothly one into the other, layer passing almost imperceptibly through layer so that it was not always possible to tell exactly what one's bearings were. Although it made his job harder, he couldn't complain. After all, much of it was his own fault. It was only demonstrating his theories.

He was awakened from this somewhat tranquil mood by the distant sound of an ageing engine.

7. UFOs—occupants and artifacts in Eastern Indiana

It was a broken-down Bedford two-tonner with a tattered canvas canopy; definitely a pre-war job. It moved slowly up the street as if searching for something. Jerry couldn't recognise the driver but, since this was his only chance of a lift, he decided to expose himself.

He ran to the fractured window and climbed carefully out to the pavement. The lorry stopped. Through the wound-down window a tired military face was presented to him. "Colonel Cornelius?"

"Well—" said Jerry doubtfully. "I think he's. . . . Can you give me a ride?"

The man had kindly but confused pale blue eyes. He was in his fifties or sixties, wearing a shiny blazer, a frayed shirt with washed out pink stripes, a regimental tie. He had a small grey moustache and thinning grey hair. "I'm Major Nye." He took a small photograph from above the driving mirror and looked from it to Jerry. "I'm to take you to Grasmere, I believe."

Jerry, trusting the major's identification better than his own memory, walked round the lorry and opened the door on the passenger's side. He put a foot on the step as Major Nye cleared various maps and documents from the worn leatherette upholstery. He climbed in and sat down, shutting the door with a slam. The Bedford's engine was still running. Major Nye put it into gear and began to back slowly up the street. "You came ashore here, did you?"

"In a manner of speaking," said Jerry.

"You knew about Grasmere?"

"I know *about* Grasmere, certainly."

"You'll be briefed there. Sorry we couldn't give you

something more sophisticated, but the Americans took their best stuff with them or else they destroyed it."

"The Americans have gone?"

"Didn't you know, old chap? Certainly. Pulled out altogether. Given Europe up as a bad job. Can't say I blame 'em. It means chaos now, of course. But, still. . . ." He stopped reversing and moved forward up the B road for Camelford. "It's going to be a struggle to get through. As you can imagine, communications are breaking down left, right and centre." He turned on the windscreen wipers as the rain grew heavier. "But so far no one group has displayed any sort of significant gain."

"Do you mean it's Civil War?" said Jerry in astonishment.

"It hasn't come to that yet."

Jerry smiled to himself. "It was always a game of Roundheads and Cavaliers for years, wasn't it? If you look at it one way."

"Oh, I quite agree with you." Major Nye was concentrating on his driving. "Come on, old girl. Come along then, beauty."

The Bedford responded with a little extra speed. Major Nye smiled. "The last lot of bombing didn't improve matters for us. There's scarcely a stretch of road left that hasn't been—" The lorry began to bump over potholes. "That's nothing compared to the destruction closer to London. Still, we'll be able to skirt London, that's one consolation." The rain crackled on the roof. In spite of the major's words, Jerry felt considerably safer in his company than he had felt for a very long time, particularly when he began to hum *The Ballad of Sexual Dependency* from *The Threepenny Opera*. The smell of petrol in the cab gradually became less noticeable and Jerry reached into his Norfolk for the ancient packet of Black Cats. He offered one to Major Nye. "No, thanks, old chap. Roll my own. I say, you wouldn't mind rolling one for me, would you?" He reached for a Rizla tin on the ledge above the dashboard and handed it to Jerry who tried to remember how to use the rolling machine, balancing it on his knees, putting paper, tobacco and filter into the rubber pad, licking the sticky edge of the paper, closing the lid and producing a fairly reasonable looking cigarette. With some pride he gave the result to the major who looked at it a little critically. "Thanks, old chap. Thicker than my usuals, but still. . . . Want one?"

"I'll stick to these," said Jerry. With his steel Dunhill, almost a match to the one he had left in the jeep, he lit the major's and then his own.

"Bloody rain," said the major. "You mustn't mind me. I've got awful habits. My wife says so. Swear all the time. India, I suppose."

There was silence for a while until they had gone through Camelford, witnessed by the suspicious eyes of the residents, and were on a road heading for Taunton and the M. Whereupon Major Nye, to Jerry's amazement, suddenly began to sing in a slight mellow voice: "Moonlight becomes you. It goes with your hair. Did anyone ever tell you how pom-pom ta-tee." He seemed unaware of his audience, peering placidly through the sheets of rain as the lorry bravely bucked along. "I'll see you again, whenever spring comes through again—through again? Something like that. Da da da dee-dee da-dum. In those old familiar places, with those old familiar traaaaa-taaaa. . . ." He went through a dozen song fragments in less than four minutes, like a malfunctioning juke box. "You're the cream in my coffee, I'm the milk in your tea." He finished his cigarette and wound down the window sufficiently to throw the butt away. "If you knew Peggy Sue. . . ." Then he seemed to remember Jerry. He opened the glove compartment to take out a large newspaper-wrapped packet. "Sandwich, old boy? Cheese and tomato probably, worst luck. Help yourself. There's far too many for me. The old ulcer. I can't eat much at a sitting. Little but often, that's the motto. Tuck in."

Jerry pulled away the paper and removed a sandwich. He relaxed in his seat, scarcely paying any attention even when three or four bright explosions lit the evening skyline to the east.

Major Nye did not seem particularly troubled, either, but regarded the explosions rather as confirmation of his earlier forebodings. "There you are," he said. "That's what the Americans have left us to handle."

"A bastard," said Jerry.

"The least of it," said Major Nye.

8. The girl next door could be a witch

There was no doubt about it, thought Jerry, there had
once been a time when he had been able to call at least
a little of the play. Nowadays even the smallest decisions
had been taken out of his hands. He yawned, searching
the grey road ahead for black patches that would indicate
shell holes. He didn't really care, because his interests were
becoming increasingly private as time went, if not on,
then at least backwards and forwards. Major Nye was
still singing. "Them good ol' boys drinkin' whisky an'
rye. . . ." Perhaps it did have something to do with his
losing faith in rock music. The best performers had
either died, decayed or fractured, leaving behind them
a vocabulary of musical ideas, lyrical techniques and
subject matter, styles and body languages which had
never been given the opportunity to mature but had, instead, been aped by the very world of Showbiz against
which they had originally revolted. And everything else
was just the same—a load of oily entrepreneurs with
their hair a little longer, their clothes occasionally a little
easier on the eyes, their language an eager combination
of professional slang and adman quasi-technical. It forced
you, whether you liked it or not, into a classical stance,
to long for a world when fiction really was stranger
than truth because there were no films, television, magazines, newspapers to prove differently, to find consolation
in the great Romantics of those far-off hazy days—
Schoenberg, Ives and Messiaen—to hang in a sticky web
of conflicting freedoms, finding an acceptable discipline
only in Art, and if you were not an artist then the only
alternative, as in Mo's case, was a nihilistic war against

the sole injustice you could identify, the tyranny of Time
and the human condition. . . .

Once again Major Nye rescued him from this sentimental reverie. "Here we are, old chap."

Jerry looked up, recognising tranquil Grasmere lake
on his left, the gigantic mock-gothic hotel which had
sheltered so many ecstatic old ladies from Minnesota before rocket fire had blown its roof away. Major Nye
steered the Bedford carefully off the road to the right
and into a small macadamised car-park surrounded by
a stone wall. A twisted sign read *Car Park For Wordsworth's Cottage Only.* Dove Cottage was to Jerry's right.
As Major Nye switched off the engine and sighed with
relief someone appeared at the gate and walked round
into the car park: a tall man of about the same age as
Major Nye but with a self-conscious dignity that was just
a little Teutonic. He wore an old-fashioned grey three-
piece suit and had a daffodil in his lapel. He was settling
a grey homburg on his distinguished patrician head,
knocking the ash from a cigarette which he smoked in
a six-inch holder, cupped in the Russian manner between
thumb and fingers.

Lost in a cavern of self-pity, Jerry remained in the cab
when Major Nye had walked through the drizzle to shake
hands with the newcomer. "Am I glad to see you, old
boy. We've been travelling the best part of two days—
rained the whole time. Nearly missed the petrol dump
outside Coventry. I'm afraid my passenger's become a
little depressed. Is your phone working? I'd like to tell my
wife we've arrived safe and sound."

"There are no lines, I fear." The man in grey spoke
softly. He had a pleasant foreign accent. "But your daughter is here."

"Splendid." Major Nye gestured to Jerry. "Time to
disembark, Colonel Cornelius."

Jerry roused himself. It was quite possible that the
petrol fumes were affecting him. He felt the need of a
pick-me-up. A Jimi Hendrix track or a few minutes of
Moses und Aron would be enough to do the trick; but he
had lost hope. He did his best to put on a more cheerful
face, opening his door, sliding to the ground, stretching
his legs and arms as he approached the pair. The rain fell
on his unprotected head. He had left his hat in the cab.

"I am Prinz Lobkowitz." The handsome man stared hard into Jerry's face. "You know me?"

"No," said Jerry. "Do you know me?" He could have ridden for ever in Major Nye's company. He was resentful that the journey was over.

"Oh, it's probably just a touch of deja vu," said Prinz Lobkowitz. "Come." He led the way up the crazy-paving path and into the cottage. "I think Elizabeth has the kettle on."

The cottage had not been used as anything but a museum for some time. The uncarpeted rooms were full of glass cases and miscellaneous objects marked "Probably Wordsworth's stick" and "The kind of pen Wordsworth would have used." Most of the genuine things had been sold off to the occupying troops years before. In a room at the back of the cottage was an ordinary table with a blue and white chintz cloth, a gas-stove on which boiled a large iron kettle, a gas-fire in the grate. Two women sat at the table, looking up as the three men entered.

Major Nye smiled. "Hello, young Bess." He embraced his rather plump and pretty daughter who wore a multi-coloured Afghan dress and who accepted the embrace with a degree of condescension.

"This is my friend Una," said Elizabeth Nye. "Una Persson."

"I think I've heard of you, my dear. How do you do?"

"How do you do?" said Una Persson.

Jerry was not sure he had ever seen a more beautiful woman. She wore a black trench-coat and beneath it a long suede riding skirt, black knee-length boots, a white polo-neck sweater. There was a cartridge belt around her waist and attached to it a holster for a large revolver. She shook hands with Major Nye and then with Jerry, giving them both a small but friendly smile. Her short chestnut hair fell into her eyes as she sat down again. She brushed it back with a long hand.

"I expect you've a good idea why we contacted you, colonel," said Prinz Lobkowitz, sitting close to Miss Persson, "but we ought to fill you in about the Scottish position as soon as possible. They'll be coming through for you shortly."

"Aha," said Jerry, looking for the radio.

Elizabeth Nye got up to pour hot water into a teapot.

"Just what I could do with," said Major Nye, rubbing his knotted hands together near the gas-fire. "This is Calor gas, I suppose, isn't it?"

"That's right." His daughter laughed. She took the pot to the table and put it down amongst the mugs and the milk and sugar already there. "Who likes it weak?"

"I'd better have it weak," said Major Nye. "Thanks, girly." He accepted the mug.

"As strong as it comes," said Jerry. "I'm afraid I've lost my memory."

"That's what I like to hear." Prinz Lobkowitz had responded to his first statement. "Eh?"

"My memory," Jerry said.

"Oh, sod it." Impatient air hissed from Miss Persson's clenched teeth. "He must be the most unreliable medium we've used. Every bloody time we need him he cops out —goes and loses his memory again."

"Sorry." Jerry was anxious to placate this lovely woman. "My mind's been taken up with my sister, you see. She's all I have."

Una Persson's expression softened. With her own hands she gave him a mug of tea. "Sugar?"

"Not for me. Just milk."

She poured a little milk into the mug.

"I don't know what I can do for you, really. I'm a fast learner, though. In some things, anyway." Jerry smiled at her, accepting the tea.

"It's not for us," said Prinz Lobkowitz. "It's the Scots. We promised them you could advise them. None of us has any experience in physics. Not yet. Not in a practical sense, at any rate."

"I've put all that sort of thing behind me," said Jerry.

Una Persson stood up and went to the window.

"I thought religion might help, you see," he continued. "If I redefined things in supernatural terms. It can sometimes work. In the short run."

He looked to them for confirmation and saw only bafflement.

"You'd better dredge up whatever you can," said Una Persson. "They've arrived."

The five people crowded to the window, staring through the trees and the ruins out towards the lake. In the centre of the lake was a small island, hilly and

wooded. Hovering over the island was a bulky hull. On
its tail-fins was painted the blue cross of St. Andrew. The
ship's entire outer skin was covered in the brilliant scarlet
sett of the McMahon clan.

"Why me?" said Jerry miserably.

"Just your bad luck, I'm afraid," said Prinz Lobkowitz.
"We're hoping that Scotland will hold, you see. Everything else is disintegrating rapidly."

"Politics?" Jerry became wary. "Is this some sort of
manipulation?"

Major Nye patted Jerry on the back.

"Cheer up, old chap. It won't be for long, after all."

"I thought I was regressing, but this—Christ!" He let
them push him towards the door.

"In the meantime," said Una Persson suddenly, a little
brisk sympathy in her tone, "we'll be helping you look
for Catherine. How's that?"

Jerry spread his hands. "Out?"

9. A Bicentennial celebration. The 1976 Guns and Ammo Annual. It's all new . . . it's informative . . . it's authoritative. . . . Start your "Bicentennial" celebration today!

Dodging and weaving as usual Jerry slithered down the mound of refuse, his kilt left behind him like a forgotten fleece where it had snagged on the barbed wire and pulled free. Below him was what remained of the road and, on the other side, the ruins of the Convent of the Poor Clares. He was relieved to see that the row of houses on the South side of Blenheim Crescent although boarded up had escaped any major damage. He had jumped ship as the *James Durie* lost height over what had been the Mitcham Golf Course, had made it as far as the Bangladeshi ghetto in Tooting, where, under the hastily invented pseudonym "Secundra Dass," he had been accepted and passed on through Brixton and as far as Pimlico before the chain had broken and he had found himself alone. From Pimlico he had to cross the desolation of Knightsbridge before he was in sight of home. Knightsbridge was the most notorious of all quarters, its inhabitants so vicious that they were feared even by the infamous denizens of Mayfair. Moreover Jerry in his kilt and turban had had the odds stacked as high against him as was possible, short of having a wooden leg as well. He had been fortunate in retaining his claymore and kris and with these weapons had been able to score himself a serviceable Lee-Enfield from a tall and muscular young lady in a silk headscarf and a necklace of black human ears.

Now, in grubby underpants, his legs running with cuts and half-healed gashes, the .303 cocked, he reached the Convent, drawn towards the blasted chapel by the faint strains of Buddy Holly singing . . . *my heart grows cold and old . . .* on a tiny cassette machine. It was a signal. The song faded and became *You've Got To Hide Your Love Away*. It could not be a trap. He relaxed by a fraction and put the rifle under his arm so that he could stoop and pull up his socks which had slipped down inside his stolen wellington boots (another prize from the lady in the headscarf). A shadow moved behind a mock Gothic window. The music stopped. Jerry raised his rifle and advanced. Pieces of broken plaster stirred as Sebastian Auchinek, in a neat set of fatigues, a Browning automatic in his inexperienced fist, broke cover, his free hand held palm outwards without much hope. His large brown eyes were wary, antagonistic, ready, as ever, for compromise. Instantly the Dixie Cups began to sing *Chapel of Love*.

"You're looking pale, Mr. Cornelius. You've lost your usual camouflage, eh? What's the matter—is the famous survival instinct shot at last?"

"I can't help the opinions people hold of me," said Jerry. "Your message came through days ago. I'm sorry I couldn't get here sooner."

"Don't give it a thought. There's not an awful lot of danger around at the moment. It's as quiet as the grave. Almost rural in some respects." He sounded wistful.

"It always was," said Jerry. "Enervating, isn't it, conventional warfare?"

"You're not fooling me, my son. I'm hip to any Pied Piper tricks." Auchinek holstered his Browning. "I'm acting on behalf of Miss Persson. As her agent. She asked me to do this."

"Still in the promotion business, then?" Jerry followed the Jew into the shadows of the chapel and found a seat on the cold ugly marble of the altar. "What sort of acts are going down with the London public at the moment?" He began to shiver. "You couldn't lend me a costume, could you?"

Auchinek was pleased with the situation. "Sorry," he said casually, "all the props are gone."

"You could lend me your guerrilla suit. You won't win the girl by making a monkey of yourself, king. Apeing her's not going to help the state of the Empire. Aaah!" Jerry opened his mouth and screeched with laughter, displaying his broken, piebald teeth.

"And you'll never get away with that material."
Auchinek shook his head. "Not these days. Tastes are
changing. The public wants sophisticated romantic com-
edy. You're offering them amateurish street theatre.
Things have come a long way since the mummer's plays.
It won't do, Mr. Cornelius."

Jerry scratched his neck. "So it is an audition, after
all?"

"Of sorts. I can help you. There might be room for a
brother and sister act in our final programme." He studied Jerry's eyes and seemed satisfied by the reaction he
received. Jerry got down from the altar. Sebastian
Auchinek turned over the tape to its reverse side. *I believe in yesterday* sang Paul McCartney, his voice finding
an echo in what remained of the roof. With a sudden
burst of malicious energy Auchinek flung the player
against the wall. It smashed at once and there was silence.
"I'm Miss Persson's manager, as you know, but I do sometimes handle other people. . . ."

"You don't have to tell me. Are you talking about
Catherine?"

"I am. My spell in the USAF. . . ."

"I don't want to know about your introduction to
black magic. . . ."

". . . proved useful in that I was able to acquire certain rights. . . ."

"I told you. . . ."

". . . and in turn come to possession. . . ."

"You're not listening. Your religious convictions are
your own. All I want to know——"

". . . of a number of flies—files—pertaining to the
activities of informants operating in this area."

"Narks? Stoolies? Squealers?"

"One of whom was a friend of yours, I believe. Gordon
Gavin."

"Flash Gordon."

"I was able to interview him, just before the big pull-
out. He knew the whereabouts of your sister. She's still
here."

"She can't be. I moved her, didn't I? I had her—I had
her—that's what I can't remember. But I was sure. . . ."

"Only the surface suffered much. The underground
sections are still almost entirely intact and functioning.

Why, there's a rumour that some of these tunnels go all the way to Lappland."

"So she was under my nose before, before, before. . . ." Jerry's head was aching badly. "Have you got her safe?"

"She doesn't look too good to me. But Miss Persson assured me. . . ."

"She's an expert at that." Images filled his poor battered head. He left the chapel and ran across to the main building, up the fractured stairs, over the demolished threshold, waist deep in lath and plaster, brickwork and shattered timber, wading towards his only hope, his goal, his faith, flailing around him as, with his last reserves of energy, he shifted muck and rubble.

"Catherine!

"Catherine!

"Catherine!"

In critical awe Sebastian Auchinek watched the wasted body of the wailing barbarian disappear in a chaos of dust.

10. High intensity colour (that's actually good for your eyes!)

"Airship? You never bin on a bleedin' airship—not since you woz a boy at ther bloody Scrubs Lane fair!" Mrs. Cornelius had a good laugh before looking down on her son and shaking her huge head, freshly permed, freshly gold. Her mouth was a handsome crimson, an exotic blossom, its tints echoed in her cheeks, contrasted by her eyelids of midnite blue, the pink powder. She belched and her breasts wobbled as she patted at her belly. "Pardon." She tugged at the waist of her cotton frock with its pattern of maroon and yellow nasturtiums. "Ah. Thass better. Wot's 'appened ter Frank?"

"He went off with the colonel, Mum," said Jerry meekly. "You didn't tell him about Cathy, did you?"

"Fink I'm daft. Silly bugger! 'Course I didn't. We don't wan' the 'ole fuckin' world ter know, do we?" Although not altogether sure what was wrong with her daughter, Mrs. Cornelius had a strong suspicion that it was connected with something scandalous. When Jerry had brought her home his mother had immediately suspected him of having attempted an abortion on her. It had been Colonel Pyat, with his connections, who had known of the fortified hospital at Roedean and arranged for the girl to be taken there. Catherine had been in the worst condition Jerry had ever seen her—more than a little frost-blackened. The hospital, however, was the best there was. The doctors had every confidence, they said, in an early revival. Jerry had had to borrow four cases of 12.77mm machine-gun ammunition from Colonel Pyat to add to his own store, and that had been for the hospital's down payment only. He wasn't sure where he was going to find the

BTR-50PK armoured personnel carrier he would need to secure the release of his sister once she was up and about. Again Colonel Pyat had been reassuring, promising that he would underwrite Jerry until the situation improved for him.

Jerry had wanted to go straight back to London from Roedean but his mother insisted on making a day of it. Frank was living in Brighton now, running a small general shop, and Mrs. Cornelius wanted to see how he was getting on.

"It 'asn't arf changed," declared Mrs. Cornelius as she stood regarding the twisted pier, most of which had tipped itself into the sea. She pointed at a distant girder. "Thass where the ol' dodgems useter be, innit."

Jerry turned up the collar of his black car coat. He put his hands deep into his pockets. It was very cold for May, although the sky was blue and clear and the water as calm as the Mediterranean. He was worried in case Colonel Pyat told Frank something which would start the whole trouble all over again. He looked back towards the darkened dolphinarium in time to see the colonel and his brother ascending the steps to the street. Colonel Pyat shook his head calling: "Nothing I'm afraid!"

"Orl I bleedin' want is a bag o' fish an' chips!" said Mrs. Cornelius with a gigantic sigh of dismay. She patted her son on the shoulder. "Up yer get, Jer'."

Jerry rose from the bench, moving his weight from foot to foot, running his tongue round the inside of his mouth. "I'm a bit worried about the lorry," he said. "What with the scavengers and that."

"It'll be safe enough where it is," she reassured him. "I wish ther bloody trains woz still goin'. Cor! Wot a cumdarn, eh?" She cast a disgusted eye over the wrecked façades, the faded signs. "Yer carn't even go on ther fuckin' beach for bleedin' bar' wire!"

Frank and Colonel Pyat arrived to stand beside them. Jerry was disturbed by the fact that Frank wore a black coat almost identical to his own. His brother's eyes were warm and cunning as if he had recently sniffed prey. "Not a chip to be had," said Frank. "Sorry, Mum. It's what I thought. Nobody's catching any fish, for one thing." He anticipated his mother's next question before she asked it. "And, of course, there hasn't been a pub open since the

ordinance. You'd better take me up on that sandwich."
He nodded towards the twitterns of the town's cold interior. "Back at the shop."

Mrs. Cornelius sighed. "I used ter love this place. It woz reelly fun. Remember ther races, Ferdy?"

Colonel Pyat, who wore a cavalry twill military style overcoat, nodded his heavy Slavic head. "Everything is gone now."

"It's not as bad as all that," said Frank. "A lot of the old residents are still here. We've quite a flourishing community, really. We've kept our identity, which is more than you can say of some. We can't offer the facilities to visitors nowadays, of course, but perhaps that's for the best—so far as the indigenous population's concerned. But you'll see. Brighton'll be back to normal before you know it."

Jerry removed a dirty handkerchief from his pocket and loudly blew his nose. Frank darted him a weary look. "Cool it, Jerry."

Jerry put his handkerchief away. "I shouldn't've thought it could have got any cooler."

For the first time Mrs. Cornelius noticed the cold. "Yore right. It's bloody freezin'. You got anyfink I c'n put on, Frank?"

"I've got some lovely coats back at the shop. Real mink. I'll lend you one of those." Frank began to walk along the front and they followed.

"Mink?" said his mother. "Bloody 'ell! You must be doin' orl right, as usual!"

"There's not a lot of call for luxury goods just now. But that'll change in time. I accepted them as barter." Frank laughed. "I must have every decent mink coat on the South Coast. I've literally got a back room full of them. The trouble is, though, that they attract rats."

"Aaawk!" said Mrs. Cornelius ritualistically.

Frank stopped and then fell in beside Jerry. "And how's life treating you?" His bleak eyes stared out to sea, giving the horizon a shifty once-over. "Getting by, are we?"

"Under the circumstances," said Jerry.

"A bit more realistic, these days, I should think." Frank was almost euphorically triumphant. He tapped his head.

"Got the old imagination in check at last. You're staying with mum?"

"I've been a bit queer," said Jerry.

"So she's looking after you, is she?"

"Well, my own place. . . ."

"A direct hit, I heard. Shame."

They were some distance ahead of Mrs. C and Colonel P now. Frank led the way up King Street. "You had your head in the clouds, you see. Now I saw the way the wind was blowing. I've got my shop. In real terms I'm probably the richest man in Sussex. Surrey, too, I shouldn't wonder. Got four Pakis working for me. Kept my head down, see, and my nose clean and here I am. I don't deny I'm well off. I don't feel guilty."

"Guilty?" Jerry had never heard his brother use the word. He cheered up a fraction. "Blimey! You must have done some terrible things. Brighton's getting to you, then?"

"What?" Frank was puzzled. "I'm happy, Jerry. Not many can say that, these days. Got my pick of anything I want. Any *body* I want." He nudged his brother in the ribs. "Some of those people'll give anything for a bit of fresh liver. Their little daughters. Eh? What! They never learned to fight, you see—only complain. I must have had every 'Disgusted' in the Home Counties in my shop! Well, I ask you!" He paused. Mrs. Cornelius and her escort were a fair way behind, labouring up the hill. "You want to work for me? Is that why you came?"

"Mum wanted to see how you were doing. I just drove the lorry."

"Your lorry, is it?"

"The colonel's. He was in the last government for a few days."

"Did all right for himself, then?"

"He reckons he was sold short." Jerry spoke listlessly as he looked at a sea bereft of boats, a sky without ships, a street without music. Catherine remained and he was helpless to give her comfort or take any direct part in her destiny. He swayed as his mother came closer. She was bent almost double, rubbing her thumb against her index finger, making peculiar smacking noises with her lips. He felt very dizzy indeed. Frank glanced at him. "You've gone all yellow."

"I'm tired," said Jerry.

"Totch-totch," said Mrs. Cornelius. "Come 'ere, yer littel bleeder. Totch-totch-totch."

Through rapidly blurring vision Jerry saw that she was addressing a small, mangy black-and-white cat in the gutter. The animal walked slowly and amiably towards her, rubbing its flank against the kerb, its tail erect.

Jerry sat down on the pavement.

His mother didn't notice what was happening to him; but the cat turned to look at him, its intelligent green eyes piercing his own.

For a moment it seemed to Jerry that his entire being was about to be drawn into the body of the cat. Then Mrs. Cornelius had pounced and seized the animal. "Gotcha, yer little bugger!"

"This is a fine time to start playing the Fool," said Frank.

Jerry passed out.

EARLY REPORTS

Many bathing deaths were reported from seaside resorts yesterday. Two men and a boy were drowned while bathing near Llanelly, and Bertie Crooke, sixteen, son of a soldier, was drowned at Exmouth. Mr. Duncan McGregor (twenty-four), a chemist, of Coatbridge, while bathing at Spittal was carried away by a strong current and drowned, despite the brave attempts to rescue him made by Mr. James Webster, of Airdrie. Two young munition workers named Griffith Robert Jones and Richard Morris were drowned while bathing at Burport.

Sunday Pictorial, 22 July 1917

The following notice announcing the adoption of a system of air-raid warnings for London by "sound-bomb" was issued last night:—The experiments made on Thursday with sky signals showed the value of sound bombs for the purpose of warning the population of London. . . . The signal will consist of three sound bombs fired at intervals of a quarter of a minute . . . having regard to the speed at which aeroplanes now travel, the warning at the point attacked can only be of a few minutes' duration.

Sunday Pictorial, 22 July 1917

The *Bourse Gazette* states that the Premier, Prince Lvoff, has resigned. M. Kerensky has been appointed Premier, temporarily retaining the portfolios of War and Marine. M. Kerensky has sent a message to Reval, Helsingfors, and other points, saying: The disturbances have now been completely suppressed. The arrest of the leaders and of those guilty of the blood of their brothers and of crimes

against the country and the revolution is proceeding. . . .
I appeal to all true sons of democracy to save the country
and the revolution from the enemy without and his Allies
within.

Sunday Pictorial, 22 July 1917

Aliens living at Folkestone and Margate have been given
notice to leave the towns . . . under a new Home Office
Order which prohibits their presence within 20 miles of
the coast. At Folkestone 130 foreigners are affected. They
must be out of the town by midnight tonight. At Margate
238 have been given three days' notice.

The Times, 5 June 1940

The trial began before Mr. Justice Atkinson at the Cen-
tral Criminal Court yesterday of Udham Singh, 37, an
Indian engineer, who is charged with the murder of Sir
Michael Frances O'Dwyer, a former Governor of the
Punjab, at the close of a lecture at Caxton Hall, West-
minister, on March 13. He pleaded "Not Guilty."

The Times, 5 June 1940

Prefabs, with people clinging to the roofs, floated past
bedroom windows at Felixstowe, where disaster arrived
when the River Orwell burst its banks two miles away.
Survivors told of nightmare screams and shouts for help
as they watched people slide to their deaths from floating
prefabs. Mrs. Beryl Hillary . . . said they were awakened
by screams. "As I looked out of the window I saw a little
girl washed off the roof of a prefab and drown." In Or-
ford Road, where the Hillarys lived, a mother, father and
two young children were drowned in a downstairs flat.
People in the top flat were rescued. Mrs. Katherine Min-
ter, of Lauger Road, said: "In the darkness all that could
be heard was the roaring of the water and the screaming
of terrified women. The housing estate was like an
ocean." . . . Two-year-old Valerie—she could not tell
nurses her surname—cried in hospital for her parents.
They are listed among the missing.

Daily Sketch, 2 February 1953

A baby girl died in a basement blaze in Sorcham Street,
North Kensington on Saturday after two passers by had

hurled themselves into the burning front room when they heard her screams.

Kensington Post, 19 February 1965

Fire danger in North Kensington has become a controversial issue between the LCC and KBC. They sharply disagree on the code of fire prevention for lodging and rooming houses. Kensington Council say that the LCC Code of Escape from Fire is impracticable and expensive. They claim it would mean an average cost of £300 per house. . . . Kensington Council have not yet revealed their own plans for fire prevention, but there is no doubt they envisage a much cheaper and simpler code.

Kensington Post, 19 February 1965

Jimi Hendrix, the pop musician, died in London yesterday, as reported elsewhere in this issue. If Bob Dylan was the man who liberated pop music verbally, to the extent that after him it could deal with subjects other than teenage affection, then Jimi Hendrix was largely responsible for whatever musical metamorphosis it has undergone in the past three years. Born in Seattle, Washington, he was part Negro, part Cherokee Indian, part Mexican, and gave his date of birth as 27 November 1945.

The Times, 19 September 1970

Part-time soldiers have been on manoeuvres with a Nazi "secret army" it was claimed yesterday. The troops were members of a Territorial Army unit. Special Branch investigators have been told that TA men linked up with a Nazi paramilitary group known as Column 88 for exercises in the Savernake Forest in Wiltshire. At least one TA officer—said to be a secret Nazi group member—is alleged to have helped to set up the operation. Members of the 20-strong TA unit thought the Nazis were another TA group. During the exercise the soldiers acted as mock terrorists, while the Nazis played the role of defenders of an important military target.

Daily Mirror, 19 April 1976

TUNING UP (4)

"What infernal bad luck!" As he walked along the deck in his glittering white uniform Colonel Pyat tossed his racquet in the air and caught it again. "We lost all our balls."

"Overboard," said Catherine, indicating the Mediterranean. She, too, wore white, a boater with a blue and white band, a simple silk shirt-waister with a pale blue broderie anglaise bodice. The skirt of the dress was cut just on the ankle of her kid boots. She and he had been playing tennis in the yacht's court, astern. "Entirely my fault. I'm terrible."

Jerry shifted his weight in the blue and white deck-chair, putting his newspaper on the matching canvas stool at his elbow. "I'm sure we'll be able to get you some more. In Alexandria, perhaps." He ran a finger round the inside of his hard collar.

"Is it far, Alexandria?" she asked him. She sat in the chair next to his. Colonel Pyat hovered, then went to stand by the *Teddy Bear*'s rail.

"Not too far." A tiny breeze found his face. He sighed with pleasure.

Colonel Pyat laid a finger on one side of his small moustache and peered out from beneath his cap. The peak shaded his eyes completely. Indeed, the only strong feature visible was his neat Imperial. "Shouldn't you be getting ready? It's almost tea time."

"So I should." Jerry rose from the canvas chair. He gathered up his books and papers. "And you, too, Catherine, eh?" He raised his Panama. "I'll see you later, then."

"Fine," said the colonel.

Jerry crossed to his cabin. It faced forward—a bedroom, a sitting room and a dressing room. It was full of light from the large port-holes on three sides, simply furnished with Charles Rennie Mackintosh designs. Even as he changed into his costume he heard eight bells ring for the dog-watch; time for tea. Slipping on his domino Jerry hurried out, making for the stern and the quarterdeck where a piano had been set up by lithe Lascar matelots. On the rest of the deck were little gilded bamboo tables with lace cloths; they had matching gilded bamboo chairs, upholstered in blue plush.

As Jerry approached the quarterdeck, racing down the companionway, he almost bumped into Miss Brunner, the governess, who made a clicking noise with her tongue before she guessed who he was. Dyak stewards, in white turbans, red Zouave jackets and blue sarongs, were setting silver-ware and tea-pots on the tables. Jerry ascended the last companionway just ahead of Bishop Beesley and Karen von Krupp (wearing her usual Brunswick coffee-coloured afternoon gown), two of his guests on the cruise, and just behind Una Persson who was smoothing the folds of her elaborate Columbine costume, gold, white and scarlet, and adjusting her own domino mask. She stood beside the piano, protecting her head with a Japanese sunshade. Jerry winked at her and sat down at the piano.

"Shall we try it, then?"

Una Persson looked at Bishop Beesley, Karen von Krupp and Miss Brunner who were arranging themselves at the farthest table, near the rail. "Why not?" she said. She cleared her throat. Jerry lifted the lid of the piano and played a few notes, exercising his fingers, folding back the flounced cuffs of his red, white and blue pierrot suit. "Where's Catherine?"

"On her way." Jerry spread his new music.

"And Prinz Lobkowitz?"

"On his way."

"Auchinek?"

"You'd know better than I, my dear." Jerry put his thumb on middle C.

"Your Mr. Collier?"

"Doubtless on his way."

"They're all arriving, the audience. Oh, I hate bad timekeeping." She folded her sunshade and put it behind the piano.

Jerry played a ¾ tango rhythm with his left hand.
"We might as well start, I think. It's only an amateur
show, Una."

She put one hand on the quarterdeck's port rail,
glanced at the smooth sea, raised herself on the points of
her ballet slippers, twirling in her three-quarter-length
skirt. She began to smile. It was the professional in her.
To encourage his companion, Jerry played a white note
glissando and began to hum the tune of their song as
Major Nye, Mrs. Nye, the Nye daughters and the Neys'
little boy, Pip, took their places at two tables near the
front. Major Nye was smiling in delight. "How jolly!"
Mrs. Nye did her best to smile, but she was not in
Una's class. The girls looked a trifle embarrassed and
the little boy seemed astonished. He wore a sailor suit,
as did his sisters. The Dyaks bent over them to take
their orders. Mrs. Cornelius, in a huge cream and strawberry day dress and a lopsided Gainsborough hat, arrived on the arm of her son Frank who wore an orange,
blue and green blazer, white cotton trousers and a yellow boater. Una began to sing in her high, sweet voice:

> *My pulse rate stood at zero*
> *When I first saw my Pierrot.*

Jerry sang to her over his right shoulder as he continued to play:

> *My temperature rose to ninety-nine*
> *When I beheld my Columbine.*

Catherine ran onto the deck, arriving just in time to join
Una. Catherine, too, was masked, dressed as Harlequin
in colours to match Una's. She had her magic wand in her
hand, Harlequin's slap-stick with which, traditionally,
everything could be transformed into something else.
They all sang the chorus:

> *Sigh, sigh, sigh . . .*
> *For love that's oft denied.*
> *Cry, cry, cry . . .*
> *My lips remain unsatisfied*
> *I'm yearning so, for my own Pierrot.*

Catherine took Una about the waist and they danced together for the last line of the chorus.

As we dance the En-tropy Tan-go!

Jerry played the chorus through again, making it more lively and giving it a strict tango rhythm now, for Auchinek had reached them. He was in white from head to foot, half his thin face covered in an expressionless white mask, the rest caked in dead white make-up, a false grey beard, huge glasses, crowned by an elongated silk hat. He was old Pantaloon, as orthodox as ever in the traditional dell'arte costume.

Una and Catherine were cheek to cheek. "Sigh, sigh, sigh. . . ." Their eyes were fixed on the audience. Auchinek went to stand awkwardly on the other side of Jerry, evidently trying to remember the lyrics. When Jerry had told him of the plan he had gone from Naples to Rome by train to buy his costume. "For love that's oft denied." Jerry stared mournfully at Columbine. "Cry, cry, cry. . . . My lips remain unsatisfied. . . ." Facing Jerry now, Una sang perhaps a mite too sardonically: "I'm yearning so for my own Pierrot." And altogether: "As we dance the Entropy Tan-tan-go!"

Colonel Pyat sat down, raising his cap in jovial, if uncomprehending, appreciation. Nearby, Frank Cornelius frowned as he tried to make out the words, comprehending all too well. He began to look a bit alarmed.

Prinz Lobkowitz came up at last, all in black velvet save for a white frill around his neck, a beribboned mandolin in his hand, his eyes merry behind his mask, as Scaramouche, and behind him was Shakey Mo Collier, panting, scrambling, swaggering as soon as he was in sight of the audience, in a gorgeously elaborate military uniform, festooned with braid, blazing with brass, a great Wellington hat on his head, sporting ostrich and peacock feathers, wearing false moustachios which he twirled rather too often, monstrous eyebrows which threatened to blind him, jackboots and sabre, a perfect burlesque bantam dandy, Captain Fracasse.

Assembled they sang the next chorus with wavering gusto:

I'll weep, weep, weep
Till he sweeps me off my feet.
My heart will beat, beat, beat,
And my body lose its heat.
Oh, life no longer seems so sweet
Since that sad Pierrot became my beau
And taught me the En-tro-py Tan-go!

Harlequin tango'd with Pantaloon, Columbine with Scaramouche, Pierrot with Captain Fracasse, until Jerry had to return to his place at the piano for his own verse:

So flow, flow, flow . . .
As the rains turn into snow.
And it's slow, slow, slow. . . .
As the colours lose their glow. . . .
The Winds of Limbo no longer blow
For cold Columbine and her pale Pierrot,
As we dance the En-tro-py Tan-go!

Frank was groaning and looking about him as if expecting attack from all sides, as if he contemplated ducking under the table. His face had turned a colour that was ugly in contrast to his blazer, but his mother merely shook her head. "Ai deown't know ai'm shewer." She was using her posh voice. "Yew cearn't unnerstand a word of the songs these days, cean yew?" She waved a tea-cake. Crumbs cascaded over her strawberry flounces. "An' wot they doin', ai wondah, puttin' on a bleedin' pentomine et Easter?" She pushed back the brim of her hat as her eye caught something in the distance. She tugged at a Dyak's jacket. "Blimey! Wot's that?"

Absentmindedly Frank swallowed his whole cake. His eyes popped. He choked. "What?"

Although they had planned another chorus, Mrs. Cornelius's cry was so loud that even the performers turned to stare in the same direction.

Sebastian Auchinek's eyes were weeping, doubtless from the toxic effects of the make-up. He removed his topper. "Where?"

"What?" said Shakey Mo, twirling a disappointed

moustachio. He had only just begun to enjoy himself for the first time since Nice.

"That!" said Mrs. Cornelius dramatically.

Miss Brunner, Karen von Krupp, Bishop Beesley and the whole Nye family rose to their feet.

"That smudge over there!" Mrs. Cornelius crammed another tea-cake into her mouth. She made a further remark, also, but it was entirely muffled.

Prinz Lobkowitz put his mandolin on top of the piano. He seemed relieved. "That's Africa."

RECAPITULATION

Mais Arlequin le Roi commande à l'Acheron,
Il est duc des esprits de la bande infernale.

Histoire plaisante des faits et gestes de Harlequin etc.,
Paris, 1585

Once, the giant huntsman was Odin, the Norse god of
the dead, who rode through the night skies seeking the
souls of the dying. Though his name was changed with
the coming of Christianity, his role did not. Often he
was thought of as the Devil himself, but in different
parts of France he was identified as the ghost of King
Herod, or of Charlemagne. In northern England he was
sometimes called Woden, while other counties saw him
as Wild Elric, who defied the Conqueror, or even as
Arthur. The phantom hounds were the spirits of un-
baptised children, or of unrepentant sinners. . . . Some
critics have pointed out, however, that their cries, as
they seek the souls of the damned, closely resemble
those of migrating geese.

Folklore, Myths and Legends of Britain, London,
1973

Filth and Noise: Portobello Residents Complain

Portobello Road Market is a disgrace say some local residents—and they are backed up by Sisters of St. Joseph's Convent. The cause is the junk and litter left by second hand dealers—the Steptoes and "totters" of North Kensington. It's not just the noise of the Borough Council workmen clearing up the rubbish that is annoying the Catholic Sisters. By day, says the Mother Superior, people throw old shoes, suitcases and other unwanted articles over the Convent wall. "The main door is thick with filth sometimes," she said. "It is quite degrading." . . . Mrs. Anna Marks, a Portobello Road shopkeeper, described the northern part of the market as "shameful." It was a disgrace to London. . . . Her husband, Mr. W. Marks, added: "I have lived here all my life—I remember when they used to drive sheep down the Portobello Road. The market has gone downhill lately."

KENSINGTON POST, 23 April 1965

1. The God from the machine

"The new century," said Major Nye, "doesn't seem awfully different from the old." He stretched his arms in his stiff drab jacket, settled his topee on his grey locks, and clumped in booted feet out onto the veranda to salute the flag as it was raised for the morning. In the fort's quadrangle a squadron of troopers in the uniform of the 3rd Punjab Irregular Rifles, a squadron of Bengali riflemen in red and dark blue, with red and yellow turbans, and Ghoorka infantrymen in gun-green and red, saluted the Union Jack. Young Cornelius was in charge of the guard. "Sir!" He, too, wore drab, with black lace and red facings, a solar topee wound about with the regiment's green, black and red colours.

"Morning, Cornelius. Happy New Year to you. Looked for you last night."

"I was still on my way back from Simla, sir. I've just had time to change."

"Of course. Any news?"

"Not much, sir."

"Ha!"

Major Nye yawned. Then he craned forward to inspect first the British and then the native troops who stood to attention on three sides of the parade ground as the bugle began its traditional call. Currently he and Cornelius were the only white officers here. He raised his eyes to the great hills beyond the walls. He had faith in his Sikhs and Ghoorkas. Secundra Dass and his Chinese allies might be threatening from the East, while Zakar Khan, the old hill fox, could be on his way from the North, with Russian machine guns and officers, but they'd

828

be no match for a couple of battalions of these chaps, plus a squadron or two of the 3rd Punjab Cavalry. Major Nye frowned.

"Cavalry didn't travel with you, after all?"

Cornelius dismissed the guard. "Yes, sir. But I was on duty, so I had to ride ahead. They shouldn't be more than an hour or two at most, sir."

"Jolly good." Major Nye moved his head. "Mind coming inside for a moment, Cornelius?"

Major Nye retired into his gloomy office. It was almost cold. On the wall hung the photograph Major Nye usually referred to as his "personal touch": a picture of Sarah Bernhardt as she appeared in her white costume in Richepin's *Pierrot Assassin* at the Trocadero in Paris on 28 April 1883, just before her marriage to M. Damala broke up. She had married Damala in London the previous year and Major Nye had been on leave at the time and witnessed it, almost by accident. Overhead the punka swept back and forth, disturbing some of the dust on the piles of papers stacked everywhere. Major Nye rarely replied to communications but he did not have the heart to file anything before it had been officially answered. "Sit down, old chap."

Cornelius sat in the rattan armchair on the other side of the desk. Major Nye removed something from his own chair before seating himself. "Had that fellow of yours in yesterday, Cornelius. What's his name? Hashim?"

"Really, sir? Did he tell you anything worthwhile?"

"Wouldn't talk to me. Wouldn't talk to Subadar Bisht. Wouldn't talk to Risaldar S'arnt Major. Would only talk to you. Trusts you, I suppose. Couldn't blame him. But he seemed to have an urgent message for you. Worried me a bit. Could mean trouble coming, eh?"

"Quite likely, sir. He was riding with the Chinese until they stopped to recoup at Srinagar. He reported their position and then returned to their camp. I'd guess that the horde's on the move again."

Major Nye frowned. "It means that Secundra Dass and his men have joined them now."

"That's the report we had while I was in Simla, sir."

"We're going to need some Lancers, Cornelius."

"Yes, sir. And a bit of artillery too, sir, I'd have thought."

"Artillery would help. Still, I feel sorry for the Chinese if our Ghoorkas get at them. They're not a fighting people, the Chinese."

"No, sir."

"Like the Americans. No good at it. They should leave fighting to the British, eh? And the Ghoorkas and the Sikhs, hm? And the Dogras and Mahrattas, what?"

"Who would we fight, sir?" Cornelius was amused, but Major Nye didn't find the question sensible.

"Why, the bloody Afridis, of course. Who else? He'll always give you a good scrap, your Afridi."

"True, sir."

"Damned true, Cornelius." Major Nye became nostalgic and querulous. "Why'd the blasted Chinese want to interfere? Waste of time. Waste of everybody's time."

"They've conquered Thibet and Nepal and Kashmir and Iskandastan so far, sir."

"Certainly they have. But they haven't crossed the border yet, have they?"

"They must be about to, sir."

"Then they're blasted fools. And Secundra Dass is a blasted fool to tie himself down with a lot of Chinese."

"They outnumber us by about a thousand to one, I should think, sir." Cornelius spoke mildly. He was trying to read a partially exposed report on the major's desk. The report was yellow, several months old at least. "If they attack while we're at our present strength, we should have quite a hard time of it."

"Certainly. It won't be easy, Cornelius. But with the Cavalry here we should do it, what?"

"It could be the largest army on the march since the time of Genghis Khan." Cornelius got up and looked through the blinds at the glinting hills.

Major Nye lit his pipe. "But Genghis Khan was a Mongol, not a Chinaman. Besides, he didn't have the British to deal with—or the Ghoorkas, or the Jats or Baluchis, or Madrassis, or the Ranghars or Gorwalis or Pathans or Punjabis or Rajputs—or the Bengal Lancers or the 3rd Punjab Cavalry—or, for that matter, the 3rd Punjab Irregular Rifles. Not just the best trained soldiers in the world, not just the bravest and most spirited, but they're the fiercest, too. Volunteers, you see. There's nothing more terrifying. more 'unstoppable,' than a force of British and Indian infantry supported by mixed Sikh and British lancers. That's why we get on with them so well—they're as civilised and no-nonsense savage as we are. It's why we get on well with Arabs, too, you know. It's why we *don't* get on with Bombay brahmins. . . ."

"The Chinese and Secundra Dass are sworn to sweep every European from Asia, sir."

"Excellent idea."

"Sir?"

"What? Ah!" Major Nye smiled in understanding. Dropping his voice he spoke slowly, as if he didn't wish to startle Cornelius. "We're not Europeans, after all. Never have been. We're British. That's why we've so much in common with India."

"They seem to hate us just as much as any other—non-Indians—sir."

"Of course they do. Why shouldn't they? Good for them. But they won't beat us."

"It seems, sir, that the Chinese. . . ."

"The Chinese are a peasant race, Cornelius. The British and their fighting Indian allies, do you see, are not peasant races. The Slavs, the Germans, most Latins, are natural tillers of the soil, makers of profits. They like to preserve the status quo above everything else. But we, like the Sikhs and Ghoorkas, are naturally aggressive and pretty rapacious. Not brutal, you understand—it's peasants make brutal soldiers. Russians, Chinese, Japanese, Americans, Boers—all peasants and burghers. The infantry, at any rate, while the cavalry are full of ideas of swagger and glory—parvenu Uhlans the lot of them, Hussars-manqués, that's what I think. Peasants —panicky butchers at best, and sometimes crueller than any Pathan—war's an insanity for them, you see, no part of their way of life—they'd rather be at home doing whatever it is they do with the cows and pigs and shops. We're cruel, arrogant, often ruthless, but we've lived by war for too long not to have become somewhat more humane in the way we wage it. We make quick decisions. We make our points hard and fast. We don't have to hate our enemies to kill 'em, we do it decently,

on the whole, with respect and economy." Major Nye
rang a bell on his desk. "Feel like some tea?"

"Thanks, sir." Young Cornelius seemed depressed,
probably because he had been up all night on the train
from Simla.

"Same goes for your Arab, your Pathan, your Sikh. It's
self-interest, it's efficiency, and sometimes it's a sort
of practical idealism, but we rarely have to work ourselves up to hatred, to find a Cause, a reason for loath-
ing those we wish to kill. Practicality—it's why we're
good at running an Empire. And as long as people
don't give us trouble, we look after 'em. The Dutch
and the Belgians, for instance, take too much out of their
colonies, and so do the French—the peasant instinct,
again, a tendency to overwork the land, you might say.
Also, of course, they were unfortunate enough to belong
to the Continent of Europe. Then there's the Cossacks. I've
a lot of respect for your Cossack, by and large, though
he's inclined to get a bit carried away from time to
time. Now if it was Cossacks we were dealing with I'd
be looking forward to a good, professional scrap, but
most Russians are tame. Most Europeans are tame.
Most Americans, God bless 'em, are very tame indeed.
I hope the British never become tame. It would be the
end of us."

"Well, I suppose if we ever lost a major war. . . ."

"It's not the winning and losing of wars that tames a
nation—it's the love of property, the acquisition of too
many comforts for their own sake, the cossetting of
oneself, that tames you. Thank God the bourgeoisie don't
run England yet, the way they run the Continent. Internationalism could ruin us. Stick to imperialism and you
can't go far wrong. A country should be in charge of its
workers and its aristocrats. Farmers, shopkeepers and
bankers have far too much regard for their cosy firesides
to be trustworthy guardians of a nation's pride or its
well-being. Your aristocrat has no respect for wealth
because he's inherited it. Your common man has no
respect for wealth because he's never experienced it. See
what I mean?"

"I think so, sir. But shouldn't the army have a
voice . . . ?"

"Doesn't need a voice if the country's being properly run. No part of the army's job, politics."

An Indian orderly entered with a tray of tea. "No fresh milk today, sir. All cows gone."

"Damn," said Major Nye absently as he reached for the pot, "that'll be their advance raiding parties, I shouldn't wonder. Better lock up as soon as the Lancers arrive, Cornelius. Post extra guards and so on. And send some sort of message to Delhi, would you?"

Cornelius accepted a cup. "Should we do anything else, sir?" Looking through the window again it seemed to him that the hills were obscured by a huge cloud of white and yellow dust.

Major Nye knocked out his pipe and picked up his cup. He chuckled as he raised the tea to his cracked lips. "Write letters to our nearest and dearest, I suppose." He lifted a white handkerchief to his sleeve and brushed away a fly. "I shouldn't think this will last too long, do you?"

2. With the flag to Pretoria

"Bleck is bleck ent wide es wide, my dee-arr," said Meneer Olmeijer comfortably, puffing at his large pipe. The tubby Boer, in khaki shirt and jodhpurs and wide-brimmed bush-hat, surveyed the tranquil plaas through twinkling eyes. "Airr you stell intirrested on de oostrrich, Miss Corrnelius?

"Perhaps . . ." she said. She had difficulty crossing the yard in her long tropical skirt. She had chosen a drab brown so as not to show the dust. Her hat, too, was brown and its brim tended to obscure her vision. "Perhaps later?"

"Cerrtinly, cerrtinly—lader or niverr—y'ave all de tame in de woahld 'ere. Yooah ön 'oliday! Ya doo whadiver ya fill lake—Liberty Krraal, eh? Heh, heh, heh!" He displayed his stained teeth. "En corrl me Cousin Piet. Efterr all, we'rre rrelitivs, ain't we?" He placed a tanned, red hand on her soft, wincing shoulder. "Ther woah's övah—we'll all be Afrikanders soon—Brridischerr oah Hollanderr—farrms oah mines." They had halted by a white wooden fence, marking the northern limits of the plaas. On their left were the huts of the native workers' kraal. Piet Olmeijer lifted a booted foot to the lowest rail; a mystical light had entered his eyes as he inspected the infinite veldt, most of which was his, won from the Matabele with blood and bibles and an inspired hypocrisy which filled Catherine with admiring awe but caused her companion, currently back in the house, considerable confusion. Una had been unable to face this morning's tour; neither, to their host's dismay, had she breakfasted. She continued to suffer,

Catherine had said when presenting Una's excuses, from the heat—but the fact was that Una, furious and frightened not so much by the condition of the native Africans as by the peculiar attitude of the whites towards them, was almost incapable now of speech in the presence of Olmeijer or his overseers. Moreover the farmer had taken a fancy to Una and had dropped several hints concerning his need for a wife and sons who could inherit all he had created. Olmeijer had told Jerry, whom he knew from Johannesburg days, that Una Persson looked strong and healthy, the sort of helpmeet an Afrikander farmer needed. Olmeijer's first wife and most of the rest of his family had contracted typhus during internment some years previously, when the Witwatersrand dispute was at its height. However, Una's bouts of ill-health, as she explained them, were causing him to relax his attention as time went on. The only unfortunate consequence of this was that gradually the farmer was beginning to speculate about Catherine's capacity for filling the role. The introduction of Christian names was, Catherine guessed, a significant step forward and, perhaps, a bold one for a widower Boer of forty sweating, self-restraining summers. It could also explain his sudden expressions of tolerance towards someone who, while they had a name that sounded comfortingly Dutch, was still an Uitlander. He had been reassured by Una herself when they had first arrived: at that point she had been anxious to recall her pro-Boer convictions in England, to disassociate herself with the gold-diggers, critical of the foreign invasion of the Transvaal, full of the romance of the Great Trek, of the courage of the Voortrekkers and their struggles against the savage Matabele. Una had always found such mythologies attractive and, Catherine thought, always sulked in bitter disappointment when the reality contradicted her imaginings. But Catherine was determined not to be critical of her friends. Una's idealism had dragged her up from despair more than once.

"Just think," said Catherine positively to Meneer Olmeijer, "only seventy years ago there was nothing here but lion and wildebeeste! And now. . . ." The veldt rolled to the horizon. "And now there's hardly any lions or gnus at all!"

"Doan't ya bileef et," chuckled Piet Olmeijer. "Ger rridin' by yerself an' find ert!"

"Well, at least there's no wild natives to worry about any more," said Catherine, still doing her best, but feeling increasingly that she was somehow betraying Una.

"Det's a fekt," agreed Olmeijer with some satisfaction. "Neow, Ah prromist Ah'd lit her see some o' da tebacca bein' pecked in da feealds, ya?"

"Oh, yes," said Catherine reluctantly. "Or the oranges, you said."

"Certainly—oah de örrinjis." He chose to detect in her manner an enthusiasm for his life and its loves. As they left the fence he reached a hand towards her but dropped it as, from the other side of the bungalow, there came a pounding sound which shook the ground and round the corner raced a tall black-and-white ostrich, its eyes starting, its beak enclosed in a peculiar harness, its broad feet stirring the dust, while on its back, whooping and giggling in a dirty, crumpled European suit, his white hat over his face, was Catherine's brother, followed by upwards of twenty grinning blacks in loincloths or tattered shorts and shirts.

"Heh, heh, heh," laughed Piet Olmeijer. "Oh, look at det berd rrun! Heh, heh, heh!" He removed his pipe from his mouth and waved it. "'Ang ern, Meneer Cornelius! Excellent!" The ostrich reached the kraal fence, stopped and then swerved, running the length of the enclosure. Jerry slipped further from the saddle, yelling with joy like a five-year-old, the loose-limbed blacks clapping and shouting. "Ride 'im, baas!"

The bird's panic increased. It began to run in circles, its long neck undulating, attempting to free itself from the halter.

"Ride 'im!"

"Hokai!" cried Olmeijer jovially. "Hokaai!"

Jerry fell heavily on his back and was dragged a short way by one stirrup before he could free himself. His face was bruised purple and yellow, covered in dust; his suit was torn and he was limping, supported by the blacks as he came back towards Olmeijer and his sister. "That was great fun."

"I don't think I'll try it now." Catherine was concerned for him. "What's wrong with your leg?"

"Turned my ankle in the stirrup, that's all."

"Foei tog!" said Olmeijer sympathetically. He spoke in Afrikaans to the blacks holding Jerry, ordering them to take him to the stoep, ordering others to capture the ostrich and return it to its pen. At the door to the house Olmeijer dismissed the boys and he took one side of the hobbling Englishman while Catherine took the other. Olmeijer was in fine humour.

"I hope the ostrich is all right," said Jerry.

"Dit is vir my om't ewe!" Olmeijer was admiring. "Ye'ave te've gets to rroide them oostriches. . . ." He remembered himself. "Excuse me, Miss Cornelius. Eouwt 'ere, wivart vimenfolk arahnd, ya git a liddel sleck wid de lengvij." They entered the large white kitchen, seating Jerry in a high-backed wooden chair. "Olly! Olly! Waar die drummel—weah de deuce es det houseboy?"

The houseboy emerged grinning. He had evidently heard what had happened. Olmeijer told him to bring cold water and towels for Jerry's ankle.

Catherine helped Jerry to remove his jacket, looking about for a cloth. "I'll clean your face."

"Nar, nar," said Olmeijer pleasantly, "lit one av der serrvants do et! Det's wod dey're paid fer, efter all!"

Catherine left the kitchen, entering a shady hall, on her way to Jerry's room to get him a fresh shirt and jacket. As she passed the door of the room she and Una were sharing, she heard her friend's voice raised in song. Glad that Una seemed more cheerful, she went in. Una was bathing. As an uncomprehending black girl poured warm water over her perfect back she rendered an old Gus Elen music hall song of several seasons before:

I wonders at th' ig'rance wot prevails abaht th' woar,
Some folks dunno th' diff'rance wot's between a sow
an' Boar!
Roun' Bef'nal Green they're spahtin' of ole Kruger
night an' day,
An' I tries to put the wrong-uns right wot 'as too
much to say. . .
W'en I goes in "The Boar's Head" pub the blokes
they claps th'r 'ands,

They know I reads a bit, an' wot I reads I under-
                                        stan's;
They twigs I know abaht them Boars an' spots the'r
                                        little game
'Cos they bin an' giv' yer 'ighness 'ere a werry rorty
                                        name!
I finks a cove sh'd fink afore 'e talks abaht th' woar,
There's blokes wot talks as dunno wot they mean,
But yer tumble as yer 'umble knows a bit abaht
                                        th' Boar—
W'en they calls me nibs "The Bore of Bef'nal
                                        Green". . . .

"Ssshh," said Catherine smiling, "he'll hear you. He's only in the kitchen. I thought you hated that song. You were saying. . . ."

"I do hate it," Una agreed, sponging her breasts, "but it's the only thing that'll cheer me up at the moment."

"You're such a pro-Boer! You could hardly get work. . . ."

"Yesterday's underdog is tomorrow's tyrant." Una stood up, taking the towel which the pretty servant girl handed to her. "That must be even more obvious on the Dark Continent, I suppose." She raised her voice and sang louder:

In this 'ere woar—well strike me pink—ole Eng-
                                        land's put 'er 'eart,
Them kerlownial contingints too 'as played a nobby
                                        part,
Some people sez we ain't got men—I ain't got
                                        no sich fears—
An' it's me wot fust suggested callin' out th' volun-
                                        teers!
Anuffer tip o' mine's ter raise a Bef'nal Green Bri-
                                        gade,
Th' way they scouts for "coppers" shows them
                                        blokes for scouts is made—
But I 'ears as "Bobs" 'll eat them Boars—an' now
                                        I twigs th'use
Of sen'din' out a Kitchener to cook ole Kruger's
                                        Goose!

Naked, Una swaggered around the room, watched by a spluttering Catherine and a wide-eyed black girl.

> *But for shootin' at th' women—well I 'opes they'll*
> *get it stiff.*
> *'Cos ain't they bin a-firin' shells at that poor Lady*
> *Smiff!*

Spontaneously, Una linked arms with Catherine and then with the servant, to march them back and forth across the carpet. "Altogether for the chorus!"

"We don't know it, Una."

> *But yer tumble as yer 'umble knows a bit abaht th'*
> *Boar*
> *W'en they calls me nibs "The Bore of Bef'nal*
> *Green" . . .*

Una stopped, put her hand on the back of the young servant's neck and kissed her full on the lips. The girl uttered a strangled yell and fled from the bedroom.

Catherine stared at her friend in despair. "What did you want to do that for, Una? You'll give the whole game away at this rate."

3. The Pathfinder

Only hours ahead of the Cossacks and the so-called "Mohawks," Una Persson reached the garrison at Fort Henry to find the place crowded with the Northwest Mounted Police and a couple of regiments who, on first sight of their dark blue and scarlet uniforms, seemed to be the 5th and 7th Royal Irish Lancers. The four high concrete towers of the fort were thick with Maxim guns. There was also a generous display of medium-weight artillery all along the crenellated walls, while circling over the pines and crags of the heavily wooded pass which the fort defended, a Vickers Vimy biplane kept reconnaisance. As she dismounted and went to look for the C.O. Una realised that her ride had been unnecessarily hasty—the plane would be able to warn the Canadians of an attack in plenty of time. The Cossacks, as usual, were not showing much caution. Her long Henry rifle in the crook of her arm, she forced her way through the lancers and mounties and ran up the concrete steps to the H.Q. building, saluting the healthy corporal on duty at the door. "Captain Persson the scout. Who's your commandant, trooper?"

He returned her salute. "District Superintendent Cornelius, at present, ma'am. Um. Is it urgent, Captain?"

She straightened his broad-brimmed hat on his head. She took a pace backward, cocking her eye at him. "You'd probably have time for a couple of choruses of *Rose-Marie* before a Cossack sabre turned you into a soprano."

He was shocked. He opened the door for her; he was still saluting. "Scout to see you, sir."

Una strode in. In the loose silk divided skirt of the Don Cossack, a wolf-skin trimmed riding kaftan, with cartridge pockets just above the breasts, an astrakhan shapka, she could be immediately identified as an irregular.

The District Superintendent greeted her: a wary wave of his gloved hand. The scarlet of his tunic clashed horribly with his young face which bore an expression of callow sternness and which suggested that he was new to the job. His accent was a reasonable attempt to give Canadian inflexions to an otherwise nondescript English accent. "You've news of the invasion?"

"They're done with Quebec and are on their way. I didn't expect to see you this far North, Jerry."

"They posted me from Toronto two days ago. I was supposed to be in Niagara Falls by now. Do you think I've been set up? Is it going to be the Alamo, all over again? Or was it the Alma?"

"Don't forget Quebec initially welcomed the Cossacks. The French always think they can control their conquerors. There wasn't any resistance to speak of. And nobody was much interested in stopping them between the time they left Alaska until they landed at Ungava. Even then you all thought they'd be content to run around in the Northwest Territory a bit until they got tired and went home. But by that time the States had started to get worried. Those are American guns out there, aren't they?"

"Mostly. They've been very good about giving us support."

"Then you've nothing to worry about. Why were you going to Niagara Falls? Honeymoon?"

"Oh, sure." He scratched his red sleeve with leather fingers. "No, I was meeting my father. I think. He's got business in Buffalo."

"I thought your father was in Mexico."

"Maybe he'll be going to Mexico later."

"Are you sure he's—?"

"No. But he says he is. It was worth checking."

"I suppose so."

"The bloody Cossacks have fucked everything up, as usual. Once they start—"

"You'll stop them. They'll never reach Kingston."

He frowned anxiously at a map of the Great Lakes. "We don't want the Americans moving in. And they will, unless. . . ."

"They've left nobody behind—the Cossacks, I mean.

The 'Mohawks' aren't a problem. As long as they all attack Fort Henry, that's it. You'll blow them to bits." She sounded sad. "You needn't worry about the States."

"It was bad enough when it was only Sitting Bull. Or do I mean Notting Hill? What's that?"

"Since Roosevelt they've had it in their heads that the rest of America is really theirs, too, that they're leasing it to a lot of incompetent relatives and foreigners on condition that they look after it properly. But in this case there won't be much more interference." She was decidedly regretful. "A shame. I'd love to see the Cossacks in New York."

"I heard that's where they meant to go. They thought the Ungava Peninsula was Nantucket."

"You could be right. They're still not clear as to whether they're in the U.S.A. or Canada. There's only one or two of them can speak any English at all—and the French 'Mohawks' can't understand the Cossacks' French while the Cossacks can't understand the French's French. Apparently the accents create two virtually different languages."

"You know a lot about them."

"I should do. I've been acting as an interpreter since Fort Chimo." She straightened her shapka. "Well, I must be on my way."

"You're not staying for the 'fun'?"

"No point. You'll beat them. They're tired, over-confident, poorly armed. They'll have eaten badly and been sleeping in the saddle, if I know them. Most will probably be drunk. They'll keep coming at you until you've wiped them out. In the meantime the 'Mohawks' will have run back to Quebec."

"They can't have come all this way without a plan."

"They got to Uppsala two years ago without a plan. They were wiped out. Four prisoners taken. It's their nature. And twenty years ago they reached Rawalpindi, couldn't find the British, hit the Chinese by accident and drove them back. Hardly anyone in England ever knew there had been a threat!"

"That was a bit of luck for someone," said Jerry innocently.

"It usually is. Well, cheerio. You're bound to get a promotion if you hang around long enough after the battle."

"I told you, I was on my way. . . ."

"I can go via Niagara, if you like. Any message?"

"If you get a chance, find a man named 'Brown.' He's staying at the Lover's Leap Hotel on the American side. Tell him I've been held up."

"Okay." She removed her kaftan. She had a buckskin jacket underneath. Hanging by a deerhide thong at her beaded belt was an old-fashioned powder horn. She reached for the horn, taking something from the bullet pouch on her other hip. "Have you got a mirror?"

He removed the map of the Great Lakes. There was a large oval mirror behind it. She inspected her face. Then, tipping a little powder onto the puff, she began to cover her nose.

4. The outcast of the islands

"I remember the good old days," said Sebastian Auchinek, his voice grumbling along with the twelve wing-mounted engines on either side of the cabin, "when there was still a sense of wonder in the world."

"That was before universal literacy and cheap newsprint." Jerry spoke spitefully. Either Auchinek or the engines began to cough. They had not been getting on since Calcutta when the Russian policeman had demanded to see their documents and Jerry had shot him.

The Dornier DoX was circling Darwin while they tried to make up their minds what to do. Nobody had expected the Japanese to strike so fast. As far as Whitehall had been concerned the problem had been whether or not to let them stay in Manchukao. When they had materialised simultaneously outside Sydney, Brisbane and other cities, pounding the settlements to bits with naval guns and bombs, resistance had been minimal. Help was on the way from Singapore and Shanghai, but it would be some time before the Emperor's armies were shifted.

"Besides," said Moses Collier from the co-pilot's seat, "it's the Aussies' own fault for being elitist. You know how eager the Japs are to be accepted everywhere at any cost. We'd better scarper, Jerry. Rowe Island's our only chance."

"It's full of bones. It's haunted. I hate it."

"No time for superstition now, Mr. Cornelius," said Auchinek with a fair bit of pleasure. "It was you who believed the story about the waters of Eternal Life with their powers of resurrection. I never did."

"You've never believed anything. A lot of people were

844

as impressed as I was." Jerry was defensive, but he responded without much spirit. "I only said I hated the place. . . ."

"That's hardly the point." Mo took a tighter grip on his controls as the plane lost height for a moment. "We've got to dump this bugger, get her repaired before she falls out of the sky. Listen to those engines!"

Jerry was looking moodily down at the Australian wasteland. "I suppose so."

"There's a couple of C-class Empire flying boats in reasonable nick there," said Collier. "I diverted them myself." Mo had spent a lot more time than any of the others in this part of the world. Occasionally he would even claim to be an Australian. "Lovely jobs. Better than this old madam any day of the week."

Jerry was sensitive about his Dornier. He would never admit that he had been hasty in acquiring it while it was still in its experimental stages. "They've got nothing like the range," he said automatically. "Nothing like."

"Maybe not, but it'll take a plane in good nick to get us to Singapore, if that's where you still want to go." Collier buttoned up his helmet strap. "What do we all thing? Is it on?"

"For me it is." Auchinek began to leave the cabin. "I'll go aft and see what the others have to say."

"See if you can get some more info out of the abo," Collier suggested. They had found a black tracker in the ruins, before they had realised that the Japanese were still present in the city.

"Can't," said Auchinek.

"He left," Jerry explained. "While we were going up. Opened the door and walked out. Said he had to find his mother and father. They'd been after an emu, apparently."

"Funny little bloke, wasn't he?" Collier glanced at the Timor Sea. "I hope he makes it."

"They're marvellous, really," said Jerry. "They can find their way through anything."

"Didn't seem to realise there was a war on." Collier hummed to himself as he made adjustments to his panel. "Number four's looking dodgy again."

"It sounds fine to me."

"Well, it's bloody dodgy. It's conked out twice."

"It missed a couple of times, that's all."

Collier sighed. "All right. Christ I wish we had some cannon with us. I don't half feel naked. We've seen a fair bit of the fleet, but what are they doing with all their bloody Fujis or Kawasakis or whatever it is they're flying these days?"

"Probably down near Sydney and Canberra or Melbourne," suggested Jerry. "This isn't a very strategic area, by and large."

"Luckily for us. Why were they hiding in the ruins when we first arrived?"

"Probably thought we were military. Hoped to take us by surprise."

"They did that all right." Mo waved his grazed arm. "Cor! It makes me want to vomit. All that fighting and no chance of hitting back. I'm joining up when we get to Singapore. Then I'll come straight to bleedin' Darwin with a great big Tommy gun. Except," he said mournfully, "that they always jam on you. Bastards, Tommies are."

"What about a Schmeiser?" Jerry was glad that only blue water and sky surrounded them on all sides now.

"You're bloody talking, me old son!" Mo whistled through his teeth. "There's even a couple of Yank machine-pistols I wouldn't mind trying. They don't have a lot of style, though, Yanks don't. Not in the military stuff. All their invention goes into the private sector. Funny that. Is it free enterprise, d'you think?"

"It's the cars I like best," said Jerry. "I'm going to miss the cars."

"They won't stop making cars just because they've got a few problems on their borders."

Jerry wasn't so sure. "I can't bear to think what the Canadians will do with Detroit."

"They might give it back. Swap it for that other place they want. Pig's Eye, is it?"

"St Paul? Maybe. It doesn't seem a fair swap, though."

"The wars can't last forever. Things are sorting themselves out already." Mo was depressing himself as he tried to cheer up his friend. "Eh?"

"It'll take ten years." Una Persson shut the door of the cabin behind her, sat down and put her elbows on the chart table.

"What's ten years?" said Mo.

"Bishop Beesley says he can see a pattern emerging already." Una toyed with a map.

Jerry laughed. "He's always seeing patterns. There aren't any. Not really. The disordered mind sees order everywhere—systems take shape from the movement of the wind in the leaves of the trees—patterns merge as the mad eye selects only what it wishes to see. Patterns are madness, for the most part. That's the bishop. He's barmy."

"Oh, come on, Jerry." Mo turned in his seat. "There's some sort of shape to what's going on, isn't there?"

"If there is, I haven't detected any."

"You've got to believe in some kind of order, man!"

"Order isn't patterns."

"It's a perfectly easy shape, I think," said Una Persson. "But it—well, it shifts. It's a prism. A classically cut diamond, perhaps. It isn't strictly linear. By selecting a linear pattern from the larger design you certainly distort things. I think that's what you mean, don't you Jerry?"

Mo belched. Then he farted. "Pardon," he said.

Jerry gave up. "All I know is that there's too much going on at once and I've had about enough. All the bleeding possibilities occurring at the same time. That's not what I joined for. I wanted a simple life. I remember. I wanted a set of nice straight tracks from A to B. And what did I bloody get? I wish I was out of it. I'm too old and this century's too familiar. Any bloody aspect of it. You can't win. Only the bloody Japanese can win."

"It's worse than that," said Una with a smirk. "Nobody wins. Nobody loses."

"That's life," said Mo Collier. The engines began to falter, to rumble. He licked his teeth.

"You're wrong. The Japanese win. It's all in inverse proportion to the amount of ego you have. These days, at any rate. The bigger the ego, the more you lose. And it's big egos make the biggest, stupidest patterns. Look at Hitler."

"I used to enjoy him," said Mo cheerfully, "in the *Dandy*. Or was it the *Beano*? Hitler?" Mo giggled. "What, that little bloke in Berlin? The copper?"

Jerry raised his hands to his head. "Sorry," he said. "I was forgetting."

5. What is art?

There were fifty keels lying at anchor over Kiev when Prinz Lobkowitz woke up and looked out of the diamond-paned window of the house he had rented near the Cathedral of St. Vladimir, with its view of the Botanical Gardens.

The artillery fire, which had been almost constant for the past week, was now only intermittent and, as a result, Lobkowitz felt a peculiar, unspecific anxiety, as one does when faced with the unfamiliar, however welcome. From several roof-tops, as he watched, rose puffs of grey smoke and he heard the crack of rifle-shots. The defenders of Kiev were firing hopelessly at the airships which swayed overhead obscuring the thin morning sunlight. It seemed to Lobkowitz that the siege was as good as over, but he could not be quite sure which side had won. Then he caught a glimpse of a German uniform on the roof and guessed that the airships, silhouettes against the dawn sky and impossible to identify from any markings as yet, were here in support of the besieging Makhnoviks, returned at last to avenge the murder of their leader over twenty years previously. They were led now by a Don Cossack styling himself Emalyan Pugachev, claiming to be a descendant of the Peasant Tsar and (incidentally) renouncing all claim to the throne in the name of the Democratic Union of Free Cossack Anarchists. Although Pugachev refused a title he was universally accepted as Hetman by the Cossacks. Now, as one of the ships turned in the wind, Lobkowitz could make out a fluttering black flag inset with the blue cross of St. Andrew. The Highlanders, having established their position north of the Clyde, had linked up with their Ukrainian brothers to push back the Russians and their

848

German mercenaries and once more establish the Ukraine as an independent state. Lobkowitz, whose sympathies were with the Makhnoviks, reflected aloud to Auchinek who had wandered in, still in night-shirt and dressing gown, smoking a briar pipe, a copy of *The Master of Ballantrae* under his arm: "Perhaps Kiev will come alive again. It used to be such a vital city."

"It won't make much difference to the Jews," said Auchinek with a shrug. "Every new government winds up promoting a fresh pogrom. It's a wonder there's any Jews left."

Lobkowitz frowned. He was forced to admit that his friend was right. "I can't see Pugachev allowing such a thing."

"Pugachev's a Cossack. Cossacks have a metaphysical and instinctive desire to butcher the members of any race originating East of the Urals or South of the Caucasus. They can't help themselves. I think they hate Jews most of all because they think of us as being a kind of decadent Tartar. Nothing to do with our habit of sacrificing Christian babies, raping Christian virgins, ruining Christian merchants or, of course, crucifying Christ. Their instinct goes back much further than that. They'll tolerate Teutons and maintain a wary trust for other Slavs who, in turn, are regarded as effete versions of themselves, but Latins belong to a caste hardly higher than the Jews. . . ."

Lobkowitz was amused. He jerked his thumb behind him at the sky. "What about Celts?"

"Honorary Cossacks. They can find many points of similarity, you see. The Highlanders were traditionally used to expand the frontiers of Empire, just as the Cossacks were sent into Siberia. From time to time they have done well in uprisings against the central government and have the same tendency to fling themselves willy-nilly into a conflict. Oh, you'd have to ask a Cossack for the rest." Auchinek scratched under his eye with the stem of his pipe. Then he scratched his nose. "I just hope the papers you got will see me through, Lobkowitz. Every time Kiev falls I get nervous. Still, I welcome it politically, this development. The Ukraine was the last major state to break free of the Russian Empire. And the Chinese have at last given up their attempts to expand their territories or to re-impose their rule on Cochin China and Korea. And if the Japanese did nothing else, they broke the chain that held the British and American colonies to their masters, without actually managing to retain a foothold in those colonies themselves. All the Empires are going down at once. It's reassuring. Did I read that the Peuhl finally took Fort Lamy?"

"I seem to recall. . . ."

"And Arabia is rising. Can it mean that the long era of Empire-building is over at last?"

"You think the world will learn to cultivate its own gardens? The wars continue. They are just as bloody."

"It will take a while, I grant you, to achieve a reasonable status quo. But Makhno's dreams may yet become the final reality. The sane equilibrium of anarchy."

Lobkowitz was impressed by this new confidence in his old friend. He was heartened. "I should work on your enthusiasm for Makhno," he advised. There was a noise on the stair. "Hello! Who's this?" The voice of his housekeeper rose up to them. Heavy feet ascended. "It will stand you in good stead."

Auchinek was grinning as the door of Lobkowitz's rooms burst open and Colonel Pyat, splendid in his white and green uniform, his boots shining with some dark liquid, came in, hastily removing his cap and gloves. "We've lost everything," he said. "I know you're not sympathetic —but those fools of peasants wouldn't listen to reason." Pyat had been acting as a go-between for the Russians and the Ukrainians. As a veteran of the Indian and Chinese campaigns he had some standing with the wilder Cossack elements and for a short time had served as one of their officers. "The Germans are leaving, so we can't even negotiate from a position of relative strength. You've heard nothing from Prague?"

"We can't help, I'm afraid," said Lobkowitz. "I might as well tell you that it's my opinion Prague will recognise the Pugachev government as soon as they have official control of Kiev."

Pyat nodded. He was fatalistic. "Then can I ask you a favour?"

"Of course." Lobkowitz felt an increased friendship for Pyat now that the man's efforts to maintain Russian rule had come to nothing.

"Make me a temporary member of your staff—until you get to Prague. I won't stay in Bohemia. I'll go on to Bavaria, where I have friends. A great many of my old colleagues are already there and apparently have been decently received."

Lobkowitz drew a deep breath. "I think I can arrange it, so long as Prague is quick to recognise Pugachev. If that happens I'll probably have enough prestige to get away with one or two irregularities. You're not, after all, who they're really after. What about your cousin, the Governor?"

Colonel Pyat was bitter. "He took the last train to Moscow yesterday evening, after he had announced that he was making me his deputy."

"That creates complications, eh?" Auchinek looked sardonically to Lobkowitz.

Pyat smiled as he shook his head. "I tore the order up. It would have been suicide to accept."

Outside, the gunfire suddenly increased its intensity and then stopped altogether.

"Then who is governor now?" asked Auchinek. He had a passion for knowing the names of those in authority.

"Cornelius accepted the job."

"But he's a known Makhnovik sympathiser!"

Lobkowitz went to the window again, staring across the frosty Botanical Gardens to the distant bulk of the new governor's palace. He laughed. "Look," he said, "the Black Flag is already hoisted over Kiev."

Pyat sat down in the large leather armchair. "The man is a blatant opportunist. He bends with every wind. I wish I knew his secret."

"Everyone envies him that." Auchinek spat into the ashes of last night's fire.

Literature and art are not the field of the literary or art critic only; they are also the concern of the sociologist, of the social historian, or anthropologist, and of the social psychologist. For through literature and art men seem to reveal their personality and, when there is one, their national ethos.

Gilberto Freyre, *Brazil: An Interpretation*

Important writing, strange to say, rarely gives the exact flavour of its period; if it is successful it presents you with the soul of man, undated. Very minor literature, on the other hand, is the Baedeker of the soul, and will guide you through the curious relics, the tumbledown buildings, the flimsy palaces, the false pagodas, the distorted and fantastical and faery vistas which have cluttered the imagination of mankind at this or that brief period of its history.

George Dangerfield, *The Strange Death of Liberal England*

. . . it is the image which in fact determines what might still be called the current behaviour of any organism or organisation. The image acts as a field.

Kenneth Boulding, *The Image*

There have been studies of the higher intellectual sphere through which ideas flowed between the two countries, but the popular sources of these ideas have largely been overlooked. Probably the major source of ideas concerning India came from fiction set in that country. "Literature is the one field of Indo-British culture which has provided a comparatively large harvest, though the average quality is not very good."

Allen J. Greenberger, *The British Image of India*

You've gain'd the victory, Rome, it will not hold;
Britain when hist'ry shall her page unfold,
In future times, where're her flag's unfurl'd
Shall prove the queen and terror to the world.
Forward at least two thousand years we'll go,
And shew what London will *be: and then shew*
A pastime Britons then will pleasure in,
A checquer'd droll, its hero HARLEQUIN.

London; or, Harlequin and Time, 1813

The formal canonisation of John Ogilvie, a Jesuit martyr, as Scotland's first saint in 700 years came a step nearer yesterday with the publication of details of a cure which is recognised as miraculous by the Catholic Church.

After years of investigation in Scotland and Rome, the Church now officially accepts that Mr. John Fagan, aged 61, of Glasgow, who was dying in 1967 from a major stomach cancer, was saved through the intercession of John Ogilvie. The priest was hanged at Glasgow Cross on 10 March 1615, for refusing to recognise the supremacy of King James I in spiritual matters.

The detailed evidence showed that almost at the moment when Mr. Fagan was expected to die, "he developed a dramatic, abrupt, and uninterrupted improvement with return to full health." A long sequence of examinations by doctors concluded that there was no possible medical explanation for the disappearance of the cancer.

Guardian, 12 March 1976

6. The Birth and Adventures of Harlequin

"Did you ever see greyer skies?" Miss Brunner had just arrived in a rattling old Ka-12 copter of the flying motorbike type, probably an experimental model. Doubtless she had been inexpertly looting museums again. Landing on the roof of a half-completed Royal Festival Hall, she had immediately turned her attention to the oily waters of the Thames where Jerry had managed to put down his own Princess Flying Boat, damaging the wings and tailplane as he had knocked over the Skylon and negotiated Waterloo Bridge. The drizzle seemed to have been falling on London for a decade; it brought a certain gleam to the overcast scene.

"Eh?"

Jerry had not been expecting her. He had come to the South Bank in the hope of finding the Dome of Discovery, but a Palestinian bomb (about the only one to hit London before the whole of their ramshackle air force had been blown apart) had left a huge crater in its place —indeed, there was no evidence that it had actually been constructed. When the Ka-12 had arrived Jerry had been bouncing up and down, clinging to a fallen girder, telling himself that this was the last time he would trust one of Flash Gordon's tips. Gordon had heard that Catherine had been transferred here from Roedean at the outbreak of the invasion, when half of Sussex had fallen to disaffected Kentish marines who had made a surprise mass attack along the whole coast between Hastings and Littlehampton. The Nursing Home, Sunnydales, had actually driven back the marines, but not before it had sustained major damage and lost over seventy per cent of its charges.

The rolled up linen blueprints of the Festival site were

already growing limp. They stuck at an angle from the pocket of his military-style camel hair overcoat. Soon they would be useful as handkerchiefs. Rain dripped from the brim of his trilby onto his cheeks so that it looked as if he had been weeping. He began to tramp away from the Hall, over cracked concrete, towards the iron framework of Hungerford Bridge.

"Eh?" asked Miss Brunner again. She hurried behind. She wore an uncharacteristic Balenciaga New Look dress in avocado green velvet over which was pulled a black duffel coat. On her feet were ponyskin boots and on her head a peculiar astrakhan cap, as if she had tried to make a concession to several different ideas of taste at the same time. "Eh?"

Jerry stopped. "Yes, very grey. A chilly era altogether, wouldn't you say?"

Having obtained her response she was satisfied, turning on him immediately. "You're being facetious." Ostentatiously she studied the river again. "Well, it's a shambles! I can't think what's got into the British Empire."

"Corruption in high places?" Jerry felt in his other pocket to make sure his cigarette cards were still dry.

"Rot!"

"I thought—"

"It's poor morale all round."

"Not all round." Jerry rubbed the water from his skin. "Some people are fighting for their liberty for the first time ever." He looked wistfully towards his ruined Princess.

Her foxy mouth snarled at him. "Liberty! How I hate it! Given the chance I intend to establish a sane element of authority in this country again. I've put all my money into land. It's land that England's made of. Land is the only thing of importance. And the one who has most land has most power to revive England's greatness. Happy people, Mr. Cornelius, are people who know where they stand. A responsible ruling class does not trade in ambiguities—it trades in facts and statements of fact. It tells people exactly what their position is and what they may do within certain well defined limits. People would rather not own land themselves, because of the responsibility. Therefore they are prepared to let those who own the land make their decisions for them. Owning land, you see, brings with it a great burden. By lifting that burden from the shoulders of the common man, by putting experienced managers in charge, we shall produce a stability this country has not experienced for fifty years. A hundred years. It is my dream, Mr. Cornelius, to reestablish the Rule of Law in Great Britain before we see 1960 again. I shall need experienced people like yourself. That's why I looked you up. You have the makings of a fine manager."

Jerry shook his head. "All I want to do is keep my head down until this floppy decade's over. There's no other way to survive it that I know."

"It's the key period, Mr. Cornelius." Her eyes were on fire. "There is still a chance for us to stem the tide, redivert the waters so that they irrigate the roots of a sane, tranquil, stable society—cottagers, villagers, townsmen and citizens all building for a common aim. Give each man, woman and child a place and a purpose and, as a consequence, a firm idea of identity—show them who the enemy is, what they must fight, and all this internal squabbling, this unhappy squeaking for revolution, will be finished with, once and for all. We reached the peak of our social evolution in 1900 and now we are devolving at a sickening rate. Can't you see it?"

"I appreciate your faith in the restoration of the status quo, Miss Brunner, but I'm not sure land values are the whole answer. I mean, by 2000 we'll probably all be living on Mars and Venus anyway, won't we? The future's in space, isn't it?"

"Space!" She was vicious. "I don't believe in space! And neither should you. Our duty is to remember our heritage—and to make our fellows recall that heritage, too!"

She was giving him a headache.

"Rockets!" he said pathetically. "Whoosh!"

She indicated the crater. "That's what rockets do. Boom!" She drove her point home: "They blow everything up."

"Yes, well, they've got to, haven't they? First?" Against her enthusiasm his logic, never very strong, disintegrated. "Haven't they?"

She moved towards him, her boots squelching. "You're very naïve, Mr. Cornelius. I'm older than you. . . ."

"I wouldn't say that."

". . . and I may seem a trifle old-fashioned. But mark my words our future lies in the yeomen of England, not in some half-baked fashionable creed of anarchistic scientific internationalism. There are too many '-isms' in the world already—and the result is Chaos. Come with me. Let me exorcise the demon of nihilism and breathe a new spirit into your troubled soul. There is only one '-ism' which will save us—the good old English penchant for pragmatism. We must reduce the number of choices facing the bewildered people of England. Choice produces confusion and confusion leads to social disintegration. And when we are strong again, strong enough to show the world that we know who we are and where we are going, we can extend the same salvation throughout the globe, bringing stability and order wherever we go. We stopped too soon, you see. We lost sight of our goals. We became afraid of responsibility—of the responsibility of Empire —we let other countries get away with far too much and, as a result, lost faith in our own authority."

"I'm still not sure about my own identity, let alone what I should be doing." As he walked on towards Hungerford Bridge Miss Brunner again began to follow.

"Strong authority produces a strong identity, personal and corporate."

"It all sounds a bit too political for my taste," Jerry told her. "I never did understand politics very well."

"But that's exactly it." They had reached the iron steps of the bridge and began to climb. The metal rang as Jerry's heels struck. She disapproved of his steel blakeys. "I hate politics, too. I'm completely a-political. I'm talking about faith—faith in one's country and its greatness —faith in common sense, in order, in justice—faith in traditional values which, say what you like, never let us down in the past." They were crossing the river now. Jerry regretted the damage he had done to his Princess. The noble flying boat was waterlogged in her starboard float and part of the wing was already under water, lifting the plane over.

"She's sinking," said Miss Brunner. "Isn't she?"

"It'll be a long time before that old girl goes down." Jerry spoke sentimentally. It was this feeling for imperfect or misconceived machinery which had got him into trouble more than once before.

They reached the opposite side of the bridge and crossed the road to the fractured Charing Cross Underground Station, where a coffee-stall had re-established itself. The embankment at this point still had its big trees, its shrubs, its nameless statues. They joined the queue of wounded soldiers and derelicts moving slowly forward until Jerry heard a familiar voice from the counter. "Garn, yer ol' bugger, toast's anuvver bloody tuppence!"

Jerry's throat contracted. His mother had returned to London. He broke from the queue.

"Eh?" said Miss Brunner, grabbing for him and missing.

He ran up Villiers Street towards the Strand as fast as he could go. At the top of Villiers Street he climbed the ruined wall of the mainline station and risked a look back. Miss Brunner was in friendly (and to him, sinister) conversation with his mother. It seemed that the most disparate people were forming alliances these days. He dropped from the wall and ran on, through Admiralty Arch, to the Mall. There were grey trees on either side of him; even the grass of the park looked grey and smelled sterile. He ran towards Buckingham Palace at the end of the Mall not because he thought he would find safety there but because its outline was the only one he currently recognised. He reached the roundabout outside the palace, the statue of the old Queen, and the fountains. To the left of the palace, the tall houses of Victoria and Pimlico looked attractive; they had hardly been touched by any of the wars. He decided to make for Buckingham Palace Road and Prince's Street, where he had once had friends, but, as he walked panting beside the railings of the palace, there came a shout from the other side and he turned his head to see a soldier in a scarlet and black uniform, a bearskin on his head, threatening him with what appeared to be a Lee-Enfield .303.

"Halt," said the guardsman.

Jerry stopped. "What?"

"Halt. 'Ow'd'yer get frew ther fuckin' barrier, chum?"

"Didn't know there was one," said Jerry. "I've been away ill."

The guardsman's brutal, bloodshot eyes narrowed.

"Stay there," he said. He called over his shoulder. "Corp!"

A corporal ran out of a gatehouse at the side of the palace façade. It was Frank. His face was pale and covered in acne, emphasised by his scarlet tunic. He grinned broadly when he recognised his brother. "Jerry! You come to see us, 'ave you?"

Jerry shook his head and was silent.

"Unlock the gate, soldier," said Frank with some relish. The small wrought iron gate was opened and the guardsman stood back to allow Jerry to enter, but Jerry remained where he was. "I didn't know you'd joined the army, Frank."

"I was called up, wasn't I? It's me National Service. You oughta be in, too."

"I've been ill."

"Well, come on! We've a lot ter talk abaht!" Frank pretended enthusiasm. "Seen Cathy, 'ave yer? And Mum? She's runnin'—"

"I know." Jerry shuffled through the gate. "The coffee-stall."

"That's right. Wiv ol' Sammy. Nil desperandum!"

"Who?"

The soldier locked the gate behind him. "Are you allowed to have visitors, then?" Jerry asked.

"Me? I'm quite an important man round 'ere, these days. I'm expectin' to 'ave proper promotion any day now. I'm the senior officer, anyway. All the others are either on barrier duty or dead or wounded."

"Who're they fighting?"

"You have been away a long time, me old son! The Miners Volunteer Force, o' course. It's a terrorist organisation, mainly from Durham and that way. They've been givin' us an awful lot o' trouble, but we'll lick 'em!" Frank opened the green-painted door in the white stone wall. They entered a small office full of dark polished wood. "Cuppa?"

"Thanks."

Frank filled the kettle from a big steel drum and placed it on a portable gas ring. He lit the gas. "Yeah. I'm virtually second-in-command at the moment."

"What? To the king?"

"The king! Do me a favour!" Frank laughed heartily

and sat down in a comfortable leather armchair beside a small coal fire. It was warm and secure. Jerry took off his soaked coat and hung it on a big hook near the door. Frank's khaki greatcoat was there, too. He sat down on a straight-backed wooden chair on the other side of the fireplace.

"What's wrong with the king, then? Been deposed has he?" Jerry rubbed his hands and warmed them at the grate.

"Deposed? 'E's bloody dead, ain't 'e!" Frank was coarser than Jerry remembered him. It was probably the effects of army life.

"Then who's in charge?"

"The church took over, didn't they? Sort of care-taking capacity until order's restored."

"The Archbishop of Canterbury or something?"

"Nar! They 'anged the poor old blighter months ago. The current boss is a bishop. Bishop Beesley. You must've 'eard've 'im!"

"Vaguely," said Jerry. He loosened a soggy tie.

"You *must* 'ave. 'E's gonna bring back spiritual values into our way of life, in'e?"

"Oh, then Miss Brunner's working with him?"

"Do us a favour Jerry! She's the one 'oo led the fuckin' miners on London, ain't she!"

"It beats me," said Jerry. He watched as Frank rose to pour water into the tea pot.

"You're dead lucky I spotted you." Frank stirred the tea in the pot. "I'll put in a word. On my recommendation you'll get a commission. Captain, at least. Bound to." Frank reached out and turned the knob of a big table wireless. There was a lot of interference but through it all came the voice of Edmundo Ros. To a rhumba rhythm he was singing his latest hit. *Enjoy yourself, it's later than you think. Enjoy yourself, enjoy yourself, it's later than you think.*

Jerry reached out for the mug Frank offered him. His hand was trembling.

"This is the chance for people like us to take advantage of the opportunities," Frank was saying, "and make something of ourselves. They need us, see."

"What for?"

"Our will to survive," said his brother. "Our terror of

poverty." His grin was savage. "Our rat-like rapacity, Jerry old lad. Our vitality. They'll pay anything for our protection."

"Sort of Danegeld, you mean?"

"Call it what you like, mate. Not that they can't teach us a thing or two about 'anging on. As soon as we've got those bloody miners off our backs—and that's as good as done, at least for the time bein'—we'll be in charge. Then we'll show 'em!"

"It sounds a bit dodgy to me," said Jerry. He was still unclear of the issues or of his brother's ambitions. "They've had a lot more experience. They'll turn on you, Frank."

"I know too many secrets."

Jerry shrugged. "Well, maybe you're right."

"Are you on, then? Comin' in with me?" Frank grinned an eager grin.

Jerry shook his head. "I'll keep moving, I think. This isn't my decade at all."

"You won't get a better opportunity."

"I'll wait and see what the future brings."

"The future?" Frank laughed. "There isn't any future. Make the most of what you've got."

Jerry scratched his damp head. "But I don't like it here."

"You never believed you'd be visiting your brother in Buckingham Palace, I bet."

"I never believed in Buckingham Palace," said Jerry helplessly. He began to smile. "And I'm not sure I believe in you any more."

"Oo, you snooty little sod." Frank glowered. His pallid lips set in anger. "You stupid, stuck-up shitty little bastard! And I was trying to 'elp you! Well, if that's the way you wanna play it. I've got powers to enlist you. And once you're fuckin' enlisted, me old son, you'll see the error of your fuckin' ways."

Jerry drew his needle-gun from a pin-striped pocket. "I think I'll have to borrow your uniform if I'm going to get through. I'll let you have it back later."

Frank was hardly aware that his life was being threatened. He stared curiously at the needle-gun. "What's that?"

Jerry said: "The future."

7. Harlequin Invisible; or the Emperor of China's Court

Jerry shrugged himself back into his frilly Mr. Fish jacket and kissed Mitzi Beesley heartily on her exposed left buttock. Mitzi twitched. Her voice from beneath the pillow was lazy. "You could stay another couple of hours. My dad won't be back yet. We haven't tried it with those bottles."

"We'd only get stuck." He made for the stairs. "Besides, you're not nearly old enough." It seemed to him, as he went down, that he was still surrounded by the aura of her juicy lust. "See you." He opened the street door.

He walked out into the Chelsea sunshine. The bishop, a popular local figure, had not done too badly for himself since the dissolution. King's Road was crowded with pretty people, with music, food-stalls, hawkers of disposable clothes, fortune-tellers, prostitutes of every possible persuasion, beautiful buttons and blossoming bows; soft bodies brushed against him on all sides, delicious perfumes swam into his nose; his flesh sang. He pressed through the throng, whistling an Animals tune to himself, on his way to The Pheasantry, which Mr. Koutrouboussis had recently purchased. There was no doubt about it, thought Jerry, Utopia had been worth hanging on for. Everyone was happy. *Here, There and Everywhere,* sang the Beatles as he passed a day-time disco; they were the poets of paradise. *Turn off your mind, relax and float downstream. . . .*

There was, Jerry found himself bound to admit, still a minority of people who would have preferred the euphoria of austerity to all this and, indeed, the King's Road was not what he would have considered his own natural en-

vironment, even on festival days such as this one. Nonetheless, if he missed an egg and chips there was always
someone to provide a fantasy of more generous proportions, with a hurdy-gurdy and a rebuilt tram or two.
If anything got to him here, then it was the self-
consciousness, absent from his own territory further north,
where hangovers of the poverty trance still operated to
the advantage of the natives. And, too, it was in King's
Road that he saw the seeds of disaster, of the destruction
of everything he held dear. He put these thoughts from
his mind and shouldered his way a little more aggressively up the road only to stop dead as he reached the
stone gates of The Pheasantry and confronted none other
than Miss Brunner. She wore a white angular Courreges
suit with shorts, white PVC boots and a white PVC
floppy hat and satchel. On her nose were huge, round sunglasses and her red hair was cut quite short. A very noisy
radio went by—*Jumpin' Jack Flash, it's a gas, gas, gas*—
so he could not hear her greeting but, to his astonishment,
he was sure she had mouthed the word "Darling", at
him. He stopped, leaned his thin body against the opposite
gate-post and sniffed at her Young Lust. "Swinging along
okay, Miss B?"

"What? Oh, yes. Fabulously. You look pretty psychedelic yourself."

"Thanks. I do my best."

"No, I mean it. As tasty as anything. Are you going
in?" She peered towards the gloom of the hallway. "You
live here?"

"I've a friend who does. Well, he's a friend of Catherine's really."

"How is your sister? That job—or did she get—?"

"She's resting at the moment."

"Frank said something."

"He's improving, then. Well, I'll be seeing you."

"No!" She placed her white plastic fingers on his arm.
"I was actually looking for you. I know we've had our
differences."

"And our likenesses. There's no need to rake up the
past."

"Certainly not. I wouldn't dream. . . . Could we have
a chat?"

"You're not trying to recruit me for anything, are you?"

"Not really. I think we've more in common than we knew." She looked distastefully down at her body. "As you can see, I'm quite 'with-it' now."

"What are you doing with yourself?"

"Ha, ha! I've been trained. I'm a fully qualified computer programmer. Shall we have some coffee?"

Jerry shook his head. "It makes me too wary, eating in Chelsea. At best I can only do it if my back's well to the wall and my eye's on the door. You know how it is."

"But there are some charming places."

"That's what I mean."

He moved into the courtyard, a zone of relative silence, and sat down on the lip of the pool. Blue, green, yellow and red water came at intervals from the fountain in the centre. After a pause, she sat beside him. "I can't remember where it was we last met," she began.

"Neither can I," said Jerry. "Perhaps it hasn't happened yet?"

"Well, yes, possible, certainly." She had lost her old confidence while Jerry had gained quite a lot. She was evidently distressed.

"I know how interested you are in science," she said.

"Not any more." Jerry tried to catch a striped fish which floated to the surface. "Sorry. Technological art now."

"Oh, well. Even better. Technological art. Yes! Yes! Good. That. Well, science is the answer, I've decided, at any rate. I thought you'd be pleased. And computers are very definitely where we are going. My backers have invested in some of the absolutely latest equipment. You'll be familiar with it, of course."

"Don't judge me too hastily. I might leave it alone. I don't fancy. . . ."

"Ha, ha. Now. . . ." She removed a pearlite case from her white bag. She offered him a cigarette. "Sobranie, I think. Are those all right?"

Jerry shook his head.

"Oh, well." She closed the case without taking one of the cigarettes herself. She looked at her Zippo lighter for some time while she continued to talk. "Anyway, you know a lot about the less orthodox branches of science, don't you? Your father—?"

"I'm afraid I've lost faith in science as anything but a pastime," Jerry said.

"You were always flippant. You mustn't say things like that, Mr. Cornelius. It is technology which will pull us out of our current difficulties."

"I didn't know we had any."

"Of course we have. All this glitter simply hides a deeper malaise. You must agree. You're intelligent. This can't last. We must think ahead."

"I'd rather not think at all." He got up and looked into the water of the fountain at the multicoloured carp. "This is where I belong. I'm happy."

"Happy, Mr. Cornelius? How can you be?"

"I don't know, but I am."

"There's more to life than drugs and sex, Mr. Cornelius."

"There's more than life to drugs and sex. It's better than nothing."

"You need a goal. You always have. This rejection of your potential is silly. You believe in science as much as I do."

"What about land?"

"It's abstracts now. It would be ludicrous to continue thinking in old terms about a new situation, don't you agree?"

Jerry became uncomfortable. "I was thinking of going into the assassination business. You know what a dreamer I am. Would it be too much of a hit and myth operation, do you think?"

"Do you believe in aeroplanes, Mr. Cornelius?"

"It depends what you mean by 'aeroplanes.'" He yearned for the cool gloom of The Pheasantry, to bask in Koutrouboussis's envy.

"A properly organised technology is the only hope for the world unless we are to plunge into total decadence and from decadence into death," she said. "If we act now, we can save almost everything of value. Don't you see?" Her circular shades were cocked at an earnest angle. "If we can somehow produce a programme, feed in all the facts, we can get a clear idea of what we must do to prepare for the future. Imagine—the whole future in a single chip."

For once Jerry refrained from the obvious response. "I'm only interested in the present." He sat down close beside her. He put a hand on her knee. "Give us a kiss."

She sighed and gave him a quick one. He found that his hand could continue up her shorts unchecked. With a shock his fingers touched her cold cunt. "Sorry," he said.

"It doesn't make any difference," she told him.

He glanced around the courtyard at the flowers. He picked at a tooth. From somewhere overhead there came a bass drone. He smiled without much interest into the sky. "Bombers," he said. "I thought we were going to have a peaceful day." They were in sight now. A large formation of F111As. "It's a free country, I suppose."

"Eloi! Eloi!" Miss Brunner became agitated. She sprang to her feet. "Peaceful? This enclave of lotus eaters? Don't you realise the world's rotting about your ears? Haven't you got eyes? Can't you smell the corruption? Can't you feel the whole world going out of kilter? Where's your sense? And all you can think of is feeling me up!"

He glanced at her from beneath embarrassed eyebrows. He felt a twinge of self-pity. "I was only having a bit of fun."

Some distance to the south, probably over Barnes, the planes began to drop their loads.

She made efficient arrangements to her clothing. She headed for the languid street, still crowded with the festive and the free. "Fun!"

He was thoroughly demoralised, more by what he had found in her trousers than by what he had done. "I'm very sorry. It won't happen again."

"That's all right." She waved a polyvinyl chloride gauntlet. "For the present."

8. The Metamorphosis of Harlequin

For the last three weeks Jerry Cornelius had remained in the roof garden of the empty department store. The roof garden was overgrown and lush; parts of it were almost impassable. Flamingoes, ducks, macaws, parakeets and cockatoos inhabited the tangles of rhododendrons, creepers, climbing roses and nasturtiums; yellow mimosa grew adequately close to the various dividing walls of the garden: and, through the ceiling below, several large roots had broken and begun to find the tubs of earth Jerry had removed from the botanical department and placed on the floor so that ultimately the plants would gain purchase here. It was his ambition to bring in increasing supplies of earth so that in time the entire store would become a jungle to which he could then, perhaps, begin to introduce predators and prey, possibly from the zoo of the store's nearby rival.

Jerry had his consolations: a battery-operated stereo record player on which he listened to traditional folk music and laid back C&W, some light reading; he could feed himself from what was left of the Food Hall and from the canned supplies in the roof garden restaurant, where he had also set up his camp bed. The restaurant was more like a conservatory now, for he had been pleased to admit as many plants as would enter. He was never disturbed. He enjoyed the novels of Jane Austen, avoided interpretation, and dreamed of safer days.

Occasionally he would creep from the upper storeys to the bowels of the building and attend to his generators, thus maintaining his freezer and, of greater importance, the central heating. He had turned this to maximum so that his plants would be encouraged to extend their roots towards the distant ground. It was his hope that eventually the remains of Derry and Toms would be preserved in a gigantic shrubbery, impenetrable save by those who, like him, understood the labyrinth. At the top of this mountain of foliage and masonry he would then possess remarkable security. Already a number of peonies were blooming in the soft furnishing department and various vines and ivies, without training, had carpeted the floors and festooned the walls of Hardware and Electrical Goods. He remained armed, but he had lost much of his caution. Aerial warfare was almost a thing of the past, the fashion having changed primarily to tanks and infantry which, ultimately, provided greater satisfaction to those who still enjoyed such exercises. London was no longer regarded as a major objective.

Jerry gathered that most of the battles were won in the world and that conferences were rapidly agreeing territorial boundaries. The Continent of Europe had apparently become a vast conglomeration of tiny city states, primarily based on an agricultural economy, with certain traditional crafts and trades (Bohemian glass, German clocks, French mustard) flourishing: forming the basis of barter between the different communities. Not that war was unknown, but it had become confined to the level of local disputes. Jerry had been unable to see this development as a wholesome one, but he supposed it suited the petit bourgeoisie who constituted, as always, the majority of the survivors. It seemed to him that in some obscure way Miss Brunner had, after all, triumphed, though through no fault of her own.

The image of a Britain become a nation of William Morris wood-carvers and Chestertonian beer-swillers drove him deeper into his jungle and caused him to abandon his books. He was only prepared to retreat so far. He was forced to admit, however, that the seventies were proving an intense disappointment to him. He felt bitter about missed opportunities, the caution of his own allies, the sheer funk of his enemies. In the fifties life had been so appalling that he had been forced to flee into the future, perhaps even help create that future, but by the sixties, when the future had arrived, he had been content at last to live in the present until, due in his view to a conspiracy amongst those who feared the threat of free-dom, the present (and consequently the future) had been betrayed. As a result he had sought the past for conso-lation, for an adequate mythology to explain the world to him, and here he hid, lost in his art nouveau jungle, his art deco caverns, treading the dangerous quicksands of nostalgia and yearning for times that seemed simpler only because he did not belong to them and which, as they be-came familiar, seemed even more complex than the world he had loved for its very variety and potential. Thus he fled still further, into a world where vegetation alone flourished and only the most primitive of sentient life chose to exist. He was thinking of giving up time-travel altogether.

Apart from the infrequent fights which would break out amongst the birds, there were very few sounds to disturb him these days as he renounced his camp bed and lay deep in his bushes, his back to moist earth, his ear-phones almost invariably on his head as he listened to the Pure Prairie League, The Chieftains and, believing that this kept him in touch with the world, Roy Harper. He was inclined not to notice when his batteries had run down and the records were playing sometimes at less than half speed. He was also inclined to fall asleep when the needle stuck in a groove and not wake for two or three days.

He was dimly aware that these long periods of sleeping were increasing but, since he felt no physical effects, he preferred not to worry about them. It was likely that his activities through the past couple of decades had ex-hausted him more than he knew. For the moment, too, he had even forgotten about his sister, who lay in her padded silk coffin in the freezer, perhaps dreaming of an even more remote past than the one he sought to create for himself.

The summer grew hotter; the jungle grew denser, and then one day, as Jerry slumbered in musty heat in a little tunnel he had made for himself in the foliage, an un-read copy of *Union Jack* for 21 September 1923 (*X-ine* or *The Case of the Green Crystals,* A Zenith Story) lying foxed and damp-stained by his limp right hand, the com-forting rumble of Centurion Thirteens, Vickers Vijayantas and Humber FV1611 armoured personnel carriers augmented the sultry tranquillity of the day, the hum of bees, the hiccuping of crickets.

The little fleet of armour came to a stop at the signal of a round-shouldered old man in the dress uniform of a major in the Royal Hussars who emerged from the leading Humber, adjusting his busby. A captain, in conventional khaki, pushed up the hatch of the Centurion immediately behind the Humber and ran over the weedy tarmac to receive orders. The major spoke a few words, contemplated the outside of the store which was almost entirely covered by thick ivy, checked the dark green interior of the main hallway, then returned to his personnel carrier. A head wearing a green, gold and purple turban raised itself over the camouflaged metal. A chubby brown face showed a certain amount of astonishment as it caught sight of the department store, which somehow had come to resemble the forgotten ruins of Angkor Wat in Cambodia. Green and gold shoulders followed the face and eventually the whole figure, small and stocky and round, stood on the surface of the vehicle, hands on hips. He was dressed in the impressive uniform of the 30th Deccan Horse, a broad sash around his waist, his sabre and pistol supported on a Sam Browne belt which was oddly functional compared to the rest of his ensemble. The major saluted and lifted a hand to help the splendid Indian to the ground then, together, they entered the forest.

The engines of the tanks and personnel carriers were switched off; silence returned. Slowly the crews began to climb from their machines and, stripped to the waist, smoke cigarettes and chat amongst themselves. They seemed to be a mixed force in a variety of uniforms— English, Scottish, Indian, Trinidadian, Jamaican and Cornish among them. Tinny Heavy Reggae began to sound from at least one turret.

The two officers reached the roof garden three hours later. They were sweating and stained, the collars of their jackets opened, their headgear askew. They searched the restaurant and the restaurant kitchens. The first thing they found was the display freezer with its pale blue contents, the beautiful smiling madonna. The major shook his head. "About the only thing he ever thought worth preserving. Poor little chap."

"They were in love," said the Indian. He tried to push

his hand down the side of the coffin to get a tub of Honey and Acacia ice cream below, but failed.

"More than that." The major sighed. "She represented everything he thought important. He believed that if he could revive her he could revive the world he had lost."

"She is dead, then?"

"As good as, old boy." The major closed the lid of the cabinet. "We'd better check the gardens now. You take the Tudor and I'll take the Spanish. If you don't have any luck, meet me back here."

They went their ways.

The major found it almost impossible to climb over the tangled branches and roots blocking the entrance to the mock-Moorish splendours of the garden where the fountains were now choked with dark green vegetation, with magnolia, over-sized tulips, peonies, poppies, sunflowers. The heavy scent from the place almost drove him back. He was about to press on when his ear detected a faint sound from his right and he looked towards the gigantic rhododendron mass immediately opposite the restaurant. Two or three flamingoes stalked from it, their pink necks wobbling, splashing on broad feet through what remained of the miniature river. But it was not the birds who had made the sound. The major moved towards the rhododendron, almost blinded by the intensity of the purple, scarlet and pink blossoms, the powerful odour of earth and decaying undergrowth. He pushed branches aside and found a low archway. He bent down and peered through the green semi-darkness. He went on his knees and began to crawl until the tunnel opened into a tiny cavern in which lay curled, foetus-like, the body of the man the major had sought over five continents.

The body was dressed in a green and khaki camouflaged safari suit, there were black Koss earphones on his head and the lead of the earphones was attached to a record deck on which Al Bowlly was singing *What a Little Moonlight Can Do* with painful slowness. On its side, near the player, was a clock, decorated in red, white and blue, and beside it a gesticulating figurine in a traditional white pierrot costume with a black skull cap, perhaps a contemporary likeness of Charles Debureau himself; near that a copy of a *Fantomas* novelette and a copy of *Le Chat Noir* magazine. The *Union Jack* was open at the beginning of the story. A box below the illustration, showing an open safe, a swirl of vapour and two men apparently confronting one another (one wearing full evening dress) read: *This story very worthily upholds the UNION JACK tradition—the tradition for really well told stories, full of character and action. It is a Zenith-Sexton Blake story, written as only the creator of the Albino knows how. If you want anything better than this you are indeed hard to please.* The major carefully picked the fragile magazine from the earth, rolled it and tucked it into the top pocket of his dark blue tunic. Then he inspected the stiff figure of the man. It was thin. The face was quite long, the lips full, the eyes, though closed, apparently large. The hair was black, long and fine, but appeared to have been dyed white at some time. There was a very close resemblance to the blonde young woman the major had discovered in the freezer. He lifted his head:

"In here, Hythloday. I've found him, poor old chap. Just made it, too, it seems. He's almost gone."

The major waited, rolling himself a cigarette as he looked down at the curled figure. There came a blundering sound from behind him and eventually a panting Hythloday crawled into view. There was not really room for all three of them. It was obvious that Hythloday at first suspected the major had been forced to defend himself.

"He's not dead, I hope. Was he violent?"

"Oh, no, no." The major smiled sadly. "As far as this chap's concerned I'm afraid violence is a thing of the past."

9. The Death of Harlequin

"Ten bloody years!" Miss Brunner was incongruous in a red and white Malay sarong, her head tied in the kind of blue turban hat popular four decades earlier. Her breath smelled of chloroform from the Victory V throat lozenges she had taken to consuming. In wedge sandals she hobbled across a green, blue and gold Kazhak carpet to the mock-Adam fireplace where old Major Nye stood looking at a collection of photographs in black and silver Mackintosh frames. Major Nye wore the uniform of his first regiment: a pale blue and yellow tunic, dark blue britches with a double yellow stripe, black riding boots with spurs, a sabre, white spiked helmet; the 8th King George's Own Light Cavalry. He had become so frail that it seemed the uniform alone kept him on his feet. He turned, blinking mildly, raising a grey eyebrow, bending his thin good ear towards her. "Eh?"

"I don't think you realise how very difficult it's been for some of us." She stared coldly at one of the marble pillars near the tall double doors. Ceramic Siamese red and black lions returned her gaze. The whole place was a mixture of oriental styles except for the original architecture, which was Victorian Greek. "I spent nine months in a Cornish internment camp for a start!"

"Start?"

"Underground bunkers. They put anything underground that will go underground. They're fond of holes, the Cornish. They're afraid of the sun."

"Ironical, in their case. They're like the Welsh. Mining you see. They love it. Like the Seven Dwarves. *Heigh ho, heigh ho, it's off to work we go. . . .*" He chuckled. "*Dig, dig, dig.* It's made them very rich these days, I gather. Tin, clay, gold and silver even. Oh, they've done it for centuries. Since before the Romans. Two thousand years at least. Give them a pick and shovel and they'll burrow through anything. It's instinctive. You have to admire them."

She had heard his racial views more than once. She sighed deeply. "Oh, yes?" She rubbed at her raw bare arm. "They're also notoriously horrible to their prisoners—including other Celts."

"True. You heard that stuff about the flint knives, I suppose, and the menhirs?"

"I saw it," she said. "I was lucky."

"Well, they've achieved their object. They don't get many unwanted visitors any more. They've a new arethyor enthroned at Tintagel at last. I got the news this morning."

"Which one won?"

"Arluth St. Aubyn, naturally." He shrugged and rubbed at his blue-veined nose. "They can't help themselves. Ancient instincts, you see, as I say. Old habits die hard."

"It seems you pulled Cornelius out in time again. He owes a lot to you."

"Someone has to look after him when he goes walkabout."

Miss Brunner glanced over to the bay windows where her old lover sat, silhouetted against the light, wrapped in a Kashmiri shawl, his eyes vacant and unblinking. "Oh, Christ," she said, "he's dribbling. And he used to be tipped as the Messiah to the Age of Science!" She shook her head in disgust.

"It's his amnesia," said Major Nye, to excuse Cornelius. "He never knows where he's going. He just keeps revisiting certain places that have some private meaning for him, some mythological significance. He's much better today. He keeps collapsing into catatonia, especially after one of the wandering spells. It can't be his sister he's looking for now. She's perfectly safe."

Miss Brunner glared into the vacant face. "There are no sanctuaries any more, Mr. Cornelius. There are none in the past, none in the future. I advise you to make the best of the present!"

"Best not to disturb him," said Major Nye. On frail legs stiffened at the knees by the boots, his spurs rattling a little, he went to stand behind Jerry's wheelchair. "All right, old son. There, there, old lad." He patted Jerry's shoulder. Since he had lost his wife and family, Major Nye had found his only fulfilment in taking care of the mindless assassin. "He never believed in the possibility of sanctuary, you know. Not for years. He disdained the idea. He was born in the modern city, you see."

"You mean he never needed security? I've known him longer than you, major, and I can tell you. . . ."

"The city was his security, with all its horrors. As the jungle is security to the tiger, you might say. When they began to destroy his city he lost his bearings completely. For a while he evidently thought that the landscape of warfare might be a substitute, but he was wrong. It's strange, isn't it, how the city grew from the town which in turn grew from the encampment formed against the terrors of the wild . . .?"

"I don't know anything about that. I was born in Kent."

"Exactly. I was born in the country. We can't possibly understand the comforting familiarity of the city to someone like Cornelius. The worse it is, in our terms, the more he feels at one with himself. Even at the end his instinct was to hide in the heart of the city, climbing to the top of a tall building for safety, reintroducing the jungle. . . ." Major Nye's voice faded. He smiled tenderly at his charge.

"He's a wild beast. A monster."

"Indeed. That's why he became such a totem to so many."

"I always considered his apparent sophistication, his affectation of an interest in science, to be a veneer." Her voice became more confident as she began to feel she and the major were on common ground at last.

"On the contrary. A creature like Cornelius takes technology for granted. It is real enough to him for it to possess a genuinely mythological significance."

Miss Brunner tightened her unlikely lips. "I never denied technology had a purpose. . . ." She frowned. "A usefulness. If handled properly. . . ."

"You tried to use it to maintain the old order. Your friend Beesley wanted to turn it against itself, to destroy it altogether. But Cornelius enjoyed it for its own sake. Aesthetically. He had no interest in its moral significance

or its utilisation. Computers and jets and rockets and la-
sers and the rest were simply familiar elements of his
natural environment. He didn't judge them or question
them, any more than you or I would judge or question a
tree or a hill. He picked his cars, his weapons, his gadgets, in the same way that he picked his clothes—for their
private meanings, for what they looked like. He enjoyed
their functions, too, of course, but function was a second-
ary consideration. There are easier cars to drive than
Duesenbergs, easier, faster, cheaper planes to fly than experimental Dorniers. He found speed exhilarating, of
course, but again speed wasn't really what he cared about.
He preferred airships to jet-liners because airships were
more romantic, he preferred Mach 3 liners and shock-
wave ships because they looked nicer and because they
hinted at an ambiguous relationship with space and time
—that was where the mystical element came in, as with
particle physics. And have you noticed how we still continue to ape the markings of animals in our clothes—particularly our traditional formal clothes? Similarly with
technology. He liked the Concorde because it looked most
like an eagle. To me it was all completely bewildering,
to you it was something that had to be tamed, to him it
was normality. He had all the primitive's respect for
Nature, the same tendency to invest it with meaning and
identity, only his Nature was the industrial city, his idea
of Paradise was an urban utopia. . . ."

"He was a snotty-nosed little back-street nihilist," she
said. "There's no point in dignifying his attitude."

"To us he was far more dangerous than any nihilist. He
was alien. He came to enjoy the bombing raids because
he was interested in what the bombs would do, what sort
of pictures they would make, even, as was often the case,
when his own safety was threatened. His will to peace
was as strong as yours or mine, perhaps stronger, but his
methods of obtaining peace were personal. They became
personal because we couldn't understand what he was
talking about. He was a friendly chap. He allowed us
all to use him. But he gradually came to realise that our
aims were incompatible. His Utopia was to us an insane
technological nightmare."

"I can't believe this sympathy of yours." She snapped.
She clacked across the carpet to the photographs. They

were all there, all his relatives, his acquaintances. "You're older than me. Your world had nothing at all in common with his."

"It probably changed just as rapidly. But I suppose it's because I know that I've so little in common with him that I can sympathise." Major Nye turned the chair slightly so that Jerry could see something of the street below, where the rebuilding work was taking place, where the bunting and the flags were going up. "Yours is an unfortunate generation, on the whole."

"I am, I hope, broadminded. But one can take for granted far too much, major."

"Not as much as poor Cornelius. He took it all for granted. It ruined him. He wasn't his world's Messiah. He wasn't the Golden Trickster. He was his world's Fool."

"Is that what he's suffering from?" She became curious, advancing again to the wheelchair, staring coldly into the drooling face. "Shock?"

"He was shown too much of the past at once. That's a theory, anyway. He hardly knew it existed before."

"And you continue to support him, you and Una Persson. Even Auchinek, who has no love for him. Why?"

"Perhaps we thought we could maintain our humanity by studying him. In Auchinek's case, at least, and in mine, you could say that we saw him as a model. In an inhospitable world he seemed to be at ease." Major Nye fingered his moustache. He sucked his lips. He dismissed the notion. "No. It's too hard for me to define. It might be much simpler than that. I need to give my loyalty to something. It's my training, d'you see. With all his faults, he seemed the best bet. He took his world for granted, just as I had taken mine for granted—not complacently, but with the sense that, drawbacks included, injustices included, it was the best of all possible worlds."

"To be quite candid," Miss Brunner began, and then was horrified to see Cornelius looking back at her through sardonic eyes.

"You'll never be that, I'm afraid," said Cornelius calmly. Then the head dropped. The lips began to drool again.

"He has these flashes," said Major Nye affectionately. She clacked toward the door. "It's disgusting. You're both as senile as one another. You need a nurse to look after the pair of you."

Before Miss Brunner could reach the doors they opened and a small black-and-white cat walked in, tail erect, followed by Una Persson who came to a halt when she saw Miss Brunner. Una Persson had her Smith and Wesson .45 in her hand, half-cocked. When she recognised Miss Brunner she smiled and uncocked the pistol, slipping it back into the holster at her belt. She wore the full uniform of a Jodhpur Lancer, for she was currently in the employ of the Maharajah of New Marwar and had come up by train from Brighton only an hour before. "How nice to see you again. And what a pretty outfit." Una bowed, the plumes in her turban nodding.

"You've certainly gone all the way, dearie." Miss Brunner was disgusted. "Did you bring your harem with you?"

"We're not allowed harems in New Marwar." Una inched past Miss Brunner and offered Major Nye a broad, open smile. "Good afternoon, Major. How's the patient?"

"Improving, I'd say."

Miss Brunner disappeared on angry heels. Una closed the doors. "It's all arranged," she said. "I do pray they won't be disappointed."

"We can only hope."

"Hope . . ." mumbled the slumped figure.

"There!" said Major Nye. "I seem to have offended Miss Brunner. I had no intention. . . ."

"I didn't know she was at liberty again."

"I'd hardly call it liberty. Apparently she plans to found some sort of mission in London, together with Beesley and that daughter of his. They've fallen on hard times, those two."

"And I didn't realise Beesley was back. Where's he been?"

"He was thrown out of Ohio, I gather. By the Sioux. Then he went to Arizona and was deported by the Navajo. He didn't have much better luck in New Hampshire, where the Elders regarded him, rather ironically, as an atheist. According to our intelligence, and it's always suspect, he spent a while in the West Indies where he managed to build up a small following, but eventually he was sent home on an emigrant ship and landed in Liverpool a month ago. The Chinese authorities sent him to us. So far the only state to offer him a home has been East Wiltshire. But he found out what happens to clergymen in Wiltshire, after their seven-year period of office. Some old custom they've revived."

"I appreciate this quest for national identity," she said, "but it does seem that most traditions were dropped for the good reason that they were revoltingly cruel and stupid."

"Well, live and let live. Things will probably settle down." He looked at the red, white and blue French clock on the mantelpiece. It was half-hidden behind the photographs. "You're about half-an-hour late. I was hoping you'd rescue me sooner."

"I dropped off to see Mrs. Cornelius."

"I thought she was coming for the festivities."

"I had something to discuss. She'll be here later."

"Still going strong, is she?"

"As always. Quite a celebrity in these parts now, and enjoying every minute of it."

"She's still with Pyat?"

"No. Pyat's working with the Poles now, over in Slough. He sees her from time to time but I think Hira—what's he calling himself?"

"Hythloday."

"Yes. I might as well call myself Lalla Rookh!" She laughed. "Anyway, he's still her main boyfriend. It gives him a lot of extra muscle in Croydon, apparently, but the Maharajah wants him to marry her and she says she's had enough of marriage, though she'd be glad of the status. She could go to Brighton whenever she liked, then."

"It's even more magnificent, I hear. Lots of gold roofs and pastel walls. Hythloday wouldn't be marrying out of caste, would he?"

"Mrs. C is regarded as high caste by virtue of being Jerry's mum. My boss has entertained her to dinner several times and been proud of the honour. She, of course, was in her element. They love her. There isn't a Sikh in Sussex who doesn't. Of course she tends to be hated by a lot of the natives who resent her privileges and think she's socialising above her station or sucking up to the masters, depending on their point of view, but that type of white will always bicker amongst themselves. I get a lot of similar spite, myself, of course."

Major Nye was amused. "They think you're a bit of an Uncle Tom, do they?"

"You could put it like that." She took a step back from Jerry as if she inspected a painting. Her uniform was primarily white and gold with a gold-trimmed scarlet sash. There was an Indian sabre at her belt and her turban was a tall one, wrapped around a spiked metal cap, matching the colours of her uniform and with some thin bands of blue to show her rank. The plumes were also a sign of rank. For Major Nye the uniform somehow emphasised her femininity and made her seem a fraction shorter than usual. "I wish he'd perk up a bit," she said beneath her breath. "They've made so many preparations."

"Officially we tell them he's been asleep?"

"Oh, certainly. But you know what legends are like. There are an awful lot of people believe that when he wakes up this time an era of peace, prosperity and cooperation between the nations will begin."

"The British nations, you mean? It was our fault, I suppose, for speaking so highly of him."

"I don't think it's that. They needed a symbol and he's as good as anything. After all, he was a lot of help to many of the independence movements, even before the civil war. Now there's scarcely one of the sixty states that doesn't have some sort of folklore connected with him. Not everything is good, of course, but most of it is. You should hear the stories the Highland anarchists tell. It's astonishing how quickly he's been worked into almost all of Britain's mythologies as well as a good many others throughout the world. As if a gap existed for him to fill. There are Cornelius legends in America, Africa, Asia, Australia, throughout Europe. He's bigger than the Beatles now."

Major Nye was pleased. He took a brass-plated tin from his tunic. The tin had belonged to his father. It was decorated with a relief bust of Princess Mary flanked by the initials M.M. while the borders contained pictures of stylised arms and ships and the names of various nations —Belgium, Japan, Russia, Monte Negro, Servia and France. In the top border were the words Imperium Britannicum. In the bottom border were the words Christmas 1914. The tin had originally contained a pipe, cigarettes and tobacco and a Christmas card from Princess Mary. Now it contained Major Nye's own tobacco and cigarette papers. He began to roll himself a tiny smoke. "You don't mind what's happened, then?"

"You think I should be jealous?"

"Miss Brunner certainly is. So's his brother."

"He was always a better entertainer than I was." Una shrugged. "And I was always a better politician. He refused to make something of himself and now the world has made something of him. There's nothing like having a common hero."

"And I'm nothing if not common," said Jerry. He blinked. "It's a bit bright in here, isn't it?"

They watched him carefully, expecting him to subside.

"What's been going on?" he asked. "You were talking about me, weren't you?"

Una shook her head chidingly. "You sneaky little bugger!"

"I didn't really take much in." He was apologetic. "Where am I?"

Major Nye seemed to grow younger by the second. He was almost dancing with pleasure. "Ladbroke Grove, old chap."

Jerry looked around him at the magnificence of it. "Must be the posh end," he said. "I never knew it very well."

"This is all new. It was built on the site of that convent. The one they bombed."

"Blimey!" Jerry shifted in his chair. It rolled slightly and he realised it was on wheels. He cackled at it. "Was I injured?"

"You could say that. You were catatonic."

"Black or white? Or both?" Jerry thought he saw a tail disappearing up the chimney. He accepted the information without question. It's a family trait. Like the Ushers. Wasn't it?"

"Like the bloody Draculas." Una Persson's amusement was admiring. "Pulled through just in time, as usual, haven't you? You've missed all the work and can enjoy all the fun."

"Oh, good." He yawned. "Is this your place, Major? Or is it a new town hall?"

"It's your palace, old son. Built by public subscription. All the British nations, bar one or two, chipped in."

"So the war's over." He stood up and the chair shot away across the smooth floor and struck the far wall. He was still a little shaky on his pins. "Well, it's very kind of them. I didn't think I was that popular."

Una hid her pleasure behind an expression of mock severity. "You wouldn't have been, if it wasn't for the fact that, for the past decade, you've done absolutely nothing. You're the stuff heroes are made of, Jerry."

"Yeah? What's London like, these days?" He walked to the huge bay.

"There's a great deal to be done yet," said Major Nye. "Those skyscrapers over there are just the beginning. They'll have high-level moving pavements going between them eventually. And gyrocopters and airships and everything. Just as you visualised it."

"The City of the Future," said Jerry breathlessly. "Is it all for me?"

"And anyone else who chooses to live here." Una joined him at the windows. "Otherwise the rest of the world's regressed somewhat, though there aren't many people complaining. This will be your monument, where past and future come together. London's independent now, too, you see. It has no authority over anything but itself. It's a free city, a mercantile, cosmopolitan neutral zone, a symbol."

"A meeting place for artists, scientists, merchants," continued Major Nye. *"In Xanadu did Kubla Khan. . . ."*

"Cor!" exclaimed Jerry. "Is it going to have a dome over it, too. A power dome?"

"If that's what you want."

"I can't just say what I want, surely? Who's the boss?"

"You are, Jerry." Una Persson's eyes were shining. "Happy Birthday."

"I get the whole of London?"

"Why not?"

"Nobody else," said Major Nye with a small grin, "wants it, really."

"Cor!" The shawl fell from his shoulders. He was still in the uniform of the 30th Deccan Horse. "'An O'Bean Utopia!" Major Nye went back to the mantelpiece and got his headdress for him. Jerry put it on as he stared through round, delirious eyes at the golden city of marvels beginning to rise from the ruins. Then he peered in the direction of the demolished Ladbroke Grove Underground Station. "There seems to be a lot of people coming up the road."

They stood on either side of him.

"We'd better get you upstairs," said Una, brushing at his back. "Onto the balcony."

"It's only fair. They'll be wanting to see you. You represent the future for them, you see. The wonderful tomorrow."

"Tomorrow? I don't get it."

"You will. They're not ready for it yet. Not personally. But it's comforting to be able to see what it will be like if they ever do want it."

Between them they escorted the astonished Cornelius from the room, through the double doors, up a wide staircase and into an even larger hall where the french windows had been opened onto the white marble balcony.

From below came cheers. A large crowd had gathered, clad in the costumes of a hundred nations, in plaids and lace; in kilts and pantaloons and britches and trousers and trews and dhotis; saris, sarongs, of silk and satin, chitons, chardors and cholees, frock-coats of cotton and felt, capes, cloaks and kaftans in moire, astrakhan, corduroy and gaberdine, bowlers, boaters, Buster Brown and pillbox caps, turbans and kaffiyehs, buskins, moccasins, mukluks, wellingtons, chuckars, brogues, slippers, sandals, plimsolls pumps and trepida in colours more varied and dazzling than the rainbow's. And Jerry saw skins of every shade, African, Asian, Anglo-Saxon, Latin and Teutonic, and the faces of all these representatives of the races were turned to him and, when he waved, they waved back.

"Hi," said Jerry in some awe, "fans."

He saw a small figure break through the crowd and move across the street. "Miss Brunner?"

Did she turn and present two fingers to him? He could not be sure, for now the procession was passing the palace.

"Bloody hell!" said Jerry. "What is it? A carnival?"

"It's in your honour," said Una with great satisfaction. "They're deputations from every British state."

"Just like the Jubilee!"

"More or less," said Una, "though things have perhaps changed a bit."

Precedence had been given to the knife-wheeled Celtic chariot driven by a lady in a sky-blue smock who hailed him with her long spear, but she was followed immediately by the ceremonial elephants, festooned in scarlet and gold, jade and silver, plumes of ostrich, peacock and bird of paradise, with intricately woven shawls, tassels and jewelled tusk rings, some of them bearing enormous howdahs on their backs—howdahs of bronze and gold or carved from rare woods and set under with mother-of-pearl. . . .

"Those belong to my master," said Una proudly, "the Maharajah of New Marwar. He's one of the most powerful monarchs in Britain."

. . . and some of the elephants pulled monstrous carriages, not unlike ornate railway coaches, the windows curtained with green velvet, the metal glowing with brilliant enamels, containing the families of the rulers of Surrey, Sussex and South Dorset. The rulers themselves, maharajas and rajas in traditional military uniforms similar to those worn by Jerry and Una, rode at the head of their lancers and their riflemen, their splendid infantry, veterans of Dorking, Bognor Regis, Lewes and Hastings, swords raised in salute to the Lord of London. Next came the mandarins of Liverpool and Morecambe, in glinting rickshaws, coaches and sedan chairs, their retainers waving dragon banners, beating gongs and playing pipes as they marched and danced their superb acrobatic steps; the great Captains of Birmingham and Bristol in vast open Cadillacs, sporting the blazing flags of New Trinidad and Old Jamaica, accompanied by masked troops playing drums of every description, by lovely black drum majorettes, by bat-men and panthermen, all style and dash. Then came the great clans of Scotland, with wailing bagpipes and rattling drums, plaids bright enough to dim the sun, the green-kilted warriors of Eire and Cymru, the Coal Dancers of the Federation of Miner's Republics, bearing their bowler-hatted Chief Executive on their shoulders; the Lancashire Free State leaders, carrying their own banner, the great red and yellow tapestry with their famous slogan *Wigan Won the War* woven into it; there were more Irish Hussars, and Scottish Mounted

Rifles, Australian Light Horse, Canadian Artillery, Welsh Irregulars, Wessex Roughriders, regiments of horse and foot from South Wiltshire, East Kent, North Yorkshire, West Wickham, all carrying flags of their states, some of them wearing uniforms whose origin was thoroughly obscure to Jerry, who knew nothing of recent history; some of the mascots and totems—skulls, pieces of furniture, sheep, dogs, goats, bulls, portraits, items of clothing, children, mummies—were equally mysterious. There were Briganti, Iceni, Trinovantes, Cantiaci, Catuvellauni, Coritani and Cornovii, with red gold bracelets and beards and braids and burnished shields of brass and bronze, with glittering M-16s on their backs, with horned helmets, huge beards and fierce eyes. There were Mercians and Northumbrians, with blood-red banners and dark helms, mounted on bucking motorcycles decorated with chrome and gold and semi-precious stones and, after all seventy-two British nations had displayed their military strength, there followed the pipe bands of Surrey and Inverness, the brass bands of Fazackerley and Bradford, the steel bands of Aston and Shepton Mallet, many of the tunes recognisable, many others hauntingly alien— a great wailing of sitars, saxophones, syrens and serpents, a banging and beating of bongos and congas and kettledrums and tablas, of gongs and cymbals, of xylophones and glockenspiels, the thrumming of guitars and mandolins, violins, banjos and double-basses, maraccas, mouth-organs, cowbells, sleigh-bells, tubular bells, songs and chants and shouts in fifty different dialects, all of them full of wild, innocent joy, for this was a celebration of peace of which Cornelius and his London were the concrete symbols.

"The king! The king!" they cried. "For he's a jolly good fellow!" they sang, and "Auld Lang Syne!"

Jerry was weeping as he waved back. He turned to old Major Nye who smiled behind his moustache.

"Am I really the king? Or just a play-actor?"

Major Nye shrugged. "Does it matter? Elfberg or Cornelius. You are their ideal. Wave to them, Your Majesty!"

Una came close, murmuring: "It's an honorary title, with very little actual power. But the honour really is considerable."

"But what are my duties?"

"To exist. It would be foolish to make a king who had any concrete responsibilities, particularly after the trouble the world's been in. It's all titular, though you do have the whole of London to play with. Anyway, nobody else wanted the job."

"Not even Frank?"

"Almost nobody else."

Jerry continued to wave. "I don't know about you, Miss Persson, but it's the best offer I've had so far."

"You've never been one to resist a bit of glamour."

"It's more the security I like."

He waved violently at the airships, keel after keel, making their stately way across the sky. "I wish Catherine could see this. Is she about?"

"She's still sleeping, I'm afraid," said Major Nye. "We didn't like to try waking her until you. . . ."

"Of course. But King Pierrot must win his Queen Columbine now. It's only right. Catherine would expect it of me. I've never let her down before. Pierrot's been waiting for centuries, hasn't he?"

Major Nye looked baffled. "I thought you were playing Harlequin?"

"I wasn't suited for the part. I changed. It was quite natural. No danger."

A shadow fell across the balcony and for a moment an expression of terror appeared in Jerry's eyes. Then it vanished. He turned, arms outstretched. "Hello, Mum."

"Cor! Wot a scorcher!" Mrs. Cornelius was sweating as only she could sweat, her huge bulk dripping with diamonds and pearls. She sported an ermine-trimmed robe of scarlet silk, a huge feathered hat. "D'yer like it? I 'ad it run up special for yer corernation. Luverly turn art, innit?"

"Lovely."

The procession was over. The sound of it began to fade near the top of Ladbroke Grove, heading towards Notting Hill.

Frank stood behind his mother. "Congratters, old son." Rage flitted in his eyes. "Feeling all right now, are we?"

The roar of the crowd below began to rise higher and higher and drowned whatever it was Jerry had been hoping to say.

10. The Mirror; or, Harlequin Everywhere

London, England: the time is Christmas Eve, probably during the nineties, and from the black night sky drop flakes of soft snow, covering roofs and walls, trees and streets, giving to the air a silence, a taste at once damp, fresh and salty; and with the flakes, from the huge darkness, there descends a fluttering, indistinct figure whose feet touch the flat top of a tall, deserted building, the new Derry and Toms. The figure darts for the shadows, even though the roof garden is closed for the season, but the footfalls, which leave light prints on the surface, together with the slap of the snow on the broad rhododendron leaves, disturb the birds there and they move in their sleep. Overhead we hear a distant bass drone, as if a flying machine departs.

Wrapped in a cloak of red velvet trimmed with green moire, the hood covering the head, a black domino mask disguising the features, the figure looks this way and that, then slips towards the exit, leaving more footprints behind it. As the figure moves, the cloak falls back to reveal the vari-coloured costume of Harlequin.

Harlequin flits down the darkened stairs to the emergency doors, takes out a key, unlocks them, pauses, as if drawing breath, then enters a side-street bustling with cheerful life: gas-jets roar over stalls and under stoves, some for light, some for heat: there are braziers, crimson and black, of jacket-potatoes and hot chestnuts; there are pans of pies, apples, toffee, cakes and fried sausages; all for sale, all cheap: fish and chips, barley sugar twists, humbugs, gumdrops, bullseyes. Huge, scarlet faces hang over the wares, shouting, laughing, crying. " 'Ot codlins,

'Ot codlins!" Father Christmas pads along the narrow space between the stalls, ringing his bell, while his costumed imps caper here and there, handing gifts to any children they meet. "Plump turkeys! Merry Christmas! Merry Christmas! Best pippins!" A sweet for a girl, a sprig of mistletoe for a boy. "Carp! Carp! Merry Christmas!" And the breath steams from their lips, muffled in collars and scarves, to join the boiling mist from the pans and cauldrons which, in turn, meets and melts with the falling snow so that the air immediately above the stalls glows like a yellow aurora. "Roast goose! Salt beef! Merry Christmas! Merry Christmas!" Dogs bark, horses neigh, children scream for the joy of it all.

Harlequin moves quickly into the broader canyon, the renewed Kensington High Street. Here, beneath arcades created by overhead pedestrian galleries climbing, step by step, into the black and white sky, among elegant towers with windows of glittering gold and silver, whose tops are lost high above, between moving sidewalks, packed with shoppers, are the warm lights of more stalls: stalls piled with vegetables, with meats, toys and sweets; stalls burdened with fowl and game, salmon and trout, pine branches, bunches of heather, holly and laurel; and behind the stalls are coffee-houses, where men and women of every nationality—Hindoos, Russians, Chinese, Spaniards, Portuguese, Englishmen, Frenchmen, Genoese, Neapolitans, Venetians, Greeks, Turks, descendants from all the builders of Babel, come to trade in London—seek the warmth alike, joining there in friendly intercourse; chop-houses, where merchants exchange Christmas gifts and clap one another upon the shoulder—"Merry Christmas!": pie-shops, whose windows are heaped with beef puddings, steak and kidney pies, treacle tarts, sweating and smoking in great white enamel basins and trays; bazaars and emporia bursting with rich, mouth-watering smells, crammed with customers still upon their Christmas hunt, while from the other side of bright frosted windows, in the public houses, comes the sound of pianos, pianolas, fiddles, harmoniums and accordions.

God rest ye merry gentlemen, let nothing ye dismay. . . .

Harlequin passes on, muffled in the cloak, head hidden

by the hood, between a little knot of boys and girls gathered round a lanthorn pole, their shadows huge on the snow, to sing:

> *Good King Wenceslas looked out*
> *On the feast of Stephen*
> *When the snow lay round about*
> *Deep and crisp and even. . . .*

Already other children stoop to gather the snow in mittened hands, knead it into balls, throw it at one another, laughing, screaming, yelling fit to burst . . .

> *Bring me flesh and bring me wine*
> *Bring me pine-logs hither.*
> *Thou and I will see him dine*
> *When we bear them thither.*

. . . Omnibuses rattle by, lights ablaze, top rails crackling like so many Christmas stars; carriages, rickshaws, cabs and cars. "Merry Christmas! Merry Christmas!"

> *Page and monarch forth they went,*
> *Forth they went together.*
> *Through the rude wind's wild lament,*
> *And the bitter weather.*

A mass of loose snow suddenly tumbles into the street, covering the children who shriek with delight and look up.

> *Sire, the night is darker now,*
> *And the wind blows stronger. . . .*

A mighty airship moves slowly between the towers, its engines idling to produce the sound of a slow, gigantic heartbeat, while tiny silhouettes look down from the yellow illumination of the observation galleries to catch glimpses of the rich world below.

> *Fails my heart I know not how,*
> *I can go no longer. . . .*

The 19.00 is bringing in the last of the Christmas mail,

proceeding with such stateliness that snow is able to form on the top of her hull; she resembles a huge Yuletide pie. The bells of St. Mary's Kensington ring out from the church in the shadow of the archway formed by two fourth-storey pedestrian roads:

Ding, dong. Ding, dong. Merry Christmas.

Mark my footsteps, good my page,
Tread thou in them boldly. . . .

Ding, dong.

And another bell joins in, held in the hand of a fat great-coated figure with a huge white cap nodding on his head, a tray depending from his broad shoulders by cords, a huge grey muffler around his neck. "Mince pies! Tasty mince pies! Merry Christmas!"

Harlequin dodges the revellers who come round the corner from Church Street dragging two or three of their number on a broad, flat sledge. The sledge is stacked high with wicker baskets, a Christmas tree, balloons and bunting. Up the hill runs Harlequin while the snow grows thicker and thicker and the traffic moves very slowly, hooting, jangling, creaking, squeaking, engines revving, horses snorting. Over-excited dogs bark and snap at Harlequin's heels. Harlequin ignores them. Old ladies pause in their black fur coats to press coins into the hands of bright-cheeked small boys. "Merry Christmas! Be good to your pa, look after your ma!" And whistling delivery lads ride their big bikes along the pavement, scoring the snow with thin black lines, swerving amiably to avoid dancing Harlequin who is almost at Notting Hill Gate where crystal towers glow green and red, black and gold, blue and silver, overlooking a plaza where a fair is in full swing, with sparking dodgems and dazzling roller coasters, merry-go-rounds and whips, rattling and banging and smashing and crackling; with rhythmic wheezing music of the calliope, with the hot smells of oil and steam and sweet cooking fat, the bawling voices from the megaphones in the hands of the sideshow men. "Roll up, roll up, roll up! Merry Christmas! 'Ere we are again! Merry Christmas! Ten for a tanner. 'Ave a go, luv. Merry

Christmas! Anyfink on the top shelf, George! Merry Christmas!" The fairground is full. Holiday-makers from the world over patronise it, for London is the centre all travellers hope to visit, the only city of its kind, where representatives of hundreds of independent nations meet to trade and to treat and to take advantage of the city's entertainments, to gape at its marvels, for London lives again as the City of the Future, a wonderland to visit but not to make one's home, rich with vice, and art, and cunning; radiant, articulate and wise. There are ships at anchor in the docks—ships from Shanghai, Toronto, Cape Town and Makhnograd, from Manhattan, Cardiff and Rangoon, from Darwin, Singapore and Freetown and a hundred states besides—there are airships at their masts over White City, bearing the flags of still more nations. The world is made up of thousands of such tiny states, most no bigger than Surrey, some no bigger than London which, itself, is independent, maintained by the pragmatism and the sentiment of a million survivors of a half-forgotten Age of Empires.

"Merry Christmas! Merry Christmas!" Down the main street, between the plaza on one side and a court of frozen fountains on the other, comes the huge sleigh with Santa Claus at the reins, drawn by six white ponies in green and black harness, with scarlet plumes on their heads, nostrils flaring, eyes flashing in the light from the huge triple globes on standards at intervals along the concourse, their rays diffracted by the falling snow. The crowd cheers. People pause to look. Harlequin crosses in front of the sleigh, just in time, dodging into the comparative peace of a narrow, north-bound street. Little houses lie on either side now and in the window of each is a splendid Christmas tree alive with candles and bunting. From the doors come the smells of log fires, of roasting goose and capon and turkey and guinea fowl, of puddings on the boil, of beef and ham and sausages and pork pies, pickles and sugar plums, carp and codlins—all enough to tempt the palate of the most jaded libertine—but Harlequin hurries on. "Merry Christmas!" call the red-cheeked old men as they turn into their gates. "Merry Christmas!" sing the housewives and older daughters, in aprons and headscarves, opening their doors to their loved ones, their friends and neighbours.

"Merry Christmas!" cries the tall airship pilot, home for the holiday, his kit bag over his shoulder. "Merry Christmas!" reply the post-man, the baker, the muffin-man.

But Harlequin replies to none of them, running on down the winding snowy street, darting in and out of the shadows cast by the sputtering lamps. Now dark figures leap from a gateway, dressed as knights, a dragon, a Fool, a Saracen:

And a mumming we will go, will go, and a mumming
we will go;
With a bright cockade in all our hats, we'll go with
gallant show!

It is the mummer's play with *St. George and the Dragon*, taking their entertainment from house to house, to anyone who wishes to see it. The Fool blocks Harlequin's path, cap and bells a-jingle:

"Alas, alas, my chiefest son is slain!
What must I do to raise him up again?
Here he lies before you all,
I'll presently a doctor call,
A doctor! A doctor! Are you a doctor, sir?"

Harlequin dodges to one side of the Fool, smiling, waving, on down the street. Harlequin comes to a cross-roads between tall buildings. High above lights still burn in windows, illuminated clocks display the time, a board flashes the schedules of the airship and the Super-Concorde flights and black shapes of family flying machines drift across the glare. At the corner, beside a lamp-post, an old man smiles at Harlequin, turning the handle of his plunking barrel-organ. A monkey in a velvet jacket and cap shivers on his shoulder. The man's voice is as old and as steady as Stonehenge. "A pleasant Yuletide to you, Arlekin."

Harlequin bows and runs on. In the distance now, at the bottom of the hill, is a glory of twinkling electric bulbs decorating a magnificent building whose front aspect dominates Ladbroke Grove. Of porphyry and jade and marble and lapis lazuli, the building is a palace from a dream, built by a genii for Aladdin. In all this magical

city there is nothing more vibrant than the Palace in the
Enchanted Dale. It glows so that, from here, it seems
the snow avoids it, or is melted before it can settle, yet
the white lawns surrounding it deny this and here, too, the
water of the fountains is frozen, reflecting all the colours
which blaze from the house. The snow has settled on the
hedges and the walls, it lies heavy on the shoulders of the
statues and the ornamental beasts, on pathways and
flower-beds, shrubs and tubs, the poplars, cypresses, oaks
and elms, all erected on the site of the legendary Convent
of the Poor Clares Colettine where so much of Old London's history was made. Set back from the bustle on the
hill, the palace seems a zone of tranquillity in all the
Christmas merriment—but there is merriment here, too.

Harlequin darts through open gates which are decorated
with Christmas wreaths, along paths, over hedges, through
clumps of trees, across lawns, to stand at last at the side
of the palace and peer through the holly-framed windows
of the ballroom where red velvet curtains have been tied
back to reveal a magnificent Christmas tree dominating a
crowded hall. The dark green pine is trimmed with globes
of scarlet and white, bunting of silver and green, a golden
star. The hall itself is hung with laurel and holly wreaths,
with ivy garlands, with mistletoe, and lit by hundreds of
tall candles in crystal chandeliers. The warmth and the
light pour into the garden where Harlequin hesitates and
studies the guests. It is a masque that Harlequin witnesses, a masque that draws the hidden figure closer as
if yearning to join. Harlequin sees all the old familiar
characters of the mummer's play, of mime and pantomime, of folklore and traditional tale—Widow Twankey,
Polichinelle, Abanazar, The Demon King, Mother Goose,
Jack Frost (a genuine albino with crimson eyes), The
Green Knight, Scaramouche, a rather lost looking Pierrot,
Hern the Hunter with his stag's antlers; a Fool, in motley with bladder and bells, Saint George, Captain Coura-
geous, Gammer Gurton, Buffalo Bill, Peter Pan, The
Babes in the Wood, Cinderella, Britannia, Dick Whittington, and someone dressed in a Harlequin costume almost
identical to Harlequin's own; Queen Mab, Prince Charming, Robin Hood, Robinson Crusoe, Sleeping Beauty, Puss
in Boots, Pantaloon, Goody Two Shoes, Hereward the
Wake, Puck, Gog and Magog, Lady Godiva, King Canute,

Blue Beard, Dick Turpin, Hengist and Horsa, The Three
Wise Men, King Arthur, John Bull, The Fairy God-
mother, Cock Robin, Father Neptune, Jack-o'-Lantern,
Sweeney Todd, Doctor Faustus, Jenny Wren, The May
Queen, Humpty Dumpty, Old King Cole, Sawney Bean,
Spring-heeled Jack, Charlie Peace, Queen Elizabeth, Mr.
Pickwick, Charley's Aunt, Jack Sheppard, Romeo and Ju-
liet, Doctor Who, Oberon, The Grand Cham, a Dalek,
Old Moore, Falstaff, Little Red Riding Hood, Beowulf,
Reynard the Fox, St Nicholas, Boadicaea, Noah and
Mrs. Noah, Jack the Giant Killer, Mother Hubbard,
Beauty and the Beast, the King of Rats, Yankee Doodle,
Nell Gwynn, John Gilpin, Baron Munchhausen, Alice,
Sitting Bull, Ali Baba, Little Jack Horner, Asmodeus,
Mother Bunch, Sinbad, Dame Trot and her cat; there
was a badger, a bull and a bear, a wolf, a cow, a sea-
serpent, a dragon, a hare, a cock and an ass, old men
dressed as young women, old women dressed as young
men, girls dressed as boys, boys dressed as girls, so that
another observer might have thought he witnessed some
innocent Court of Misrule.

Harlequin held back from entering, partly because of
the false Harlequin within, partly because in all that
company only Columbine was not present. Laughter
washed from the hall as a band played a sprightly Lancers and the guests danced in long columns, up and down
the ballroom, round and round the tree, clapping and
whistling, leaping and pirouetting, fingers on hips, wrists
raised, bowing, prancing, arm in arm, hand in hand,
shouting with merriment and good humour: the ballroom
shook to their feet as figures in elaborate silks and velvets, in laurel, in Lincoln Green, in cloth-of-gold, in brocades, in motley, in animal heads, in scarlet and black
moleskin, in hoods, capes, cloaks, tabards, doublets and
hose, in leather and lace and living plants and flowers, in
painted wood and padded fur and polished metal, masks
and powder, cosmetics, wigs and false noses, silver- and
bronze- and gold-gilding, whooped and giggled and bent
their bodies in the ritual of the dance.

The windows rattled, the log-fire blazed, the candles
flickered, the creatures of folklore, mythology and fable
capered and shouted. Harlequin retreated.

"Better the myth of happiness," Harlequin murmured, "than the myth of despair."

Then Harlequin had slipped away, to climb nimbly up a trellis at the side of the palace, swinging onto a balcony and through a window already open. Snow blew into the darkened room as Harlequin closed the window and drew from a sash wound twice about the waist a traditional wand, crossing rapidly to the white bed in which lay a golden-haired girl dressed in a daffodil-yellow ballet costume—Columbine, already masked, but pale, breathing sluggishly, fast asleep. Harlequin seemed sad, looking down on the girl for long moments, cocking an ear as the music rose from below, hands on hips, indecisive. Then Harlequin skipped a few steps, almost involuntarily running to the door to look out—a wide landing, a marble balcony, the ball below—back again to the bed, taking one of Columbine's cold hands, kissing it as a single tear crept from beneath Harlequin's domino and fell upon the flesh. And where the tear had fallen it appeared that the skin grew warmer and that colour spread along the bare arm to the soft shoulders, the neck, the wonderful features of Columbine.

Then Harlequin kissed Columbine upon her gentle lips, stood up and placed the tip of the wand upon her breast and Columbine opened her eyes. They were blue. They were bright. They were kind.

"Merry Christmas, my own, dear Columbine."

"Merry Christmas."

There came a noise from the marble landing beyond the door. Two guests—Britannia and the mock-Harlequin —went by. Harlequin moved to close the door, hearing a little of their conversation and smiling at its familiarity.

"He'll always fall on his feet, it seems—but I think he knows he hasn't really earned the position." Britannia spoke sharply, trying to adjust an uncomfortable sword and shield carried in one hand so that she might with the other clutch her punch. The shield was decorated with a Union Jack and the motto: *Honi Soit Qui Mal Y Pense*. She supported an elaborately plumed helmet of engraved silver and red horsehair, a scarlet and gold coat, with epaulettes, and her skirts were made up from the old arms of Britain: lions and harps for the most part.

"He thinks he has," said quasi-Harlequin peering over

the balcony and almost losing his triangular hat, "that's the worst of it. He's all cocky again, as usual—never seems to realise how much other people protect him."

"You can't say you've actually protected him, Frank." Britannia was amused. "I, on the other hand, did my level best to look after him. . . ."

"I've offered him dozens of really good opportunities in the past, Miss Brunner."

"I suppose that's where we both went wrong. All the opportunities were in the past. . . ."

Singing rose from the hall below:

> *Peace on Earth! How sweet the message!*
> *May its meaning bless each heart,*
> *And today may all dissension*
> *From the souls of men depart.*

Britannia accepted the false Harlequin's arm. "I suppose we'd better join them." They began to descend the wide staircase.

"Merry Christmas!" cried Major Nye in the armour of St. George (he had always felt a strong sentimental enthusiasm for *Where The Rainbow Ends*). "Merry Christmas, Miss Brunner! Merry Christmas, Frank." He waved an arm which clashed faintly. "Food at the buffet. Anything you like. Drinks at the bar. Hot punch. Name your grog!" His pale eyes twinkled. He clanked back into the milling crowd.

"I suppose all this devolution has its virtues, after all," said Miss Brunner. She dropped her sword. Frank picked it up for her. "I, of course, was a firm believer in centralisation. However, your brother ruined that. We were partners at one time, but there was a division."

"I remember," said Frank, "I got shot!"

"Did you? Poor boy. Now I'm reconciled. I'm a school-teacher these days, did you know? For the Maharajah of Guildford's children actually. Seriously, I'm beginning to think that it was a good idea to slow the pace, absorb things better. There isn't much of the century left. Of course, we still have the moral superiority, don't we?"

Frank turned his masked face so that he could see the buffet. He licked his lips.

"It's a bit mediaeval, I suppose," continued Miss Brun-

ner nodding agreeably to Bishop Beesley as he went by
with Mrs. Cornelius in tow. Bishop Beesley had come
as Widow Twankey, Mrs. C as Mother Bunch, "but none
the worse for that, by and large."

"Yeah," said Frank with a certain relish, "they're
thinking of re-introducing the Black Death next year."

"This isn't really the season for cynicism, Frank,
dear." She drew him towards the tables. "Now, what
shall we have?"

Frank picked up a plate. "What about some devilled
bones?"

"Spare ribs, aren't they? I suppose it's appropriate."
She began to gnaw.

Mr. Koutrouboussis arrived at the buffet panting and exhausted. "Phew! You need a lot of energy for this!" He
had come as Aladdin's wicked uncle, Abanazar, with a
dark, pointed beard fixed to his chin and heavy robes of
green satin sewn with gold astrological symbols, a monstrous turban on his head. He studied the fowls, the cold
meats, the blancmanges, the jellies, the flans. "It all looks
so delicious." He handed a plate to Prinz Lobkowitz who
wore an Elizabethan Oberon costume and whose mask
glittered with real gems. "We've met before, I think.
Merry Christmas to you."

"And to you, sir. Our host seems a trifle under the
weather." Prinz Lobkowitz chose some olives.

"Perhaps hosts never can enjoy themselves as much as
their guests. There must be so many anxieties. Were you
at the last party?"

"During the Peace Talks? An absolute disaster."

"Doomed to failure, one could argue. A worthy attempt."

"To maintain the old order. Isn't that what most Peace
Talks are about?" Prinz Lobkowitz smiled. "It's a natural
enough instinct, surely."

"Ah, you would know better than I about such things."
Abanazar rubbed his hands and picked up a dish of
plums.

"It is true," said Oberon, "that I have been a politician
all my life, and an idealist for most of my career, if the
search for perfect compromise can be dignified by the
description of 'ideal.' "

"It is better than anything I ever possessed," Koutrouboussis told him sadly, spooning at a plum or two, "save for a passion, once, for a young girl. But she evaded me, though for some time she was mine. Do you understand women, Prinz Lobkowitz?"

"Oh, women, women, there are far too many different ones. You speak of the romantic kind?"

"I am not sure. Romance remains a mystery. I enjoy power, however. Women are said to admire men who enjoy power."

"They use them often enough, that is true, to further their own romantic dreams. The more a man loves power for its own sake, the less he interferes with their fantasies, while at the same time he is able to indulge them. Such relationships were once quite common, when I was younger. They seem to work excellently. And yet you have never experienced one, with all your ships and oil?"

"Never. I suppose I was too direct. She obeyed me, but only up to a point. She disappointed me. She would not commit herself as much as I had hoped."

"There you have it. She saw you as committed to your power and therefore thought she would be free, that she need not give too much of herself to you. It was you, Mr. Koutrouboussis, who disappointed this young woman."

The Greek tugged absent-mindedly at his false beard. Parts of it came away in his fingers. A peculiar knowing light burned and faded in his dark eyes. He fumbled in his robes and withdrew a cigarette case, offering it to Lobkowitz, who declined. "I wanted her very much." He said again: "She evaded me."

"My friend," said Prinz Lobkowitz sympathetically, and chewed a pickled walnut.

A large crowd was now approaching the table. Prinz Lobkowitz and Mr. Koutrouboussis wandered away.

Sebastian Auchinek arrived with Mitzi Beesley. Sebastian Auchinek was not quite right as The Demon King, though the costume itself was splendid, with a long pointed tail and real horns. He held his pitchfork gingerly, anxious not to hurt any of his fellow guests. Mitzi Beesley was a depraved Peter Pan. "The English have always needed queens," he was saying. "They are useless without them. Queens created the Empire, after all."

"Half the greatest explorers were—" began Mitzi.

"I'm not sure that's quite what I meant."

Mitzi giggled. "But Mr. Cornelius isn't a queen. He's a king. Or is he a king *and* a queen?"

"His trouble is that he's all things to all men—and women too. Perhaps he doesn't know himself. It's probably the secret of his success."

"He doesn't seem too pleased with that success." She craned to catch a glimpse of a darting white costume.

"I agree he seems ill."

"Hello, father," said Mitzi. "You make a lovely widow."

"Thank you, child." Bishop Beesley was a picture of dignity in his flounces and ribbons, his huge hat, his rouge. He had already been twice mistaken for Mrs. Cornelius. He continued his conversation with Colonel Pyat, a Saracen King in golden armour. "My motives were questioned probably because I was always a trifle unorthodox. I hoped to show people the way—back to decent standards. I did my best to be up to date at all times. I did not reject technology, nor did I turn my back on drugs."

Mo Collier, as Robin Goodfellow, had been standing at the bishop's elbow. "I read one of your sermons. It was great. *Cocaine in the Treatment of Sinus Infections.* Remember?"

"Not too easily."

Mitzi joined the conversation, glad to help her father. "It was just before *Salvation through Sugar,*" she said. "The Mars Bar Messiah, they called you." She became sentimental, recalling former greatness. "The Orange Fudge Oracle. The Chocolate Cream Cleric. The Hershey Bar Bishop. The Man Who Brought the Tootsie Roll into the Pulpit. The Turkish Delight—"

"There was so much to do," said the Bishop. "Some of the details have become a trifle hazy now."

"Sort of set into the blancmange of the past." Mo was in a rare philosophic mood. "Stuck to the sides of the great jelly mould we call Life."

"The Smarty Saint," continued Mitzi. She began to pant. His eye had fallen on her.

Dazed, Mitzi dropped back. To escape the dreamy Robin Goodfellow beside him, Bishop Beesley gathered up his skirts and followed her.

Mo was tasting some cream. Dubiously he licked his

lips. "Does it go off?" he asked a nearby Karen von Krupp, who said, without taking her attention from her companion, "That'll be your epitaph, Mr. Collier."

". . . but I can't hope to survive for ever in this environment," Miss Brunner was telling Karen von Krupp, who wore her Beowulf outfit rather well, in spite of her age and frailty. "All I wanted was to create a little peace and quiet for myself. People kept interfering."

"Ja," said Karen von Krupp. She was quite drunk. "Ja, ja, ja."

"Simplification had always been my goal. Naturally, I had to synthesise a great deal of information. The world had to be broken down into the proper bits in order to produce a programme suitable for processing by a reasonably sophisticated computer. . . ."

"Ja, ja," said Karen von Krupp. "Ja, ja, ja."

"You thought she embraced the world," Professor Hira (as Polichinelle, with peculiar protruberances on chest and back) was no longer calling himself Hythloday. He was talking about Miss Brunner, unaware that she was behind him. Mr. Smiles knew; he looked awkward as The Green Knight. They had made him leave his green-painted Shire horse with its blood-red bridle in the stables where, unbeknownst to him, it was fighting with the two lions which had drawn Miss Brunner's chariot as far as the front door. "She did not! She crushed it, forced it into a little square box; packed it in a hurry, too. Some try to understand the world, while others seek to impose their understanding on it. Unfortunately, Mr. Smiles, these latter folk are those least equipped to perform the operation. Like Frankenstein, my dear Mr. Smiles, they produce a monster."

"I'd considered coming as Frankenstein." Mr. Smiles brightened behind his black beard which he had, unsuccessfully, also tried to dye green, "but I gathered it wasn't suitable. Too modern or something. Or too general? And yet Doctor Who is here. Is everyone supposed to be part of British folklore tonight? Frankenstein, I should have thought. . . ."

"I think so." The little Brahmin physicist was disappointed in his audience. "Although I'm Italian, aren't I? Pulcinella? Punch?" He chuckled. "Or Vice, if we're get-

ting down to basics. We're all part of the same zany Cav-
alcade, eh?"

"I'm not sure about that. They made me leave my
horse outside."

"Harlequinade, then. Where is Harlequin?" Professor
Hira sought about him in the crowd. "Or what about
Masquerade? Or is it a Morality Play? You're the English-
man, Mr. Smiles. You tell me what it is we're in!"

Mr. Smiles sipped his spiced rum. "God knows," he
said. "A bloody madhouse."

Mrs. Cornelius had somehow got hold of part of Old
King Cole's costume. She still wore her skirts of green
and brown, but she had a crown askew on her head, a
white beard hanging around her neck. She spotted Hira
and was delighted. "Oo! There yer are! Where yer bin
'idin', eh?"

Punch blushed.

"I jest bin talkin' ter Robin 'Ood," she confided to Mr.
Smiles, putting a hearty arm about her lover, who gasped.
"I arsked 'im where 'is mate wos—you know, ther monk."
She screamed with laughter and her crown threatened to
fall off her head altogether. "As usual I got me pees an'
kews mixed up. Where's yer mate? sez me, Wot mate's
that, madam, sez Robin 'Ood, Oh, yer know ther one, I
sez—Wot's 'is name? Then I remembered, you know,
didn't I? Triar Fuck? sez me. Then Robin 'Ood straight-
ens up like a telegraph pole. Forgive me, madam, 'e sez,
but I don't believe as 'ow I 'ave the where-wival!" She
flung back her head and just saved her crown as she
shook with mirth. "Get it? See? Robin 'Ood ain't a bloke
at all. It's a bloody woman, innit! Ah, har, har, har! They
always bloody are in fings like this, ain't they?"

Professor Hira was baffled as usual but he managed to
laugh with her through long practice. "He, he, he. Oh, very
good!"

Robin Hood herself strode by, equally baffled, causing
Mrs. Cornelius another outburst. Lady Sue Sunday had
lost Helen Sweet again.

"It's traditional, see," explained Mrs. Cornelius to Professor Hira. The band had begun to play an Irish jig. "Oo,
come on!" She seized her lover and dragged him back towards the tree where most of the guests were dancing
again.

Lady Sue found Helen Sweet, as Little Red Riding Hood, talking to Simon Vaizey. The elegant playwright had almost not come, since he wanted to wear his own Pierrot costume, but he had compromised and come as the Fool. ". . . Through dreaming towns I go, The cock crows ere the Christmas morn. The streets are dumb with snow," he was saying to a rapt Helen. "I've long since given up any hope of finding *my* Grail, dear. I haven't the brains. Well, God give them wisdom that have it; and those that are fools, let them use their talents."

"I'd suggest you try using them elsewhere, Mr. Vaizey," said Lady Sue jealously. "Nice to see you again. I'd heard you were dead."

"I couldn't miss the party, could I?" Simon Vaizey stole away.

Jerry Cornelius, moving gracefully amongst his guests, bowed his Pierrot bow, elaborate and strange, passed Simon Vaizey and winked, reached his seat of honour. In his black and white Pierrot costume, his make-up, he bore an aura of sadness with him which no amount of capering and smiling could dispel. He sat down with a sigh, long and limp in the marble chair at the farthest end of the hall, just below the musician's gallery, from which dripped bunting, laurel, holly and ivy, so that he was half-hidden by decoration. Above his head the band was playing traditional music—fife, tabor, pipes and the beat of the snare dominated everything while the guests whirled about the tree in a haze of green and gold, scarlet and silver. He was feeling that loneliness most painful when one is amongst friends; and there was more than a touch of his old self-pity. He pursed cherry lips and whistled, against the harmony above, a Commander Cody and His Lost Planet Airmen song, *I'm down to seeds and stems again blues.* . . .

"Merry Christmas, Jerry!"

Flash Gordon found him, brushing aside the bunting, sympathetic and unwelcome as usual. His hot, dog-like eyes were about the only recognisable thing behind his thick make-up, his long golden wig (he had come as Lady Godiva). "You'd have been much better as Harlequin, Jerry." Evidently he believed that his friend was sulking. "Somehow the part doesn't suit Frank."

"I used to be," Jerry crossed his billowing legs, "but

Harlequin somehow metamorphosed into Pierrot. It happened in France, I think. Don't ask how. I used to believe I was Captain of my own Fate. Instead I'm just a character in a bloody pantomime."

"It's not too bloody now, at any rate." Flash always tried to look on the bright side. "Everyone's cultivating their own gardens. I didn't tell you about my new strain of peas, did I?"

"I was never much interested in gardening," Jerry told him, doing his best to be friendly to Flash.

Flash laughed. "No! You liked blowing things up. You and Mo Collier. Blowing things up."

"Of course," Jerry continued, "I'm grateful for what everyone's done." He reached out to pat a slightly hurt Flash on the heavily sweating right hand. "But all I wanted was Catherine back. They could have had everything else. There's no point without her. It's all my fucking fault, Flash."

"You shouldn't feel guilty." As someone whose main relish in life came from feeling guilty, Flash was unconvincing. "You shouldn't blame yourself."

"I'm just pissed off. I've ruined it, as usual. I can go anywhere I like in the city. Do anything I like. See anyone I like. Disguises are easy. Nobody bothers me. But all I want to do is stay at home and make love to Catherine."

"Well," said Flash speculatively, "you could always. . . ."

Jerry shook his head. "It's not the same."

"I'd agree with that!" Flash's eyes grew rounder and hotter with reminiscence. He realised, suddenly, that he was being selfish and did his best to return to more general topics. "They say that's the trouble with Utopia. You get bored. While there were big countries to fight, or big corporations, or just very powerful people, it was easier to be an individual." He sighed artificially. "Now everyone's an individual, eh, Mr. C? It's taken a lot of the fun from life, I'll tell you."

Jerry was surprised to find himself agreeing with Flash. He nodded. "It's horrible, winning. With everyone on your side. It makes you edgy. And I've run out of things to do."

"You've done a lot for everyone. I'm grateful. We're all grateful."

"It's nice of you to say so, Flash," Jerry looked down as a small black-and-white cat rubbed its thin body against his leg. He picked it up and stroked its head. It purred. He smiled.

"That's what you need," said Flash encouragingly. "A pet. You've cheered up already."

"I love it." Jerry spoke in some awe. "That's what I need. Love."

"Everybody loves you, Jerry. Well, almost everybody."

"It's not being loved, Flash, that's difficult to come by. It's loving."

"You love everyone. Everything."

"That's my trouble. Oh, I wish I could find a way to wake Catherine up. She was my lodestone. Past, present and future. Reality, if you like—myth, too—of hope, of reconciliation, of peace and freedom." He had to raise his voice for the music was growing louder and louder, the shouts of the guests noisier and noisier. "She's my ideal, Flash. Nobody else will do. Have I said all this before?"

Flash came closer, to make himself heard. His breath was warm in Jerry's painted ear. "Not in so many words. You've been a good brother to her, Jerry, in your own way. You've looked after her, even though she hasn't been able to give you much in return."

"I was willing to destroy the world for her."

"That's real love all right," said Flash. "That's the test, isn't it? Still," he smiled nervously, "I'm glad you didn't."

"I thought I had."

"Oh, not you, Jerry. Never!"

Jerry put his chin on his fist. Pierrot defeated.

"I'll go and get something to eat. Do you want anything?" Flash moved away, rubbing at the make-up on his face. "This stuff's going to bring on my blackheads something rotten. See you later, Jerry."

Gathering his blonde locks about him, Flash sidled for the buffet tables.

Jerry saw Harlequin break from the dancing crowd and run towards him. "You ought to get a spot of grub down you, Jerry," said Frank. "You're looking like the bloody phantom at the feast. Enjoy yourself, boy! What price entropy now, eh?"

"Oh, piss off," said his brother, and stroked his cat.

Frank seemed unmoved by Jerry's rudeness, perhaps because he was very drunk. His mask was higher at the left than at the right, his hat was too far back on his head. "You're not sleeping enough, these days, are you?" He staggered and leaned against the back of Jerry's marble chair. "You ought to try to get a bit more shut-eye. Mind you, you shouldn't need that much, considering all you've had in the past. . . . On the other hand, sleep isn't cumulative, you know. That's the irony, isn't it? Tiredness, of course, is. You get worse and worse. That's what's wrong with speed. Less and less real, in a sense. You've been pushing yourself beyond the limit. All these new schemes . . . these potions you've been cooking up in your lab. . . ."

"You don't look that well, yourself."

"I've given too much of myself away, Jerry. It was always my trouble."

"You've never given anything away in your life. Sold it, more likely. Blood and souls. . . ."

"Steady on, old son. Noblesse oblige!" Frank burped. "Pardon." He was gleeful, evidently sensing that he had got through to his brother. "I could let you have something to get you moving again. A few mills of—hic—tempodex." He made a plunging motion towards his arm. "Back on your old form? No danger!"

"I'm all right here. If you could find a drug to perk Cathy up, that'd be more useful. After all. . . ."

"No recriminations! We agreed. Anyway, it's not in my interest, is it?" Harlequin smirked. "Not with you in your position and me in mine. Now, if you were to give me more power. . . ."

"I haven't got any bloody power!"

"Well, influence, then. . . ."

"You can't transfer influence, Frank."

"I dunno. I've been experimenting. . . ."

"I wish I'd never bought you that chemistry set when we were kids. It's been nothing but trouble." Jerry stared moodily over his brother's head. The music had stopped again and the guests were surging towards the buffets and bars, parting like the Red Sea on either side of the tree. "This is all your fault. Not mine."

"Oh, come on now. Do me a favour, Jerry. You were

the one with the big ideas. It was just carrying on the family business. What's born in the blood is bred in the bone. We're all victims of history."

"That's why I was trying to get rid of history." He rose from his throne, now that he could see a clear path ahead, and left his brother standing beside the chair, running a grey hand over the cold stone.

"You want to get yourself a proper job, old son," called Frank. "This is no work for a man!"

Jerry ignored him. Already the guests were beginning to move back into the centre of the ball-room. His mother approached, holding a plate on which an entire trifle staggered. " 'Ere yer are, Jer'—wanna bit?"

"No thanks, mum."

"Good fer yer." Evidently she had been sick down her dress and had cleaned it inexpertly with the beard she now held in her other hand.

Prinz Lobkowitz rescued him. "What a nice little cat. What's its name?"

"Tom," said Jerry, "I think."

"And the costume! Perfect." Prinz Lobkowitz quoted knowingly, probably Verlaine.

> *"Ce n'est plus le rêveur lunaire du vieil air—*
> *Sa gaieté, comme sa chandelle, hélas! est morte,*
> *Et son spectre aujourd'hui nous hante, mince et clair.*
> *Et voici que parmi l'effroi d'un long éclair*
> *D'un linceul.*
> *Sa pâle blouse à l'air, au vent froid qui l'emporte,*
> *Avec le bruit d'un vol d'oiseaux de nuit qui passe,*
> *Ses manches blanches font vaguement par l'espace.*
> *Des signes fous auxquels personne ne répond."*

"Oh, I wouldn't say that," said Jerry. He pushed on, the crowd growing denser. Major Nye leaned against a pillar talking to Karen von Krupp, St. George in conversation with Beowulf. "The British, you see, have an ability to shuck off their civilisation in an instant and become, for as long as it suits them, wild beasts. It is the secret of their survival—it is what makes great explorers, mountain climbers and killers. They do not belong in Europe. They never belonged in Europe. Their instincts have always led them to more savage parts. It was civilisation brought the British down—as civilisation crept across the globe like rabies, they were forced to turn on one another and, for a long time, make a savage environment of their own land. You take my meaning?"

"Ja," said Karen von Krupp, "ja, ja, ja."

A great mound of vegetation, Jack-in-the-Green, that had been Herr Marek, the Lapp priest, was confiding in a whisper to Cyril Tome, who was now setting puzzles for children's television and who had come as a somewhat anaemic Hern ("more a Hernia," as Lady Sue had said to Helen Sweet when they had arrived). "I've been haunted, you see, for years by the knowledge that I am the slave of a machine existing somewhere underground. It has forced me to simplify my language so that it can communicate with me better. I *could* attack it by using complicated and poetic language, but it takes reprisals, killing or maiming not me but my friends—in railway accidents, planes and car crashes, lift failures, and with electric shocks. I have to think of others, but I must warn them, somehow, too. In order to do this I have resorted to complicated subterfuges. . . ."

"Merry Christmas!" Mitzi Beesley raced past, pursued by her grunting father. "Now," he breathed, "now we'll see!" He had his skirts to his knees as he chased her. She disappeared behind the tree.

"The failure of the second half of the twentieth century was to absorb the achievements of the first half," said Dick Whittington (ex-prime minister M. Hope-Dempsey), "particularly the rarer malt whiskeys." He was speaking to Eva Knecht, also a principal boy. She had come as Prince Charming. "You are drunk," she said. "Would you like to tie me up?"

Jerry could see that the party was beginning to lift. Stroking his cat he continued on his way through the throng and reached the wide stairs just as the band began to play Doctor Hook's *Queen of the Silver Dollar*.

It was a beautiful Christmas, thought Jerry. The nicest he had had. Slowly, he mounted the stairs, pausing to look back at his happy guests, at the snow falling outside. It was getting quite late. He looked for Frank in the hall, but the Harlequin costume was nowhere to be seen. He shrugged and continued up the stairs, tripping once over his long satin trousers.

He had reached the landing and was on his way to his own apartments when he heard a noise from behind Catherine's door. He paused, made to enter, then changed his mind. Almost in panic he began to run along the landing to his own rooms, dashing through the door without bothering to put on the lights, dumped the little cat on his bed, and went to the trunk in his study, rummaging through it rapidly until he found what he wanted. "Wait here," he told the cat. It was best to take no chances.

Needle-gun in hand he returned to Catherine's room. "Who's in there?" He kicked open the door and walked in.

Frank stood at the end of Catherine's bed. He had removed his mask. He had a loaded hypodermic in his hand. He was looking tired and ill, like a sick vulture. "I don't feel very well," he said. "Look. She's woken up."

Catherine, in contrast, was in the peak of health. Her skin glowed, her eyes were bright, if a little dazed. She and Una Persson were propped on their pillows, in one another's arms. Catherine was entirely naked, her Columbine costume scattered across the floor. Una was naked save for her Harlequin's mask. She did not seem to realise that she was still wearing it.

Frank fell to his knees. Una pulled a smoking S&W .45 from under the bed-clothes. "I'm sorry, Jerry. I've shot your brother. He was going to. . . ."

"That's all right." Jerry put his needle-gun in his baggy pocket. Joy mounted within him, slowly. "How long have you been awake, Catherine?"

"Not long. Una woke me."

"I'm very grateful, Una," he said, "for all you've done."

"Ugh!" groaned Frank from the floor. "She's two-timing you, Jerry. Ugh! Both of us!"

"I don't think so," said Jerry, smiling tenderly at both of them. "Are you?"

"I must be going." Una Persson's smile was just a fraction late, but it was a good, brave one. "Leave you two alone."

"Oh, no," said Jerry. He sat on the bed beside her, still looking at Catherine. "Please stay."

Una stroked her hair. "I was just saying goodbye." She

looked at her wrist. "What's the time? My watch has stopped."

"About midnight, I think."

"Good. I can catch the last flight out."

"You're welcome. . . ." Jerry said.

"Ugh." Frank's voice was fainter.

"I'm still a working girl, you know." Una climbed from the bed and, walking around her victim, began to pull on her own Harlequin costume. "I'm sorry about the mess."

Frank groaned. His chest was crimson.

Una tucked her slapstick into her sash. "I didn't mean to kill you. It was the shock. You shouldn't have dressed yourself up like that. I thought you were me for a moment. What were you trying to achieve? Imitation isn't art, you know, Frank."

Unclean blood fell down his chin. "Merry fucking Christmas," he said, "you bitch. Both of you. All of you." Clutching himself he began to sidle across the floor. "Oh, fuck. Oh, fuck."

"He'll be all right, I expect," said Catherine to reassure Una. She reached out and took Jerry's hand, squeezing it. Jerry sighed. "He's always making a lot of the things that happen to him."

Frank reached the door and crawled through it into the light of the landing. "God help us, one and all."

Una went over and closed the door. "You'll want to be alone. I've told her everything you've done for her, Jerry—and all that's happened." She bent to fluff at his ruff. "Pierrot wins Columbine, at last. It's taken hundreds of years."

Jerry could see that Una was close to tears. He stood up and helped her on with her red and green cape. "Let me know if there's anything I can do."

"Your work's over," Una said, "but mine's not finished yet. Otherwise I'd give you a run for your money. Pierrot couldn't wake her, you see. Only Harlequin has the power to do that. Pierrot has no power—only charm." She kissed him briskly on the cheek. "Cheerio, you little bugger." She paused by the bed and bent to kiss Catherine's lips. "Merry Christmas, Columbine."

"Oh," said Catherine. She looked from her brother to her friend.

Una reached the window, opened it and stepped through. Cold air filled the room. A few flakes of snow settled on the sill. Then she had gone, Harlequin returned to the night, and the window was shut. There came a sound, like the crying of hounds, but it was either made by the guests below or came from the traffic in Ladbroke Grove.

In the ball-room it seemed that the Christmas Party had taken on fresh life as wave upon wave of laughter rose up to them. "Merry Chrissmas Merry Chrissmas!" they heard their mother shout. "Merry fuckin' Chrissmas!"

Then the music started up and the palace shook to their dancing feet.

Jerry pulled off his huge trousers but kept his flowing blouse and his skull-cap on. He knew how much his sister liked it. He got into bed. He touched her vibrant skin. They embraced. They kissed.

From outside, from below in the whiteness of the garden, a light voice was raised for a few seconds in song:

For in you now all virtues do combine—
Sad Pierrot, brave Harlequin and lovely
    Columbine. . . .

There sounded a bass drone, then silence.

Jerry rolled into his sister's soft arms and the two were joined together at last.

"Catherine!"

"Jerry! Jerry!"

A crack of light appeared from the door as it was pushed open and a small black-and-white cat entered. It jumped to the foot of the bed and began to wash liquid from its paws. It looked up at them and purred.

All in all, thought Jerry, it was going to be a very successful season.

EARLY REPORTS

What wonders now I have to pen, sir,
Women turning into men, sir,
For twenty-one long years, or more, sir,
She wore the breeches we are told, sir,
A smart and active handsome groom, sir,
She then got married very soon, sir,
A shipwright's trade she after took, sir,
And of his wife, he made a fool, sir.

The Female Husband, c. 1865

Old England, once up a time,
  Was prosperous and gaily,
Great changes you shall hear in rhyme,
  That taking place is daily.
A poor man once could keep a pig,
  There was meat for every glutton,
Folks now may eat a parson's wig,
  For they'll get no beef or mutton.

What Shall We Do For Meat! c. 1865

Now the trial is o'er, and the Judge did say
Mistress Starr, you have lost the day,
And five hundred pounds you'll have to pay
  For tricks that are play'd in the Convent.

Funny Doings in the Convent, c. 1865

All the world will mount velocipedes,
  Oh won't there be a show
Of swells out of Belgravia,
  In famous Rotten Row;

Tattersall's they will forsake,
    To go there they have no need,
They will patronise the wheel wright's now
    For a famed Velocipede.
The dandy horse Velocipede,
    Like lightning flies, I vow, sir,
It licks the railroad in its speed,
    By fifty miles an hour, sir.
        The Dandy Horse; or, The Wonderful Velocipede,
                                              c. 1865

Three men they say on that fatal Friday,
    At four o'clock on that afternoon,
Those villains caused that explosion,
    And hurried those poor creatures to their doom.
They from a truck took a barrel of powder,
    A female, Ann Justice, was there as well,
And in one moment death and disorder
    Around the neighbourhood of Clerkenwell.
        Awful Explosion in Clerkenwell, c. 1865

I am the famous dancer, Harlequin.
I've shown my postures and my grace sublime
In every epoch and in every clime.
Wherever Youth and Beauty gaily meet
I am the dancing pattern of their feet.
        Harlequinade, c. 1865

The myth of the golden past gave way to the myth of the
golden future but, for a short time in the 90s and then the
1960s we enjoyed the myth of the golden present.

        M. Lescoq, *Leavetaking,* c. 1965

TUNING UP (5)

"Who are we today, then?" Miss Brunner leered at Jerry over her pint. "Che Guevara?"

Jerry hesitated at the door of the Blenheim Arms. The pub had a special extension for the evening. It could stay open until midnight. It was very noisy. It smelled strongly of mild beer. It was packed with celebrants. It was warm. "Happy New Year," he said. He closed the door of the local behind him.

"That suit's very light-weight for the weather, isn't it?" His brother Frank took Miss Brunner's lead. "On our way to Bermuda, are we?"

"I don't feel the cold," said Jerry. He knew that he looked smart in the suit, even if it was rather thin, and he hadn't bothered to wear an overcoat because he was only popping into the pub from across the road where he was staying with his mother. Gradually, however, he became self-conscious. He approached the bar. They were all in tonight. All facing him. Mr. Smiles wiped froth from his moustache. "The trousers are a bit baggy, aren't they?"

"They're meant to be baggy." He felt in a pocket for some money. The pocket seemed the size of a sack.

"Stop taking the piss out of him," said Catherine. She wore blue denims and a dark green sweater with a picture of Dr. Hook and the Medicine Show on the front. "I think it's very sexy, Jerry." She opened her shoulder bag, looking for her purse, but Mo Collier was ahead of her. He waved a fiver at the barman. "Usual?" he asked his friend.

"Why not?" Jerry had forgotten what his usual was. He was attempting to regain lost ground by cultivating an air of insouciance. He looked Miss Brunner up and down: black strap-overs, fishnet stockings, skirt just above the knee, square-cut jacket with heavily padded shoulders. Perm. Earrings. "That's a sweet costume. Are we going as historical figures? Where did you hire it?" He was lame.

She shook her head in genuine disappointment. "This gear cost a fortune and you know it. You can do better than that."

But she tugged for a second or two at the back of her jacket and raised his spirits.

Frank said anxiously, looking at his wrist-watch: "We'll have to drink up. The coach'll be here any minute." They were all going down to Brighton to celebrate New Year's Eve at Mr. Smiles's new hotel. He had spent the last ten years in Rhodesia, where he had made a fortune, and was anxious to renew old acquaintanceships. Frank wore a red polo-neck sweater, purple bell-bottoms and a black velvet blazer-style jacket. He held a double gin in one pink hand.

"Still teaching at St. Victor's, then, are we?" Jerry asked Miss Brunner. "Having our way with the tweenies?"

"That's defamation if ever I heard it." She spoke without much conviction, almost amiably. Even though she had been prosecuted for her sexual activities at the school she had not only managed to get off all the charges but had somehow managed to become headmistress of St. Victor's Primary School. Her attempts to re-introduce corporal punishment, though, had not been all that successful. Increasingly the parents of the children were from the upper middle classes—people who had moved into the district as their incomes declined, who sustained their position in the world by selling their houses in Chelsea, South Kensington and Belgravia for large profits and buying cheaper houses in North Kensington, with the result that rents had risen all round, though the authorities tended to be warier of residents who might now be the sons and daughters of rich people, or literate radicals, rather than working-class youths. There were distinct, if superficial, improvements. Black men were hardly ever beaten up in public by the police any more (this distressed the new arrivals) and the police had increasingly come to see their new role as the protectors of Rate Payers from

Non-Rate Payers (those whose rates were included in their rent and paid by the landlord). Street fighting in North Kensington had declined and street music and street theatre had increased, but the police did not discriminate between these activities: all were likely to cause annoyance to the Public (Rate Payers) and were dealt with with equal ferocity. According to the methods favoured by the individual officer, friendly banter would be employed, an attempt to "jolly" the victims into giving up without a struggle, or outright threats and violence would occur from the start. Miss Brunner approved of the police's new attitude but mourned the days before parents became sophisticated and could now recognise, pursue and pillory the poor paedophile. Not everyone gained from the New Liberalism. Ten years before, hardly anyone had ever heard of her particular passions, except her little charges and their hopeless parents who had been content to recognise her authority, as they recognised all authority, with a dumb and wholesome fear and, amongst the more spirited, like the Cornelius children, a little primitive and easily handled blackmail. As well, the older and more knowing they became, the less interest she took in them. The seventies were increasingly difficult years for Miss Brunner. In her opinion children were growing up far too early.

"I still fink 'e shouldn'ta moved me wivvout arskin'," Mrs. Cornelius was complaining. She sat at a little corner table, behind two pints of stout, talking to Colonel Pyat who sipped his vodka and nodded intensely at almost every word. He was dressed in an old fur coat, part of the stock of second-hand clothes at his Elgin Crescent *Glory of St. Petersburg Vintage Fur Boutique* which was doing such excellent business, these days; time had given him wealth, a seamed and baggy face, a decadent dalmatian, which wheezed on a leash at his feet. Mrs. Cornelius had recently been given accommodation in the basement of a house in Talbot Road and was shortly to be moved to an identical basement in the house in Blenheim Crescent whose second floor she had occupied for so many years. Frank had sold the family flat for a handsome sum to a young doctor and his wife and had told his mother that the council would be bound to find her a new home when they saw the condition of the basement, which was very damp. However, it had not taken her long to get comfy and now she didn't really want to move. She wore a vast ragged coney coat, a present from the colonel. She saw Jerry at the bar and waved him over.

" 'Ullo, Jer'—yore lookin' very dapper—they put yore dole money up? Har, har, har!" She shook, looking to the others for confirmation of her drollery. "Her, her, her, ker-ker-ker-ker. . . ." She had developed the local cough almost to perfection. Jerry picked up his whisky and swallowed it down. His mother felt in her handbag and produced a tenpenny piece. "Ker-ker-ker—shu—hu—shove some—ker-ker-ker—money in the juke box love. 'Ere yer are!"

Reluctantly he came over to take the coin. "What d'you want to hear?"

"Oh, you know best. One o' yore fav'rites. Wot abart that 'Oo lot?"

"Don't like 'em any more."

"Rollin' Stones, then."

"They haven't done anything worth listening to in ages."

"Chuck Berry!"

"Come on, mum! He's gone completely commercial. Years ago."

"There must be someone yer like, Jer'. Ya used ter 'ave all these 'eroes."

"They've all gone off. Or died." His smile was wistful. "I haven't got any heroes any more, mum—at least, nobody you can hear on the average juke box. Not these days."

"Well, give us some Gary Glitter. I like 'im. Or Alvin Stardust. Or the Bay City Rollers. They're like ther Beatles, ain't they?"

"Why not?" He pushed his way through the crowd to the glowing juke-box. He put the money in and pressed buttons at random. He returned to the bar and gave his mother a thumbs up sign as Paul Simon began to sing something miserable and only barely revived.

"Oh, I like this," she said, "it's one of the old ones, innit?"

A plummy voice rose to challenge the music. The Bishop was drunk again. "We gather today to celebrate the deaths of enemies and to mourn the deaths of friends. . . ."

"Go on, Dennis!" shouted Mrs. Cornelius. She was always kind to the old has-been.

"'E must be on 'is ninth creme de menthe," said Mo Collier, grinning at Jerry. Ex-lay preacher and boy scout leader, Dennis Beesley had once run the local sweetshop but had sold it years before. Rumour had it, he had eaten all the profits. He had taken part in many neighbourhood activities, had organised the North Kensington chapter of the Monday Club, been chief representative for the Union Movement, the Empire Loyalists, and until lately, the National Front. He was still regarded by some residents as a political sage, in spite of the mysterious scandal which had led to his being expelled from both the Boy Scout movement and the National Front. His daughter Mitzi, who had looked after him since his wife had run off with a black Methodist preacher from Golborne Road, was also in the pub, being chatted up as usual by half a dozen or so of the lads, though she was showing more interest in the owner of the nearby all-night supermarket, Mr. Hira, known as "The Professor" because of his constant references to his university degree.

Dennis Beesley continued his oration, cheered on by several regulars. ". . . to execrate those whom we hate and to praise those whom we love. From the highest and noblest of motives are brotherhoods such as ours formed so that we may comfort one another, huddling close, turning our backs on the terrifying darkness of Eternity, lifting our quavering voices in hymns of praise to the Great Idea, the Desperate Hope." He raised green liquid to his full, sticky lips. The red blotches under his cheeks clashed badly with the creme de menthe. He drew a breath. "My dear friends, let us now kneel to stroke one another's heads, to murmur reassurance, to pretend to divine commitment, to rage, for a short while, against the Unacceptable, to complain of our wrongs, to seek scapegoats for our own shortcomings, to protect the indigenous people of these isles against the encroaching hordes of the Children of Israel, against the Yellow Peril, the Black Invasion, the Asian Tidal Wave, the Red Menace, the Brown Betrayer, the Olive Exploiter and—and. . . ." He frowned as he drained his glass.

"And the Great White Whale," suggested Mr. Hira, putting his arm round Mitzi's waist. Mitzi rubbed herself against him. Beesley burped. "Thank you," he said. His flesh turned to a shade of green much paler than his drink.

He shut his mouth suddenly and rolled urgently towards the lavatories.

"Hurry up," Frank called after him, "or you'll miss the coach."

"Such a shame," said Miss Brunner. "They ruined him, unfrocking him like that—or un-knickerbockering him, is it? The elders made far too much of it. He was only after their bullseyes."

"Definitely the post-war answer to Walt Disney," Major Nye was saying enthusiastically to Catherine. "I love him. I've enjoyed them all. Ten Thousand and One. The Clock and the Orange. Barry Lindsay. He can do no wrong in my eyes."

"I've always thought his pictures have everything except a good director," said Jerry, not for the first time.

"Yes, I know," said Catherine. "You've mentioned it before." She meant no harm, but she crushed him. He drank another whisky.

Mrs. Cornelius came flat-footed to the bar. " 'Ow old's that Miss Brunner nar? She was a stoodent teacher, wa'n't she, w'en you woz at school? Must be fifteen years, eh? Still at St. Victor's, is she?"

"Still there." Miss Brunner had heard her. "I'm headmistress now, you know."

Mrs. Cornelius was admiring. "I've got ter 'and it ter yer." She winked at Miss Brunner and jerked her thumb towards her son. "Carn't yer do somefink abart 'is appearance? 'Ain't yer still got some inference over 'im? 'E used ter be such a smart dresser—all the trendy colours, all bright an' sharp. Nar look at 'im. Looks as if 'e's garn on a bloody safari! Looks like a bleedin' clarn at ther circus wiv them trahsers! Ah, ya, ha, her, her— ker-ker-ker-ker!"

"The world caught up with me," said Jerry, "that's all. Anyway, I never liked going with the crowd."

His mother hugged him and stopped herself coughing. "There, there! Don' let yer ol' ma git yer dahn. No offence meant, Jer'."

"None taken, Mum."

"That's the stuff. There's not a lot o' 'arm in yer, Jerry. I'll say that!"

"What you drinking, then?"

" 'S'all right—ol' money-bags is payin'—'ave one on

the Fur King o' Elgin Crescent! I did okay stayin' wiv 'im, eh?"

"You certainly did."

"I've never gone short o' beaux," she said. "Whatever else 'as 'appened ter me. Men've orlways fancied me. An' I, I've gotter admit, 'ave orlways fancied them." She shifted on her massive legs. "Ker-ker-ker."

"I don't know how you do it, mum," he said as she shouted for service. "You'll still be going in a hundred years."

"Two bloody 'undred!" She winked at him. "Vodka, port an' lemon an' whatever 'e's 'avin'," she told the barman. She indicated her son.

"Double brandy, please," said Jerry. He thought he might as well get something out of an evening which had so far been more than a little depressing.

"Is 'at right," said his mother, "abart you goin' off all them pop stars yer used ter like?"

"They never fulfilled their promise, did they?"

"An' Georgie Best and Muhammad Ali and them others?"

"Same went for them. They all seemed to let me down at the same time."

"Funny, reely, wiv Caff talkin' up with all that, nar. Wot yer like nowdays?"

"Nothing much. I've lost faith in heroes."

"Ah, well. Yer orlways did 'ave yer 'ead in the' clards. Come darn ter Earf a bit now, eh?"

"Looks like it."

Catherine put her arm through his. "Don't needle him, mum. Everybody's picking on him tonight."

"She wasn't," said Jerry. "Not really."

"Buyin' 'im a bloody drink, wa'n I?" His mother was defensive. "You wos orlways too protective to'ards 'im, Caff. Let 'im stand on 'is own two feet—'e's old enough an' ugly enough nar!" But Mrs. Cornelius was smiling as she carried the vodka and port back to her table.

Jerry sipped his brandy. He offered the glass to her. "Want some?"

She nodded and took the drink. "You comin with us to Brighton?"

"Depends how pissed I get. It's the worst New Year I've ever had. I feel so lonely. I'm really depressed, Cath."

"That's not hard to see. Whenever you wear the wrong clothes for the weather I can tell. Clothes are a dead give-away, aren't they, to how a person's feeling? If you like we can go back to my flat. I don't particularly want to spend God knows how long in a smoky coach, singing rude songs—besides the roads are almost impassable, apparently. Heaviest snow of the century. We could see the New Year in together."

"What about your girl friend?"

"She's working. Gone abroad for a few days. She knows about us, anyway." Catherine squeezed his hand.

He was profoundly grateful. "Why not?" he said casually.

The door of the pub opened and cold air blew in. There was a glimpse of the frozen street. A bulky figure stood there. He was dressed in a vast dark overcoat, with a black muffler over his face, a fur cap on his head. In the odd light from the pub the tall dog at his side seemed to have red ears and eyes.

"We're off!" cried Frank with delight. "Off into the countryside. A-hunting we will go. Tantivvy, tantivvy!"

Jerry saw a small black-and-white cat run from the warmth of the bar into the chill of the street and had an impulse to stop it, but the newcomer was shouting now:

"All aboard what's going aboard!"

Hooters, whistles, rattles clattered and cawed and shrieked as, baying, the party surged out into the old year's last night.

CODA

But Harlequin's domination has waned. . . . In the modern world he is pale and lost, the frustrated Pierrot. Columbine has become a gold digger, Pantaloon is gaga, and the Harlequinade itself which used to be the core of the Pantomime, the mythical world into which all waited for the particular scene to be transformed, is now separated off as a quaint little period piece.

Randall Swinger, *The Rise and Fall of Harlequin,*
Lilliput Magazine, December 1948

Overcrowding—The Increasing Stress in North Kensington

North Kensington's Golborne Ward is the most severely overcrowded area in all London. Here 40% of the people live at a Housing Density of more than 1½ people a room. Kensington is one of the four London boroughs in which "signs of increasing stress can be seen through the effects of overcrowding." These are some of the stock facts to emerge from the Milner Holland report on housing in London.

KENSINGTON POST, 19 March 1965

MRS. C. AND FRANKIE C.

"They say in the paper that we are on the brink of a new Ice Age," said Colonel Pyat hopefully, casting a gloomy, Slavic eye over his ranks and ranks of old fur coats, evening capes, stoles, cloaks, hats and gloves. Spring had just arrived and with it the normal slackening off of business which always depressed him. He had long-since ceased to believe in the future.

"Stop broodin' yer silly ol' bugger an' 'urry up," said Mrs. Cornelius cheerfully. Her old eyes glittered behind a barricade of cream and powder. "Ker-ker-ker. We still got ter call fer Frank." Out of loyalty she wore his latest gift, though the weather was unusually mild. They were on their way to the People's Spring Festival, organised by local community leaders on the Westway Green below the motorway flyover to the west of Portobello Road. Mrs. Cornelius was excited. It was to be Jerry's first public appearance with his rock and roll band, The Deep Fix.

"Mind you," she said as an afterthought, "these fings orlways start late, if at all. Still, it's up ter us ter be on time, innit!"

"I hate it," grumbled Pyat. "Jungle music. Teddy boy noise."

"Cor! You are art o' touch, incha!" She snapped her fingers and rocked from side to side, wafting lavender water and scented powder. "Y've gotta be wiv it these days—trendy, far art, too much, rock an' roll!"

She swayed through the door into Elgin Crescent. It was a busy Saturday in the market. Colonel Pyat glanced viciously at the Indians, with their cheap cheese-cloth shirts and dresses, who were doing such a roaring trade.

There was the usual confusion of locals trying to shop in
a hurry while visitors moved slowly and uncertainly along
the narrow street between the stalls, wondering why so
many people scowled at them. Most of the money they
brought to Portobello Road stayed in the district for the
few hours that the antique-dealers and stall-holders remained there. Colonel Pyat followed Mrs. Cornelius
from the shop, locking the door carefully behind him.
He, too, wore an enormous fur coat. The day was miserably bright and sunny.

Together they pushed their way up the Portobello Road,
through the trinket-sellers, the street-musicians, the pur-
veyors of craft-goods, the racks of denim and cheesecloth,
the mass-produced patches and buttons and belt-buckles,
the green-grocery stalls, the sellers of Indian metalware,
of beads, flutes, drums, posters, army uniforms, handbags
and purses, weapons, Victoriana, until they reached
Frank's shop, which was currently dealing in stripped pine.
Frank waited reluctantly outside, holding a brass candle-
stick in each hand, part of his old antique stock. "If I
sell 'em for that," he told a small man in a pork-pie hat,
a camera and a black blazer with four metal buttons on
the cuff (evidently a German), "I shan't make any profit,
shall I?"

"Fifteen?" said the German.

"Sixteen," said Frank, "and that's final."

"Done," said the German awkwardly.

"You're so right," said Frank accepting the money.
"You won't regret it. That stuff appreciates, some of it."

"Come on, Frankie," said his mother, pulling at him.
"Yer can't stop dealin' can yer, yer littel cunt?"

He was offended. "At least someone in this family's
making their own living."

They trekked on until they reached the railway arch
and, immediately after it, the motorway arch, where
dozens of small stalls were set out selling the accumulated
junk of the twentieth century. They skirted the stalls even
as their eyes automatically shifted across the wares, rounding the corner to the big patch of grass where a crowd of
young bohemians and their children had already gathered
outside the graffiti-smeared walls of one of the motorway
bays. This bay had a chicken-wire fence strung between
its columns and a sign, already much attacked by weather

and local children: WESTWAY THEATRE. Within the bay old railway sleepers had been arranged in banks to form seats. On the wall behind the seats were three murals, one by Cawthorn, one by Riches and one by Waterhouse. Somehow the murals had escaped the ravages of the rest of the theatre which had long-ago collapsed as a result of calculated lack of local government support. The Council had been reluctant to allow the project in the first place and had made sure it would not flourish by bringing in an administrator from outside the district and making sure that he had no power, no money and no encouragement. After a while enthusiasm had broken down into a classic series of disputes between a variety of splinter groups and an attempt to produce a free theatre for the district had failed. But, for the first time in over a year, it was to be opened—or had been opened—by the people who had originally started the scheme with their free Saturday concerts featuring Quiver, Brinsley Schwartz, the Pink Fairies, Henry Cow, Mighty Baby, Come to the Edge and Hawkwind, until the police, in support of seven Rate Payers, had managed to put a stop to them—and Jerry and his band were to have their chance at last.

Mrs. Cornelius, with the dignity of one who was related to an artiste, Colonel Pyat in tow, Frank in the rear, went through the gates, calling out to her son who sat dreamily on the little stage trying to put a new plug on his amplifier lead. " 'Ere we are, then! Give us a number, lads!"

Mo Collier grinned at her in some shyness. He had plugged in his bass and was plunking at it. No sound came from his own amp. He turned a couple of knobs and a screeching rose and fell. He made another hasty adjustment. " 'Ullo, Mrs. C. You're a bit early, aincha? We don't start till 'alf-past two."

"It is now exactly a quarter-to-three," said Colonel Pyat. He tapped his wristwatch as if it were a barometer.

"Sod," said Jerry. He looked through the chicken wire at the gathering crowd. Behind it a number of policemen were beginning to line up. He finished with the plug and fitted it into the board. A red light flickered on his amplifier. He was surprised. He took his Rickenbacker electric twelve-string over to the amplifier and pushed the jack-plug lead into the socket. He played a chord. Mo winced. "We'd better tune up."

Terry the drummer suddenly came to life behind his kit and played an erratic roll before subsiding again. He looked like the dormouse in Alice in Wonderland. They had all had several tabs of mandrax and had become very stoned to help quell their nerves for their performance. Jerry began to pluck at his many strings, staring vaguely at Mo, who plucked back. Gradually they got their instruments into some kind of uniform tuning. Mo nodded towards the centre of the stage where hardboard had been placed across a gap (there had been two attempts to burn down the theatre during disputes between different radical groups). "Watch out for the 'ole, man."

Jerry nodded absent-mindedly. He was visualising the enthusiasm of his public. He had a glazed, harried look.

"All right, Mick Jagger," shouted Frank in his poshest voice, "let's hear you!"

"Ker-ker-ker," said his mother.

Jerry approached the microphone and began to chant into it. Nothing came through the PA. He staggered back towards the amplifiers. Elsewhere various people were fiddling with other pieces of faulty electrical equipment. Jerry had a word with his friend Trux, who was holding a wire in one hand and scratching his head with a screwdriver.

"Ker-ker-ker."

People were beginning to file into the theatre now, although the stage was so arranged that the band would play facing the people who sat outside on the grass. Some of the organisers of the event had not yet turned up. There had been a problem involving fresh disputes with a group of Rate Payers; the organisers could be seen on the far side of the green, gesticulating, deep in conversation with a number of middle-aged men and women with arms folded in front of them and expressions of extreme distaste on their faces as they looked first at the crowd and then at the stage. Once or twice a policeman wandered over and talked to a long-haired man in a fairisle pullover or had a word with a thin-lipped Rate Payer.

Jerry went behind the stage into the connecting bay, which served as a dressing-room. He was beginning to feel much better. He accepted a joint from a girl whom he remembered vaguely. Her name was Shirley Withers and she had offered him a warm look such as he had not received for a very long time. He felt taller, slimmer, more handsome. He grinned at her. A promising grin. He began to move with some of his old grace, the guitar resting casually on his hip. He went back on stage and plugged in again. He played a fast twelve-bar progression. He knew he was playing well. He nodded to Mo and Terry and began to jump up and down as he played. Some people were already clapping and cheering.

Mo put a final turn on his A string and inclined his head in a brief bow. Mrs. Cornelius, Colonel Pyat and Frank Cornelius sat down in the front row. Jerry did not look at them. He was looking at his Fame.

Unexpectedly, they all started more or less together, going into a fast, standard boogie rhythm. Jerry danced towards the mike. He had never felt so happy. At last he was able to emulate all his earlier heroes. Perhaps he could become a hero himself, only he wouldn't let people down the way the others had. The crowd was his. He stepped up to the mike and opened his mouth.

The crowd roared.

It was the last thing he heard before the floor gave way beneath his feet and he fell into the shallow pit below.

He was far too drugged to feel any real pain, or even much concern, as he lay on his back looking up at the dim patch of daylight above, at the broken Rickenbacker on his chest, listening to the waves of laughter and applause from the audience, to Mo's bewildered bass, to Terry's inappropriately determined drum solo. Then he passed out for a moment or two.

He felt sick and miserable when he woke up. Shirley Withers was in the hole with him. She was trying to lift him upright. He saw his mum peering over the edge.

"You okay, Jer'?"

"I'm fine. I can carry on now." He knew his chance had disappeared.

"Your guitar's *ruined*," said Shirley. "Have you got another?"

He shook his head. He got to his feet, the pieces of smashed wood still hanging around him by the strap. He climbed out of the hole and blinked. The police had closed in on the crowd. A fight had started. Two panda-car constables were already on stage. Frank was talking to them.

"Pigs!" shouted Jerry weakly. He turned to Terry. "Keep playing. Keep playing."

"They turned the power off," said Mo. He sat down cross-legged and buried his head in his hands.

"Don't let them stop your music!" Jerry addressed the confused crowd. "You've got rights. We've all got rights."

"No need to make any more trouble, sir," said one of the constables. "How's the head?"

"Piss off!" said Jerry. "It's a plot. Why'd you bloody have to interfere?"

"We've had complaints. I've nothing against this sort of music myself. I like it. Not that you could play any now, could you, old son?" He indicated the broken Ricken-backer. "So there's not a lot of point in making a fuss."

"I haven't had a go yet," said Jerry mournfully.

His mother moved to his defence. "Lay off the poor littel sod—it was 'is turn to do 'is act. 'E's bin waitin' years fer ther chancest, an' you 'ave ter go an' spoil it!"

The constable backed away from her. "We didn't damage the stage, madam."

"Pigs," said Mrs. Cornelius with some relish. "Mother-fuckers!"

"It's all right, mum," murmured Jerry.

"I'm on your side entirely," Frank was saying to the other constable. "If I had my way I'd ban this sort of thing altogether. I'm a Rate Payer."

"Put 'em all up against a wall and shoot 'em," said the constables with relish, then, as one of the organisers approached, "I'm really sorry about this. We're just doing our duty."

"Are you sure you're okay now?" said Shirley. Her eyes were worried rather than warm.

"Fine," said Jerry, "um. . . ."

She anticipated him. "Got to go now. See you around. Bye, bye."

"Bye, bye," said Jerry.

"You were very good," said Mrs. Cornelius. "Wan'e, kernewl?"

But Colonel Pyat, a huge, frightened hamster, was already on the other side of the barrier and making for home.

"I'm a Trader *and* a Rate Payer," Frank continued. "I've lived here all my life. I remember when this was a quiet, decent neighbourhood."

Mrs. Cornelius gurgled sceptically. "Wot? Oh, yeah. So fuckin' quiet yer couldn't get a bloody taxi ter take yer 'ome. They woz shit scared o' Nottin' Dale. They wouldn't drive yer beyond Pembridge Gardens! An' the coppers used ter patrol in threes. I remember one year they barricaded the Nottin' Dale coppers in their own nick and they couldn't git art till the people let 'em art!" She eyed the constable with fond speculation. "We woz famous in them days," she said, "for bein' fierce. They're all soft nardays—coppers *an'* yumans."

"Listen," said the policeman with some heat, "they wanted to send the SPGs in—then you'd 'ave known what for!"

"Took pity on yer, did they?" said Mrs. Cornelius contemptuously. "Ruddy little squirt."

"Now, then, madam. . . ." He reddened, seeking support. "Arthur. . . ."

With a quick, cunning movement, Mrs. Cornelius stuck out her varicosed leg. The constable yelped and fell head-first into the hole. Mrs. Cornelius took her son by the arm. "C'mon—let's go an' 'ave a cup a tea. Yer'll make it yet, Jer'—I know yer will."

The sleepers and the dope had begun to take effect. Jerry's eyes were watering. As his mum led him off the stage, he burst into tears.

AUCHINEK

Sebastian Auchinek's expensive white suit thoroughly out-
shone Jerry's cheap one. They sat together, side by side,
on a long deep tan ottoman, in Auchinek's elegant,
sparsely furnished, Sackville Street office. Big windows
admitted cool sunlight as if it were exclusive to the establishment. Auchinek was hatless. Jerry wore a broad-
brimmed fedora. "Sam Spade? Right?" said Auchinek
pointing at the hat.

"Philip Marlowe," Jerry told him. "*The Long Goodbye.*"

"Right! Beautiful." Auchinek returned to his commiserating mood. "But they're not cheap, are they, Ricken-
backers?" He spoke reverently. "£500?"

"About that," said Jerry. He had got his guitar from a
friend who had done Sound City's entire stock in 1973,
loading two pantechnicons in half an hour on a Sunday
morning in July.

"And," said Auchinek smiling, "of course it wasn't
insured?"

"No."

"You people!" Auchinek wore a waistcoat of pale blue
leather, its edges trimmed with metal studs, a lilac shirt, a
yellow cravat. Somehow all he seemed to lack was a green
parrot on his shoulder. "So, Jerry! What can I do you
for?"

"I wondered if you could get us some gigs. We did very
well at the Westway, until the accident."

"Heavy rock?" Auchinek rose sadly and went to his
desk. He looked significantly back over his shoulder as he
picked up a black plastic box which looked as if it had
cost much more than anything in silver. "Heavy rock? It's

not my scene. Solo singers, yes. Orchestras, yes. Boy and girl singing acts, yes—soul trios, quartets, quintets, sextets, septets, octets, yes, yes, yes, yes. Soul, soul, soul, soul— that's your basic day-to-day demand anywhere in the country or on the Continent, Las Vegas, you name it. Soul isn't just a popular fad—it's the genuine commercial music of a decade. Black or white, it makes no difference. Country music, rock and roll groups, reggae— nothing compared to soul. Jerry, you haven't got a bad voice—make it sweeter—get together with some other guys, maybe some gals, and do some harmonies—a good funky bass, a touch of wa-wah, even a taste of fuzz, nobody's objecting to that. It's fine, gives it body, texture— do you know how many records I've produced myself? —you don't have to give up your principles, just alter your angle a little. Mainly it's the songs, see." He began to sing in a low, lugubrious voice, hunching his shoulders, awkwardly moving his hips. "Baby, baby, baby, you broke my heart in two—now two hearts beat as one, but they're not having any fun, 'cause both those hearts belong to me! See? Lovely stuff." He made a cryptic windmilling motion with his arms. It was on the strength of this motion that Jerry, for the first time in his life, had developed racial prejudice while watching *Top of the Pops*. He had discovered that he hated black people. Then, after another week or so of watching several similar acts, he decided that he hated white people, too. Now he was hating Jews. He wondered just how much disharmony *Top of the Pops* was responsible for. It was surprising what music could do for the racial situation. However, he was desperate enough to continue trying to reason with Auchinek, his only contact in the commercial music business.

"I can't do it. But we thought of this idea—Music from the Spheres—astronaut music that's come from the stars —it's a good gimmick. We tell the kids it was given to us by space people, see. Like *Chariots of the Gods,* you know."

"*Gramophones of the Gods?* Jerry, a gimmick's as good as the thing it's promoting. Okay—yes, good gimmick— but did the astronauts send us soul music? Maybe they did. You prove it. If the music isn't soul—if it isn't what people want to hear—it doesn't matter how good

a gimmick you've got. It's the Number One Rule, Jerry.
I've told you before."

"But that stuff's just so much Muzak. It's piped music
for supermarkets. People didn't want to hear the Beatles
till they heard them, or Hendrix, or The Who."

"They heard them—they liked it—therefore it must
have been what they wanted. My point!"

Jerry accepted the Camel Auchinek offered him. "But
mythology, see? Everyone's into mythology. I was reading
this book—*The Mythical History of Britain*—yeah?"

"Fabulous. . . ."

"It reckons we're all descended from the Trojans. . . ."

"Trojans? I thought we were all descended from
Martians. Maybe Trojans was their word for Martian?"

"You're probably right," said Jerry.

"So what about the Martians?"

"An album—the mythical history of England up to the
present day."

"So?"

"Couldn't you interest someone?"

"Certainly I could interest someone. With my muscle,
Jerry, I could interest anyone. Fabulous history of England?
—fine—as rock music—the sort you like?—not really—
as folk music?—who cares?—as soul? Very good! Good
orchestrations, nice lyrics, nice arrangements, easy swinging rhythm—lovely—but King Arthur? A soul opera of
King Arthur? Maybe, maybe. You are thinking of King
Arthur? Like Wakeman? That's nice, the Wakeman. Exactly what I'm talking about. But it's been done. Can it
be done again? With a new angle? Well, maybe. But
Wakeman isn't The Miracles, if you see what I mean. A
market, I grant you. A good market. But not a really solid
market. Not so safe as soul. So what else were you considering? Let's spell it out, eh? Talk it through. Fine? Trojans? Who's heard of Trojans, these days?"

"We could make it Martians, as you suggested—gods as
astronauts, the Bermuda Triangle—something up to date.
The same stuff—but more modern. . . ."

"Yeah, but that's mythology—the Bermuda Triangle is
science. You don't want to get them mixed up, Jerry.
There's too much confusion already in the world today.
Still, not to split atoms, eh? Okay. Martians. Bermuda Tri-

angle, Scifi, right? Far out. Okay, the market's getting big enough to stand it. Super. Fab. So far so good. So we have a Soul Opera about the Bermuda Triangle——"

"Or Jaws Superstar," said Jerry wildly.

"Sharks? Sure, maybe. Giant sharks. Up-dated Moby Dick, with good music. Why not? We do a film. We all go out to Bermuda for a few weeks. Why not? Sure. Come to me with something on tape, some notes. Good. I'll listen to it. I'll take it down to the country with me. If I like it, I'll sell it. Can I say more?"

"But I need a new guitar first. If you could lend me the bread. . . ."

"You still have that Equity card since I got you the film extra work?"

"Yes."

"Then I can help you earn some money. Una's new show."

"Playing guitar?"

"They don't need a rock guitarist. Not another one. A good part. The show's about Frankenstein, see, and what it means in moral terms today—beautiful songs." His hands windmilled over one another.

"But I haven't had any acting experience."

"You don't need it."

"And I can't sing soul songs."

"You don't have to. You yell. Rock and roll experience is perfect for this part. You scream. You jump up and down. With these teeth in. You get three appearances, maybe more. A night, I mean."

"Who am I?"

"Who are you? You're the vampire. I should have thought of it before. I apologise. Okay? Want it? The pay's good. Get your name on the programme. A start in a career. Look at 'Hair,' how many people made it from that! Look at 'Jesus Christ Superstar'? And 'Godspell'?"

"Oh, blimey," said Jerry.

"Contacts. You'll have a new guitar in no time. A break. Una'll be delighted."

"You hate me, don't you," said Jerry.

"Hate you? What's hate? I disapprove of you, because you're a talented boy who doesn't know what's good for him. You frustrate me, Jerry. You do. You frustrate me very, very much. So what's it to be? The vampire? Or back to busking on a borrowed banjo? Down the garbage chute or up the golden escalator?"

"I'll try the vampire," said Jerry.

PERSSON

"'You were splendid," Una Persson leaned over a drowsy Catherine and lit Jerry's cigarette for him. She climbed across their bodies to be on his left. They all lay together in Una's king-size four-poster. It was early afternoon. "You're a natural actor." Una was talking about the movie rushes she had seen earlier that day at the studios. The film was her own first starring role (a remake of *Camille*) and by encouraging Jerry (who played Armand's friend) she seemed also to be encouraging herself.

Lying between the two women Jerry was in his element. His emotions were mixed but all pleasant. He felt they were three sisters sharing a delicious conspiracy, that he had two mothers, two concubines, two loyal friends; moreover he became still more cheerful when they ganged up on him, to take the piss out of him, to dress him up, to have their way with him. Perhaps it was their affection for each other which turned him on most, the fact that they were able to relax with him and therefore make him relax in turn. They enjoyed going out together, forming a little exclusive club whose erotic secrets only the three of them would ever know. Depressed, they were able to comfort one another; happy, they were able to infect one another.

"And you're better than Garbo." It was true. "Much better. You're a bit like her in looks, but your range is greater."

Una lay back on her pillows, fingering her breasts as she absorbed his praise.

"You can out-act anyone, Una." With a luscious sigh Catherine ran her soft hand down her brother's chest and

937

stomach. "Ah! I don't know how I get the work at all! I can't act for toffee. Still, six weeks in panto's better than nothing. We start rehearsals next month. It's hard to get into the Christmas spirit in September, mind you." She rubbed her own stomach. It rumbled. "Cor, I'm starving. Breakfast time."

"It'll be tea-time soon," said Una. "I've been working since six o'clock."

"I'll get some tea, then," said Catherine agreeably, running fingers through tangled blonde hair. "Did you pick up the tickets from the agent?"

"Three one-way Class 1 berths on the *Alexander Pushkin* sailing next week for New York. We'll have to fly back."

Catherine put her dirty feet on the white carpet, stood up and took her pale brown Janet Reager negligée from the back of the door. "It'll be nice to see the old house again. And a good time to go." Like her brother, she shared with Una an enthusiasm for American Gothic wooden houses.

"Will they let us sleep in the same cabin?" Jerry asked as his sister left. "Do you think?"

"I've arranged it. They think we're ballet dancers. It's okay."

"That's the Russians all over. One rule for the ballet dancers and another for everyone else. I wonder what it'll be like." Jerry's Russophilia was only equalled by his romantic love for the United States. He could think of nothing more marvellous than travelling to one place on a ship belonging to the other. He had often remarked on the strong similarities between the two nations and believed this similarity to be the cause of their rivalry.

Una indicated the print on her wall. It showed the famous 18th century actor John Rich in his role of Harlequin. The caption above the print read *Harlequin Dr. Faustus in the Necromancer* and below it was a verse:

Thank you Genteels, these stunning Claps declare,
How Wit corporal is yr. darling Care.
See what it is the crowding Audience draws
While Wilks no more but Faustus gains Applause.

"I told them we were putting on a new production,"

Una said, "but I didn't tell them you were playing Columbine."

Jerry patted his stomach. With success, he was expanding.

"I'm not sure I'll get into the dress. Can't I be Harlequin or the Pierrot?"

She shook her head. "It's not your turn."

He giggled as she took him in her arms.

NYE

"You're Nöel Coward, if you want to be." Major Nye stiffened his shoulders. "I can't say fairer than that. You've the figure, now that you've lost a few pounds, the voice, the looks—or can have. What d'you say, old chap?"

It would be Jerry's first real star part in the West End, but he remained reluctant to begin a new commitment. Una would be back from America soon and Catherine would have returned to the provinces. If he took the role it would mean quite probably that they would not be together for several months.

"I don't know an awful lot about the thirties," he said.

"Twenties, actually, this setting. *Bitter Sweet* with an all male cast. As he'd have liked it himself. You're not worried?"

"Not about that. So it's Brylcreem and six inch fag holders, eh?"

"That's a bit superficial, old boy, but you've got the mood—it's what the public's desperate for. . . ."

Major Nye had become an impresario late in life, with his run of successful nostalgia shows on stage, screen and television. Series like *Clogs* and *Mean Streets,* set during the depression in Northern towns, had shown people that things had been worse than they were now and taken their minds off their current troubles, while musical versions of *King of the Khyber Rifles, Christina Alberta's Father, A Child of the Jago* and *The Prisoner of Zenda* were all still running in West End and Broadway productions, as well as in touring companies (Catherine was currently playing Rupert of Hentzau in one of these).

"The traditionalists are going to be a bit upset," Major

Nye continued, pausing by a railing and staring out to sea. He had come down to Brighton especially to meet Jerry who was just finishing a run as Harlequin Captain MacHeath in the revived *Harlequin Beggar's Opera* which Jerry had himself suggested to Major Nye after Una Persson had given him the idea. The revived full-blooded pantomime was just one more of the major's successes in England and America. "But we're used to that by now—and we're doing more for them than anyone else, even if we do take liberties occasionally. Still, it's the literary bods do the complaining, not the public, and it's the public that matters, eh?"

"Every time," said Jerry. He waved. Elizabeth Nye, the major's daughter, who had first interested her father in the stage, was running along the promenade to meet them. She was playing Columbine Polly Peachum to Jerry's Harlequin. "Hello, Jerry. Hello, Daddy. Is lunch still on?"

"If you're interested, my dear." He looked questioningly at Jerry. "Spot of lunch, then?"

"Lovely," said Jerry. "Have you asked Sebastian about this?"

"No need to bring in agents until the last minute. They only confuse things. I didn't know you were still with him."

"He's useful," said Jerry. "Anyway, I feel sorry for him. His musical interests have taken a turn or two for the worse."

"He didn't move with the times," said Major Nye. "Lived in the present too much, in my view. Couldn't see that the wind was changing. Of course, I never expected anything like this myself. I started, you know, doing modest little music hall evenings with amateur performers. Now we're dragging up every damned traditional entertainment since Garrick's day—and before. We'll find we've got mass audiences for *Noye's Fludde* next season, at this rate."

"The eighteenth-century satirists thought the Harlequinade was going to be the death of the theatre." Jerry had pursued his usual research. "They thought Shakespeare and Jonson were done for—pushed out of business."

"Nothing ever kills off anything else," said Major Nye

comfortably, pointing his stick at Wheeler's across the road. "Nothing invented ever dies. Fashions change. But it's always there, waiting to be revived according to the mood of the times. History is retold by every generation, always slightly differently—sometimes very differently. Funny stuff, when you think about it, Time."

"I've never thought about it," Jerry said.

A BUNDLE

Jerry sat in the studio mock-up in his elegant evening dress smoking a sophisticated cigarette, copying his successful Coward role but looking more like a Leslie Howard, sardonic, quizzical, as he turned to the camera and said:

"Once upon a time it meant something to be the owner of a car. It put you above the common herd. Now Rolls-Royce brings back meaning into motoring. . . ." The camera pulled away from the close-up in order to show the whole scene ". . . with the mini-Phantom."

"Cut," said Adrian Mole, the director. "There's a phone call for you, love. That was beautiful. All right, lads and lasses, you can go home now. Everything's perfect."

Jerry climbed from the cramped seat and moved stiffly from the studio. In the office one of the bright, competitive girls who worked there handed him an instrument. "Hello?"

The voice was indistinct, accented, anxious. Colonel Pyat.

"Your mother, Jerry. She is not at all well. She wants to see you."

"Is she in hospital? St. Charles?"

"No, no. She wouldn't let them take her. Still in Blenheim Crescent. You haven't been to visit her lately and I think she's upset."

It was more likely that Colonel Pyat disapproved of him, thought Jerry. "Thanks, Colonel. I'll go and see her right away."

"I've looked in, but I have the shop to run. I'm all alone, you see."

"Don't worry. Has the doctor been?"

"I haven't spoken to him, yet. But I think it's serious. She could be—oh, well, you had better look for yourself."

"Does Frank know?"

"Frank, too, has his business. He's going to try to pop round this evening. Catherine we can't find."

"She's on tour." Jerry was surprised by his lack of annoyance, his spontaneous feeling of concern for his mother.

The evening clothes were his own so he did not need to change. He went straight to the car-park where he picked up his real Phantom. He nodded to two young girls who recognised him as he drove into the street. It was surprising how popular he had become since he had allowed Auchinek to give him the "conventional" image. It offered reassurance, of course. He touched the stud to lower his window and threw his Sullivan's cigarette into the street. He looked bitterly at his eyes in the driving mirror. He had always hated reassurance. Reassurance was death.

He reached Shepherd's Bush and headed up Holland Park Avenue, turning eventually into the maze that was now the Ladbroke Grove area, all diversions and one-way streets, coming at last to Blenheim Crescent. Opposite his mother's basement, which was identical to the one she had temporarily removed to in Talbot Road, was the fortress of the new housing estate, built on the site of the Convent of the Poor Clares and named after the order (Clares Gardens, though no garden was in evidence anywhere). He found a space close to his mother's flat and parked. All the meters had been smashed, though he didn't benefit, however, since he had his resident's parking permit. He still lived in Kensington, in the more exclusive Holland Park area. He locked his car carefully, knowing the habits of the local kids, and descended the makeshift wooden steps of the basement. The wooden door was unlocked. He went in, recognising the familiar, comforting smell of mildew and stale food.

"Mum?"

A fairly feeble cough came from the back room, where she slept. He made his way through the debris of her living room, with its ancient furniture, its scattered magazines, its unwashed crockery, its dead flowers, and entered the bedroom which smelled of disinfectant, camphor, moth-balls, rose-water, lavender-water, urine, stout and gin, a combination which never failed to fill him with nostalgia.

She lay in the iron-framed bed, beneath several quilts, propped on a variety of dirty cushions and pillows, in full make-up, so that it was impossible to tell from her skin how she was, though her eyes were uncharacteristically dull.

"Hello, Mum. Not too good, I hear."

Somehow her jowls and her baggy pouches seemed to be one with her disintegrating cosmetics and gave the impression that the face beneath it all was that of a child. She had rarely seemed so pathetic. He drew up a cane-bottomed chair and sat beside the bed. Because it was conventional, he held her hand. She pulled it away with a throaty chuckle. " 'Oo'd'ya fink I am—Littel bloody Nell?" Her coughing began strongly but quickly grew faint. "Ker-ker-ker. . . ." She reached, unable to speak, for the glass on the bedside table. He handed it to her. She drank. It was neat gin, Jerry guessed, by the smell on her breath as she handed the glass back.

"I've 'ad it, Jer'," she said. "You know 'ow old I am?"

She had always kept it a secret. He shook his head. She was delighted. "An' yer never will," she said. "Know 'ow old you are, do yer?"

"Of course I do. I was born on 6 August 1946."

"Thass right. They let orf ther bloody A-bomb ter celebrate. Most people on'y ever got fireworks—an' they 'ad ter be pretty fuckin' posh, an' all!" She eyed his costume. "Nice. I orlways knew you'd make it, in the end. You an' Caff. Frank's doin' okay, too—but 'e never 'ad much imagination, did 'e? Not like ther rest've us."

"Yeah," said Jerry, nodding. He took out his silver cigarette case, offering it to his mother. With some difficulty she removed a cigarette and put it between her lips, drooping as always. Jerry lit it. He lit another for himself. She coughed a little but soon stopped.

"Well," she said, "I'm dyin'—it's why I was so keen ter see yer. Got yer in'eritance, in I?"

"Oh, come on mum, don't be daft." He tried to smile.

"'Besides, you haven't got a penny. It's all gone on wild living."

"It *'as*, too!" She was proud. "Every bleedin' shillin'. They didn't need no bloody inflation when I was arahnd!" A brief cough and Jerry thought he saw her wipe blood from her lip.

"Shall I go and fetch the doctor?"

"No point." She tapped the side of the mattress. "There's a box under me bed. You know—me box. You 'ave it." She reached into her several layers of cardigan and nightdress and removed a key from her bosom. She pressed it into his hand. "Open it later. There's yer birf certificate in there an' a few ovver fings, but not much. Yer farver. . . ."

He passed her an ash-tray, a souvenir from Brighton, so that she could put her cigarette down while she coughed.

". . . wanna know abart 'im?"

"I didn't think you knew much."

"More 'n I've wanted ter tell up ter now. I got a lot of it from me mum and me sister." She chuckled and the dewlaps shook, threatening to break away and fall on the quilt. "Bloody funny story. It goes back ter the year dot. I dunno wot 'e'd be—yore great, great gran'dad, maybe —any'ow 'e was born abart 1870 an' married this, er, Ulrica Brunner. Ker-ker-ker. They 'ad these kids—where is it?" She felt under her pillow and withdrew a sheaf of tiny slips of paper, sorting through them. "Ah. I've bin workin' it art, see. Yeah. Katerina, Jeremiah an' Franz. Well, Katerina married this Hendrik Persson geezer—a Dane or Dutchman or somefink—but on'y just in time— she woz awready up ther spart—by guess 'oo—"

"Jeremiah," said Jerry with a sinking feeling. He had come to expect coincidences in life since he had begun to study the history of the Theatre.

"Yeah," said his mother. Then she realised what he had meant and shook her head. "Nar! Not 'er bruvver—'er *dad*." She winked at him. An ancient owl. "Give us some o' that Lucozade love. And put a drop o' gin in it." He poured some of the yellow liquid into her gin glass. She sipped. "Ur! Innit 'orrible? Well—ker-ker-ker—Katerina 'ad 'er baby an' this Persson feller thort it wuz 'is an' corled it, believe it or not, Jeremiah—in honour of 'er dad, see? Well, Franz marries a cousin corl'd—" she picked another slip of paper from the sheaf—"Christina Brunner, right? An' they 'ave some kids, one of which is anuvver Cafferine, an' Jeremiah goes ter live wiv 'is married sister an' from wot me mum sez they 'as it away an' a little girl's the result—anuvver Ulrica. Then 'er bruvver goes ter Russia or somewhere an' changes 'is name ter Brunner or Bron or maybe Brahn, see. Any'ow 'e meets this Cafferine Brunner later an' they gets married, not knowing then that 'e's 'er uncle. They 'ave free kids they corl Frank, Jeremiah an' Cafferine an' 'e goes off again, back ter Russia. Frank marries a Betty Beesley, Jeremiah marries some German bint name o' Krapp, an' Cafferine marries a cousin corled, believe it or not, Cornelius Brunner, an' she got one in the oven off 'er bruvver before she trips dahn the aisle. In the meantime Ulrica's grown up an' married anuvver Russian corled—this is funny—Pyat, but, from wot we worked art, she'd 'ad a kid by *'er* dad an' it was brought up fer years wivart knowing its mum an' dad till someone tells it—it's registered, see, as Frank Brunner. Eventually Frank Brunner marries Jenny Beesley an' they 'ave two boys an' a girl. The girl does well for 'erself, goin' on ther stage, legit, an marryin inter the foreign royal fam'ly—Princess Una von Lobkowitz, no less. An' then ther boys marry a Mary Greasby an' a Nelly Vaizey an' settle darn in Tooting or somewhere sarf o' ther river, but Jerry's a widower in ther meantime, wiv a fair amarnt o' Krapp money, an' there's two kids—Alfred and Siegfried—'oo 'ave ter change their name ter Krapp an' go an' live with ther fam'ly in Germany, while Jerry comes back ter England an' marries a Greek girl, daughter of ther shippin' millionaire Kootiboosi or somefink. They 'ave free kids—Francesca, Joacaster an' Constant—an' live up Campden 'Ill somewhere. Francesca marries a bloke called Nye an' goes art ter India wiv 'im where she dies in childbirth—one son, Jeremiah. Joacaster marries a cousin, Johannes Cornelius, an' goes art ter Sarf Africa, an' they 'ave a little girl, an' Constant marries a Katerina Persson an' they 'ave a little girl an' all, 'oo's up ther stick a monf after 'er first period, if wot I 'eard wos right, with 'er dad's daughter, Honoria—which *might* be me—in fac' I'm pretty sure it is. Well, you know a bit abart yore dad—'e wos

moody—'e married me, I'll say that, though a good deal
older'n me, but corled 'imself by 'is secon' name, Jeremiah, for ther weddin' an' I never woz sure it was legal
—'e scarpered o' course an' fer a long time I thort it
woz 'cause o' ther coppers. Anyway, you free come very
close tergevver, though yer might not 'ave all been 'is, or
any of yer—yer could've bin 'is bruvver-in-law Frank's,
'oo I sor a lot of 'cause e'—ther one wot married me—
was orlways travellin' or lockin' 'isself away—or, I must
be honest, *my* dad's, if it woz me real dad or me mum's
—the ol' goat. 'E wos a kernewl, too, yer know, in
Mexico, it woz, an' ovver places. Any'ow me sister Doris
married a bloke corled Dennis Beesley (an' I sor a fair bit
o' 'im while she woz doin' war-work an' me ovver sister,
Renie, married yore little mate Mo Collier's dad Alf—
nice bloke 'e woz, killed in Germany 1946, somefink ter
do wiv ther black market, wannit? Anyway, there woz a
lot've ups an' darns rahnd abart that time an' I don't
blame meself, though no one'll ever know exactly 'ow oo's
related to 'oo—except we're as sure as eggs related—we
woz orlways a close family. Sammy, 'oo died, was Alf
Collier's bruvver, an' they 'ad a Brunner, a Persson an'
a Cornelius or two in there somewhere, an' all. Well,
ther's on'y a few *main* fam'lies in this distric', ain't there?
Like over in Nottin' Dale they got abart free clans—
'Arrises, Sullivans an' Kellys—it's ther same wiv ther Corneliuses, Cornells an' Carnelians rahnd 'ere—along wiv
ther Brunners, Perssons an' Beesleys, though they woz
never much compared ter ther Corneliuses 'oo really run
these blocks for a 'undred years or more—since the Convent woz built an' there was on'y that an' the Elgin 'ere a
'undred years ago or so. An' they did well for themselves,
some of 'em."

"Where did they come from, Mum?" Jerry asked. "Ireland? There were a lot of Irish moved in here, didn't they
—because of the convents?"

"Some finks Ireland—but this area's orlways 'ad a
lot o' immigrant in it—Dutch, Italian, German, Swedish,
French—it's a common name. English an' all. Wot abart
that fer a tale o' scandals, then? Incest on top a bloody
incest, eh? D'yer believe it?" Her eyes glittered.

"Every word," he said. "I'm glad it's cleared up the
mystery of my birth."

She bawled with laughter. "Yer sarcy sod! Ker-ker-ker."

"Others did well for themselves, did they?" He frowned. His mother never took him seriously.

"Oh, yers. One got a knight'ood, one opened a department store, anuvver started a rest'rant—gold mines, ships, factories, greengrocers—yer've on'y got ter name it! There wos a doctor or two an' all—an' some of ther girls married inter the English aristocracy. They spread all over, ther Corneliuses!" She gasped and laughed again. "Like muck! Like a fuckin' plague, eh? Har, har, har, ker-ker-ker-fuck!"

Blood really was coming from her mouth now. Jerry helped her sit upright. Her body shook. Her skin sagged is if she shrank within it. "Oh, fuckin' ell. Oh, fuckin' ell, Jerry. 'Ere, did Caff tell yer?" She struggled. Her eyes ran with tears; her make-up smeared. She looked like an eight-year-old. She was full of fear. "Did she? Don' let 'er 'ave it, Jer'."

"Have what, mum?" He was distracted, holding her in one arm and trying to reach for the glass of Lucozade with his free hand. "Eh?"

"Ther baby. . . ." Her frame reared in his grasp. "Yore fuckin' bastard baby." She began to cough but was too weak. Her body quivered. The fear fled. She grinned. "Yer got ter larf, incha?"

"Drink this, mum. I'll go and get the doctor." He was weeping. He knew she was dying.

She cuddled against his chest, like a baby animal. She sighed. It took him a few moments to realise that she had not breathed in. She grew cold. He kissed her stiff, lacquered hair, the powder of her face, and then he was calm, standing up, pulling the sheet to her chin, kneeling to feel under the bed and pull out her box.

It was too dark to see properly in the bedroom and he did not like to turn on the light. He carried the cheap wooden writing chest into the other room and put it on the table in the window. He looked out, over the top of the area, through railings at the blocks of new flats. He shrugged and used the key to open the box. It folded back into a surface on which one could write, each half of the surface being the lid of a section. He pulled up the top flap, using the little loop of string his mother had nailed there, in place of the original tag. There was a bundle of papers amongst the cuttings of advertisements, beauty treatments, anecdotes his mother had accumulated or inherited from her mother. They stretched back more than a hundred years, to 1865. He took out the bundle and set it aside. He opened the bottom flap. There was a fairly new book there which he had bought while researching his part of a year or two earlier. It was called *Pantomime, A Story in Pictures,* by Mander and Mitchenson, published in 1973. He was puzzled. It was not like his mother to keep any book, let alone this one. Perhaps she had intended to sell it. He turned his attention to the bundle. He was very close to breaking down.

He fingered the papers, secured by rubber bands. He turned to call back into the cold, dark bedroom. "Don't worry, Mum—old Corneliuses never die—they just fade into someone else. There's too bloody many of us, eh?"

He was certain that he had heard her chuckle. He jumped up and went back to look into the bedroom, but she had not moved. She lay dead in her bed.

He returned to the table. He pulled the bands from the bundle. The bands were so old that they had perished and fell away beneath his fingers.

He found some photographs, very faded, of himself and Frank and Catherine when they were children. They had been at Brighton and had had their photographs taken in a booth, poking their heads through holes above cut-out figures so that it looked as if they were three Pierrots, with children's faces and adult's bodies, on the pier. Their mother, standing beside them, looked far more innocent than her children, just as she looked now. She had been thinner, then, too. He found a marriage certificate for his mother's wedding. *Honoria Persson married to Jeremiah Cornelius at the Parish Church in the Parish of Tooting in the County of London on 22 July 1944 according to the Rites and Ceremonies of the Established Church after Banns by me, Wilfred H. Houghton, Curate.* At least he seemed legitimate, he thought. He could find no birth certificate for either his mother or the three children, though she had said his would be there. Perhaps she had been thinking of the marriage certificate. He found ticket stubs for his first appearance at the Prince of Wales Theatre as the vampire in *Soul of Frankenstein,* which had run for a week. He found ticket stubs for Catherine's early appearances in the Jupiter Theatre repertory company, where she had met Una Persson and Elizabeth Nye. There was a Royal Premiere programme for *Queen Christina*, the successful follow-up to *Camille*, which his mother had attended in full regalia, outshining anything the Royal Family could produce. There was a programme for *Twelfth Night*, decorated with a Heath Robinson jester and a phrase from the play—*A great while ago the world begun, With hey, ho, the wind and the rain. But's that's all one, our play is done, And we'll strive to please you every day*—in which Una Persson had appeared as Viola and he as Sebastian. There were a number of other programmes and tickets, all of them connected with the careers of himself or his sister. There was a film company hand-out, giving the synopsis of a bad science fiction film in which he had appeared for a few seconds, as an extra, and on this had been scrawled a peculiar doodle, apparently in his own hand. He could remember nothing of it. He held it closer to the light from the window, trying to see if it made any sense at all. As he lifted it, his brother's staring face appeared, grinning at him with comforting malevolence.

Jerry got up from the table and went to let Frank in. He opened the door, lifting the handle so that it would not scrape on the floor as it usually did. "She's dead," he said.

"Catherine?"

"No, Mum."

Frank made a small, unpleasant sound and went to check.

Jerry again picked up the dirty hand-out:

He screwed it up and let it fall on the floor, then he

called goodbye to his sobbing brother and left the basement, climbing aboard his Phantom, on his way to find Catherine. He turned on the stereo. The Beatles were singing *Hello, Goodbye* again. The sky was dark grey. He switched on the windscreen wipers. It was raining heavily. He, too, had begun to cry by the time he reached Greyfriars Bridge, on his way to Blackheath, the bearer of bad news for the mother of his unborn son.

—MICHAEL MOORCOCK
Notting Hill
April 1976

APPENDIX I

The following is reprinted from *The Nature of the Catastrophe,* London 1971:

This chronology begins with the convenient date of 1900, but there is evidence to support the existence of a Jerry Cornelius even in pre-Christian times (the first significant reference, of course, is the famous one in Virgil!) just as there is evidence to say he did not appear on the scene until much later. We are not here suggesting, for instance, that a child of one year could have been a spy during the South African War. The chronology merely lists well-supported references to Cornelius. It does not propose that they can possibly refer to the same individual!

The Compilers

1900
18 December
 Birth of a boy, christened Jeremiah Cornelius, at the Bon Secours convent, Guatemala City. Mother died: father unknown. He lived in the convent until the age of about six when he was transferred to a monastery school some distance from the city. (Letter to David Redd of Haverford West from Sister Maria Eugene of the Bon Secours convent, who died in 1960.)

1901
25 January
 Boer War double agent known as "Cornelius" caught and shot by a party of Boers under Commandant Pre-

torius, about two miles west of Jericho, Transvaal. (Despatch from Pretorius to Kruger.)

1903
9 April

Log of the SS *Maureen Key* reports picking up an English-speaking seaman in Bay of Biscay about noon. Seaman was adrift in small boat and was incoherent. Name: Jerry—possibly Cornell or Carnell, Carmelion or Cornelius. Was handed over to port authorities in Bilbao but disappeared shortly afterwards having stolen a coat and a piece of meat.

14 October

Catholic mission in Djelfa, Algeria, contracts plague of unknown origin and all die. Scrawled on the side of the confessional are letters JE CORNELIU, plainly recently written by the monk who had been acting as Confessor when overcome by the disease. (*Le Monde Catholique*, 30 October.)

1904
24 January

Programme of the Empire Theatre, Leicester Place. The Grand Spectacular Tableau, No 7 on the bill—"The Treasure Island of Monte Cristo": the part of Edmund Dantes played by Mnsr. J. Cornelius. At No 10 on the bill Mdlle. Marguerite Corneille, Comedienne.

14 October

The St. Petersburg uprising. A list of arrested "foreign elements" issued by the Okharna (secret police) includes a Jeremiah Cornelius (thought to be a pseudonym). It is unclear whether he was deported or executed. (Burns Collection.)

1905
November

Reports from the Carpathian Mountains in Rumania that a bandit—"perhaps an Englishman"—called Jeremiah Cornelius has been operating there for more than a year, organising several bandit gangs into a single force. (Records of Transylvanian Central Police Bureau now at the Austrian War Museum, Vienna.)

1907
16 February
Reference to a Jerzy Cornelius in list of thirty prisoners tried by military court as Socialist Democrat terrorists, St. Petersburg. All found guilty and shot. (Burns Collection.)

8 July
Rouvenjemi, northern Finland. A gang of criminals thought to be Russian nihilists rob several banks, a post office, several shops and are thought to have escaped by train. One suspect, a Russian Jew calling himself Bronsky, claimed that the leader of the gang was known only by the name of "Cornelius". The Russian thought the leader was probably a Swede. (*Dagbladet*, Sweden, 12 July.)

8 October
"A young man of well-bred appearance, speaking Danish with a French accent, giving the name of Jeremiah Cornelius and his country of origin as Australia, formally accused of indecent assault by Miss Ingeborg Brunner at the 11th Precinct Police Station, Göteborg, last night. So far police have failed to arrest the accused." (Despatch sent by Thomas Dell to *Sydney Herald*.) The story was not published, although a subsequent cable informed the newspaper that Miss Brunner had dropped the charges. (*Sydney Herald* correspondence files.)

12 November
The journal of Yüan Shih-k'ai, Commissioner of Trade for the Northern Ports, China, notes the employment of a Captain J. Cornelius, described as "an American soldier of fortune", to "help in the training of officers for the Peiyang Army", Tientsin. It appears that Yüan Shih-k'ai's commission was later countermanded, but that an appeal to the Empress Dowager reinstated Cornelius, though his position with the Peiyang Army became poorly defined. When, in 1909, Yüan was dismissed from office, his American protégé, on leave in Shanghai, disappeared.

(*The Journals of Yüan Shih-k'ai*, edited with an introduction by Prof. Michael Lucy Smith, Collett Press, 1942.)

1908
19 February

Calcutta. Aurobindo Ghose of the extremist Nationalist Party records that Tilak, leader of the party, sent "a Eurasian called Cornelius with a message" to Congress leader Gokhale, a moderate. Gokhale never replied to the message which, Ghose thought, contained some suggestion of a secret meeting, but Cornelius was later arrested in a waterfront brothel where he had disguised himself as a woman. He was charged with the attempted assassination of Gokhale's close associate, Shastri. "A meaningless action," comments Ghose. There is no reference to the result of any trial. (Ghose, *India's Lost Opportunity*, Asia Publishing Co, Bombay, 1932.)

13 April

Afghanistan. Despatch from Colonel R. C. Gordon commanding 25th Cavalry Frontier Force. Rumours that dissident hill tribes are united under a quasi-religious chief who appears to be of European or Eurasian ancestry and is referred to variously as Elia Khan, Shah Elia or Cornelius. "A tall man with burning eyes who rides better than any tribesman and who has already cost us some fifty men, including three lieutenants and our Risaldar Major." Colonel Gordon asked for reinforcements but died with the rest of his post when it was wiped out two days later. (Michelson, "Lords of the North West Frontier," *Strand Magazine*, April 1912.)

1909
30 March

A man known only as "the English assassin Cornelius" is arrested in Innsbruck after hurling a bomb at the Kronprinz Frederik of Statz-Pulitzberg whose horse reared in time so that the bomb missed and exploded in the crowd. The assassin later escaped under circumstances which indicated help (or even orders) from someone highly placed in the government. (*Daily Mail*, 2 April.)

17 May

Secret dispatch from Captain Werner von K. (probably Koenig) dated Linz, 17 May, to Ludendorff of the German General Staff, Berlin: "I am sending to you Herr Cornelius, who has convinced me that he can supply much exact information concerning our good neighbours!" (Records in Berlin Military Museum Document PRS-188.)

1910
29 January

Gustav Krupp writes to his chief ordnance technician Fritz Rausenberger: "You were quite right to employ the Herr Doktor Cornelius. His efforts have contributed greatly to the speedier development of our new gun. Please convey to him the firm's congratulations." (Krupp correspondence files.)

1911
22 May

Passenger list of the SS *Hope Dempsey,* leaving Southampton 22 May, bound for Rangoon, via Aden, Karachi, Bombay and Madras, gives a Mr. Jeremiah Cornelius (who later disembarked at Port Said).

August

Sir James Keen, an amateur archaeologist exploring ruins in Chad, reports meeting a fellow Englishman in the town of Massakori. "A tall, youngish chap, very brown, affecting native dress and living, apparently as the sheik's chief lieutenant, with one of the tribes of armoured nomad horsemen. He was civil, but reticent about his origins, offering me only his local name, which I did not catch. However, I learned the day after he had left that he was regarded by the French as one of the most painful thorns in their sides and that the garrison at Fort-Lamy had orders to shoot him on sight, no matter what the circumstances. I was informed that his name was Gerard Cornelius and that he was a deserter from the Foreign Legion." (*The Lost Civilisations of Africa,* Harrap, 1913, p. 708.)

2 November

Report of Lieutenant Kurt von Winterfeld, command-

ing a company of Protectorate Troops stationed temporarily at Makung on the Njong River, Cameroons, states
that a European called Cornelius was shot while attempting to steal the steam launch serving the garrison. He had
passed himself off as a German trader in order to board
the vessel, but von Winterfeld suspected that he was an
English spy. His body fell into the water and was not recovered. (*German Imperial Year Book for 1911.*)

1912
7 March

The Bight of Biafra. The *Santa Isabella,* a Portuguese
schooner, hailed by a European sailing a dhow. The European gave his name as Cornelius and offered to work
his passage to Parades, the ship's home port. In Parades
Cornelius was believed to have transferred to the *Manité,*
an American barque bound for Charleston via Boston.
(Log of the *Santa Isabella.*)

1 June

Captain Simons of the *Manité* records loss of the seaman Cornelius overboard three miles off Nantucket in
heavy seas. (Log of the *Manité.*)

13 November

Discovery of a cabin, recently built, on Tower Island,
Galapagos, by crew of an Indian fishing boat blown off
course and seeking shelter. No sign of cabin's occupant.
Indians frightened, left island as quickly as possible after
one of them, a half-caste known as "Cortez", had taken
an empty metal box bearing the lettering "Asst. Comm.
J. Cornelius, Sandakan". (Journals of Father Estaban,
San Lorenzo mission, San Domingo, Ecuador.)

27 November

An English engineer Jeremiah Cornelius offers his
services to help in the completion of the Panama Canal
but cannot produce satisfactory references. He is not employed. Later, parts of the canal near Cristoban are dy-
namited. Colombian guerillas are suspected. Manager of
the Company hears rumours that Cornelius is working
with the Colombians. (Records of the Panama Canal
Co.)

1913
5 April

United States troops in Nicaragua attacked by a well-organised band of "nationalist" terrorists in several areas around Lake Nicaragua. US marines in Granada are wiped out and all arms, including several artillery pieces, stolen. Interrogation of suspects reveals that the terrorists are said to be led by an American, Jerry Cornelius. (Records of US Marine Corps.)

30 October

Peking. The missionary Ulysses Paxton mentions a conversation between himself and Liu Fang of the Methodist Episcopal Church. Referring to the possible conversion of the military leader Feng Yü-hsiang (later to be known as the "Christian General"), Liu told Paxton that a certain "Father Cornelius" had been responsible for Feng's interest in Christianity. Neither Paxton nor Liu knew of a missionary of that name in the area, though Liu had heard it said that the so-called "White Wolf," a remarkably intelligent and powerful bandit leader who had taken to roaming north-central China in the wake of the Second Revolution, was rumoured to be an ex-Catholic missionary called Kang Na Lu ("Acting with High Resolve") or Cornelius. (*Devil against Devil* by Ulysses M. Paxton, Grossett and Dunlap, N.Y. 1916, p. 179.)

1914
Summer

The White Wolf, pursued by Feng's and other armies, is killed in Shensi during a pitched battle between his men and "government" troops. Feng weeps beside the corpse and repeats the name "Cornelius" over and over again. "Later he ordered the body burned, but it had been stolen, presumably by survivors of the White Wolf's band." (*North China Herald*, 25 August.)

1915
May

Rumours of the White Wolf's reappearance in Kansu. In Kungchang Mission, Father King, an American priest, lends rail fare to a fellow missionary, Father Dempsey, who claims to have been the captive of a bandit gang.

Father King notes the initials J.C. on the other priest's bag. Father Dempsey claims that the bag belonged to a fellow missionary, Father Cornelius, who was killed by the bandits. Father Dempsey boarded train for Haichow and Father King comments on his surprising fitness, his apparent youth, his brilliant eyes. (Letter to Father King's sister, Maureen O'Reilly of Brooklyn, 8 June.)

3 August

During the famous Okhotsk Raid (thought to be inspired by Germany), two of the attacking gunboats were sunk before the defender's batteries were put out of action. The commander of a Russian launch heard the name Cornelius shouted several times during this engagement and gathered that this was the name of the officer in charge of the raid. He assumed the name to be German (although Germany continued to deny responsibility for the raid long after the end of the war). Upon the surrender of the garrison, the attackers disembarked, imprisoned all military personnel, and looted the city of most of its food, treasure and arms. The name Cornelius was heard by civilian witnesses who thought it referred to the tall man in elaborate Chinese dress who wore an ivory mask, carried no weapons, and appeared to supervise the pillage of Okhotsk. (*Report of the Official Committee Investigating the Fall of Okhotsk*, St. Petersburg, March 1916, pp. 306-9.)

1916
4 February

Sale by Henrik van der Gees of Samarana, Java, of his estates (inc rubber plantations and tin mines) throughout the East Indies. To: Mnr. Jeremiah Cornelius, a Dutch banker. The estate was the largest singly held property in the East Indies and was sold for a disclosed sum of eighteen million guilders. (Samarana Land Office records.)

17 August

The Cornelius estate made a public company, the managing director being a Francis Cornelius, believed to be the brother of the purchaser who has returned to Rotterdam. The chairman is given as a Herr Schomberg of Sourabaya. (*Die Gids,* Batavia, 20 August.)

1917
14 July

Parish register for St. Saviour's Church, Clapham, records the marriage of a Captain Jeremiah Cornelius, RFC, to a Miss Catherine Cornell, respectively of Nos 32 and 34 Clapham Common South. Captain Cornelius was on a forty-eight hour leave and returned to France immediately after the marriage. (Note: There is no record of a Captain Jeremiah Cornelius having served with the Royal Flying Corps.)

1921
6 May

The Interior Department of the USA leases naval oil reserves at Teapot Dome, Wyoming, to the Jeremiah Cornelius Company of Chicago. Various accusations in the press (notably the *Philadelphia Enquirer*) concerning the allegations that the founder of this company is none other than "German Jerry" Cornelius, a notorious racketeer often considered to be a more dangerous, though less notorious, character than Dion O'Banion, of which he is a known associate. Thomas Redick of the *Enquirer* disappears, presumed killed. The Cornelius Company continues its activities, although it denies any connection with criminal elements and claims that its president is "travelling in Europe." (*American Mercury*, 15 October 1923, p. 38.)

1922
1 March

The Munich Riots of February-March. Arrested as a "socialist agitator" by the police, a J. Cornelius. Tried 3 March and imprisoned for thirty days before being expelled from Germany on his failure to produce papers proving his citizenship. (Munich Court Records.)

September

Route of Greeks from Asia Minor by Kemal Pasha greatly facilitated by the tank company commanded by Major Cornelius, a South African soldier of fortune. (*Daily Mail,* 3 October, *The Sin of Pride* by Victor Manning.)

December

During the March on Rome a Geraldo Cornelius prominent in the Fascist take-over of power (for a short time he was editor of *Il Popolo d'Italia*) until assassinated "almost certainly on Mussolini's orders" in December of the same year. (*Threatened Europe*, J. P. H. Priestley, Gollancz, 1936, p. 107–8.)

1923
July

Lithuanians capture Memel from the French garrison installed by League of Nations. "The plan was successful almost entirely because of the work of the Dutch adventurer Cornelius." (French commander quoted in *Le Figaro*, 12 August.)

1924
21 January

Death of Lenin. A suspicion that he was assassinated on Stalin's orders voiced in the English-language *Exile* (14 February), a White Russian newspaper published in London and aimed at arousing sympathy for the émigré cause. Count Birianof wrote: "Various Russian expatriates were approached by those who were plainly agents of the Bolsheviks and told that they would be given the opportunity to 'eliminate' the Red leader. It was so plainly the kind of trap we have become used to that all émigré organisations gave orders to their membership to pay no attention to the schemes. However we have reason to believe that a Levantine gentleman, originally of Kiev and familiar in the Whitechapel area as 'Cornelius the Nihilist' made it known that he would be willing to do the deed. Whether 'Comrade' Lenin died of natural causes (a guilty conscience, perhaps?) or whether he was killed, we shall probably never really know. However, if he was killed it was almost certainly by Cornelius acting on the orders of General Secretary Joseph Vissarionovich Dzhugashvili (who prefers to hide behind the name of 'Stalin')—a man with a greater lust for power than even his fanatical master knew! And what has happened to the nihilistic Jew? Dead, himself, by now, if we know anything at all of Bolshevik plots and counter-plots."

1926
27 February

Otto Klein shot on the steps of the Regensburg Opera House. After preliminary investigations, Regensburg police ordered the arrest of a tall, dark, slender man of about thirty going by the name of J. (possible Johannes) Cornelius, a known member of the NSDAP. (Mackleworth, *The Return to Barbarism*, Gollancz, 1938, p. 18.)

18 April

Ernst Auchinek tried for the murder of Klein; strongly denies that he has been known as Cornelius or that he has any connection with the NSDAP. He was hanged a month later. (Mackleworth, ibid, p. 22.)

1927
22 November

Leon Trotsky records a meeting with "the man generally known as 'Cornelius'" in Siberia, where they were both exiled. "I was curious to meet this mysterious fellow, of whom I had heard much from Stankovich, in particular. He was undernourished and poorly dressed for the winter, but his eyes were hot enough to melt snow and he seemed singularly self-contained. I met him only for those few short moments before he was led away, but I had the impression that he was almost enjoying his imprisonment." (Letter to Manfred Schneider, 5 June 1930.)

1928
April

Mount Chingkangshan, between Hunan and Kianri. Mao Tse-tung has retired here after his recent defeat of September 1927. He is joined in the spring by Chu Teh, who brings with him an occidental sympathiser called Cornelius. Mao and Cornelius discuss tactics for several days and Mao is much impressed by the man's knowledge of China, as well as his grasp of Communist theory and its application to the special problems of China. Mao offers Cornelius a position in the army he is planning to reform, but Cornelius disappears that night and there is some suspicion that he may, after all, have been a spy of the Kuomingtang. (H'ang Lean-li, *Two Paths to Freedom*, Routledge, Kegan Paul, London, 1940, p. 807.)

January–December

All Cornelius properties sold up in US and Britain.

1929
November

Wall Street Crash. "Situation not improved by the sudden pulling out of Cornelius interests from many major companies." (*Wall Street Journal*, 26 November.)

1931
December

Japanese invasion of Manchuria. British minister in Tokyo telegraphs London: "Would suggest preparedness re rumours Japanese aided by English fascist associated with Russian émigrés here. Could prove embarrassing for us as basis for potential propaganda. The Englishman is said to be called Gerry Cornelius. Suggest you ascertain origins, etc, and speedily cable any information to here." (6 December.) The telegram was acknowledged but its contents ignored. (*Imperial Policy in the Far East, 1909–1939*, C. W. Nolan, Samson and Hall, 1950, p. 506.)

1932
12 April

Body of a young man about thirty found in Thames near Hammersmith Bridge. Several stab wounds in the throat. A gold and ormolu striking watch marked *Thos. Tompion, London, 1685* on its inside case and on the inside of its outer case *Jerry Cornelius from his dear friend Southey, Keswick 08*, the only object discovered on the body. The engraving is of little help in identifying the body since it evidently cannot be addressed to so young a man. Records show that no such watch has been reported stolen. No further evidence comes to light and the case is closed for the moment. ("London Keeps Her Mysteries", *Union Jack* magazine, August 1934.)

1934
1 July

Secret message from Himmler to Hitler on morning after extermination of Roehm and SA supporters: *All cleansing operations successful. Only the Jew-lover Corne-*

lius remains to be tidied away. (*Night of Terror,* Barry Hughes, Scion Books, 1951, p. 64.)

1935
March
One of the "freelances" used by Mussolini in the Abyssinian campaigns of March is listed as Cornelius, a Dane. (*The Times,* 29 March.)

10 August
Arab Nationalists meet in Cairo for the third Secret Congress at which Comintern representative is present. Representative used name "Cornelius". (Adad, *Arabia Reborn,* Daker, 1962, p. 76.)

1937
18 December
Palestine. Jews and Arabs clash outside Qasr-el-Azak. British special patrol discovers corpses morning of 18 December. Among the bodies are those of two Europeans. One carries a revolver of unusual design and with no maker's name or registration marks. An inscription on the barrel reads "From Catherine to Jerry". The other corpse is that of a woman, very like the man in features and colouring. She has a similar gun with the inscription "From Jerry to Cathy" on the barrel. "The odd thing was that they seemed to be fighting on opposite sides." (Report of Lieutenant Robert Gavin, Special Police, Palestine, quoted in Fennel and Harvey's *British Political Policy in the Middle East 1900–1950,* Benson and Bingley, 1958, p. 569.)

1938
14 September
Madrid. "An offer was made through a Dutchman called Cornelius to supply us with 5,000 Mauser rifles and about a million rounds of ammunition. The Dutchman also offered tanks, planes and so on. We believed that he must be representing a foreign government but he insisted that he was an independent dealer. He demanded 50,000 dollars (US) for his 'wares' which, of course, at this stage we were unable to raise. We learned later that he had sold the guns to the Falangists and that they had proved to be

in a dangerous state of disrepair and caused a number of casualties before being abandoned. We concluded that the Dutchman had unconsciously done us a favour in preferring to deal with our enemies and we drank his health!" (Palero, *The Betrayal of Spain,* Independent Publishing Association pamphlet, 1948, p. 12.)

1939
5 January
Czech Ambassador in Copenhagen writes to his government in a despatch: "I strongly recommend that you accept Herr Cornelius's terms and ensure speedy delivery of the arms he mentions." (A. P. Peters, *The Day before Doomsday,* Viking, NY, 1960, p. 56.)

3 March
Ivan Jeczakowski, the Polish industrialist, acting as agent for his government, pays two million American dollars to the Brazilian arms dealer Geraldo Corneille on delivery of fifty British Mk 1 infantry tanks, in Warsaw. (A. P. Peters, ibid, p. 72.)

6 July
Passenger list for the SS *Kao An,* a Panamanian passenger steamer, leaving Southampton, includes a Mr. and Mrs. J. Cornelius, a Miss Christine Brunner, a Mr. S. M. Collier and a Mr. Gordon Ogg, all bound for Macao.

22 September
The British tanks sold by Corneille to Poland develop technical faults and are abandoned after one engagement with the German Army near Lodz. "We placed too much reliance on them. They seemed to fall apart around us," reports the colonel in command of the regiment. (A. P. Peters, ibid., p. 106.)

1940
20 August
Assassination of Trotsky, Mexico City, by a Russian using the name of Jacques van den Dreschd of whom Trotsky had written just before his death: "He claims to be a friend of Cornelius, whom I met briefly in Siberia. At certain times I felt they could almost have been brothers

—particularly about the eyes." (Letter to Maria Reine, August 1940.)

1946
Summer

Nuremberg War Crimes Tribunal. During their trials von Ribbentrop, Goering and Streicher speak repeatedly of a witness who will come forward in their defence. He is referred to sometimes as "Herr Mann" and sometimes as "Cornelius." After being sentenced to death, they claim that Cornelius has betrayed them. Unsuccessful attempts are made to trace "Cornelius" but the only person of that name seems to be one of Himmler's astrologers believed to have committed suicide soon after the Fall of Berlin. (*The War Crimes Trials, Nuremberg and Tokyo* by Walter P. Emshwiller, Reilly & Knap, NY, 1949, p. 1003.)

1948
11 February

Assassination of Gandhi. Police seek "a one-armed man called Cornelius" in connection with the crime. Cornelius believed to be an Eurasian living in Delhi. There is some information suggesting that he was a collaborator with the Japanese in Burma and that he has an Indian wife. All investigations prove fruitless. (Mehda, *What Killed Ganhi?*, Indian Publishing Company, Bombay, 1954, p. 40.)

1949
14 March

Jerusalem. Israeli commanders interview a captured Egyptian spy Cornelius. He dies during questioning. (Uncorroborated report in *Freedom*, 12 October: *The Needless Agony* by Sandra McPhail.)

1953
May

Kenya. "One of the captured Mau Mau who had almost certainly been involved in the massacre of the Gordon family claimed that they had been led by a white man who had dyed his skin and posed as one of them. This man, said our prisoner, had been directly responsible for the rape of the two younger girls and their subse-

quent dismemberment. Several stories of this kind were
circulating at the time but no evidence ever came to light
to confirm or, for that matter, deny the rumours, though
one of the Mau Mau leaders came up with the name of
Jerome Cornelius, a businessman of Afrikaaner extraction,
who had been lost in an aircrash the year previously. If a
white man was directing Mau Mau operations in the
Muranga district—which seemed to us highly unlikely, to
say the least!—he must have made himself scarce soon
after our big operation of June and July when the Mau
Mau were virtually wiped out for the time being." (James
B. Bayley, *The Darkening Continent,* Union Movement
pamphlet, 1956, p. 7.)

1954
3 June
  Angkor Wat, Cambodia. The bodies of five French soldiers discovered in a temple. They had been tortured. The
sixth soldier was still barely alive. The torture was evidently the work of Cambodian terrorists calling themselves the Cambodian Liberation Army. Before he died,
the sixth man claimed that the terrorists had been led by
a European whom they called Cornelius (*Campaignes en
Cambodie,* Versins and Henneberg, Gallimard, Paris,
1963, p. 98.)

1955
18 July
  Algeria. French intelligence contacts FLN officer who
uses the pseudonym "Cornelius" and gives information
which leads to the death and capture of nearly twenty important members of the FLN. (Peter B. Saxton, *The Sun
is Setting,* Howard Baker, 1969, p. 103.)

30 July
  Nicosia, Cyprus. Eight Cypriot terrorists are captured
by British troops in the Hotel Athena. Before the captives can be transported to prison a counter-attack takes
place and they are rescued. The only survivor of the raid
is Corporal John Taylor who says that the raid was led
by a masked man whom one of the captives addressed as
Cornelius. (*Daily Sketch,* 1 August.)

1956
October

Suez Crisis. "It was rumoured that Eden had received a report from a Foreign Office man in Cairo called Cornelius. The report advised immediate occupation of the Canal Zone. This report, so it was said, was what finally decided Eden to give the necessary orders." (Sir Hugh Platt, *The Defence of Suez,* Collins, 1960, p. 17.)

10 November

Budapest. Russian and Hungarian secret police seek an Englishman believed to have taken an active part in the uprising of 23 October. He is sometimes called Cornelius. For a while the police place much importance on his capture and interrogate all imprisoned foreigners as to his whereabouts, but suddenly stop their investigations and no more is heard of him. (Richard Geiss, *They Went to Hungary,* Hodder and Stoughton, 1958, p. 400.)

1958
September

China's Great Leap Forward. European refugees cross from China to Hong Kong. Among them is a Jeremy Cornelius, half Chinese, half English, who disappears before he can be vetted by the authoritires. *(Hong Kong Times,* 21 September.)

1960
Spring

The Ladbroke Grove Murders in London. Within three months eight women disappear. All live in Ladbroke Grove. Two of them are found dismembered in the grounds of a disused monastery in Kensington Park Road, the others are found in Hyde Park. All corpses have the initials J.C. carved on their foreheads and the work is thought to be that of a religious maniac. The last corpse found has the slogan "J.C. loves C.B." carved into its back. Moses Collier, a labourer, confesses to the murders but further investigations and questions prove that he is mentally unbalanced and could not have been responsible for any of the murders. The case remains unsolved. (R. W. Eagen, "The Killer's Mark," *Weekend,* 4 July 1966.)

1961
Summer

The war in the Congo. White mercenaries fighting for the Congolese are commanded for a while by a Major Jerry Cornelius apparently a Belgian deserter. Later Cornelius disappears, believed killed by UN troops. (Alexander Charnock, *Twilight of Africa*, Hutchinson, 1965, p. 607.)

1962
20 November

The Cornelius Realty Company of Key West buys large areas of land in Florida at a time when values are relatively low because of the Cuba Crisis. After the crisis is over, the company resells the land at 100 per cent profit and then dissolves. (*Business Month*, January 1963.)

1963
24 November

Dallas, Texas. Police seek a Jerry Cornelius in connection with the assassination of President Kennedy. It is believed that he is an associate of Lee Harvey Oswald and a young man known only as "Shades." The young man, it is rumoured, was heard boasting in a Houston bar that he was Kennedy's killer, not Oswald. After a fruitless investigation Police conclude that Cornelius and "Shades" are inventions of Oswald. (*Time*, 11 December.)

1964
Spring

Sudden take-over of various large department stores in London and London suburbs by the Torrent Group of Companies. The Torrent Group is described as a partially owned subsidiary of the Cornelius Development Corporation of Chicago. (*Business Journal*, 15 June.)

1965
Spring

The Deep Fix, a pop group, go to No. 1 with *Felt for You, Velvet for Me*. "There's few would argue that lead guitar Jerry Cornelius is the group's real guv'nor and maybe the best white blues guitarist ever." (Chris Marlen, *Melody Maker*, 19 April.)

30 June
Bomb explodes in Alford Street, Dover, Kent. Several bodies found but none identified. The house was owned by a Mr. J. Cornelius, believed to be one of those killed. (*Kentish Times*, 5 July.)

14 August
Thailand. A meeting of Chinese trade representatives with Bangkok businessmen. The intermediary is a "Mr. Cornelius," a Belgian industrialist. (*Eastern Trading News*, 25 August.)

22 September
Death of a youth in Kilburn, stabbed in broad daylight in High Street. A gang of youths was seen running away from the scene of the crime. An identification bracelet on the young man's body gave the name Jerry Cornelius. Police asked relatives or friends of the dead man to come forward but so far nobody has done so. (*West London Times*, 29 September.)

1967
12 December
"Police raided a flat in Chepstow Villas, Notting Hill Gate, last night and seized what they described as the biggest ever drug cache to be found on private premises. The occupant of the flat, a Mr. Jerrold Cornelius, escaped from custody and has not yet been found. The police wish to interview him in connection with their enquiries. The drug cache included marijuana, hemp, cocaine, heroin and purple hearts as well as methadrine and dexadrine." (*Guardian*, 13 December.)

15 December
Conference of Black Panther leaders in Kingman, Ohio. Minister for Special Activities is given as Jerry Cornelius—"something of a mystery man even in Panther circles." (*Newsweek*, 20 December.)

1968
13 January
The highjacked TWA Boeing 707 which crashed in the sea off Trinidad had a J. Cornelius listed among its pas-

sengers. There were no survivors. (*International Herald Tribune*, 15 January.)

17 December

Multiple crash on the M1 motorway near Luton. One of those killed in the Phantom V he was driving (and which was in head-on collision with an articulated truck) is a Jerry Cornelius, described as "a young fashion designer." (*Sun*, 18 December.)

(*Note:* Although the compilers have discovered other references to people who might be Cornelius since the last entry above, they have not yet been able to check the authenticity of these references and therefore prefer not to include them as yet.)

APPENDIX II

"What's the hour?" The black-bearded man wrenched off his gilded helmet and flung it from him, careless of where it fell. "We need Elric—we know it, and he knows it. That's the truth."

"Such confidence, gentlemen, is warming to the heart."

The Stealer of Souls, 1963

"Without Jerry Cornelius we'll never get it. We need him. That's the truth."

"I'm pleased to hear it." Jerry's voice was sardonic as he entered the room rather theatrically and closed the door behind him.

The Final Programme, 1968

APPENDIX III

The captions to chapters in this novel are advertisements and headlines taken from the following sources, most of them published 1975-76:

Jane's Weapons Systems, Interavia, Official Detective, Crime Detective, True Detective, Official UFO, Guns and Ammo, Titbits, Weekend, the Guardian, the Daily Mirror, Horology Magazine.

The first four chapter headings referring to Harlequin are taken from productions staged between 1716 and 1740 by John Rich at Lincoln's Inn Fields and Covent Garden. The fifth is from Charles Dibdin's Covent Garden production, Christmas 1779. These classic pantomimes consisted of a dramatic "opening," in which the main characters all wore oversized masks, on a theme usually taken from folklore, Romance or Classical Mythology— and which lasted for the first quarter whereupon, at a moment of tension in the plot, the characters would be transformed magically into members of the Harlequinade, to act out their parts in a fantastic, musical, satirical and symbolic manner and bring the whole entertainment to a satisfactory resolution. There were some 400 pantomimes of this kind staged in the 170 years between Rich's first production and the start of the modern pantomime which began to take its place from the 1870s and had almost completely superseded it by the 1890s.

The Broadsheet quotes at the beginning of the Coda section are almost all taken from John Foreman's excellent two-volume collection of facsimile broadsheets *Curiosities of Street Literature* (London 1966).

Muzak is a trade name for piped music used in restaurants, supermarkets, bars and other public places.